LEGENDS REBORN

THE COMPLETE SERIES

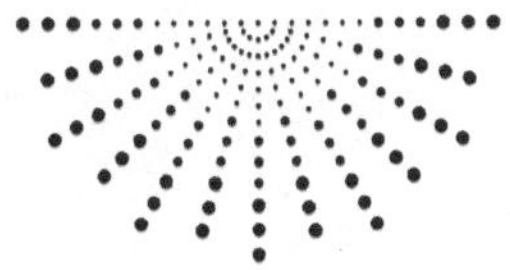

EVA CHASE

INK SPARK PRESS

Legends Reborn: The Complete Series

This is a work of fiction. Any resemblance to actual persons, living or dead, or actual events is purely coincidental.

First Digital Edition, 2018

ebook ISBN: 978-1-989096-22-2

Paperback ISBN: 978-1-989096-23-9

Created with Vellum

MAGIC WAKING

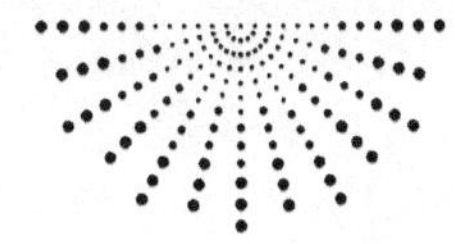

LEGENDS REBORN #1

CHAPTER ONE

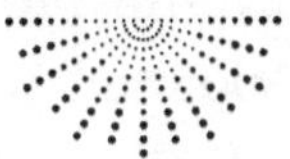

The day I found my king started with a stomachache.

I stretched on my bed amid the tangle of blanket and sheet, still waking up. The warmth of the sunlight streaming through the narrow window soaked into my skin, but the knot in my stomach didn't loosen. I knew what it meant. My heart thumped.

Today, after twenty years, four months, and six days of searching and waiting—not that I'd been counting or anything—I was going to set eyes on *him* again.

I rolled over and caught sight of a creature I was much less enthusiastic about.

A gloom was lurking under my computer desk. No one else would have been able to distinguish that patch of thicker darkness within the regular shadow, but my magic-touched sight could make out even those mindless scraps of dark intent. I grimaced.

The gloom crept along the wall. When I breathed in deep, its presence prickled at the back of my mouth. Just one couldn't do much damage—and wouldn't bother trying to damage any ordinary human being—but set a whole crowd on the attack and no one would laugh. I'd witnessed swarms like that more times than I cared to remember.

They were the vermin of the dark fae, so I dealt with them the way I'd deal with a cockroach or a rat—extermination.

I sat up in the bed and snapped a twig off the weeping fig in its pot beside the window. A whisper of the living energy nestled inside the wood tingled against my fingers. It would fade by the end of the day, but in the meantime, it held power.

I raised my hand and pointed it at the gloom. My fingers clenched around the twig. "*Darkness begone,*" I murmured in the archaic English of my first existence.

A spark lit within the patch of shadow and spread across its body. In less than a second, it ate away my unwelcome visitor.

The twig had gone dry and dead against my palm. I tossed it into the base of the pot. Technically, I didn't have to be up for another hour, but there was no way I could relax now.

I paced the room and grabbed a pair of jeans and a sweater from a basket of folded laundry. My hair resisted the ponytail I finger-combed it into. Several brown strands slipped free to drift across my face as I ducked to retrieve my sneakers from under the bed.

So what? I was going to see my king today.

No, I wasn't as ready as I wanted to be. I still hadn't figured out how to fix this mess I'd gotten us into—this repeated cycle of lives lived and cut short. I wasn't even sure I could avoid my past mistakes, escape what had happened last time—

My throat constricted. Catching that thought before it could blossom, I balled it up and tossed it away. I'd never been completely ready. But we *were* both still living. At least I'd accomplished that much.

I knelt to pluck several more twigs off the fig's outer branches, stuffed the handfuls into my pockets, and opened my closet.

My wands waited in a shoebox I'd stuffed under winter boots and a spare blanket. I ran my fingers over the smooth sticks. The magic I'd worked on them had sealed their life inside—if I'd left them out in the sun, they'd have started sprouting leaves. I tucked the birch one into my backpack.

To find a pair of gloves, I had to dig through my remaining moving boxes. But it wasn't just glooms and other dark rabble my king would need protection from.

It was also me.

I jammed a thin cotton pair into my back pocket and stepped out of my bedroom, my pulse still jittering.

Priya, my roommate, stood in the kitchen. She was spreading jam on a piece of toast. Her head of sleep-rumpled black hair bobbed up at the sound of my door, and a smile leapt to her face.

"Good morning, Emmaline!" She waved the knife at me with her usual frenetic grace. "Want eggs? I was just thinking I'd fry some up to go with my toast."

No one else called me "Emmaline" except my mom—I always told acquaintances and teachers to stick to "Emma." But Priya had seen my given name when we'd been filling out the lease and declared it one of the most beautiful names she'd ever heard. Somehow I hadn't had the heart to tell her I found it incredibly stuffy. In her cheery voice, it did sound kind of pretty.

I was already smiling back at her despite the twist of impatience inside me. Priya's boundless enthusiasm made it difficult to be irritated at her, which was probably why we were tentatively becoming friends. I hadn't been in the habit of making many of those—in this life or those prior.

"Thanks, but I think I'll stick to toast," I said. "Leave the jam out?" Food derived from animals didn't always sit well in my stomach. No need to add to my supernatural indigestion.

Priya chattered about an article she'd read for her politics course and her theories about the latest episode of a TV show we'd been watching while I gulped down my quick breakfast. Normally, I'd have contributed more. As I swallowed my last bite, Priya tilted her head.

"Something's bothering you," she said. "What's up?"

I might not have been perfect at hiding my emotions, but I had centuries of practice at lying. After all, there weren't many situations in which I *could* be truthful about being the reincarnation of a legendary sorcerer. People tended to get twitchy about even one part of that equation.

Downplaying worked better than flat-out denial. "It's nothing major," I said with a shrug. "Lab report due for a prof who seems like a tough one."

Priya nodded, accepting my explanation unquestioningly. No amount of practice stopped the little jab of guilt I felt at seeing that.

"I'm sure you've got it in the bag. You work *too* hard."

"New school, new expectations," I said. "I'll worry less once I'm into the swing of things."

I tugged on my gloves as soon as I stepped out onto the street. Thank the light the October weather was just nippy enough that wearing them didn't look totally bizarre. My gaze flitted over the streets the whole way to campus, my skin prickling at every shift in the breeze. I couldn't be sure of anything about *him* except he'd be the same age as me. He might not even be a *he* in this incarnation. Unlike me, with my regular flipping back and forth, he usually arrived male, but I could never be sure.

When my eyes hit him, I'd know him, no matter what.

At the edge of campus, a broad lawn stretched toward the sprawl of three- and four-story buildings, the older old-fashioned brick ones skirted by modern concrete additions. The view sent a jolt through my chest, even though I'd seen it dozens of times now.

It was the same image that had swam into my head and prompted me to transfer here for junior year—after skimming through page after page of internet search results before figuring out where my capricious psychic ability was pointing me.

My nerves jumped every time someone new walked by me, but I went through classes, lunch, and more classes without any revelations. I ducked into the change room to prepare for fencing practice with more than a little relief. Feinting and parrying would burn off some of my tension.

"Advanced learners, split off into pairs to spar," Coach ordered after the warm-up exercises. I nodded to the guy standing next to me. We stepped to the side and began a conversation between our training blades. With each tap and dodge, a grin crept farther across my face behind the dark mesh of my protective mask.

Once upon a time, I could have been called clumsy, especially when asked to handle a weapon. That was exactly why I'd decided to take up fencing when I had the chance. After many lives worth of drills, the moves were starting to come naturally to me. I was stronger and more coordinated than I'd ever been.

Which didn't mean I was infallible. My partner lunged, I swung to block his strike, and a low, rolling laugh carried from the doorway several feet behind me. The sound smacked into me, knocking the breath from my lungs. My arm wavered, and my opponent's saber caught my hand. My fingers twitched apart as I yanked them out of the way. My own saber flipped through the air and nearly speared the guy standing in the doorway.

He stepped back without a flinch. My weapon clattered to the floor. The guy raised his eyes. They were a blue so striking I could identify it even at a distance, so deep it was almost indigo. He gave me a cocky smile and ran his hand over his sun-streaked blond hair. The muscles in his arm flexed against the sleeve of his fitted raglan shirt.

Every muscle in *my* body had frozen. Recognition sang through my every cell on a level beneath thought, beneath memory.

A level the guy in front of me clearly wasn't aware of yet. No hint of shock crossed his face. I looked no different to him than any of the other fencers in our training gear. While *I* was born knowing who we were, my spell kept my king's memories locked inside his mind... for now.

"I hope you're normally more coordinated than that." He

nudged the saber back toward me with his foot. "I don't want to have to worry about being impaled every time I come into the room."

An echo of his voice from our first lives rang through my head. *Gods, you're more likely to impale* me *than the enemy.* Those words had been spoken in affectionate jest, not this guy's distant cool. The quiver of excitement that had been racing through me dimmed.

This incarnation of my king was a jackass.

The difference was so jarring I couldn't help bristling. "My coordination is infinitely improved when people aren't making sudden loud sounds in the training area," I said. "And you could simply not come in."

He hesitated, blinking at me. Before I'd spoken I bet he hadn't even realized he was talking to a girl. I took advantage of his silence to stride over and retrieve my saber.

Two other figures were peering into the room beside the new guy—the friends he'd been laughing with. A lanky black guy, who had a couple inches on my critic's already-formidable height, elbowed him with a rakish grin. A willowy girl with pale auburn tresses stood at Mr. Blond's other side, hugging her cardigan over her gauzy maxi dress. She squeezed his forearm in apparent reassurance, and something wrenched in my chest.

She was his girlfriend, no doubt. Well, why *wouldn't* he have a girlfriend with those looks? That was a good thing. His off-putting attitude was a good thing. Every reminder I could get to keep my distance, emotionally and physically, was a gift.

I existed to be his mage, to get him out of the snarl I'd created with my magic. Anything more risked us both, as I'd had ample opportunity to discover before.

That pinching in my chest was not jealousy. Not even a little bit.

"Have fun, Darton," the rakish friend said with a playful salute. "Return to us with all your parts intact." The girlfriend shook her head at him, and they headed off. The new guy—my king who didn't yet know he was my king—strode in to talk to Coach. I studied his shadow to confirm no glooms were tailing him and rejoined my sparring partner after Coach ambled over.

Darton. Funny how in every life something of our essence wove even into the names each set of parents granted us. A sound or a syllable carried from our origins.

At least by all appearances, he hadn't started to wake up on his own. As long as I could keep it that way, I had time to finally set things right.

My blade rapped against my opponent's, and Coach's voice traveled to my ears. "You're here to become a better quarterback?" His tone was skeptical and amused.

"I want to up my game," Darton said. "Coach Michner says my weakest area is dexterity. Fencing sounded like an enjoyable way to work on that. Is that a problem?"

"No," Coach said. "We don't have any requirement that you're devoted to the art. I *will* expect you to respect it—and to show up for practices on time."

A smile curled my lips behind my mask. Darton sounded a tad chastened in his reply.

"Right. Of course."

Coach believed in fencers staying fully suited up for practice so we were as comfortable as possible with the equipment we'd wear in competition, so they walked off to get Darton prepared. I felt his movements through the room with a faint tickling over my skin. My sparring partner disarmed me twice. I'd just paused to take a breath and regroup when Coach headed back our way, Darton in tow.

"Emma is one of our most experienced members," Coach was saying. "Since you two have already 'met,' I'll have her lead you through the basic warm-up."

My back stiffened. He often asked senior members to teach the junior ones, but it hadn't occurred to me he'd come to me, now, with this. Sodding hell. Darton was already eyeing me. If I acted cagey for no obvious reason, I'd draw his attention even more.

If I was careful, the risk of skin-to-skin physical contact was minimal. The other risks, which had to do with the heart pounding away in my chest, I'd just have to deal with.

I drew myself up straighter and tucked my one bare hand deeper into my sleeve. "Sure, I can take him through the paces."

Darton raised his eyebrow at me. "Don't worry. I'll keep up."

He did, which was a relief because it meant I didn't need to get close to adjust his position. It was also an annoyance, because I could hear him getting smugger with each comment he tossed out. He'd been a master with a broadsword way back when. It wasn't surprising he'd pick up fencing quickly. But that didn't mean I had to like how this unaware incarnation talked about it.

"So why do people get into this as a hobby anyway?" he asked when we paused after the first set of exercises.

"You mean if they're not just using it to make them better at some other sport?" I said. "Fencing is a sport too, FYI."

He'd pulled his mask up, so I saw the disbelieving face he made. "You can't say it's the *same*. And it's not as if you're likely to end up in a sword fight outside this room."

I restrained myself from asking how often he got into tackling fights with people off the football field and motioned for him to turn so we could start a two-person drill. "Some of us find the practice enjoyable regardless of how 'useful' it is. If you commit, you'll find it's intensive training for the body and the mind. You're not going to feel the full effect if you come at it like a tourist."

To give the guy credit, he took that critique in stride. He followed my instructions through several parrying sequences in silent concentration.

"Maybe I will get more into the training for its own sake," he remarked. "Now that we're on to the actual fighting, I can see the fun factor."

He chuckled and picked up his pace. Did he really think ten

minutes of practice was enough to justify pushing a senior student's limits? My king might have always been talented, but he'd also had some humility.

I matched Darton beat for beat. Back and forth, back and forth—

He broke the pattern. His saber swiped at my padded shoulder.

My pulse stuttered, but I kept my footing as I sidestepped. I whipped my blade around his and flicked it up. His saber slipped from his grasp. It clanged to the floor at his feet much as mine had half an hour ago.

"Hey," he protested. I lowered my blade, leaving my mask on. Coach was already sending some of the other members off to the change room. We were done here.

"You *never* start sparring without getting your training partner's okay first," I said. "And if you don't want to make a fool of yourself, get the basics down before you start escalating."

I stalked away before Darton could say anything in response. My legs had gone shaky.

How was I going to keep enough distance with him hanging around fencing practice three days a week? I'd found my king all right, and he was already proving more trouble than glooms and visions combined.

CHAPTER TWO

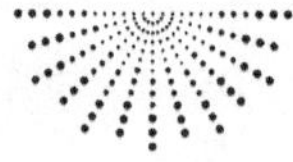

"Since when are you into football anyway?" Priya asked. She leaned back against the bleachers with a knowing smile. We were sitting near the top where I figured the players on the field would be less likely to notice us. The October wind tugged at the jacket I'd pulled on over today's sweater. For a "windbreaker," it wasn't living up to its name.

I hunched my shoulders against the early morning chill. "I enjoy sports." That was true, in moderation. "I just thought it might be fun to try something new."

"Like freezing our asses off watching our home team face off against itself?" Priya's smile widened. The cool weather didn't seem to faze her at all.

"I heard they're pretty good." Also true, from my hasty research last night where I'd dug up whatever I could find out about Darton's schedule. "I figured I'd check them out before I commit to watching a whole game."

"Mmm," Priya said. "Now I think we're getting somewhere. *Check them out*, huh? I don't suppose there's any one particular hunk of manhood down there you're focusing on?"

I wrinkled my nose at her. "No. They're all the same to me."

Technically, I wasn't here to *check out* Darton on the field. I was just… keeping an eye on him. As long as the soul inside him stayed dormant, the glooms and various other lesser creatures of darkness wouldn't be drawn to him. But I needed to figure out what his normal looked like and be around often enough to notice when he *did* start to awaken. If he woke up and the glooms caught on first—

I swallowed hard. It was not going to happen that way this time.

Football practice had crappy timing, but it was one of the few places I'd be able to observe Darton without sticking out like a sore thumb. And without catching his attention. I'd already done that far too well in fencing practice yesterday. Thank the light for masks.

Here, at least fifty other spectators were scattered throughout the stands—mostly friends and girlfriends of the players, I guessed. The rakish guy and the willowy girl who'd followed Darton to fencing club were sitting on the lowest tier with a few other guys who must have been part of Darton's larger entourage.

On the field, Darton broke from a skirmish to dash across the goal line. "All right," the willowy girl shouted with a clap of her hands. "Nice one, Art!"

My head twitched at the nickname. She called him *Art*, did she? I wouldn't be surprised if all his friends did. That was almost funny. And yet, it made my gloved hands clench. I tucked them deeper into my pockets.

I had no claim on him, not the kind she might. I couldn't let myself *want* that kind of claim. Even when I got that wish fulfilled, it only ever made our lives fall apart faster.

Priya tossed her dark hair back from her face. "*I* had a crush on one of the wide receivers for a couple months last year. I went to a bunch of games so I could… *appreciate* his performance. It's nothing to be ashamed about. We're only human after all. If there is a guy down there you think you might like to know more about, you can always pick my brain."

I considered her offer as the players rearranged themselves into a new formation. Maybe Priya did know something useful. She'd been at this school two years longer than I had, after all. I'd just throw her off the scent a bit.

"What's the story with the guy with the bad leg?" I nodded to the running back who'd started limping about fifteen minutes into practice and was now on the bench massaging his calf.

"Marco Castaneda," Priya said. "Sophomore. Everyone thought he was on track to making quarterback until he got twisted up bad in a tackle halfway through last season. He was out for the rest of the year. I guess he got the okay to give it another shot. Either way, he'll be fine. I've heard his real passion is computers, and he's already got a gig lined up with Google."

I laughed at her speedy recitation. "You really do have the deets. Okay. How about linebacker number fifty-one?" The large, dark-skinned guy appeared to be the most boisterous on the team, bouncing off the ground and bellowing a victory cheer whenever his side in the practice exercises "won."

Priya cocked her head. "That's Tommy Franklin. He's a senior but only joined the team last year. The guys were kind of standoffish with him until he started hosting parties at his apartment, but now he's everyone's fave."

"Are you sure you were just 'checking out' and not actively stalking these guys?" I nudged her teasingly, and she bumped her shoulder back against mine in retaliation. The moment felt so blissfully normal—like I really was just a college junior joking around with a friend I wasn't keeping any deep dark secrets from— that the next question rolled off my tongue without any hesitation at all.

"What about the quarterback, then?"

I didn't think I'd let my voice or my expression change, but

Priya's eyes immediately sharpened. She glanced at the field and then back at me. "Oh, is *that* who you're hung up on?"

I gave her my best bewildered look. "Why are you fixating on him? You didn't think I was head over heels for Marco or Tommy."

"It's a sixth sense." Priya waggled a finger at me. "I'd ask why *you're* fixating on him, but it's really not that hard a question to answer. Darton Rowe, star quarterback and all-around golden boy. He's good looking, rich, dean's list worthy, and a respected athlete —what's not to like?"

With a resume like that, no wonder he was cocky. "Maybe he's the one *you* have a crush on," I muttered.

"Had," Priya said. "And nope. My guy graduated, more's the pity. But I can still applaud your excellent taste in men. I'm pretty sure Darton is single right now, you know. He's got a rep for being a bit, ah, picky, but I bet you could turn his head if you tried."

She contemplated my face with an intentness that made me squirm. "I'm not interested in turning his head," I insisted, although the "single" remark had grabbed my attention. I couldn't see how to ask about the girl cheering him on from the stands without giving away my interest.

It shouldn't matter anyway.

Priya arched her eyebrows at me. I waved her skepticism away and swiveled back toward the field.

Practice was wrapping up. The coach had called a huddle, but several of the guys were already taking off their helmets. Darton's hair caught the sunlight even damp with sweat, flaxen strands glinting amid the darker gold. It was almost the same shade in this incarnation as it'd been when I'd first met my king, all those centuries ago. My mouth went dry.

The coach finished talking, and the guys jogged to the edge of the field. The spectators around us started getting up. Darton's friends gathered around him as he gulped from a bottle of water.

I pushed to my feet, swung my backpack over my shoulder, and turned to head to the opposite end of the bleachers, where I could climb down without risking crossing paths with him. The less he saw me without a fencing mask on, the better.

Priya grabbed my arm. "Where are you going?" she said, her voice low. Her eyes gleamed. "You should go down and say hi! Look, he's coming right this way."

Darton and his entourage were ambling along with the apparent intention of skirting our side of the bleachers. I shook my head. "I don't want to say hi, Pri. I'm not into him. Really."

She gave me a light tug. "Oh, come on. Don't chicken out on me. I can tell you're at least curious. He won't bite."

I wasn't so sure about that, given he'd come at me with a blade yesterday. And it was beside the point.

"I've got to get to class. Maybe another time." I made a mental note *not* to let Priya invite herself along next time.

"Emmaline," Priya pleaded. At the same moment, a guy a few rows below us dropped his phone with a clatter. He swore loudly. Darton, who was just coming around the stands with his friends, glanced up. My pulse stuttered. One flick to the right and his gaze would hit me.

I spun around and jerked against Priya's grasp—just as she let me go of her own accord. "All right, all right, have it your way."

The unnecessary force I'd put into breaking free propelled me backward. I stumbled, and my back slammed into the rusty guardrail. It must have weakened over the years after holding up however many drunken sports fans, because it didn't hold *me* up. With a squeal, the bar popped out of its frame. I tumbled past it over the edge.

The twenty-foot drop to the ground didn't give me a whole lot of time to think, so it was a good thing I'd had centuries to hone my instincts. My heart lurched, but my lips spat out a few quick words. One of the twigs in my pocket disintegrated.

The pillow of air I'd called into being caught me. I still hit the ground, but the impact jarred my body without breaking any bones. If I'd cushioned myself any more, it would have been obvious to anyone observing that something unnatural had happened.

My breath had jolted out of me. My head spun. I blinked at the grass beside my face as my awareness caught up with my instinctive reactions.

Well, that was one way to make a quick exit.

Someone was yelling. Multiple people, actually. I pushed into a sitting position, and a rush of dizziness washed over me. Before I could find my bearings to stand, the one guy I'd been trying my best to avoid leaned over me.

"Are you all right?" Darton asked. From the flush on his face, he must have run over. His friends and a few other players were coming up behind him.

I groped for my inner poise. "Um. Yeah."

He offered his hand to help me up, but I was already scrambling to my feet. My legs wobbled. Damn it.

Darton caught my arm to steady me, and I had to stiffen to keep from flailing away like a maniac. Heat washed through my body. Only two layers of fabric lay between his bare hand and my skin. Two thin shields holding off disaster.

I stepped backward, and Darton let go. He was eyeing me with concern. I met those intense blue eyes for as little time as I felt I could get away with while appearing convincingly stable. "I'm okay." I was reaching for an excuse to hightail it out of there when Priya dashed over from the stands. She'd taken the longer, safer route down.

"Thank God!" She came to a stop beside me and looked me up and down. "I was terrified. The school needs to do better maintenance on those bleachers."

"No kidding." I rubbed the elbow that had taken a sizable portion of the impact. My hip was aching.

Priya's attention shifted to the guy in front of me. An unnerving spark lit in her eyes.

"Thank you for racing over so quickly to help," she said to Darton in her most chipper voice. "I'm Priya."

"Darton." He gave her a brief nod, but his gaze slid right back to me. Expectantly. Oh, swine crud and cattle sod. I *really* shouldn't have let Priya come with me.

I could have admitted we'd already met. But maybe he'd never figure that out. If he found out now, it was only going to fix my face more firmly in his memory.

"Emmaline," I said quickly, hoping he wouldn't make the connection to the "Emma" Coach had directed him to yesterday. "And yeah. Thank you. I, ah—I've got a class to get to—"

"Then you'll want this." Darton's rakish friend scooped up my backpack, which had rolled a few feet away, and handed it to me with a sly grin. "I'm Keevan. Kudos on the impressive fall. You took it like a champ."

I wasn't entirely sure that was a compliment. "Thanks."

Darton frowned. "Are you *sure* you're okay? If you need a hand getting to the campus medical center…"

I couldn't help being touched by his refusal to let the situation go, as inconvenient as it was. The guy wasn't a total ass. Nevertheless, I didn't want his hands anywhere near my vicinity. That kind of touching was severely inadvisable.

"One-hundred-percent injury free." I took a step to the side to show off my now-steady feet. "Guess I was lucky."

"Really lucky," Darton's maybe-girlfriend murmured.

Darton's frown turned puzzled. The back of my neck prickled.

My voice. The fencing mask would have muffled it a little, but that didn't mean he *couldn't* notice the similarity. I had to get out of there before he put two and two together.

"Well, ah, hopefully we won't meet this way again." I offered a brisk wave of my hand and took off.

I'd only made it two steps before Priya caught up with me. She leaned in conspiratorially. "At least you did get to talk to him. He knows who you are now. That was a pretty memorable entrance."

"Yeah." That was the problem. Even if Darton didn't connect the girl who'd fallen from the bleachers to his sharp-tongued fencing partner, he'd recognize me now. My responsibilities had gotten ten times harder in the space of a second.

CHAPTER THREE

THE CRUSHED HIMALAYAN salt rattled into the glass bowl. I opened the baggy of dried ague root and poured it over the rough crystals. The faintly tart odor tickled my nose. I kneaded the powder and salt together. The damp afternoon breeze drifted over me, but the hedge at the edge of the campus grounds held the worst of the wind away from my spell-making.

The pages in the leather-bound book spread open beside me fluttered. They were crisp and yellowed, knowledge recorded more than a hundred years ago in some other life I only retained a few hazy memories of. I'd retrieved it from my storage locker an hour ago. My recollection of my lives after the first might be hazy, but the magical beacons I'd set in place each time always led me back to my stash of scribblings.

Looking at those stacks of supplies and journals, the oldest of them long since crumbled, always left me cranky. They made a thorough record of my failures. All the lives cut so short because I'd slipped up somewhere. All the lifetimes in which I hadn't been able to untangle the spell that was drawing the dark rabble to us and keeping us locked in this cycle.

Not again. This time, I'd do everything right.

I pulled a wand from my bag and pointed it at the mixture in the bowl. The words in the old tongue rolled from my throat. *"When fae darkness crosses, witness and tremble."*

A shiver ran through the wand and up my arm. The tingle of life in the stick dulled. Soon, this wand would be nothing more than dead wood, which was why I'd brought backups.

I straightened up and scanned the grounds. I'd picked a spot secluded enough that no one would have seen or heard the details of my preparations, but a group of girls—freshmen, I'd bet, by their giddy nervous energy—was ambling down the drive toward the entrance. A couple of them shot me curious glances.

I had the entire property to circle. No way was I pulling that off without drawing some notice.

Normally, I'd have waited and cast magic like this on a Monday in the wee hours of the morning, after the weekend partiers were finally asleep and before the early birds were up for breakfast. But now that Darton was somewhat aware of my existence, I needed protective measures in place that *didn't* require having him in my line of sight. I was just lucky that it appeared he mostly studied, worked out, and slept on the college's grounds.

I was going to have to come up with other plans for his away games and for Thanksgiving, when I figured he'd probably make a trip home. If we survived that long.

For now, I just needed to avoid looking so sketchy that someone called campus security. I studied the traffic roaring along the road on the other side of the hedge, as if I were waiting for a specific car, until the girls had passed me by. Then I gestured the wand toward myself and muttered a few words to deflect attention.

The wand's core shuddered and crumbled. The last of my words tugged right into my body. It was too late to reach for one of my spares. Sod it. I pushed the thump of my pulse and the light of life that flowed through my blood into the casting. A prickle raced over my skin, and the light around me rippled. I tossed away the dead wand.

No one would give me a second glance now. And if I'd put a day or two of this body's life into the casting, oh well. I wasn't likely to make it to old age anyway.

I grabbed one of the other two wands I had on me and palmed a handful of the herbed salt. "*When fae darkness crosses, witness and tremble,*" I murmured, sprinkling the mixture in a thin trail on the ground. I walked ten paces, sprinkled some more, and repeated the incantation. The wand twitched in my hand with each casting. It wasn't practical to lay the salt in a completely unbroken line, but if I kept the gaps small enough, any passing glooms—or more dangerous creatures of darkness—would trigger the warning.

My second wand died in my hand about halfway around campus. I'd expected to get more out of it—I must not have sealed that one well. I paused to catch my breath. Even when I used the energy in the wands to charge my magic, the focus necessary tired me out after a while. I might as well take a moment to check on a project of sorts I'd started before my encounter with Darton.

A gloom was squirming amid a clump of trees near the campus border, not far from the athletic department's track. "Hello, Carl," I said. Not that glooms had names, but it looked like a Carl to me. The clot of darkness roiled as it pushed against the magical binding I'd laid around it.

I brushed my hand over the sealing spell and frowned. The woven energy was starting to fray, worn down by the gloom's struggle to escape. It might take years, but the spell would eventually crumble and let this shred of darkness go free.

Balls. I'd hoped that new combination of words, herbs, and wood might create a permanent effect. Back to the drawing board. There had to be a way I could re-seal our true enemy that didn't rely on mine and my king's lives maintaining the balance.

There had better be, or I was never going to break this eternal cycle, not without freeing that enemy and bringing on my king's final death.

"I'm sorry, but I don't think we can stay friends any longer," I informed the gloom as I drew out my final wand.

"*Darkness begone,*" I muttered, and Carl contracted into nothing. I turned away, my chest tight.

I'd captured the greatest dark fae of them all once. I'd kept her sealed away from humankind for fifteen hundred years. I *had* to be capable of doing it again, just a little differently.

Of course, it would have helped if I understood how I'd managed to create the first seal. I hadn't exactly been thinking clearly in the moment.

I charted a course past a couple making out against a maintenance shed, around the track and the bleachers where the railing that had broken off was now tied with yellow caution tape, and back to the hedge. Only a handful of salt remained when I reached the main entrance. I tipped that into a small silk bag and tied off the ribbon that closed it.

A tremble ran down my back as I raised the wand to lock the last bit of the incantation in place. I'd pushed myself to lay down the casting quickly, and I was paying for it now. But it was almost done. I'd handled far worse.

"*When fae darkness crosses, witness and tremble,*" I said one last time. The quiver of energy in the wand snuffed out. I shoved some of my own life's power after it. My nerves wrenched—and that was when the vision hit me.

They never came quietly. The world before me tore apart with a rush of spiraling darkness. My stomach lurched. The shapes before my mind's eye whirled as if I were falling… tumbling straight down toward a sprawl of forest.

Toward a small grove of trees surrounded by the patches of vibrant autumn reds and yellows. The vision slowed, and I stared. Blackened patches spread across the branches where the bark had disintegrated. The leaves that sprouted from them dangled brown and shriveled. The grass that was matted around the trees roots lay limp and gray. A chill permeated the air through the grove, so thick it penetrated the body my mind had left behind.

I shivered, and a fresh rush of darkness loomed like a fog rolling over me, icy cold as it spread down my throat and into my lungs—

I came to on my back on the campus lawn, gasping for breath. For a few seconds, the blue sky stretched above me struck me as impossibly bright, fake as plastic. I dragged in the cool, clear air and coughed.

My visions never offered much help, either. I had no idea where that cluster of trees was or when it would matter. I didn't even know what their existence signified. All I could say in the wake of the dread still crawling over my skin was that whatever had harmed them meant to do the same to me and all other things living.

When I was growing up—the first time, centuries ago—I'd only ever gotten brief flashes of feeling, barely even an image, there and then gone. So when my first *real* vision came, knocking me off my feet and flooding my mind, I couldn't ignore it. I saw a young man, fair and strong with the sun glowing off his face and the walls of his castle behind him, and I knew it was time to go.

My father wasn't so sure, even though he'd always said I was to volunteer my service to the king's son—eventually. "I thought we would wait until you were a little older," he told me. "The prince won't be king for some time yet. There's no good to come from rushing in."

"It's not rushing," I said. "I need to go, now." The vision had told me that as clearly as if it had spoken words. Whatever purpose I was to carry out, it was meant to begin, and I didn't have much patience for dithering. In that way, at least, I was completely my father's son.

In the end, Father nodded his pale head, squeezed my shoulder —we were never a hugging sort of family—and wished me luck as I packed a few possessions to bring with me.

I set out with total certainty, even though I knew sod-all about the current king and the son I intended to serve. My light fae community in the woods did not mingle much with humankind. Father had told me generalities—that the king was the most respected in generations, that nearly everyone considered him to be fair but firm, and that his son, though only a year older than me, had already started making a name for *him*self with his willingness to pitch in when ordinary folk were in need. That was the limit of my understanding.

My feet, seeming to know where to take me without any consultation needed, carried me to a town a few hours' ride from the castle. I came across a group of townspeople assembled in a courtyard on the outskirts. The prince's golden hair gleamed in their midst.

He was in the middle of explaining his plan to stop a gang of marauders who'd been thieving along the highways. His hands swept with passionate gestures mixed with the occasional joking remark, and his audience listened in obvious awe. I'd missed most of the explanation—he was just finishing.

The townspeople dispersed with enthusiasm. A few of the locals took note of me, the stranger in their midst, with wary glances. I hesitated at the edge of the courtyard. The prince walked apart from his guard to examine a cart that might have been part of his plan, so I pushed myself forward.

I strode up to him and dropped to one knee, bowing my head. "Your Highness," I said, "if I might speak with you."

The prince let out a sound somewhere between a cough and a laugh. "Of course, good fellow. Speak as much as you wish. But I'd rather you did it standing face to face with me."

His smile, small but warm, told me he meant that, so I got to my feet. "I've heard many remarkable things about you and your father," I told him with a directness that probably should have embarrassed *me*. "I admire the way you look out for your people and the good you've already done for them. I've traveled a long distance in the hopes that I can be of use to you. I'll take on whatever job you'll assign me, as long as it helps you with your work."

He blinked, and I had enough wits to realize my compliments had affected him, even as well as he'd kept his composure. I hadn't realized yet how rarely the over-awed ordinary folk spoke to him directly or how measured his father was with praise.

I hadn't quite decided during my journey there whether I should reveal my magic right away or slowly hint at it. I didn't have many skills that would be useful to a prince otherwise, but magic was the domain of my fae heritage, not my human side, and I'd heard enough stories to be aware that even the best people sometimes responded… poorly to what they didn't understand.

But the prince didn't ask for any proof of my skills. He clapped me on the back, grinned, and said, "With an attitude like that, I'm sure we can find plenty of ways for you to contribute. For a start, how about we carry these casks of wine to the inn? No one will think much of my generosity if I don't provide a drink to go with the meal I've arranged."

Was it the grin and the light it brought into his eyes? The way he went straight to *we* as if we were already allies? Or maybe the fact that he'd not only come to the town to deal with the marauders, but had also gifted them with a feast as well? All three combined, no doubt. In any case, I'd looked back at him with a grin of my own, and just like that, if I was being honest, I'd already prepared to follow my king-to-be to the ends of the Earth.

Fifteen hundred years later, I sat up on the grass beside the campus entrance and pressed my hands against my face. So many years had passed since that day, and yet I could still bring the taste of that wine and the tenor of his voice back in an instant.

I'd followed my liege so much farther than the ends of the Earth since then. I'd watched him die and followed him into death a hundred times. And still, the closest thing I had to answers were ominous visions that might as well have been blotches in a Rorschach test.

"It can't keep going like this, Arthur," I said to the ground, to the air, to the soul locked inside the unknowing young man sitting in a classroom right now. "We *have* to end it."

If only I had the slightest idea how.

CHAPTER FOUR

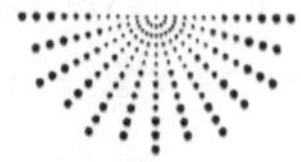

My sparring partner lowered her foil. "Normally you'd never let me through like that. Where's your head at, Emma?"

I grimaced behind my mask. "Sorry. I'll try to stay more focused."

We resumed our stances. I stepped forward with a testing feint, but my mind still wasn't completely on the duel. A significant sliver of my attention stayed trained on the open doorway to the gymnasium—the one Darton hadn't yet walked through, even though practice was halfway over.

I'd managed to keep tabs on him here and there over the last week. There hadn't been any signs worthy of alarm. I'd watched him head into his Modern Social Theory course a few hours ago. So where in darkness was he? He'd shown up on time for the last three practices.

I might not have been so edgy if the chill of that creepy vision of the rotting trees hadn't still been hanging over me.

After a few quick back-and-forths, I found my rhythm enough to score the winning point. I lowered my saber and rolled my shoulders, sweat beading under my uniform.

"I'm going to grab a drink," I said, and my partner nodded.

In the hall, I pushed up my mask and gulped from the water fountain. I was just straightening up when a familiar baritone voice carried from around the corner. My heart leapt, and I tugged my fencing mask back on.

Whoever Darton had been talking to must have headed in a different direction, because he came around the corner alone. I should have ignored him and walked back into the gym. Unfortunately, my tongue had other ideas.

"Practice started forty minutes ago," I said.

A challenging glint leapt into his eyes, but his expression was otherwise regretful. "I know. I had to talk to a professor who has limited office hours, and the conversation went long…" His mouth curved at a teasing angle. "Were you hoping you'd seen the last of me?"

"It seemed like a possibility." I hadn't forgotten how uninvested he'd acted when I'd led him through the warm-up that first day.

He cocked his head. "Do you figure I'm the type to just give up on things?"

Was he goading me or bothered I might think that? His deep blue eyes fixed on mine even though he couldn't have made out more than the vague shape of them through my mask, and a memory flashed through my mind. A memory of a young man not that much older than the one in front of me adjusting a crown that hadn't yet sat easily on his head, but with eyes as intent and his jaw set firm as he'd prepared to speak to his people. My chest clenched.

"I'm reserving judgment for now," I said as tartly as I could manage. "It's Coach's opinion you should be worried about."

I headed to the far end of the gym on my own. Better that I stick to solitary practice for the rest of the hour in my current state of mind.

Even as I ran myself through a series of footwork drills, my gaze kept drifting to Darton. Maybe I'd been a touch harder on him than he'd deserved. Coach had obviously accepted his explanation with full grace—he was taking Darton through some of the paces. And the flexing of Darton's muscles, the careful attention with which he moved, told me he was putting every effort into following Coach's directions accurately. When he slipped up, he didn't laugh it off. He immediately tried again.

Something about his stance at certain moments looked off to me, though. I couldn't quite pinpoint the problem. A sort of stiffness when he turned at the waist? Or was I just making up excuses to study that well-built body even longer? I tugged my gaze away.

"All right, folks," Coach called out. "Great work today." He turned to Darton. "I can stay a little longer if you want to make up for your lost time."

"Thanks," Darton said with what sounded like honest gratitude. "I'd appreciate that."

I left my mask on until the last moment, hurrying into the change room as soon as I'd set it on the rack. I intended to leave surreptitiously as I had every practice before, but when I slipped into the hall a few minutes later, I nearly bumped into Darton's willowy, auburn-haired maybe-girlfriend. I caught myself just shy of colliding with her. She glanced over, and her face lit with recognition.

"Oh! You're—it was Emmaline, right?"

Swine crud. I pasted on my most agreeable smile. "Actually, I prefer Emma." I might as well set that much right.

"You're still okay after that fall?"

"Completely. I probably used up my luck for the year."

She chuckled, a heartier sound than the airy giggle I'd have expected. "I'm Izzy. You're in fencing club? I didn't realize you already knew Darton."

And straight into dangerous territory we went. "I didn't," I said quickly. "I mean, we hadn't really talked. He hasn't been around that long."

"Right, of course." She smiled back at me, so genuinely that guilt tweaked my gut. Not enough that I didn't wish this conversation was over, though.

Izzy looked toward the gym doorway, where she'd probably been headed. The sound of tapping blades drifted through it. "I thought practice would be over by now. Darton promised he'd look over a project of mine."

My gaze followed hers as I reached for an excuse. Coach was taking Darton through some of the footwork exercises I'd been doing earlier. I opened my mouth—and Darton hesitated with that stiffness at his waist again. The words I'd been going to say halted in my throat. There *was* something wrong. I edged a little closer, keeping enough distance that I didn't think he'd get much of a look at me if he happened to turn this way.

"He got here late, so he's just getting a little extra practice in," I said in answer to Izzy's last comment. My eyes stayed trained on Darton. Was that a bit of a wince as he stepped to the side?

Izzy ambled right up to the doorway. "It's more complicated than I realized. I mean, I thought fencing was mostly about what you did with the sword, not so much your feet and all that."

"Everything about your stance supports your weapon," I said automatically. I'd only heard that from Coach about a thousand times. "Anyway, you can't expect an opponent to stay still, so you have to know how to move after or away from them."

"Of course." At the corner of my vision, Izzy's pale cheeks pinkened. She was pretty in the gentle, doe-eyed manner my king had often been drawn to. A question I really had no business asking fell from my mouth.

"How long have you two been together?"

"Oh, we're not—I mean, we *were*, for a little while, but that was last year." Izzy rubbed her mouth. "We gave it a try, but it turned out we're better as friends."

I stifled the spark of relief that shot up inside me at that revelation. It didn't make any difference to what I had to do. And *she* still wanted more than that. The longing quivered off her as she gazed into the gym. She was waiting for her second chance.

"Sorry," I said. Suddenly, I really was. It was only a matter of time before Darton started waking up, and then he wouldn't be the guy she'd fallen for anymore. If I didn't get my act together and figure out how to get us out of this cursed spiral, she wouldn't have him as *anything* for much longer than that. "I just assumed."

"No, it's fine," she said with a little laugh, but then her brow knit. "It isn't at all *dangerous*, is it? The fencing? To be going at each other with swords and all…"

I had to laugh at that suggestion. "Not anywhere near as dangerous as football. Between the masks, the gloves, and the padding in the uniforms, we're well protected. And the training weapons aren't even sharp. It's not really *fighting*, just sport." Which maybe was why I could stomach it better than the swordplay of long ago.

"Well, that's a relief." Izzy shook her head. "Football is kind of scary, isn't it? Concussions and sprains. But there's no way he's ever giving *that* up. Boys!"

Coach had added the movements of the epée to the footwork exercise, and darkness take me if Darton wasn't picking it up like a pro. He moved with an elegant precision I wouldn't have anticipated from a football player, but then, he wasn't just that. Darton was a king at his core, even if he didn't know it yet. In that moment, it radiated from his every movement. Watching him made my breath catch.

Coach swung around to the right. Darton moved to copy him —and stumbled. He halted, his chest heaving, and my breath stopped altogether. Izzy leaned forward, the furrow on her brow deepening.

"What happened?" Coach said, his even voice bouncing off the high ceiling.

Darton made a face. "I don't know. I don't think it's because of the training. I've been feeling a bit—since this morning—"

He pressed his free hand to his abdomen, slightly to the left, just below where his rib cage would end. I swallowed hard. Icy fingers clamped around my heart. No. It couldn't be.

"I must have bruised a muscle or strained something without realizing it during yesterday's game," Darton was saying. I stepped backward. My legs wobbled, and Izzy's gaze darted to me. My expression must have given away a little of my horror, because hers softened with concern.

"Are you all right?"

"Yes," I choked out. "I just remembered something I need to take care of. I'll see you around."

I took off before anything else could tumble out of my mouth. The chill seeped through the rest of my body as I hurried toward the outer doors. In the back of my head, I was still seeing Darton standing there with his hand pressed to his side.

To the spot on his side where, hundreds of years ago, the Darkest One had driven her shadowy blade in to the hilt. The ring of her cackle as my king's body had slumped echoed through my memory. A red splotch had clawed across the fabric of the tunic beneath his split chainmail, dark and deadly, at the same time the color had leached from his face. And I'd hurled out the words, conjured the power, that had set everything since in motion.

That moment was where it all ended, and where it all began. But none of his past incarnations had shown a physical connection to that past injury. I'd have noted it somewhere in my stacks of decaying journals if he had. It didn't make sense.

Unless we were facing a greater threat this time around.

CHAPTER FIVE

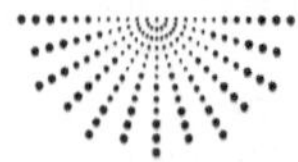

THE PUNGENT HERBAL scent of the incense filled my nose. Sitting cross-legged on the hardwood floor of my bedroom, I leaned over the smoldering sticks in their bowl and breathed deep. Energy whispered from the twigs I'd placed in a circle around me. I straightened up, set my hands in my lap, and closed my eyes.

"*The mind's eye,*" I murmured in the old tongue. "*From here to there. Let me borrow, let me see.*"

I dragged in another breath and exhaled it long and slow. My awareness drifted upward with the air I expelled. Up and out, through the plastic and brick of the apartment wall, across the rising dawn—and into the head of a sparrow perched on the building's roof.

My sense of my human body faded. I was a bird standing on spindly legs, beady eyes giving me a panoramic view of the city. At my mental nudge, the sparrow spread its wings. With a few flaps, it was soaring on a cool air current toward the outskirts of the city. I urged it higher until I could make out the nearest patches of forest in the distance.

I knew what I was looking for—that cluster of death-touched

trees that had chilled me in my vision. The image had clearly been a warning. I *didn't* know if it was connected to Darton's odd, echoing discomfort, but it seemed at least a reasonable guess. Something had affected him in a way I'd never seen before, which suggested a malicious power greater than any we'd encountered in our repeating lives. The sort of power that might leach the life from a grove of trees with its presence alone.

I really hoped they were connected. Because that was my only lead, and I had no bloody clue how I was going to help him if it didn't pan out.

The sparrow glided over the first stretch of trees. The autumn colors had swallowed up almost all the green. I guided the bird downward until it was skimming just a few feet over the canopy of leaves. Branches and shadows flickered beneath us as the wind warbled around the feathered body.

The grove should be easy to spot—a patch of gray amid the brighter leaves. It would stand out even more sharply with the sparrow's ultraviolent sensitivity. I swiveled its head, taking in the entire forest.

We soared over the field on the other side with no luck, so I nudged the sparrow to the west. This search was only going to work if the malicious presence was nearby. It ought to be—magic was difficult to sustain across a distance. I supposed if it were strong enough, it could be affecting Darton from halfway across the country.

As if glooms and the rest of the lower dark rabble weren't trouble enough. What in light's name did this thing want with Darton? How had it even latched on to him?

I needed those answers, but I suspected I wasn't going to like them.

The sparrow crossed highway, farmland, and another stretch of woods. Fatigue crept through its sinewy muscles along with a pinch of hunger. I didn't want my sight-riding to harm it. Time to find another mount.

I reached out again, and my mind caught on a crow balanced on an electric cable strung across a nearby field. A shiver of distaste ran through my awareness—scavengers and I didn't always get along—but its larger wingspan would get me farther, faster. I focused on it and leapt.

The crow had an itch under its left wing. I let it scratch at that with its beak, and then I tugged it into the air. We shot up toward the clouds so I could reassess my course.

Nothing below drew me with any urgency. I turned us north, because that was where the patches of forest looked the thickest. As the crow swooped toward them, the memory of the vision's chill crawled through me.

Yes, north *felt* right.

The crow had crossed one span of forest and just soared over another when an unpleasant prickling shot through its body and my mind. The bird veered closer to the treetops of its own accord. Its small heart raced in its chest.

It had sensed something I couldn't. We were being pursued. Something, somewhere, was tracking our movements and closing in.

The crow landed on a branch near the peak of an oak tree. It stood there, stock still, amid the shifting shadows of the leaves swaying in the breeze. I held there with it, waiting, watching.

A crow wasn't typical prey for any predator. Whatever was out there… was it after the crow because of *me*?

A familiar, unnatural chill seeped over the crow's wings, numbing its muscles. *No.* I pushed it forward in a burst of feathers. Fly, fly, fly. Under branches and around trunks, now higher, now lower, left and then right. I didn't know how to dodge our pursuer when I had no idea where—or what—it even was, but I wasn't going to give it an easy chase.

The crow trembled as it flapped its wings, fear and the physical strain of our headlong flight sapping its strength. I could have let it go. Could have released it and let my awareness snap back into my body in my bedroom. If whatever was hunting us caught the bird with me in it, I couldn't be sure it wouldn't hurt me too.

But I wasn't ready to flee. The thing chasing us had the same horrible presence I'd felt in that grove of trees. I'd come here hunting for *it*. I needed to know more.

I couldn't ask the crow to give up its life to that cause, though. It dove between two pines, and I sensed a rabbit nibbling at a sapling's bark down below. With a bolt of thought, I jumped from the bird into that furry body.

The crow flapped away overhead. For the first several seconds, amid the jitter of my thoughts, I kept my consciousness balled tightly in the rabbit's head. The animal's eyes weren't much use to me, but its nose might be. No immediate impression of my pursuer came to me. Was it still fixated on the crow?

If it had found me here, maybe I was close to its lair.

I suggested to the rabbit that it needed to seek out a spot that smelled of rot. The bunny left off its nibbling and loped forward across the tree roots. It paused, and paused again, testing the air with a quiver of its nose. A tendril of something sour and decaying twined with the scents of dry soil and pine needles. *That way*, I told it. *Follow that trail.*

I kept it close to the tree trunks and the scattered bushes and ferns between them, to stay as sheltered as we could. But we hadn't stumbled on anything meaningful yet when the rabbit abruptly froze. Its nose twitched; its body went rigid. I couldn't tell what it had sensed, but it obviously wasn't anything good.

A branch creaked somewhere behind us. The rabbit bolted. Its feet thumped over the dry soil as fast as the patter of its heart. Before I could regain control, it had darted into a hollow beneath a granite bolder.

The rabbit spun around to brace its hindquarters against the back of the hollow. Nothing stirred outside. I watched the opening, my mind as still as my host's body.

I couldn't take on much of an enemy, not with only my mind

and a rabbit's body. Fully casting without the ability to speak was impossible, and what magic I might be able to summon non-verbally was slight. But my pursuer's lair had to be close. I couldn't give up. Not when this thing might be hurting Darton even worse tomorrow.

I crouched there in the dark, sharing the rabbit's hope that if we laid low, our pursuer would back off—or at least wander far enough away that I could explore farther. The rattle of the animal's pulse and the tension wound through its body stirred a memory up from the depths of my history.

The bark of the tree trunk bit into my back through my thin tunic. I pressed against it harder. The tramp of footsteps carried through the forest, far too close for comfort. Especially because they were the footsteps of men who very much wanted to kill me... and the prince braced against a different tree about ten feet away. My hands clenched tight at my sides.

It was my fault. I'd persuaded Arthur to take a little time for himself, just this once. Not that he'd done a very good job of it. He'd claimed we were going out for a ride, the king's son and his ever-present attendant, but within half an hour, that ride had turned into a series of village calls. I hadn't minded the excuse to get off the normally placid mare he'd stuck me on—horses never took well to me, and she'd gone entirely skittish—but I didn't see how asking after ill farmers and taking notes on grain stores was for himself.

And then, along the road between the third village and the fourth, six members of the marauding gang the king's soldiers had mostly managed to suppress earlier that year leapt out in an ambush. Just our luck.

I didn't remember exactly how we'd ended up in the woods, without our horses or our weapons but alive for the time being. Between the clang of swords and the rearing of my horse, the fall and my overall panic, I'd lost at least ten minutes in a blur. But now the four men Arthur hadn't managed to dispatch were prowling through the forest, intent on finishing the job they'd set out to do. Which I suspected involved our heads ending up on sticks.

I glanced over at Arthur where he stood braced and ready even without his sword, his gaze distant as he followed the sounds. He had to be thinking he never should have listened to me, that I'd pretty much gotten him killed with my well-meaning badgering. A pang filled my chest. In another minute or two, unless some miracle dropped out of the sky, I'd have to ensure he wasn't killed by using my magic, so blatantly he'd have to recognize it as a supernatural power.

I hadn't shown him even a hint of it yet. We'd never talked about the fae or otherworldly powers. I might save him only to have him banish me from his sight, execute me, or…

But there was no question which outcome, his death or mine, would be worse.

I curled my fingers around a slim branch low on the ash tree that hid me and looked at the king's son again. He met my gaze this time with a smile and a nod, small but confident. The pang deepened even as some other tension inside me released.

He didn't blame me for our predicament. Not even a little.

That knowledge gave me the courage to move. I snapped the branch and shouted into the air. A wind whipped through the forest. I stepped from behind my tree in time to see it pummel our attackers onto their backs. The gleam of Arthur's sword leapt into my mind. I reached out and called to it. The blade shot through the underbrush from wherever it had fallen to land at the prince's feet.

My pulse thudded in my ears. I turned toward Arthur. He was staring at me, his eyes wide. Then, before a new sort of panic could take hold of me, a grin stretched across his face.

I slipped out of the memory into an ache of homesickness. Gods, we'd come so far since then. I wished I could have smacked down my current pursuer with a surge of conjured wind.

It had been quiet out in the forest for a few minutes now. I directed the rabbit to edge a little closer to the opening.

It took one step, and the view of the forest outside caved in on us.

The boulder above us fractured and crumbled. A shudder of magical power hit the rabbit's skin with a rush of frigid air. The animal scrambled backward, and I threw myself out of its head. My awareness snagged on a robin gliding between the trees.

Not giving it a chance to adjust to the change in management, I urged it onward, upward, fast. The air shrieked behind me. My pursuer had tracked my leap.

The robin swerved to the left, dipped, and dodged. I gathered myself again. An invisible force swept through the branches ahead of me, twigs snapping and leaves browning in its wake, and walloped the bird in the face with a cold fist of power.

My host spun, head over wings, and my mind jerked out of it.

I came to slumped on the floor of my bedroom. The incense was still smoking in its bowl. The twigs in their circle around me had disintegrated into dust—all except one. I raised a hand to my forehead, which was pounding. My stomach had twisted.

I hadn't found our enemy's lair, but I'd gotten enough of a taste of its power to know what we were dealing with. That hadn't been any lesser fae creature stalking me—oh, no. The clout of that strike —that had been pure fae magic. Only higher fae could wield the energies of the world with that much strength and precision.

And only one sort of fae did so with such a chill.

A full dark fae had come here, seeking my king. A dark fae who'd hurt him from miles away and been prepared for me to come searching for it. Everything I'd seen had the flavor of a mercenary.

I drew up my legs and rested my head on my knees. It couldn't know exactly where Darton was or it wouldn't be lurking around a forest on the other side of the state. I just had to keep it that way. The dark rabble I could handle, but we'd been lucky not to draw the attention of a full dark fae in any of our previous reincarnations. If this mercenary came calling directly, I might not have any hope of stopping him before he had taken what he wanted.

CHAPTER SIX

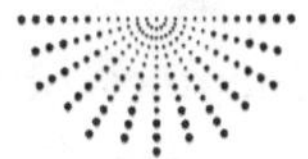

I OPENED my bedroom window to disperse the smoke from the incense, and a knock sounded behind me. "Emmaline?"

Priya's tone was so urgent that I dashed to the door. "What's up?" I said as I opened it.

Priya gave me a relieved smile, but she looked me up and down as if checking for injuries. "I called you, like, four times, and you didn't say anything."

Bat crap. "Sorry," I said, a lie automatically leaping to my tongue. "I had headphones on, music going. I didn't even hear you."

Priya tipped her head, her nostrils flaring. Could she smell the incense? But even if she could, there wasn't anything weird about incense.

This was why I preferred not to do any extended magic in the apartment. It was always a tricky trade-off, making sure I had a few direct connections to the modern world while maintaining a space for my stranger habits. Not for the first time and undoubtedly not the last, I wondered if I should have gone the roommate route after all.

The important thing was keeping up the illusion that everything was normal. I shifted forward, and Priya stepped back to let me leave. I hadn't eaten anything that morning, since sight-riding came easier on an empty stomach, but now my stomach was asserting just how empty it was. It gurgled insistently despite my lingering dread.

Priya trailed behind me into the kitchen. "So everything is all right?"

"Sure." I walled off the memory of that cold, invisible presence in the back of my mind. *No, nothing is all right, not at all.* "Same as usual." *Other than the fact that for the first time in fifteen centuries, an actual dark fae has fixated on my king's supposedly hidden soul, and I haven't even been successful at saving him from glooms the last several dozen lives.*

Her mouth twitched into a frown. "You've just… Well, you've seemed kind of distant the last few days. Like your mind is always someplace else. I know we haven't been friends that long, but you know you can talk to me if something is bothering you, right?"

The genuine worry in her voice squeezed my heart. We might not have known each other long, but she was a good friend. One of the best I'd ever had since I'd started this repetitious cycle. Or at least she would have been, if I could have let her.

Instead, I had to keep lying.

"There's nothing. Really." My smile felt stiff, but I hoped she wouldn't notice. "Just, you know, the course load is picking up, lots of assignments to stay on top of. Nothing more serious than that."

She exhaled, still eyeing my face. "If there ever *is* more than that, I'm game. I can keep an open mind. Just try me."

Yeah, right. *Oh, well, in that case, let me tell you all about how I'm a hundred-times-reincarnated wizard, and I've got a king to save from an evil fairy creature.* Ha.

I was never going to be able to say anything like that to her. Or to anyone else—not my parents, not Coach, not the sort-of friends

I'd left back home. I never could. This was how it always happened. I found my king, and the rest of my current existence fell to pieces.

I turned away to open the fridge. The pressure in my chest sharpened into an ache. But I had centuries of practice at holding my tongue.

"I'll keep that in mind. You know, there's nothing here I'm really in the mood for. And you're right that I haven't had much time to hang out. Do you want to go grab brunch at that place down the street that has the hash browns you're always raving about?"

Priya's face brightened. "That's an invite I'm never going to turn down!"

Her gaze lingered on me for a second longer, though, before she headed for the coat hooks to get her jacket. And I knew she didn't really believe I was all right, no matter what I said.

But then, could I blame her? I didn't believe it either.

❦

"Come out, come out, wherever you are," I murmured under my breath. The campus green stretched out before me, and the gloom had to be around here somewhere. In my pocket, the salt in the pouch trembled again.

I skirted the fine arts department's small theater building, walking faster when the trembling intensified. Following the magical signal was like a game of Hot-and-Cold once I got in the general vicinity, but at least glooms moved at a leisurely pace. The other two I'd caught in the last week had barely drifted past the edge of school property before I'd found them.

I made for the parking lot up ahead, but before I was even halfway across the green, the trembling rose to an outright jitter. My gaze snagged on a hazy fragment of darkness rippling through the tiny interconnected shadows formed by the blades of grass. It jerked to a halt and then crawled onward in a slightly different direction.

Hmm. This one wasn't so leisurely. I hurried after it, finding I had to speed-walk to keep pace. Since my encounter with the dark fae mercenary this morning, I'd meant to try out a new containment spell on the next gloom I came across, but this might not be the best one for the job.

It looked almost… purposeful. Where was it heading? I could have cast it away right then, but getting the answer to that question felt more important.

The gloom continued in its swift, halting course across campus —back around the theater, between two of the residence buildings, darting from shadow to shadow. My fellow students wouldn't have been able to make it out, but they could see *me*. A few guys I passed shot me odd looks when I stopped abruptly as the gloom hesitated. Then it was off again.

We left behind the residence halls, passed the physical sciences building, and reached the edge of the college's central courtyard. An uneasy prickle crept over my skin. A memory stirred in the back of my head—and not one I wanted to return to. It was the last thing I'd seen in the life before this one—a young man's face twisted in pain and rigid with death as a swarm of glooms roiled around him.

One couldn't do much damage, but a bunch of them? Oh, yes. I didn't understand why the gloom was behaving so oddly, but I didn't like it. Maybe I was better off exterminating it before it got into any real trouble.

I palmed one of the twigs I'd stashed in my clothes this morning—and a jovial voice ran out from across the courtyard.

"Hey! It's Emmaline the Indestructible. She can give you some answers."

My head jerked up, and my eyes locked with the deep brown ones belonging to Darton's rakish friend Keevan. He grinned as he sauntered toward me. Izzy was right behind him. And there was

Darton between them, laughing at something Izzy must have said. My pulse skittered.

The gloom had brought me straight to my king. It shouldn't have been drawn toward him at all, not when the soul inside him was still completely dormant.

My hand clenched around the twig. I couldn't start muttering and pointing at what would look to the three of them like empty air now that they were watching me. When I stepped forward to meet them, I moved in front of the gloom as I went. At the same time, I focused on the twig against my fingers and pictured an invisible wall sprouting from the ground around the gloom. My fingers tightened. The twig crumbled. My wordless spell shivered into place.

The magic wouldn't be very powerful, but it would keep the dark vermin contained—and away from Darton—for at least an hour or two. Way more than enough time for me to get out of this situation and deal with it properly.

"You seem to be keeping better balance today," Keevan said teasingly.

Izzy elbowed him. "Don't bug her about that. I bet Emma has better coordination than you with all that sword practice."

Darton's head snapped up at that, and my heart flipped for a completely different reason. "Sword?" he said.

"In fencing club." Izzy gave him a look that clearly said she thought he was being dim. She didn't know he hadn't made the connection yet. But that last bit of anonymity I'd held on to had just disintegrated. Darton's expression tightened as understanding followed by embarrassment and consternation shifted over it. His gaze held mine, more a glower than a glance now.

I offered a tiny shrug, and his mouth twisted. He wasn't going to admit he'd been unaware in front of his friends, of course. Too much pride for that. But I could tell I was going to be hearing about this at our next practice.

At least Izzy seemed pleased to see me. "We keep bumping into you," she said, smiling. "After two years of never meeting—it must be fate or something!"

Well, that was one way to look at it. "I wasn't here the last two years," I said, grateful I had a solid excuse that wasn't—*I just started stalking the bunch of you. Well, only one of you.* "I just transferred in."

"Oh, where from?"

That part was going to be trickier to explain. I briefly considered lying, but given my luck in the last ten minutes, I had the feeling I'd end up caught in it somehow. "Yale," I admitted.

Darton had stood still and silent through the exchange, but he couldn't keep his mouth shut at that. "*Yale?*" he repeated. "You got into Yale and decided to come here instead?"

I bit my tongue. *Yes, I did. For* you, *you arse.* "Are you only here because *you* didn't get into Yale, then?"

His glower returned. "It's family tradition." His tone implied he could have gone to Yale if he'd really wanted to. From what Priya had said about his grades, it might be true, so fair enough.

"Well, I didn't have any family tradition," I said. "It was a good school, sure, but something was... missing."

That wasn't even a lie.

"Which begs the question." Keevan waggled his thick eyebrows. "Did you find that something here?" He waved his arm at the sturdy but not especially impressive buildings around the courtyard.

My eyes twitched, but I managed not to glance at Darton. "I'm not sure yet."

Maybe something of that truth seeped into my voice. At the edge of my vision, Darton was still focused on me, but more considering than glowering now. As if he were contemplating how or why I might have ended up here, near him, at all.

I didn't want him wondering about that.

I turned to Keevan. "What answers were you talking about that you thought I could give?"

"Right!" He nudged Izzy. "Get her to do the survey, Iz. Maybe she'll have something more interesting to say than the bunch of us."

Izzy grimaced and pulled out the clipboard she'd tucked under her arm. "I'm supposed to ask people these questions for a presentation for one of my English classes," she explained. "You really don't have to."

"It's fine." Once we had that over with, maybe they would leave so I could finish taking care of the gloom. I resisted the urge to check behind me, where it should still be lurking beside the bench where I'd trapped it.

"Thanks." Izzy retrieved a purple pen she'd lodged behind her ear and poised it over the paper. "What's your major?"

"Double major, biology and chemistry," I said. Suddenly, all three of them were staring at me again. I'd gotten that a lot even at Yale. Apparently I didn't look the part of a scientist.

"That must be a lot of work," Izzy said. I suspected that remark wasn't part of the survey.

It wasn't, really, between the baseline sensitivity to living systems that my fae heritage had given me and the fact that I'd taken pretty much the same courses in every life since I'd survived long enough to make it to college, but I couldn't exactly tell her that. Better if they didn't think I was even weirder than I'd already come across. "Yeah, it is, but I manage."

"My older sister is doing her Ph.D. in physics here," Keevan put in. "The science department is hardcore. Kudos."

Izzy adjusted the clipboard. "I guess most of your assigned readings for school are nonfiction?" I nodded, and she checked something on the page. "How about recreationally? Do you read books or magazines that aren't for school?"

"Sure," I said. "Some."

A dark flutter of movement caught my eye. I swiveled as if checking my backpack for something and glanced at the bench. My body tensed.

The gloom was edging closer to us. It was edging *over* the

protective boundary I'd sent around it, toward the part of the bench's shadow that touched that of the nearest building.

My spell had been hasty and wordless, but it should have been strong enough to repel any regular gloom for more than a few minutes. Any *regular* gloom. This one had also made for Darton as if it'd been searching for him. If it pulled itself free of my trap completely, it could get to him in a matter of seconds. And if it touched him and recognized the magic twined through his spirit, we'd be totally screwed.

I turned back to Izzy to make an excuse and froze. She wasn't looking at me anymore. She was peering toward the gloom. Her brow had knit, as if something about the scene puzzled her. Her pale fingers clutched the clipboard. A shiver ran through me.

If she'd fully made out the gloom, recognized a patch of darkness was moving of its own accord through the shadows, she'd have looked terrified, not just confused. But she was seeing *something* when she shouldn't have noticed anything at all.

This was all wrong. Where had a gloom gotten enough power to overcome magical barriers and trigger human senses?

If Darton hadn't been standing right there, I might have tried to examine it further, to learn what I could about it. But he was, and my king came first, always. I couldn't risk him.

"You know what?" I said quickly, "I've actually got to get to— to the library. I seem to have left my notebook there."

Before anyone could comment on that feeble excuse, I spun in the general direction of the library, grabbing a few twigs from my pocket as I did. At this point, I didn't trust just one to do the job.

With a dip of my shoulder, the strap of my backpack slipped off as if by accident. It thumped on the ground, and I swung my arm in a motion a little too broad to just be snatching after it, letting the noise of its fall swallow my murmur. "*Darkness begone.*"

Light flared inside the gloom's filmy form. It blinked out of being. The anxious weight in my chest relaxed.

"You're not making a very good case for being coordinated."

Darton hefted my backpack before I could reach for it properly and held it out. I accepted it from him, letting the dust of the twigs I'd sapped the energy from fall from my other hand. His gaze seemed to catch those fragments. Couldn't I catch a single break today?

"It's a good thing I'm not really concerned about proving anything to you, then," I retorted, and hurried away before I could blow my cover any more than I already had.

CHAPTER SEVEN

"Stop here," I said to the taxi driver. "This is good."

The cab pulled to a stop on the gravel shoulder of the narrow highway. The driver took in the sprawl of forest beside us and then looked back at me, his brow furrowed. "Here?"

"Yep." I checked the price on the dashboard console and handed him a wad of bills that covered it twice over. Having savings accounts that had been collecting interest for decades made certain parts of my repeated lives a lot smoother. "I'm meeting some friends for a camping trip. Thanks for getting me all the way out here."

The driver fanned the bills and gave a slightly sputtered laugh. "All right. Have fun!"

I couldn't blame him for his initial hesitation. According to the maps, the woodland I stepped out in front of stretched across hundreds of acres, most of them rarely disturbed. Because the forest's inhabitants made sure they weren't without humans even realizing they'd been magically persuaded.

I set off into the brush. My hiking boots crunched over the first fallen leaves of autumn. The fresh, dry scent of soil and wood should have been refreshing, but my stomach twisted. After the convoluted journey by large bus, then smaller bus, and finally the taxi that had gotten me here, it was almost lunchtime. I fished out the cheese and veggie sandwich I'd packed, but I'd only gulped down half before the twist turned into a knot.

It wasn't only hunger weighing on me. After all, this was no recreational hike. I stuffed the rest of the sandwich into my satchel and tramped on over the uneven earth.

The boundary tingled over me as I crossed it. The magic laced through it would have turned back any normal human with some unconscious sense that they needed to be elsewhere. I shook the itch off in an instant and kept walking, my head high and my feet steady.

They'd know who I was. They'd greet me when they took a mind to.

It only took a few minutes. Three luminescent figures shimmered into view ahead of me, as if out of the streaks of sunlight penetrating the canopy above us.

Light fae and dark fae were named by their natures and affinities, not by their appearance. Life energy glowed through the skin of the three fae who came forward to meet me, but that skin was pale gold on one, ebony on another, and bronze brown on the third, in the middle. He stepped ahead of the others. The faintest beam of sunlight set his coppery hair gleaming and shone in his hazel eyes.

The fae bowed slightly at his thin waist, which told me he was a hell of a lot younger than me. I might have several centuries on most of them in spirit, but only the newest fae recognized that seniority when it came packaged in my regularly changing human form.

"You are welcome here, Son and now Daughter of Eóghan." His voice was so silvery I could almost see it shining. "What is it you seek?"

The fae only ever mentioned my father. My mother, the human

woman who'd carried me for nine months and birthed me for the very first time, had never counted to anyone. Even to my father, she'd been more of a tool than a person. I wasn't even sure he'd bothered to find out her name. He'd been far more concerned about picking a mate with the appropriate physicality and brains. By the time it had occurred to me to ask, he'd already forgotten… if he'd ever known.

The way the fae raised their children, with each child belonging to the community at large, I hadn't even realized how strange that was until I'd entered Arthur's world.

The other two young fae flitted around me, their eyes wide. Had they ever even seen a human form up close? As the human world had expanded in population and power, the fae had withdrawn in turn. At least that had made it easier for me to avoid running into any dark fae who might be familiar with my history —until now.

"I need to talk to one of the elders," I said. "There's a dark fae active nearby, and I'm concerned."

The trio gathered together to murmur to each other. I crossed my arms over my chest as I waited. They might have been more comfortable if I'd used their overly formal way of speaking, but I didn't have the patience for it these days.

"I will return with guidance," the one who'd spoken to me before said. He glided away. The pale man darted away into the sunbeams like a leaping spark. The ebony woman hesitated, peering at me with nearly round eyes.

"I've heard so many stories about you," she said.

Light deliver me. "I doubt more than half were true," I muttered.

She shook her head. "Even if only that—I can't imagine, so many lives, in so many places. Not just on these lands, but across the ocean too. Is it very different there?"

My jaw tightened, but I resisted the impulse to tell her to leave me in peace. At least her childlike curiosity was a more enthusiastic welcome than I was likely to get from many others here.

"Human beings are very similar on a whole in every place," I told her, "while still being very different from each other. It's part of what makes them interesting."

"Have you seen—what is it called, where there is sand without end?"

"The desert?" I supplied. "You can see that right here if you just go farther south. The temperature shifts take some getting used to, but there's no shortage of sunlight, that's for sure."

"Well, I haven't traveled much beyond the enclave. Yet." She glanced down at her hands, which she'd twined in front of her. "Do you really find that—"

"Sunki." The coppery-haired fae returned in a flash of light. His voice was mildly chiding. "Our guest must come speak to Chimalis now."

The young woman shrank back so swiftly that I said, in as warm a voice as I could manage, "It was nice talking with you," if only just to annoy the other guy.

I followed the coppery-haired fae deeper into the forest, past tree trunks that glimmered with the outlines of doors. The homes they opened into, built and hidden by sorcery, would be far larger than the trees appeared capable of containing. The magic I'd bent my mind to studying and needed tools to fully use came to the fae as easily as breathing. Which made it even more irritating that they never used it for anything other than their very narrow priorities.

This forest was thriving, so what did it matter to them if another was being chopped down to make room for a subdivision, or if pollution was saturating the air everywhere else? What did it matter to them if this human king or that human president did well or poorly by his people?

My father had been different. He'd thought beyond his enclave. But even he hadn't been prepared for the commitments I'd been willing to make outside his kind. He'd wanted a child with human blood to ground it against the characteristic light fae flightiness and distraction, but he hadn't considered that his fae influence and teachings might not be enough to always sway that blood to his way of seeing things.

My guide stopped in a small clearing where sunlight pooled from a gap in the canopy. A table had been conjured there, set with sparkling cups of juice and cut fruits. They still offered me the basics of hospitality, at least. I sat on the oak stool.

The moment my rear touched the wood, another fae emerged from the forest. Like all her kind, she was lithe and elegant. But the fae did age. All the light fae looked a little faded around the edges to me, but as an elder, Chimalis was becoming nearly translucent, right to the core. As she passed into the pool of light, I could make out the darker shadows of the forest behind her through her glowing form.

She rested her tan hands, the slender fingers grown inhumanly long, on the table, a subtle reminder to respect her age and the status that came with it.

I bowed much as the young fae man had to me. I might have insulted her, or else those undoubtedly watching this meeting, by not prostrating myself lower—but then, if they were going to see me as a being unworthy of their full respect, why should they expect me to perfectly follow their customs?

"Daughter of Eóghan, what name do you carry now?" The elder fae's voice had the same translucent quality as her body, as if it came from much farther away than the other side of the table. Her misty blue eyes darted over me, never quite settling on one spot.

I wasn't sure if the question was politeness or a sign they didn't recognize me as who I'd once been enough to call me by the name my father had given me, but I'd rather they used my current human name anyway. "Emma."

"I'm told you come to us on this day with worries."

I nodded. "I've seen evidence of dark fae powers in the area. I believe a mercenary has set his sights on my... charge. He's attempted to do us harm. And on top of that, I ran into a gloom yesterday that was unusually strong."

"The darkness does shift," Chimalis murmured.

Right. I plowed onward. "My own ability to investigate is limited. I was hoping someone here might have sensed or heard more about what's going on. Why the mercenary is here. What his goals are." Beyond destroying my king, presumably.

The elder shivered on her stool. Her eyes went even more distant. "There are strange stirrings. A winter chill well before the winter."

A typical light fae answer. I bit back my impatience. "Do you think the Darkest One could be exerting some influence after all this time?" Dread gnawed at my gut at the thought.

Chimalis tipped her head to one side. "I have no sense of it. She is imprisoned far. Her sprouting is young. No point is fixed."

Was *that* answer supposed to be helpful? Swine crud, the New World fae were even loopier than the ones back in Britain. This was why I hadn't come out here earlier. But desperate times called for desperate measures.

"Can you tell me anything about the strange stirrings or the chill?" I said. "Or how to push them back, suppress them?"

"We can only know the shadows are longer than they once were, and the air grown colder," Chimalis said. "We keep to the enclave. The dark fae keep clear of us."

I frowned. "For now. If one is gathering power, making moves against *me*, he might decide to do more damage beyond that. He's obviously an enemy of the light."

"If he comes to us, he will find it impossible to do harm," the elder said placidly. "That is *why* we remain here. Tell me, daughter of Eóghan, why do you not give up your quest and stay here with the people of your soul?"

My spine stiffened. "I can't."

"Nothing prevents you. This wrenching from one life to the next so often, it's unnatural. It must cause you much pain. I can see it has." Her eyes sharpened, fixing for a moment on my face. "You know the darkness does not come for you. The other, he was a pillar once, but now he is nothing. Let them have him. Let your wandering end."

"My father believed it was important that we thwart their plans," I said. "That it was about more than just one human life. Why would the dark fae want him so badly if he doesn't matter more than that?"

Chimalis bowed her head. Her fine, shimmering hair slid over her narrow shoulders. "Eóghan had many wise ideas, but many odd ones as well. He did not always see as he should. Sometimes destruction must sweep through to bring new life from the ashes."

"Well, I'm not willing to risk who knows what kind of 'destruction' with fae philosophy as my only guarantee it'll end well." My voice shook. I shut my mouth and inhaled, collecting myself. "*I* was one of my father's odd ideas. The only reason I exist is so he could send me to unravel the darkness gathering around Arthur. I have no intention of giving that purpose up."

"You have so much loyalty to one long passed?" Chimalis asked with what sounded like honest curiosity. "You would continue to act as his tool?"

I bristled, gritting my teeth. She had never met my father and was in no position to judge him. He'd had uses for me, yes, and he hadn't always agreed with my decisions when they veered contrary to his intent, but he'd loved me. I knew that.

Anyway, it wasn't *him* I was staying loyal to. It was the soul still living inside that rather difficult man back on campus. My hand fell to my pocket, feeling the pouch of salt there. I was probably too far away from my magical alarm system for it to work. The risk hadn't been worth it. The light fae had nothing useful to tell me. I was on my own, as always.

I stood up. Now that I'd confirmed as much, I'd better get home.

"If any of you *do* see signs of dark fae stepping beyond their usual practices, I'd appreciate a head's-up. I'm sure you could figure out where to find me."

Chimalis nodded, but I didn't really believe she or the others would seek me out. They kept to their enclave, as she'd already said.

How can they just sit by? I'd ranted to my father more than once, after it had become clear the Darkest One herself had some stake in my king. *They're lucky the dark fae have never yet taken a mind to slaughter* them, *or there'd be none of you left.*

You don't understand, he'd said in that slow, knowing voice of his. *That carelessness is our strength. The dark powers only understand order and certainty. They can't cope with the unexpected. And we always have chaos on our side.*

I'd never felt especially comforted by that response. The light fae's chaos simply meant they never pulled their heads out of their asses long enough to notice there might be problems worth applying it to.

"May your path be ever lit," Chimalis said. It was the light fae's standard farewell.

I gave her another truncated bow. "And yours in turn."

Arms tight at my sides, I marched back through the forest the way I'd come. I didn't need a guide to show me to the road. Then it'd be another mile or two before I made it to anywhere I could expect a cab to pick me up.

I'd nearly crossed the enclave when a slim figure flitted out of the trees toward me. The ebony-skinned fae who'd peppered me with questions earlier—Sunki. She bowed to me, more deeply than the others had.

"Might I speak?"

Not more questions. "Please make it quick," I said, suppressing a groan.

She took my instruction to heart. Her words tumbled from her tongue. "I listen to the animals. They have felt the darkness rising. Tendrils of it, sweeping like water grass in a stream, without aim."

"Searching," I said. She dipped her head. So the mercenary

didn't know exactly where Darton was yet. That would explain why he hadn't traveled closer.

"And it feeds the glooms and the other lesser creatures of darkness," she said. "They grow fatter, and they follow the threads."

Creatures, plural. My gut twisted. The gloom I'd seen wasn't just a fluke. The dark rabble was absorbing the mercenary's power—and he was *sending* them searching for us? Lovely. But at least knowing that gave me a better chance of getting in his way.

"Thanks," I said, meaning it.

Sunki bowed again and tucked her hand behind her back. "It was such an honor to speak with you at all. If I could offer a gift that might make some small difference..."

She reached out to me, her fingers clasped around the hilt of a dagger. The power sealed inside it quivered through me. I caught my breath.

The blade, thick and lightly curved, was nothing more special than tarnished silver. But the holly-wood handle, polished smooth and carved with spiraling vines along the hilt, radiated life energy into my palm when I took it. Enchanted—live wood, like my wands—but from the feel, it had been made to hold the entire essence of the tree it had been cut from. It would have taken me months of concentrated effort to create a weapon like this.

"Thank you," I said again. A flash of a smile crossed Sunki's face. She gave me one last bow and slipped away.

I turned the dagger in my hand as I walked on. The shiver of its energy stayed with me, but as the awe of seeing it wore off, the knot in my gut remained.

It was a true gift, sure. A powerful weapon against the dark. I could slice through a gloom or any other piece of the dark rabble without drawing on any magic of my own. But only one at a time. And only those lesser beings. One half-fae wizard and one enchanted dagger were far from enough to take on the army of dark fae creatures this mercenary was empowering.

CHAPTER EIGHT

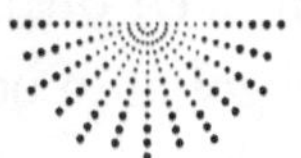

I'd gotten in the habit of arriving at fencing practice early so I could be suited up before Darton came around. I wasn't prepared to see him standing in the hall outside the gym door when I came around the corner. A little jolt ran through me, excitement and anxiety intertwined.

He'd been leaning against the wall with an open book in his hand. At the sound of my footsteps, he looked up, lowered the book, and pushed himself fully upright.

The way the lines of his body moved inside his fitted clothes set off a warmth inside me I had no control over. It really wasn't fair. My hand tightened around the strap of my backpack, but I kept walking steadily over.

"Emma," Darton said with a tip of his head.

"Darton." I stopped, longing to continue into the change room, knowing we were going to have this conversation sooner or later. I might as well get it over with.

"You really could have told me." His voice was light, but his indigo-blue eyes held mine intently.

"Told you what?" I said. "'By the way, I'm talented at both

losing my grip on my saber *and* falling off tall objects'? It didn't seem like vital information."

He looked as if he were biting back a grimace. "I wouldn't criticize the way you handle a sword *now*."

I shook my head. "It's not that big a deal. And if *you're* going to get better with those 'swords,' you might want to get ready for practice."

He paused, his gaze still fixed on me. If he didn't stop paying me so much attention, I was going to be flushed on the outside too, where he could see it. I turned toward the change room.

"Partner with me for the two-person drills?" Darton asked.

A persnickety part of me wanted to say no, just to irritate him. The weakest part wanted to ask why he'd made the request, with a little-too-much hopeful anticipation at the thought of his answer. I tensed against that hope, but I didn't say no either.

He was reaching out to me of his own accord. I could protect him far better from the threats I hadn't anticipated if he liked me. If he trusted me. Taking the stealthy route was impossible now anyway.

I'd just have to keep a tight rein on my impulses. I knew better than to entirely trust myself.

"Sure," I said, short and simple, and pushed past the door.

My heart had started thumping, but it slowed again when I slid on my mask. My little shield to ensure he didn't notice an accidental stare or an expression I'd rather stayed hidden.

And I needed it, because after our conversation in the hall, my awareness of his presence had only heightened. I felt each of his movements during the warm-up like an echo of my own, even though he was at the other end of the line.

"All right, folks—partner up," Coach said. Darton made a beeline for me as if he'd been just as aware of my position in the group as I'd been of his. I clamped down on my pleased shiver at the thought, lifted my mask to acknowledge him, and immediately tugged it back down.

Coach called out the first drill, and Darton stepped into the correct stance without hesitation. Even if he didn't see fencing as a serious sport, he'd obviously been paying attention. We shuffled back and forth in a rehearsed rhythm. Jab, parry, jab, parry. He drew in a breath, and just from the shape of it, I could tell he was smiling behind the black mesh.

"So you're a football fan?"

"What?" I said.

Darton chuckled. "You were watching the team practice that morning before you took your fall."

Oh. Of course. I'd steered clear of the stands ever since I'd had to introduce myself to him there. I shrugged around the motion of my saber. "Not really. Priya's the one more into it." From what she'd said, that had been true. Last year, at least.

"Priya?"

"My friend who was there with me." I peered at him through my mask. He'd remembered me but not her, even though she'd pushed the introductions? Well, I was the one who'd made the more dramatic *entrance*. There was no need to read more into it than that.

But if he wanted to talk through the drills, I had my own subjects to bring up. "How has your side been? It looked like you'd injured it the other day."

Darton's arm dipped, just slightly, but enough for me to know he was remembering that pain. The ghost of a deeper pain he couldn't have remembered yet.

"It's not bad," he said, which told me it wasn't *gone* yet. "I don't think there's any real damage."

How the heck could I ask about the discomfort in more detail —whether it was continuous or periodic; if the latter, what pattern there was to when it showed up—without sounding obsessively concerned? Before I'd figured that out, Coach ordered us to switch drills. Darton and I repositioned ourselves a little farther apart, our arms extended.

I tapped my blade against Darton's, and he began retreating from my mock charge. "Watch your footwork," I said automatically, like I would have any other beginner I was paired with. "Your front foot should be landing on the heel."

"Are you sure you're the best person to be advising on proper footwork?"

His tone was teasing but cocky enough to raise my hackles. I might like him better than I had on our first meeting, but he still had some jackass in there.

"I guess you'll find out if you ignore me and end up on your arse," I retorted.

We reached the wall and headed back in the other direction, me retreating now.

"So you just up and left Yale?" Darton said between slightly ragged breaths. "I bet your parents raised hell over that."

"Not really. They trust me to know what's best for myself." My gaze lifted to his face. For the first time, I found myself regretting the masks. "Are you only here because of *your* family?"

"Well, no."

We paused at the opposite wall. As if having sensed my wish, Darton shoved up his mask and swiped his sleeve across his face. Uncertainty had softened the usual cockiness in his expression. Something about this topic got to him.

Before I could scrutinize him further, he pulled the mask back down. "I know they wouldn't have been *happy* if I'd gone somewhere else. And my parents are covering most of the tuition— I'm not sure they would have anywhere else."

"There are these things called scholarships, you know." I motioned him backward to continue the drill. "Did you grow up near here?" *Do you have family around who you might go visiting sooner than I've planned for?* I wasn't sure exactly what I'd do if he ventured closer to the mercenary's territory, but it'd be nice to have a little warning.

"Upstate," he said. "Not close enough that I can drop in to do laundry like Keevan does. Where are you from, anyway?"

Not close enough he was likely to head home at random. One small concern I could cross off the growing list. "Here and there," I said. "We moved around a lot."

The truth was my parents had lived in the same house on the outskirts of Boston since before I was born. But I'd lived so many lives all over this continent and others, and accumulated so much random knowledge during them, that it was easier to pretend I was worldly in a more mundane way.

"You're a bit of a vagabond," Darton said in the same cocky-teasing tone as before. He almost sounded like he was... flirting with me. My pulse skipped, and an answer more honest than I would have preferred slipped out.

"Not by choice."

At least a little of my weariness must have slipped out too, because Darton fell silent. His advance when we switched directions didn't feel quite as aggressive as the last.

"It's pretty brave, changing your plans like that," he said after a moment. "I mean, a lot of people would think you're crazy to leave after getting into a place like Yale."

"I gathered that from your reaction when I mentioned it," I said dryly.

"I'm trying to give you a compliment."

"Well, maybe you need to try harder." Bugger it, *I* was flirting now. A smile had crept across my face, not that he could see it. I dropped the banter. "It's not that difficult to make a decision like that when you know for sure what you need to be doing with your life."

"Okay, drill time is over," Coach said from across the room.

Darton stopped, his saber drifting to his side. "And what is that?" he asked. "Biology and chemistry... Something to do with medicine?"

"You could say that." I was focused on saving lives, in a very specific sort of way. The question about what he wanted to be doing leapt to my tongue, but I caught it. My throat tightened. Hearing him talk about dreams I'd know he almost certainly wouldn't get to reach would only be painful.

Darton glanced across the gym. Coach had started instructing a small group of the beginner students. The senior fencers were pairing up to spar or working through some additional solo exercises on their own. Darton should have gone over to join the beginner group, but he turned back to me instead.

"Would you do me the honor of sparring with me? I'd appreciate the benefit of your expertise, and I'll do my best not to make a fool of myself in the process."

The teasing note hadn't entirely disappeared, but his voice was mostly serious. It held an echo of our first practice together, when I'd chided him for taking that swipe at me. An unspoken apology for that misstep.

Longing swelled in my chest—to accept that apology and his request. I swallowed hard.

I wanted it too much. I wanted to keep talking with him, not just to earn his trust and find openings to protect him, but just for the sake of knowing him better, being near him, feeling he'd chosen my company. But I couldn't forget what a mess I could make if the bare hand at my side brushed his even for an instant. Accidental contact during the controlled drills was easy to avoid. While free sparring with a novice? It was a much bigger risk.

"Maybe another time," I said before I stepped away. But I couldn't pretend I didn't see the way his shoulders stiffened, just a little, as if I'd slapped him.

CHAPTER NINE

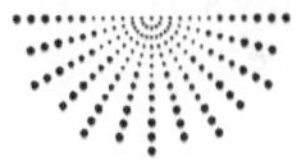

I'D BEEN a dedicated enough trainee for the last month and a half that Coach didn't blink when I stepped out of practice ten minutes early. I walked into the women's change room like I normally would have, headed straight out the door into the hallway, and ducked into the men's side.

The room smelled like floor polish and boy sweat. Wrinkling my nose, I scanned the benches. The clothes Darton had been wearing when he'd confronted me sat in a pile on one beside the wall. I pulled out the baggy of supplies I'd brought. Casting actual magic on anything of his was a bad idea—our dark fae mercenary might sense the resonance that would result. But plenty of things had their own power without my adding any oomph to it.

I grabbed his shoes. Brown suede sneakers—I could approve the style and the convenient texture of the material. Hopefully these were the ones he mainly wore. I could trust the average guy not to have a wide variety of shoes. I rubbed the sides and soles with the mixture of powdered salt and herbs I'd blended this morning. It wouldn't be enough to repel a really determined gloom, but it'd discourage most of them from getting too close.

When I blew at the sneakers, the visible powder drifted away. The suede showed only a faint scuffing, not so much I thought Darton would notice. I set the sneakers down and hightailed it out of there before the rest of the fencing club retired from the gym.

Between that and the large ring of enchanted salt I'd spent all yesterday laying down through town, I could rest a little easier even when Darton ventured a little off campus. But only a little. It wasn't enough. The mercenary's magic was reaching him somehow, if only with that vague pain. I wanted to cut it off completely.

I stewed over the problem as I changed. A salve, maybe. I could tell Darton it was for sore muscles—a special formula I'd brought a few containers of from back home. He might have warmed up to me enough to take it already. I could cook up something that really would soothe aches and pains while also providing a barrier against magical interference.

Perfect. Now I was imagining him rubbing his hands over his naked limbs. I yanked my head out of that daydream and hurried for the door.

"Emmaline!" a cheerful voice greeted me the second I stepped out. Priya was waiting in the hall. I'd been so busy worrying about Darton that I'd forgotten she often stopped by after practice on Mondays to walk home with me. She had an elective in the same building those afternoons.

For the first few seconds, her grin lifted my spirits. Then her smile turned sly. She hooked her arm around mine and tugged me down the hall, leaning in conspiratorially.

"You didn't tell me he joined fencing club. Sneaky girl. Please tell me you've made a move on him by now."

My face heated. And this was exactly *why* I hadn't told Priya about how often I was now seeing Darton.

"I haven't, and I'm not planning on it," I said. "I don't want to."

"Don't lie to me. I saw how you looked at him when he heroically came to your rescue."

"I don't want to make a move on him," I repeated firmly. I

wasn't even lying… if we were only counting the decisions I made in my head and not the rest of my body's desires.

Priya sighed. "Fine. But we *are* going to sit down and have a talk about the problems with being all work and no play someday soon. Speaking of hangouts, what do you want to cook tomorrow?"

We usually handled our meals separately, but as we'd moved from roommates to tentative friends, we'd reserved Tuesday nights for what Priya called "girl time." We made dinner together, picked a movie to watch or one of her video games to play, and just relaxed. Deciding what to cook was a key component of the fun. Priya always wanted to experiment with new flavor combinations, and I liked to take on recipes that challenged my chemistry skills.

"There was that soufflé recipe we decided to hold off on last time," I said. "The one with the yam. Or if you're up for something spicy, I stumbled on a lamb curry with cream recipe that sounded good. Unless you had something else in mind?"

"Maybe, but I'm not sure it's up to your standards of difficulty." Priya gave me a teasing nudge. "Show me the curry one. I could go for lamb. It's my turn to do the grocery shopping, right?"

"Yep." Thankfully, because my other cooking project was going to take up most of my non-school time in the next twenty-four hours.

I found the bookmark on my phone and handed it to Priya as we walked. Newly fallen leaves scattered the sidewalks, dappling the pavement yellow and red. The crisp sunlight beaming down from the cloudless sky lit them up. The breeze that licked over my hair was tart but not outright cold.

This was my favorite part of fall—the colorful, refreshingly cool beginning. I wasn't all that fond of the end, when the trees had turned into skeletons and the leaves to rotting mush.

Would I get to see that end before my own came again? My chest clenched at the thought of starting over, waiting through all those childhood years, playing the game of being a regular human being, until I crossed paths with my king once more.

It used to be easier. We used to be reborn within a mile of each other. I'd find him sooner—but then he'd start to wake sooner, the darkness would descend on him sooner, and we'd both die sooner. So, okay, that hadn't been an ideal scenario either. But the time it took before the magic drew us back together stretched longer each time. I didn't like to think of what that might mean. What if someday I stopped finding him altogether?

Nope. Not following those depressing thoughts today. Maybe the mercenary would give up once I had my new protections in place and bugger off. Maybe the gods would reach down from the sky and tell me what the hell I'd been thinking when I'd cast this spell in the first place. Hey, a wizard could dream.

At the apartment, I hustled into my bedroom to pop open the bin of supplies I'd hauled back from my storage locker. Priya had said she was going out to meet with a study partner after she ate, and then I'd have the kitchen to myself.

I retrieved and sorted the ingredients I'd need, pummeled the ones that needed grinding into submission, and carried everything out into the main room after I heard the front door click shut behind Priya. Making a salve that was effective for its declared purpose and my own secret ones was going to take several steps, but at least the work kept my hands and my mind busy. Less room to fret about what I'd do if this plan didn't work after all.

I was stirring the second pot, the steam dampening my bangs so they stuck to my forehead, when my phone rang where I'd left it on the counter. My parents' home number came up on the screen. I hesitated, but they were due for a call. I was going to need to talk to them soon if I didn't want *them* fretting. My stomach sank as I hit the accept button.

"Hey," I said in a false-chipper voice.

"Hi, honey," my mom said. "Is this a good time for us to chat?"

There probably wasn't going to be a truly good time again in this lifetime. I exhaled. "Yeah. This is perfect."

I wanted to talk to her—I really did. But there was so much I *couldn't* talk to her about now. This part of the cycle, the part where everything in my current life started falling apart, wasn't easy even in the crummy family situations I'd been born into sometimes in the past. And my parents in this life weren't crummy at all. What I'd said to Darton was true. Through my childhood oddities and the decisions I couldn't explain, they'd always accepted and supported me. Just hearing Mom's gentle voice sent a stab of homesickness through me.

I might never see them again. I'd known that when I'd said my good-byes in August, but now, after everything that had happened in the last two weeks, that possibility felt far too likely.

"Is everything still going well at the new school?" Mom said. "I guess you must be into midterms now."

The potion in the pot was starting to thicken. I stirred harder. "Yep. Everything's going great. I aced my first two."

"Well, congratulations. You know we're so happy that the move has worked out for you, even if we don't get to see you as often."

"Five more weeks to go until Thanksgiving." I managed to keep my voice breezy, but I had to change the subject. "Did you get that problem with your art supplier worked out?" Mom ran an interior decorating business.

"Oh, I had to cut those ties, but I found a new company that seems more together." I could almost hear the shake of her head. "I've got to look out for my own customers, you know?"

"Of course."

I kept the conversation focused on what she and Dad were up to as I took the pot off the element to cool and mixed in a few additional ingredients. Finally, Mom said, "I know you're working hard to start off on the right foot there, but don't forget to take some time for yourself now and then, all right?"

The comment echoed Priya's about all work and no play. I bit my lip, wondering what she'd think if she'd known I'd already skipped four classes in the last week while trying to stay on top of my other, more pressing responsibility. The one she'd never know about.

"Of course, Mom." I swallowed hard. If the situation escalated quickly, I might not even get another chance to *talk* to her or Dad. "I love you."

"Love you too, hon," Mom said, and then the salt in my pocket jittered against my thigh. I froze.

"I, um, actually have to get going," I said quickly.

"Is something wrong?"

Yes. So bloody much. "Nope, just got another call I was expecting coming in. A boy." She'd like that.

"Oh, well, don't let me keep you then." She chuckled, and then she was gone from the line.

I dropped my spoon and rested my hand over the fabric. The salt trembled against my fingers. I closed my eyes, absorbing the sense of it. The gloom had crossed the barrier I'd laid in the southwest end of town, heading east. Not too close to campus. Maybe it would do me a solid and head back in the opposite direction?

I'd barely had time to hope when a vision socked me between the eyes. An image flashed into my mind: Darton leaning against a bar stool with a beer glass in one hand, the reddish glow of the pub lighting tinted his sun-streaked hair and tanned skin. The grin on his face was probably melting the knees of every female person, and possibly some male, in a twenty-foot radius.

The vision faded as quickly as it had hit me, and I grasped the edge of the counter. My heart was racing and my stomach churning with the certainty that the spot I'd just seen was exactly where the gloom was headed.

CHAPTER TEN

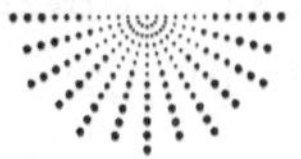

THE SALT in my pocket jumped the second I stepped out of the cab into the ruddy lights of the pub. The gloom was close, but I'd gotten here fast enough to cut it off. Thank the light I'd caught the name of the place on Darton's coaster.

No one I recognized was standing near the front window, but I pulled my jacket's hood farther over my head anyway. Following the jittering in my pocket, I ducked down the alley toward the back of the building.

I emerged into a small, little-used courtyard. The aged wooden bench behind the pub was missing its middle backboard, and a tang of rotting garbage seeped into the cool evening air from the dumpster on the other side. Thin streaks of light from the streetlamps trickled into the space from the adjoining alleys.

But nowhere near enough light to deter a gloom. The one I'd come for was just slinking along the wall of the restaurant opposite the pub. My hand clenched around the twig I'd been carrying since I left the apartment.

I couldn't get down to serious business yet, not with Darton so close, but I should have at least a few minutes to myself back here in the dark. I'd trap the gloom, conceal myself, and wait until after closing when I could count on working uninterrupted. If the dark fae mercenary had lent this bit of vermin his magic, I might learn something about him from it.

"*Still you'll stay*," I murmured. The twig went brittle against my fingers. The gloom jerked to a stop where it had been wavering across the cracked pavement toward the pub. That minor enchantment would hold it in place while I completed the full binding spell.

I drew a vial of ambergris oil from my bag and sprinkled it on the ground in a circle around the scrap of living shadow, speaking the incantation under my breath as I went. Then I pulled out a wand. "*Through flesh, not bone*," I said as I pressed the oak tip to my left palm. My skin split with a stinging pain. Blood welled up along the thin line I'd drawn. I squeezed my hand into a fist, winced, and let drop after drop fall along the ring I'd marked with the oil.

With the circle complete, I clapped both my hands together three times. I bowed my head, ready to call out the final threads of magic from the wand.

"Hey!"

The voice rang out through the darkness from just a few feet behind me. I fumbled with the wand and jerked it behind my arm. When I turned, a far-too-familiar figure was emerging from the shadows of the alley. My pulse lurched. I stepped between him and the circle I'd drawn —between Darton and the gloom that had come looking for him.

The guy I'd seen in my mind's eye less than half an hour ago peered at me and then beyond. My shoulders stiffened. Swine crud and cattle sod. Of all the people who might have wandered back at here at this exact moment, why had it needed to be *him*?

Darton squinted at me in the dim light. "Emma?"

He must not have recognized me until just now. He must've heard my clapping hands and come over to see who was back here.

Down the alley, the pub's side door was slightly ajar, spilling an amber glow into the space.

"Darton." I kept my voice as even as I could. If he'd waited just a couple more minutes to come out for a smoke or whatever his original purpose had been, I'd have completed the spell. I could have made my excuses and left. Yet again, he'd caught me in the middle of business I couldn't leave unfinished.

"What are you doing?" he said.

A fair question to ask someone lurking in an abandoned courtyard, but that didn't mean I had to like answering it. I managed to maneuver the wand into my bag while gesturing with my other hand to distract him.

"A friend of mine's cat got out of her house a few days ago. I was walking by and thought I saw it run back here. I guess it took off faster than I could catch up."

A lost-pet scenario tended to provoke sympathy rather than suspicion—and it wasn't unbelievable. I really had chased after a runaway puppy of my cousin's down an alley back home when I was fifteen.

What I'd forgotten to consider was the state of my hand.

"Are you *bleeding*?" Darton took another step toward me. I dropped my palm to my side before he could try to examine it—to *touch* it—and groped for an excuse.

"I tripped, running after the cat. It's nothing. Just a scratch." I pulled my gloves on, hiding the wound.

Darton still looked skeptical. That was no good. I needed him to leave.

"What are *you* doing back here?" I asked pointedly.

He motioned vaguely toward the pub. "I just needed to duck out for a second. It gets… stuffy in there after a while." He paused. From his stance and the way he drew in his breath, I gathered he wasn't outright drunk but definitely a bit buzzed. "Funny, it seems like everywhere I go these days, there you are."

I crossed my arms. "I don't know. From my perspective, it's the other way around."

"Touché." He gave me a slanted smile. "I guess I invaded your fencing club first."

He didn't back off on his present invasion, though. He ambled over to the bench and sat down. Then he gave me an uncertain glance.

He didn't know how I felt about him, obviously. He wasn't sure whether our banter had been friendly, tolerant, or maybe even only irritated on my side. To be fair, it had kind of been all three.

He ducked his head, running a hand through his hair. There was something so lost in his expression, just for a second, that my heart squeezed. But I might still have resisted if his arm hadn't lowered a moment later so that his elbow could press against his side. That fatal spot. The mercenary was still getting to him.

I had no salve to give him yet. The best I could offer was my company, which for whatever reason, he seemed to want. And I did feel awkward standing there. So I meandered over to the bench and perched at the opposite end, leaving a space between us.

Darton rested his arm on the top of the bench as he turned toward me. "You seem like a person who knows her own mind," he said. A little of his usual cockiness had come back into his tone.

"I don't know if I'd say that. There's far too much of it to keep track of."

His brow knit, and then he laughed. "And you're truly weird, you know that?"

I scuffed my shoe against the gritty concrete. "I've been told once or twice."

"I just meant—like you talked about changing colleges. You know what you want to do, and how to do it, and you don't let other people's opinions get in the way."

"Hmm," I said. "I've just learned that if there's something you want, other people's opinions *shouldn't* matter. Unless they know something you don't."

He nodded. "See, you say that, and it totally makes sense. But I've never heard anyone put it that way before. I can honestly say I've never met anyone quite like you."

I couldn't hold back my guffaw at that. I tried to cover the sound with a cough, but Darton caught my amusement anyway.

"You don't believe me?"

"No, it's not that. It's… never mind." I shook my head. No, he'd never met anyone like me, except all the dozens of times he'd met *me* before. But, gods willing, it'd be a long time before he could get that joke.

If we were going to chat, I'd rather we keep off the topic of me. "Is that a problem you run into a lot?" I added. "People's opinions getting in the way of what you want to do? Your friends don't seem all that judge-y, at least from the little I've talked to them." Keevan and Izzy had been friendlier to me than Darton had.

"Well, no, not my close ones… but I don't think even they would necessarily understand everything." Darton paused. That distant look came over his face again as he gazed across the courtyard. "Was that part of transferring schools hard for you?" he asked abruptly. "Leaving your friends behind?"

I shrugged. "There were people I enjoyed hanging out with now and then, but honestly, I'm kind of a loner."

A smile tugged at his lips. "You do give off that vibe. But you were with that friend of yours the other day. You came with her to watch a football practice even though you're not really into the game."

Why were we talking about me again? "Priya came with the apartment," I said, but even as the words came out, I didn't like how flippant they sounded. Pri deserved more than a careless dismissal. "And we get along well. I like her. But I don't need some huge social circle. Friend quota filled."

"No room for more then?" Darton teased before I could turn the conversation back to him.

A not entirely unpleasant prickle ran down my back. He was flirting again. I eyed him. "I decide that on a case-by-case basis."

"Sure. There are lots of ways you could vet potential candidates. Test their science knowledge. Check out their fencing skills…"

"I don't know. That could be a good idea." I'd meant to bounce his joke back at him, but my mind spun off in another direction. *Wouldn't* it be nice if I could set up a series of trials and have people clamoring to prove themselves? Not for me, but for him. My king had once had people competing to stand by his side and protect him back in our first lives. It'd certainly been convenient, even if they hadn't succeeded in the end.

It wasn't as if the job I'd done of protecting him had worked out all that well either.

Darton pointed a finger at me. "You're plotting something. I can tell."

"Nothing to do with you," I said airily to cover the bald lie.

He laughed. "I don't know if that should make me less worried or more." His gaze sharpened again. Those dark blue eyes caught and held mine. "Do you really not have anyone in your life who's important enough to miss?"

I pulled my gaze away. My throat had tightened. "My parents, I guess. But, you know, they're my parents."

And him. Always him. The person he was meant to be—the person he'd become, over and over. The person I still had to save—properly, this time.

Not that I could say anything like that to him in his present state.

"Emma," Darton said. Emotion colored his voice, raw and open, and I couldn't bear to find out how he was looking at me or to respond to whatever weakness he thought he'd discovered in me. So I let myself be a coward, keeping my eyes trained on the shadowy ground.

I didn't see him reaching out.

His fingertips grazed my cheek as if to brush my hair back from my face. I flinched away—too late. The spark of the contact, bare skin to bare skin, was already flaring into my brain. Memory flooded my head, almost as vivid as a vision.

The king's son, now king, settled his crown on his head. He never looked totally comfortable wearing it in those moments when it was just the two of us before he stepped from his private chambers to greet whichever people had assembled to await his presence. Before them, as if by magic, the gold circlet would become as much a part of him as the dimple in his cheek when he shot a smile my way.

Today, that smile was slightly grim. "Have you seen any definite sign of a problem?"

I shifted on the padded chair. Bird chatter and joyful voices carried from outside. They didn't penetrate my uneasiness.

"No. But I know something is coming. I can feel it, Arthur. The fae all but confirmed it."

He nodded, the sunlight from the arched window catching on his bright hair. "I'll keep my eyes open, but I need to do this. The people need it, after all the fighting... Whatever happens, we'll face it, as we always do."

Did he fully believe that? I knew I didn't. But my king didn't have my instincts, hadn't seen my visions. And there amid the whitewashed walls and opulent fabrics of his chambers, it might have been hard to imagine anything could go wrong. Not here, not now.

But it would. It would.

The king stepped away from the mirror toward the door, and before I quite knew I was going to move, I'd grabbed his hand. He stopped and looked back at me. The shadow of our earlier argument crossed his face. I braced myself.

"Your Highness," I said, and then, because that sounded far too formal for what I meant to say, "Arthur. I just... I want you to know how much it's meant to me, to be able to serve you as long as I have. After everything we have faced, and no matter what happens next, there's nowhere I'd rather be."

His jaw twitched. The fear he'd been suppressing flickered in his eyes and melted away. He squeezed my fingers, and my pulse skipped. "Thank you," he said. And—

Darton scrambled off the bench. The sudden motion jerked me back to the present. He backed away, his eyes wide and his face pale. His hands shook as he tucked them under his folded arms.

"I've got to—" he said, catching himself on the verge of a stammer. I pushed to my feet, my stomach knotting. That touch would have sent a bolt of memory through him too, but one even stronger than the one that had hit me, because it was the first he'd ever had in this life. Because he couldn't have been remotely prepared.

It would have felt intensely real and yet absolutely alien. I didn't know *what* he'd seen, which part of that first life had hijacked his mind, but hijacking was the only word for it. He couldn't know I'd had anything to do with that strange sensation, but that didn't mean he'd want to be experiencing a mental breakdown in front of a relative stranger.

"It's getting late," he finally said without meeting my eyes. Then he swiveled on his heel and hurried down the alley toward the street.

My body ached to run after him, but I held myself back. One sliver of contact had only just cracked him open. If I didn't touch him again, he'd wake up by increments. Slowly.

Normally, I could have counted on having at least a week or two before his aura seeped through enough to draw the glooms directly to him… but the ones the mercenary had lent power to had been drawn to him already. I was going to have to stick extra close to him from here on—without him thinking I'd turned into a full-out stalker.

I pressed my hand to my forehead and dragged in a rough breath. All wasn't lost. I still had ways I could at least try to protect him. I'd known this moment would eventually come.

I just hadn't expected it *tonight*.

There was no time now for extended experiments. I scowled at the gloom I'd trapped and fished out my wand. *"Darkness begone,"* I snapped. The creature dissipated with a faint popping sound. I spun and jogged to the street, hailing a cab on my phone as I went.

CHAPTER ELEVEN

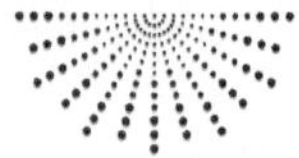

Darton set off toward the football field in the hazy dawn light. He looked paler than usual but otherwise no worse for wear. A damp breeze tickled across my neck where I was watching him from under the awning of a campus cafe. I tugged my jacket tighter around me.

No more glooms had shown up overnight, but I wasn't counting on that luck holding. Now that my king's spirit had started waking up, there was no point in aiming for subtlety. I'd chucked the salve in the garbage last night. I had a spell that had served me well in the past, one that would create a sort of bubble around Darton that should at least slow the super-powered glooms down. Give me a chance to dispatch them before they got close enough to taste him.

If they got that first taste, the situation would be cocked up even without a fae mercenary breathing down our necks.

Unfortunately, the spell came with two problems. The first being that I needed part of Darton's physical essence to work the casting. And that wasn't the sort of thing I could just go up to a person and ask them for.

The second problem was I had to cast the spell right on him, in his presence, over the course of several minutes. The previous times I'd used it, it had been after Arthur's soul was awake enough to know who both he and I were. I hadn't figured out yet how I was going to pull it off without Darton deciding I was insane.

One challenge at a time.

I'd just drained the last of my bitter coffee, grimacing but grateful for the caffeine kick, when Keevan emerged from the residence building. My magical digging into school records had told me he and Darton were roomies—and that he had class at eight on Tuesday mornings.

As soon as his lanky frame had disappeared, I got up and headed for the residence building's entrance. The heavy stealth enchantment I'd cast over myself itched like a thick wool sweater, only one that covered me from head to toe. I hurried up to the third floor, around the corner and halfway down the hall, to Darton and Keevan's room. The students I passed brushed right by me as if I wasn't there.

By the time I reached the door, my skin was outright burning. Maintaining full invisibility was a pain in the ass. *"Open,"* I whispered to the lock, and then darted into the room.

I kicked the door shut behind me and shook off the stealth enchantment with a sigh of relief. I'd rather cast it again when I had to leave than conduct my search with it gnawing at me. Both guys should be occupied elsewhere for at least another couple hours.

The room was laid out in typical dorm fashion: a bed, a desk, and a shelving unit on either side. A glance at the shelves told me Darton's side was the left, where football strategy manuals squeezed up against politics, sociology, and law texts, and a bunch of novels that looked like legal thrillers. The lack of trophies and other badges of honor surprised me. He kept his things pretty spartan.

I pulled back the covers on his bed, but it appeared he was a bit of a neat freak in general. Not a single stray hair remained on his pillow or beneath his sheet. I frowned and smoothed the navy duvet back into place. The guy had to at least have a brush somewhere.

A caddy with shower supplies sat at the back of his desk, but it didn't supply me with a hair either. I shifted through the books stacked next to his computer. My hand paused over what looked like a sketchbook.

Darton *drew*? That didn't fit my impressions of the guy. I eased the sketchbook out of the stack and flipped it open.

The first several pages revealed nothing remarkable. He had some skill, but most of the pencil drawings looked unfinished, abandoned before he'd given them a real effort. Most of them were figures: a professor at the front of a lecture hall, a guy I thought was Keevan making a wild gesture, Izzy sitting at a table with the end of her pen pressed to her lips.

That last image gave my gut a little twist before I turned the page. Then my breath stopped completely.

He'd drawn *me*. From memory, obviously, and not an exact likeness by any means, but there I was in my fencing uniform, sabre in hand and mask in the other, my dark hair pulled back in my habitual ponytail. He'd barely marked my mouth, as if he hadn't been sure what expression to give me, but my eyes were carefully drawn. They peered from the page as if in thoughtful contemplation.

There were a couple more after. Lighter, hastier sketches: me standing by a tree, my arms crossed and hair lightly windblown—a memory from when Izzy had been doing her survey?—and a close-up of my face, the paper worn where he'd drawn and erased and drawn again, unsatisfied with the sharp line of my cheek, the slant of my jaw.

A shiver tickled through me. I shut the sketchbook and tucked it into place on the desk. My chest had gone tight.

He'd noticed me. He was intrigued. I could have guessed as much from our conversation last night.

There was always a connection between us. How could there

not be, after the history we'd shared? It was never enough, though. I couldn't let myself dwell on it, let myself hope it meant more than it did. I wasn't going to be that selfish or that careless again.

A narrow basket wedged between the desk and the bookshelf caught my eye. Laundry hamper—jackpot!

I pawed through the small heap of clothes and found a polo shirt with a few gold-blond hairs clinging to it. I plucked them off and dropped them into a cloth bag. Then I dropped the shirt, turning to go.

The door swung open.

I froze. Keevan froze too, staring at me from the doorway. "*Don't see me, never did,*" I spat out over the thudding of my heart.

The air contracted around me, and a splintering pain jabbed through my nerves. All the twigs I'd hidden in various pockets crumbled to dust.

Keevan blinked. His forehead furrowed. "Art?" he said. He stepped inside tentatively, his gaze searching the room. He probably still had the sense that something was wrong, even if he couldn't remember what he'd seen to make him think so.

I dodged him—he'd still feel me if I touched him—and sidled to the door, managing to dart out just before he pushed it closed. It thudded nearly as loud as my still-racing pulse. I stopped in the hallway, recovering my composure.

That had been much closer than I liked. I'd lost at least a week of life casting that spell so suddenly, unprepared.

And now I was out of magical materials. I hurried down the hall. I'd have to find a suitable tree on campus and relieve it of several twigs before I could even think about casting Darton's protection.

The clinking of test tubes and rasping of pens over paper settled my mind. I bent over my own notebook, studying the final results in the chemistry apparatus I'd set up for the day's lab. The acid gave off a pungent, soapy smell. As I wrote out my observations, a plan finally started to form in the back of my mind.

I needed to be within ten feet of Darton for the protection spell to work, but a physical barrier wouldn't affect my ability to cast. It was the middle of the afternoon now—hardly anyone was in the dorms. When he finished the second of his back-to-back lectures, I could conjure a little sleepiness in him, nudge him into taking a quick nap, and sneak into the room next to his to cast the spell through the wall.

It'd take a lot of energy, but he'd never have to know I was even nearby. I could pull that off.

"Emma," Professor Kapoor called as I was passed his desk on my way out. I stopped. Uh oh. Had I forgotten an assignment amid the last two weeks' distractions?

He lowered his voice. "You missed our last class," he said. "And you looked somewhat… out of sorts when you came in today. If you don't want to talk, I'm not going to press, but I wanted to at least ask if everything is all right."

My face heated. I hadn't realized my angst had been that blatant. But I was touched by his concern, even if it meant I was going to have to lie to yet one more person in this life.

"Everything is fine." I forced a smile. I might not make it to even one more of these labs after today. "But thank you for asking."

"Okay," Professor Kapoor said. "You obviously have a lot of talent for this work. I try to support that when I see it in a student. If you ever do need extra time because of outside circumstances, please come talk to me."

A lump rose in my throat. By the light, how I wished I could get that kind of offer in the area I really did need extra time. "I will."

At least I had a plan now. I could make this work. My confidence crept back as I meandered over to Darton's lecture hall. His class wasn't over for another half hour, so I just staked out a secluded spot down the hall from the room and breathed slow and even to steady my nerves.

The minutes ticked by, but the door didn't open. Neither Darton nor his classmates emerged. Odd. When the next class of the afternoon started arriving and heading inside, I peeled myself off the wall and strolled over.

The seats in the hall were empty except for the few scattered students who'd shown up for the next one. My stomach dropped.

What the hell had happened? Had the professor let them out extra early—or taken them on some sort of field trip? Or maybe the class had been outright cancelled.

It didn't matter. The result was the same—I had no idea where Darton was now. And no way of knowing where he might be before he decided to head back to his room for the night.

The campus was big. I didn't have much hope of simply stumbling on him, even though I'd managed to when it *wasn't* convenient. I checked the library, the football field, and the sandwich place he and Keevan appeared to be addicted to. No luck.

I wandered until I reached the front gate. The shadows were lengthening as the afternoon stretched toward evening. Tension wound through my gut.

I knew the soul of my king nearly as well as I knew my own. Now that it had started to stir inside Darton, I could reach out to it through my magic and know exactly where he was. The trouble with that approach was that connecting with him would release a little of that energy into the air. Any gloom tasked with searching for him would latch onto it in an instant.

I wavered for a minute, but then the glooms made my decision for me. The salt pouch in my pocket quivered. A gloom had drifted over one of my boundary lines—north of here.

It wasn't on campus yet, but I couldn't even say for sure Darton was still here. I slipped a twig into my hand, closed my eyes, and exhaled the ancient words. *"Where are you, my liege?"*

The awareness of him hit me like an elbow to the ribs. About a mile away, on the exact opposite side of campus.

Way too close to the gloom I'd sensed.

A knife of panic cut through me. My legs were already striding forward when my eyes popped open. I pushed myself into a run.

As I crossed the first major courtyard, the salt pouch jittered again. Two glooms—no, three—no, *four*. The first had been coincidence, but these had been drawn by my call. Damn it. I ran faster, ignoring the odd looks the other students were turning my way.

I could have run faster if I'd brought my magic into play, but I wasn't sure I'd make it to Darton if I put on a public display that obvious.

My sneakers thudded over the pavement. I dashed down the paths between the buildings, across a field, and around the horticultural department's conservatory. The salt vibrated at a continuous if erratic rhythm. I didn't have the wherewithal to keep count or track where each impulse was coming from. My chest was aching by the time I stumbled to a halt at the end of the garden on the other side of the greenhouse.

Darton was there, all right. Keevan and one of his other friends too. Darton was pointing out something in a sheaf of papers to them as they ambled between the beds of half-wilted flowers. Izzy had wandered a little apart from the boys to eye the glossy apples in a hunched tree. Some other students were laughing as they kicked around a hacky sack to my left, but they weren't the company I was worried about.

No, what concerned me were the five glooms crawling across the garden from various directions—converging on the spot where Darton now stood.

Before I could spring forward, before I could do *any*thing, three of them drifted right against his legs.

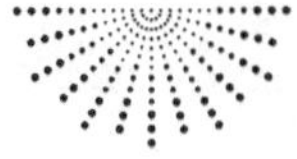

No! The protest echoed in my head, but I didn't let it escape my mouth.

I could still fix this. As long as none of the glooms drifted back to their master to report what they'd found, we were safe. Relatively speaking.

The glooms were too far away for the fae dagger I'd stuffed in my bag to be of any use. I palmed a handful of twigs and cast a quick distraction spell over me to divert casual attention. In the few seconds that took, the glooms that had touched Darton whirled around and rippled away across the garden, hugging the patches of shadow along the flowerbeds. The two latecomers twisted around his ankles and quivered giddily.

"*Darkness begone,*" I whispered and jabbed my hand toward the closest gloom. It wisped apart into the air. Another had just streaked past Izzy's apple tree. Her head jerked around as if she'd seen it from the corner of her eye. I pointed and spoke the dispelling words again.

One of the two latecomers tumbled across the wilted flowers

toward me. I exterminated it with a mutter and a slice of my arm. Two left.

That pair had darted in the opposite direction, farther away from me. I skirted a rose bush, the lingering floral perfume cloying in my nose. The leading gloom whipped between the thumping feet of the hacky sack players, and I managed to throw my magic across the distance after it. The effort drained the life from all but the last of my twigs.

The last gloom had flitted out of view beyond the ring of students. I hurried after it, my heart pounding. There—it was making for the hedge at the far end of the garden. I grasped my final twig. My arm jerked up.

And a body rammed into my side.

I tripped, my feet tangling, and hit the ground. The hacky sack player who'd dashed backward into me stumbled and swayed around. He raised his hands, his face flushing red.

"Sorry! Crap. Are you okay?"

I didn't care about his apology or his question. I scrambled onto my feet and groped after the twig I'd dropped. Where was the gloom? I threw myself around his group, toward the hedge.

Nothing but bare, regular grass and leaves met my gaze. My heart plummeted.

It was gone.

It was gone, and it had touched Darton before it had fled. Tasted the soul inside him and the magic that bound it there. Escaped to carry the message to every creature of darkness that might be eager to share in that tasting. Which experience told me was an awful lot of them.

We might be dead before our mercenary even got here.

My throat had constricted. I fought to swallow. The guy who'd bumped into me had followed me.

"Hey," he said. "Is everything all right?"

Why the hell wouldn't people stop asking me that?

"Yes," I bit out. "Fine." Other than the part where everything was absolutely wretched. The sun was sinking behind the conservatory. When night fell, all the creatures of the dark rabble would be at their fullest power—and I'd be at my weakest.

And it was all my fault. Something in the spell I'd used to sustain our lives and bind the Darkest One away spoke to the lesser darkness. Maybe they sensed a thread of their highest master in it. Or that Arthur's spirit lived on in defiance of her. Whatever the case, they would try to do what she had failed to—wipe him from this world. They'd nearly succeeded more than a hundred times over.

I'd failed him again. We'd barely even come together in this life and I'd already failed him.

My fingers tightened around the remaining twig, not that I had much use for it now. I glanced over at Darton. He was still laughing away with Keevan and the other guy, his back to me now. The distraction spell had been enough to stop him from noticing me even in my collision with the hacky sack guy.

Izzy had come up beside him. Her hand rested on his arm with a familiarity that dragged the feelings I'd been suppressing—and *really* didn't have room for right now—into my chest. I gritted my teeth.

I wasn't going to give up yet. The protection spell I'd planned wouldn't repel the glooms now that they'd had a taste of the king's spirit, but I could shred any that came near him. Over and over, as long as it took, until I figured out a new plan.

Of course, that meant *I* had to be near him too.

Darton and his friends headed toward the edge of the garden. I shook off the distraction spell, pushed aside my doubts, and propelled myself forward. I'd made it halfway over before the sound of my feet must have caught Darton's attention. He was the first of them to look my way.

Our eyes met. In that first instant, I saw an echo of last night's bewilderment. My steps slowed. He blinked, and just like that, he looked more like the cocky, assured guy I'd met in the middle of fencing practice.

He said something to the others and headed my way while they continued across campus. Whatever he wanted to say to me, he apparently didn't want them hearing it. I stopped and let him come to me.

He halted a few feet away from me. "Emma."

"Darton."

"So we run into each other again," he said. "Are you looking for another lost cat?"

His tone was teasing, but his gaze stayed wary as he waited for my response. Was he suspicious of me or worried he'd offended me?

"No," I said, and found my mind was too scattered to produce a halfway decent excuse. "Just stretching my legs. Too much time sitting in class today."

He nodded and lowered his eyes. "Thank you. For sticking around with me while I was rambling last night. I must have had more to drink than I realized."

The tension in my body eased. He was only worried. Well, why would he assume some weird vision that had popped into his head had come *because* of me?

Even if I'd been fairly useless in the last ten minutes, I could at least do this one thing for him. "It was fine," I said, offering him a slight smile. "I think I kind of like little-bit-buzzed Darton."

He raised an eyebrow. "*Only* that Darton?"

"I'm withholding judgment on the sober one pending further information." I gathered my nerve. "Maybe—partly in the interests of collecting said information—the bunch of us could grab dinner? If you all don't have something else lined up." I motioned to his friends, who'd just reached the conservatory.

Darton hesitated, but before I could think my suggestion had come out badly, a grin sprang onto his face. "Sure. I don't think we'd nailed anything down for tonight. Let me see what everyone's up for."

I let out my breath as he loped away to check in with his friends. Suggesting a group hangout had felt like a safer bet than trying to convince him to spend the whole evening with me alone.

My phone buzzed. I pulled it out and winced.

At the grocery store, Priya had texted me. *Was it ground or whole coriander we needed?*

I'm so sorry, I typed back. *I'm going to have to bail on dinner.* My fingers hovered over the screen. This once, going with the truth was probably the excuse she'd take the easiest. *I'm going out with Darton and his friends.*

A string of winking and thumbs-up emojis blew up my phone. *Go you! It's about time. Hey, I'll clear out for the night. Don't want worries about thin walls giving you an excuse not to seal the deal.*

It's not a DATE, I replied. Gods, even over the phone, she'd managed to make me blush.

Sure, sure. It's all good. I've been meaning to drop in on my cousin anyway.

There was no point in arguing with her. I shoved my phone into my bag and turned toward Darton's group.

The moment I looked their way, Keevan and Izzy waved to me. They turned and walked away as Darton strode back over. A prickle ran down my back.

"It turns out they've got someplace else to be, so it's just the two of us, I guess." Darton cocked his head. "If you think I'll be good enough company on my own."

Sod it. It practically *was* a date. I willed my legs not to start backing away.

I could handle this. I could keep myself in check. I *had* to—for Darton and the king he didn't know he was.

"I guess we'll see," I said, reflecting his casual air back at him. "If you start boring me, we'll just have to get some drinks into you."

CHAPTER THIRTEEN

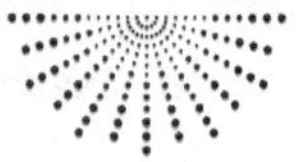

"And *then*," I said, sweeping my arm for dramatic effect, "after all that trouble, they come running across the parking lot to realize they've been chasing the wrong bus the whole time. It's a bunch of high schoolers partying after prom, not the band."

Darton tipped his head back as he laughed. "God, Emma, I wish my parents had stories half that entertaining.

I smiled, running my finger through the sheen of condensation on the outside of my beer mug and making a concentrated effort not to ogle the slope of his neck from his throat to the V-neck of his sweater. My goal for the evening had been to keep Darton entertained enough that he'd want to stick around. So far that was working out, although I'd had to dig into my admittedly large stash of hippie-dippy stories from my parents' pre-parental escapades.

The campus bistro we'd ended up in was warm and bright enough to be falsely comforting, with a jangle of country music carrying over the chatter around us. Darton had eaten his way through a burger and fries and was now on his third beer. As far as he knew, I was on my second. Actually, I'd surreptitiously enchanted them into colored water. I wasn't going to risk impairing my own judgment any more than sharing the warmth of his presence did on its own.

"What did they do when they figured out the mistake?" Darton asked.

I leaned back in my chair. "My mom always gets a little vague at that point. I kind of suspect they talked their way onto the bus and partied like teenagers until the chaperone noticed and tossed them off.

"My dad was the kind of college guy who'd have been watching the hippies having the time of their lives and silently plotting how he'd 'show' them once he was rich." Darton took a swig from his beer and set it down on the wooden table with a thump. "He managed the rich part. I don't know if any of the kids who had more fun than him ever cared."

"And here I figured he must have been captain of the football team," I said lightly. "So you're not following in his footsteps?"

"Well… Same school, same major, same projected career path. I'm not straying very far."

"It seems like a pretty sweet path." Earlier in the evening, Darton had mentioned he was pre-law. Apparently his dad was a big-time corporate lawyer. "Nothing wrong with that."

A shadow crossed Darton's face. "Is life supposed to be that easy?"

I hesitated. I hadn't anticipated the shift in his mood. "What do you mean?"

"Honestly?" He looked at his beer mug instead of me. "I wish I could feel the way you do. Like I knew where I wanted to go with my life, to be sure I'm heading in the right direction and not just coasting along. This probably sounds like entitled whining, but no matter what I do… I always have this gnawing impression that it's not enough. Or not important enough."

A pang of sympathy filled my chest. That was the Arthur in him. The knowledge he was meant for greatness, as present as if it were written into his DNA.

He had been great. I just hadn't managed to preserve him in the time he was meant for.

"Why not do something that does feel important?" I said gently.

"I try." Darton laughed again, but this time without much humor. "But once I get going, nothing ever feels exactly right."

Because the sense of direction that's compelling you is fifteen hundred years out of date.

"You know the one thing I've done that feels like a real accomplishment?" he went on. "When I was twelve, my little sister fell in the pool. No one else was around. I jumped in and got her out. Did CPR and managed to get her breathing again. She'd have drowned if I hadn't moved that fast, if I hadn't remembered all that first aid training I learned in Boy Scouts."

"Saving someone's life is *definitely* an accomplishment."

"Yeah." He rubbed the back of his neck. "But I don't know how I'm ever going to do anything better than that. So is that it? I was at my best at twelve? Like I said, I know this sounds stupid. I'm not normally this woe-is-me. But I really do admire that about you. The certainty you have. Maybe that's why I like talking to you— hoping some of it might rub off on me."

He gave me a smile that was a little more relaxed, but I could still see the longing in the depths of his eyes. My throat tightened.

A real friend would have been able to comfort him. Reached across the table and squeezed his hand. Told him he'd find his way. But even with my gloves on—"My hands get cold all the time," I'd told him when he'd teased—I didn't want to take the chance of even that small physical gesture going wrong. And I couldn't bear to lie to him that blatantly.

He wasn't going to find his way—not as Darton Rowe, not as his father's son.

I could say *something* true, at least.

"I think I've given you the wrong impression," I said. "I knew what I wanted to study in college. With most other things... I have no idea what direction to go in. I just keep trying and hoping I'll eventually stumble on the right thing."

Darton bobbed his head, but I suspected he thought I was humoring him more than empathizing. He beckoned our waitress as she slipped by. "Check?"

My heart lurched, my gaze jerking to the window. It was fully dark outside now. No more glooms had come hunting Darton yet, but they'd be on their way. How was I going to keep him safe for the rest of the night? I couldn't expect him to stay up into the wee hours just chatting with a girl he barely knew.

The waitress dropped the receipt on the table, and Darton pulled out his wallet. I grabbed mine before he could try to pay for both our meals.

"Where are you heading now?" I asked as we waited for our change. I could have tried staking out his dorm room within a concealment spell, but that wouldn't help if the glooms seeped through the outer wall or the window or—

"I've got practice tomorrow morning," Darton said. "I should probably call it a night. But I'm glad we did this, Emma."

"Me too." I could lose him tonight, just like that. It all came down to the next few minutes.

He stood up to shrug on his jacket. I scooted to the end of the bench and scrambled to my feet so hastily my heel snagged on the table leg. I wobbled, and Darton caught my arm. My gaze fixed on his bare hand against the fabric of my shirt, and inspiration hit.

He wanted to be a hero. Deep down, that was what he'd always wanted.

I waited until we'd stepped outside and he turned to me to say his good-byes. The chill of the night air twisted around me. I braced myself. My gloved hand closed around his.

"Don't go."

I relaxed the careful control I'd been keeping over my expression, my emotions, and without even trying, nervous tears sprang to my eyes. Darton took one look at me and frowned.

"What's wrong?"

"I…" I sucked in a breath. "My roommate is out of town. It'll just be me at home. I don't know if I'll be okay on my own. I'm sorry, I realize it'd be a huge hassle, and I wouldn't ask if I knew anyone else I could—"

"Hold on." Darton looked confused, but at the same time, a heat had crept into his voice that did something funny to my stomach. "Are you asking me to come back to your place and spend the night?"

Darkness take me. That wasn't how I'd meant the request to sound. "No," I said quickly. I didn't have to fake my embarrassed stammering. "I mean—yes, I'm asking if you'd stay, but—on the couch, not, like, *sleeping together.*"

Darton eased his hand from mine to run it comfortingly up my arm. Sparks shot over my skin at the contact, even with the layers of my jacket and shirt in between. Oh, some part of me very much wished I had meant the proposition the way he'd first taken it.

"What's going on, Emma?" he said.

I made myself stare him right in the face and let the last memory of my last life swim up out of my consciousness. The broken and bruised body the dark rabble had left behind when they were done with him, because I hadn't been there like I should have been. A different man, but the same one.

"I don't think it's safe." My voice trembled of its own accord. "I'd just… I'll feel so much better if you're there with me. Just this once. Priya will be back tomorrow."

Darton's expression softened. "Okay. You've got nothing to worry about. I'll be there. It's not even that big a deal."

You don't have a clue. I smiled gratefully, blinking back the tears. Now how was I going to deal with the other half of the problem?

CHAPTER FOURTEEN

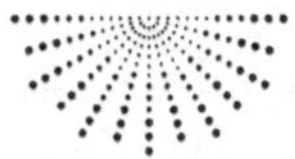

Darton snored. It wasn't a particularly obnoxious snore, at least
—just a low rumble that rose and ebbed with his breaths. After
several minutes, I started to find it somewhat comforting, mainly
because it told me he *was* still breathing.

I'd managed to put off any questions Darton might have had
after we'd gotten to the apartment by bustling around making up
the couch and thanking him profusely every time he'd opened his
mouth. Ducking into my bedroom with a minimum of socializing
had fit my frightened act, thank the light.

Of course, my fright wasn't entirely an act. I sat on my bed as
Darton washed up and hunkered down on the sofa, tracking his
movements by sound. My hand rested on the salt pouch in my
pocket.

Not even a gloom had trailed Darton here. So far. In some
ways, that worried me more. I'd have expected one or two that had
been in the area to have headed this way by now.

But these weren't glooms following their normal impulses. The
mercenary wasn't just lending them power. He was also controlling
them. To what end?

When Darton had been snoring long enough that I felt sure he was staying asleep, I inched open my bedroom door. I couldn't see him from that angle, but the thin light from the streetlamps beyond the living room window outlined the back of the couch, the entertainment unit, the kitchen island, and the front door. Settling myself on the hard floor where I could keep watch, I opened my bag and pulled out the supplies I'd been hauling around.

Maybe the spell I'd planned wouldn't hold off any gloom eager for the king's essence, but it might still slow them down a little. And damn it, I needed to do *something*.

I measured out the herbs on a silver plate, laid a circle of twigs around them, drew the symbols, and added the stolen hairs. The words of the incantation whispered over my lips. I closed the door just for a minute to light a flame on the plate. Then I blew the acrid smoke toward the living room, willing it through the door, across the floor, and around Darton's sleeping form.

There. It might not buy me more than an extra minute or two, but even a second's grace could make the difference between life and death.

I studied the shifting shadows in the main room and contemplated my next steps. If none of the dark rabble had come for Darton by morning, I could probably allow him a little distance by daylight. My salt warning system was still in place. It was the nights when he needed protection the most.

I grabbed my laptop. With a little magical finesse, I made my way into the college residence records. Ah. There was one empty room in Darton's building, scheduled for repairs after its original occupants had bashed several holes into the walls. Lovely. But useful. I could camp out there until I came up with a better plan.

I redirected the repair order and cloaked the record of the room so it wouldn't show up if someone else searched. Amazing how anything and any place could nearly cease to exist if it wasn't visible on a computer screen. And people thought *magic* was creepy.

Dawn light started to creep through the windows. My salt pouch lay still. I bit my lip, rubbed my hand over my weary face, and allowed myself to crawl into bed to snatch a couple hours of much-needed rest.

Sleep sucked me down into a deep, black void. In the midst of it, a vision unfurled, too stark to be just a dream.

Two trees swam into view, their trunks leaning so one crossed in front of the other like an X. My heart was thumping hard, the taste of adrenaline filling my mouth. Grit dug into my palms. *Give them hell,* a gruff voice I couldn't place hollered. A flare of heat seared over me.

I woke up with a jolt, my pulse still thudding. My head felt as if it'd been stuffed full of wool. I turned my bleary eyes toward the clock and swallowed a groan.

No more sleep for me. Darton had practice in an hour.

I pulled on a clean shirt and jeans and pawed briefly at my hair before shoving it into its usual ponytail. I stepped into the main room already debating how to best wake Darton up. He struck me as the sleeping-in type.

It threw me for a second when I found the couch empty and a very-awake Darton standing in the kitchen, stirring something in a pot on the stove. His hair was sleep rumpled in a way that provoked a tug of fondness in my gut.

A sweet, bready smell crept into my nose. My mouth watered. But the scene was far too domestic. Too cozy. The tug inside me turned into a painful twist.

"What are you doing?" I blurted out before I could catch myself.

Darton turned and gave me a sheepish smile. "Good morning. I, ah, hope you don't mind—I poked around in the cupboards and saw the bag of oats in there. When I was a kid and home sick from school, my mom always made me oatmeal. There's something kind of comforting about it. I figured maybe you could use something like that."

Right. Because of how I'd freaked out in front of him last night. I managed a smile. "Yeah. Thank you."

"You're right on time," he said, more confidently now. "I just added the sugar." He spooned the thick mixture into two bowls and shot me a glance as he checked a couple drawers before locating the cutlery. "Fifteen kinds of tea and only instant coffee is a travesty, just so you know."

"I don't even drink the coffee," I admitted. "That's Priya's. I prefer being eased into alertness rather than kicked in the head."

"Hmm. With that attitude, you must have drunk the wrong coffee." He arched an eyebrow teasingly as he carried the bowls over to the table. "I'll forgive you if you tell me the truth about whose book that is."

He nodded to the corner of the counter by the fridge… where one of my historical romance novels was sitting out. My cheeks warmed. I'd been reading it while making dinner a few days ago and totally forgotten it since. At least it was one with a subdued cover, no blatant man chest or cleavage on the verge of bursting out.

"That's mine," I said shortly. "I like them more for the historical parts than the romance."

A total lie—though I did *like* the historical context, as wrong as the authors often got the details.

Darton grinned. "Ah-ha! So you do have at least one vice."

The conversation ebbed when I joined him at the table. We ate in silence, Darton gulping the instant coffee he'd resorted to between bites. He'd done a decent job with the oatmeal, actually— a little on the sticky side, but cooked well and with a lot of sugar— but it sat heavy in my stomach.

I liked seeing him sitting at my table. Liked the little teasing comments. But I couldn't have this, not really.

I forced down everything in my bowl, grateful he'd only filled mine halfway. As I set down my spoon, Darton leaned his elbows onto the table and fixed me with that inescapable indigo-blue gaze.

"Emma," he said, quiet and serious. "Are you going to tell me what you were so scared of last night?"

Somehow, I'd let myself think I'd successfully evaded this conversation. Since I was done eating, at least I didn't choke.

"I don't really want to talk about it," I said.

His eyebrows rose. "You had me spend the night on your couch to protect you and you're not even going to tell me why?"

I had you spend the night on my couch so I could protect you. Obviously, I couldn't say that. Instead, I hedged. "It's personal. I really appreciate that you stayed. Thank you. Priya will be home soon, and everything will be okay."

I wished. But at least I'd circumvented the most immediate potential disaster.

Darton shook his head. "No. I want to know what's going on. I think you owe me that much, Emma. I saw how worried you were. Do you think you're in danger? Has someone tried to hurt you?"

Going along with that story would have been the easiest route in the moment, but it would only lead to complications. He'd want to take the matter to campus security or even get the police involved. I'd have to pile on lie after lie when I had more important things to focus on.

"I just don't do well at night on my own," I said. "It's not about anything that's happening right now."

"Bullshit. Something was going on last night. It freaked you right out."

I shrugged. "Maybe it looked that way to you, but that's not true. I'm sorry I made a big hassle for you. You want vices—there's my big one. Okay?"

His jaw set. "No, it's not okay. And it's not about you making a hassle for me. Staying wasn't a big deal. It *is* a big deal if you're in trouble."

The look he was giving me, so full of concern, did a number on my heart. I fumbled to find a response, and he reached across the table toward me.

His bare hand reached toward mine.

I jerked my arm back with a lurch of my stomach. Oh, no. This was too close, too intense. I needed him out of here, now, before any hope I had of keeping him safe unraveled.

I pushed away from the table and picked up my bowl. "Don't you have practice to get to?" I asked as I walked it over to the sink.

"I can skip one to help a friend."

My throat tightened. The words I was about to say burned in it, but I didn't see any other way.

"Your *friend*? You barely know me, Darton."

"I know you well enough," he insisted, standing up.

I summoned the chilliest tone I had in me. "I don't think you do at all. My roommate took off unexpectedly. I was nervous about being on my own all night, so I glommed onto you. You were there. That's all there was to it. That doesn't mean I want to start exchanging friendship bracelets."

Darton stiffened. "Don't do this."

He was never going to want to talk to me again after this, at least not until he woke up enough to understand why I'd had to push him away. But it was probably safer for both of us if I stuck to lurking around the edges of his life until that time. I'd already gotten too tangled up in his for either of our good.

"Do what?" I said, throwing my hands in the air. "Tell you the truth? I thought that's what you were asking me for."

"Emma."

"Just *go*. You'll find lots more kittens up trees to make you feel like you're doing something important with your life. You don't need me."

I suppressed a wince as the words fell from my mouth. I'd cut a little deeper than I'd planned.

Darton's expression shuttered. He strode across the room, grabbed his jacket off the hook, and set his hand on the doorknob. But even then, he gave me one last look.

I stared back at him defiantly, my teeth clenched to keep my chin from trembling. He yanked open the door and stormed out.

CHAPTER FIFTEEN

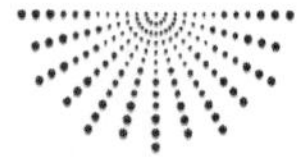

THE DOOR BANGED SHUT. A sob broke from my throat. My fingers closed around the kitchen counter as if I needed it to hold me up.

It'd be all right. I'd had to do it. I'd had to hurt him so I'd have some chance of preventing a far worse outcome later.

I stood there until my shakiness subsided. Each breath drew in the sweet smell of the oatmeal he'd cooked for me. An ache lingered in my chest, but I had to ignore it.

I needed to give Darton a head start before I followed him onto campus. *He* couldn't know I was sneaking into his residence. I had to focus on that. Focus on the real danger here.

First, I tugged on my gloves. No matter how strange I looked, I was *not* going without them in Darton's presence again. Then I headed into my bedroom to grab my duffel bag.

In went a crapload of magical supplies to supplement the ones already packed in my knapsack, followed by the sleeping bag I'd thankfully brought from home. There probably wouldn't be much furniture in a vacant dorm room.

A change of clothes. Some snacks from the kitchen, in case I got hungry in the middle of my surveillance. No pizza deliveries possible.

I zipped the bag shut and leaned over it. My head was spinning. Two hours of vision-interrupted sleep was really not enough to put me at my best. But I'd just have to make do. Once I was set up in Darton's residence building, I could sneak in a nap.

I pushed myself upright—and a quiver ran through the pouch of salt at my hip. My hand dropped to it.

The quiver didn't stop. It heightened, jittering erratically, as if it were being jerked from rhythm to rhythm at a frantic pace.

My pulse stuttered. I threw myself to the window.

The day had turned overcast while Darton and I were eating breakfast. Only thin sunlight washed over the street outside. And amid the dull shadows of the buildings and cars, clots of darkness were streaming by. Dozens of glooms.

All of them heading toward campus.

There were too many of them, coming too quickly. How could they—

I knew before I'd even finished thinking the question. My dark fae enemy was behind this. The mercenary had held the dark rabble in check, and then sent them at us in a horde.

I scrambled for my backpack. A wand. The light fae dagger, which I shoved into my pocket where I could reach it easily. I tossed the pack over my shoulder and clenched the wand in my hands.

I couldn't outrun the glooms. I'd just have to hope no one was around at this early hour where I planned to descend. I knew exactly where Darton should be.

Closing my eyes, I pictured the building and the lawn. *"Like the wind, carry me,"* I said, and snapped the living wood of the wand in half.

A whirlwind of energy whipped out from it into the core of my body. My ribs shuddered, and my lungs seared. Everything emptied from my head but blackness and a roar of sound. With a lurch, I found myself stumbling on the grass at the north end of the football field. The athletic building loomed in front of me.

I'd barely made it in time. Patches of shadow were swarming across the field toward me. I grabbed the dagger in one hand and another wand in the other.

"*Darkness begone!*" My voice rasped, my throat still sore from the teleportation spell, but a wave of light split through the glooms. It shredded them apart across the field.

The salt in my pouch hadn't stopped quaking for a second. There were more coming—so many more.

The wand had gone brittle in my hand. I tossed it away, and it disintegrated where it hit the grass. Pulling another from my bag, I ran for the athletic building doors. The dark rabble could be approaching from all sides. I had to get to Darton to protect him.

My sneakers squeaked on the waxed linoleum floor inside. Where were the locker rooms? My gaze flicked over the signs as I pounded down the hall. There—the women's... and the men's. I burst inside.

Male voices and laughter echoed between the lockers. The guys in the row closest to the door, each in differing stages of undress, stopped to gape at the girl who'd charged into their midst. I dashed down the aisle, ignoring the startled shouts that rang after me.

Darton mustn't have arrived much earlier than I had. He was standing beside an open locker three rows down, the sweater he'd worn to my apartment crumpled on the bench beside him, his shoes kicked off. His hands were just falling to the buckle of his jeans. I skidded to a halt at the sight of him—in all that muscular, bare-chested glory—and his head jerked up. His arms flinched to his sides.

"*Emma?*" he said, his expression incredulous. "What the—what the *hell* are you doing here?"

For a split second, I entertained the idea that we might make a stand right here in the locker room. But even with the bright florescent lights beaming overhead, shadows pooled beneath the benches and along the bases of the lockers. The dark rabble would find plenty of paths to travel along.

"We've got to go," I said. A shout and a yelp carried from another row. I spun around as a shape like a jaguar made from shadow sprang from the wall. It landed on the end of a bench, smashing the wood to splinters, and swiped a paw at a guy who'd been too shocked to fully dodge. He stumbled backward with a cry of pain.

Shit.

"*Darkness begone,*" I hollered at it, flinging the wand out to encompass any creatures already in the room. Then I lunged forward and grabbed Darton's wrist.

They were after him. If I got him away, they'd leave everyone else alone.

"Come *on,*" I said. He stared blankly at me. His head jerked around at the screech of claws cutting through metal. I hauled on his arm. "We have to go, *now!*"

I dragged him into the aisle just as another creature of darkness rounded the opposite end. Darton flinched at its lupine snarl and spun around. I didn't have to drag him quite so much to make it to the doorway.

"W-what is going *on?*" he sputtered. I tugged him down the hall the way I'd come. "Where are we going?"

A good question. My mind whirled and latched onto an answer. "The track." Open ground, too flat to hold sheltering shadows. The dark rabble might not be frenzied enough to cross that much ground yet.

A dark beast leapt at me from the doorway. I swiped at it with the fae dagger, and it winced backward, its form splintering into the air. Another swing of the blade scattered the glooms crowding around the entrance.

Darton's jaw was still slack, but I didn't have to pull him after me on the way outside. Apparently he'd seen enough to want to get away without further prodding.

We raced across the grass to the broad ruddy swath of the track. Darton crossed his arms over his bare chest with a shiver. The chill of the morning air bit into my own face. I glanced at the sky, and my heart sank.

The sun was merely a spot of light glowing through the clouds. It wasn't going to be enough.

I stopped halfway across the track. "This is crazy," Darton was saying. "Oh, God."

The dark rabble had followed us, as I'd expected. Glooms and larger creatures of darkness rippled out of the athletic building and across the campus grounds, surrounding us in a wave. My stomach lurched.

I'd never seen so many coming for my king all at once. He'd died before under the weight of a tenth this many. But the mercenary had obviously inflamed their urge to destroy. And now they'd caught wind of their prey.

The first few creatures to reach the edge of the track hesitated. My fingers tightened around the hilt of the dagger. One by one, they crept forward into the dim sunlight.

I reached to my bag to grope for another of my wands. We needed a place that we could flood with full light from end to end. Where near here— Oh. Yes, that could work.

But as I dragged the wand out, my grip on the polished wood wavered. Darton was staring at the dark rabble approaching us, but when I paused, he looked over at me. His face was white, his eyes wide. And I was about to frighten him even more.

The cat was already out of the bag, wasn't it? If we survived, there'd be no coming back from this, no convincing Darton I was some ordinary student, regardless of what I did next. And if I didn't act now, our chances of survival were nil. I inhaled sharply.

"Darkness begone," I shouted with every bit of desperation in me. The wand cracked apart between my fingers as light blazed

through it. A rush of brilliance seared across the field. The glooms and their dark companions shuddered and vanished.

Darton swayed on his feet. "What the hell?" he managed to say. As if I had time to explain. I set my gloved hand on his back and shoved.

"This way," I said with a gasp for breath. "*Run.*"

CHAPTER SIXTEEN

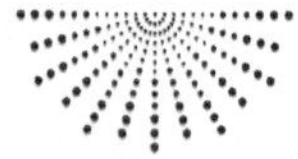

DARTON DIDN'T NEED a second push. We tore around the athletic building. I pointed across the green toward the campus theater. "There. We have to make it there."

More glooms and other dark creatures were creeping around the edges of the buildings and stalking across the grass. A few of the students strolling to their early morning activities caught sight of them and bolted for the theoretical safety of the nearest doorway. Others froze like rabbits in a hawk's shadow.

"Get out of here!" I yelled at them as we raced by. That was enough to break most from their dazes. But they didn't all dodge fast enough. One of the creatures leapt between a couple and knocked them to the ground. An enormous snake-like beast slithered past a girl who'd tripped in her panic, snapping its tail against her legs. She cried out in pain. My gut twisted.

If we could get into the theater building and clear everyone else out, the dark rabble would congregate there. Away from the bystanders who never should have been drawn into this conflict.

A winged shadow dove at me from above. I slashed upward

with the fae dagger, but the creature's filmy talons raked across my forearm before the light energy sliced through it. A sharp burn radiated through skin and muscle. I hissed in a breath, yanking my arm to my belly. My sleeve gaped open, the flesh beneath where the creature had touched it turning dead and gray.

Darton glanced over and blanched even whiter. "Are you going to be all right?" he said, his voice ragged from the run.

"Let's hope so," I muttered.

We reached the theater doors just as the dark rabble surrounded us. I spun around with a swing of the dagger, scattering the closest forms, and Darton heaved open the doors. Inside, I dove for the fire alarm.

The pulsing blare echoed down the hall and rattled my ears, but it'd get anyone else in here to leave. Darton had halted behind me, waiting for my cue. I took off toward the main auditorium, and he followed at my heels.

"You have to tell me what's going on," he said. "What *are* those things? You knew they were coming. How did you… do whatever you did that killed them? *Where* did they come from? What do they want?"

"All you need to know right now is that if they catch us, they'll kill us." I yanked open the auditorium door. "If we survive the next hour, I'll explain the rest."

We sprinted up the aisle to the stage. I swung myself onto the wooden platform rather than bothering with the stairs. As Darton clambered after me, I dashed into the wings.

The light controls had to be around here somewhere. I ducked between the curtains, a dusty smell tickling my nose, and caught sight of a broad black panel covered with switches. Bingo! Thank the light this school wasn't artsy enough to have an ultra-complicated setup.

My hands whipped across the panel to snap all the switches on. The lights crackled overhead and flooded the stage with light from every possible angle. Darton swayed in the mist of it, blinking and probably momentarily blinded.

The breath rushed out of me. I'd done it. The entire stage was lit so thoroughly not a single shred of shadow darkened the floor.

I hurried across the polished wood to Darton's side. The fire alarm wailed on. I tuned the racket out as well as I could as I peered beyond the stage. A couple of the lights had been pointed toward the area at its foot, so I could make out the front row of seats, but beyond that, the rest of the auditorium blurred into a black mass.

A gloom rippled along the edge of the light as if testing how much its shadowy body could tolerate. It flinched away into the deeper darkness. More shapes shifted across the tops of the chairs and the fringes of the aisles, but nothing ventured out far enough to become fully visible.

My shoulders eased down, but the rest of my body stayed tense. My gambit was working—for now. More glooms and dark creatures would be converging on us with every minute we stood here. It wasn't as if we could live on this stage for the rest of our lives. I was going to have to come up with a more permanent solution. But at least I had space to think.

Darton had started to pace. His steps took him close to the edge of the stage, and he veered to the side abruptly. The muscles in his bare shoulders flexed. He only stilled when a creature with a knobby head sank its jaws into the cushion of one of the chairs and ripped out a chunk of fabric and stuffing.

"What. The. Hell. Are those things? What is going on? Why are we in here? Shouldn't we, I don't know, call the police or something?"

A laugh burst out of me. It sounded so hysterical I clamped my mouth shut. Breathe. In and out.

"The police don't have any clue how to deal with a situation like this," I said. "These are the things that go bump in the night, Darton. Creatures people have pretty much forgotten really exist thanks to our modern-day 'advances.' But they never really went away. They just got quieter. Until they see something they want."

"What are *we* going to do about it, then?"

I grimaced. "I'm *trying* to figure that out."

Darton fell into an uneasy silence. I scanned the auditorium again. One of the snake-like creatures slithered along the edge of the light in an undulating line. Another shadow beast pawed at the lit floor by the end of an aisle. The thing on the seatbacks was still wrenching shreds of stuffing out of the cushions.

A mass of glooms lurked behind the distinctive creatures. I couldn't tell how many had already gathered in the blackness, but their presence grated against the light fae essence woven into my soul. My fingernails dug into my palms.

The fire alarm trailed off, and the hum of the overhead lights filled my ears. I tipped my head back, eyeing them. A glimmer of an idea sparked in my mind. I'd used up most of my living wood, but electric energy was still energy. Running through those manmade machines and wires, it didn't hold the natural power to kill the dark rabble on its own, but I could channel it through *my* natural body with a little effort, convert it into conjured sunlight

"Stay there," I said to Darton before he could launch into more questions. I swapped the dagger for one of my few remaining wands and stalked closer to the front of the stage. Inhaling deeply, I raised one hand toward the lights. I pointed the other, holding the wand, at the darkness.

"*Stream fast, stream far, and burn,*" I commanded, and jerked the wand.

A bolt of crackling brilliance shot from the stick's tip and blazed across the first several rows of seats. Every dark creature in its path dissolved. So did the wand. I flicked the crumbled wood from my hand and reached into my bag for another.

The flash of light had revealed the rest of the theater, all the way to the writhing mass of darkness that was blotting out the seats and the walls, as even more poured inside. In the few seconds it took to pull out my next wand, the dark rabble surged forward. It filled the space I'd just cleared as if I'd accomplished nothing at all. Behind me, Darton swore.

There had to be a limit to them. They couldn't keep coming forever in these numbers. But I didn't know how many the fae mercenary might have drawn from distant grounds to serve his purpose. We might have an entire continent's worth of dark rabble to deal with.

"*Burn,*" I called out, propelling another sizzling wave over the creatures in the shadows. My hand shook as the electric energy flowed through me, but I managed to throw light nearly halfway up the auditorium this time.

The luminescence faded, and the rest of the monsters swarmed forward. Were they at least a little thinner where they squirmed by the base of the stage? I reached into my pack. Three more wands. A bunch of twigs. Was that going to be enough?

Two of the spotlights flickered. Not so much that the glow on the stage visibly dimmed, but the jitter caught my eye. I glanced up at them, and a few more quavered. My back stiffened.

I'd only turned them on, what, ten minutes ago? Fifteen? No way should the bulbs be burning out just like that. I'd drawn my power from the wires, not the bulbs themselves, and I could still feel the electricity streaming through the cables. Something else was going on.

I stepped closer to Darton.

"What?" he said.

"The lights." Another flickered, and then another. A ripple of darkness crossed them in a shuddering chain, just as my sense of the electricity hiccupped. My mouth went dry. "They're eating through the electric supply."

"*What?*" Darton repeated. He raised his hands as if he thought he could fight off our attackers with his fists.

If I could find them… If I could pinpoint the spot where they were working at it…

I extended my awareness into the space around us, beyond the walls and below the stage floor. The thrum of electricity buzzed against my nerves. Where was it stuttering?

I followed the hitch in the energy down into the ground and out… to where a pack of the dark creatures had burrowed down into the lawn beside the theater. I winced at the feel of their shadowy teeth and claws scraping at the cable and the wires within.

Sparks danced behind my eyes. The stage lights wavered and dimmed. *No!*

I groped for a wand and opened my mouth, the words to blast light across that distance and shred those creatures into nothingness already rising in my throat—

Every bulb above us snapped off.

In that first instant, in the sudden black, my mind blanked with shock and horror. The emptiness of the dead lines laced through the building, the fixtures overhead dulled of light, echoed through me. With a rising hiss, the wave of monsters barreled toward us.

The sound of our impending doom sent my mind spinning into action. Darton grabbed my arm, his tight grip both protective and seeking protection.

I could still touch the sputtering flow of electricity in the far end of the cable the creatures had split. I could reach it, pull it, if I extended myself far enough, and bridge the gap they'd cut.

My fingers closed around my last three remaining wands. No time to second-guess—no room for moderation. I knew, even as I swung my arm, that either I took every creature in and around this building down in this fell swoop—or we were dead, because I wasn't going to be conscious to try again.

"Come to me and burn," I hollered, heaving at every particle of electricity in the line with all the life inside my body.

The energy walloped me across the back of my head and ripped through my chest, tearing the breath from my lungs. A brilliant sear exploded around me, as if the sun itself had fallen through the theater's roof.

My vision filled with the yellow-white glare. Inside my head, everything went dark. My knees gave, and then I knew nothing at all.

CHAPTER SEVENTEEN

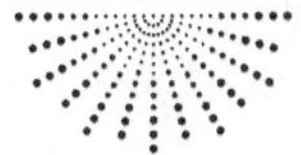

A SHADOWED FIGURE stood by the decrepit carcass of a cabin in the woods. Tall and lanky with black hair and pale skin—but it was a paleness that seemed to swallow the light that touched it, leaving a haze of darkness in its wake.

Just as the light fae exuded a natural glow, the dark fae dampened any radiance in the air. They deepened shadows and drained the vibrancy from everything around them.

The figure turned, revealing a masculine face, a profile of harsh angles. His lips curled with a smirk.

"I feel you spying on me, would-be protector. But you are not here. Your magic is not here. What will you do to me, hmm?"

His low, ringing voice washed over me. I couldn't move. Couldn't answer. My limbs, my tongue, were someplace else.

Somewhere I was needed. I had to get back.

"Nothing, yes," the dark fae mercenary—who else could it be? —remarked. "Poor thing. You'll just have to watch as my shadows claim my prize and carry him back to me. I can't believe it took me so long to stumble on the two of you. The one you're guarding is a great one. I can feel that there's nothing the darkness I honor would appreciate more than the chance to devour every hint of his soul. And I *will* deliver him to her."

No. I had no throat to force the word from.

"It's just a matter of time. I'm sure we'll see each other soon—for as brief a moment as you manage to survive the meeting."

The dark fae laughed, a hollow sound, and the vision fell away. I spun into a thicker blackness, the chill of his words wrapped around me. *Devour every hint of his soul.*

If the mercenary captured Darton—if he wrenched my king's soul from that body in whatever ritual sacrifice he had planned—he might destroy not just Darton's life but whatever was left of Arthur's.

My thoughts whirled and blurred. Then my eyes blinked open to a panicked face lit by an eerie glow.

"Emma!" Darton's grip on my shoulders tightened. I was lying flat on the floor. No, not the floor—the polished wood of the stage where we'd made our stand. My back hurt, probably because I'd fallen on it when the effort of that last casting had knocked me out.

I'd given up at least a year of this mortal life with that one blast. Maybe two. Not that it mattered if we didn't live through the next few hours.

I pushed myself into a sitting position. "I'm not sure—" Darton started to protest, but I ignored him. An ache ran down my spine and up the back of my head. I forced myself to think past it.

"Are they gone? The glooms and the—the creatures that were trying to attack us. They're all gone?"

Darton nodded. The light shifted over the planes of his face. It was streaming from a cell phone screen—he'd turned his on and set it on the stage beside us. Otherwise, the auditorium was dark, but also still. If any of the dark rabble *had* remained, we wouldn't be having this conversation.

"Are you all right?" Darton said. "You've been passed out for a couple minutes. We should get you to the health center—"

"No!" I shoved myself onto my feet, swayed, and managed to steady myself as Darton grabbed my elbow.

The dark fae mercenary wasn't planning to give up. He'd be sending even more of his minions after us. And if they caught Darton…

"We can't stay here. More of those things are coming."

Where could we go? Anywhere in the city, we'd be putting even more innocents in the line of fire. I needed more supplies. Damn it, I needed time to prepare.

The light fae enclave. They would take us in if I forced the issue—if I pressed hard enough on the allegiance they owed to my father. I didn't know if they'd actively *help* us, but at least if the mercenary and his creatures found us there, the fae would be able to defend themselves.

"We have to go." I motioned for Darton to pick up his phone. "We can stop at your dorm room and my apartment to grab essentials, and then—" I wasn't sure about the bus schedule. Where was the closest car rental place? I'd burned away all the dark rabble within a large distance, but there was no telling how much time we had before the next wave hit us.

"Emma, stop." Darton's hand clenched around my elbow. "I'm not going *anywhere* until you explain what's going on. I don't understand any of this. What those things were. What you did to get rid of them. Why they came after you in the first place. Who you even *are*."

I looked at him in the thin light. The fear he was trying to cover leaked into the twitch of his eyes, the sharp slant of his mouth. He wanted to be strong, because that was what he did, what he'd always done. But he couldn't take on this problem, not really, not when he didn't even have a clue what we were up against.

I couldn't keep lying to him. We weren't getting anywhere if he didn't believe enough to fight for his life alongside me instead of fighting *with* me.

"They aren't coming after me," I said. "They're coming after you."

Darton's forehead furrowed. "What? I've never seen anything like those… bogeymen before in my life."

"Not in this life," I said as evenly as I could manage. "This isn't your first one. Do you remember the other night outside the pub? An image rushed into your head—a scene that would have felt unfamiliar but also… as vivid as if it belonged to your past. That was a memory, Darton. A memory from the first life you lived, more than a thousand years ago."

His expression had frozen in place. He shook his head. "That's crazy."

"It sounds crazy when I have to lay it on you all at once, but that doesn't mean it's not true. It's the whole reason I'm *here*. You made a dangerous enemy in that past life. An enemy who's still making trouble for you, one way or another, even now. I've been trying to keep you safe."

"We'd never even met before *I* decided to join your fencing club," Darton said.

I laughed weakly. "Darton, I told you I left Yale to come here because I knew I had something else I needed to do with my life. That was finding you. Believe me, I'd have gotten here earlier if I'd known where to go before then."

The skepticism in his face hadn't softened. If anything, he looked more incredulous. "*You're* crazy."

Bloody hell. We didn't have time for a debate. The passing seconds gnawed at me.

But all the same, my body balked. I knew what I had to do. But the more he woke up, the more easily the mercenary would be able to track him.

I dragged in a breath and yanked off my right glove.

"I can show you. When that memory hit you the other night, it was because you touched me, skin to skin. We're connected, and the contact triggered that connection. We can make it happen again. It's easy."

I held out my bare hand. Darton stared at it. For a second, I thought he was going to turn and stalk off, that I'd have to force the waking on him.

His jaw flexed. He slid his hand down from my elbow to fold his fingers around mine.

A little jolt raced up my arm, even though I'd been fully prepared for his touch this time. My own memories trickled up, much more gently than the ones that would be racing into Darton's mind. His eyes glazed over as I watched. He was hardly even here.

The impressions of a time long past washed over me, and I let them come. The image swelling inside my mind was totally out of tune with our current situation—bright and happy. By the light, how I wished our lives had stayed that simple.

The prince and I lounged at the edge of his estate's orchard—a moment of rest after a long, hard ride. There was something wonderful about feeling, if only briefly, that we were two ordinary young men simply sharing a summer's day. My muscles were aching, true, but the brilliant warmth of the noon sun made up for that. It beamed down on us from above and radiated from within the golden stalks of the scratchy bale of hay we were leaning against. The rich, dry smell filled my nose.

"So what can you do with this magic of yours?" Arthur said casually.

"Whatever you like," I said, flushing with eagerness for his approval. "Are you hungry?"

I gestured to the nearest tree and murmured. A large, ripe apple snapped off its stem and sailed through the air to hand in the hand Arthur extended. He tossed it up, caught it, and chuckled. Then he bit in, as if it were a fruit gathered by completely normal means. A knot in my gut I hadn't noticed loosened.

That memory blurred into another.

My prince dragged me into the castle's stables. Our feet clattered over the straw-strewn floor. Swine crud, I thought as I hurried to keep pace. Not another ride.

We came to a stop in front of one of the stalls. A bay mare with wide, dark eyes peered out.

"There," Arthur said, as if I were supposed to know what was going on.

"What?" I said.

"She's yours." He reached to rub her nose. The mare whickered with a contented hum. "The seller trained her specifically as a child's horse— all patience, no skittishness. Since you ride about as well as a small child, I figured you'd suit each other."

His tone was teasing but his gaze intent as he stepped back. I eased forward, braced for the mare's reaction. Every animal sensed my fae heritage, and every domesticated horse I'd encountered so far had objected to it with rolling eyes and stomped hooves.

But this one didn't shy away from my reaching fingers. I held my breath as I scratched her chin. She emitted the same pleased sound she had for the prince. He looked exceedingly pleased with himself, but I didn't mind. My own face had split with a smile I couldn't contain.

He'd gone out of his way to find a horse I wouldn't dread handling, even though his family already owned dozens. He'd arranged this gift just for me. For me and all that damned time we spent riding together.

I opened my mouth to ask the mare's name…

The memory shifted again.

I was lying on my back on a camping roll, cool air on my face and lumpy ground beneath me, gazing at the night sky. A campfire crackled beyond my feet. Beside me, the man who was now my king waved his hand toward the stars.

"What do you think they are, really? All those lights we only see when the sun is away."

I tilted my head, considering. "Maybe they're suns too, just farther away."

"That must be awfully far. Do you suppose people will ever travel all that way? Perhaps by using magic like yours?"

I snorted. "I don't know, but I'm sure that's nothing we'll ever see. It's looking to be a long day tomorrow. Go to sleep, my liege."

Arthur harrumphed, but he rolled onto his side, his back to me. I studied that back in the dim light of the fire. Exhaustion hazed my thoughts. As if of its own accord, my fingers crept across the short distance between us and rested on the fabric of my king's blanket.

The warmth of his body beneath bled through the wool at the faint pressure. My heart thudded. Arthur didn't stir. He probably hadn't noticed. I wasn't sure whether I wanted him to or not.

No, I did. I wanted him to—

I jerked my consciousness out of that memory into the present to find my pulse thumping here too. Okay, that one had delved a little deeper than I'd have preferred.

Darton's grasp on my hand had faltered. With relief, I decided he must have seen enough. I tugged my arm away, breaking the contact.

Darton shuddered, blinked, and the glaze faded from his eyes. They fixed on my face as intently as if he were looking straight through my skin and skull to the mind that had lived alongside his so many times before. His lips parted.

"Merlin?"

CHAPTER EIGHTEEN

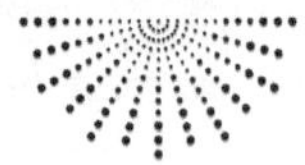

Hearing Darton say my name—my first name, my true name—sent a rush of warmth through me that I should have been prepared for, but wasn't. I bowed my head, my throat suddenly tight. "Your Highness."

"*Merlin.*"

He grasped my shoulder and pulled me to him, clapping one arm around my back. My breath hitched at the feel of that bare, sculpted chest against my body, but I hugged him back, clenching my hands so my fingers didn't brush his skin again. A tremble ran through him as he held on to me. What memory had he seen?

Enough to convince him, at least.

It felt good, being that close to him. Breathing in the citrusy fabric softener smell that was only Darton's and the earthy, masculine musk that had belonged just as much to Arthur.

It felt good because this embrace meant more to me than it ever would to him. My heart squeezed.

"Darton," I said.

He stepped back, his expression abashed. "Sorry. I just... I still don't understand, not really, even though I know... What is going on?"

I drew myself up straighter. "Look, I know it's a lot—it *is*—and that's exactly why I can't get into every detail right now. The most important thing you need to understand is that there are dark powers that want very much to kill you, and they know you're here now, so we have to leave. The faster we get moving, the harder it'll be for them to track you. Once we're on our way, there'll be more time to talk."

"Okay," Darton said. "But I expect you to explain *every*thing."

I nodded. "I promise. Now let's hurry."

I gave Darton five minutes to pull on a new shirt—as much as I enjoyed the eye candy, I'd rather he didn't get hypothermia—and to stuff a few essentials into a bag in his dorm room.

"How long will we be gone for?" he asked as we ducked out of the residence building and started to jog across the courtyard. "*Where* are we going?"

"To the first question, I'm not exactly sure." We were going to be lucky to survive more than a couple days with the dark rabble this close on our heels, but I wasn't going to tell Darton that, not this early in his waking. "But if you need more basics, I've got money. We just need to stop by my apartment so I can grab some supplies, and then there's a place I think we might be safe, south of here. I need to check the bus schedules. Maybe we'll have to rent a car."

"If we have to go somewhere farther than we can walk, Keevan would help. He's got his own car."

"No," I said firmly. "It's safest if we're alone. I don't want to bring him into this mess."

"Bring me into what mess?" said a voice just behind us.

I swung around, my pulse skipping. Keevan and Izzy, her arms crossed tightly over her chest, stopped a few feet away from us. They'd obviously just caught up.

"What are you doing here?" I blurted out.

"What are *you* two doing?" Keevan demanded. "We heard…" He paused, looking almost embarrassed now. "Well, we heard that there were some sort of *monsters* chasing Darton—that he ran off— so we came looking to make sure he was okay and to figure out what the hell everyone is *on*."

His gaze dropped to my arm. To the slashes in my jacket and the slivers of dead gray skin that showed through it. The shadow creature's wound didn't hurt anymore, because there were no nerves left in the spots where its claws had raked to feel anything. I tugged my sleeve to cover them, and his gaze flicked up to meet mine.

"There *was* something after you." Shock had colored his tone. He hadn't believed it when he'd said it before. "And—now you're talking about taking off somewhere?"

"It's hard to explain," Darton said, which was easy for him to say when even he didn't really understand.

"You can't get involved," I put in. "There are monsters, yeah, if you want to call them that, and they're dangerous. But once we're out of here, they shouldn't hassle anyone on campus. So you're better off here."

Keevan frowned. "This is totally wacko, but Darton's my best friend. If something dangerous is going down that could hurt him, I'm not hanging back to protect myself. You need help, I'm there, Art. You gotta drive somewhere? Name the place."

Izzy nodded, looking scared but determined. "Everything he said. I saw the way the lawn looked behind the athletic building… I don't want whatever did that getting to Darton. I'll do whatever I can."

I suppressed a groan. We didn't have time for an extended argument. And having the use of a car would make the next few hours so much easier.

Keevan could drop us off by the enclave, and then I'd send him right back here.

"All right," I said to Keevan. "We *could* use your help. Thank you." I glanced at Izzy. "But that's just for the car. You've got to stay here."

"No way." Her hands dropped to her sides, balling into fists. "There'll be something I can do."

"Izzy," Darton began. She shook her head, her chin set.

I sighed. "Fine, fine. The whole gang can come. Why not? Keevan, you and Izzy go get your car and meet us at my apartment."

As soon as I'd given them the address, they hustled off. Darton loped along beside me the rest of the way across campus. I could tell from the way his jaw worked that he was simmering with questions, but the dark rabble's attack must have shocked him enough that he was wary of distracting me.

Inside the apartment, I strode straight to my room. Darton leaned against one of my bedposts as I stuffed a few final items into the duffel bag I'd already mostly packed. Then I organized the equipment I was keeping on me. Fae dagger in my pocket, the hilt jutting out for easy access. A wand tucked into my belt loop. That was as good as it was going to get.

I turned toward the doorway. At the exact same moment, Priya stepped into it.

I froze. I hadn't even heard her approaching.

Her gaze darted through the room, taking in the bulging bag I'd just slung over my shoulder, the bewildered guy beside me, and the tension that must have blared from my own expression. "What's going on?"

"Nothing important," I said. Guilt gnawed at my stomach at the lie, but it was for her own protection. "We were just leaving."

I moved toward the main room, but she blocked the doorway. "For how long? You look like you've packed half the bedroom."

My hand tightened around the bag's strap. "I'm not sure. But we really do have to get going."

Priya finally stepped to the side, but she grabbed my arm when I tried to pass her. "Emmaline. What happened? You're acting so weird. Don't say it's nothing. It's obviously not."

The sense of time slipping away from us loosened my tongue. "I can't get into the details, but something bad is going down, and Darton and I need to get out of here for… a while. You don't need to worry. I know what I'm doing. I'll make sure my half of the rent gets paid."

"I'm not worried about the *rent*." Priya stomped her foot. "Geez, Emmaline. Where are you going? How are you getting there?"

"One of my friends is picking us up in his car." Darton's voice sounded creaky after his long silence. I appreciated him speaking up for us, but not the way Priya's eyes narrowed at that statement.

"Oh, so *his* friends are allowed to know what's going on?"

"It's not like that. Pri…"

Priya tugged me a little to the side. Her voice dropped. "I'm not blowing smoke up your skirt. If something's gone wrong, I might be able to lend a hand."

She raised the sleeve of her sweater, calmly and deliberately, just high enough for me to see the leather band wrapped around the brown skin of her forearm right below the elbow. A leather band that was etched with lines so familiar my heart stopped. I stared at them and then at her as she shook her sleeve back down. Priya gazed back at me steadily, her mouth pressed flat.

She was wearing a fae armlet, marked with fae runes. Where the hell had my sweet, bubbly roommate from the suburbs of Seattle gotten *that*?

And how had she known *I'd* know what it meant?

"I think we have a lot to talk about," I said. "But not right now." I sucked in a breath. Screw it. "Come on. Let's hope Keevan's car has room for five."

A grin stretched across Priya's face, so brilliant it was as if I'd invited her on a road trip to Palm Beach and not to flee some unspecified mortal danger. She clapped her hands, bounded into her bedroom, and emerged with a large satchel before I'd even walked the whole way to the front door.

"Do you really think it's a good idea for her to come too?" Darton murmured to me.

"No," I said. "I wanted it to be just you and me. But it looks like I'm not getting much choice in the matter."

A honk carried from the road below the living room window. Our ride was here. I just hoped it wasn't the last one we took together.

CHAPTER NINETEEN

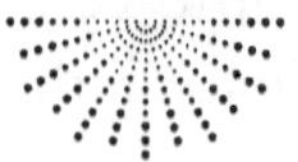

THE BACKSEAT of Keevan's red Toyota wasn't the largest space I've ever been squeezed into. I'd taken the middle spot between Priya and Darton so I could see through the windshield while still having Darton within immediate reach, and while she was thin as a whip, I was so close to him that I felt every slight movement he made. The solid muscles in his arm pressed against mine. The thump of his pulse echoed through his body.

With my gloves on, I wasn't too worried about accidental skin contact. The problem was more how much I wanted that contact purposefully.

Inside the boy I was becoming fond of in his own right, my king was stirring. It had been far too long since I'd spoken to him outside a memory, since I'd been able to look into his eyes and know he knew exactly who he was looking back at.

My mind darted to the last memory I had of his weight over me, caressing hands, and tangled sheets, some two lives past. A flush I really did not need to be dealing with right now flooded my skin. I bit my lip and focused on the map I'd brought up on my phone.

Keevan filled the car with the buoyant melodies of a classic pop radio station for the first couple hours of the drive. As we neared the state line, the reception started to break into static. He switched it off. The quiet that followed felt ominous. Apparently not just to me, because after a minute, he cleared his throat.

"So. Emma. I'm hoping I speak for us all when I say I'd really like a little more explanation about shadowy monsters that can rip through locker room benches, and how we're going to make sure they don't rip through us."

My throat tightened. I'd known I was going to have to tell him and Izzy something. The truth—part of it, at least—was easiest. If they didn't believe me, that was their problem.

"There are fae living in the world," I said. "Some of them are a lot like us, like people, but most of them are more like animals, or even less conscious than that."

"Fae," Izzy repeated. "You mean *fairies?*"

"Not like something out of a Disney movie." I rubbed the streaks of deadened flesh on my left forearm. "They're just part of… another side of the world that people have mostly dismissed these days. Anyway, there are two kinds—light and dark. The light loves chaos and energy and the dark loves order and stillness, so they tend to be at odds. Although there are few enough left that they don't get in each other's way too often anymore."

"Order versus chaos," Keevan said. "It sounds like we should be on the dark's side."

I smiled thinly. "I wouldn't recommend that. Life is chaos, and nothing is quite as orderly as deathly oblivion. So you can guess which direction each side likes to push the rest of us toward."

A nervous giggle slipped from Izzy's mouth. "Okay, in that case, I'll vote for light."

Darton shifted, the brush of his knee sending a fresh tingle of warmth up my leg. "It's the dark ones that came after us, right?"

I nodded. "Came after *you.*"

"Why would they want Darton?" Keevan said. "I mean, he's a

great guy and all, no complaints here, but I didn't think he was such a big superstar that he'd have fairy things knocking down his door."

That was the part I didn't think it was wise to get into. There was no way they were going to wrap their heads around *that* truth, even if I'd wanted to get into it.

"You could say he's got a connection to someone who has caused a lot of trouble for the dark fae in the past," I said. "An ancestor, a *long* time in the past. They're very good at holding on to grudges. And now they've noticed he's around."

"And they want to… to kill him?" Izzy's voice dropped with the last two words.

"That's the general idea."

"What are you going to do about it?" Priya asked, the question simple and soft. She hadn't questioned my story at all. How much of what I'd said had she already known? I eyed her, my shoulders tensing. We *really* needed to have a talk—a private one.

"We're heading to a light fae enclave," I said. "It's about another hour from here, if the traffic doesn't interfere. I don't know how much they'll help us, but just being around them will make it harder for the dark rabble to find Darton again."

Izzy turned in her seat to peer at me. "And how do *you* know about all this stuff? Are you one of—"

"No," I said quickly. Better to keep that part of my explanation simple too. In a literal sense, the life I'd been born into was completely human, spiritual heritage aside. "I've been friendly with the light fae for a while. It's a long story. They'll let us in. That's all that matters."

Darton's friends fell silent. I couldn't tell whether they were merely absorbing what I'd said or wondering what to do about the lunatic in the backseat.

At least I seemed to have stunned them out of asking anything else. What they thought about it didn't matter.

Darton's hand crept over his thigh to clasp my fingers. My heart squeezed as I returned the pressure. He was here with me. Confused and torn, no doubt, but here, and that was all I really needed.

The roads I directed Keevan down grew narrow and lonely. Finally, I had him pull the car off onto a large patch of grass facing a little wooden shack that served as a fruit and vegetable stand during the warmer months.

"This is as far as we can go by car," I said. "Darton and I will walk the rest of the way. I really appreciate the drive and the company—but the rest of you should head back now. I don't know for sure how long we'll be safe here, but the dark fae shouldn't hassle anyone else on campus now that we're gone."

"Nuh-uh," Keevan said firmly. "This may be the wackiest story I've ever heard, but that's more reason to stick with it to the end."

"But if Izzy—"

Izzy shook her head. "I can handle a walk in the woods. Let's go."

My gaze slid to Priya, whose slightly arched eyebrow was all the answer I needed from her. Biting back a groan, I glanced at Darton. He spread his hands as if to say, *What can we do?*

Not much, apparently. I could have bound the bunch of them to the car, but I couldn't force them all the way home. If they were out here at all, they were safer with me.

I sighed and motioned for Darton to open the door.

The fae weren't likely to appear to me when I had human company, but my recent visit here had left me with a concrete sense of where the enclave began. We'd tramped maybe a mile and a half into the forest when a tingling passed over my skin. I stopped and scanned the trees before giving a short bow.

"As the daughter of Eóghan, I request sanctuary for myself and my friends from Chimalis of the light fae. We swear to do no harm. Our need is urgent."

Energy rippled around us. Izzy shivered, pulling her cardigan tighter around her. The young fae man who'd greeted me on my last arrival shimmered into sight beside one of the trees, and she gasped. Next to me, Darton's jaw dropped open. Keevan let out a low whistle.

Priya just stood there, cool and casual, as if this were old hat to her.

The filmy, gleaming figure stepped forward and bowed lower than I had. "Daughter of Eóghan, you are welcome here. Your guests must stay in this spot until you've discussed the matter with Chimalis, but they will come to no harm from us."

That was very different from promising to *protect* my friends. I hesitated, reluctant to leave Darton behind, but I'd known our abrupt arrival would require additional smoothing over. Bracing myself, I followed the sentry deeper into the enclave.

The young fae led me to the clearing where I'd met Chimalis before. The same table and chairs awaited, with cups of the cool, nectar-laced tea the light fae enjoyed.

This time, I didn't sit. I wasn't interested in having a relaxed chat.

A few torturous minutes ticked by before Chimalis glided out to meet me. Two other elders, not quite as old or translucent as she was, flanked her. I went through the motions of a formal greeting, but impatience gripped my chest.

"The trouble I came to speak to you about before—it's gotten worse," I said. "The dark fae pursuing us sent an onslaught of dark creatures after us, and he lent them enough power that they made the charge in clouded daylight. He spoke to me in a vision. I believe he's attempting to please the Darkest One. Her influence is seeping from her prison somehow."

"We heard word of a shadow passing," Chimalis acknowledged —whatever the hell *that* was supposed to mean. "But it has not extended far. An ocean is safety enough."

My hands clenched. Didn't they care what dark fae did in their own lands? Didn't they care what *might* happen if the Darkest One shook off her bindings even slightly?

Of course, Chimalis and her brethren here might never have faced the Darkest One when she moved freely. Most of them wouldn't have even been born before I'd sealed her away all those centuries ago. But now the mercenary was right on their doorstep.

"It isn't safe enough for Arthur and me," I said. "The dark rabble nearly killed him. Their master means to try again."

"Then that which was to pass will find itself completed."

"He wasn't *supposed* to die," I snapped. "I made a mistake. If I'd cast properly... but that's beside the point. The dark rabble is tracking him now. We couldn't stay where we were living. Will you allow us to put ourselves under your protection?"

The three elders drew back to murmur to each other. I shifted from foot to foot as I waited.

Chimalis turned to me. "The boundaries of our home may obscure the trail. We offer you lodging and sustenance here in respect to your father. But I will not ask my own people to put themselves at risk if the danger comes upon you here."

I inclined my head. I hadn't really hoped for a more generous offer, as much as I'd have welcomed it.

"With luck, it won't come to that." But I knew just how much luck we'd need to keep the dark mercenary away. It wasn't as if Darton could live his life out in the forest anyway. If we were going to have any hope of surviving longer than the next few days, extreme measures were required.

"I need something else," I said. "Is there anyone here who could advise me on how to kill a dark fae?"

The glow that imbued Chimalis flickered, as if the idea of death offended her very essence. Well, it probably did. She pursed her lips. The man at her right stepped back, his mouth curling with disgust. The other woman crossed her arms over her chest.

"The path of life flows onward with our blessing."

I grimaced. "I know, I know. But *this* life wants to cut short a whole lot of other lives. Doesn't that make any difference to you?"

"It isn't done," the man said. By which he'd meant, they hadn't done it. I gritted my teeth.

"If your journey takes you away from the light, it is not in light you will find the answers," Chimalis said in her not-at-all-helpful way. "Now, to accommodate your—"

A crystal-clear voice pealed from amid the trees. "Wait!" A young fae stepped out—the tall, ebony-skinned woman who'd given me the dagger now stuffed in my pocket. Sunki. She must have heard about my arrival and come to watch the meeting.

She bowed low to the elders, quivering. Interrupting them had been a major breech of decorum. "May I speak? I have information that may be of use to our guests."

Chimalis's stance had gone rigid. "Sunki, you forget your roots. This is a discussion for those long grown."

The young fae shrank back, spun, and darted away into the trees. Sod it. Just with that one sentence, she'd given me more reason to hope than anything these "wise" old husks had offered.

Well, they'd already given their word that we could stay, and they hadn't been likely to offer more. I gave the elders a swift bow. "Thank you for your kindness." Then I hurried after Sunki, not caring if I'd offended them.

Her form had already started to haze away into the streaks of sunlight. "Sunki!" I called, and she stopped. Her pale eyes fixed on me and widened. She dipped down.

"Daughter of Eóghan."

"Emma will do," I said. "I want to hear this useful information of yours."

A smile crossed her face. "I can't answer the question you asked, but I listen to the tales that pass this way. I've heard there's a human who hunts the dark fae. Near the great gouge in the earth, it's said he lives."

The great gouge... "The Grand Canyon?"

She shrugged. How would she know? She'd never left this forest.

"All I know is what I just told you," she said, "and that he lives where two trees cross. I'm not sure how old the stories are, or whether he's even still living, but perhaps he would know what you need."

Where two trees cross. My mind leapt back to that vision in my brief sleep this morning—to a dark crossing of trunks flashing before my eyes. My pulse skipped.

"Thank you," I said, meaning it so much more than I had when I'd said the same words to the elders. The vision had been showing me the way, and Sunki had offered the vital clue to piece it together. There *had* to be someone there who could help me defeat the mercenary.

Now I just had to find out if any other fae had heard more of this story, because I didn't like our chances of trying to track down a single house around the entire Grand Canyon.

CHAPTER TWENTY

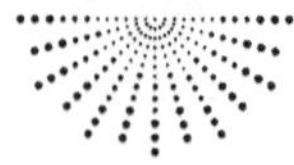

KEEVAN TIPPED his head to study the cup of nectar tea one of the light fae had offered him. The waning afternoon light filtered through the trees around the clearing we'd settled in and glinted off the pale liquid. Its steam carried a tangy sweetness.

"Do the 'standard' rules apply around here?" Keevan asked in his usual joking tone. "Isn't there some trick about how you're not supposed to eat fairy food or you'll be stuck in their world forever?"

"The fae do have that power," I said, "but it's not automatic. And I'm sure this bunch has no interest in kidnapping us."

They'd prefer we left as soon as possible was more like it. But the information I'd been able to scare up so far was slight. Sunki had brought me around to speak with the fae who were willing to entertain my questions, but while a few others did remember hearing about this human who hunted dark fae, only one had recalled anything more than she had.

"I crossed paths with an elder on a scouting venture south of here a few years ago," that young man had told me. "She spoke of the hunter in passing—said there was talk he lived near a town of petals, by the east end of the gouge."

Not the most helpful tip. A town of petals? Presumably that was human information filtered through at least three layers of a telephone game slanted by the light fae tendency toward metaphor and vagueness. I might be able to work with it, but I needed a map, and my cell phone didn't get any service out here.

When I'd made it back to the clearing, the shadows had been growing long. If we tried to make it to the car, the sun might set before we got there. My fatigue was already wearing on me, and I'd rather spend the night here than on the road with who-knew-what lurking in the shadows. The fae would just have to put up with us until morning.

Sunki had promised to inquire farther afield. Maybe she'd bring me something more concrete. For a fae, she wasn't bad.

Keevan took a sip of his tea and grimaced. "Well, that is… interesting." He leaned against the broad oak he was standing by. Near his feet, Izzy took a bite of the baked roll she'd been brought. Their gazes roved through the clearing, watching the shimmering forms of the fae ambling around.

"How long will we wait here?" Izzy said. "Is there a point when we can assume this dark fae thing has decided to leave Darton alone?" Her eyes had gotten even wider since we'd entered the enclave, but she was sitting with a calm I couldn't help admiring. Was that what had attracted Darton to her—the quiet composure behind her flower-child looks?

She wouldn't keep that composure long if I answered her honestly. The mercenary had no intention of leaving Arthur's soul alone now that he'd gotten my king in his sights.

"I have to find a way to stop the dark fae so he can't keep after Darton," I said. "And I'm working on a strategy for that."

On the other side of the clearing, Priya had fallen into conversation with a couple of our hosts. The glow they exuded glinted off her dark hair, flickering as they laughed in twinkling tones at something she'd said. Priya grinned back at them.

She looked completely at home, as at ease as she did in our apartment. My stomach twisted.

Keevan waved his half-empty cup toward me. "So who exactly was this ancestor of Darton's who got him in all this trouble? That's got to be quite the story."

Yes, and not one I had any interest in sharing. "I'll leave it up to him whether he wants to tell you about it," I said, which seemed a fair answer. My attention was still fixed on Priya. There was no point in putting *that* conversation off any longer. "Are the two of you all right for now?"

Izzy nodded, and Keevan gave me a pensive look but a thumbs-up as well. I stalked across the clearing with a small weight lifted from my chest. I hadn't wanted Darton's friends along—it was their own fault if they were uncomfortable—but I felt a little protective all the same. This place wasn't my home any more than it was theirs, but at least I understood it.

Priya's shoulders tensed before I'd made it halfway to her. She made some comment to her fae companions, and they brushed hands with her before they slipped away. The knot in my stomach tightened. That was an awfully familiar gesture for a fae to offer any human.

I came to a halt in front of her. "What's going on, Priya?"

She looked at me for just a second before lowering her eyes. "I thought, while we're here, I might as well make friends."

"You know what I mean. You know *how* to make friends with them. You've got that—" I motioned to her arm. "That band with the runes. You're not going to convince me this is your first experience with the fae. I'd be surprised if it's only your *tenth*."

"Emmaline." She sighed and rubbed her mouth. Then she raised her head. "Don't be angry. It was better that I didn't tell you before. You wouldn't have understood."

"Understood what exactly?"

"I grew up with the fae," she said. "An enclave not that far from Seattle—that part wasn't a total lie. I never could get them to tell me how I'd ended up there as a baby, whether my parents had left me or they'd abducted me or what." She laughed haltingly. "Sometimes I got the impression they didn't totally remember. But they kept me until I was eight, and I kept visiting after they managed to bring me back into the human world."

I stared at her. "You're a changeling. Not in the usual direction, but…"

She shrugged. "'Foster child' is more how I'd describe it."

"That doesn't explain why you ended up rooming with me. Why you didn't tell me. By the light, Pri, you must have known I was working magic. You had to have sensed something was up with me before today."

Her gaze darted away from me again. She sucked in her lower lip. Then she said, quiet and careful, "I knew everything."

I'd tried to anticipate what she might say, but that statement stopped me in my tracks. All I managed to spit out was, "*What?*"

A glitter of fae wildness sparked in her eyes, so distinctive it was a wonder I'd never made the connection before. Eight years raised by them—that would leave a mark. But how could I have guessed?

"They knew about you," she said. "My enclave—well, *all* the light fae know about you. The daughter of Eóghan who lives over and over, tied to the long-dead-but-never-dying king. They knew the dark creatures come where you appear. It worried them. When you transferred, they asked me to, well, to keep an eye on you. To watch what was happening."

It took me a second to recover my tongue. When I did, it felt laced with ice. "You were spying on me."

Priya winced. "It wasn't like *that*. They only wanted me to be able to let them know if there was danger coming that they should prepare for. Obviously concern about outside affairs isn't common across all enclaves." She shot a critical glance at the clearing at large.

Oh, no. She wasn't changing the subject just like that. "That still sounds like spying to me. Especially when you didn't tell me.

When you pretended you didn't have a clue what I was worried about. You did know, didn't you? Why I was so distracted?"

"I guessed." Her eyes fixed on mine again. "I didn't know how to tell you, Emmaline. But I always thought maybe I could help you, even if that part didn't seem to matter much to the fae. I still think I can help. Why do you think I came with you?"

I shook my head. "I don't know. Apparently I don't know much of anything."

"We've really been friends," Priya insisted. "I didn't *pretend* to enjoy hanging out with you. I didn't pretend to care that something was going wrong."

"It doesn't matter." Sure, she hadn't pretended—but she'd cared because she'd wanted to know what to tell her fae family. All that time she'd chummed up to me, tried to draw me out, without ever sharing the most vital piece of information about herself, or that she already knew so much about me—

I backed up a step.

"Emmaline," Priya started.

"No," I said. "Not right now. Maybe not ever. You don't get to hide something that big from me and then act like nothing's changed two seconds later. People don't work like that."

A lump had risen in my throat. I whirled and strode away before she could protest further.

I should have known better. I shouldn't have cared as much as I had. Trying to make friends had never worked out well for me— why should that change now?

CHAPTER TWENTY-ONE

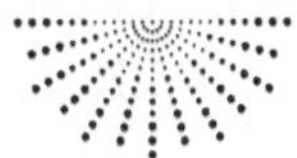

My feet carried me straight to the only person I'd ever been able to count on in any of my lives. Darton had wandered apart from the others earlier for some space to think, but I'd been aware of his presence the entire time, laced through the whispers of fae magic that twined in the air.

He was sprawled on the coarse grass in a smaller glade, gazing at the clouds streaking across the sky. A few of the light fae hovered amid the trees around him. Arthur's host was as much a curiosity as I was—*long-dead-but-never-dying*, as Priya had put it—and they weren't at all afraid of *him*.

I frowned at them and made a jerking motion with my hand. A shudder of irritation ran through their glow of life, but they retreated, leaving us to the bird song and the cool tickle of the late afternoon breeze.

"May I join you?" I said.

"Sure," Darton said, sounding a little dazed. "Why not?"

Offering him as much distance as I could in the small space afforded between the trees, I sat down on the grass a couple feet from him and leaned back on my elbows. A disconcerting sense of déjà vu stole over me. So many days and nights my king and I had stolen a moment to recline and contemplate the sky that stretched above us.

I pointed to a particularly puffy bit of cloud. "What do you think—a rabbit or a mitten?"

Darton gave a choked laugh. "Just like old times," he said, and I knew a sliver of one of the memories he'd glimpsed.

"It's a lot to take in," I said. "I'm sorry I had to lay it on you all at once. Usually the revelation is a little more… gradual."

"But you've known all along."

I nodded. "I need to, if I'm going to look out for you. And you *don't* need to, not right away. As soon as that part of you starts waking up, the dark rabble can sense it."

Darton frowned. "Why do I even still matter to them? I mean, whatever I might have done… before, that was centuries ago, wasn't it?"

"I don't know," I admitted. "I don't even know why you were so important to them in the first place." I didn't know why my father had wanted me to seek out the prince and future king all that time ago. But something had tied the Darkest One to Arthur's future.

"So we've lived and died, lived and died, over and over again? Do you always manage to find me?"

"The spell I cast—you were dying, and I was trying to stop that from happening—ties our souls to this world and to each other. The bond has frayed a little. I used to be able to count on finding you while we were still children. But it always brings me to you before too long."

"Before I start remembering on my own."

My throat tightened. In all but the unluckiest circumstances. "Usually. Yes."

He rubbed his forehead. "This seems so insane. If I hadn't seen —felt—whatever those memories were… I can hardly believe it anyway."

"As long as you believe you need to stay far away from the dark rabble and not get killed, that's all that really matters."

"Well, that's inspiring."

"Hey," I said. "I'm here to be your wizard and your defender, not your life coach."

A laugh sputtered out of him, one that sounded more authentic than his last effort. "Am I going to remember any of the lives other than my first one?"

"I don't think so." Maybe if I kept him alive long enough, just this once, we'd find out. "You never have before. So just assume they were all full of me being brilliant and saving your arse repeatedly."

"Do *you* remember them?"

"The earlier ones have faded. With the more recent ones, I've retained a few fragments." A pale body set upon by shadows. Any humor I'd summoned fled me. "And I keep written records, as well as I can."

Darton set his hands behind his head to cushion it. "Were you watching me from the beginning—after you transferred? I don't remember seeing you until a few weeks ago."

"I hadn't 'found' you until you walked into fencing practice," I said. "Our paths hadn't crossed. But I knew you when I saw you."

His smile turned teasing. "So that's why you were so 'friendly.'"

"I was making the best I could from the situation handed to us," I retorted. "It's hard, you know. I don't *want* to wake up that part of you and bring the dark forces down on us. But I've got to stick close enough to you to be ready when you start to wake up of your own accord. Sometimes I don't get the balance quite right."

Darton was silent for a moment. Then he said, abruptly, "Isn't it lonely?"

I looked at him, but he was still staring at the sky. "What?"

"For you," he said. "Living over and over again, knowing who you are, not being able to tell anyone. Not even me, when you first meet me. That's an incredibly big secret to have to shoulder."

"Technically, you keep secrets and shoulder burdens," I informed him.

He shifted over on the grass so he was close enough to elbow me. "Have you always been annoyingly pedantic?"

"Yes," I said, deadpan. "You love it. You just haven't remembered that yet."

He shook his head, but I could tell he was fighting a chuckle. "Well, whatever the correct terminology, I stand by the observation. And I'm sorry if I made things harder for you."

His sympathy tugged at a soft spot inside me. I scooted a little forward so I could lie all the way back on the grass, imitating his pose with my arms bent behind my head. "I appreciate that," I said. "If it makes you feel any better, as far as I recall, you haven't made it particularly harder than usual this time around."

"It does, actually." He exhaled. "So what was I really like back then? Are all the legends true? Was I as great as they say?"

He was trying to keep his tone jaunty, but a note of yearning rang through it, so heavy with need I hesitated before choosing my words.

"The legends are almost entirely fiction," I said. "No Lancelot, no questing after holy grails, your table was not round. Those are literary inventions built up around the small scraps of the real history that survived the ages. But the one thing the tales do get right is that you were a damned good king. And I think I was in a position to judge that accurately."

He made a noncommittal sound. "What is that judgment based on?"

What was it not? A rush of past moments poured through my mind.

"You were compassionate," I said. "Always looking out for your people. But smart about it. You knew how to weigh the good of the many over that of the few, when it came down to that. The country was at war when you were crowned, our neighbors vying for territory and the local lords beginning to squabble in the wake of it, and you managed to unite them against the common enemy. That was always your commitment—to establish peace and maintain it. To let people live without fear that their fields would be razed or their homes ransacked. I'm not going to lie and say everyone was happy, but a lot more were happy after you than had been before."

"That does sound pretty great," Darton murmured.

"It was an honor to stand beside you." I looked at him again. His face was less than a foot away now. My heartbeat kicked up in tempo with a yearning of my own, one I couldn't entirely suppress. "Then and since and now, still. Always."

This time, he turned to gaze back at me. I couldn't read the emotion in his eyes, but I recognized it. I'd seen a glimpse of it that night behind the pub. The night he'd touched my cheek and started waking.

Before that memory could act as a warning, Darton moved. He rolled onto me, bracing his weight on his forearms. In an instant, his body covered mine from the chest down—not crushingly, but firmly enough that I lost my breath all the same. I stared up at him, at that face that was becoming familiar in its own right. In that moment, it held an expression I'd known for fifteen hundred years, set with passionate determination.

His fingers stroked over my hair with a gentleness that felt contradictory. I still couldn't breathe, not with the feel of him against me as I'd tried not to remember it just a few hours ago, different and yet the same. Not with his eyes searching mine so intently.

"Tell me to stop." His voice came out low and almost harsh as he tried to tame the tremor in it. "Tell me you don't want this too."

My lips parted—he'd given me the words I needed to say—but the lie was too big to work quickly from my throat. At my silence, Darton bent down and caught my mouth with his.

His kiss was everything I always wanted, hot and fierce, as if he were trying to fit ten kisses into this one. A shudder of longing— for more, for anything he would give me—ran through my body.

My hand swept into his hair of its own accord and pulled him even closer. His lips coaxed mine apart to deepen the kiss. The taste of the nectar tea he'd drank earlier slipped from his mouth into mine, and a memory swam into my head.

"She's just... she's lovely." The prince paced his chamber, his shoes rasping against the stone floor and muting when they hit the rug. "That hair of hers, like a dark waterfall, and those eyes, so fathomless... I can hardly think of what to say when I'm with her."

"I think you should scratch 'poet' off your list of possible careers, Your Highness," I remarked with a touch of rancor I hadn't intended.

"Yes, yes," Arthur said. The wave of his wave dismissed my joke without so much as a smile. "I thought, maybe, there was some way you could help. With your particular skills and so on."

A chill passed through me that was deeper than the cool autumn air. "Are you asking me for a love *potion, Arthur? You can forget about that. Do you have any idea how unconscionable—"*

"No!" The prince's eyes widened with horror. "Oh, gods, no. I would never— Do you really think that of me?"

I didn't. But then... "I've never seen you moon over a lady like this before," I pointed out. "How am I to know how that might have addled your mind?"

He snorted, some of his usual humor returning. "I admire her. I'm hardly addled. I simply thought you might be able to offer something to bolster my confidence. So I can remember how to find my tongue when I have a chance to talk to her."

The rancor inside me clenched at my chest. Why did I feel so uneasy over such a simple request? I shook the discomfort off. "All right. That much I can do. First, we must—"

Darton's lips brushed over mine again, and I yanked myself out of the memory and away from his kiss in the same motion.

"We can't do this," I said tightly, tipping my head to the side. "Please get off me."

Darton blinked at me, his eyes hazy. Still immersed in whatever recollection this physical contact had stirred up in his head.

Then his gaze cleared. He shoved himself off me and scrambled upright. An ache ran down my body at the loss, but that was exactly why I'd had to stop this interlude. That and—

"You feel it." Darton wavered on his feet. "You kissed me back."

Oh, my king. I felt whatever you did and so much more. I pushed off the ground, shaking away bits of stray grass that clung to my clothes.

"Every time we touch directly, the contact wakes up more memories in you," I said. "And the more that part of you wakes up, the louder it calls to the creatures tracking you. Do you really *want* them finding you?"

"I thought we were safe here."

"Not completely. Not forever. I'm not taking that risk."

Darton's jaw clenched. "What if *I* want to take it? Every time… There's so much I'm missing that I don't know, that I don't understand. Maybe it's worth the risk to fill in those blanks."

"Everything you could remember, I already know," I said. "Nothing could be worth it."

"But what if *I* want to understand—"

A shout echoed through the forest. I tensed, and Darton's mouth snapped shut. A shriek split the air, so panicked it turned my blood cold. I leapt up.

"The dark rabble is here," I said. "They've already found us."

CHAPTER TWENTY-TWO

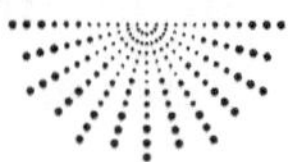

"What?" Darton said, but the paling of his face told me he knew exactly what I was talking about. I hurried to the edge of the glade. More shouts rang out, mingled with a startled hiss, a cry, and the rustling of fae legs flitting through the underbrush.

I couldn't see any sign of the attack. The dusk was deepening with a chill in the breeze that stung my skin. Glints of light darted between the trees in the distance.

Darton came up beside me, and I held out my gloved hand to keep him a little behind. My heart thumped.

The dark fae had found us here so quickly. The enclave had barely provided any shelter at all—or the mercenary had so much power he could track even the slightest hint of Arthur's essence, even when obscured by other energies. I bit my lip.

My first and only real concern was keeping the man beside me safe. We'd managed to fend the dark rabble off so far. They were *not* taking him here.

"I need my bag," I said. I'd dropped it in the clearing where I'd left our other companions, not expecting to have any immediate use for it. I caught Darton's hand with my left and brandished the fae dagger with my right. "Come on."

"I thought we were protected here," Darton said as we hurried through the thicker forest. "Isn't that why we came? Can't these other… fae do anything?"

"I'm sure they're trying. I didn't expect this, but things are a little different this time around." I tugged him faster. "It's not just the shadow creatures after you. There's a full dark fae directing them. That hasn't happened before, at least not recently enough that I have a record of it. Obviously I underestimated the danger."

Darton's jaw tensed. "And those things out there—they still want to kill me."

No. They wanted to carry him back to the dark fae mercenary so he could perform whatever ritual would dedicate Arthur's soul to the Darkest One. But I was not letting that happen, so knowing that wouldn't do Darton any good.

"Yes," I said instead. And then, because I was, "I'm sorry."

Darton's eyes flicked to me, startled. "No. Em, don't even think you have anything to apologize for. It's because of you I'm alive right now at all."

More of the light fae streaked by us as we plunged into the clearing. Their forms were little more than wavering sunbeams amid the dusk. They streamed this way and that, some toward the hollers still carrying from the edge of the enclave and some fleeing away. Others whirled around us as if they couldn't decide which tack to take.

"What's happening?" I called out to them. "How many creatures are out there? Can you hold them off?"

None of them slowed long enough to answer me.

"Darton!" Izzy leapt to our side and grasped Darton's arm. Her cool had vanished, not that I could blame her for that. She trembled as she clung to him. Keevan bounded over, slapping his hands together as if eager for a fight, but fear shone in the whites of his eyes.

"What the hell is going on?" he said. "I'm guessing it's not good."

Priya came up behind me. "The enclave is being attacked by glooms and shadow beasts. Part of the pack that came after you on campus, I'd guess."

Izzy outright shuddered. "What do we *do*?"

I'd already crouched down by my duffel bag. I snatched out a few wands, shoved the extras into my back pocket, and retrieved a bag of crushed salt to supplement their power. I didn't have enough hands to hold all of that and the dagger too, but salt didn't require a skilled touch. I held it out to the others.

"The dark creatures don't like salt. It won't keep them off us completely, but you can make them back off for a moment if they get right in your face. And then I'll take care of the rest."

Keevan reached for the bag, but Darton got there first. He tore the corner open. I straightened up and swung the duffel over my shoulder.

"Are we going to *have* to go face to face with these things?" Izzy's voice quavered. "I thought—"

Chimalis materialized in the middle of the clearing. She glided over to us, the filmy edges of her body rippling. Her expression was profoundly sad but unshakably firm. I knew what she was going to say before she opened her mouth.

"The creatures of the dark have sought you out here," she said. "We are doing what we can to slow their progress, but we are not prepared for combat of this magnitude. You must go, and then they will leave us too."

And I was sure this burned through any favors I could ever have expected to beg from them, in this life or the next several, assuming I got that far. Oh well. At this point I'd be happy just to be around that long in the first place.

I glanced at Darton, as if to reassure myself he hadn't vanished in the second my attention had been elsewhere. "We have to get to the car."

Chimalis nodded. "We will attempt to clear a path to the humans' road. But you must move quickly. It is a long way and holding against the dark tires us."

"Okay." I sucked in a breath. "Let's move. Fast. Everyone, follow me."

"May your paths be ever lit," Chimalis murmured. She was already drifting away. The farewell had never sounded more ridiculous than now as we hurried off into the dark ahead.

"This way." Sunki appeared ahead of me and beckoned. "I'll help as much as I can."

We sped up to a lope, crossing the uneven ground between the trees as quickly as we could without risking a fall. Our feet thudded over the packed earth. More and more light fae blinked in and out of sight amid the trunks on either side of us. The dark rabble must have been too deep in the shadows for me to make them out.

Good. Let them stay there.

I'd barely had time to think that when a light fae man toppled onto the ground ahead of us. Izzy shrieked. Glooms twisted around his limbs and neck. A pained grunt escaped him.

Priya dashed forward. I twitched my wand without pausing to think. "*Darkness begone.*"

The patches of shadow clutching at the fae man blinked away into the air. He heaved himself upright with a rasp before throwing himself into the forest again. I swallowed thickly.

Whatever Chimalis had said, some of her kind were fighting hard. Fighting for us. Even though this was our war, not theirs, and we'd brought it to their doorstep.

We hustled on. Other glooms started to trickle through the lines of fae defense. I jerked my wand and sliced out with my dagger, destroying them one by one. The tingle of energy running through the wand's wood began to fade, but it wasn't gone yet.

A shadow creature shaped like a giant hawk swooped down at Darton out of nowhere. "Art!" I shouted automatically. His head jerked up. Izzy staggered backward, and Keevan swore.

Before I'd even spat out my casting, Darton tossed a handful of salt into the air. The creature recoiled. My spell hit it, and it burst apart into the air.

My wand crumbled in my hand. Keevan stared at my now-empty fingers. "Is that a bad sign?"

"There's a reason I brought backups. Keep moving!" I pulled another wand from my pocket. My pulse raced in time with our feet. I caught Sunki's eye. "Is it just the lower creatures?" I said. "Has anyone seen an actual dark fae?"

She shook her head. "He comes like a shadow, here and yet not."

More fae vagueness, but I thought I knew what she meant. Our pursuer had imbued these creatures with his power, but he had stayed distant. A bit of a lazy one, apparently. But then, given the army he was commanding, I supposed he could reasonably afford to take it easy.

"Can't you cast the same spell you did in the theater?" Darton said. He panted as he ran. "Blast them all away as far as we need to go?"

A hoarse laugh slipped out of me. "If I have to, I will. But I prefer not to go around knocking years off my life left and right." And if I threw out that much energy and failed, then I wouldn't be conscious to protect Darton or the other three tagging along.

"You mean—" Keevan started.

At the same moment, another creature, this one in a wolf's form, knocked over one of our fae defenders and sprang through the trees at Darton.

I dropped my wand to clutch his arm and yank him backward as I leapt in front of him. My hand whipped out with the fae dagger. Its blade sliced through the creature's neck. The shadow wolf crumpled, spilling darkness across the brush.

The trees ahead were thinning. Hope thrummed through me alongside my heartbeat. "Have your key ready," I said to Keevan as I hauled Darton faster. My hand slipped from his arm. He groped after mine, and his fingers closed around my wrist where my sleeve had ridden up during the fighting. Skin to bare skin.

A spark shot through my nerves. Sod it. Getting him out of here mattered more than keeping his soul in its slumber. I let him hold on as we rushed forward.

Darton stumbled, but he stayed on his feet, his grip tightening. Priya dashed around to his other side. She looked ready to grasp his other arm if she needed to.

Impressions of past times welled up in my mind, but the blare of adrenaline kept me moving, focused on the present. The memory played out in the back of my head, echoing the panic of our mad flight.

My king was standing in the western field, his head bent close to a man I didn't recognize. He was tall and long-faced with tan skin and slate-gray hair, his shoulders slightly hunched. The man motioned with his arm, and my hand tensed against the edge of the castle window where I'd stopped to glance outside.

The shadows on the ground near him had twisted, as if drawn to his movement.

I scrambled over the windowsill and jumped. The air rushed past me. Some witness below gasped as I plummeted, but I'd already muttered the words to cushion my fall. My plunge slowed, and I hit the ground with only a light jarring of my knees. And then I was running.

"So you can see," the dark fae man was saying, "it is merely a matter of—"

"Your Highness," I blurted out, stumbling to a halt beside them. I hesitated to be as familiar as to grab my king's arm in front of a stranger, but there were other ways of getting his immediate attention. I threw myself prostrate at his feet, which was the last thing I'd ever have done in any normal circumstances.

As Arthur well knew. He crouched in an instant. "Whatever is the matter, Merlin?"

"You must come," I said, my head still low. The ground smelled of

rich earth and summer grass, but a trickle of the fae's deathly chill seeped into my nose. "Back to the castle. Now."

The urgency in my voice must have convinced him. I scrambled upright as he tossed out a brief apology to his companion, and then he was hurrying with me to the gate I'd leapt over in my charge from the window.

"Tell me what's the matter."

"Not here." Not in the yard beyond the gate, not in the castle hall, not until I'd slammed the door to his chambers shut behind us.

I spun around to face my king. "That man you were talking to was not a man. If you see him or anyone like him again, you must stay away. Don't talk to them. Don't even look *at them."*

Arthur frowned. "He hardly seemed a threat, especially on that scale."

"He wouldn't. He wouldn't want you to see it. They're a part of my old world, not yours. You have to trust me, Arthur. There's nothing so dangerous on all the Earth as a dark fae who wants something."

A heap of glooms spilled out into our path, and my mind jerked fully out of its reverie. Sunki cried out a few words, but only a few of the creatures quivered apart. Damn, the light fae around here really didn't go in for much combat training, did they? I guessed they rarely saw the need for it.

The faint smell of asphalt reached my fae-touched senses. We were almost to the road, to the car. I took in the sprawl of glooms rippling along the path toward us, Keevan and Izzy drawing up short, the stretch of woodland between us and our goal. My stomach balled. I had one wand left in reach, no time to dig in the bag for more. Between that and my own power, could I manage this much while staying conscious?

I didn't have much choice but to find out.

I tugged my arm from Darton's to snatch up that last wand and thrust it forward. "*Burn and banish,*" I shouted with a heave of power.

A blaze of light washed from my body and the wand. It

careened across the brush and seared through the mass of glooms and whatever else lurked amid the trees. My legs wavered. It was *my* elbow Priya had to catch. But she did.

"Are you okay?" she asked.

"Yes." I jerked my arm back, my head spinning. "I just bought us about a hundred yards' grace. Let's not waste it talking."

We took off at a sprint. Izzy let out a choked sound of relief at the sight of the car. Keevan hit the unlock button, and we dove in different doors, me pushing Darton ahead of me.

Sunki pressed her ebony hand to the window, and I nodded my thanks as I barked out the order.

"Drive!"

CHAPTER TWENTY-THREE

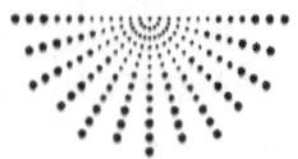

"So…" Keevan said after the car had been roaring down the lonely highway for several minutes. "Should I assume those shadows with minds of their own can't outrun a car?"

"They can't if you're driving this fast," I said. "So, you know, definitely keep that up."

"Aye, aye, Captain." His joviality sounded so forced I didn't think any of us believed it. "And where exactly are we driving *to* now?"

I shifted, squeezed between Darton and Priya on the backseat's worn faux leather again. "I'm trying to figure that out. For now, keep heading south."

I skimmed my fingers over my phone's screen. Where was the east end of the Grand Canyon? Gods, that had *better* be what the fae had meant by the "great gouge."

Eastern Arizona. *Here we go.* I zoomed in on the map.

Priya leaned over, her narrow shoulder bumping mine. "What are you looking for? Maybe I can help."

My back tensed. "That's all right," I said, sharper than I'd intended. But then, I wasn't even totally sure what she was still doing here. Making sure she saw this entire disaster through so she could make a full report?

Darton sank down in his seat, gazing blankly at the one in front of him in silence. He rubbed his jaw. "I saw something."

"What?" My attention was still focused on the map. Petals… Petals… I hoped that word hadn't been too literal. Arizona might be dry, but I was sure there were still plenty of gardens around.

"In my… um… when I grabbed your arm," Darton said hesitantly, as if even he weren't all that sure about what he was trying to say. "You said there was nothing from before that you didn't know about, but I don't think you knew about this."

"Anything I wasn't present for, you'd have told me about. At least if it were important."

"Because I was so hopeless without you?" A little drollness had come back into his voice. I guessed he wasn't totally shell-shocked.

"*True friends don't keep secrets,*" I said. "*Your words.*" Ones I hadn't lived up to quite as fully as my king would have liked, but I'd been as open with him as I could without threatening the greater priority of his safety.

My finger stilled over the screen. Just beyond the eastern tip of the canyon was a little dot of a town named Peddleton. *A town of petals.* That was exactly how the fae would have bastardized a name like that in the telling from one to another.

"Okay," I said. "There's a man who lives in Arizona, probably near a placed called Peddleton, who knows how to take on the dark fae better than I do." *I hope.* Light willing, he'd at least be *alive* and not long dead from a story decades old. "We're going to pay him a visit and see what he has to say. We should be able to stay on this highway for a while yet."

Keevan gave a jerky nod. Beside him, Izzy sat with her shoulders stiff against the seatback. A grayish bruise I hadn't noticed before marked the back of her hand, which was clenched against her leg.

One of the glooms had brushed against her hard enough to do damage.

Darton prodded me with his elbow. "Apparently at times I was more of a 'do as I say, not as I do' type, because whatever I was doing in the place I saw, the one thing I remembered for sure was that I was worried you'd find out I'd come there. So I doubt I was in a hurry to tell you about it."

My head snapped around. He'd never mentioned a memory in which he was hiding things from me in any of his past lives… at least not the ones I could remember or the moments from those previous I'd been able to note down before the end. Granted, he didn't often have the chance to recover more than a fraction of that first life before the shadows took him, and me with him.

"Where *were* you?" I asked.

"I don't know." Darton frowned. "It was a long, narrow room with lots of shelves covered in bottles, all different colors. It smelled like dust and… kind of like my mom's herbal tea. My mom now, I mean. I haven't—" He cut himself off, his gaze darting to his friends at the front of the car as if he'd only just remembered them. "You know what I mean."

And you barely knew your mother then. The queen had passed when Arthur was two. But his description recalled a place I could identify. Ffion's workshop—the alchemist.

"What were you doing there?"

"I didn't remember that much," Darton said. "It was just a glimpse and a feeling… But it felt important. I was hoping whatever I was going to accomplish there would fix something. For you, I think."

I'd been the one who stepped in to fix the problems my king couldn't solve, not the other way around. I hadn't *had* any problems except the ones that continually arrived at his door.

Unless… unless he'd known. Might he have thought an alchemist could cure me of *that* sentimentality? My throat tightened.

Arthur had never mentioned a visit to Ffion's workshop to me —I was sure of that much.

Darton ducked his head. "Anyway, I thought we could... try again? And maybe I'll see more, get a better idea of what I was up to."

"You can't control what will surface," I said. "Not with any accuracy. You can try to focus on the other memory, and maybe that'll tug one up that's related, but especially this early, when there's so much still buried—"

"What the *hell* are you two going on about?" Keevan broke in. "All this stuff about memories buried and surfacing—and you're talking as if you've known each other for ages. What am I missing here?"

Priya glanced at me, but she kept her mouth shut. I groped for an answer. The thought of getting into the past lives of legendary kings made my chest clench up. How well was *that* likely to go over, even given recent events?

But I already had a thread I could use in the vague explanation I'd offered him and Izzy earlier.

"I told you that Darton is connected to a past ancestor that the dark fae clashed with. Some of that man's memories have passed along to him. And I have a comparable situation through an ancestor of mine, who helped back then, which is why I'm here to help now. Sometimes it can feel as if the things that happened back then really did happen to us."

"Uh-huh." I couldn't tell if Keevan bought my half-lie or if he simply didn't have the bandwidth to push harder. "So you're having old-timey memories, Art? That sounds pretty psychedelic."

"It definitely feels weird." Darton let out a stilted laugh. He was going to need more practice with the lying thing. He adjusted his weight next to me, bringing me back into all-too-clear awareness of his closeness. The citrusy smell from his shirt tickled my nose. I swallowed the flicker of desire down—and he rested his hand on my leg just above my knee, palm up. His voice lowered as he bent his head beside mine.

"I think we should try. Right now, we need all the information we can get, don't we?"

It was hard to believe I was making the clearest decision ever with his breath heating the side of my face—the lips that had been pressed against mine less than an hour ago nearly brushing my ear —but I gave it a champion's effort. The thought that my king might have been keeping secrets gnawed at me. Just a brief touch, just hands, wouldn't stir the soul inside Darton that much.

And it wasn't as if the mercenary and his dark army weren't tracking us quite closely already. I wasn't sure we *could* make the situation much worse.

"Just for a minute, then."

I pulled off my glove and laid my hand over his. His fingers twined with mine, his skin dry and warm. A fluttering energy ran up my arm and shivered around my heart.

Sights and sounds of past times rose in the back of my mind, but I kept my awareness firmly focused on my current body. On the feel of Darton's hand and the pressure of the seat belt across my chest, the headlights streaking across the darkening road ahead of us, Keevan's staccato breaths, the rustle as Izzy swiveled to peer at us, her mouth flattening before she turned to face the road again. I wanted to stay here, in the moment, so I could detach myself before this experiment carried on too long.

Darton's fingers gripped mine. His head bobbed with the motion of the car. The new memories springing up in his head would become less intense each time, but he'd only experienced a few so far. He'd still barely be aware of anything around him in the thick of one. It'd take several more of these moments before I could hope he'd be able to talk to me during one.

One minute slipped by and then another, and Darton stayed lost in his recollection. His lips twitched. His eyes opened, and I drew my hand back. The deep blue of his irises glinted when he looked at me.

"That really was a waste of a good boot," he said, incredulous and amused.

A laugh burst out of me. I clapped my hand over my mouth to try to contain it. Yes, that had been… quite an adventure. Darton grinned, clearly pleased with himself for provoking that reaction in me.

"So not a very helpful memory then," I said when I'd recovered my self-control.

"I tried, but…" He spread his hands apologetically.

Keevan drummed his fingers against the steering wheel. "Okay. Look. Darton, I'm in this for however long you need me, but I just can't—it doesn't make sense. I don't know."

Darton's face fell. "Keevan, man, I—I don't know either. What do you want me to say?"

"Is there anything you *can* say that'll let me wrap my head around this craziness?"

Silence filled the car. Keevan grimaced. "Yeah. That's what I thought."

"Does it have to make sense?" Priya said softly. "Can't you just believe there are some things in the world that don't, not in the way you're used to?"

"I don't know." Keevan's voice sounded broken. "Beasties made from shadows and magical ancestor connections and… I don't know."

My jaw set. This was why I'd wanted to go it alone. Priya, at least, had some clue what she was getting into. Darton's friends couldn't have imagined this by half. And the fact was that this race across the country might very well be a suicide run. They hadn't agreed to witness that.

I had to protect Darton. I didn't have the capacity to take responsibility for anyone else.

"You can drop us off at the next town," I said. "We'll figure something out. We can rent a car, grab a train or a bus, whatever's there. It's okay. You've already done a heck of a lot."

Izzy jerked around so abruptly I had to suppress a flinch. She stared at me. "We should leave Darton with *you*? It doesn't matter what your ancestors or whoever did. You don't know him, not really. And he doesn't know you. It's—it's your fault he's mixed up in all this stuff, isn't it? Maybe we should drop *you* off."

I could only stare at her. Her normally gentle features had gone rigid with resolve. Darton's eyes widened.

"Isabel…"

"Don't 'Isabel' me," Izzy snapped. "You're in danger, and it started when she came along—and the farther she makes us go, the worse it gets."

My hands balled at my sides. "I'm trying to get him *away* from the danger. Could *you* have blasted away the things that came after him on campus? Or ripped up the glooms back there in the forest?" How the hell did she think they'd have made it out of there without me?

Her gaze turned dagger sharp. "Would they have *been* there if you hadn't? If we hadn't followed you out here into the middle of nowhere?"

"Darton is the one they're following."

"We only know that because you've said it," Keevan put in. "Izzy is right."

Did they even have eyes? Light above, I should never have agreed to let them come.

"I trust Emmaline," Priya said. "I've known her longer than any of you. I know she's telling the truth."

Keevan guffawed roughly. "We don't know *you* at all."

"*Stop it.*"

Darton's voice cut through the car, ragged but unyielding. Everyone else shut up.

"You know me," he said. "You came all this way because you were worried about me. I can't tell you how much I appreciate that, from both of you. A lot of what's going on seems crazy to me too. But Emma is on our side. On *my* side. Even if you don't trust her yet, trust me enough to know what I'm talking about. I wouldn't say that if I wasn't sure."

He squeezed my knee, and it was hard to say whether it was that contact or the passionate defense he'd just given me that sent more heat through my body.

Izzy sucked in her lower lip. Keevan rubbed his hand over his forehead.

"We're going to need to sleep at some point," Izzy said finally. "It's getting late. We can at least do that, can't we? We'll all be thinking clearer after we've had some rest."

"Anywhere we stop, we give the dark rabble a chance to catch up," I said.

"If we don't stop for that, we'll end up stopping because we've crashed into something, and we'll really be stuck then. I know there's no way I'm getting any sleep in the car. After everything today…" She shoved her hands through the auburn waves of her hair. "It's going to be hard enough in a bed."

I couldn't say I didn't sympathize. My awareness of the dark army closing in behind us jittered through my nerves even when I wasn't directly thinking about it. And Keevan looked worn out already. But…

Darton's thumb ran up and down the side of my leg. "Can't you set down some sort of magical protection?"

"Not exactly." Nothing even a mere gloom couldn't leap right over in their current super-powered state.

But I could cast down another line of salt, a supernatural trip wire that would give us warning when the dark rabble was close. I stared down at the phone map, the lines of the roads blurring and re-sharpening before our eyes. At our current pace, we'd reach Peddleton in the wee hours of the morning, when we couldn't exactly drop in on strangers to make inquiries anyway.

I let out my breath. "All right. But it's not *that* late. I'd like as much of a head start as we can get. We should be well into Utah by midnight. I'll switch off with you at the wheel before then if you need it, Keevan. At midnight, we'll look for a place to stop off for the rest of the night."

My gut had twisted as I made the concession, but Keevan's shoulders sank down and some of the tension left Izzy's face. Apparently I wasn't getting rid of them. I hoped I could keep working around them.

CHAPTER TWENTY-FOUR

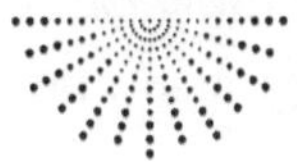

"Why here?" Keevan asked, frowning at the sprawl of low fields on the other side of the windshield. The highway light on the post where we'd stopped lit the grass with an eerie yellow glow.

I held up my phone. "The motel is another ten miles down the road. If I lay down a line here, we'll have plenty of warning—and time to get going—if the dark rabble catches up with us before morning."

Keevan's frown didn't budge, but he didn't say anything else, just swiped his hand past his drooping eyelids. He'd insisted on staying at the wheel, but now, at just past midnight, he looked too exhausted to argue about anything. Izzy nodded where she was curled up in the passenger seat.

Darton pushed open his door, the hinges squeaking. "I'm coming with you."

That suited me fine. The car wouldn't be much protection if the glooms were closer behind us than I'd have guessed.

"Grab the salt," I said with a nod. Then, to the others, "This shouldn't take too long. Try to relax for a bit."

Keevan slumped in his seat.

"Are you sure I can't—" Priya started, her expression beseeching, and I cut my gaze toward her.

"Do you know how to work magic? Because if you do, you should have been using it when we were running out of the enclave."

Her mouth twisted. "No. Well, I'll shout if anything bad starts going down here."

It wouldn't. If the dark rabble came, they'd come to Darton and me. They didn't give a sow's arse about the three people we were leaving behind in the car.

Our elongated shadows wavered in the lamplight as we tramped over the ditch and into the thicker darkness across the field. I peered to the north. Had I seen an unnatural movement, or had that just been a trick of my own weary eyes? The night stayed still and blank, but my pulse kept skittering. The mercenary had already surprised me more than once. We'd cut it far too close too many times.

Darton seemed more interested in the sky, where a dappling of stars peeked between the streaks of cloud. I made for a skeletal electrical tower that stood about a quarter mile from the highway, and he kept pace. After a minute, he glanced over at me.

"Did you and Priya have an argument I missed?"

"Yes," I said. "But I'd rather not talk about it."

"Fair enough." He shifted the bag of salt in his hands. The fine grains hissed against each other. The wind licked over us, chilly and laced with the scents of dry earth and dying grass. It reminded me of the chill the mercenary carried around him even in my visions.

"Have you had any more of that pain?" I asked. "In your side, where it was bothering you before?"

Darton tipped his head as he considered. "Not today. Not that I can remember. I guess I should be glad it's not acting up even more with all the dashing around we've been doing."

I was glad for that, but I didn't think it was a coincidence. The dark fae must have been using the moment of Arthur's near death to seek out his essence. He might not have known the significance, only felt some impression from the Darkest One that had guided him. But he didn't need to search for Darton like that anymore. His creatures had all the scent they required.

For a moment, we walked in silence, but then Darton cleared his throat. "When you were using your... abilities, getting us out of the forest, you said something odd. Is it true that doing magic takes away from your life? The more you do, the sooner you'll die?"

"Yep." I didn't have to force the breeziness of my answer. After shaking hands with my physical mortality a hundred times, it was hard to get emotional about it. "It hasn't really mattered. It's not as if I'm ever around anywhere near long enough to die of old age."

Darton's stride faltered with a sudden hitch. He caught himself. "What happens to me if something happens to you?"

"Oh, you don't have to worry about that. I go when you do, not the other way around."

He stopped dead then, and I could have smacked myself. Between my fatigue and the stress of the last few days, I hadn't watched my words. Mortality might be a well-worn concept to *me*, but Darton had never thought about death with that much familiarity.

His face looked gray in the wan glow that barely reached us this far from the road. His gaze didn't waver from mine. "So how long do we normally make it?"

"Keep walking," I said. "We don't want to waste time." When he didn't move, I grabbed his forearm and tugged. He came along, his posture tense.

I dragged in a breath. How to put this without provoking a total existential panic? "I told you before it's taken longer each time for you to wake up on your own. The dark rabble never comes after you before you know who you are. So when you became aware at a younger age, we had fewer years to live. At the beginning, we wouldn't have been more than kids. More recently... From what I can remember and what I've recorded, in the last century or so, the oldest birthday I've made it to is twenty-two."

"Twenty-two," Darton repeated in a hollow voice. I felt him doing the calculations. Our birthdays would be within a day or two of each other. A year and a half—that was how far off twenty-two was. As if we had much chance of making it even that far with the mercenary breathing down our necks. A shiver ran down my back, as if that breath had touched me right now. I walked faster.

We reached the foot of the electrical tower. Darton passed over the salt when I reached for it, but he stood rigidly. His jaw worked.

"I always try to extend that time," I said. "I try everything I can. You have no idea how many—" My voice caught. I swallowed. "But there's only one of me, and who knows how many thousands of glooms and the rest."

"Yeah."

I didn't know what else to say, and there wasn't really time for delays. I drew out the spare wand I'd brought with me—gods, how was I already running low on those?—and pointed it at the bag of salt. During the drive, I'd mixed in the necessary herbs. I murmured the incantation to command the salt to react to any shadow creature's crossing.

Darton stirred out of his daze as I headed toward the car, sprinkling the salt along the ground.

"What am I usually doing while you're working your magic and so on?"

I shrugged. "Not a whole lot. Offering emotional support? Our enemies are my kind, not yours. It was my spell that got us stuck in this cycle. I'm the one who has to untangle it."

"So I was a great king, but I'm utterly useless now."

"You're not *useless*," I said. "I'd imagine you could do plenty more important things if you had the chance to. We just—we all have separate roles. The magical arena is my domain."

His voice dropped. "I feel useless. You've been the one doing all the work here, Emma. I'm barely managing not to get in your way."

The pain in that admission squeezed my heart. My mind darted back to our conversation in the restaurant yesterday evening. The lack of direction he'd talked about, that *need* to know he was contributing something important to the world.

How much harder must that desperation be hitting him now, watching me battle forces he could barely understand, telling him it was all for his sake? No wonder he was groping after a fragment of memory, a slight chance he might offer *some*thing I couldn't.

"I doubt it'll make you feel any better," I said, "but I will point out that if I hadn't cocked up the spell in the first place, we wouldn't have to be fending off the entire dark rabble instead of focusing on the sorts of things you *will* be great at again. At least useless is better than active ruination."

"Don't say that," Darton said with more force than I expected. With a tone that sounded almost like my king's. "You've done so much—back then and now, while I—God. Last night. Even then, I thought you wanted me there to make *you* feel better, but it was for me, wasn't it? You were scared for *me*." He paused. "Did you sleep at all?"

With his eyes intent on me, I found I couldn't lie. "A couple hours. After the sun came up. The dark rabble can't move as quickly in daylight."

"*Two* hours!" he burst out. "You've been going all day on two hours of sleep? How are you not falling over?"

"Practice." I dug out another handful of salt. "And staying alive is an excellent motivator. I probably will fall over when we get to that motel." His question stirred up other memories from this morning, though. "I'm sorry about afterward, just so you know. I was only being mean because I needed you to leave so I could get the rest of my plans in order. That was before I knew that whole army was coming for you right then."

"That's the last thing you need to apologize for. God." Darton shook his head. "So we really are running for our lives."

A laugh sputtered out of me. "Have you only just figured that out?"

"I don't know. None of this has seemed completely real, to be honest. It's still sinking in." He raked his fingers through his hair. "What do you figure our chances of making it past twenty-two are this time around?"

My throat closed. Darton gave a hoarse chuckle. "That bad, then. Okay."

"Honestly," I said. "I didn't think we were going to make it out of the theater, so I'll be grateful for every hour farther we're still living."

CHAPTER TWENTY-FIVE

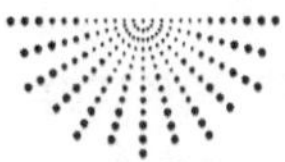

I ONLY GAVE myself a minute in the motel room shower, even though I'd left the new pouch of salt on the counter where I expected to hear it rattling if it stirred. But between that short interlude and a quick change of clothes, I walked out into the main room feeling infinitely less manky than when I'd walked in.

Darton was sitting on the second bed, flipping through channels on the tiny flat-screen TV. He switched it off when I emerged and turned to face me. The eye contact alone was enough to send a little tingle over my skin. Sharing a room with him felt dangerous in a totally separate way, but if the dark rabble arrived, I couldn't risk having even one wall between us.

"I tried to call my parents," he said. "Only got voice mail."

"Well, it is pretty late." Almost one in the morning now. But I could understand him hoping for one last conversation before his probable death. A lump rose in my throat. "If you want to shower, you should do it now. We don't know how quickly we might have to leave."

He got up and crossed the room. I stepped to the side to clear his way, but instead of heading to the bathroom, he stopped in front of me. His gaze locked with mine.

"I've been thinking."

"Always a hazardous activity," I joked, partly because the husky note in his voice had amplified the earlier tingling.

He took a step closer—close enough that if he'd stretched out his arm, he could have touched me. My pulse thumped.

"Darton—"

"I've been thinking," he interrupted, "that I need to dig up more of that one memory and find out what I knew that you didn't. And I've also been thinking that the deepest I've gotten into my memories wasn't when we were just holding hands. It was when we were kissing."

My skin flushed from head to toe. "What's your point?" I asked as innocently as I could manage.

He moved forward, and I backed up—right into the wall. He set his hand a few inches from my head, leaning on that arm. He bent toward me, and if I'd thought his voice was husky before, now it was low enough to melt me.

"You have fifteen hundred years of accumulated wizardly wisdom, Em. I think you know what my point is."

Of course I did. And it was just like him to find a way of presenting this proposition as if it were an act of heroism.

If he'd had any clue how much every particle in me was screaming for me to touch him, trail my hands up his chest, pull his mouth that last short distance down to mine—but I'd been down that road before. It never led anywhere good for either of us.

My body stiffened. Darton hesitated. He straightened up enough to give me room to breathe. His eyes searched mine.

"You said before that we shouldn't because it'll make me more of a beacon to the dark creatures. But those things are obviously following me wherever I go anyway. The more I remember, the more I'll be able to pitch in. So is there something else stopping you? If you really don't—if it's *me*—I wouldn't force the issue."

"No," I broke in. "I know you wouldn't. It's not that. I just—" *I know how much it hurts to act out a love beyond any you'll ever return.* As if I could say that to him. "All those hundreds of years of keeping my distance so I didn't wake you up early—it's a hard habit to break."

He cocked his head. "Has it normally taken a lot of effort to keep your distance from something like this?" He made a vague gesture between himself and me. "Do we often…"

Memories flitted through my head—other sets of hands, other eyes, other mouths, traveling over other bodies I'd inhabited. "Sometimes," I hedged. *Almost always if I let it happen*, would have been the truth. We were inevitably pulled toward each other. But how easily *he* gave in to that desire depended somewhat on what sort of body *I* was in. "There's a connection between us, magic and history."

And I'm never sure how much you come to me merely because of that rather than any real wanting.

Darton's gaze dropped. I felt the imminent question and braced myself.

"Is it strange," he said, "being a woman, now, when, before… At least if I'm remembering correctly…"

"You are," I said, "and no. The specific bits that come with any physical body, male or female, never mattered all that much to me even before this swapping started. I'm Merlin. That's all I need to know. Wherever my soul ends up, I'll still *be* Merlin, so I'm not much fussed as long as I'm human. A lemur or a warthog or something I'd take some issue with."

He paused. "Do *I* go back and forth too?"

I had to laugh at his uncertain expression, feeling a little relief. I'd take uncertainty over disgust or abhorrence any day. "Not much. Apparently yours is a man's soul through and through. It's only been a few times, I guess when circumstances threw fate for a bit of a loop… You do make an interesting woman on those rare occasions, as I recall."

"Hmm." He looked down at himself, at the shape of the space between our bodies. I held my breath as I waited to see where this line of thinking would take him. Whether he would be the one to stiffen now and draw back from me.

Instead, he said, "This isn't just about who we were before, though. This is about Darton and Emma too."

I guessed that was how he needed to frame what he was feeling to get around the memories in which he wouldn't have thought of me that way even for a moment. But I couldn't help asking, like prodding a canker sore, "Are you sure?"

"Well, maybe I can't be sure how mystical connections or whatever might be affecting me." His voice dropped again. "All I know is that there's been *something* there from the beginning. From before I even saw your face behind that fencing mask. A spark. A partly antagonistic one at the start, maybe…"

He smiled, and darkness take me, he did have a smile worth every wonder known to humankind.

"You are so… enigmatic. In an intoxicating way."

"Those are some nice SAT words there," I said.

Darton shook his head, still smiling. "You know what? I think I like you even more, somehow, when you're putting me in my place. I like that you do it. I like *you*. I *want* you. So what if I don't know exactly why? Does anyone with anyone? Does it *matter*?"

As I gazed at him with the raw honesty in his words washing over me, it didn't. Not in that moment, at least. Because he was right—the dark rabble was hot on our trail no matter what we did. Because that memory he was chasing really might be useful to us. Because his remarks from an hour ago were still ringing through my head—*I'm utterly useless now*—and I wanted him to be able take them back almost as much as he did.

We'd already come this far. Giving in always felt almost as good as it hurt.

My answer came out in a whisper. "No. I want you too."

A gleam lit in those indigo-blue eyes. Darton leaned in. The tip of his nose brushed mine. He traced his free hand down my side, and my pulse pounded even harder.

"You want this?"

"Yes," I murmured, lost in his gaze.

His palm settled on my waist. He tugged my hips forward to meet his. "And this?"

"Yes."

His head dipped. His breath teased over my lips. "And—"

Good gods, enough of this torture. I clutched the back of his neck and pulled him to me.

Our mouths collided in a crash of heat and tongues. I couldn't kiss him hard enough, deeply enough, to feel satisfied. My hand slid to cup his cheek, to trace down his neck and over those football-player muscles I hadn't gotten to properly explore when they'd been on view before. An urgent, needy sound worked itself from Darton's throat. He pressed me against the wall, kissing me back just as fervently.

But then the forcefulness of his lips eased. He kept kissing me, so gently the tenderness of it made my heart ache, but I knew his mind had come unmoored. I stayed there with him, trading breath for soft breath, waiting for him to come back.

His mouth drifted away from mine to tease along my jaw. He grazed it over the crook of my neck. Then he paused with a shaky inhale.

"You really were terribly, terribly bad with horses, weren't you?"

A giggle jolted out of me. "Despite your best efforts."

He nuzzled my hair, nipped my earlobe, and blazed a scorching path to my lips. We'd only kissed once more before I felt him fade a second time.

I let my mouth linger against his for a moment, and then I just held him. He hugged me back as if I were his anchor amid the rush of ancient history. His thumb stroked up and down my spine. I buried my head in his shoulder, soaking in the mingled scents of citrus and earth in the warmth of his body.

He was far away right now, but that distance meant my king was returning to me, bit by bit.

His embrace relaxed, and he bowed his head next to mine. "The whole flashback thing does make hooking up a little tricky, doesn't it?"

I snorted. "It's early days. You'll get better at staying present."

"With practice?" he suggested hopefully.

As tempting as that idea was, I knew it was time to stop. Under the giddy thump of my pulse, the ache in my chest was growing. And there were logistics to consider too.

I swatted his arm. "I think we've had enough of that tonight. I would actually like to add to that two-hour store of sleep I've been running on."

"Well, I can't argue with that." He smiled against my cheek. "I got back to it. To the memory, in the alchemist's shop. I remembered enough this time to know that's where I was."

I pulled back to watch his expression. "And?" Whatever he'd recalled couldn't have changed his opinion of me if he was still making hook-up jokes, but I'd tensed all the same.

Darton's gaze drifted away as he slipped back into the memory. He frowned. "He was showing me pieces of... glass? I think. Round ones, laid out on the workbench."

That image tugged at my mind with a vague sense of familiarity. *Had* he mentioned this moment to me in another life and I'd simply not had the chance to record it?

"What were they for?" I asked.

"I'm not sure. I'm going to have to try to bring up more next time. I had the impression, the bit I fell into, that he and I had already discussed whatever my purpose was. But I know I was excited about what he'd told me. I was going to make something easier for you, something you'd been worried about." His brow furrowed. "There was a man I'd talked to who'd frightened you. The alchemist was saying that he'd never seen 'one,' that he could only rely on 'fairy stories.'"

My skin turned cold. "Not a man. A dark fae. You never told me you went to Ffion to ask about them."

Was that why this memory had surfaced for him now—because of the mercenary's magic that had already touched him?

"I think I wanted to handle the situation by myself," Darton said. "Make less work for you. Or something like that. I just wish I remembered how the hell a bunch of glass shards was supposed to accomplish that. You don't have any idea?"

I shook my head. What were the chances a human alchemist who'd never even seen a dark fae had held some secret knowledge that would defeat them? It was grasping at straws.

"We'll try again if we can't find out anything from this hunter the light fae talked about," I said, more for Darton's benefit than because I had any real hope we'd find our answers there.

CHAPTER TWENTY-SIX

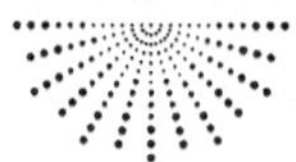

THE POUCH of salt in my pocket shuddered. I jerked awake.

A thin gray light seeped through the gap between the curtains beyond the red glow of the clock. It was six fifteen. We'd made it to morning, if not with a whole lot of sleep to show for it. I blinked blearily, and the salt jittered again. My body jolted into full awareness.

I shoved off the comforter and leapt out of the bed. "Darton, we've got to go. Now."

A defiant muttering filtered through the pillow his face was buried in. He pushed upright with a groan. He'd taken off his sweater to sleep, and his undershirt showed off his muscular arms and chest to full effect.

I yanked my gaze away. This was not an appropriate time to be getting distracted.

"The sooner we leave, the better," I told him. "Get dressed."

I ran to the bathroom to relieve myself and splash cool water on my face. When I returned, somewhat revived, Darton was standing outside the bathroom door, his sweater and shoes on. His face looked sleep worn, but his eyes were alert.

Alert and somber. His voice came out with a rasp. "I was dreaming. I don't remember it all but— I don't know whether they *were* just dreams or real."

I paused. "What did you dream?"

His head bowed. I was about to order him to hurry up or leave it for later when he brought his hand to his abdomen. To the spot on his gut where he'd felt that pain before. My pulse hiccupped.

"The woman," he said. "The dark fae? Who killed me. She stabbed me here?"

I swallowed thickly. "Yes. But she didn't *kill* you. You're not dead. You've lived more lives than she ever will. I stopped her."

For the time being, at least.

"Right," Darton said, but the shadow in his expression lingered. I wanted to say something more comforting, but comfort wasn't my specialty even at the best of times. And right now, we had barely any time at all. I gripped his arm with what I hoped was a reassuring pressure.

"Do your business, fast. I'll get the others. If you've got more questions, we'll get to them once we're on the road."

The benefit of holing up in a random motel in between nowhere and nothing was we'd been able to get rooms right next to each other. I rapped on the door of the one the other three had shared. On the other side, someone—it sounded like Priya— cursed, and someone else—Izzy, no doubt—gave a resigned-sounding yawn. It was Izzy who opened the door a few seconds later, tugging on her cardigan.

"Already?" She ran her hand through her pale auburn waves to untangle them.

I nodded. "It's not bright enough yet to slow the dark things down much. If we're lucky, we've got fifteen minutes before the first ones turn up—but we might not be lucky."

She darted off to grab her things. Keevan slunk past the door without glancing my way. Darton strode over, his cowlicks ineffectively tamed with water.

When Izzy and Priya emerged onto the concrete walk, Keevan was nowhere to be seen. "He went into the bathroom a few minutes ago," Izzy said with a frown.

Darton stepped inside and knocked on the bathroom door. "Come on, Keev! Let's get a move on."

He didn't answer. My chest clenched. What if he was having second thoughts? Or third or fourth thoughts, really. He'd acted pretty fed up with me and my stories last night.

Izzy bit her lip. Darton banged on the door again, loud enough that Priya winced—and finally Keevan jerked it open.

He stood there on the threshold of the room, looking blankly at Darton. The blood vessels stood out in his eyes, and his dark skin had a grayish cast. He listed to the side.

Izzy's eyes widened. "Are you okay?"

"I'm fucking tired," Keevan grumbled. "It took me forever to get to sleep. If I even did. Feels like I was staring at the ceiling and then you were knocking on the door."

I felt bad for him, but sympathy wasn't going to keep Darton alive. "We're going. Are you coming?"

His gaze focused on me. "Yeah," he said roughly. "Of course. Yeah."

"You're not in any condition to drive," Darton said.

Priya raised her hand. "I'm feeling pretty good. I can take over for the morning." She looked at me. "It's not too much farther, right?"

My instinctive reaction to her offer was skepticism, but we'd already wasted too much time. I stuffed the twigs in my pocket and hefted my duffel. "Fine. Keevan, try to sleep some more in the car."

Priya's driving did reflect her personality, but not as worryingly as I'd feared. She worked the gas and took her turns with a brisk, carefree air that suggested nothing could possibly go wrong—and the car went along with it. As we pulled onto the highway, I thought I made out a flickering darkness in the distance behind us. I pulled a few twigs from my duffel bag, but after a minute or two, we'd left even that hint of pursuit behind. For now.

The sun rose higher, burning off the darker, longer shadows the dark rabble preferred to travel along. I eyed the sky through the windshield. Hardly a cloud touched the blue. We should pull away from them quickly. At least while we could drive fast.

We reached Peddleton midmorning and cruised down the main street, which was a blink-and-miss-it type of deal. The vegetation was sparse too. "We're looking for two large trees leaning together to make an X," I said as we looped back around town. I hadn't seen anything like that. We trundled around the outskirts and ventured out along the back roads without any luck.

"Any idea where to from here?" Priya asked.

"No," I admitted. My stomach knotted. The sun would have slowed down the dark rabble, but with the mercenary's lent power, they'd still be on our trail. With each circle of the countryside we made, they were drawing closer.

A lark swooped past the windshield. Izzy squeaked in surprise, and I went still. There was a more efficient way I could search. But I'd be leaving myself totally helpless in the car.

My body balked. Priya veered down yet another side street. A stand of poplars fluttered leaves in the breeze. Still nothing. Keevan sighed, and my fingers tightened around the twigs I was still holding.

It was better to leave myself to the mercy of Darton's friends than to the dark rabble, wasn't it?

I reached over the seatback to fumble with my duffel. My groping hand found the incense I'd stuffed in one of the smaller pockets.

"I'm going to do some magic," I said to the car at large. "I need to find the place we're looking for. I won't be able to talk to you while I'm doing it. Just keep driving around. Hopefully it won't take very long." I handed the stick of incense to Darton. "Hold this?"

He took it. I lit the end with my lighter and lay the twigs across my lap and around me. It wasn't as formal a circle as I preferred, but it'd do for a quick flight.

I sank back against the seat and closed my eyes. The herbal smoke of the incense filled my nose. I breathed it in and murmured the sight-riding incantation under my breath.

My mind lifted from my body, through the roof of the car, and up toward the sky. A robin was just darting past. I leapt into its head.

The world with its sprawl of interlocking roads and stubby buildings stretched beneath me. I urged the bird higher, turning to scan the ground below. The wind buffeted the robin's wings and pushed it even higher, and its gaze caught on a wave of motion far to the north.

The shadows were shifting. Even from that distance, the bird's eyes picked up the shiver in the dark spaces amid the scrub and farmland. Its muscles tensed at the sight.

Oh yes, the dark rabble was coming for us.

I nudged the bird around to swoop in a broad circle well beyond the edge of town. Where were those damned trees? The robin's gaze flitted over fences and billboards and—

There. I tugged it to the left, and the crisscrossing trunks of two old elms came more sharply into view. My thoughts twitched with excitement, but I held myself within the bird and took in the entire landscape. A tingling in the back of my mind told me where the car that held my body was. If we turned here, and then there... Yes. That would take us to those trees and the squat gray building set down the dirt drive behind it.

I released the robin and plummeted. My spirit fell back into my body with a lurch, and my eyes popped open.

The stick of incense Darton was holding had burned an inch down. He was staring at me, his expression tensed. At my other side, Izzy let out a sharp breath. Keevan had turned in the front seat, his face looking even grayer than before. When I met his gaze, his eyes jerked away.

"That," he said in a creaky voice, "was really creepy."

"What *happened* to you?" Izzy said. "You went so still... Priya honked the horn at a dog, but you didn't move even then. It was like you were just gone."

Because I was gone. But given how shaken up everyone looked, I didn't think confirming that would help matters.

"I was vision-riding," I said. "It's no big deal. And I know where we need to go now. Priya, take the next left. Then a right three roads down."

Darton let me pluck the incense from his fingers. I snuffed it out against the canvas of my duffel and tucked the rest away. No point in wasting it.

I'd settled into my seat when Priya made the second turn. A giggle slipped from her lips.

"Well, what do you know?"

Just ahead of us, the two elms leaned past each other against the hazy blue of the sky. Keevan let out a sputtered chuckle. Priya eased on the gas.

The building that stood a quarter mile down the potholed driveway looked more like a large garage than anything I'd have called a house. The ground between the trees and its walls and all around it was barren, just dry dirt and a few patchy shrubs.

Priya drove up the driveway and stopped the car in front of the building. The engine's growl was still fading when a door in the side swung open.

A tall man with a mane of white hair and a hawkish nose stepped out. He raised the shotgun he was carrying, but not quite high enough to aim it at us. Just to show he could if he decided to.

I motioned for Darton to get out so I could. He emerged holding his hands up in submission. I rolled my eyes at him and scrambled out onto the dusty earth.

"What are you doing here?" the man demanded in a gravelly

baritone. He took a step forward, out of the building's shade. The sunlight caught on a spider web of scars etched across his cheeks and chin, nearly as pale as his hair. "I don't have any business with strangers."

I eased in front of Darton. "I'd appreciate it if you made an exception. I've been told the man who lives here knows how to kill dark fae."

Beside me, Priya opened the driver's door and slipped out. She peered at the man with a curious tilt of her head. Keevan and Izzy didn't stir, but I couldn't blame them.

The man's jaw clenched. He squinted at the bunch of us, his narrow gaze lingering on me and then Priya. Did the traces of our fae association cling to us in some way his eyes could perceive?

He shifted the gun in his hands. For a second, I expected him to point it at us after all, but he lowered the muzzle toward the ground.

"Back the car up to the trees, and then come in. This sounds like an inside conversation."

CHAPTER TWENTY-SEVEN

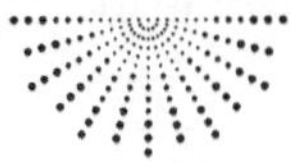

"So you *do* know how to kill these things?" Keevan jumped in. His shoulders had straightened and the color had come back into his face as he'd gulped down the cereal our host—who went by Jagger—had offered us. I'd only just finished my truncated story of why and how we'd ended up at the building behind the crossed trees.

Jagger rubbed his chapped lips where he was standing by the fridge. The rest of us were sitting around a polished oak table in a kitchen that was a lot neater than I'd expected given the grungy exterior. One wall was concrete, but the other three looked like regular plasterboard, painted pale yellow, and the bowls felt like real china. No windows in the place, but light streamed down on us from panels that covered the entire ceiling, bathing us in a steady, thorough glow. It banished all but the most tenacious shadows.

Seeing that had set me a little more at ease, but the glimpse I'd gotten of the dark rabble rippling toward us from upstate lingered in the back of my mind. The milk residue in my mouth turned sour. I shifted on the hard wooden chair, waiting for the fae hunter's answer.

"It depends on what things you mean," Jagger said. "The first thing you've got to know is I've never actually killed a *fae*. Not the human-looking kind. The amount of power those sort have…" He shook his head with a rough chuckle.

My heart sank. Fingers tensed around my spoon, I gathered myself to probe further, but Keevan beat me to it again.

"Would it be a wild guess to say it looks like one of them tried to kill you?" He offered a goofy grin.

Jagger's hand twitched toward the interlacing scars on his cheek. I cleared my throat sharply.

"Forget that. What we really need to know is what you can tell us about hunting any of the dark creatures and about fending off the fae at the very least."

"That I can do," Jagger said. "The lesser dark creatures—the things you're calling glooms and the ones like animals—that's what I hunt. Those I've killed."

Izzy lifted her head. "Those are the things that have been after Darton so far. If we just knew how to get those to stop—"

By the light, could they not leave the conversation to the people who knew what the hell they were talking about?

"It's a dark fae that's urging the rabble after Darton," I interrupted. "The mercenary is lending them power—they wouldn't be half as much a threat without him behind them. We'll need to deal with him. But the strategies may be similar." I studied Jagger's spare, wiry frame. "Do you have magic?"

Few full humans did, but he might not be full human any more than I was.

Jagger gave me a crooked grin. "Nah. I leave sorcery out of it. The drill is simple. Natural light destroys the dark. On open terrain, a flamethrower with a proper flint will do the trick. You've just got to amp it hot enough."

Our mercenary, like most fae-kind, had seemed rather attached to his woodland habitat. "And when you don't want to burn down an entire national park?"

"Now that used to be a complicated matter of lures and traps. But some ten years ago, new findings started coming down the pipe."

"Down the pipe?" Priya repeated with an arch of her eyebrows.

"There are a few of us hunters scattered around," Jagger said. "We check in and exchange strategies over the internet."

"Wait," Darton said, sounding more bemused than he had any right to be when I was trying to figure out how to keep him *alive*. He poked my arm. "You could have just Googled the answers and saved us the road trip?"

"Of course not." I'd searched the internet in this life, even though the new tech felt more byzantine than the language I spoke magic in. It never hurt to dig around a little in case some human development revealed new secrets. I hadn't found any chatter about fae that remotely aligned with my reality.

Jagger leaned back against the wall. "We keep our communications private. The better not to have any thrill-seekers interfering. In any case, one of us discovered another way to make use of the sun. Solar energy can be captured in cells and passed on to a focused light source. The process only gets more efficient every year. I've got several guns soaking up the rays on the roof right now."

"Sun guns!" Keevan said. "So if we get ourselves a bunch of those—"

I cut him what I hoped was a silencing glance. We didn't have time for joking around.

"Do those really work?" I asked. "Even with the battery as a stepping stone?" My focus might have been on the biological and chemical sciences, but I knew enough about physics to understand the basics of solar power. Electrical light on its own could repel glooms and their kin, but it didn't outright harm them. I'd only managed to use the electricity in the theater by transforming it through the magic in my living body.

Jagger nodded. "The effectiveness fades the longer you keep the energy trapped in the cell. It's best for daylight hunting in dark areas, or evenings. But we've found ways to amplify the effect using crystals inside the chamber to keep the light bouncing around until we're ready to fire. That extends the usefulness somewhat.

"And the solar panels are helpful in other ways." He motioned to the ceiling lights. "But even if you caught a full dark fae amid daylight, and you'd just charged my best gun a moment ago, I don't think you'd do more than annoy it."

"That's a start," Keevan said, but my stomach had knotted.

I didn't need a *start*. I needed an end.

Jagger pointed at me. "It's Emma, right? Come with me. I'll show you what I've got."

The others started to get up, but I waved them down. "Finish eating. Who knows when we're going to get another chance to. I'll handle the shop talk."

Jagger led me down a brightly lit hallway to a narrow flight of stairs that stopped at a short ladder and a hatch above. We climbed out onto his roof.

Other than the small concrete square where the hatch opened, the entire surface gleamed with glossy black panes baking in the sun. A rack of guns, mostly rifle-sized, stood at the edge of the bare spot. My gaze immediately leapt from them to the landscape around us, but the shadows of the telephone poles and the sparse vegetation on the other side of the road lay still. For now.

Jagger hefted the largest weapon—practically a bazooka. A narrow pane ran down the top of its length, presumably feeding sunlight into whatever battery he'd hooked it up with.

"It functions a lot like a regular gun," he said. "Not that you look as if you've played much with those either. You squeeze the trigger, and the seal on the end opens. The crystals at the back focus the light into a beam straight down the muzzle. Aim it well, with fresh light, and you can shear apart a gloom. Or wound one of the bigger creatures enough to get it in a better position for torching."

I took the gun from him. The metal shape felt awkward in my hands, so much heavier and bulkier than a wand.

"So is this a calling that passed down through your family?" I said. "Why do you keep it up? The dark fae and their creatures don't bother much with humans these days."

"Not much, but they do, if you know how to look for the aftereffects," Jagger said. "They're vermin. I exterminate them."

The sentiment echoed my own so well I could accept it. But he hadn't answered the first part of my question. He'd tried to speak casually, but a thread of tension in his voice had rung with a deeper familiarity. I looked at the interlocking scars that creased his face.

"Who was it you couldn't save?"

Vermin might kill even an ordinary person if they were pushed into a corner. If they saw that person as a threat.

Jagger's mouth pressed flat. "You didn't come here for my personal story. What you need to be asking is why you're so intent on getting *your* friends killed."

I blinked at him. "What? I'm here to *protect*—"

"The one fellow. I caught that. But what business did you have hauling the other three into it? They're lambs. They haven't got a clue. And you're driving them into the slaughter."

"I didn't want them here," I protested.

"Then why are you still with them?" He glowered at me. "You know what you need to do—what you should have done instead of all this racing around while the shadows ran you ragged. Go straight to that fae. Take the battle to him—just you, no bystanders. You dictate the terms of engagement so they work in your favor, and you take him down with whatever magic you've got. If that's not enough, I'll give you the tools."

I swallowed hard. Maybe he was right. I could have insisted on leaving Keevan, Izzy, and Priya behind so many times, but I hadn't. We needed an end, yes, and it was up to *me* to provide it. But—

"I don't know if I'll have enough to stop him even then," I admitted.

Jagger grunted. "From what I can tell, from that story I know isn't the whole one, you know your enemy better than I could. You figure it out. Or you die. But make it just you."

He jerked his chin toward the gun. "Keep that. And this." He fished a plastic fob out of his pocket and pointed across the dusty ground to a smaller building I hadn't noticed, about a hundred yards behind the one we stood on.

"I've got a van prepped for hunting. Mounted with solar panels and lights. It'll give you a safe haven during the night and a way of blasting the creatures to kingdom come if you time things right. That I'll want you to bring back, if you can."

"Thank you." My fingers closed around the fob. My heart thudded. Was that really all there was to it? I took what I had now and made the best I could out of it?

Did I have much other choice? Coming here had been my only lead.

"If you take this thing down, it'll be an honor to have contributed," Jagger said. "I haven't heard of a dark fae stalking a human like this in my lifetime. Not a trend I'd like to see restarted." He paused. His eyes narrowed as he peered toward the road. "And it looks like you'd better get a move on. Trouble's coming."

I turned to follow his gaze. The edges of the shadows around the crossed trees and Keevan's parked car undulated with a surge of scurrying glooms. My back tensed.

Our time was up.

CHAPTER TWENTY-EIGHT

Jagger grabbed another of his sun guns and stalked across the solar panels to the edge of the roof. I followed him, stepping gingerly on the brittle black sheets. The thin shadows of the telephone pole lines along the road were squirming as the dark rabble wriggled and crawled along them, shrinking to avoid the sun.

"They can't make it to the house by daylight," Jagger said. "No matter how long the shadows get. I set up the property and maintain it to ensure that much. But you'll want to be well on your way before dusk sets in."

I glanced at the sky. My stomach clenched, my fingers tightening around the gun I was still holding. "I don't think we've got even that much time."

Jagger frowned. "It'd take more cloud than that little thing to—"

The fluffy white streak I'd spotted drifted in front of the sun, and the beams lighting the ground dimmed slightly. Enough that with a heave and a surge, flits of darkness shot across the open ground between the crossed trees and Jagger's home. They landed, roiling around each other, in the slice of shadow along the eastern wall.

The grizzled man's jaw had gone slack. "Well, hell. I've never seen them attempt that before."

"It's the mercenary." I hurried across the roof to the east side. "He's sending them extra power. And they're already very keen to get to us—to Darton."

Jagger hesitated a beat before he stalked after me. "Who *are* you?" he demanded.

I'd skipped the whole reincarnation part of the explanation, along with any mention of exactly who Darton and I were connected to, just like I had with Darton's friends. I didn't see how it'd do us any good to get into it now. Instead, I shouldered my gun.

"It's complicated. Show me how this thing works?"

Jagger shook his head at me, but he raised his own weapon. "I've never seen this many swarm together at once either. It'll be like shooting fish in a barrel."

He took aim and pressed the trigger. The seal on the tip flipped up, and a streak of brilliant light cut through the shadow below us. The beam must have hit a gloom, because the edges of the thicker, churning darkness shuddered. The rest of it crept along the edges of the wall as if seeking a crevice to slip in through.

A shiver ran down my back. It was just that wall standing between them and my king.

"Can we only pick them off one at a time?"

"If you try to widen the range, you dilute the light too much to destroy them," Jagger said. "Believe me, you're not the first one to wonder."

"What about that flamethrower you mentioned?"

"Oh, I've got a few tricks up my sleeve if it comes to that."

The forms of the dark rabble squeezed together so tightly I couldn't make out where one creature ended and another began. I aimed haphazardly, figuring I had to hit *some*thing, and pulled the trigger. A puff of shadowy dust dispersed into the air.

Jagger hefted his gun. We fired again and again, but the shadowy mass barely thinned. A thicker cloud grazed the sun, and more shadows raced across the yard to the house. Jagger's hands didn't waver, but his shoulders had gone rigid.

The shade beside the house was swelling with dark vermin now. They swarmed across the wall with a hiss that raised the hairs on my arms. I lowered my weapon. Whatever defenses Jagger had prepared, he'd obviously never imagined facing an onslaught like this.

"I'm sorry," I said. "They're here because of us. We can make a run for it. They'll follow us once they sense we're moving."

Jagger grimaced. "This is a matter of principle now. And they'd smother you before you made it two steps to the van, the way they're coming on. I said I had other tricks, didn't I?"

"I never thought I'd need to use this in the middle of the day," he went on, striding across the roof to a control box protruding beside the hatch. "But it'll take out the lot of them. Give you some breathing space for your escape."

He twisted a knob. A *whoosh* of energy vibrated through the air, and the ground along the border of the building burst into flame. A wave of heat surged over me. I flinched backward with a yelp.

The writhing shadow against the wall burned away with a high-pitched cry that sounded disturbingly like a scream. The shade around the trees and telephone poles frothed as if in sympathy.

I eased back to the edge. The flames crackled in a translucent orange line about two feet tall, all along the base of the building. The sharp smell of burning gas prickled my nose. I let out a shaky chuckle.

"I'm starting to see why you don't have windows."

"If it keeps them away, I'm happy." Jagger came up beside me and studied his handiwork. He smiled. "I've never actually had to put that system to use before. For all my preparations, nothing much ever bothered coming out here for *me*."

I ignored the hint toward his earlier question. "And hopefully they never will. So… how do *we* get past the fire to make a run for it?"

"I wanted to confirm that it'd work. Now you go down and grab that boy of yours and whatever else you brought. The other three kids you can leave here with me. They'll be safe enough if you're right about the dark varmints clearing out once you're gone."

"I—"

He fixed me with a steely look before I was even sure what to say. "You *leave* them. It's bad enough they're here for this."

I shut my mouth. My gut twisted. He was right—of course he was right. I should have been that firm to begin with, instead of putting so many people in danger who'd never needed to be.

"Holler when you're ready to go," Jagger went on. "I'll shut off the flames, give the varmints a chance to get cozy by the house again. Then I'll fry 'em quick while you make a dash for the van. If you run fast enough, you'll get there before they recover."

"Can you keep the fire going long enough for that?"

"It's fed by a county gas line. Unless the supplier runs out, I think we're good."

"Okay." I hustled to the hatch and scrambled down the ladder, ignoring the heavy thump of my heart.

In the kitchen, Priya was still sitting at the table, examining the pale grain of the wood as if she could read stories in it. The others had gotten up. They paused in their puttering around the room when I burst in. Keevan glanced at the gun I was holding. His eyebrows leapt up.

"Now that's what I'd call fighting equipment."

Izzy peered at the empty space around me. "Where's Jagger?"

"Taking care of things so Darton and I can get out of here," I said. My duffel was still sitting behind my chair where I'd put it down. Thank the light I'd brought it in instead of leaving it in the car, even though Jagger hadn't found anything in there useful to his methodology. I heaved it across my back and turned to find four pairs of eyes staring at me.

"You and Darton?" Keevan said. "What about the rest of us?"

"Emma," Priya started.

"They've found us again," I said before she could go on. "The dark rabble. They're going to keep finding us. But it's Darton they're following. I've got… I've got the beginning of a plan. As soon as we're out of here, you three can head back to campus. You should be able to make it there before you even miss Friday's classes."

"That's not the point," Keevan said.

"How are we going to know that you two are okay?" Izzy put in.

We probably won't be. "We have phones. I appreciate everything you've done to help, but it's only going to get rougher."

Keevan looked to Darton. "You get a say in what happens too."

Darton opened his mouth and hesitated. "I don't even completely understand what we're up against. If Em thinks we're all better off—"

Jagger appeared in the doorway. The way he clutched the frame, his knuckles whitened, made me tense.

"Emma…" he said. "I need you to look at something."

A chill ran down my spine. I grabbed Darton's wrist and gave it a squeeze. "Be ready, by the door." I dropped my duffel there and jogged to follow Jagger to the roof.

Up in the open air, he walked to the front of the building and pointed toward the road. It didn't take long for me to figure out what was worrying him. A little plume of dust shot up from an unnaturally dark splotch amid the shadow beside one of the telephone poles.

"What are they doing there?" he said. "I don't like the look of it."

"They're digging," I said. "Maybe they think they can get at the building from underneath?"

Jagger's stance relaxed. "They'll be disappointed then. This place is standing on solid cement."

Watching the flurry of motion around the hole stirred up a memory. My heart sank. "It might be something else. When they came after us on campus… they dug down to the electrical line and cut it."

"My entire system is internal," Jagger said. "From these panels straight to my private generator."

But it wasn't electricity they wanted to avoid. The acrid tang of burning still hung in the air. I leaned forward. The flames were sizzling on along the wall.

"You said the gas line is a county one. Hooked up to a supplier somewhere else."

Jagger glanced at me. "Do you really think—"

The line of fire below us sputtered. Jagger's face paled nearly as white as his scars. He swore.

"Go. Go *now*!"

He pushed me toward the hatch, but I was already running. The crackle of the flames fizzled out with a faint *pop* before I'd even made it to the opening. I clambered down the ladder and dashed for the door.

Jagger's footsteps thudded behind me. We froze at a creaking that echoed throughout the entire building.

"What the hell is that?" Keevan's voice carried from the kitchen.

I didn't want to tell him the answer I was almost certain of. A fresh swarm of dark creatures had surged up against the building— and they were pushing on that wall with all their might.

Another creak reverberated through the space, rising to a groan. Jagger laughed, so hollowly my skin turned even colder.

"Oh, no. They're not beating this one," he muttered. He nudged me toward the kitchen and grabbed a bundle of fabric from one of the cabinets as he followed. He thrust it at me. The coarse material settled so heavy in my arms I might have thought it was waterlogged if it hadn't felt completely dry.

"It's no good for any of you to stay in here now," he said to me. "But you know what you have to do once you've got some distance from that horde."

"Jagger," I started. The groaning intensified, and the interior walls trembled. Darton and the others stepped closer to me.

Jagger shook his head at whatever he thought I'd been going to say. "I can get all of you out of here safe. You just have to listen. I'll shout, and then you've got to run. Five seconds, as far as you can make it in that time. Then you throw yourselves down on the ground with that tarp over you. No messing around. Got it?"

"What—"

He grasped my shoulder to cut me off. "I don't know what you're doing, but it must be worth an awful lot if they're that desperate to stop you. Good luck." Then he sprinted off down the hall.

Darton caught my eye. I lifted my shoulder in confusion, my throat tight.

"You heard him. Does everyone have everything they need?"

Keevan gave a jerky nod. Izzy clasped her hands together in front of her. "What's happening out there?"

I was saved from having to answer by Jagger's bellow from somewhere deep within the house.

"Now, get going. And give them hell for me!"

The words from my vision. My pulse stuttered. I shoved open the door and tugged Darton with me. The others spilled out into the sunlight in our wake. I pointed to the building Jagger had said held his van. "That way."

We bolted for it. Priya counted out the seconds with a gasp of a voice.

"Five, four, three, two, one…"

"Down!" I shouted and tossed myself to the ground, dropping

my bag beside me. I wrenched and kicked at the thick black material of the "tarp" so it billowed over us. "Everyone get under. Hurry!"

I pulled it over my head. Darton's breath was harsh beside me in the sudden dark. My own hitched. "I just—" Izzy's voice murmured somewhere too my left.

A *boom* thundered through the air. The ground shook beneath us, and Izzy's comment turned into a squeal of pain.

CHAPTER TWENTY-NINE

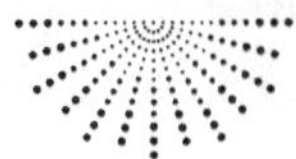

HEAT SEARED OVER THE TARP. I cringed beneath the plastic-feeling fabric, my skin aching at the pressure. Then the temperature dipped again, in time with the clatter of objects hitting the ground around us.

Two heartbeats passed before I found the courage to pull back the tarp. I pushed myself upright. The others shifted around me and froze as they took in our surroundings.

The tufts of grass around us were scorched black. Thirty yards away, the building we'd fled spat up smoke from its burning ruin. The walls had collapsed in, the roof burst off in a rainfall of gleaming black fragments. Flames crawled across the interior walls now exposed.

My jaw had dropped. "Jagger?" I shouted, scrambling to my feet. The acrid smell of the smoke filled my lungs, and I coughed. "Jagger!"

No one answered or stirred amid the wreckage. Nothing moved except the warbling flames.

Because the blast had destroyed all of the dark rabble that had been nearby too. Jagger had known it would.

He'd given us our head start by whatever means he could.

I choked up, remembering that last squeeze of my shoulder. *Good luck*, he'd told me. I knew what he'd say now. *Don't stand around dawdling. Get yourself gone.*

He'd sacrificed so much for us. For me. The least I could do in return was make sure that act had been worth it.

"Come on," I said hoarsely. "We don't have a lot of time."

I offered Darton a gloved hand to pull him up. Priya was already standing, peering at the smoking building. Keevan swayed onto his feet.

"My car," he said. My gaze shot to the Toyota beside the crossed trees. Both the trees and the car were blackened now, the Toyota's hood split where a chuck of concrete had hit it. The windshield had shattered in on the front seats. I grimaced.

"We're not going anywhere in that now. But Jagger left us something better."

I jogged the rest of the way to the garage and shoved open the door. The others gathered around me as I eyed the gray van with lumpy fixtures all over its sides and top. Izzy was holding her arm bent against her stomach. Her forearm was blistered red.

"I didn't get all the way under the tarp in time," she said in a thin voice at my startled look. Her eyes gleamed with tears she was trying to blink back.

I swallowed hard. This—her injury, Keevan's ruined car, maybe even the disaster of Jagger's home—was my fault. My fault for letting Darton's friends come this far. My fault for letting them come at all. Jagger had been right. Whatever little help they'd offered, it didn't justify the danger I'd put them in. It wasn't fair to them when they didn't understand.

"I've got witch hazel in my bag." I shoved my duffel toward Priya. Anyone raised by the light fae should at least be able to recognize that. "Let's get going."

Jagger had given the key and the responsibility to me, so I heaved myself into the driver's seat of the van. Darton climbed in beside me. The other three piled into the back. As Priya rustled through my bag, I stared at the spread of controls on the dashboard, as complicated as the fixtures outside. None of them were labeled. Jagger obviously hadn't imagined he'd been loaning this vehicle out when he'd customized it for his hunting expeditions.

That I'll want you to bring back, if you can. It didn't look as if there were anyone left to bring it back to.

My fingers clenched around the steering wheel. Then I shifted the one stick I did understand and reversed us out into the sunlight.

"Here," Priya murmured behind me. Izzy gasped. My roommate must have slicked some gel over her burn. I turned the car toward the drive, watching for returning glooms or worse.

"When we have a moment to stop, I should be able to at least mostly heal it," I said.

"With magic?" Izzy let out a choked giggle. "No. No, that's okay. I don't want *that.*"

The firmness of the last statement set my nerves on edge. I turned right, away from Peddleton and whatever trail we'd left leading into town. The clouds that had screwed us over not long ago had drifted on, leaving the sky stark blue around the blaze of the sun. Small blessings. I wished we'd had them earlier.

"Where are we going?" Darton asked quietly.

Yes, it would probably be best to have a more concrete direction than just *away.* I dragged in a breath. Hog's balls, what I wouldn't give to stop and rest my head for a second. But I didn't know how many dark vermin Jagger's last-ditch effort had destroyed or how many others might be homing in on my king right now.

The van cruised by a desolate farm, a gas station-slash-family diner, and a sign announcing we'd entered another county. "Emma?" Priya said.

"I'm thinking." Jagger had said I should go after the mercenary by myself. Confront the dark fae on my own terms. What other choice did I have? Maybe I could summon enough magic to at least stop the mercenary temporarily until I figured out a better plan.

I couldn't confront him until I knew where he was.

I had a sense of the dark fae from my sight-riding last week, from that brief vision when he'd spoken to me. With the right tools, I could figure it out. But a phone app wasn't going to cut it.

"I need a map," I said. "I'm going to track down this mercenary and turn the tables on him."

"Are you sure that's a good idea?" Keevan said. "Can't we, like, call the police or the FBI or something?"

"Do you think the police have any idea how to combat fae magic? I *wish* it were that easy."

"So there isn't any faerie enforcement agency?" His voice was so strained the question didn't even sound like a joke.

"No," I said. "We're on our own."

We rumbled into another town. I veered over to the sidewalk outside a general store and motioned to Darton. "You come with me. Everyone else, stay here. I shouldn't be more than a minute."

The dusty shop had a rack of maps by the far end of the counter. I grabbed the largest one that covered the territory I needed, and then a couple more in case the mercenary hadn't lingered in his little clump of dead forest after all.

As we stepped out of the store, a shudder of darkness down the road caught my eye. Glooms were slithering along the edge of the sidewalk just a few blocks away. My pulse stuttered.

"Get in, get in!" I pushed Darton toward his door and dashed around to mine. The second I'd dropped into the seat, my foot was on the gas pedal.

I was going to *have* to stop at some point to work the magic I needed. I scanned the passing landscape as we tore out of town. Jagger had the right idea, setting his home apart from everything else that cast a shadow. The light fixtures on the van should help me with that.

I didn't trust the matted, yellowing grass or the uneven sprawls of gravel that allowed too many tiny shadows. And I wanted more distance from the approaching dark rabble too. I pushed the van as fast as I dared go. For several minutes, we roared along the highway.

We passed through another small town. A large hardware store came into view up ahead, with a huge asphalt parking lot beside it. A store-closing sign was draped across the darkened windows, and the lot was empty. And completely flat.

I yanked the wheel and turned off the road. "Uh, what are we doing *here*?" Keevan said.

"It's the safest spot for avoiding the shadow creatures," Priya said with more assurance than I was comfortable with yet. "No shade for them to creep up on us. As long as the sun stays uncovered."

"Are we going to count on that?" Izzy peered through the window, her brow knitting.

"And are we just going to *sit* here?" Keevan added.

I parked in the middle of the lot. "No," I said shortly. "I'm working on the rest. First, I need to figure out these lights…"

I jabbed at the buttons on the dashboard. Radio—soaring classical music, *so* not what I'd have expected. Air conditioning. Front lamps. Ah, now we were talking. A flood of brilliant light washed away the van's own shadow beyond the hood. Smiling, I pressed the other buttons around that one. Then I stepped out to survey the result.

Light glowed all around the van's sides and across its underbelly. No shadow "varmint" was getting within ten feet of this thing. As long as those panels on top held the sun's power, at least.

I grabbed my duffel from Priya and carried it and the maps to a spot a few feet in front of the van, within the flow of light but enough apart from everything else that I could clear my head. I opened the map that covered the area around the college, spreading it on the ground. Then I dug in my bag for some material to inspire my connection to the mercenary.

Oaks. The trees he'd been living among had been oaks. My hand closed around an appropriate twig.

"What are you doing?" Izzy asked.

"You could call it dowsing," I said. "It sort of is. But I'm going to need to concentrate, so no more questions, all right?"

I pulled off my glove and drew out the fae knife. The skin on my palm split with just the slightest press of the blade's tip. Bracing against the sting, I dug it a little farther until a few drops of blood pattered onto the map's surface. Closing my eyes, I clutched the oak twig in that hand. My memories of the dark fae and his lair swam up in my mind. I tugged at the energy inside the twig and my own body.

"*On paper as real, bring me to the one I seek,*" I murmured in the old tongue.

My eyelids lifted. The lines on the map were quivering. The twig in my hand shivered with them. Then it twitched in one specific direction. I let my arm follow that pull, repeating my incantation under my breath. A trickle of blood seeped down over the bark. The twig jerked and jerked again, until my hand was poised over a green patch on the map some hundred miles northeast of the college.

The twig rammed downward, so swiftly I almost lost my hold on it. It tapped the paper, smudging it with my blood. My fingers tensed.

Right there. That was where our enemy was lurking. Relief and dread coiled together in my stomach, cool and jittery.

The twig crumbled to dust. I wiped it away, accidentally smearing blood on the hip of my jeans. "Okay," I said, gathering the map. "We'll need to—"

I turned and halted at the expressions on my companions' faces.

Priya looked normal enough. Who knew how much fae magic

she'd witnessed before? But Darton and his friends were watching me with wide eyes.

Darton seemed to recover first. "You're still bleeding," he said.

I glanced at my hand. It wasn't a deep cut. Hardly worth expending more energy over. I tugged my glove back on and sheathed the dagger. "I'll be fine."

"The map *moved*," Izzy said. "You *talked* to it."

Well, not exactly, but I didn't see that getting into the finer details of magical practice was going to help anyone.

"Yes," I said. "I do magic. I cast a spell, and now I know exactly where this menace who's after Darton is. But I've got to get to him before his shadows catch up with us again. So—"

"No."

Keevan's voice was so raw my gaze shot to him. He'd crossed his arms over his chest. His eyes flashed when mine met his. "This is enough. I'm done."

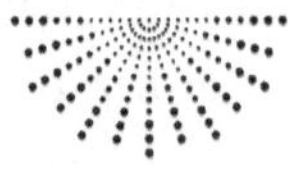

Keevan's declaration was met with silence. None of us seemed able to speak. "What?" I managed finally. "Why now?"

Keevan flung out his arm in a vague gesture that encompassed my blood-dappled map, the van, and the distant building we'd seen eaten by flames. "I've told you before that I don't understand this. I don't like it. And things just keep getting crazier. That guy—he might be *dead*. My car practically got blown up too. You're cutting yourself up and making maps come to life…"

"I didn't *enjoy* any of that."

"I don't care!" Keevan said. "I just know I'm in way over my head. No regular human being can do the stuff I've seen you do."

"You've lied to us," Izzy said in a low voice. "Haven't you? Or at least there's a lot you've decided not to tell us. What you *have* told us doesn't really add up."

When I opened my mouth to protest—to pile more lies on top of the earlier ones—Keevan held up his hand. "I don't care about that either. If there are things you feel we can't handle, that you've got to keep to yourself, fine. But I can't keep tagging along like I'm cool with this either. You made it clear you think we're dead weight anyway."

When I'd almost left everyone but Darton behind at Jagger's place. The shock of the explosion had temporarily bound our little group back together, but he was right. I'd already been thinking about where to drop them off on the way to the mercenary's lair. I didn't want to try to explain any more of my history than I already had. I didn't even know how *I* was going to deal with the dark fae, not really, let alone stop him from slaughtering everyone around me.

And yet the idea of them leaving wrenched at my chest.

"We can at least give you a ride back to campus," I said. "Your car—I mean, I'll cover the cost for you to replace it, but in the meantime—"

"Let's not get into that," Keevan said darkly. "I saw a bus terminal in town. I've got my credit card. You paid our way down here; I can manage to get myself back."

Izzy studied me, her pale eyes steady and her chin high. "You don't really want us to stay, do you?"

She stood there so unbending it was hard to believe I'd ever thought she was soft. I found I didn't know what to say. Which was ridiculous, because all I'd wanted from the beginning was for them to take off.

"Right," she said when I didn't answer. Her gaze slid to the man beside me. "Darton..."

"You don't have to go along with this craziness, man," Keevan broke in. "Those things are probably chasing *her*, not you. Let's just get out of here."

Darton reached for my arm, a gesture that warmed and tore at my heart at the same time. A couple days ago, those two had been his closest friends. I'd ripped a chasm between them in just twenty-four hours.

But then, what were the chances he'd survive to miss them all that long?

"I told you before," Darton said. "I trust Emma. I know she's telling the truth. If I went with you, without her—none of us would make it back to campus."

Keevan threw his hands in the air. "Fine. You know my number. If you need bailing out, I'll come. It's her I'm done with, not you."

He stalked off toward town. Izzy's mouth twisted. When Darton glanced away from her, her shoulders stiffened. She turned and hurried after Keevan.

"I'm sorry," I said. "I—"

Darton shook his head. "It's not your fault."

I was pretty sure it was. Whether I could have avoided this situation without getting us into an even worse spot, I didn't know, but I was the one who'd brought us here.

Priya cleared her throat. She'd hung back during the argument, but now she caught my eyes and jerked her head to the side.

"A word, Emmaline?"

I wasn't particularly keen to hear her assessment of our present circumstances, but I followed her a little apart from the van and Darton anyway. The sun beat down on our heads as heat rose in an echo from the asphalt beneath us, roasting us from both directions. The oily smell of the baking pavement turned my stomach.

Priya stopped. "Why have you been so angry at me?" she said abruptly.

My eyebrows twitched upward. "Because… you lied to me the entire time we've been living together? You were spying on me?" How could she ask that?

"You lied to me about an awful lot of things, because you thought I was safer not knowing. How is that different?"

"I didn't know you had any idea the fae even existed!" I burst out. "You knew *exactly* who I was and what I was going through. Of course it was different."

She cocked her head. "What would you have done if I'd told

you, even hinted at my association with them? Would you have opened up to me then?"

I tried to imagine it. If I'd seen the armlet with the runes during a casual conversation, if Pri had made an offhand remark about the fae, how would I have reacted?

Panic. I'd have been out of that apartment searching for a new living situation before the dust had settled.

I wasn't angry with her just because she'd lied. I was angry also because I didn't trust the fae, any of them, light or dark, and I would have assumed she'd do more harm than good if she interfered. I still wasn't sure of her motives. But I *was* sure I'd earned the right to that distrust at least a hundred times over.

"No," I said, "but that doesn't make it okay that you were sneaking around, sending back reports or whatever to your enclave. It doesn't matter how important *you* thought keeping an eye on me was. I should have had the choice."

Priya gave me a small smile. "Do you really think I came all this way so I could make a report? Gods, Emmaline, the enclave would have been happy just to know you'd taken the king and all the trouble that surrounds the two of you farther away from them. I knew who you were because they asked me to watch you, but that's not why I agreed to do it."

"Well, why then?" I demanded. "You thought you could 'help' fix a problem *I* haven't been able to in fifteen centuries?"

"Maybe," she said. "And maybe you're right to make fun of that idea. But it wasn't just that either. Do you know what it's like to spend the first eight years of your life with only the fae for company? No, wait, you do. You have to know how it is trying to live in the human world with so many things in your head they'd never believe, so many quirks you never realized were quirky..."

She laughed, a little raggedly. "I've never had any real friends. Any time I started to get close with anyone—as a kid, as a teenager —I'd always accidentally mess it up. By being me. By being weird."

"Yeah," I said quietly. I did know what that was like. It was why I'd stopped really trying to make friends dozens of lives ago.

"I thought it'd be different with you," Priya went on. "Because you were kind of like me. And you know what? It was. You never looked at me like I'd grown a second head or backed off because of some vibe I didn't mean to give off. You were fine with me being me. I was just waiting until I could contribute somehow, until what I knew about the fae might be useful instead of just a secret… We could take them on together, I thought. And neither of us would have to keep going at it alone."

The strain in her voice made my throat close. "Pri…" I said. "It's not that easy. You can't just decide that someone should trust you and then expect that to be all it takes."

She raised her head. "Maybe not. But I don't think it's as hard as you're making it either. I don't know whether it's just that you've gotten so used to only having yourself or that you actually *like* being the only one taking a stand, but you're screwing up, Emmaline. You aren't the only one who cares about him." She pointed to Darton.

"It's not the *same*," I started, but she cut me off.

"You aren't the only one who cares about *you*. But you keep shutting us down, shutting us out. And maybe we haven't been through everything you have, maybe we can't do the same things you can, but I think everyone who was in that van has strength, and you've shut that out too."

My hands clenched at my sides. "It's up to me! It was my spell. It's my duty. He was *my* king."

"But not just yours," she said. "Look, I know you've got a lot of trouble ahead of you. I just needed to say that. Do you think you'll find something for me to do? Or are you going to ditch me the next chance you get, like you tried to back at Jagger's?"

I didn't know what to tell her. "I've always handled things alone. Do you know how to kill a dark fae? Because if you do, you should have spoken up before Jagger blew up his home."

Priya's expression dulled. "Okay. What Keevan said about phones and all that applies to me too. But I don't want to stick around if I'm only going to get in the way."

She set off in the same direction the other two had headed. Keevan and Izzy had already disappeared amid the buildings. I stared after her, my stomach churning.

Good riddance. No more stupid arguments, no more trying to explain the inexplicable. Just my king and me, the way it always had been.

Darton studied me as I marched back to the van, but he didn't comment on Priya's departure. "What now?" he asked. Ready for whatever I told him.

"We track down that dark fae," I said. "Let's see what we've got to work with." I tugged open the van's back doors and clambered inside.

A restless urge quivered through me. I stalked along the wall, running my fingers over the equipment mounted on it. More sun rifles, set by the windows to absorb power through the glass. A couple of bigger but stumpier contraptions I guessed were flamethrowers, with tanks of gas to refuel them. A hazmat suit of the same tarp material that had protected us from the explosion. Skids of protein bars and shakes—fuel for us.

Nothing that told me I could destroy a dark fae so eager to destroy us first.

I paced back and forth and then sank down at the edge of the floor by the doors. I'd meant to hop out, but the moment my butt hit the worn carpeting, my heart sank with it, and I couldn't move another inch. I rubbed my hand over my face.

"Hey," Darton said. "How can I help? What do you need?"

Nothing, I meant to say. *Just give me a minute to think.* But when I opened my mouth, a swell of anguish choked off the words. I closed my eyes.

I needed my king alive and safe, finally. I needed him to know who I was, completely. I needed not to have to go through this horrible cycle all over again. I needed at least the certainty that if I failed, we *would*.

My first instinct was to swallow those thoughts. That wasn't how I talked to Arthur. I didn't let him see when I was struggling. He was always carrying too much of a burden on his own. I had to be the strong one, the capable one, the one who knew how to get things done and who had unshakable faith we'd see our purpose through. That we could keep going.

But Priya's accusation was still ringing in my head. *You keep shutting us down, shutting us out.* She'd hit the mark better than she'd realized. I shut *everyone* out, even the man who'd stood beside me from the beginning, who'd owned my heart for centuries. I'd thought that was being strong, but it suddenly felt ridiculous.

I'd never been stronger than my king—in some ways, maybe, but overall? Back then, if I'd told him I was worried he'd bend under pressure, he'd have laughed at me.

I couldn't quite bear to look him in the face. When I opened my eyes, I found myself focusing on the whorls of his sweater. My hand trembled, but I reached out and grasped his shirt anyway. My voice came out ragged.

"I need *you*. I need you here, like this, knowing me, believing in me... I don't want to have to start over. I don't want to have to wait another twenty years before I can get just a few days of being with you properly. I—"

The words broke around the fear that was too large to express. My chin wobbled. But before I could even finish panicking over how Darton would respond, his arms came around me. He pulled me into a tight embrace, his thighs pressing against my knees where I sat on the floor of the van, his head tucking next to mine. His earthy scent surrounded me.

"I'm here," he said. "And I'll fight with everything I have to stay here. I know you. I know what you can do. I know what *I* can do, even if I've got a lot more catching up to do. We'll find our way out of this."

Tears burned in my eyes. I blinked them back, tipping my face to his shoulder.

I needed him, and I had him. I should have known that. Whatever the quality or extent of his romantic feelings for me, my prince, and then my king, had always been my greatest friend.

The tender feelings were there too, though. Maybe it was selfish, but I needed that reassurance as well. I lifted my head, my cheek grazing his, and traced my fingers up the line of his jaw. Darton leaned into my kiss.

His mouth brushed against mine with a gentleness I hadn't felt from him before. He kissed me slowly, almost cautiously, as if he weren't sure how I'd respond. As if this were the first time, feeling each other out, rather than the mad rush of the last two times we'd collided.

Those earlier encounters had felt desperate, attempts to squeeze as much contact into a few fleeting seconds as we could. The way he touched me now, the slight shift of his lips—a little closer, a little deeper—the tentative foray of his tongue, gave the impression he was trying to stretch out this moment for as long as it could last.

When a memory swam up through those breathless sensations, I didn't fight it. I let it sweep over me and carry me back to the time when we'd been our best selves—before I realized I wasn't falling into one of the good times after all.

CHAPTER THIRTY-ONE

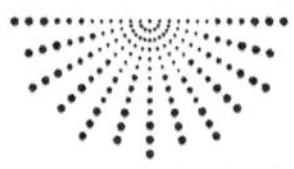

The light was wrong. Normally when I woke up, it was streaking across my feet from the narrow window near the foot of my bed. Now it filled the room around me from several directions in a warm glow.

A room that was much larger than mine had ever been. And the mattress beneath me was much softer than I preferred, wafting a faint, familiar-but-not-that-familiar lavender scent from the herbs woven into the stuffing. Because it wasn't my room or my bed.

The weight I'd only just registered against my waist shifted—an arm, wrapped around me. A nose brushed the back of my neck as breath spilled down my back. My own breath caught with the shudder of my nerves.

I was in my king's room. In my king's bed.

I had a fuzzy recollection of stumbling in here late last night after a full day's riding, having followed Arthur out of habit. Of looking around in my exhaustion and not wanting to move another step, but nonetheless saying I should take my leave. And of my king, with a careless yawn and a fatigue-slurred voice, telling me not to be silly. That his bed was big enough for five, so it could surely fit one scrawny wizard as well as himself. That I'd better not snore.

I didn't think I'd snored. More importantly, I wasn't sure how Arthur had come to be pressed against me in this morning embrace when as far as I recalled, we'd fallen asleep at opposite ends of the bed.

Most importantly, as much as I longed to revel in this moment and the tenderness with which he held me, I had no idea how he was going to react when he *woke up and realized what he'd done in his sleep.*

I lay still. My pulse thudded. Could I slip out from under his arm without disturbing him? Would he be upset if he woke up alone, without understanding why I'd disappeared?

Could I dare to hope he might be pleased *to find us in this position?*

I'd barely had time to entertain that possibility when Arthur stirred —and flinched away from me. His arm thumped the mattress. I swallowed hard and made a show of stretching as if I'd only just woken too. As if I had no idea what position he'd just removed himself from.

Arthur sat up on the other side of the mattress. "Merlin," he said, "get your lazy body out of my bed. Don't you have your own?"

His usual teasing tone held a sharp note that jabbed at my heart. I scrambled up. "My apologies, sire." I dipped into a bow, watching for my deference to light a spark of mischief in my king's eyes.

They stayed dark. His body—bare except for his underclothes—had tensed. I jerked my gaze away before I was tempted to appreciate his physique.

"We've got a lot to do," he said. "We've returned victorious. I think I'll declare a festival day. You can go make up some effects for the celebration, can't you?"

"A festival?" My stomach lurched. "We defeated one enemy, Arthur, but I don't think you should—"

"I'm really rather tired of hearing what you think I shouldn't do." Arthur shoved himself out of the bed on the opposite side, his back to me now. His voice had turned all sharp, no teasing. "I think I've proven I can defend myself. Everyone here could use a day to unwind, not least of all me. Off with you. Get on with it. I don't need you hovering."

"Arthur," I said tentatively, and his head whipped around.

"I said go," he snapped.

I winced and hustled to the door. Down the hall to the staircase, and on into… a van in a parking lot with Darton leaning over me, his breath stuttering against my cheek.

"I'm sorry," he said before I had a chance to center myself in the present. "I'm sorry. Don't go, Merlin. Don't ever, ever go."

My heart flipped over. What memory had *he* come out of? I'd never threatened to leave him, not seriously, but maybe there'd been a time he hadn't known I didn't mean it.

"Arthur," I said, clasping my hands behind his neck. "You idiot, I have stayed with you for fifteen hundred years and never once regretted it. If it's fifteen hundred more, I'll still be there with you on whatever's left of this wretched planet."

His laugh was a tattered sound, and then he was kissing me again, hard now. He pushed forward, and my knees splayed around his thighs until the heat of him burned against me from mouth to groin. A choked sound of encouragement broke from my throat. His tongue swept into my mouth, his hand pushing under my shirt to cup my breast. I arched into him, whimpering as his thumb flicked over the nipple. His other arm tugged me even closer. The feel of him between my legs, so hard, made a giddy shiver race through my core, nearly melting me.

I tangled my fingers in his hair, kissing him with all the passion he'd provoked in me, and he met me with a needy groan. His thumb stroked over my breast again, his other hand trailing down to the waist of my jeans. Gods, yes. We were in the back of a near-stranger's van in an open parking lot, but what did consequences matter when death was only two steps behind us? I wanted him. I wanted *all* of him.

His fingers slipped down to traverse the boundary of my panties—and then stilled.

The pressure of Darton's lips eased back. His body rocked

against mine in a faint rhythm that nonetheless electrified me, but he wasn't fully there. Another memory had taken him.

I sighed and scooted back an inch to let the pressure *inside* me dwindle. Then I laid a kiss at the base of his throat just above the collar of his sweater, because I could. Because I wanted one more taste of him before this interruption brought us back to the more urgent business I couldn't afford to ignore.

After a minute, Darton's head drooped. He caught my shoulders to steady himself. A flush spread across his cheeks, but a different sort of eagerness lit his expression.

"I think I know what Ffion was telling me."

I straightened up. "You got back into that memory?"

He nodded. A smile slid across his face, assured and yet with the childlike pleasure of a boy who'd just beaten all his friends at a difficult game. I wanted to kiss it, but I needed to hear what he'd learned.

I nudged him, and he stepped back so I could stand up.

"I don't know exactly how or why I got there," he said. "I wasn't trying to this time—ah, being focused on other things—but maybe it's because I've been thinking about that memory so much in general?"

"That could have primed you," I said. "But it doesn't really matter. What did you *see?*"

"Lenses," Darton said, as if that explained everything. When I looked at him blankly, he waved his hand. "The pieces of glass Ffion was showing me—they were lenses. Clear sections cut to concentrate the light that passes through them. Like a magnifying glass or, I guess, the crystals Jagger was saying he uses in his guns."

"Lenses," I repeated. My gaze slid across the parking lot and stuck. The shadows beneath the posts and chains that surrounded the lot were squirming. More glooms were creeping along the cracks in the sidewalk to join them. My pulse hitched. Our recent tear across the state hadn't bought us more than half an hour. How long would we be able to stay ahead of them?

I pulled Darton around to the front of the van. "So how were these lenses supposed to help you? What did Ffion expect you to do with them?"

"He was just demonstrating. He said that from what he understood, if you wanted to take on a creature of darkness, you'd need as strong a light as you could gather. And the right lens could concentrate light into something even more powerful than what comes directly from the sun."

That wasn't a strategy I'd given much consideration to, but then, taking down the lesser creatures with a twig and a couple words was less hassle than messing around with a magnifying glass.

"I can concentrate it with my magic too," I said. "Get in. We can't stay here any longer."

Darton climbed into the passenger seat, but his eyes were still vague. "Sure, but what if you used *both*? You can only put out so much power before you drain yourself, right? But if you pushed yourself to your limit, and we used the right lenses to amplify that effect even further... We could hit this dark fae harder than you could have managed on your own."

He might be right. I looked at my hands as I walked around to the driver's side, trying to picture channeling magic-drawn light through circles of glass.

"Ffion was saying the effect should be even greater with multiple lenses," Darton went on. "If you could hit the dark thing from all sides with concentrated light so it had no way to escape."

An image sprang into my head—a blaze of light bouncing through gleaming shards and striking a center point—one after another, as if forming the spokes of a giant, searing wheel. The power of that idea radiated through me. My father's voice rang up from my memory, with words that no longer felt absurd. *The dark fae can't cope with the unexpected. And we always have chaos on our side.*

I hopped into my seat and fumbled for the key fob. "Okay, but... where are we going to get lenses that do what we want?

Dollar store magnifying glasses aren't going to cut it. We'll need the most concentrated light possible. And we're going to need them *soon*." The entire border of the parking lot was jittering with living shadows now. I frowned at the row of switches that would shut off the van's protective lamps. Then I noticed Darton watching me with a funny little grin.

"What?"

He shook his head, the grin staying. "You're so… you. It's always spectacular watching you in the planning zone."

The compliment and the grin were doing something funny to my stomach, but now wasn't the time. "Well, when you're done admiring, maybe you could pitch in with the brainstorming?"

"Lenses…" He rubbed his chin. "High quality ones built for a specific purpose. Maybe some sort of scientific supply store? Except I think I'd need a degree in physics to know exactly what to ask for." He paused, and then started to laugh. "That's it!"

I started the engine. "You're going to complete a B. Sci. in the next two hours?"

"No. Keevan. His sister's in the physics department, remember? I don't know if she's done any optics work herself, but she probably at least knows someone who has or where that kind of equipment would be kept."

I glanced the way Darton's friends had gone, my body tensing. But the clench of my gut I braced for didn't come. Instead, I felt more as if a weight had lifted.

Keevan had wanted to help. He'd wanted to be there for Darton. If we went ahead with this plan, he really could be.

It was a long shot, but what else did we have?

"I know you've been hesitant to let them get involved—" Darton was saying.

"No." The image of the beams of sunlight shooting out in their spokes flashed through my mind again. Chaos was the strength of light's side. And the people who cared about Darton, about me, they were his strength. Our strength. I flicked off the panel of lights and hit the gas in the same movement. "Let's go. We're going to need everyone."

&

As we raced out of the parking lot, a clump of glooms hurled themselves at the side of the van. They smacked it hard enough to rock us. I gritted my teeth and pushed the pedal to the floor. We roared onto the street, swerving to get on the right course, and barreled toward the bus terminal.

"I'm sorry," Darton said abruptly.

"For…?"

His mouth twisted. "For not telling you about talking to Ffion and what he told me, back then. I don't know everything that went into that decision, or what might have been going through my mind afterward. But right then when he was telling me… I *really* wanted to come to you with the whole solution worked out. To show you I could fight that battle beside you instead of leaving it in your hands. Maybe I never had the chance to pursue that strategy before…"

Before he'd died. Or nearly, at least. My throat tightened.

"It's all right," I said. "I know you would have. You couldn't have known how it would all play out. They're my kind—more than they are yours, at least. That's why it was my battle. Why it still is. Remember that, okay?"

He nodded, but he didn't look satisfied.

Before I could emphasize the point, our destination came into view up ahead. A bench stood by the curb outside a little ticket office barely wide enough for a door and a window. Izzy and Priya were sitting at opposite ends, and Keevan was pacing on the sidewalk behind them.

I pulled the van over and slammed on the lights, ignoring the stares of a couple passing by. We'd put hardly any distance between us and the dark rabble. I had to make this work, and I had to do it *fast*.

Keevan's head had jerked up. He stopped moving as Darton and I stepped out. Glooms wriggled through the shadows between the buildings and under the awning of the shop next to the ticket office. I held out my hand to keep Darton close to the van.

"You're still here," he said to Keevan.

Keevan smiled crookedly. "The next bus heading in the right direction doesn't come through for another couple of hours."

Priya stood up. "What's going on?"

Izzy stayed on the bench, her back stiff, but she'd turned her head to watch the conversation.

"We have a plan," Darton said. "A good one, I think. And—"

"Darton," Keevan said, sounding fond but deeply exasperated.

A gloom prodded the edge of the van's glow. *Fast.* It wasn't Darton who needed to make amends here. I stepped up beside him. My nerves were skittering, but I made myself speak.

"We can get into the details later. First, I need to apologize. To all of you. For shutting you down when you wanted to help, and for lying. You're right. There's more going on than I've told you. It's only because I didn't want to make things even more confusing for you, but still, that's on me."

Keevan folded his arms over his chest. "And why are you saying this now? Did you figure out something you need us for after all?"

He obviously intended the question to shame me, but I didn't see any point in avoiding that fact. "Actually..." I said. "There is a favor we want to ask from you. And I'm starting to think the key to stopping the dark fae that's after Darton might be all of us working together. If the way I treated you before is a deal breaker, okay. But I am sorry. And this is what you wanted, isn't it? To be there for him?"

"We want to know what's really going on too," Izzy said, fixing me with her cool gaze.

"Not a problem. I can lay it all out for you on the drive up." I motioned to the shadows, which were starting to roil as the dark rabble gathered around us. "We can't get into it here. The things after Darton are already catching up."

Izzy's gaze followed my gesture. She jumped up with a flinch, her face paling. Keevan glanced over too. His eyes widened as he took in the shapes amassing in the shadows around us. He swore under his breath and took a step back.

"I want to get Darton away from here," I said—firmly, to stop my voice from quivering. "I don't want to be standing here with those things so close at all. I'm only taking the risk of talking to you because of how important I think it is that we have you with us."

"I'm in," Priya said. "I'll drive so you can concentrate on the storytelling."

Keevan shifted his weight, his attention still fixed on the dark creatures. "I don't know."

Damn it. "Look, I can't promise you're going to believe me," I said. "It's going to be pretty obvious *why* I didn't want to tell you everything by the time I'm done." Something in me balked, but I'd get over that hesitation. I drew in a breath and let magic seep into my words. "I swear you'll get the whole story. I owe all of you that much."

"Come on, man." Darton clapped him on the arm. "I want you with me for this. If nothing else, it'll be a great adventure."

Keevan's laugh sounded strained, but at least he'd laughed. His shoulders eased down a notch.

"All right. It beats waiting for the bus. But the verdict is out on exactly how much more I'm getting involved until I hear this story."

CHAPTER THIRTY-TWO

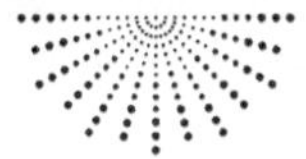

UNSURPRISINGLY, there were a lot of questions when I finished laying out the entire tale. Well, several seconds of bewildered silence that reverberated through the van, and then the questions.

Keevan, sitting at my right in the backseat, pointed at me. "So *you*," he said in an understandably skeptical tone, "were a wizard. *The* wizard—the world-famous Merlin. Pointy hat and robes and all?"

"No pointy hats and robes only on special occasions," I said dryly. Now that the whole story was out there, the tension inside me had dispelled as well. I'd given them everything I could. What they made of it was out of my hands. "And I'm *still* a wizard. I'm still Merlin. I'm just inhabiting a bunch of other people along the way."

"And Darton—" At my left, Izzy's gaze shot to the man in question.

"I was a king of mythic proportions," Darton supplied from the front passenger seat. He'd drooped a little as we'd talked. How much sleep had he managed to get last night? "No one finds that harder to comprehend than I do, believe me."

"You're telling me you've actually *seen* stuff from back then?" Keevan said. "Like, royal pronouncements and jousting and all that?"

Darton's mouth twitched with a hint of a smile. "I haven't gotten to jousting yet, but yeah. I've seen a lot now. I don't believe Em's story just because she said it. I *wouldn't* believe it just because she said it. But it's hard to argue with what's going on in my head."

"What about Lancelot and Guinevere and whoever else? Are we going to run into them too?"

"They never existed," I said. "A lot of embellishments were added to the myths over the years. I recommend forgetting everything you've heard. It wasn't even that exciting a lot of the time. There was a mind-numbing amount of politics, which honestly is mostly people sitting around and talking—or maybe, if you're both lucky and unlucky, shouting—at each other."

"I can support that assessment," Darton put in.

Keevan shook his head. "Well, I don't know. Unless *I* start having visions, it's kind of hard for me to think you're not just pulling my leg."

I looked at him pointedly until he met my eyes. "Yeah. So now you know why I started with the edited version of events."

"It doesn't matter, does it?" Izzy's voice was so low I couldn't tell how much she believed. "Who you were before, I mean. Whatever's going on, those things are after Darton. We know that for sure." When Keevan started to speak, she raised her voice. "We do, Keev. I've thought back to yesterday, when we were running for the car, a lot. You must have seen them too. They were leaping right at *him*—they weren't after Emma."

"I've only known Emmaline for a few months," Priya said from the driver's seat. "So I can only vouch for her that far. But I do know the light fae all talk about the king the Darkest One couldn't quite kill and the fae-blooded one who saved him. That really happened."

"Fine," Keevan said. "Duly noted. Crazy story or not, we need to take down this dark fae thing. I got the impression you have some shiny new plan to accomplish that?"

Darton laid out what he'd seen in his visions of his visit to the alchemist's workshop. He straightened up as he talked, enthusiasm livening his expression. He looked and sounded so sure he'd found the key that my own spirits started to sink.

We were hurtling forward, following the theories of a man who'd never encountered a dark fae. Maybe Arthur hadn't told me about the lenses back then because he'd tried the idea out somehow and found it ineffective, at some later time Darton hadn't recalled yet.

"So will you talk to your sister, Keev?" he said. "All we need are those five lenses. Then we're set."

Izzy hugged her arms tighter around herself. "Is it safe for us to go back onto campus?"

"The dark creatures that came through yesterday morning should have cleared out by now. But Darton and I should keep our distance just in case." I glanced out the window. "If we manage to drive through the night, switching off at the wheel, we'd be almost home by sunrise. We can find somewhere to park and get a little sleep with the solar-powered lights going, then stop by campus and grab what we need. It'll be a couple hours to the forest where the mercenary is staked out. For the plan to work, we'll want to have plenty of daylight left."

"Donielle is going to wonder what the hell I've got going on, you know," Keevan said. "But okay. It's not like I hassle her for favors very often. I'll call her now so she's got time to work things out on her end before we get there." He raised his fist in the air. "Let's do this thing. Let's kill a dark fae!"

He fished out his phone, and I slumped back against the seat. My earlier dread crept up.

Let's kill a dark fae! As if it would be that easy.

We were really going to do this. I was going to drag three uninvolved, ignorant people straight to a dark fae who was eager to spill human blood. How could we possibly surround him without him catching on? What ridiculous part of me had thought the image in my head could become reality?

Jagger's chiding voice ran through my memories. *What business did you have hauling them into it?* I clasped my hands together on my lap, but my pulse thudded on.

Maybe he was right. Maybe attempting this wasn't making up for past mistakes, but the biggest mistake I'd made yet.

❧

The back of the van didn't make for comfortable sleeping, especially with the dawn glow and the light of the built-in beams seeping through the windows. And even more especially with the memory of what lay beyond that light lingering in my head.

The last time I'd looked out, the shadows had been churning around the van throughout the dirt lot we'd pulled off into. We were driving right back through the mass of them that had been pouring toward us. One wrong move, one failed power cell, and we'd all be dead right now.

My pulse rattled through my veins. Darton and Priya, who was sharing the back with me, had nodded off almost immediately, exhausted from the long drive. Izzy hadn't stirred where she'd nestled on the backseat under one of the wool blankets I'd bought us. And Keevan, who'd tipped back the front passenger seat as far as it would go, was snoring in a faint, whirring rhythm.

I dipped my hand into my duffel and pulled out a stick of incense and a handful of twigs. As quietly as I could, I lay out the twigs, lit the incense, and set it on the floor by my face. I murmured a brief chant under my breath. My body slackened as if I were asleep too. My mind drifted up through the van and out into the open air.

The dark rabble was still gathering, prowling, amid the shadows beyond the beams' reach. I hesitated, weighing the risks. I didn't like leaving Darton here without my direct protection.

But I liked the idea of leading all four of my companions to their deaths even less. I pushed myself up into the air and caught on a swallow flitting past.

The bird couldn't fly as fast as I wanted to travel. I needed to be finished this mission before the alarm went off in the van to wake the others. The swallow's beady eyes spotted a truck on the highway, and I sent it swooping down into the bed. We rode there until the driver made a turn in the wrong direction. I urged the swallow up and onto another vehicle going the right way.

I felt as much as saw when we'd reached my destination. I compelled the swallow into the air again. The haze of the dawn had burned away in the wake of a clear, crisp day. I circled the farms near the edge of the wood. This part of my scheme I didn't enjoy at all, but there wasn't any way around it.

A middle-aged man was leading two horses out to pasture. He walked at a strolling pace that suggested he didn't have anything particularly urgent to do today. That was probably the best option I'd get. He latched the gate, and I sent the swallow diving. I propelled my consciousness out as the bird swerved above the man's head—and then I dropped into him.

Taking up temporary residence in another human being's head felt a lot different from taking over any other sort of animal. Sharper thoughts whispered around my awareness with flickers of images and emotions. I hummed silently into them, willing them quiet, willing them still. Putting the man's mind to sleep.

Then I walked him out of the farmyard and into the woods.

My impressions of this unfamiliar body were muted. I tested my reflexes as I strode along. My limbs moved with only the slightest hesitation. And when I plucked a twig from a bush I passed, I conjured a ball of light from it with a few quiet words.

All right. I had a physical presence. I had my magic. The dark fae mercenary lurked somewhere amid the trees ahead of me. If I could find some way, some weakness, here on my own, I'd make sure he wasn't lurking anymore before I left.

I brushed the man's fingertips over the tree trunks, reaching for the life inside them. So much energy that could be turned into power. How much could I channel into one blast without burning through my own life? It wasn't any good destroying this one enemy if I left my king alone to face all those who would come after.

I had to try. Whatever it took. If the dark rabble took Darton for themselves, at least Arthur's soul would still go free and we'd get another chance. The mercenary might end us completely.

A metallic undertone permeated the air—the smell of the dark fae's lair. The bird chatter faded. The only sound that remained was the rustle of autumn leaves beneath my host's feet.

I stopped when the graying branches of a tree showed through the autumn foliage up ahead. The mercenary was here somewhere. Resting during the day, like a vampire of legend? I wished a stake through the heart would be enough to do the job. I gripped a smaller branch on the sapling next to me and snapped it off.

Maybe a stake *would*. If I could draw enough sunlight through the gaps between the thinning leaves overhead and into this stick, then drove it into his chest...

I took another cautious step—and a chilly voice rang out beside me.

"Ah, the king's would-be protector."

The words seemed to coil in the air like smoke. I jerked around. The lanky, blunt-nosed figure I'd seen in my brief vision smiled at me—a smile that could have cut steel. He stood in the darkest shadows where two pines brushed against each other, his presence congealing the shade even darker.

Okay, not sleeping. I clenched my host's hand around my makeshift stake, fighting for calm against the racing of the man's pulse. I had some advantage. The mercenary hadn't been prepared for me, at least not to kill me on sight. All I needed was a brief opening.

The dark fae looked me up and down. His lip curled in apparent disgust. "This is not the guise I expected. Not only do you commit yourself to those organisms, but you wear their bodies too. I couldn't stand it."

It had been so long since I'd talked to a dark fae that I'd forgotten how insultingly they spoke about people. They saw humans as no different from the deer and the hares that roamed the woods—living beasts with no power and little awareness. They saw humans as *less* than that, really, because at least the other creatures still recognized magic as something real.

I shifted back on one foot, closer to the nearest patch of sunlight. I needed that energy if I was going to make use of any opening I got. "Both sides of my nature have served me well," I said.

"Have they?" The dark fae peered at me, and the tremor of his presence tickled over me. By the light, how young he was—like a sapling, bendable and untested. Stewing with his eagerness to take up this quest for his imprisoned ruler. A ruler he couldn't ever have met. Did he even know who I was, or was he working completely off the vague impressions he'd sensed from her?

A flicker of confidence sparked inside me. "In ways you couldn't understand," I said, just to keep the conversation going.

"Hmm. You've fended off my underlings longer than I anticipated. But I haven't tried all that hard yet. Perhaps tonight I'll come for your king myself."

"You can try." I took another step toward the sunlight. A young soul would be easier to sever from this world than an older one with its roots sunk deep. If I just—

The mercenary whipped his arm at me with a burst of shadow, so abruptly I had only an instant to try to dodge. The dark energy hit my host in the gut. My borrowed body doubled over, a burning ache spreading up through his chest. I forced the man backward, stumbling.

Okay. Not so weak a soul. I had to—

Before I'd even drawn a breath, the dark fae hurled another blast of magic at me. I managed to heave myself sideways, but my mind cringed at the sear of cold. The man's body reeled deeper into the shadows.

No, no. I needed the light.

My host's lungs wheezed as they squeezed air up a suddenly narrow throat. The man I'd borrowed, who I'd sworn I'd return safely, was one blast from dying even if I'd survive.

The dark fae marched forward, and I threw myself with very little grace toward the nearest patch of sun.

My spirit sighed the second daylight hit my face. I would have gasped for joy if I'd had the time to. Instead, I whirled myself around to meet the mercenary's next attack.

"That worthless animal body," he sneered, raising his hand again. I braced myself, pulling the sunlight into me, its rush of energy far too pale before the surge of darkness the mercenary was gathering.

A swallow dove out of the trees, snatching at the dark fae's hair —and he didn't even blink. My swallow? Had some of my purpose rubbed off on it?

But what did he care? It was just one more useless animal to him.

Two thoughts collided in my head: Attempting to kill the dark fae on my own would almost certainly end with me dead and him perky as ever. But he'd just given me the answer I needed to end this for real, if not at this exact moment.

The mercenary slammed a fatal wave of his magic toward the man's body. My fingers tightened around the stick.

"*Light be my steed*," I cried out. The branch crumbled, and sunlight blazed down around me. It swept my borrowed body off its feet, shooting us away from the onslaught and my enemy.

The dark fae let out a wordless shout, and then I was gone. The bolt of light flung the man through the woods and dropped us in a heap at the base of the farm's fence.

I sprawled there for a moment, waiting for my host's heart to settle and confirming no appendages were broken. His tailbone might be bruised, and he'd have a strange burn mark on his belly when he "woke up," but the damage could have been much worse. It *would* have been, if I hadn't gotten us out of there when I had.

I gave his mind a soft pat and pushed myself out of him. The pull of my body dragged me back toward the van—toward the greater trial that still lay before me.

CHAPTER THIRTY-THREE

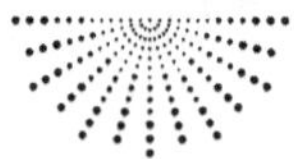

I DROPPED BACK into my body with a sharp inhale. My eyes burst open. The stick of incense on the floor released only a thread-thin line of smoke from what was now mostly a streak of ash.

A chill had pervaded the van—or maybe I just felt the cool of the morning more deeply after my confrontation with the dark fae. I shrugged my blanket higher over my shoulders.

"Em?" Darton murmured behind me.

I hesitated. Could I avoid a conversation if I pretended I was asleep?

His clothes rustled as he shifted. "You went away somewhere, didn't you? Like before, in the car."

I rolled over to face him. He looked back at me, hair rumpled and eyelids heavy. My heart thumped with pained affection.

If only we could just run. Drive this van to the ends of the earth, always one step ahead of the dark rabble and their masters.

It was impossible. Even if escape had been that simple, we couldn't sustain a life of driving all night, every night. We'd run ourselves ragged, and then we'd make a mistake, like always. And as soon as the mercenary made good on his threat to come for my king directly, we'd be screwed regardless.

No, if my little trip had convinced me of anything, it was that we needed to stop the dark fae as soon as possible.

"I'm back now," I said softly.

"Is everything okay?"

I shrugged, and he made a face. Easing a little closer to me, he lifted his hand to brush a stray hair from my cheek. The same gesture he'd made the first time we'd touched. Now I didn't have to flinch away. The graze of his fingers sent a fleeting warmth over my skin.

"You won't go off on your own for real, right?" he said. "We'll stick to the plan?"

Guilt pinched my stomach. He couldn't know how "real" the attempt I'd just made had been, but maybe he guessed. Maybe he knew me that well by now. At least I could honestly say, from here forward, "I'm not going anywhere. We're in this together."

Darton inclined his head, touching my waist with a nudge I understood. I rolled over, and he scooted even closer to spoon me. His face tucked against my hair, his arm around my waist. Like that moment long, long ago, except this time, he did it consciously, willingly.

The ache around my heart expanded. I closed my eyes against a sudden burn of tears. Exhaustion washed over me. The last thing I felt before I tumbled into sleep was the brief press of Darton's lips to the back of my neck.

The shadows along the edges of the wood lay still—for now. I pushed away from the van's window where the others were still peering at the forest. We'd parked on the gravel shoulder of the two-lane highway across from the farm where an undoubtedly now-rather-bewildered man lived.

"We've got an opening," I said, grabbing a canvas bag. "Let's take it while we have it."

Keevan straightened up as much as the van roof allowed. "So it's just the dark fae guy we'll need to watch out for?"

"He sent all the dark rabble he could reach after us, and we left them behind again this morning. But they'll catch up with us fast, so we've got to get moving. There might be a few newcomers in the forest, but they won't bother the rest of you anyway."

"Very comforting," he muttered, but he dropped his phone and watch into the bag when I held them out. Izzy and Priya chucked in their electronic devices too.

They made an odd trio, like members of some sort of new age club, all dressed in similar tunics and trim pants. While Keevan had visited his sister on campus, I'd taken the rest of us shopping at the hippy-dippy place just south of downtown. We were wearing clothes made entirely of natural fibers and dyes.

"Your armlet too," I said to Priya. I'd never sensed any fae energy emanating from the rune-etched leather, but that didn't mean a full fae with sharper sensitivities wouldn't. She shoved up her sleeve to grab it and tossed it in.

Izzy rubbed her arms. "This mercenary—you're sure he won't notice us creeping around?"

"The dark fae—and even the light fae, to some extent—see humans as part of the animal world. And themselves as something higher." My mind darted back to that moment in the woods when the mercenary had ignored the swallow's dive without so much as a twitch. The sneer in his voice when he'd talked about my host's body. My mouth twisted.

"You've got nothing artificial on you now," I went on. "He'll sense there's something living moving around, but you won't seem any more significant to him than if you were a bird or a mouse. Especially when he'll have Darton and me to focus on."

At least, I hoped that was true. I pulled my hair back from my face into its habitual ponytail. "Are you all ready?"

Priya nodded. Keevan clapped his hands with a shake of his shoulders. "Let's get this over with."

"Okay. Stay close to the point I showed you and spread out in a circle around that. Make sure you stop at a spot that's getting some sun through the canopy. With the branches getting barer, that shouldn't be too hard. Then just sit still until I call on you. We'll be about ten minutes behind you to give you time to get settled, but I don't know how long the fae will take to come."

I followed the three of them out of the van and around the side, but I stopped at the edge of the ditch. As soon as I entered the forest, the mercenary would sense my presence.

Even in the early afternoon, the autumn breeze had a cool edge to it. The smell of damp leaves on the verge of rotting filled my nose. Keevan tipped his head, and he and Priya tramped off along the shoulder toward the trees. Izzy hesitated.

"Emma," she said quietly.

"Yeah?" Please, no last-minute doubts. I'd had enough of my own.

She lowered her head, her hands tight by her sides. She looked smaller somehow without her usual flowing skirt and cardigan.

"You and Darton, "she said. "Whatever there is between the two of you, because of whoever you were before... You're more than friends, aren't you?"

Her tone was even, but I heard the thread of underlying tension. My stomach knotted. She cared about him a lot. I couldn't help remembering the jealous twinges I'd felt when I'd thought our situations were reversed.

"The connection between us, because of our history, is pretty intense," I said, which was as close to agreeing as I was comfortable getting.

"You've been trying to save him all this time. You've kept following him, protecting him, *dying* for him, over and over..." She glanced up at me then, peering into my face. "There isn't anything you wouldn't do for him, is there?"

"No," I said honestly. "There's not. But, Izzy—"

She shook her head. "It's okay. We weren't even—I knew there wasn't much chance we'd get back together like that, even before you were in the picture. Maybe it's better being sure that we won't. I can't compete. That's just the way it is. And thank you. For doing all this for him—and for letting me do what I can too."

I groped for an appropriate answer, but I guessed she hadn't expected one. She turned and headed after the others with a brisk, steady stride. I waited until the forest had swallowed her up, and then I climbed back into the van.

Darton was crouched by the seatbacks, examining my runed dagger. Oblivious to the conversation I'd just been having about him, apparently. He raised his head and waggled the dagger as I came over.

"Do you think this will help us at all against the mercenary?"

"It makes dispatching glooms easier, but it's not going to have much effect on a full fae. Anyway, I'm going to need to focus all my attention on channeling the light through the lenses."

"Is it all right if I carry it then? I feel strange being the only one not contributing."

"Giving you a lens wouldn't really add to the effect when you'll be standing right next to me," I said. "But you're contributing in other ways."

"I'm the bait." The words came out a little flat.

"Well, that's one way of putting it." It was probably the most accurate way of putting it, but I didn't have to admit that.

He stood up, stooped beneath the low roof, and cupped my cheek to kiss me. Soft, sweet, and over far too quickly. He was probably trying to avoid getting caught in another memory.

"I would have let you hold on to the knife without any extra persuasion," I said.

He grinned. "I know. The kiss was for me."

Oh, he had no idea how wrong he was.

We clambered out. The sun shone high overhead, beaming

strong enough to pierce the gaps in the forest's canopy. That was all I needed to see.

"How much longer do we wait?" Darton asked.

A wild impulse I blamed on desperation flitted through me. "Kiss me again, and then we'll be good to go."

I'd thought he might laugh the request off, but he immediately leaned in. He pressed his lips to mine, hard, nudging me against the side of the van. I lost my breath, lost everything in the sensation of his body against mine. He rested his hand on my waist as the kiss deepened. Then his lips stilled, just for a second. He kissed me again, so thoroughly a whimper worked its way out of my chest.

Our breaths were ragged when he drew back. "You're right," he murmured into the space between us. "The memories do get easier to balance."

"Lucky you." I gave him a playful swat and pushed him toward the forest. We set off side by side. "What did you see this time?"

"Nothing all that revealing. You used to keep twigs in your *hair* sometimes. It really looked absurd. But I appreciated it that time those glooms snuck into my chambers. Assuming that was just the one time."

"There were a few times," I said. "After you talked to that dark fae I warned you about."

"I don't suppose if we asked the dark fae today why they want me so badly, he'd tell us?"

I guffawed. "Ah, no. Anyway, I don't think he *knows*. He's not old enough to have been around back then. He'll never have communicated with the Darkest One directly, not in any coherent way. He's just been able to sense that she still has it in for you after all this time."

On that cheerful note, we treaded into the forest by the stark white trunk of the birch I'd pointed out to the others earlier. I snapped handfuls of twigs off the brushes and saplings we passed and stuffed my sleeves with them.

After several paces, we stopped in a spot where the sun streaked to the forest floor. A bird called overhead. The leaves hissed with the rising of the breeze. Not a rustle from our companions sounded. I had to assume they were waiting as promised.

"I'm here, dark one," I shouted. "And I've brought what you wanted. Are you going to come and get him? Or are you too afraid even when he's right at your doorstep?"

A gloom slunk toward us. I bade it begone with one of my twigs, and the filmy creature blinked out of existence. Darton shifted his weight beside me.

"Really?" I called out again. "You're not even going to come talk to me? I think we've got a few things to hash out. But if you're really going to leave this job to the rabble instead of *earning* the honor you want so much…"

Nothing stirred amid the trees. I swallowed thickly. This plan got us nowhere if I couldn't taunt the dark fae into coming to meet us.

"Isn't there anything else he wants that he'd come for?" Darton asked under his breath. "Other than me dying, I mean."

"Oh, he doesn't want you just dying, not in any old way." That was the one last-ditch trick I was keeping buried deep in my back pocket. If our scheme fell apart, if the dark fae got the upper hand, I'd have to kill Darton before he could. Free my king's soul to follow the cycle onward to its next iteration. The thought nauseated me, but the alternative… "It'll only count as the sort of victory he wants if he wrenches your soul from your body directly."

And possibly ensured it never inhabited another body again.

Darton's back stiffened. I didn't have time to ask him what about my words had bothered him specifically—I hadn't told *him* just what sort of victory the mercenary was after—because at that moment, a shrouded, pale-faced form stepped between the trees several yards away from us.

The mercenary halted there and peered at us with his silvery eyes. I tensed, ready to throw up a shield if he tried to attack us from afar.

Right now, he was still too far away for *our* attack. I needed him inside our circle, at least twice as close to me as he was now, to be sure.

"What is this game?" he inquired in his icy voice.

"It's not a game," I said. "It's a challenge. One you're apparently too cowardly to meet."

"As if I can't tell you have some ploy you're attempting to engage."

I shrugged. "Apparently you believe I *could* hurt you, or you wouldn't be worried about any 'ploys' I might have prepared."

A couple more glooms glided toward us. I took them down one after the other with my gaze still fixed on the mercenary. My heart beat faster. How much longer did we have before the full force of the dark rabble caught up with us?

"I simply have no need to take the risk," the dark fae replied calmly. "In a few hours, dusk will creep in. And my underlings will have caught up by then, if not earlier. They can spring the trap *and* destroy you and your king. Light always fades, and then darkness remains."

The dark side's favorite refrain. He hadn't moved even an inch toward us. I fidgeted with the twigs in my sleeve and dipped my other hand into my pocket to close my fingers around the lens. But I had no use for it if I couldn't count on the others to have a direct line of sight to our target. Could I ask them to move to a different position without him catching on? Or—

"I wouldn't be so sure about that," Darton said.

My head jerked around. The dark fae let out a cool chuckle. "And what do you mean by that, Unburied King?"

Darton lifted his chin, the dagger clenched tight in his hand. "I mean I could kill myself right now, and then you'll have no chance at the glory."

I stared at him. "*Darton.*"

He turned, thrusting the dagger toward me. "Do it. Slit my wrist. Deep enough that I could bleed out. I trust you. Let's see how long he hangs back there in the shadows after that."

Every part of me recoiled at the thought. I'd been prepared to kill my king, but not until the last hopeless moment. But as Darton gazed back at me, his jaw set and his expression so determined, I realized he was right. If he were dying, the dark fae would have to act. Have to come forward to finish the job. And then we'd have him.

If I made the cut with enough care, we'd have time. I could heal Darton after. He'd said he trusted me. It could work.

He'd still be bait, but he'd be making a difference in his own way. I knew, looking at him, the echoes of conversations past in my head, how much that meant to him.

Still, I balked. But the mercenary didn't. From the corner of my eye, I caught the snap of his arm as he whipped a blast of magic toward us.

My fingers clutched a clump of twigs. "*Wood be my wall!*"

A translucent barrier shot up in front of Darton and me, shuddering as the bolt of dark magic crashed into it. The impact reverberated through the air into us. I stumbled, and Darton caught my wrist.

"Em," he said. "Merlin. Let me do this. Now, while it can still matter."

While we still had any chance at all. Sod it. Darkness take them all. I snatched the dagger from his grip. The dark fae was already swinging his hand to hurl another assault.

I gritted my teeth and sliced the blade across Darton's left wrist.

A gasp broke from his throat. Blood spilled down, brilliant against his tan skin, against the green and yellow of the grass and leaves it pattered onto on the ground. I'd forgotten how stark red arterial blood was, all but glowing with oxygenated life. My lungs constricted.

Darton stepped back and sagged against a tree trunk. "Here I am," he said to the dark fae. "Come and get me."

The mercenary had lowered his hands. A sickening hunger shaded his face. Darton's blood streamed on, the coppery scent filling the air. My stomach churned. I slid the lens out of my pocket, hiding it against my palm.

The dark fae took one step forward. Another. His eyes had brightened even as his expression had tensed.

"You really did it," he said, horrified and awed at once. "He'll die."

"Yes," I said, forcing the words from my throat. "And you'll have no part in that."

A sharp little grin split his face. "Oh, but I still can."

He threw himself forward, balling dark energy in his hand to wallop me when he broke through my shield. Which he would have—if I'd let him get that far.

He was two steps away when I jabbed out my hand with the lens, pointing the curve of it toward him. The dagger fell from my fingers. I thrust my other hand toward the sky, to the gleam of the sun above me.

"*Light of life to me and mine,*" I hollered, and heaved down every fragment of light I could reach, wrenching it into me and out through the lens.

All the twigs still on me disintegrated in a burst of dust. The blaze of sunlight shot through the lens and struck the dark fae square in the chest, just as he shattered my shield.

The mercenary flinched and spun as if to reel away. "Pri!" I yelled, and a figure shot up amid the trees at my left, holding out her own lens. I focused my attention on the beams of sunlight glowing over her and yanked down again. The light condensed into a point that hit the lens and pierced the mercenary in mid-stagger. He lurched in the other direction.

"Keevan!" I cried out. "Izzy!" Another figure standing, then another, and all the light I could summon streamed down toward them to those little circles of glass, until I could barely see anything through the searing haze inside my head.

The dark fae shrieked. The pressure squeezing under my skin made me want to shriek too. But we were hitting him from all sides with ever-expanding daylight, and he had nowhere left to turn.

"I am for my master," he spat out around a groan. "I am for the greatest one!" The power coursing through me started to ebb as my strength sapped away. My vision flickered, but the mercenary's body was spasming. With a choked sound, his shadowy soul broke apart.

The pieces split from his chest and hissed away into the rushing sunlight. His body crumpled.

I swayed. In the moment before I hit the ground, I was aware of nothing but a frantic babble of voices around me.

Keevan reached me a second later. He hauled me up. My head spun, but my gaze narrowed in on the flow of blood coursing over the forest floor.

"Arthur." I threw myself down beside Darton. He tipped his head to the side as I grabbed his wrist.

"I don't even feel that bad," he said in a slightly singsong voice that didn't inspire much confidence. "A little… floaty, maybe, but really—"

"Shut up," I rasped, leaning close to the gouge in his skin. Priya thrust a snapped-off branch into my hand. My fingers closed around it. I pulled at the life within it, every shred I could summon, from the green center into my spell. *Mend and seal and see him well.*

My anatomy textbooks and studies long ago had etched the layout of arteries, tendons, and layers of skin into my memory. I closed my eyes, seeing them knit back together in Darton's wrist. Darton let out a stuttering sigh of relief.

"Holy fuck," Keevan said.

The effort drained the last of my energy. The branch crumbled through my fingers, and I pitched forward into my king's lap.

CHAPTER THIRTY-FOUR

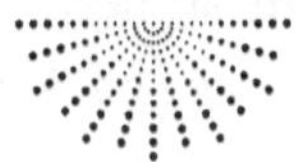

"Here she comes," Keevan said. I blinked and found myself
staring up into Darton's face.

I was still lying partly on his lap, the back of my head resting
on his thigh. He looked way too worried about *me* for someone
who'd asked me to all but kill him not that long ago.

"How long was I out?" I asked, my voice hoarse.

"A few minutes." Darton smoothed a shaky hand over my hair.
"Are you okay?"

I pushed upright, ignoring four noises of protest around me.
My head swam with a momentary dizziness and my joints
throbbed, but I could live through that.

"I'll bet I shed another year, but I can survive without that.
Who needs old age anyway?"

Izzy let out a startled giggle. Keevan looked around. Toward the
body of the fallen dark fae. It had shrunk where it lay as if deflated,
the pale face already blotchy with rot.

"We did it, right?" he said. "We… we killed it. Him."

"We stopped him from killing Darton," I said with the proper reframing. "You were great. All of you. We did it." A slight hysterical laugh bubbled up from my chest. "We really *did it.*"

"Woohoo!" Priya shouted. Keevan pulled me to my feet. To my surprise, he gathered me into a rib-crushing hug. Then he stepped back and pumped his fist. Darton shifted to get up, and Izzy darted in to help support him. I let her maneuver him to his feet. Her face fell just a little when he waved her off. But watching him stand, straight and mostly steady, she smiled.

"Come on," I said. "Let's get back to the van. We'll have more to worry about if we stick around here much longer." The dark rabble's strength and urgency would have faded with the mercenary's death, but their momentum would keep carrying them this way unless something else diverted them.

We stumbled between the trees and out onto the field beyond them. I fell in step beside Priya.

"Thanks," I said. "For getting me that branch when I was healing Darton. I wasn't thinking clearly enough to grab one myself. And I'd probably have taken two or three years off if I'd worked that magic without it."

She bumped her shoulder gently against mine. "You needed it. I could give it. That's how friendship works, right?"

A little of my previous hesitation prickled through me, but this time, I pushed it aside. "Yeah. So we're still friends?"

She beamed back at me. "Still friends."

We stopped for a moment outside the van. The undiluted sunlight poured over me. I soaked it in, reluctant to leave it for the shelter of the vehicle. In the rabble's normal state, daylight should be more than enough to protect us.

Darton came up behind me and wrapped his arms over mine. He leaned his head against my shoulder.

"You saved me again."

"I do seem to make a habit of it."

I was starting to relax back into him, allowing myself at least one minute to revel in our temporary reprieve before I considered the dangers still ahead of us, when Izzy flinched.

"There's one coming," she said. I followed her gaze. A gloom was rippling along the shadow of the farm's outer fence.

And Izzy had still been able to see it.

I stiffened in Darton's embrace. "What's wrong?" he said quietly.

"She shouldn't be able to see the dark vermin at all now. Not without the extra power the mercenary was sending them." Was it just taking more time than I'd expected for his energy to fade? Or was something more going on? The dark fae's last words, calling out to his master, rang through my head, and my stomach twisted.

He'd sensed her and her desires from across the ocean. There was no reason to assume that was a fluke.

"The Darkest One has been regaining some of *her* power," I said. "More than I realized. If she's getting stronger, all the dark creatures will too."

If she got strong enough, my binding might not be enough to hold her.

"Hey." Darton pulled me closer against him. "We'll get through it. No matter what happens. We've got this."

His touch and his words sent a shiver of memory through me —an echo of my king's voice as he'd stood before those crowds of lords and peasants alike and addressed them with one of his stirring speeches. The confidence that had come so naturally to him mingled with the strength of Darton's arms around me now. A lump rose in my throat. I tipped my head back against my king, my best friend, my sometimes lover, and opened myself to the sensation rising inside me.

For the first time in a long while, despite the peril I suspected lay ahead of us, I felt a spark of true hope.

MAGIC WAKING - BONUS SCENE

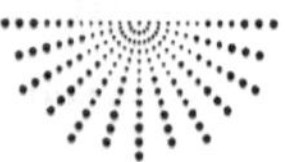

DID you wonder what memory Darton fell into that left him pleading with Emma not to leave before they made out in the back of the van? This bonus scene shows the events from the end of chapter 30 through the beginning of chapter 31 from Darton's point of view...

She needed me. That thought kept ringing through my head as my mouth melded with Emma's at the back of the van. The wobble that had crept into her voice came back to me, and I eased closer, deepening the kiss, wanting to show her just how much she had me.

We'd been through hell in the last two days and it looked like there was more hell ahead of us. I couldn't avoid recognizing just how much of that hell was thanks to me. In that moment, I'd have given just about anything to take her away from this whole ordeal.

Did Emma have any idea how much I'd needed her? Not just to use her magic to blast away the creatures that were eager to take a bite out of me, which she'd done plenty of. But also to make sense of the cluttered impressions that were starting to flood my mind: that sense of being me, *Darton*, law major, football player, follower of my father's legacy, but also at the same time *Arthur*, prince and then king over a domain I'd only caught glimpses of.

I'd be so lost without her. Without him? Because she was also the Merlin of my memories. I still didn't feel totally confident trying to reconcile those two personas, stubborn and sarcastic though they both were, so I pushed that thought away and let myself sink deeper into the kiss. Into the heat of her mouth and the gentle pressure of her hand where she'd gripped my sweater and—

And away into another of those frustratingly insistent memories.

This bed was damned comfortable. To be fair, it always was, but as the first hazy tendrils of awareness slipped through the haze of sleep, I found myself particularly contented. I was tucked against a warm presence from head to toe, the bright sharp scent like a pine forest in full summer sunlight filling my nose—my favorite smell, really. I started to shift my weight, to scoot a little closer.

And then I woke up enough to register who that smell and that warmth belonged to.

My body jerked back automatically, my arm wrenching away from my wizard's slim waist and smacking the mattress between us. I pushed myself to the opposite side of the bed—the very large bed, what in God's name had I been doing all the way over there pressed up against Merlin when I'd had all this space for myself? What in God's name was he doing anywhere in this bed to begin with?

Those questions drained away along with most of the blood from my face when I realized I was experiencing a rather standard morning reaction down below. Lord help me, he hadn't felt that part of me pressed up against him, had he?

My wizard was stretching his knobby arms and yawning as if waking up here were the most normal thing in the world. I vaguely remembered him stumbling in here after me last night and looking as though he'd collapse if he walked one step farther, and it seeming perfectly reasonable to offer him one side of my bed to collapse on. But that wasn't— I hadn't wanted— I'd never asked for—

And he was still just sprawled there, his tunic riding up to show the pale skin of his taut belly—

"Merlin," I said, fighting to keep my tone light. "Get your lazy body out of my bed. Don't you have your own?"

The wizard leapt off the mattress as if it'd been on fire. "My apologies, sire." He bowed down so ridiculously low it'd have been more respectful if he'd just stayed standing straight. When he did straighten up, his rumpled tunic had drifted back into place. That wild hair of his was even more mussed than usual. Did I need to paste a comb to his hand? A couple of quick swipes with my own hand might do it—

My fingers balled. Merlin peered at me for a second before his gaze darted away. He could tell something was wrong. He always saw far more than anyone really should.

Damn it, this was nothing. Put it aside, Arthur, and get on with the day.

Get him out of this room so I could have a moment to myself.

We'd come home triumphant. That one war was done. What more excuse could we need for a little distraction?

"We've got a lot to do," I said. "We've returned victorious. I think I'll declare a festival day." *Yes, there, perfect.* "You can go make up some effects for the celebration, can't you?"

Merlin's eyes jerked back to me, so puzzled and worried that my stomach knotted. "A festival?" he said in a hesitant voice. "We defeated one enemy, Arthur, but I don't think you should—"

Oh, for heaven's sake, could he not see I needed this one respite from… from everything?

The retort spilled out before I'd thought it through. "I'm really rather tired of hearing what you think I shouldn't do." I pushed myself off the bed with my back to him, not wanting to see the pained expression he might be making now as he thought of all the ways he'd had to protect me over the last weeks… months… years. All the ways he might still have to protect me. My jaw clenched. "I think I've proven I *can defend myself. Everyone here could use a day to unwind, not least of all me. Off with you. Get on with it. I don't need you hovering."*

"Arthur..."

I couldn't stop my head from snapping around. "I said go."

The look on Merlin's face, the flinch as if I'd slapped him, echoed into me with a stab of guilt. He'd already spun and rushed out the door. As it thumped shut behind him, my hand dropped to my side, my arm going slack.

Why had I barked at him like that? He'd only been expressing exactly the concerns I'd have expected him to. There were more battles ahead. And I couldn't say I'd have made it through the ones before without my wizard—my most loyal subject, my best friend—by my side.

God knew he deserved better from me than the attitude I'd just shown him. How had this turned into such a muddle?

I strode to the doorway, but when I opened it, he'd already disappeared down the stairs. He could be anywhere in the castle now. Probably wherever he thought he'd be least likely to run into me any time soon. I closed my eyes, gripping the side of the door—

—and I was braced against Emma at the back of the van, her soft cheek grazing mine as my breath hitched out. As the past collided with the present, my head spun, and the guilt I'd felt in that moment centuries ago bubbled up my throat. The apology I didn't know if I'd ever given before tumbled out.

"I'm sorry. I'm sorry. Don't go, Merlin. Don't ever, ever go."

And she was here. He was here. Emma and Merlin, fingers intertwining at the back of my neck, voice wry.

"Arthur. You idiot, I have stayed with you for fifteen hundred years and never once regretted it. If it's fifteen hundred more, I'll still be there with you on whatever's left of this wretched planet."

I couldn't have asked for a better answer. A laugh wrenched out of me, and all I could do was kiss her again, with every bit of affection, every bit of need, I had in me.

SOUL'S BLADE

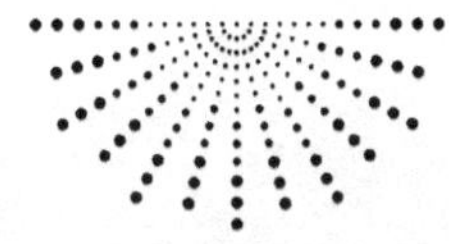

LEGENDS REBORN #2

CHAPTER ONE

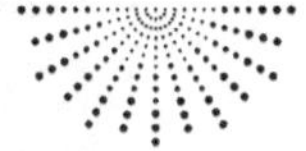

AFTER KILLING my first dark fae, there hadn't been much to do other than head home. The five of us were piled into a van tricked out for fae-hunting, which I'd borrowed from a man who was probably dead. It didn't make for the most peaceful atmosphere.

And yet, for a couple hours squeezed in the backseat beside the young man I'd risked everything to keep alive, that space somehow felt cozy. Priya, my roommate and tentative friend, was humming cheerfully at the wheel. Darton's friends—Izzy at his other side and Keevan in the front—looked relaxed for pretty much the first time since we'd taken off on this chaotic road trip nearly three days ago.

Darton himself had his arm around my shoulders. I'd let myself lean against his well-muscled chest, where the rise and fall of his breath could remind me at regular intervals that for all the mistakes I might have made in the recent weeks, I'd done one thing right. I'd saved this incarnation of my king from a fate that might have destroyed his soul completely. And I'd wiped myself out rather thoroughly in the process, so this position was totally acceptable.

Even great wizards needed a break from time to time. By all

appearances, the guy who was also my liege liked taking my weight for a change.

Possibly I liked it too. The heat of his body seeped through his cotton shirt to the side of my face. He smelled like warm musk and the earth of the forest where we'd confronted our greatest enemy— of this life, at least. I closed my eyes, soaking it in.

"You should spend the night at my apartment again," I said. "Even with the mercenary gone, the glooms will be on the prowl for you. Tomorrow we can figure out the best long-term plan."

"That works for me." His thumb stroked over my hair where it lay against the nape of my neck, just barely skirting skin-to-skin contact. Just barely avoiding jostling loose from his mind another memory of his original life. I swallowed hard, resisting the urge to nestle even more closely against him.

The more memories he awakened, the easier the glooms could find him. I'd risked a lot when I'd thought we were pretty much goners anyway, but I was going to have to go back to my usual, more cautious ways now.

Priya pulled up by the campus gates for Keevan and Izzy, who lived in the residences—and didn't have to worry about the dark rabble cutting *their* lives short. Keevan gave us his usual rakish smile. "It's been real... and also completely bizarre. Thanks for a wild ride, Emma. And I'd better see you soon, Art." He saluted to Darton and me with one dark hand and hopped out.

Izzy squeezed Darton's arm. "If you need anything..." She glanced past him to where I'd straightened up. "Either of you. Just let me know, all right?"

There wasn't a whole lot an ordinary mortal could do against a fae enemy, even a mindless scrap of darkness like a gloom, but then again, she and Keevan had proven themselves awfully useful in the past day. I wasn't going to forget that. I nodded.

"All right."

She swept her pale auburn waves back from her face and slipped out. The breeze made her loose trousers ripple around her legs like one of her usual flowing dresses as she walked into the lengthening shadows of the evening. She looked like a wavery, flighty girl, but that shell hid a will strong as steel.

"And onward," Priya said, spinning the wheel. Technically she was an ordinary mortal too, but raised by the light fae like a changeling, which one had to guess was why she'd taken our recent adventure so much more easily in stride.

As she turned onto our street, a sense of relief settled over me. Home. We were almost home. And in that home was my bed, where I could properly rest my weary body for the first time in far too many days. I started to sag into Darton's embrace again—and my gaze caught on a movement in the shadows.

I jerked upright. "Stop!"

Priya didn't ask questions. She hit the brake hard. I pressed my hand to the window, staring at the buildings beyond. "What—" Darton started, and I motioned him quiet.

We'd stopped just a couple doors down from our apartment building. In the shadows along the edges of its neighbors and between them, thicker patches of darkness were creeping. Glooms. Some of them drifted aimlessly, but others slunk through the shadows toward the same place we'd been headed. And the shade in front of our building was rippling with them. My heart sank.

"The apartment building is full of glooms."

"What?" Darton said. "Why would they go there?"

I bit my lip, my mind whirling. "The mercenary summoned them all back to him, but most of them hadn't made it close to the forest when we destroyed him. All that extra energy and sensitivity he was lending them died with him. So they must have gravitated toward the closest place where they sensed your essence, if they could sense it at all. And for a bunch of them, that was here. This is the last place you spent an extended amount of time before we took off."

He'd been in there several hours, sleeping on the couch and

then having breakfast, just before the first wave of them outright attacked.

Darton stiffened. "Will some of them have gathered on campus then? Keevan—"

I shook my head. "Keevan will be fine." Even though he shared the dorm room where Darton had slept most other nights in the couple months before now. "They're not going to hurt anyone if they don't see any point in it."

"They tore up the campus plenty on Friday."

"Because the mercenary had them all stirred up, and because those people were between them and you." Because it was him they wanted—just him. Or rather, my king's soul lodged inside him.

"Speaking of which," Priya piped up, "it looks like we're not keeping quite a low enough profile."

She was right. A few of the glooms had changed direction. They wriggled along the edges of the shadows on the road just a few feet from the van. My body tensed.

The daylight was already fading. In a handful of minutes, it might be dark enough for them to make that final leap to us.

"Are we just going to run again?" Darton said. The frustration in his voice reverberated through me. I frowned at the creatures lurking beyond the window, and a sense of resolve rose up in my chest.

"No," I said. "The mercenary did us a favor. Now we've got a whole bunch of the local glooms collected together in one spot. I'm better off taking care of them all now rather than giving them time to scatter."

The fewer I left in our vicinity, the longer we could go before enough amassed to truly threaten Darton again.

I pushed open the door and stepped onto the pavement. Before I had a chance to tell him to stay in the van, Darton had shoved himself out the opposite door. "Darton," I said, but he didn't so much as hesitate as he strode around the van to join me.

I felt absolute loyalty to my king, but I could still note that at times he displayed an idiotic lack of self-preservation.

He halted in the thin sunlight beside me. The dagger one of the light fae had given me—the dagger I'd forgotten he'd been holding onto—glittered in his hand. He squinted at the shadows.

"I can see them, just a little," he said. A reminder that the glooms *were* still slightly super-powered, thanks not to the mercenary but to other dark stirrings I didn't like to think about. Otherwise only my fae-touched sight would have been able to make them out.

"And they can see *you*." I motioned at him to get back. The glooms were churning in the shadows now. More were starting to seep from the edges of the windows and doors on our apartment building.

Swine crud. I darted to the young maple growing in a plot of soil set in the sidewalk, part of the town's initiative to "keep the streets green." Right now it could keep me supplied with fresh twigs so I could work my magic.

"So what are we going to do?" Darton said as I snapped off finger-lengths of wood from the lowest branch. "Are you sure you're up for another—"

The sun dipped just a sliver lower, and the nearest glooms sprang.

A cry broke from my mouth, but Darton's reflexes kicked in. His hand whipped through the air, slicing the fae dagger across the patches of darkness leaping at him. At the touch of its blade, they shattered into the air like burst balloons.

Darton stumbled backward with a rough inhale. "Okay," he said. "I guess I should be glad for all that fencing practice after all."

I wasn't sure if it was his time in fencing club or a deeper instinct that had guided his hand, but it didn't much matter now. More glooms were pouring out of the apartment building and rippling across the road. I waved Darton out of the way and smacked my palm against the trunk of the young maple.

"Sorry," I murmured to it. And then, to Darton, "Be ready to catch me." The last thing I needed was to split my head open on the sidewalk when I fainted. And I could already tell a faint lay in my future.

I closed my eyes, reaching my awareness into the tree, into all the living energy thrumming beneath its bark. The bright green pulse of it shimmered against my eyelids. I sucked in a breath, and yanked, hard, thrusting my other hand forward at the same moment.

"*Darkness begone,*" I called in the ancient tongue that was my first language.

The tree's life ripped through my body and shot out from my hand. It blazed across the street, searing through every gloom in its path. Searing through the walls of the buildings and on into the rooms and hallways, eating up the glooms there too.

Lights blinked out in apartment windows with the tinkling of popped bulbs. A startled yelp carried from the main doorway. A woman walking her dog stopped in her tracks, gaping at me, as the tree trunk turned cold and dead against my hand.

A chill rushed through me too. My head spun. My legs crumpled, and the world around me fell away into blackness. Yeah, I might have pushed myself a *tad* too far.

My eyes blinked open what felt like ages later, although judging from the faces leaning over mine—Darton's and Priya's—I hadn't been out for more than a couple minutes. They looked concerned but not panicked. Darton was gripping my shoulders. I staggered as I tried to push myself to my feet, and his hold tightened.

"Em," he said. "Take it easy."

"Are you okay, Emmaline?" Priya asked.

I swiped at the sweat that had beaded on my forehead and gathered myself. Not a single gloom remained around us that I could see. But we had a different sort of company now. Several of our neighbors had emerged from the apartment building. The woman with the dog was talking to one of the men and pointing at me.

I didn't normally blow my cover quite this blatantly. In the last few days, stealth had mattered a lot less than survival. Concealment was another habit I was going to have to get back into.

"We'd better go," I said.

"Inside?" Priya said. "Where do you want to stash the van?"

I shook my head. "Not here. I mean, you should go home. You'll be fine. But even if I exterminated all the glooms that were in the apartment, they'll have left their mark all over the building. It's not safe for Darton anymore." I gave another heave and managed to balance on my legs this time. Which was a good thing, because apparently I was going to have to wait a while longer before I got that sleep I'd been looking forward to.

"Come on," I said to Darton, suppressing a yawn. "Back in the van. We'll grab a hotel room for the night and figure the rest out in the morning."

Because if I'd learned anything about the dark fae over the years, it was that there were always more.

CHAPTER TWO

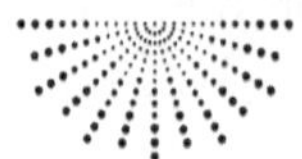

I'D SWEAR the beds in the hotel room we stepped into half an hour later were just begging to be collapsed into. Unfortunately, my work wasn't quite done.

I dragged in a lungful of air that smelled like ambiguous floral freshener. "Sit down," I said to Darton. "We've got to make you harder to find."

He sank onto the second bed. It was a good bed, no squeak or creak, just the faint rustle of the duvet. I'd chosen the hotel well, at least.

"I thought that the... glooms, and the other dark things, were only following us because of the mercenary," Darton said. "Now that he's gone—"

"No such luck. They're always drawn to you once you start waking up. They've gotten us plenty of other times before"—*every* other time before, to be exact—"without any of the higher fae involved. It just usually takes them longer to gather enough numbers to do real damage. I'd rather avoid them even knowing where to gather for as long as possible."

"How can you do that?"

I dropped the duffel I'd carried up from the van onto my bed and unzipped it. The twigs I'd gathered earlier today would still hold enough life to be useful. By tomorrow, I'd need a fresh stash.

I snapped several of them, letting loose the sharp green smell from within, and lay them around me on the floor.

"I can cast a spell that'll dampen the impressions your soul gives off. It should keep them from noticing you unless one brushes right past you. And there are ways we can make it less likely they'll do that too. Give me the dagger."

He handed it over. I ran my fingers over the polished wooden handle. The living energy sealed inside it wouldn't last forever, but at least it wouldn't drain simply with the passage of time, only through usage. It was the one helpful thing my light fae sort-of brethren had given me in this life.

I stepped closer to Darton and raised the blade to carefully slice off a small lock of his gold-blond hair. He looked up at me, but I didn't let myself meet his eyes. My skin was already tingling with the awareness of his presence, of the privacy this room afforded us. I couldn't afford those kinds of distractions.

My fingers closed over the golden strands I'd cut off. I brought the dagger to my palm and dug it into the flesh. Darton winced as the blood welled up.

"I hate seeing you do that, Emma."

"Says the guy who had me slice open his entire forearm a few hours ago." Remembering that moment, the rush of blood after, made my stomach go wobbly.

"Hey," he said. "I'm pretty sure that move saved the day."

It had. But I'd hated doing it all the same. I'd hated knowing that if the gambit didn't work, if it didn't draw the dark fae mercenary into our trap, I'd just killed my king.

I sucked in my lower lip. "Well, this move might save us a whole bunch of days if I do it right. And doing it right needs some wizardly blood. Now stay still."

He sat stiffly upright as I squeezed the locks of his hair against the cut on my palm. Words in the old tongue rolled from my mouth in a steady whisper. I grabbed one of my few remaining wands—cedar, that was a good fit for my purpose—and dragged the tip across my bloody hand.

"I managed to get rid of some of the glooms with the dagger," Darton said. "Even though I don't have 'wizardly' anything. Maybe I should keep it on me from now on, in case you're not around to save my skin. Unless there's a better weapon I could use?"

"One brief battle and you're already wanting to upgrade your weaponry?" I teased. "If we have the time, I can try to make you something better. Just keep in mind we're talking a *lot* of time. It took me a couple years to get Excalibur ready."

He perked up at that. "Excalibur was real?"

I ignored his question as I drew a circle around him with the wand. "*Like mist conceal, and never reveal.*" I repeated the chant again and again, and finally pressed my palm, blood-smeared and hair-flecked, to Darton's forehead. He twitched, but managed to restrain a full flinch.

The threads of my magic wove around him. Around the soul I could feel like a pulse of energy beneath his skin. Another magic lingered there, tangled so deeply in his essence that I couldn't pick apart where one began and the other ended. But it was that spell that had kept returning him to life, in new bodies and new times, after each time the creatures of darkness had overcome us.

A shiver of some other sensation—thicker, almost stuttering—ran through the pulse. I'd felt it before, casting magic this closely on his past incarnations. My brow knit. That part, it didn't feel like my king. Was it some sort of damage that had come with the wound he'd been dealt, that would have caused his first and only death if I hadn't intervened?

If it was, it didn't really matter. It hadn't changed over the centuries, and as far as I could tell it hadn't harmed either of us in any way.

I let the chant fall from my lips again, and then I pulled back my hand. "You can wash off your forehead now. Sorry. I know it's kind of gross. And yes, there was a real Excalibur. I haven't paid enough attention to the more modern tales to know whether the reality would meet your expectations, though."

Darton got up and ambled over to the bathroom. He left the door open so we could keep talking.

"Did I really pull it from a stone?"

My lips twitched upward. "No. That's just fanciful thinking. I commissioned it from the best craftsman in the kingdom, and I worked magic over it for those two years until it was so attuned to your soul it was almost magic itself. When you held it, it was as if it was part of your living body, your life energy glowing right through it."

"Sounds pretty intense." Darton splashed water on his face. "I don't suppose we could pick *that* up for the next time the glooms come calling?"

My smile turned into a grimace. "No. It was lost. In all our early lives, I never got old enough to go looking for it properly, and by the time I did, I had no idea where it'd ended up. I've asked around among the light fae over the years, but no one's had a clue. At least not one they could be bothered to tell me."

"This isn't what you expected, is it?" he said, coming to the doorway. Damp strands of hair framed his handsome face. "From the spell you cast, when I was—when that really powerful dark fae tried to kill me. You wouldn't have wanted us to be stuck in some weird cycle of getting attacked by the glooms and the rest, dying and being reborn, over and over."

"No, I didn't." Suddenly I felt twice as exhausted as before. "I told you before, I only had a split second to act, before the Darkest One would have done even worse to you. All I know is I threw out all the magic I could summon with the intention of keeping you alive, keeping me with you so I could help you stay that way, and keeping the Darkest One as far off as I could manage. And I guess it did all those things. But... this isn't how I'd have wanted it to go."

It had been a very long fifteen hundred years, let's just say.

Darton rubbed his mouth. I was getting to know this version of my king, his quirks and habits, well enough to see whatever he was about to say mattered to him a lot.

"So is this what our lives will be from now on?" he said. "Running and hiding and fighting when we have to?" His voice came out strained.

Oh, my king. Oh, the young man carrying him. My stomach twisted.

If I'd been more careful last week, he might not have even started to awaken yet. He might have lived on in full, blissful ignorance for another year or more. I couldn't give that back to him, but I'd do whatever else I could.

"No," I said firmly. "You'll go back to classes tomorrow. I told you we'd figure out a more permanent solution, and I meant that. You should have a normal life... for as long as you can manage it. And I think we can manage it at least a little longer."

And maybe between guarding him and dealing with whatever glooms wandered our way, I'd finally find a way to untangle that hasty spell of centuries ago. To release us from the cycle of lives and deaths the Darkest One was bound up in too—without letting her go free.

Okay, so I'd been trying to do as much for most of those centuries and hadn't gotten close before, but it was at least *slightly* possible. A wizard was allowed a little hope.

The pressure of all my responsibilities settled over me. I couldn't restrain a yawn this time. My eyelids had started to droop. I might have swayed on my feet. Slightly.

Darton's expression softened. Gods, he could melt me from across the room with just one look like that.

"Get some sleep, Em," he said gently. "You've saved my hide at least three times in the last twenty-four hours. I think you've earned it."

"Well, if you're going to make it a direct order, my liege," I mumbled, and climbed onto the bed. I didn't bother with sheets or duvet. The second my head hit the pillow, I was out.

❧

My king followed me into sleep. Somewhere in the depths of my slumber, a memory from our first life together swam up, vividly sharp.

The fire crackled in the hearth, the pungent scent of pine smoke drifting through the air of Arthur's bedchamber. The light flickered over the smooth-shaven face of the newly crowned king. He leaned forward in his brocaded chair and lifted the crown from his head. Holding it in his hands, he studied it as if he'd never looked at it before.

"Is everything all right, sire?" I ventured from where I sat on the other side of the hearth. Normally I wouldn't have been hesitant to speak. But up until five hours ago, I'd served a prince, not a king. And I'd never seen his expression quite like this. Set and yet somehow uncertain.

"What if I can't do it, Merlin?" he said, quiet but steady.

"Do what?" I said. "Order people around? Make sure those people have food and work and relatively few other people trying to kill them? Debate with the lords about how exactly they should do those things on their lands until your head aches? I'm pretty sure you've been doing all of that for a rather long time already."

A hint of a smile darted across his lips and was gone. "It's different. Before I was one of many voices. Now I'm the last one. The final decision-maker."

"Right. Because you had so little authority when you were just the crown heir. I wish you'd told me that earlier, so I could have ignored you when you dragged me on all those sodding horse rides."

He rolled his eyes at me, the least king-like gesture I could imagine.

Yet somehow Arthur managed to make even that look regal. My pulse stuttered. Damn him.

No, damn my foolish heart.

He lowered his head to consider the crown again. "I just want to do right by them. I want to do right by all the people in this realm. What will happen to them if I fail as a king?"

I kicked out my legs and crossed my ankles as if this conversation was nothing more than shooting the breeze. "I suppose some other fellow will come along who wants to take on the job. Hopefully one who's generous with his food and his wine."

Arthur shot me a look. "Are you implying I haven't been generous enough?"

"Of course not. You are exactly the king I came here to serve." I dug a twig from my pocket and cast its energy toward the dancing shadows along the wall. They shifted into human-like figures, bobbing their heads down in a bow. "And look, I've brought a whole bunch of minions who think you're the best thing since spoked wheels too."

This time, the smile that crossed his face stayed. "Merlin," he started.

"Sire," I said. "You were a great prince, and you'll be a greater king. Do you really think I would waste my talents around here if I didn't believe that?"

He chuckled, and the last of his tension left his shoulders. "No, I suppose not."

When he hefted himself to his feet, I stood as well, ready to take my leave. But instead of dismissing me immediately, Arthur moved toward me. He clasped my shoulder. The warmth of his hand bled through my tunic, and my breath caught.

"I'm still not sure how I was lucky enough to end up with you at my side," he said. "If I've been great, it's in large part thanks to you."

"I'll be sure to remind you of that the next time you propose we go riding somewhere," I tossed out, but the heady sensation in my chest had tightened into a knot.

I'd never told him the full story of why I'd sought him out. I didn't even know the full reason. But I knew my father had raised me for this purpose, to watch over Arthur, not just for the king's protection but for my people's as well.

He'd never said it outright, but I knew it all the same: Something about the man before me had made my father afraid.

CHAPTER THREE

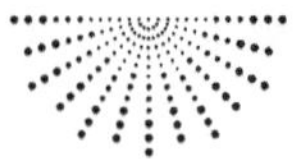

SOMEONE WAS SHAKING MY SHOULDER. My eyes popped open, my fingers grasping instinctively for a twig, a wand—anything with power that might be in reach. All they caught on were the folds of the sheet now draped across my shoulders.

Darton was leaning over me. I pushed upright, shaking off the last shreds of sleep. "What's going on? Is there a gloom? Did something happen?"

"Hey," Darton said, raising his hands. "Everything's okay. My first class today starts at eleven. I thought it'd be nice to grab breakfast with you before I left. I wanted you to at least know I was heading out, anyway. We haven't had a chance to talk about what precautions you think I should be taking now and all that."

"Right." I blinked at the clock, which insisted it was quarter to ten—in the morning, obviously, given the bright autumn daylight streaming through the hotel room window. My head felt muggy, as if it'd filled with rain clouds while I slept. I rubbed my eyes. My mouth tasted like ash and sour wine, even though as far as I could recall I hadn't consumed either in a rather long time. "When did I go to bed?"

"Like, seven last night." Darton frowned. "Should I have woken you up earlier? I didn't mean to throw you off somehow. It just seemed like you really needed the rest."

"No, no, it's okay. I'll be all right." My body was catching up after those three days of barely snatching more than a few hours rest here and there, not to mention the multiple intensive castings on top of that. I probably could have happily slept until *tomorrow* morning. But I wouldn't be much use to Darton unconscious.

"So you haven't seen anything at all that was unusual or made you concerned?" I checked.

Darton shook his head. Then he paused. "I did have a dream—one I think was actually a memory. I'm not sure if it meant anything significant."

"Well, now that you've mentioned it, you might as well tell me the whole thing."

He sat back on his own bed, his gaze going distant. "I was lying on... I guess a mat, in a big tent. And I had the most awful pain in my side. Not where the Darkest One—" He cut himself off with a gesture to indicate the spot below his rib cage where the greatest of the dark fae had dealt her would-be fatal wound. "Higher, just below my shoulder. Anyway, it burned like hell."

"If you were in a tent, it was probably a battle wound," I said. "In the last few years, one of our neighbors decided they liked what you'd done for your kingdom so much they wanted to take it for themselves. You were not on board with that idea. And you were right there with the army driving them back. You were never one to stand aside while others were fighting on your behalf."

Darton nodded. "You neither. You were there. I mean, as the Merlin before. You were chanting something that made the burning ease off. And you had some paste you mashed onto the spot—something to help it heal, I think. I'm not sure. I was kind of hazy by that point."

"Hmmm," I said. "That doesn't really narrow it down. You did have a habit of getting yourself injured alarmingly often during those battles. Probably because you were always running to the front of the fray with that sword I enchanted for you."

Darton's brow furrowed. "I think it must have been a really serious wound this time. You were... very upset. I swear you sounded like you were holding yourself back from crying at one point. Or maybe that was just in my head."

A lump rose in my throat. I could think of two or three times I'd felt that panicked over one of my king's injuries. I hadn't realized he'd ever noticed how frantic I got when I wasn't completely sure I had the skill to save him. He'd never mentioned it afterward. Never pointed out that my reaction was more intense than one would generally expect from an attending wizard patching up his liege. But then, we'd also been friends.

He'd been my only real friend. And more than that too. Had some of that other emotion shown through without me realizing?

I swallowed the lump and made myself shrug as if it wasn't of any significance. "Well," I said in my best flippant tone, "if you'd kicked the bucket on me, I'd have been out of a job. Finding another would have been incredibly inconvenient." My stomach gurgled. "And I think we'd better get that breakfast before *I* kick the bucket out of hunger. Just let me take a quick shower first. I'm wearing more of the road than I'd really prefer to."

It was more than breakfast I needed. I had to come up with some sort of plan. I stepped into the hotel bathroom's glass-walled shower stall and turned the water control to close to the hottest setting. The near-scalding water battered my skin. I scrubbed soap over it, my mind spinning off in other directions.

I had my standard techniques. The spells like the one I'd cast on Darton last night, or the salt boundaries I'd laid down before to alert me when a gloom came near. Simply staying near him, ready, as much as I could worked to a certain extent.

But those strategies had never been enough in the long run any life before. And I wasn't likely to make any progress on untangling the spell that both bound us in these repeating existences and drew the darkness back to Arthur's soul if I was standing guard over him every minute of the day.

My thoughts slipped to Jagger—the man who we'd ended up connecting with while fleeing from the dark fae mercenary. A man who'd hunted fae himself, at least the lesser sort. It was his van parked in the hotel's underground lot.

He'd blown up his entire home to kill off an onslaught of glooms and buy us the time to get out of there. We hadn't seen him since. I didn't see how he could have survived the explosion. It was hard for me to imagine the gruff, no-nonsense man with his silvery hair and face etched with scars giving up just like that, but maybe he hadn't seen it as giving up but giving over. His life for ours.

The thought made me uncomfortable. I turned off the water and grabbed one of the towels, directing my mind to more practical matters.

Jagger had given me some new ideas. Ones I hadn't considered, thanks to technology that grew by leaps and bounds while I was busy getting through yet another childhood. Solar panels could capture sunlight and contain it for at least a little while, to use as a weapon or as a shield. In a dire situation, we could make use of the flame throwers the van had come equipped with. I wasn't sure how I could adapt the fae hunters' science to Darton's everyday life, though.

The old ways might be old, but I knew them through and through. The mercenary had been a fluke. And now that our battle with *him* had destroyed a sizeable population of glooms and other shadow creatures, it might be months, even years, before enough amassed again to cause any real damage. We could start with the basics, and I'd build a consolidated strategy from there.

I was still mulling it over when I stepped back into the main room. I gave my hair one last swipe with the towel, tossed that onto the bed, and combed my fingers through the damp strands. Then I noticed the way Darton was looking at me.

He was sitting on the end of his bed, shoe in hand as if he'd been about to pull it on, but he'd frozen. His gaze was fixed on my face with an expression like he was surprised to see me. Like I hadn't been right here talking to him all of ten minutes ago.

"What?" I said, lowering my hands.

A hint of a flush crept into his cheeks. He lowered his eyes, but they leapt back up to me the second he spoke.

"You just—something about your hair, and maybe the light— You almost look like you. Like Merlin."

His voice came out low. Was I imagining it, or was there an almost *husky* note in it? As if he were pleased by what he saw?

The sound sent a tingle over my skin. It seeped right into my chest with a flutter of hope I should have suppressed. But I could also be idiotic at times, especially when it came to my king and my heart.

I took a step closer, tilting my head in whatever approximation of *coy* I was capable of, and let my own voice drop. "Do you like that?"

Darton blinked. For a split-second, I really thought he was going to reach for me, grasp my hand and tug me to him the way he had more than once in the last few days, with desire hazing his eyes. Then he rubbed his mouth and really looked away, with a muffled laugh.

"It wouldn't make much sense if I did. You were a *guy* back then."

The words raked through me, scraping open a scabbed over pain I really should have left alone. I sucked in a tight breath and formed some manner of smile.

It wasn't only the rejection, although that was the sharpest part of the hurt. Hearing him say those words rubbed me as wrong as if he'd said I'd been a genius horseman or a force of darkness. I hadn't felt particularly like a "guy" back then, any more than I felt particularly like a woman now. I was Merlin. This body's parts or that one's, it wasn't of much consequence to me.

But this wasn't the time of a debate on that matter. I wasn't sure my king would ever understand. *He* was too solidly a man.

A man who had clear tastes and preferences.

"I was *me*," I said simply, and moved to my duffel bag. The sting of humiliation kept prickling through my chest. I dug out my last wands and transferred them into the backpack where I could keep them more easily at hand once we left the room. I'd look for a tree or a shrub to claim some fresh twigs from on our way out. And sometime very soon I'd need to make a visit to my storage locker, although that too was becoming depleted of supplies much more quickly than I'd prefer.

Thank the light, Darton didn't push the subject. He watched me in contemplative silence. His phone pinged with an alert, and he picked it up.

I hefted the backpack over my shoulders. I'd have to keep a proper distance from him from here on. In the last couple days, with our next death nipping at our heels, I'd let my sense of caution slip. What did it matter if he woke up a little, if my heart broke a little, if we were going to die an hour later anyway?

I'd given in to the want in his eyes and his voice. We'd kissed, we'd touched—we might have done more if those early memories hadn't thrown him off course every time the skin-to-skin contact had continued more than a few minutes.

Thank the light for *that*. Because we weren't dying, not yet. I could control myself. I'd done it before, if not always *well*.

"Who is it?" I asked. A report from Izzy or Keevan, maybe? Darton had already typed out a response to the texts.

"My little sister," he said, with surprise and clear affection. "Asking for tips for her college applications. And she wants to come down here to visit and check out the campus."

CHAPTER FOUR

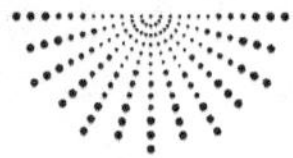

"So this barrage of glooms just never stops?" Izzy said. "They keep coming after Darton—Arthur—you know, over and over, until..."

She trailed off uncertainly beside me as I twitched my wand toward another meandering gloom. *"Darkness begone,"* I murmured.

A magical spark ate away the scrap of darkness, leaving nothing.

Keevan stood a little ahead of me, and Priya had paused at my other side. I'd found a chunk of time in the middle of the day when they were all free, and now they were rearranging themselves around me as we patrolled the campus, blocking my wizardly activities from view so I didn't cause another public stir.

The breeze whipped around us as I scanned the grounds. The chill in it stung my cheeks. By all appearances, we'd cleared out the central square of any remnants of the mercenary's dark forces.

"Yeah," I said. "But reducing the gloom population buys us more time. We just want to make sure none of that population runs into Darton first."

I directed us toward the athletic fields. Technically *I* was supposed to be in class, but my Organic Chemistry lab didn't feel particularly pressing when various glooms were still drifting around campus. The fresh alert boundaries I'd laid down this morning weren't going to give me any warning of dark creatures already within them.

"That's where the cleanup crew comes in." Keevan rubbed his hands together. "Is it just glooms, or are there more of those weird shadow animal things around too?"

I couldn't tell whether the thought made him eager or nervous. Maybe a little of both. "There aren't so many of those in the world in the first place. And they're more averse to hanging out around people when they aren't... motivated to do so. They probably wandered back to their original haunts as soon as the mercenary stopped pressing them."

A shadowy form wriggled through the corner of my vision. I corrected myself. "Most of them, anyway. Over here."

My grip on my wand tightened. I strode toward the snake-like creature of darkness, gathering the life energy inside me too. Exterminating the bigger beasties took more magic than the glooms. I *really* needed to get back to my storage locker and retrieve more of my stashed wands.

How many did I even have left there? I'd burned through more in the last week than in at least five past lives before now. But it had been worth it. My king and I were still here.

And being mildly tired and stressed about supplies beat fleeing for our lives any day.

"*Darkness begone*," I muttered at the shadowy snake, pushing an extra umph of energy through my wand. The beastie disintegrated before it could slither around the corner of the building it'd been hugging—and so did the wand. Hog's balls. I wiped the grit from my hand onto my jeans and reached for another.

My last one. After this, until I made it to my storage locker, I'd be relying on scavenging living wood from the local trees.

Izzy's head twitched. "There's something," she said, pointing with her chin.

There was. Another gloom was skirting the stands by the football field. She'd noticed it from twenty feet away. My gut clenched as we headed over.

Priya was tracking it with her gaze. "You can still see them too?" I said to her.

She shrugged. "I could always see them a bit. Just, like, a sense of them—you couldn't really call it *seeing*. I must have picked up a sensitivity growing up in the enclave."

With all those light fae around her. That did make sense.

"The feeling's definitely gotten more muted since we got rid of the mercenary," she added. I guessed it wasn't too hard for her to figure out what I was worrying about. "And it doesn't look as if anyone else is noticing them."

A couple of freshmen strolled right past the gloom without a flinch, even when it darted into the girl's shadow to trail along behind them. I flicked my wand toward it before they carried it any farther away. A couple of whispered words, and it was gone.

The tension in my gut remained. "Can *you* see them at all now?" I asked Keevan.

We started to circle the stands so I could check the shade beneath them for hints of movement. Keevan cocked his head. "Only a bit. Like, if you point one out, and I focus really hard, I can get a sense of the shape of it. So maybe I always could have and I just never knew to try before." He nudged Izzy with his elbow. "Izzy's always been the sharpest one in our bunch."

Izzy rolled her eyes. "I don't remember noticing them before you showed up, Emma. But I guess maybe I wouldn't have made the connection. The first few times I got a sense of one, it was just a shadow that seemed *off* somehow, but I couldn't explain why."

I didn't know whether that should reassure me or not. She didn't seem to have any trouble identifying the things now. She *had* been burned by one in our earlier travels. I'd healed the wound, but maybe the close contact had increased her sensitivity. Or was it simply what I least wanted to believe—that a different dark force was now lending them power?

"Don't sell yourself short," Keevan said lightly, grinning at Izzy. "I was going around without *any* clue there were little bits of darkness coming after Darton."

"I don't think a talent for noticing dark faerie things is going to do me a whole lot of good anywhere else," Izzy replied.

"Oh, you never know. You could carve out a new little niche for yourself."

Izzy shook her head with a laugh. Keevan's grin widened, his eyes so bright you'd have thought it made his whole day to have amused her. He kept watching her, his normally jaunty expression turning almost tender, when she turned to make some comment to Priya. I glanced from him to Izzy as the realization settled over me.

Oh. How had I managed not to see *that* all this time?

To be fair, I'd been rather preoccupied with the whole not-getting-killed thing for most of the time I'd been around the two of them. And it didn't look as if Izzy had noticed the shade of longing in Keevan's expression either. I guessed her excuse was still being hung up on Darton. Not that I could blame her there.

"What's the sack for?" she said to me then, startling me out of my speculations. My fingers had twisted into the fabric of the empty, herb-rubbed bag I'd been carrying under my arm. I forced them to relax.

"If my plan works out, it'll be for containing one of the glooms. When we've pretty much cleared the campus, I'm going to bag one of the last ones. They're useful for testing spells on."

Keevan perked up. "Spells for destroying dark fae?"

"Spells for binding them," I said. "If I break the spell I cast way back when that's kept the whole dying and being reborn cycle going, Darton—and I—could live a normal life with what we've got now. But that magic has also been keeping the very powerful dark fae who tried to kill him imprisoned where she can't hurt us or anyone else."

"So if you free the two of you, you free her too," Priya filled in.

"Right. And then even if removing the spell meant the glooms weren't drawn to him anymore, which I'm not sure of, she'd probably pick up right where she left off." I grimace. "I need to come up with a spell that'll keep her bound without our souls being tied up in it. But we're talking about a fae tens of times more powerful than that mercenary we only barely managed to stop. It's not easy."

"And you can't just adapt the original spell?" Izzy said. "I guess you'd have done that already if you could."

"Yeah." It seemed easier not to mention that I wasn't entirely sure how I'd cast that spell in the first place. It certainly hadn't turned out the way I'd been imagining in my surge of panic as I'd raced to my king's side all those years ago. "I'll just need a place to keep my test subject. I don't really want to be keeping a gloom anywhere near Darton."

If one of my experiments failed and the vermin got a taste of him during its escape, we'd have a new onslaught on our doorstep in days.

Keevan rubbed his angular jaw. "Can't you stash it in that dorm room you're going to be squatting in?"

Before everything had gone to hell last week, I'd found a room in Darton and Keevan's residence building that had been left vacant while waiting on repairs and magically taken it off campus records so I could use it for myself. It meant I'd be closer on hand if something went wrong in the night, but—

"That's still closer than I feel comfortable with. I don't want to take any chances."

"Hmm. What you need is a place like Jagger's."

He waggled his eyebrows as he said it, but it wasn't actually a bad idea. Jagger's home had been a fortress against the dark fae: set apart from anything that cast a shadow, drawing all its power from solar panels, bordered by gas jets that could burn off any of the dark rabble that approached it. Forget experimental glooms—if I could stash *Darton* away someplace like that...

No. For one thing, even Jagger's setup hadn't stopped the dark rabble when they'd been stirred up enough. And more importantly, there was no way Darton was agreeing to that big a disruption of his life. I was supposed to be helping him get back to normal, at least for a little while.

"You could keep it in your old room in our apartment," Priya said. "I don't mind taking on a new roommate."

My lips quirked up, but I shot her a questioning look. "Are you sure?"

She waved off my concern. "You said you'll still pay your half of the rent, after all. I can keep an eye on it. I'll be happy to help."

Some of the tension inside me loosened. One of the biggest ways this life differed from most of the ones before: I had actual friends this time around. Friends who really did want to help. And maybe the circumstances Darton and I were facing now weren't all that different from what they'd been before the mercenary. I'd brought us back to baseline, hadn't I? Which might be as close to normal as we could ever get.

No more glooms lurked under the bleachers. I zapped away a couple we came across lingering near the campus theater building where Darton and I had taken a stand at the start of this whole mess, but it was looking as if the pickings were getting thin. Good. I was more than ready to be done with them.

"Loner at ten o'clock," Priya said, motioning to a patch of darkness wriggling along the hedge by the horticulture department's garden.

The last time I'd been out this way, a bunch of hacky sack players had been using the garden as a playing field. Now that stretch of autumn-shriveled greenery was empty except for the gloom and a guy with hunched shoulders cutting through—late for class, based on his hurry. I veered a little to the right so he could pass before I got down to business.

He ducked through a gap in the hedge, swung left—and hesitated.

His whole body stiffened for a second, his gaze fixed on the spot where the gloom was lurking. My skin went cold. His brow knit. He blinked, and then shook his head and hustled on. I watched him go, my spirits sinking.

It wasn't just Priya and Izzy. It wasn't just sensitivity brought on by experience. That guy had no connection to the fae at all, no reason to be "sensitive" to their kind. The gloom should have been completely imperceptible to him. And yet it had clearly drawn his attention.

"He didn't really see it," Priya said. "He got an impression, but not enough to be sure of himself."

"Small comfort," I muttered. It didn't matter what about the gloom had caught his eye, only that it had. And I couldn't blame that fact on the mercenary's powers now.

I tugged the sack out from under my arm. I might need that new binding spell for more than just creating a more stable life for me and my king. The mercenary had sensed the Darkest One's intentions. With each new piece of evidence, I couldn't ignore what my instincts were telling me. Even with our souls still bound, she was stirring. Which meant she might break free on her timetable, not mine.

"Okay," I said, shaking the bag open. "This one I'm taking with me."

CHAPTER FIVE

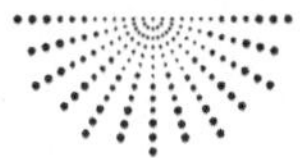

Just to be clear, I loved my parents, even if they were only the most recent set in a long line spanning centuries. They'd given me my space when I'd needed it. They hadn't freaked out too much over all the quirks you'd expect to see from a child growing up with a knowledgeable wizardly soul merged with her body. They'd always shown they had my back when I needed them there. That being said, they sometimes had the worst timing ever.

My phone's ringtone jangled, and I scooped it up from the cafe table with a jerk. I didn't want to distract Darton from his little sister—or draw her attention to my presence watching over them. They were sitting on the other side of the campus cafe, but it wasn't as if I were invisible. Or inaudible.

"Hi, Mom," I said quietly.

"Hello, dear," Mom's warm voice carried through the line. "Is this a good time to talk? You sound a little strange."

"No, no, I'm fine." I cleared my throat. Darton hadn't even glanced over. That was good. He knew I was here, of course, but I'd rather he forgot I was as well as he could. He hadn't seen his sister since the summer, and a normal visit wouldn't include a wizard bodyguard hanging around. "I'm just doing some reading on campus. I don't want to disturb anyone talking too loud. What's up?"

"Oh, I texted you a question over the weekend and didn't hear back, so I wanted to make sure everything was okay over there."

She'd texted me? I must have missed it amid all the chaos. "I don't think I even got that message," I said. "What was the question?"

"I found a box of your old high school notebooks. I wanted to make sure you didn't have any use for them now before I put them in the recycling."

Darton's sister—Audrey, he'd said her name was—ducked her head as she giggled at something he'd said. She had her back mostly to me, but I'd seen enough to know they looked a lot the same. Her hair was a matching wavy golden blond, her figure tall and athletic. The jacket she was wearing proclaimed that she was a member of her high school track team.

Darton smiled back at her over his cappuccino. Then a woman brushed past the back of his chair, and he tensed as if restraining a flinch.

He'd been jumpy all day. Considering recent goings-on, I couldn't blame him for being a tad nervous about his sister's visit, but I'd hoped it might give him a welcome change of pace. A sense that things *could* go back to normal. I was here to make sure nothing got out of hand, after all. And I'd only seen a couple of lingering glooms since clearing the campus earlier that week.

"Don't worry about it," I told Mom. "I don't need that old school stuff anymore. Go ahead and get rid of them." Any notes I'd made that were of real importance, I had stashed either back at the apartment I'd shared with Priya or in my storage locker.

"All right," Mom said. "Sorry if I'm hovering a bit. I'm still getting used to you being so far away."

I smiled with a pang of bemused affection. "It's not like I visited more often when I was at Yale."

"No, but I could drive to see you in a few hours if I wanted to."

Thank the light she hadn't been able to just drop in to check up on me over the last week. Trying to explain even half of the stuff I'd been up to would have taken some major mental gymnastics.

"So are you going to tell me more about this boy?" she added.

My shoulders stiffened. My gaze leapt to Darton automatically. "Boy?"

"Don't pretend you don't know what I mean," she said in a teasing tone. "The last time we talked, you had to get off the phone because a boy was calling. You think I can't tell from your voice when it's someone important?"

Oh. I'd almost forgotten I'd used that excuse. I'd actually needed to get off the phone so I could run off to protect Darton from a rambling gloom. I rubbed my mouth, my chest constricting. My relationship with my fellow college student and long ago king was one more in the long list of things I couldn't talk to her about. That list was only going to keep getting longer now that my liege was waking.

"He's just a friend," I said. The standard stall.

"Hmm. Is that all you want him to be?"

"*Mom.*"

"It's just a question."

I rolled my eyes, but I couldn't help smiling again. It was such a regular, Mom-like thing to say. As if I *were* a regular college student making eyes at a cute classmate. "We'll see," I said. "I promise I'll tell you if anything major happens."

That doesn't involve magic, reincarnated souls, or faerie beings, I added as a silent addendum.

The waitress brought Darton and his sister the sandwiches and fries they'd ordered. When Mom said her good-bye, I settled in at my table for a long haul. My stomach gurgled. I should probably get myself something to eat too.

As I signaled a waiter, a familiar face appeared by the cafe window. Keevan raised his eyebrows at me, changed course, and strolled inside.

I suppressed a sigh as the lanky guy ambled over to my table. Keevan hadn't always been my biggest fan—he'd kind of outright blamed all the trouble we were in last week on me. But then I had been lying about quite a few things to him, so I guessed we were even there. And he'd helped plenty since then.

Keevan glanced over and noted Darton's presence before dropping into the chair across from me. "You look like you could use some company. Is this some super spy wizard stake-out?" He grinned.

"I'm just making sure Darton has nothing to worry about other than showing his sister around campus," I said. "He didn't exactly like the idea of her running into a bunch of glooms or worse."

"I thought we took care of all the glooms and other beasties on our patrol."

I shrugged. "We got most of them, at least. But, you know, he's pretty protective of Audrey."

Not that long ago, when we'd been getting to know each other —before he'd known who either of us really were—he'd told me the story of how he'd saved her from drowning in the family pool when he was nine. Dragged her out and performed CPR on her until she started breathing again. He'd thanked Boy Scout training for his quick thinking and the ability to pull it off, but I figured some credit should be given to Arthur's ingrained determination too.

I don't know how I'm ever going to do anything better than that, he'd said, talking about how aimless he'd been feeling in his life recently. My fingers curled around my coffee mug. We hadn't talked about those feelings since. Since he'd found out he probably had less than a couple years left of this life, because of the soul he was carrying and the dark forces intent on claiming it.

"So he asked you to put him on surveillance for the day?" Keevan said.

"Yeah. Did you figure I was just stalking him for fun?"

He spread his hands. "I don't know. *You're* pretty protective of *him*, in case you haven't noticed."

"For good reason," I muttered, and took a sip of my tea.

A bluster of autumn leaves gusted past the window near Darton. His arm jerked, knocking into his cup. Audrey's hand shot out. She managed to catch the glass just before it tipped over the edge of the table.

Darton laughed, making an awkward gesture as if joking about his clumsiness, but his sister's brow knit. If I could see the strain drawing lines at the corners of his mouth, she had to too.

Keevan's smile had turned crooked. "Aw, come on, you love it. Saving him, getting to be his defender. Don't tell me you don't."

"I don't love the fact that I need to." I sure as hell wished Darton could have relaxed right now. But then, we'd only been back for a few days. The truth was still sinking in.

"Fair." Keevan shook his head. "I really don't get the relationship you two have. It's like you're soul mates or something, but then at the same time you're... whoever you already were, right now. At least he is. Because he only just got onto the whole Arthur thing, right? You've known who you are all along."

I tensed again, despite my best efforts. "I have," I said. "But the kind of body, the kind of brain I'm in has some influence. I still had kid-like impulses when I was a kid and all that."

"Really? I would have liked to be around to see that."

Maybe you will, I stopped myself from saying. *If I don't come up with a brilliant solution to all our problems in the next year or two, we'll be dying and starting all over again. Although maybe the second part only if we're lucky, given how things have gone in this life so far.*

Keevan leaned his elbows onto the tabletop, looking over at Darton again. "It must be hard for you, huh? Even now. You know all this stuff that he's hardly even remembered yet."

"I'm kind of used to that part of the cycle."

"Yeah, but..." He turned his gleaming eyes on me. "It's not just about doing your job or whatever. You've got a personal stake. You haven't followed him around all this time, going through all those deaths, just 'cause you worked for him once upon a time."

Maybe he didn't know what a sore spot he was poking, but my hackles rose all the same. A retort fell out of my mouth before I'd had a chance to think it through. "And why do you follow Izzy around, Keevan?"

His mouth snapped shut. Oh, so there were ways of shutting him up. But I didn't feel particularly vindicated, watching the slump of his shoulders. Keevan and I had our differences, but he wasn't a bad guy. *He'd* only been looking out for Darton, in his own way.

"It's not that pathetic, is it?" he said hoarsely. "I don't—I mean, I try not to—"

"It's not," I broke in. "I didn't even notice until a couple days ago. I'm sorry. I shouldn't have brought it up."

He rubbed the back of his neck. "I guess I shouldn't have been hassling you about Art either."

"I get it," I said. "I know it's a weird situation. I'm not used to having to help people outside of it understand how it all works."

"Yeah." He looked at his hands and then back at me, his expression suddenly serious. "I've been glad when it's felt like there was something I could do that might make a difference. But I don't really know how I fit into his life anymore. How do you keep a friendship with someone who's... becoming someone else? Can you?"

I turned that question over in my head. "Who Darton is—his personality—he's always *been* Arthur. He's not becoming someone different, only realizing why he is who he is. Before, he just didn't know the history, why he felt certain ways. So he's not going to change that much."

But my throat had gone tight. *Who* Darton was might not change a whole lot, but his priorities had already taken a major shift. I didn't know how much longer there'd be room for friendship, honestly. I'd never been able to find much space for it in my own lives. And I had no idea how to tell Keevan that, or if I even should.

"I can't help thinking—" Keevan started, and a dark twitching caught my eye. My back went rigid. Keevan fell silent, following my gaze.

In the shadow under the order counter, a dark fae creature was creeping in Darton's direction. Its long, sinewy body and pointy head brought to mind a weasel—a big one. My hand dropped to my shoulder bag, to the wand I'd been carrying in there.

I hadn't gotten any warning. It must have already been within my protective salt lines. We'd missed this one in the other day's trawling of campus.

It was just the one, though, and it didn't look as if it had much sense of purpose. It was moving vaguely toward Darton, but it hadn't turned its head in his direction once. Maybe it simply sensed something potentially intriguing awaited in the room, with no real idea what.

I had time. I could do this slow and careful, with a minimum of disturbance.

"Keevan," I said, readying myself to stand, "could you—"

I meant to ask him to go over and say hi to Darton and his sister, so they'd be otherwise occupied while I dealt with the shadow vermin. But apparently Darton had been watching *me* more closely than I'd realized. Before I could even finish my sentence, his head jerked toward me and from there to the dark creature. Then he was pushing upright with a rasp of chair legs against linoleum.

"Art!" His name burst from my lips as I scrambled to my feet. He was already moving, heedless of my protest. The fae dagger I hadn't known he was keeping in such easy reach glinted in his grasp. He dodged the other diners and lunged down to slash the blade through the shadow creature's head.

I'd only managed to take a couple steps toward him when his blow hit. The creature shuddered and disintegrated around his strike. Darton straightened up, a breath stuttering out of his mouth.

His sister had gotten up too. Audrey stared at Darton, her face paling beneath her tan. Her gaze dropped to the knife.

"What are you doing, Darton?" she said. "What *is* that?"

Darton took in his sister's expression, and the determination etched on his face faltered. He jabbed the dagger into its sheath and shoved it in his pocket. I took another step toward them, my pulse thudding. Was there anything I could say that might reassure him or her or both of them?

Darton's gaze shot to me. His jaw tensed, and he gave me a brief shake of his head. One swift movement, and a sensation like clenching fingers squeezed around my heart.

He didn't want me getting involved. Did he think I'd make the situation even worse?

He hadn't even trusted me to take care of the creature for him.

Keevan came up beside me. Darton turned to his sister, touching her arm, saying something in a low voice. She was frowning. Her chin trembled when she answered.

I could have calmed her, at very least. Suggested an alternate explanation for her brother's bizarre behavior. But even though Darton's mouth had twisted with guilt, he didn't look at me again. It was like he wanted to pretend I wasn't even there.

I'd wanted that, before. But I'd also wanted him to believe he could count on me.

"What's going on with Art?" Keevan said in a hushed voice.

"I don't know," I said.

Audrey strode off to the restrooms. As soon as the door closed behind her, I couldn't hang back anymore. I hurried to Darton's table. He'd sat back down, his shoulders slightly slumped.

I leaned over beside him. "What are you doing?" I demanded under my breath. "I was going to take care of the creature. That's what I'm here for."

Darton blinked up at me. Another flash of guilt passed through his eyes. But his mouth set.

"Then why hadn't you? You'd seen it, and you were still sitting there."

"It wasn't an urgent threat. I was getting ready to handle it in a way that wouldn't freak your sister out. Isn't that what you wanted?"

A choked laugh slipped out of his mouth. "I want to know she isn't going to get hurt a lot more than I'm worried about freaking her out."

"I wouldn't have let her—*or* you—get hurt."

He looked back at me steadily. His voice wasn't angry or accusing, just softly matter-of-fact. "How do you know that for sure? They got past you in the end all those lives before, didn't they?"

A chill settled over me. I'd *seen* in his jumpiness that he hadn't felt safe even with me here, even if I hadn't wanted to admit it.

Why should he trust me? Hanging around near him, laying down warning lines—those were all the same strategies I'd used in the past. In the past, when a fae mercenary had nonetheless managed to target him and nearly kill the both of us. And, as he'd rightly pointed out, in all the lives with all the deaths before that.

I'd been trying not to interfere too much, but *he* was going to screw up the normal life he wanted if I couldn't give him the confidence that I'd be ready when he needed me.

"I know," I said around the tightness in my throat. "I can do better this time. I'll show you."

CHAPTER SIX

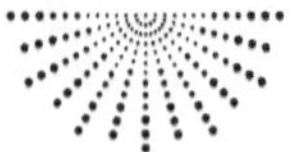

I STARTED to tense as I turned Jagger's van off the two-lane highway onto the local road that led to the construction site. I hadn't told Darton much about what to expect. Hadn't wanted to give him the wrong impression in either direction if I chose the wrong words.

He looked a little tense himself, but he straightened in anticipation when I turned again, onto the driveway. The fur ruff along the hood of his bomber jacket rustled against the seat. I studied his expression as he took in the view through the windshield.

The place wasn't much to look at yet—not that it was ever going to be a beauty of a house. I was going for function over style all the way down here. Construction tarp drifted across the unfinished walls of the single-story structure. They hissed in the breeze as we stepped out.

Darton tapped his foot against the sprawl of hard concrete. "This is an interesting take on lawns."

I glowered at him. "Grass makes shadows—shadows the dark rabble can hide in. We can't count on the desert heat baking the plant life away like Jagger could, so a concrete yard seemed like the safest bet."

I wasn't taking any chances there. The ground thirty feet from the house on every side was solid, flat cement. A chalky smell hung in the cool air. The construction team had only just finished pouring it yesterday. Beyond the edge of the concrete stretched yellowed fields, nothing thick enough to provide a lot of shelter until they reached the farmhouses or the patch of forestland some half a mile away.

Darton turned, surveying the grounds. "How much of this land is yours?"

"Ours," I said automatically, even though technically I'd paid for it. But I'd kept my accounts, the ones my careful records and magical beacons led me back to life after life, mainly to fund whatever my king might need, so really the money was his as much as mine. I hadn't done much to earn it in over a century, other than let it sit and snowball with interest. "The full lot is about a couple square miles."

Darton gave me a startled look.

"It wasn't *that* expensive," I said. "Just some old fields no one had found much to do with in a while. I guess the soil isn't great for farming."

He shook his head and ambled over to the house. "I can't believe you pulled this all together so quickly."

I couldn't tell whether he was awed or uncomfortable. "Hey, after a little magical finessing at the permit office and double pay for the construction company, everyone was happy to lend a hand."

The corner of his mouth quirked up at my breezy tone. Okay, that seemed like a step in the right direction.

"I took a lot of inspiration from Jagger's house," I said. We stepped through the open doorframe. "The roof will be mounted with enough solar panels to keep us off the grid. We're in cell tower range, so no need for a home line anyway. And they've built in a similar trick with the gas fire along the walls. I had a tank installed to supply those pipes so we're not dependent on an external line."

We'd learned last time around that the dark rabble would dig right down to interfere with electricity and gas if they needed to.

The interior walls were finished. The first room we stepped into was an open concept living space, kitchen at one end and a big living room at the other. My hands twisted where I'd clasped them in front of me. "There'll be lots of room to have people over. I mean, anyone you feel comfortable inviting. Keevan and Izzy, at least, will understand."

Darton nodded. "It's a lot more space than the dorm room, that's for sure."

I still couldn't quite read his tone. He'd never have expected to end up moving a half hour outside of town into some crazy anti-fae house.

"I know it's not the most convenient change ever," I said. "But whenever you're here, you'll at least be able to relax. No gloom is going to get close enough to this place to sense your presence here, so they won't start being drawn into the area like they might be if you keep staying in the dorm. I can recast the dampening spell every morning before you head out."

"What's this?" Darton motioned to an interior door that already had a deadbolt mounted on it. A strong one.

"That's our dark rabble trap," I said. "If any of them *do* come calling and make it past the other protections, there's an opening that'll look like an easy way to slip in. But they'll end up dropping right into a little enclosure in there, where I've got solar-powered lights and lenses set up to blast them from all sides with concentrated sunlight."

He chuckled. "Whoever you got to draw up the plans for this place must have thought you were insane."

"I... might have used a little magical persuasion to get past that problem too." I nudged him on down the hall with my gloved hand. "This door leads to the garage, where we'll have the van ready to go in case things get dire. I'll make sure it's fully outfitted and gassed up at all times, so you'll have those protections on hand whenever we're on campus too. And these are the bedrooms."

I nudged open an interior door. Sunlight filtered through the translucent tarp that covered the spot where the far, exterior wall would be. The room was at least twice as big as the one Darton currently shared with Keevan. "Three of them, so you'll have space that's totally your own, and we'll have extra in case we have guests who need to stay over. They each have their own en suite bathroom."

"You didn't want to have to argue about who gets the first shower?" Darton suggested with a wry smile.

I elbowed him. "I figured you'd want some breathing room. Obviously it all looks pretty dull right now while it's empty. You can pick out whatever furniture you want. I'm happy to give you final say with the common areas too—I don't care much as long as there's something comfortable to sit on. And—"

"Em." Darton turned toward me, so close that all at once I couldn't breathe. It was just me and him in the hall, the wall at my back and him in front of me. The scent of him, citrus and earthy musk combined, washed away the chalky smell and the pinewood tang of the freshly cut wood. He touched my waist. The heat of his hand traveled through my sweater.

"You've gotten all this set up for me," he said. "Because I said you weren't doing enough to keep back the glooms?"

A lump rose in my throat. I clamped down on the urge to shift closer to him, to feel that warmth all through my body. "I should have made more changes earlier. I should have started working on something like this the moment we got back. There are other possibilities to protect you here, or when you're away from here, that I need to do more research on, but— We got a second chance. I'm not going to screw that up."

He bowed his head. His nose nearly brushed my forehead. My pulse hitched. "Darton."

"I wasn't really angry with you the other day. You know that, right?" He swallowed audibly. "I didn't mean to make you feel you weren't trying hard enough. I wouldn't be *alive* if it wasn't for you. I was just wound up—having Audrey there right after those things were raging all over campus—"

"It's okay," I said. "You were right. I don't want to ruin your life... but I've got to do everything I can to make sure you have one in the first place. And my old strategies only got us so far. I've got to use everything I can."

"Em." His voice dipped. "What about *your* life?"

A strained laugh tumbled out of me. "I can worry about that when I've fixed the mess *I* made."

"The mess you made that also kept me alive."

"In about the least practical way possible."

"I'm pretty sure it still counts." His thumb traced an arcing line across my side. An eager shiver ran over my skin in its wake. I clenched my fingers to stop them from reaching for him. He wanted Emma. He wanted the woman he saw when he looked at me right now. And he might not even have wanted her without the magical bond between our souls twining through his feelings.

He hadn't wanted Merlin, not like that. He didn't want *me*.

"Any way I can help," he said. "Anything I can do that lets *you* worry less, you have to tell me. I should be protecting myself at least as much as you are."

"That's not how this works, Art."

He caught my head as I started to shake it, his hand carefully touching only my hair. The gentle caress was still enough to send a flood of longing through me.

"The hardest thing," he said, "is going to be spending all those nights out here with you, and not even being able to kiss you."

"We talked about this," I said, trying to sound firm even though my will on this subject at this moment felt about as wobbly as Jell-O. "The more you wake up, the harder it'll be to mask who you are. Killing the mercenary bought us some time, but we've still got to be careful."

"The memories that came back to me before ended up helping us."

"Yeah, well, we can't assume we'd get that lucky again. And you'll keep remembering more on your own. There's just no good in speeding up the process."

He lowered his head until his breath tickled hot past my ear. "It's only if we literally touch, skin to skin, that it stirs up the memories, isn't it? There's no reason... that we couldn't..."

His thumb stroked higher, skimming the swell of my breast through the fabric. My breath hitched. For a second I was caught up in the thought of all the things it was possible to do, possible to feel, without ever touching skin directly.

Then the image flashed through my mind of Darton in the hotel room, his incredulous expression when I'd asked if he liked being reminded of my original body.

I scooted to the side, away from him and his warmth. Darton's gaze followed me, his smile falling.

"I don't think that's a good idea," I said quickly. "It's too easy to get caught up in the moment, to forget what we're not supposed to be doing."

He inclined his head, accepting. But when he met my eyes again, his were searching.

"Are you sure that's all it is? If something else is wrong—if I've done something—"

But he hadn't. It wasn't wrong for him not to want all of me. Telling him how I felt... That would only lead to more pain for me and guilt for him. Neither of us needed that.

"No. It's just being careful." I forced a smile. Sod it. I should never have let us mess around as much as we already had, and then we wouldn't have even been having this conversation. "If I can finally get all that old magic sorted out, then we'll have no restrictions at all."

I meant to walk back to the open ground, where I'd be much less tempted to sway in my resolve. But I took all of three steps, and my vision fractured. My knees gave.

"Emma!" Darton shouted. That was the last thing I knew before my mind blinked away from him and the partly constructed house.

Streaks of shadows shot past my awareness. I couldn't tell whether I was looking forward or up or down, only that I was tumbling in that direction with no way of stopping. The shadows parted around a dark pool surrounded by jagged gray-brown rock. Its surface churned with thicker shadows. My stomach lurched, and then I was plunging through it.

After the first shock of chilly rushing water, I fell away into an open space beneath. A space where a person could breathe, but I could sense with every fiber of my being that each breath would feel suffocating. As if the darkness gusting around me would fill my lungs if they'd been there with me, clog my throat. The edges of the shadows twisted into figures, faces, bits of scenery. They flicked out at me as my vision carried me onward.

A sense of recognition settled over me. I'd heard of this place. Hadn't ever been there—hadn't ever *wanted* to be—but the details matched. The question was, why had my clairvoyant impulses decided to take me on this little tour of dark spaces?

The question had barely flitted through my mind when I arrived at my answer. The vision spun me around. I felt as if I stumbled, although I had no limbs to stumble with. Then I was staring at a gleaming length of metal twined with fingers of shadow.

The vibrations of magic woven into the sword's core tingled over me. I'd have recognized it from that even if the binding on the grip, the touch of filigree on the hilt, hadn't jolted my memory. My awareness reached for it instinctively—

—and I jerked awake on the newly sanded floorboards in the unfinished house. My head was resting on Darton's knee. He exhaled in a shaky rush as I pushed upright. I stopped, one hand braced against the floor, the other pressed to my forehead. The wave of dizziness rose and ebbed.

"Are you okay?" Darton said. "You weren't even—at least, it didn't look like you were doing any magic, and out of nowhere you just... collapsed."

I rubbed my eyes. The image of the sword was still dancing behind them. "I had a vision. They come like that sometimes. No hello and how are you first. Not much of a good-bye either."

"Like the vision that told you to switch colleges so you'd bump into me."

I nodded.

He studied me. "What did you see this time? Do we need to be worried?"

I must have looked bad. I closed my eyes and opened them again, and managed to get to my feet. "No," I said. "Actually, in some ways it's good. I know where your sword is now."

"My sword... Excalibur?" He leapt up after me. "We can go get it then. It'll be one more way to defend ourselves."

"Ah, well, it's a little more complicated than that. The place where I saw it, as far as I know it's back in Britain. And I'm not exactly sure where in Britain it is. What I do know is it's not any place a person generally wants to go. It's..." I hesitated. "Imagine that all the nightmares you ever dreamt decided to start a club where they shared tips on the best ways to torment you. That's not really a place you'd want to hang out for any amount of time."

"Oh." Darton couldn't disguise the disappointment in his voice. "Then we're just going to leave it there?"

"I don't know." I grimaced. "When I get a vision, it's usually telling me something I need to know."

What the hell was coming for us now, that we'd need Arthur's soul-bound sword to get us through it?

CHAPTER SEVEN

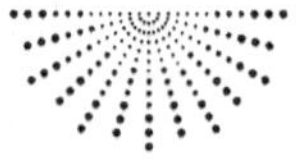

I STOPPED by the door to the dorm room I'd taken over and cast a quick distraction spell on myself. Tweaking the school records bought me a lot of wiggle room, but I wasn't going to get away with squatting up here for very long if students started noticing me coming and going. I rolled the stiffness out of my shoulders, grimacing at the air mattress I'd been sleeping on.

Just a couple more days, and the new house would be finished. Then I could sleep on a proper bed—in a room that didn't have a half-a-foot-deep hole in the wall from some party boy on a bender.

The bag of salt I was carrying hadn't alerted me to any dark rabble entering the building during the night. Still, the back of my neck prickled as I headed down the residence building's stairs to Darton's floor. I had enough protections on and around this place that I should have known minutes before anything with malicious intentions got close to him... but it was hard to feel completely certain of his safety before I had him in my sight.

No one gave me a second glance as I emerged from the stairwell. Exactly as I liked it. The distraction spell itched at my skin, but I left it on. I didn't want anyone noticing me following Darton either. *He* knew I'd be keeping an eye on him, but none of the other students would realize my stalking was sanctioned.

Bodies jostled around me, dodging me without taking note of me on any conscious level. The hall smelled like clashing perfumes and laundry someone *really* needed to take home to their parents' washing machine. My nose wrinkled. I wasn't going to miss this aspect of dorm life either.

Down the hall, Darton emerged from his room. Keevan stepped out behind him. The rakish guy made a sweeping gesture with his hand, teeth flashing bright on his dark brown face, and Darton started laughing. He gave his friend's shoulder a playful shove.

A twinge of fondness ran through me, watching the two of them. Watching Darton looking like a regular college guy. Then my stomach twisted. There wasn't going to be any more early morning teasing once we moved into the new house, at least not between him and Keevan.

Well, they'd have lots of other time to horse around. And it wasn't as if Darton had a problem with my company. His gaze slid past his friend and found mine amid the dorm hall chaos. Even with the spell, his soul knew mine well enough to spot me. He smiled, and the ache in my stomach dissolved.

They headed for the main doors, and I ambled after them, leaving plenty of distance. Darton's morning Law and Political Theory seminar was at the same time as my Developmental Biology lecture, so after I'd seen him into that building safely, I might actually continue my own studies today.

I wasn't the only person who knew Darton's schedule by heart. Izzy was standing near the bike rack just outside, a wool jacket buttoned over her typical airy cotton dress and her pale auburn hair drifting with the breeze. She waved to the guys, but to my surprise, her gaze slipped past them, searching.

For me? I muttered under my breath to disperse the distraction spell, and her eyes brightened. She moved to fall into step with me as the boys continued across campus.

"Hi, Emma." Her brow knit. "It is okay to keep calling you that name, right?"

"After twenty years of hearing it, it feels just as much mine as the original one. Don't worry about it." I glanced sideways at her. The furrow between her thin eyebrows hadn't left. "What's wrong?"

"I..." She rubbed her mouth, her head dipping down. "I'm probably just being silly. But after everything this weekend..."

"It's fine," I said. "Whatever it is, I want to know. And even if it's silly, I promise not to tell you I think so."

Her lips twitched with a faint smile. "Okay. It's just that I saw this guy last night. There wasn't anything *obviously* strange about him. He was, like, normal height, normal build, normal brown hair, normal clothes, you know. But when I looked at him, I got this uncomfortable feeling. A lot like the feeling when my eyes catch on one of those glooms."

A chill traced down my spine. "You saw him *here*? Around the college?"

"No." She shook her head firmly. "I was out at a restaurant on the other side of town with some friends. I saw him standing across the street when we were waiting for the taxi to get home. And that was all he was doing—just standing. I might just be extra jumpy. It was late. Lots of regular shadows." A nervous giggle slipped out of her.

"Did he do anything at all while you were there?"

"No. Nothing weird. He stood there for a minute like he'd stopped to think about something, and then he walked off. I tried to act like I hadn't even noticed him—no one else did—but I don't know if he realized he'd bothered me." She looked up. "Do you think he's someone we'd need to worry about?"

"From what you've said, the only thing I'm concerned about is the vibe you got from him. But I'd have to see him myself to know for sure." I sucked in a breath. "If he gave you that feeling, it *could* have been a dark fae. And obviously we don't want another one of those lurking around here. I'll see what I can find out. Thank you for telling me."

"I thought you should know." She brushed her hair back from her face. "I've got to get to class. If I see anything else—"

"Let me know, right away," I said with a nod. "Text me if you're not sure where I am."

She meandered off down one of the side paths. I continued trailing after Darton, who'd parted ways with Keevan while I'd talked to Izzy.

My hand dropped to the salt pouch in my pocket. The lines I'd laid down across and around campus should have alerted me if even a gloom had passed over them, let alone a full dark fae. I closed my fingers around the pouch. My awareness drifted into the tendrils of magic between the salt there and the crushed crystals of it scattered along the ground in every direction.

The lines lit up in my mind—a circle around the residence building, an extra sprinkling along the border of Darton's room, wider circles around the core of the campus, the outer buildings, the farthest edges of the college grounds. They all shone with power, unbroken. No, nothing had passed this way without my knowing.

Maybe it really was just Izzy's nerves getting the best of her. But I didn't feel comfortable counting on that.

Darton disappeared into his seminar room. I hesitated outside. Then I turned and headed in the direction of the science buildings —but not to go to my lecture.

I'd spent some time examining the physics course offerings in the last few days. There was a class on electromagnetics right now I'd been considering sitting in on. With Izzy's news, that course of action suddenly felt a lot more urgent than keeping my grades up.

Thankfully, it was a big class. I slipped in just as the professor moved to the lectern and nabbed a seat right at the back. As her staccato voice pealed through the room, I dug out a notebook and pen.

Jagger and his internet buddies had come up with strategies for tackling the dark rabble that had never occurred to me. For all I knew, they hadn't taken things far enough. Simply combining my magic with sunlight and lenses had allowed us to overcome the fae mercenary. If learning a little physics would give me more options —better options—I'd switch majors in a heartbeat.

Maybe I should have started with a more beginner level course. I hadn't studied physics since high school, and some of the professor's talk about voltages and directionality went over my head. Still, I dutifully jotted down every term and idea that sounded like it might pack a punch. I could look up simpler explanations later.

A manmade current shouldn't affect the dark rabble directly, but if I could figure out how to turn it into natural energy without draining my own power converting it... I really should have paid more attention to this side of science before.

Machines and electronics with their orderly circuitry had always given the light fae side of me a vague discomfort. They seemed much more to the tastes of the dark realm. But it was hard to picture a sizzling current of electricity and not see an element of chaos there. My fault for letting those old prejudices divert me.

By the time the lecture finished, my head felt heavy with unfamiliar concepts. I'd filled five pages with my messy scrawl. Well, that was plenty of homework for the day.

I ducked out ahead of the main rush of students, hurried for the entrance—and almost ran right into my Organic Chemistry professor coming out of an office.

Professor Kapoor stepped back with an automatic apology. Then his gaze focused on my face. His eyebrows drew together as he realized he knew me. "Emma."

"Professor." I bobbed my head, wondering if I could get away with making a run for the doors. I had the feeling that would cause more problems than it fixed.

"I haven't seen you in a couple weeks now," he said. "I have to admit I've been concerned. We're getting into the core material for finals—you've missed a key lab—"

"I know," I said quickly. "I'm really sorry. I just— Things have come up. Ah, family things." That was almost true. At this point my king was more my family than anyone else. "I had to take some time away."

"I can make some allowances for extenuating circumstances, but only if I'm aware of them. Do you have a moment to talk now? I may be able to arrange a repeat of the lab, and there are readings you'll want to get to as soon as possible."

He motioned for me to follow him, but my legs locked in place. Dread squeezed around my gut.

Who was I kidding? Sure, I could go along with him and pretend my absence had been a temporary anomaly. But I'd be wasting his time and mine, wouldn't I?

I knew my priorities had shifted. I couldn't be attending labs and doing course readings when I had an entirely new field of study to master, glooms to fend off, a possible dark fae to watch out for... And those priorities weren't ever going to shift back, not unless I failed and started over in a whole new life, waiting for the moment I encountered my king again.

Darton might be able to hold onto most of his normal life for a while longer, but my "normal" life—it was over. It had been over, really, the instant I'd set eyes on him in fencing club. There was no use in denying that fact.

I swallowed hard. "I really enjoyed your class, Dr. Kapoor," I said. "But I'm actually—I'm just here tying up some loose ends. Unfortunately I won't be attending any classes anymore."

Professor Kapoor's eyes widened. "It's okay, really," I said before he could start in on any questioning. "I'll pick up my studies again when I have the chance." *Most likely, in a whole new life and body, but let's not get into that.* Then I turned heel and took off. As long as I kept my gaze forward, nothing I lost could bother me too much.

CHAPTER EIGHT

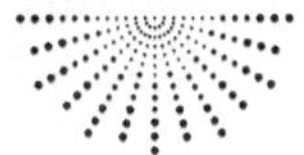

THE PAVED YARD around the new house might not have been pretty, but it made a decent training ground.

"You want to keep your body behind the dagger as much as possible." I moved into a defensive stance for Darton to model, my sneakers rasping over the concrete. The pose wasn't that different from one I might have used while sparring in fencing club—other than my current weapon was a chopstick. "To make it as difficult as possible for them to get close to anything except the blade. One or two glooms on their own won't be able to do you much damage, if they even try to. But if they get a taste of your presence, we'll have them calling a whole new horde down on us in no time."

"Right," Darton said. "No getting touchy-feely with the shadow creatures."

I rolled my eyes at him, and he grinned. With a gloved hand, I pushed his arm so he bent his elbow. I was keeping as much of *my* body covered as possible to avoid any "touchy-feely" between us. Not that every inch of my skin wasn't fully aware of exactly how close we were standing.

"Don't extend your arm all the way," I said. "You want to have the flexibility to jab a little farther if you need to."

Darton took a few experimental swipes with the light fae dagger. It flicked through the air, the silver blade gleaming in the late afternoon sunlight. He lowered his hand. "A dagger doesn't let you keep your enemy at much of a distance, does it? Is there any way you could enchant one of those fencing swords for me?"

"Oh, yeah, because you wouldn't draw *any* attention at all walking around campus brandishing an epee or a sabre."

He grimaced. "Point taken. I have gotten a few weird looks just from people noticing the dagger. It's hard to keep it totally out of sight."

"You shouldn't have fighting so much on your mind anyway," I said. "You're not equipped to really tackle any kind of fae creature. This practice is just to make sure you're as prepared as possible in an absolute emergency. Those things are magic, and it takes magic to really defend against them."

"Hence the request for magical weaponry. But I get it, I get it." Darton tucked the dagger back into his pocket. "I do feel better knowing I have *some* way of at least slowing those things down if I need to. I seem to remember I did a fair bit of fighting on my own, no magic involved, way back when, though—and I was pretty good at it too."

"Yeah, you were, I'll give you that. But those battles weren't against fae."

And in the later battles, he *had* had magic on his side, at least in his blade. Sometimes in other ways as well. A memory trickled up from one of those early skirmishes of Arthur's rule, before the extended conflict had really weighed down on any of us. I let it wash over me.

I was hanging back from the main force of the fighting, as usual, next to my sack of freshly snapped sticks. Dragging the life energy from them one by one and letting them crumble into dust, I blinded that soldier with a flash of redirected sunlight, tangled this one's feet with a sudden eruption of grass, and set a group of them off balance with a gust of wind. My lungs strained with the effort, but I didn't hesitate for a second.

If I'd tried to outright kill any of the men, the energy that bent to my will would have recoiled. Setting them up for our soldiers to land their blows didn't offend my fae nature, though.

In the midst of a fray, I could always track exactly where my king was fighting. Excalibur gleamed with an unearthly light, brighter with the determination in Arthur's soul powering its swing. Man and weapon moved together as one being. He swung, sliced, and parried as if it weighed half what the huge broadsword truly did.

Shouts and clangs echoed across the field. Our men fell back, shields raised to fend off a shower of arrows. I grabbed a handful of sticks and whipped the projectiles aside with a cutting breeze.

Our enemies on the ground surged forward. One lunged with his spear at a solder who'd stumbled in his momentary retreat. The young man whipped up his arm, but his grasp on his short sword was wobbly. It fell from his hand when he blocked the first blow. The enemy soldier raised his weapon to strike again.

And Arthur was there. The spearhead glanced off Excalibur. The enemy soldier growled and spun around, thrusting his weapon toward my king's side. Arthur neatly batted the spear away, sidestepping—and opening his back to another soldier who'd just whirled toward him.

His name caught in my throat. I didn't have time to grasp more than the few remaining sticks still in my hands. "Shove them, gone, away," I gasped out, and shoved my hands forward with all the energy in those sticks, wrenching more from within me.

A blast of air rammed into both of the soldiers swinging at Arthur. It propelled them right off their feet with a jerk. They hurtled through the air, disappearing among the trees where the archers were hiding.

The effort yanked at my soul. I teetered and almost fell, my vision hazing. Someone caught my arm. The medic who helped me tend to the injured after each battle had come up beside me.

"Merlin?" he said.

I shook my head, as much to clear it as to say I didn't need help. My legs steadied. I heaved a breath and snatched up another handful of sticks.

When we'd finally sent what remained of the enemy force running, I'd all but forgotten that moment of over-extending myself. My king hadn't.

"Merlin." Arthur grasped my narrow shoulder and spun me around. His tawny hair stuck up in sweaty tufts and dirt smudged his sunburned face, but even so, there wasn't much I'd rather have looked upon. Until I realized those bright blue eyes were narrowed with anger. And that the anger was aimed at me.

"I heard you almost fainted from a casting," he said, still holding me in place. "Right after the last volley of arrows."

"I'm fine," I said quickly. "I was *fine."*

"You nearly burned yourself out tossing the men I was fighting into the woods."

"I was fine," I repeated. "And I was saving your life, Your Highness. You're welcome."

His jaw clenched. "I didn't need saving, Merlin. I can handle myself. You're supposed to be looking out for everyone, not focusing your energy on me."

"And I was doing that almost the entire time. Forgive me from preventing your imminent skewering when I had the chance."

"I wouldn't have been skewered. I've already got a bloody enchanted sword, Merlin. What was the point of all the effort you put into that if you're not even going to let me use it when I need to? I can't lead these men if you're stepping in the way."

Ah. There was the heart of the matter. I should have known. Any inclination I'd had left to banter fled me. I touched Arthur's arm.

"I overreacted," I said. "I didn't have much time to think, and I used a lot more punch than the situation required. I apologize for that. But you've been getting plenty of use out of that sword of yours all the same, and having it doesn't mean you can be outright careless. You can't lead anyone if you're dead. It doesn't make you invincible."

His expression softened slightly. He sighed. "I know that, Merlin."

But I'd wondered if he really did. And now, watching Darton rest his palm against the hilt of the dagger, testing how quickly he could draw it, I was almost glad that damned sword was far away in the last place I'd ever want to pay a visit. It had been a great weapon, sure, but I didn't need my king getting ahead of himself in the confidence department. A tool was only as effective as the person wielding it.

An engine's growl carried across the fields. It was almost dinnertime.

A taxi turned up our drive and deposited Priya in the yard. She hustled over, hefting a grocery bag bulging with supplies for the meal we'd made plans to cook. Her eyes widened as she took in the house. The big white block of a building seemed to glow a bit even in the fading daylight.

I motioned her to the front door, Darton following us. "Come on in."

She stepped inside, gawking at everything. "Wow. You really decked the place out nice, Emmaline."

"I figured there were some ways I didn't want to imitate Jagger," I said. "If we could potentially end up holed up in here for a while, there's something to be said for comfort."

Darton and I had squabbled—mostly playfully—until we'd settled on a pair of plum leather sofas, an assortment of dark-stained wooden tables and cupboards, and wool rugs thick enough to dig one's toes into. The old-fashioned styling of the furniture didn't entirely match the house's modern design, but given that the people living here were two old souls in modern bodies, I couldn't say it wasn't fitting.

The aspect I enjoyed the least was the lack of windows—but light willing we wouldn't be in here much during daytime hours anyway. Priya peered up at the broad electric fixtures, which beamed thanks to our stored solar energy. "You copied his approach to lighting."

"Yeah, well, windows make for too easy an entry point for anything really determined. And the solar energy is fresh enough that these lights would put off any gloom, at least."

"Only glooms?"

I smiled. "We've got other methods for anything bigger. This place is both technologically and magically enhanced."

"You've got one up on Jagger there, then," Priya said. Her expression turned more serious. "It's too bad he didn't have any wizards around to make his place extra secure."

My chest tightened, thinking of the smoking ruin of his house. "Yeah."

Darton leaned against the kitchen island, his pose casual but his gaze intent. "You said you need magic to really take on the dark fae. Couldn't you teach other people to cast spells and all that?"

He wasn't ready to let the idea of taking on the dark fae himself go yet, clearly. Could I teach people like him, he meant.

"What, open a wizarding school?" I teased. "No. It doesn't work that way. I can only work magic because I'm half fae. I was *born*—the first time—with the ability to bend the energy of life and light. Less ability, because of the human half. That's not something you can teach. At least not in any reasonable length of time. I think there have been people who've managed to reach some level of connection... but only after decades of concentrated study."

"Oh." His tone did only a passable job of hiding his disappointment.

"That's not completely true," Priya put in. "Anything living can use its *own* life energy, right? If it gets worked up enough or whatever. My fae guardians had stories about people or even animals pulling off some great magical feat by sacrificing their lives."

I looked at her balefully. "Yes. Technically, under the right circumstances and with the right mindset, you can turn your life into power if you get yourself killed. But since our main goal here is making sure Darton *doesn't* get killed, that's not really a strategy of much use to him."

She shrugged. "I was just being thorough."

I didn't think Darton needed any *more* self-sacrificing ideas getting into his head. He was frowning now, his gaze distant. "It's not a big deal," I told him. "You don't need to do magic. You've got me. That's the whole reason I'm here."

"It's not that." He rubbed his mouth. "I feel like I already knew that, about the sacrificing and the magic. But not from you—this you, anyway. I can't remember who told me, or when."

"It could have come up in some conversation in our first go-around. Don't worry about it. It doesn't help us anyway."

To my relief, Priya redirected the conversation. She took one more look around the room with a happy sigh. "Well, I'm definitely going to have to start visiting on a regular basis. Shall we get cooking?"

She dumped her bag on the kitchen island. I ambled over to join her, bringing up the recipe on my phone.

Darton peered at the bag's contents. "Need any help with dinner?"

I shooed him off. "I learned a very long time ago that kings and kitchens don't produce the greatest results. Or at least not this king." At his mock wounded look, I gave him a gentle shove. "Go relax. That's another skill you could use some practice at."

Darton pretended to huff, but a minute later he was sprawled on one of the sofas, channel surfing on the TV mounted over the fireplace. Priya and I got down to work, washing and peeling and dicing. As the frying pan sizzled and the smell of frying garlic and onion filled the air, *I* started to relax. I liked the house, but for the first time, it really felt like a home.

Maybe this new normal, one I could share with people who knew what I was and who I could trust with that knowledge, would be pretty good after all.

I got to float on that feeling for maybe five minutes. Then the pouch of salt in my pocket shuddered.

I froze with the spatula poised over the pan. Priya's head jerked around. "What?"

At her voice, Darton turned off the TV and sat up. I rested my hand over my pocket. The vibrations of the warning spell tickled through my palm.

It was the boundary around the edge of our property that had been tripped.

"Something's come into the yard," I said, my heart thudding. "Chances are it's just a wandering gloom. The outside lights should put it off."

"What should we do?" Darton asked.

"*You* don't do anything." The last thing I wanted was him charging out there hoping to play hero.

I waited, fingers still pressed to the pouch. The boundary would trigger again when whatever it was left. Or if it crossed the line I'd laid down just a few feet from the walls. The line it *shouldn't* be able to cross if it was only one of the dark rabble. But then, the rabble that had come at Jagger's house shouldn't have been able to hit him as hard as they had either.

The salt didn't stir. The hiss of the frying vegetables filled the room, no other sound breaking it. My hand tightened around the spatula. I offered the utensil to Priya.

"I think I'll take a quick look, send it on its—"

The salt all but jumped from its pouch, and a *clang* cut off my voice, reverberating through the walls. My pulse hiccupped. I spun around, my hand flying to the wand I'd stuffed in my back pocket. Darton sprang up, tensed.

"The sun trap," I said. "We caught something." I strode to the hall. The way the trap worked, whatever it'd caught had probably already been burned away. But my stomach still knotted as I grasped the door handle.

Darton and Priya had followed me. "Stay back," I told Darton. "Let me take a look first."

He nodded, but he'd already drawn the fae dagger. I put my hand out to emphasis my request and tugged open the door.

My fingers slipped from the handle. I sucked in a breath, my jaw going slack.

The interior walls of the sun trap were completely reflective, to bounce the solar-cell light at any intruder that triggered it. But the material I'd picked worked like a one-way mirror—from the outside, I could see in. And what I saw standing in that octagonal case wasn't a gloom or a shadow creature but a man.

No, not a man. A dark fae. Light blazed at him from all sides, making him twitch and shiver. His thin lips had drawn back in a grimace. His dun brown hair stood on end, and his knobby fingers dug into his arms where he'd hugged them over his chest. And clots of shadow churned in his hooded eyes.

Those eyes looked straight at me, even though he shouldn't have been able to see me through his side of the wall. They tracked me as I pushed myself to step inside. My heart battered my ribs. The trap hadn't killed him yet, but it was clearly torturing him. The thought darted through my mind to set him free, send him off with this as a warning.

But I couldn't shut off the trap without giving him full freedom to use his power. And if his intention had been honorable, presumably he'd have knocked on the door rather than trying to sneak his way in.

His face contorted further. The wand wavered in my hand.

He opened his mouth, and a snarl of a voice carried through the wall. "Merlin. I knew it was you."

"What the hell?" Darton said. He and Priya had edged through the door I'd left open in my shock. The dark fae cut himself off with a low muttering I couldn't make out. A casting. *No.* My arm jerked up. "*Blaze, burn, sear him clean,*" I shouted.

My will and the wand wrenched at the energy in the solar cells.

I caught a glimpse of the dark fae grinning a twisted grin at me. Then light flared inside the trap, so brilliant I was blinded. My vision stuttered. The wand crumbled. My legs wobbled as I gave over a fragment of my own life to the spell.

The light faded, the panels on the trap walls cutting out. Only the regular fixture on the ceiling kept glowing.

Nothing remained in the trap except a mound of sunken flesh and fabric.

CHAPTER NINE

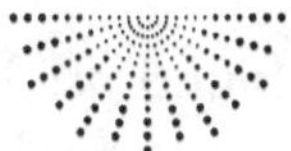

THE LIGHTS in the house's common room beamed over me just as brightly as before, but the warmth didn't penetrate my skin. The smell of our unfinished dinner only made my stomach ache. I paced from the kitchen island to the nearer sofa and back, passing the spare wand I'd retrieved the second I'd stumbled out of the sun-trap room from hand to hand. The smooth, firm oak wood in my grasp was just grounding enough to stop me from spiraling into utter panic.

"*Two* full dark fae in the space of a month," I said. "This shouldn't be happening. It's *never* happened. Nothing worse than the dark rabble has ever bothered with our past incarnations."

"That you remember," Darton said tentatively.

"I would have left notes if a full fae had come calling before." Unless it'd turned up and immediately slaughtered us before I'd had the chance to write down a record. Which I supposed was possible. But I *did* still have at least vague memories of our last several deaths, and none of them had come about that way.

I pinched the bridge of my nose. "There might even be three. Izzy said she saw a man who gave her a strange vibe. He could have been the fae we just burned up—she said he had brown hair—but we don't know that."

Darton had stiffened. "What? Izzy never mentioned that to me. *You* never mentioned that to me."

I waved off his implied complaint. "You didn't need to know. She wasn't sure, and I had no reason to be—and there wasn't anything you could have done about it anyway. We were already set to move in here."

"How do you think he found us? I thought that spell you cast would stop the dark fae from noticing me?"

"The lesser dark creatures," I said. "The ones we usually have to worry about. I'm only half fae, and not even in that body anymore —if a dark fae comes looking, I can't completely hide you, only divert them for a bit. They've just never come looking before. Maybe this one was a friend of our mercenary. Maybe he mentioned what he was hunting." He just hadn't seemed like the type to have close friends—or to want to share his prize.

"Well, he's gone, right?" Priya said, her voice halting. She'd looked a bit shell-shocked since I'd ushered them back out here. She shifted on her feet as if testing how well each could hold her weight. "You took care of the problem. Nothing to worry about."

Without her usual cheer, the reassurance fell flat. I got the impression she was hoping I'd pick up the thread and reassure *her*. "Other than disposing of the mess in the trap? For now. After this, we can't assume there aren't other dark fae who know about Darton too. But how long is it going to be before another one comes? Before one comes sometime we *don't* have a handy way of overcoming them?"

"We stopped the mercenary without needing any special traps," Darton said.

"With a plan that required the coordination of five people and you nearly bleeding to death. That's not something I can whip up in the spur of the moment. As of now, there's nowhere you're really safe except for in this building."

And I wasn't even completely sure of the house. The sun trap had needed my assistance to overcome the dark fae's defenses. I hadn't gotten much of a chance to evaluate my opponent.

The mercenary we'd fought before had been a young fae, strong and determined, but without the resilience and wisdom of age. If a fae much older than him heard of Arthur's presence and took a mind to come after him—if more than one of them came at the building at once—if they found a way in that wouldn't shunt them into the trap—

Darton crossed his arms over his chest. "Well, I can't stay in here forever."

"You can't go wandering around out there when we don't even know what we're facing." I swept my hand to vaguely indicate the vast world of dangerous unknowns outside.

"That wasn't how this was supposed to work. I've got classes, I've got football practice and games. I'm not giving up my entire *life*."

Priya had ducked her head, but at that she raised it a little. "It'd be better than not having a life at all, wouldn't it?"

The overhead lights gleamed off her eyes, and she winced. I paused, momentarily distracted from my other looming concerns.

"Are you okay?"

"Yeah, I just—" She rubbed her temple. "This headache hit me out of nowhere. Must be all the excitement." She managed a weak smile. "Sorry I'm not more help."

"No, it's okay," I said. "Why don't you go lie down in the guest room? You can grab painkillers from the bathroom cabinet in my bedroom if you want them."

She nodded and shuffled off in the direction I indicated. I waited until she'd disappeared behind one of the doors before I turned back to Darton. I drew in a breath to steady myself.

"She had a point, you know. 'Having a life' is only relevant if you're actually alive."

Darton grimaced. "And being alive is only relevant if I get to have an actual life."

"I know. You're right too." I stepped closer and touched his elbow. "We did take care of the mercenary before, and the trap did stop tonight's fae before he could do... whatever it was he wanted to do. So I won't ask you to never set foot outside these walls again. I just want a little time to get my bearings. There's obviously even more going on than I'm aware of."

My thoughts slipped back to the mercenary's death nearly two weeks ago. *I am for my master*, he'd called out as the sunlight burned him away. *I am for the greatest one.* The Darkest One, he had to have meant. With Priya's comments about sacrificial magic lingering in my mind, I had to wonder if he'd meant those words as more than just a final statement of defiance. Had he managed to lend her power? Or passed his power on to others he knew were on the way?

Darton's stance had loosened slightly, opening to me. His voice was still hesitant. "And what does 'a little time' mean, exactly?"

"You take a few days off," I said. "I can conjure you up a doctor's note or whatever you need. I'll work on some new ideas I think might bear fruit and watch to see what else comes our way. And then we'll talk again about what makes sense. I promise I'll do everything in my power to make sure you can leave here again without taking your life in your hands."

"Come on out, Shirley," I said, shaking the sack. The glooms didn't actually have names, as far as I'd ever heard, so I figured there wasn't any harm in me giving the ones I dealt with one of my own choosing. And this one struck me as a Shirley through and through.

The scrap of darkness I'd collected on campus several days ago crept from the mouth of the bag and hesitated. We were stationed in a patch of shadow cast by a patio umbrella I'd placed in the middle of the concrete yard. Bright morning sunlight beamed all around it. The nearest neighboring shadows were hidden in the short grass several yards away. There was nowhere for the gloom to escape to.

It wriggled along the edge of the shadow unhappily. I pawed through the tools I'd brought out for my experiments. My fingers closed around the handle of the taser.

"This is going to hurt me more than it's going to hurt you," I informed the gloom, although I was pretty sure it wasn't going to hurt either of us. Mechanically generated electricity seemed unlikely to have any more effect than mechanically generated light: unpleasant but not actively destructive.

I muttered at my finger to open a split in the skin. A little blood would lubricate the magic. I mashed the bead of red liquid into the sage leaves on the ground. Then I whipped them in a circle around the gloom, flicking on the taser as I did.

"Bind it, hold it still."

The electricity crackled. The gloom twitched. With a quiver in the air, the magical barrier I'd cast solidified around it. The dark vermin bumped up against the invisible wall and retreated.

I touched the barrier and frowned. No, mechanical electricity hadn't added any oomph to my casting at all. It felt the same as if I'd cast it normally. And the electric surge obviously hadn't bothered the gloom all that much either. I murmured to dismiss the spell. Okay, on to the next option.

I picked up the piece of amber, big enough to fit solidly in my palm, and the rabbit skin with fur intact. After several swipes of the stone across the fur, the space between them crackled faintly with static. Not a lot—I didn't enjoy the thought of just how much fur and stone I'd need to generate the kind of power I was probably going to need to take on a full fae—but enough for me to test it out.

"Bind it, hold it still," I cast again in the old tongue. I pressed

my bloody finger into the sage leaves just before tossing them around the gloom again. My other hand scraped the amber over the fur and raised it to smack into the sage.

An electric sizzle shivered into my hand. The air popped.

The gloom spasmed and wisped away.

Cattle sod. I stared at the spot where it had been for a moment and then lowered the stone. Well, I could obviously say *naturally* generated electricity and the dark kind did not get along.

The new magical barrier had still snapped into place, even though there was nothing left for it to contain. It had a sturdy feel to it the first one had lacked. But I'd lost my test subject in my zeal. Oops.

I shoved my supplies into the bag that wasn't much use to me until I found another gloom, and stood up. I could lay bait that would draw glooms this way, but the thought of encouraging the dark rabble to investigate our little shelter here made me cringe.

Drive out a ways, set the trap, and gather a few—that's what I'd need to do. While I was waiting, I could figure out how to amplify the effect I'd just generated. A barrier that would hold a gloom in place wasn't going to do sod all against the Darkest One.

Maybe I'd gather enough dark vermin to experiment more with the destructive aspect too. If more full dark fae *were* headed our way... we'd need all the defensive options we could get.

I lowered the patio umbrella and reached for the post to heft it under my arm. A prickle ran over my skin. I paused, my head jerking up.

The fae sensitivity I'd inherited from my father—the first one, long ago—drew my gaze to exactly the right spot. The spot where a tan figure with a mane of blond hair crouched in the distance, where the field beyond our yard met a stretch of forest.

My body tensed, but I'd already recognized he wasn't an enemy. At least not the typical sort. The sunlight beamed off him, setting off a shimmer in the air around him. I could almost see the fence posts through the edges of his form.

He was fae, but not dark. My kind—the light. Not that I'd been getting along all that well with their sort recently either. The last time I'd gone to the nearest light fae enclave, I'd ended up bringing a hoard of dark rabble to their doorstep. They hadn't been especially pleased about that.

And, being fair, I'd *never* gotten along with the flighty, erratic extended family my father had brought me into. The *flighty* and *erratic* parts are plenty of reason right there.

This one's wits clearly weren't any brighter than most of his kind. Even though it must have been obvious I'd spotted him, he was still hunched down as if he figured I might forget I'd noticed him if he simply didn't move. I mentally rolled my eyes.

"Hey!" I called, heading toward the field. "This property belongs to me, the daughter of Eóghan. If you have business here, you should speak to me about it."

The fae man flinched. Then he blinked away into the sunlight as if he'd never been there. I stopped in my tracks, watching, but he didn't reappear.

He'd flitted off to wherever he'd come from, I had to guess. My fingers clenched around the neck of my sack.

Were the light fae spying on me directly, now that Priya was no longer reporting back to them? Or was he watching this area for some other, darker reason?

I wasn't sure which was worse.

CHAPTER TEN

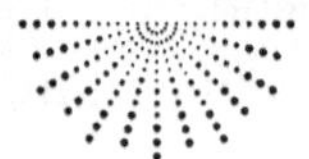

"I come bringing coursework and takeout," Keevan announced as he sauntered into the house. "You don't have to thank me for the first part." He handed Darton the assignments he'd gone around to pick up and waggled a plastic bag crinkling with containers of Thai food. The tangy smells of curry and lemongrass wafted from it.

"And here's the stuff you asked for, Emma." Izzy held up the padded case she'd carried in. "Keevan's sister helped us out. Lenses, copper wire of different sizes, assorted batteries." She looked at me a little curiously. I motioned for her to set the case on the floor.

Priya edged inside behind the others. Her gaze lingered over the main room as if she hadn't already seen it, but she didn't move from the door.

Had the drive up been awkward? Priya didn't know Keevan and Izzy other than from our bizarre road trip fleeing the mercenary's dark rabble army last month. But when I'd mentioned to her in a text that Darton's best friends were dropping by, she'd immediately jumped at the chance to tag along. Maybe she was still feeling nervous after our encounter with the dark fae the last time she was here.

Darton moved to help Keevan lay out the cartons of food on the table. I grabbed plates from the cupboard. "How's the new car working out?" I asked Keevan.

His old one had been ruined beyond repair when Jagger had, well, blown up his own house. A fair bit of the blast had hit the car. Since I was the one who'd gotten Keevan dragged into that mess, I'd given him the money to replace it.

"It's great!" he said. "Runs better than the old one. I should get you to destroy my things more often." He gave me an easy grin to show he really did mean the joke in good humor.

Izzy had wandered into the living room area. She studied the walls and the ceiling. "Is this place rigged to explode like Jagger's was? Darton said you modeled it after his place. But I've got to say it looks a lot cozier in here."

"It's got a few tricks," I said. "Hopefully none we'll have to use."

"Come on," Keevan said. "Better eat while the food is all hot."

Izzy headed over to the kitchen, but Priya was still standing in the narrow space of the front hall. I went to meet her.

"Hey, Priya."

Her head twitched and turned toward me as if I'd startled her. She blinked with a jitter of her eyelids. "Hey."

I frowned. "What's up?"

"Nothing. Nothing." She flexed her shoulders and fixed her eyes on my face. "I was just thinking. What's new with you since I was last here?"

That was a remarkably casual question considering what she'd seen that last time.

I shrugged. "Not much. I think some of my experiments might be heading in a productive direction, but I've got a lot more work to get through before I'll have satisfied any of my real goals." I started walking to the table, and Priya followed me. "I did want to ask you—I saw a light fae hanging around the property yesterday morning. Have you had any contact from your enclave—anything mentioning one of them coming out this way?"

Her gaze had wandered to the sofas. I waited a moment, but it was as if she hadn't heard me. I cleared my throat. "Priya?"

Her head jerked around with the same stiff movement as before. "Oh. Sorry. No, I haven't heard anything from back home. I can try to get in touch and see if they're up to something. I do still have a bit of sway with them."

"I'd appreciate that. Even if it isn't one from your enclave, if they know anything, I'd like to know it too."

I tugged out a chair for her to sit beside me. Keevan and Izzy had already settled in on either side of Darton. Priya hesitated for a second and then lowered herself into the seat.

She wasn't acting like herself, that was for sure. Something had to be wrong. I didn't think she'd appreciate me interrogating her in front of the others, though. Maybe I could get her apart for a little one-on-one talk after dinner.

We all dug in. I stuck to the vegetarian dishes, since my stomach was already tight with tension. Meat didn't always sit well with my digestive system, another lovely feature of my light fae heritage.

Within a minute, Keevan had Darton laughing. My liege relaxed in his chair even more as Izzy related a story about her unpredictably wacky Post Modern Literature professor. Watching them, I let out my breath, releasing some of the tension with it.

Darton had survived being stuck in here for the last two days. He could still enjoy himself. With the new supplies, I could hope that I'd be able to come up with a protection spell I'd feel happy— or at least, happy enough—with tomorrow. I'd promised him I'd get him back to his regular life as soon as I could.

Priya spooned just a little of the pad thai and green curry chicken onto her plate, and what was there, she only picked at. I couldn't actually say for sure she'd eaten more than a couple bites when Keevan leaned back with a groan. He patted his belly. "Okay. One more bite and *I'll* explode."

Izzy giggled, and he flashed a brighter smile her way.

I started gathering the empty cartons. Darton stood to help me clear the table. Priya stiffened and then leapt to her feet.

"I'll help!" she said brightly.

She grabbed her plate and mine, and darted around the table to set them in the sink. As Darton followed suit, she spun around toward him. I paused, my gaze fixed on her, a creeping sensation running up my back.

There was nothing to worry about. It was just *Priya*, for light's sake. But every instinct was telling me that something here was very, very wrong.

"Darton," I said, not knowing what I was trying to warn him against, only that I needed his attention on me. That impulse might have been the only thing that saved him. Because just as he swiveled to look at me, Priya jabbed her hand toward him.

Her hand that was suddenly clasped around a thin, glinting blade.

Darton's sudden movement threw off her aim. The knife sliced across Darton's side rather than plunging straight in. Darton made a choked sound and stumbled to the side.

"What—whoa!" Keevan said, grabbing his friend. Priya lunged forward, blade swinging. Before she'd made it even a full step, I was already spitting out words. My intent wrapped tight around the life energy inside me.

"Up and over, bring me there."

A surge of air propelled me over the table. I flung myself at Priya, catching her just as she slashed at Darton's chest again. My arm smacked into hers. I wrenched her down toward the floor, grasping one wrist and groping for the other. A whine wavered from her throat as I wrestled to keep her down. She stabbed and kicked, faster than I could keep up with.

The thin blade severed my shirt sleeve and cut into the flesh beneath. Pain lanced through my forearm. I sucked in a sharp breath and fumbled with my free hand for the twigs in my pocket.

My fingers closed around them. "*Still and steady, hold her,*" I gasped out. Priya's body froze beneath me. She stared up at me, wide eyed, her lips parted around her panting breaths.

"What— What the *hell?*" Keevan said.

I pried the knife from Priya's hand. It was plain steel, but sharp enough that I nearly nicked my finger at the slightest graze. Not one of ours. She'd brought it with her. To do *this?* To try to gut Darton right here in our kitchen?

My gaze shot to him. Darton had sagged against the kitchen island, his hand pressed to his side. Red was streaking across the fabric of his shirt.

"Get something on his wound," I said quickly. "Stop the bleeding."

Izzy sprang into motion. She grabbed the nearest hand towel. I wanted to leap to his side, to seal the cut with my magic, but I didn't dare let go of Priya. I had no idea what she might be capable of right now.

"Priya?" I said. Her eyelids fluttered and her expression stuttered. Then her lips twisted into a mocking grin.

My stomach lurched. I'd seen that grin before. On the face of the dark fae in our trap, in the moment before the light had destroyed him.

The moment before I'd *thought* the light had destroyed him. He'd been casting. And Priya had been in the room with me, despite my warnings. I should have been more firm about them, clearly.

I gave an hour or two of my life into a brief muttering of a spell. "*Light, come.*" A glow sparked between my thumb and forefinger. I lowered them to Priya's face. The grin jerked away. She flinched, recoiling as much as my hasty binding spell allowed.

"What's wrong with her?" Izzy said. She was hovering near Darton, who'd taken the hand towel from her and jammed it against his side. I didn't see any blood seeping through it yet. The cut mustn't be dangerously deep. But I was hardly happy about him doing any bleeding at all.

"It isn't Priya," I said. "Not really. She's being sight-ridden." I'd done the same myself, with animals and occasionally people—casting my soul from my body into another when I needed to take action in disguise.

When *I* had, though, I'd always had my own body to come back to. The dark fae man had made a more permanent leap. The signs had been so subtle I'd missed them, but thinking back, the clues fell into place: Priya's sudden if mild aversion to the lights, her stiffness with her body as if finding it unfamiliar, her general distraction.

He must have hidden, partly dormant in the back of her mind, over the last few days. Slowly gathering control for when he'd get his chance at Darton.

I narrowed my eyes. "How did you get here, Dark One? Who sent you?" I didn't need to ask *why* he'd been sent. The same reason the mercenary had come after us, obviously: to kill Darton, to steal Arthur's soul, in the hopes they could free the Darkest One.

The spirit inhabiting Priya's body lay stubbornly silent beneath me. I brought my conjured light close to her again, right up to her eyes. She grimaced, a hiss of pain escaping her.

"How did you know to come here?" I demanded.

"That's no business of yours," she bit out.

"I can put you back in the light box, you know," I said. "The cells have been charging all day. Lots of fresh sun-powered light for you to bask in."

Tension trembled through Priya's body, but I didn't see the slightest waver of the fae's resolve in her face. I wasn't likely to get answers by tormenting him. He could have tried to bargain for his life the first time he'd been in the sun trap, but he'd focused on fulfilling his mission instead. He mustn't have expected to make it much farther than this alive.

There were other sensitivities I could press on. Dark fae were known for their pride.

I eased back a little. "Well, seeing how you've reacted to my magic gives me enough of an answer. You clearly don't have enough power for any higher fae to consider enlisting your services. A lone wanderer who happened on a lucky scrap of information, desperate to get some attention, huh? It's pathetic, really."

Keevan made a choked sound, half amused and half disbelieving.

The fae twitched in Priya's body. "You know nothing."

"I know what I'm looking at," I said calmly. "A helpless soul trapped in a human body. How degrading. You lowered yourself to this state only to be captured by a wizard who's barely half-fae at this point. If any other dark ones do hear about this, they'll be laughing in your memory."

"*I'm* laughing," the fae snapped. "To think of how swiftly you'll fall, Merlin. I see no greatness in *you*. And the only fate awaiting you is dire. Rhedyn won't rest until your body and soul are ground to dust."

I froze. *Rhedyn*. I hadn't heard that name in anything but my memories in centuries.

Before I'd recovered from my shock, the fae spat out a few hasty words in his own tongue. My binding spell cracked. Priya's arm lashed out—but not at me. It rammed her hand into her mouth, as if the fae meant to choke her on her own fingers. As if all that mattered now was taking *one* of us down with him, regardless of who.

My pulse lurched. "No!" I smacked the glow I was still holding against Priya's face. She flinched, her muscles going just slack enough that I could wrench her arm away from her mouth. Her lips started to move, and I slapped my own hand across them.

"*Seal them, tight and true.*"

She struggled under me, shoving her knees at my stomach,

swinging her free fist. Keevan sprang in, grabbing her other arm. I pinned her legs under mine, crossing my ankles. *"Still and steady."*

Her body stiffened once more. Her mouth stayed pressed shut as she glared up at me, my spell holding it closed and shutting off the dark fae's primary route to magic. The time for talking was done. Out here in the open, at least.

I sat back on my heels, my breath rough in my throat. "All right," I said. "To the light box it is."

CHAPTER ELEVEN

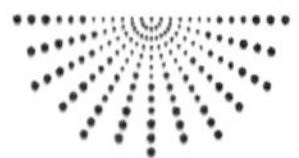

Darton was waiting in the hall, leaning against his bedroom's doorframe, when I emerged from the sun-trap room. He straightened up and came to meet me as I shoved the deadbolt back over.

"How is she?"

I swiped my hand past my aching eyes. My head was muggy, and my mouth felt as if I'd been licking ashes. I wasn't sure what hour of the morning it was, but it was definitely way past the time this body would have preferred to be sleeping. This brain, too.

"I think the fae's spirit is burned out of her now," I said. "But I'm having her sleep in the trap until I can test immediate sunlight on her tomorrow, just to be sure." After all, I'd thought I'd destroyed that dark fae once before and been wrong then. My gaze dipped to his side, to the spot where I'd healed his wound a few hours ago before I'd started the more intensive rounds of my interrogation. "How are you?"

Darton's arm dipped closer to his abdomen. "There's nothing left except a twinge." Then he attempted to smother a yawn.

"I assume Izzy and Keevan went home?"

He nodded wearily. "They would have stayed if I'd let them, but I told them the company would make it harder for you to concentrate."

"You didn't have to wait up either. Come on. You should be in bed." I nudged him back down the hall toward the bedrooms.

He went, but slowly so that I'd walk beside him. "I wanted to know right away if the fae said anything else—about how he found us. About what they want."

"They want what they've always wanted," I said. "For whatever reason, their queen has a special interest in you, Your Highness. And it seems her influence is seeping out of her prison more than it ever has since I sealed her away."

"Is that what he said?"

I grimaced. "No. I had to infer. I tried questioning more, adding some... pressure, with the lights, but after a point I just wanted him out of Priya. Before he could try to hurt her, or any of us, again. The dark fae have a high tolerance for pain and a deep dedication to those they recognize as their superiors. I was lucky I got anything at all out of him."

Darton stopped at the end of the hall and turned to face me. "You seemed upset when she—he—mentioned that one name. Raydin?"

"Rhedyn," I said, knowing he might not even be able to pick up the subtle difference in pronunciation. My chest tightened. "Yeah."

"Who's he?"

I pushed my hair back from my face. "She. She was one of the Darkest One's oldest and most trusted underlings. We clashed a few times, back in my first life. And it's partly her fault you and I are in this whole mess. I was busy fighting her off when the Darkest One attacked you, or I'd have been able to intervene faster." Maybe stopped the fatal stabbing completely. At very least had a handful more seconds to figure out what sodding spell I was casting.

"She *was*. Past tense?"

"I— " I sighed. "I thought she was dead. Or sealed away with the Darkest One. By the time I was living to an old enough age to start asking around in the enclaves back 'home,' no one had seen or heard word of her in decades. But apparently this particular life is full of unpleasant surprises."

My head drooped. Hogs balls, I was tired. And not just of tonight. If Rhedyn was still alive, if *she'd* sent this dark fae after us... how many more were on their way? How much worse were our lives about to get? Because I couldn't for a second believe they'd get any better, not if she was on our trail.

And who else would her minions hurt? My thoughts went to Priya, curled up on the floor of the sun trap with the pillow and blanket I'd brought her, her face tight with exhaustion. I swallowed hard.

"Hey." Darton touched the side of my head tentatively. I let him draw me to him. Let myself breathe in the familiar citrusy-earthy smell of him, soak up the warmth in the rise and fall of his chest. Ignored the skip of my heartbeat. I could take comfort from him. There was nothing more than friendly in that. And light knew I needed it right now.

"You're doing everything you can," Darton said. He stroked my hair, sending a shiver I should not have enjoyed so much down my back. But it didn't loosen the clenching in my chest.

"I knew Priya was acting strangely. I knew the dark fae had been trying to cast something when I destroyed his body. I should have considered, checked, made sure..."

"You've had kind of a lot on your mind, Em."

My hands balled against his shirt. "That's no excuse. Protecting you from the dark fae—that's my *one* job. If I can't manage even that—"

"You did." Darton's arm tightened around me. "I'm okay. Priya's going to be okay. You kept all of us safe."

"But you almost weren't. And I don't even know for sure that she is. He could have done anything to her after she walked out of here with him inside. I have no idea what she's been through that she hasn't been able to tell me yet. If he'd managed to kill her, I'd never have known. And she didn't even need to *be* here. She only wanted to help me."

My throat constricted around those last few words. I'd learned a lot from Jagger in the very short time I'd become acquainted with him, but there was one piece of advice he'd pressed on me that I hadn't listened to: Keep my friends and Darton's out of this mess. He'd said the right thing was to take care of anything to do with the dark fae kind myself.

I knew that wasn't entirely true. I'd only managed to stop the mercenary because I'd trusted Priya and the others to stand beside me. But maybe Jagger hadn't been entirely wrong either.

Darton bowed his head next to mine. "I'm sorry," he said hoarsely.

I frowned. "What have you got to apologize for?"

He drew in a breath. A quiver ran through his body, so quickly I probably wouldn't have noticed it if I hadn't been leaning against him. "Maybe you would have noticed what had happened to Priya sooner if I hadn't been griping about missing a few football practices. You were trying to protect me from a guy who wanted to *kill* me, and I acted like you were the problem."

"No. No." I pulled back to look at him. The anguish on his face wrenched at me. "I get it. It was a totally normal reaction. You've hardly had time for the situation to sink in. You've only *known* who you are, what we're up against, for a few weeks. You wouldn't be you if you accepted everything I said without ever questioning it."

His gaze slid away from mine. "I could have picked a better time to be questioning. Maybe this is new to me, I've seen what the dark fae can do. I remember... enough. You've been doing everything you can to keep me and everyone else safe, like you always do. I *know* that. So the last thing I should be doing is making it harder for you. Whatever you think we have to do from here on, whatever measures we need to take—"

"Art," I interrupted. My fingers curled into his shirt. I waited until he met my eyes. "I don't want to ruin the life you have here, if I can help it. I've never wanted to. We'll figure out the best balance we can. If you don't like the sound of any strategy I propose, I want you to tell me."

"And get in your way? We've seen how well that works out. Your best friend possessed, me getting knifed in our kitchen…"

Another brief tremble passed through him beneath my hands, and the clouds in my head parted with a sudden understanding. Darton was feeling guilty about what had happened to Priya, yes, and worried about me overextending myself, like always, and he had to be nearly as exhausted as I was. But it was more than that. He'd also been a hair's breadth from dying this evening.

Even a few weeks ago in the forest when he'd asked me to split open his arm, we'd still been the ones in control. Tonight, if I'd been a second later with my warning, if Priya had moved a smidgeon faster, the evening might have had a very different ending. And of course Darton was even more aware of that than I was. He was the one who'd been bleeding against the kitchen counter.

His former memories weren't solid enough for the idea of death to feel like more an inconvenience than a true *end*.

"That wasn't your fault," I said. "And we survived it."

"This time."

"Art."

His expression had gone terse, his eyes almost dazed, not quite meeting mine. "What am I really contributing here? You've got all your magic. I have no soldiers to command, no lords I hold sway with, not even a goddamned sword."

"*Art.*"

"Why exactly am I still worth all this trouble—"

I couldn't think of a single thing to say that would break him out of the downward spiral of emotion. But there were other things I could do with my mouth, and other ways of shutting a person up.

I yanked him toward me at the same time as I raised my head to press my lips to his.

Somewhere inside me, I'd had intentions of moderation. One quick kiss to startle him away from those uncertain thoughts. There was no need for more than that.

But the second my mouth caught his, a raw, needy sound escaped him. His fingers slid into my hair, tracing sparks over my scalp. He kissed me back, hard, and just like that, I was lost.

One of his hands traveled down my side to grasp my waist and pull me tighter against him. His lips coaxed mine apart, his tongue tangling with mine. For an instant, his hold started to slacken. A memory taking hold. But he must have managed to keep some awareness, because the next instant he was spinning me to brace me against the wall, his body hot against me from mouth to thighs.

I teased my fingertips up the back of his neck and received an eager hum as my reward. A memory of my own tickled up in the back of my mind: coming across a pond after a long day on the road with the then-prince, Arthur deciding a swim was just the thing to cool off and pulling me in too. Bright sun, chilly water, laughter bouncing through the air. I held the images at a distance as Darton tilted his head to kiss me even more deeply.

The faint remembered sensation of lapping water mingled with the slide of his palm up my torso to cup my breast. A whimper broke from my throat. By the light, how I'd missed this. How I'd missed *him*. Even if it wasn't everything I'd ever wanted, it was a hell of a lot.

Did it really matter, waking him up more, if we knew now the mercenary hadn't been a fluke? The second dark fae had found us despite my best efforts. And my king wanted this, wanted me. Right now I didn't care how or why.

His lips left mine to press a scorching kiss to my jaw, my neck. A gasp of encouragement slipped out of me. He touched the wide collar of my sweater, easing it down over my shoulder by torturous increments as his mouth followed the same path. When another memory surfaced, I was too caught up to resist it. The sensations it carried bled over the brush of Darton's fingers, the gentle nip of his teeth.

This corner of the king's private audience room was dusty. Someone should really have a chat with the cleaning staff about that. I tugged my nose as I leaned against the cool, whitewashed plaster, warding off a sneeze.

I wasn't even really supposed to be here. I'd tagged along with Arthur to answer his father's summons for lack of anything better to do, but the king had given me one brief narrow-eyed look and told Arthur they had matters to discuss alone. The prince had twitched his eyebrow upward at me before he'd turned to follow.

He was the one I took my orders from, so I'd cast a quick distraction spell over myself and followed. But the spell and the dust combined in a rather uncomfortable itch, and if I did sneeze, I could forget about blending into the shadows.

King and son had sat down on the rather stiff-looking chairs with their brocaded cushions near the room's large window. The heavy curtains had been tied to the sides, so sunlight washed over them. It gleamed off Arthur's hair and the matching gold of the king's crown. If he was wearing that for a private talk with Arthur, he meant business.

"I noticed you spent a great deal of time with Lady Lorena during the visit last week," he said.

"She makes excellent conversation," Arthur replied.

The king smiled. "Is that your only interest? I'd say she's also fine to gaze upon."

Arthur shrugged, with a careless air I could see through even at a distance. I wondered if his father knew him as well as I did. My prince had given me little sense of his childhood family experiences, but these days the two of them barely saw each other outside of official functions and occasional chats like these.

"She's pretty enough," he allowed.

"I bring up the subject only because you must remember that now

that you're of marriageable age, any young woman you single out, even briefly, will be subject to speculation."

Oh. So that was the purpose of this conversation. I resisted the urge to fidget. If I could have turned off my ears, I would have.

"I know better than to be compromised in any way, father," Arthur said.

"That's not all I mean." The king shifted in his chair. His smile faded. "You must also be conscious of the impression it gives others. You will want to make a suitable match before long, and the appearance of interest in a... less than suitable lady may discourage your better prospects."

"I suppose you have a list of those you'd consider suitable."

Arthur had kept his voice light, but his father gave him a sharp look. Apparently he had a better read on his son than I'd have guessed.

"You'll want a wife. You'll want heirs. And you'll want to make your choices to offer them the most advantages you can."

"I know," Arthur said. "Have I ever failed to meet my duties yet?"

Despite his casual tone, his back had stiffened slightly. An ache crept through my chest. For him, for whatever he might have wished for himself that he couldn't allow himself to have. And there might have been a deeper pinching too, at the thought of a partner in marriage coming to stand by Arthur's side. Being there to hear his worries and celebrate his triumphs, while I— Where would I be then?

I squashed that worry. I could serve Arthur all the same either way. That was what I was here to do. It was ridiculous to fret about the inevitable future. Even if—

I careened back into the present. The pinching sensation still radiated through my gut, reminding me of all the things I'd known I could never have, even if back then I hadn't yet admitted to myself I even wanted them.

Gods, would I never learn my lesson?

Darton's fingers dipped to the border of my bra. My hand shot up to catch his. I scooted out of his embrace with a shaky breath.

"Emma?" Darton said, peering at me. He gripped my hand as if unwilling to release that one last point of contact. My name of this life from his lips solidified my resolve. Yes. Emma. That was who he was seeing. That was why this could never work.

"It's been a long night," I said. "I don't think... we can make the clearest decisions right now. And I need to be ready to look after Priya in the morning."

The first point, I think he might have argued. At the second, he inclined his head. His gaze, when he lifted it to mine again, still looked hungry. So hungry it sent a tingle through me even as my discomfort jabbed deeper.

"We'll talk tomorrow," he said. He kissed my knuckles and turned to his bedroom.

I wandered into mine with my pulse still thumping, wondering what I could possibly say to him tomorrow that would satisfy us both.

CHAPTER TWELVE

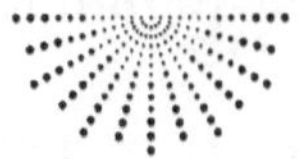

MAYBE BECAUSE I was a throwback in a nearly literal sense, attempting to navigate the internet always gave me a headache. I squinted at the computer screen as if I could persuade it to accomplish want I wanted simply through the power of my will. So far that technique wasn't paying off so well, but I wasn't sure anything else I'd tried had been all that productive either.

Give me a clear path, a database with boundaries to navigate or a specific fact to track down, and I could magic my way there. What I was attempting to ferret out today was a lot more vague.

I adjusted my position on the smooth leather cushions of the sofa. This forum I'd stumbled on seemed like a halfway decent possibility. I signed up so I could post the message I'd been leaving all across the World Wide Web.

My concentration didn't stop my ears from picking up the faint squeak of Darton's bedroom door opening. My shoulders tensed. I'd woken up a couple hours before him, but I didn't feel any more ready to try to follow up last night's encounter. I hit the post button and navigated onward, trying to pretend I had nothing else on my mind as he padded down the hall toward the common room.

He leaned onto the top of the sofa, nothing but a thin white undershirt covering his upper half. I was definitely not thinking about how covered—or not—his lower half might be. The flex of his muscular arms against the wooden frame provided plenty of distraction already. Especially when my mind far too easily tripped back to those arms pulling me to him less than ten hours ago.

"What's this?" he said.

"A somewhat half-assed plan." I made a face. "If Rhedyn is assembling any sort of dark fae force, I was thinking people like Jagger—the other hunters he said he stayed in contact with around the world and traded information with—might have noticed. And they might know something we could use to come up with a less half-assed plan."

"You know how to get in touch with them?"

"Well, no, that's what makes this part half-assed. He said he talked to them through private channels, but they've got to spend some time on the regular internet too, right? So I'm posting a plea for help here and there, in the hopes that one of them happens on it and takes it seriously." I motioned toward the screen. "I've mentioned a couple things no one who's never encountered a real fae should know. That should give me a little cred."

"Sounds reasonable." He glanced back toward the hall. "Have you checked on Priya?"

"Yeah. She was okay this morning. Definitely no more dark fae hanging on in her head." My stomach knotted, remembering the way she'd thrown her arms around me when I'd opened the sun trap and pronounced her free. The shakiness of that relieved embrace. The choked apologies.

I'm so sorry, Emmaline. I was there and then I wasn't, he just shoved me down, stole my thoughts away... I knew he was going to try to hurt someone. I knew and I couldn't do anything.

As if her inability to fight off a foe so much more powerful than her was somehow to blame, instead of my carelessness. When I'd tried to reassure her, she'd shaken her head and refused to listen.

"We had breakfast together, and then I called her a cab to get her home," I added. "I think she was more than ready to get out of here."

"Who wouldn't be?" he said with a short laugh.

When I glanced up at him, his smile was more wry than bitter. I still couldn't stop myself from saying, "What I said last night, about making sure you don't give up the life you've had—I meant that. It's still possible that the dark fae was lying to unsettle me, or that even if more are coming we can put them off..."

I couldn't say I believed either of those possibilities to any large degree, and probably Darton guessed as much. He reached over to tuck a strand of my dark brown hair that had escaped its habitual ponytail behind my ear. His fingertips barely grazed my cheek, but every nerve in my body sparked all the same.

"I meant what I said last night too. You do whatever you need to do. I'm not going to fight with you about it. I trust you."

I met his dark blue eyes, all the parts of last night I'd been trying to avoid thinking about leaping back into the front of my mind.

He trusted me. And I was about to lie to him—again, about the same thing I'd been lying to him about for fifteen hundred years.

At least I could say it was the only thing I'd ever outright lied to him about, omissions notwithstanding. The contents of my heart weren't *really* in his rights to know anyway.

"Everything... after that conversation," I said. "That was my mistake. I didn't mean—"

Darton swallowed audibly. "I get it," he broke in. "Emotions were running high. Neither of us was thinking completely straight. I mean, not that I minded, but..."

"But until we know exactly what we're dealing with, it's still safer the less woken you are," I filled in. *Yes, that is absolutely the main and only reason I'm going to be avoiding kissing you again.*

"Then I guess there's nothing more to say about it for now."

"No," I agreed. Not for ever, either.

He straightened up and ambled to the kitchen, but I was left with the uneasy sense that we hadn't resolved anything at all.

❧

The early November chill had left the grass all along the edge of our massive paved yard in a sorry state, wilted and yellowing. The wind whispered over the limp blades as I circled the grounds. Nothing moved on the field between the concrete and the forest and farmhouses on the other side.

No light fae had shown themselves since I'd spotted that one man a few days ago, but they might have simply been keeping more distance. Or using magic to disguise themselves that was subtler than my half-human senses could detect.

Of course, it wasn't the *light* fae I was particularly worried about.

I was just coming around the back of the house when my gaze caught on a darker splotch amid the yellow-green. My legs locked. I scanned the field, but there was still nothing in view except me and the ripples of the wind.

I stepped tentatively onto the grass. Several paces from the concrete, a swath of blades lay dead, brown with rot. And not just a random swath. The grass had been withered in the shape of a rune.

The void. The blankness of death that to the dark fae was the most perfect sort of order.

A chill deeper than the bite in the looming winter ran down my back. With the noon sun shining brightly overhead, I didn't feel an immediate danger. I'd waited until the morning's clouds had cleared precisely so that I'd know I had the sun's energy to defend me if it came to that.

But another dark fae had been lurking around our home. Leaving his or her mark for me to find. Taunting me with the death he wished for me and my king.

I rubbed my arms and swiveled back toward the house. We'd had enough of games. If Rhedyn was out there, I wasn't going to wait to see what else she might have in store for us. There had to be a way to bring the battle to her.

Darton was in his bedroom, probably keeping up on his assignments, so I didn't have to explain myself when I strode straight through the common room to mine. I ducked into the expansive closet I'd included in the house's building plans.

I hadn't moved all of my materials out of my storage locker. I needed to know the essentials—my old journals, basic magical materials—would be there for me to recover in my next life, if I got that far. But since the possibility of even a next life was starting to seem thin, I'd brought several crates of supplies back here to stash them closer at hand.

The lid of one and then another creaked as I shoved them open. My fingers closed around baggies and bundles of dried herbs. Lavender, feverfew, anise. I couldn't compel a vision to come, but with the right combination of ingredients, I could encourage one.

Of course, I didn't want just any vision. I'd have to give it some direction.

I set the herbs burning in a bowl on the floor and sat down beside it. Leaning against the footboard of my bed, I closed my eyes and reached back into my memories of my first life to my first encounter with Rhedyn. The images surged up, drowning out my awareness of the room around me.

The pine smell of the woods tickled my nose, but that wasn't what had set the rest of my nerves prickling. Heavy branches blocked most of the dwindling sun, leaving the forest beyond our clearing hazed with an early evening.

I couldn't see anything lurking between the trees. Couldn't hear anything over the stomping of the horses' hooves and the clatter of cooking pots being arranged by the fire. But I knew, with a sensation that wriggled right through my bones, that our camp of soldiers was not alone.

My king came up beside me and set a hand on my shoulder. "You look disturbed, Merlin. More so than usual, I mean."

I shot him a narrow look, and he smiled at me, but with a certain amount of weariness. We'd been on the road, clashing with forays of hostile forces, for over a month. And we didn't have any idea when that battling might end.

"Ha ha, sire. There's nothing for you to worry about. But I think I might take a walk."

"I'd suggest you take a sword with you if I didn't know you're as like to cut your own arm off."

I would have prodded Arthur with my elbow if that hadn't seemed too familiar a gesture with the men he commanded all around us. "Good thing I have more efficient ways of defending myself then. Why don't you go polish that sword I charmed for you?"

Before he could come up with a retort to that, I set off through the woods. I didn't know exactly where I was going, but the prickling under my skin amplified as I moved farther north. So I kept walking that way.

The sounds of the camp faded. Shadows drifted around me. One flickered, and my head jerked toward it.

A woman stood in the deeper shade beside the broad trunk of an elderly pine. The edges of her ash-blond hair and tan skin blurred into the shadows. She was a dark fae, and from the depth of those shadows, one who'd spent a long time on this earth. My hand leapt to the wand tucked into my belt.

She smirked at me, her eyes glinting like polished obsidian. "What do you think you're going to do to me, halfling?" Her voice was low and smoky.

"Whatever I need to," I said. "Although if you move off of your own accord, I won't have to do anything at all."

She shrugged. "I'll do your pet king no harm tonight. He's far too important for trifling with, isn't he?"

There was something mocking in the words, but I didn't understand what she was implying. The dark fae didn't see any true importance in human rulers. But they had shown a periodic and odd fascination with Arthur's family, my father had told me.

"What's so special about him to you, that you're following him around just to gape at him?" I asked.

She tossed her hair dismissively, but then her body stilled. Her eyes had focused on something beyond me. I turned.

The movements of the camp were just barely visible between the trees. On the side of the clearing nearest us, Arthur was demonstrating an effective angle with which to swing a blade to one of the novice soldiers.

Excalibur gleamed in his hands even in the waning light, charged as much by the strength of his soul as the sun. Ah.

"You appreciate my handiwork," I said.

The dark fae's eyes twitched back to me. She smirked again, but this time it was more of a grimace. No, she did not like the look of that sword at all, as much as she was trying to hide her reaction from me.

That was good to know. All the months I'd spent working over that blade suddenly seemed more than worth it.

"Don't think too much of yourself," she said coolly, and sliced her hand through the air with a few muttered words. Pain cut across my side like a frigid razor. It dug into my lungs. I—

—opened my eyes with a gasp for breath in my bedroom fifteen hundred years later.

Yes, thank you, I would prefer to skip the part of that memory where I rolled around on the forest floor in agony for an hour. I *had* managed to cast a hasty counter-spell, but it'd still taken that long before my efforts had dulled Rhedyn's assault enough to allow me to stand. She'd been—she *was*—a powerful dark fae indeed.

The smoke from the sizzling herbs had coated my mouth and

throat. My thoughts seemed to slosh in my head. Good. I had to chase that woozy feeling.

I leaned over the plate and inhaled even more smoke, until my lungs burned with it. Then I slumped backward.

"Sight beyond sight, sight beyond sight, show me what I wish," I murmured in the old tongue. Over and over, keeping my mind focused on Rhedyn's smirking face, on the tang of pine, on the creeping forest shadows. The words and the memory blurred together. My tongue thickened. The back of my head opened up into spiraling darkness.

I fell away from the room and down, and down, until I felt as if I'd flipped feet over head. I blinked, but the darkness didn't clear.

My plummet slowed. Sounds reached my ears: the sharp *plink* of drips hitting a metal surface. A rumble like a distant passing train. And a voice, unfamiliar and yet with a cadence that sent a shiver of unpleasant recollection through me, muttering too low for me to make out the words. The same few phrases, chanting. Like I had been, just a minute ago.

Magic.

A damp chill seeped through me. The water dripped on. I tried to turn, to orient myself toward the voice, to move close enough to see the speaker. My mind-sight hitched, and the vision shattered.

I jerked back into the awareness of my body. The sensation of dampness crawled over my skin, even though the air in the room around me was crisp and dry. I rubbed my hands over my arms to dispel the goose bumps.

I was home. Home and as safe as I could be anywhere. But all at once I couldn't shake the impression that doom loomed over us as closely as a thundercloud on the verge of bursting.

CHAPTER THIRTEEN

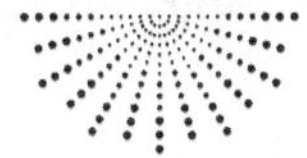

"He *promised* he'd come," Priya said, shifting her weight from one foot to the other. "But then the light fae don't exactly have the best sense of time, do they?"

"That would be the understatement of the century." I swiped my hand across my mouth and glanced around us.

We'd been standing a few paces from the front door of my and Darton's house, waiting, for nearly half an hour. It should have been a day worth enjoying—clear sky, birdsong in the air, that air a tad warmer than the past week—but everything seemed to rest on our overdue visitor. "Do you know *how* he'd be coming, or from which way?"

She sighed. "Beats me. He insisted he'd meet us here."

"Should we go inside and find something else to do until he shows up?"

"I don't know if he'll bother knocking on the door if he doesn't see me. You never know how weird they're going to be about human stuff." She glanced sideways at me. "Or sort-of human stuff. However we'd classify you. Hey, have there been any other signs of the dark fae around since we talked yesterday?"

"Other than the rune markings they've been leaving every night for me to find in the morning?" I said. "Well, they haven't tried to confront me or to get into the house. I guess what happened with the first one scared them off." Or else they were preparing for a larger assault than I'd anticipated. "You've been okay, since... since all that, haven't you?"

"Never better," Priya said cheerfully, but her smile looked a little stiff. Of course it would take more than a few days to get over being possessed.

"If you ever need to talk, or anything," I said, and trailed off uncertainly. I had centuries of practice at keeping my distance from everyone other than my king, because there'd never been anyone I could be myself around. Practice at being a good friend, not so much. And most regular friendships never included a problem quite like this.

"It's fine, Emmaline. Really, it is."

I still didn't totally believe her, but Priya's tone was gentle enough that I let the subject drop. And then there wasn't any more time for conversation, because a slender young man with gleaming bronze skin blinked into view on the drive.

"Ohanko!" Priya said, and bounded over to meet him. I trailed a little beyond. The light fae smiled at Priya, but his stance was wary. When his gaze shifted to me, he went still, staring as if in disbelief and awe.

Wonderful.

"Yes, it's really me," I said dryly. "The great Merlin in the flesh, if not the stuff I was originally born with."

The fae had the awareness to look chagrined, which put him ahead of about ninety percent of those of his kind I'd talked to in the last several centuries. "I didn't mean— I've heard a lot of stories, but I never thought I would meet you," he said in a melodic tenor. "It's remarkable what your magic has accomplished."

Okay, give the guy another point. The last light fae I'd had an extended conversation with had used words more like "unnatural."

"This is Ohanko." Priya wrapped her hand around his elbow. "He was basically my brother, when I was growing up in the enclave. Ohanko, Emmaline. Or Merlin, I guess."

Ohanko dropped into a deep bow—full respect for my soul's accumulated age. I bobbed my head in return. "It's a pleasure to meet you. Do you want to come inside?"

He glanced down at the pavement, which he didn't look entirely comfortable standing on. "I'd rather not close myself off, if that's all right."

"Sure, sure, no problem. Here, we can sit in the field if you'd like that better."

We ambled over to the grass. Even though it was still just as wilted as a couple days ago, Ohanko sank down onto it with apparent relief.

"Priya says you know something about the light fae guy I saw spying on us last week," I said.

He nodded. "He was one from my enclave to the north. We did not mean to... 'spy.' We were merely concerned and wanting to monitor the situation as well as we could."

"And what situation is that, exactly? Me and my king hanging out here."

"Oh, no. Your business is your own. Our concern lay with those who might not see it that way. About a week ago, we became aware that a large number of dark fae had arrived from across the large salt water." Ohanko motioned vaguely to the east.

To the Atlantic? I tensed. "How many is a large number?"

He cocked his head, considering. "Perhaps a dozen. And they all immediately made their way in this direction."

An uncomfortable prickle raced down my back. A dozen full dark fae coming after us from across the sea—from my and Arthur's homeland, I had to assume—was more than I'd ever imagined I'd have to deal with.

It wasn't just our homeland. It was Rhedyn's too. I doubted that was a coincidence.

"Have you gotten any sense of a leader among them? Or of whom they might be directed by?" Had she herself made the journey?

"No," Ohanko said. "Their actions have made little sense to us. Our scout observed them arriving in the forest nearby. Then, one was swallowed by your home. And all but one of the others drifted away in a sun's span."

Even the most with-it of light fae leaned toward metaphor. I suppressed my impatience. "So there's one still here." The one who was decorating our field so enthusiastically. "And the others left at least a few days ago, after we caught the first guy in our sun trap? Where did they go?"

"The one that has lingered has a purpose we have not seen. The others left so quickly our scout did not track them. They are not all together, at least. When so many come together, we were able to feel their arrival. One or two dark fae on their own, at a distance, may as well be shadows."

So they could be anywhere. I supposed I should be relieved they weren't still scheming altogether, but my stomach was churning. They had to be up to something. Something inspired by what they'd observed of our little fortress here? There was nothing good that could come of that.

Ohanko had lifted his gaze toward the house again. "Where is the king?" he asked. "He *is* here, with you?"

"And safer inside rather than out." Especially with one of those dark fae still lurking around, leaving us vaguely threatening runic messages. I grimaced. How the hell could I give Darton any piece of his regular life back when there could be more full fae lurking around any corner? "Is that all you can tell me about the dark fae?"

"I wish I could be more helpful," Ohanko said. "But because Priya has asked, I will join the scout in surveying the area. If I hear or see anything new, I will bring it to you."

"Thank you. I appreciate that." I got up, my mind already spinning off in other directions. I couldn't count on the light fae just happening upon crucial information. Maybe it was time for a little vision-riding of my own—in a less permanent, non-destructive way, of course. "I think I need to look into this further in my own ways."

Ohanko inclined his head and then dipped into another low bow. I returned it with a brief bob and headed for the house. Priya paused for a moment to say a few last words to her foster brother. She jogged after me and caught up just as I was pushing open the front door.

"What do you think they're up to?"

"I don't know," I admitted as we walked into the hall. "But there are ways I can try to find out."

Darton came out of his room at our voices. "Did Priya's... friend come? What did he say?"

"Nothing that's of a whole lot of use to us yet." I waved Darton aside, striding down the hall. "I'll let you know when I can—"

My phone jangled. I stopped and pulled it out of my pocket. It was Dad's number—his cell phone, not the home line.

If it had been Mom, I might have let her go through to voice mail and caught up with her later. But Dad hardly ever called me. *You can't have a proper conversation unless you're face to face*, he'd said more times than I could count. Usually our only direct communication between visits was him texting me the occasional gif or meme he found particularly amusing.

I raised it to my ear. "Hello?"

Dad's soft, dry voice carried into my ear. "Oh, hi, Emma. I just needed to... Your mom's had a bit of an accident."

I'd already started to brace myself at the fumbling hesitation in his words. At his last statement, my stomach dropped. He wouldn't be calling me about it if it were just a *bit* of a concern. "What? What happened?"

"Well, she— She's okay now, or at least the doctors say she will be."

"Dad. What. Happened?"

He made an uncomfortable sound. "You know how steep our driveway is. She was backing out to make a client call, and it seems the brakes lost power. The car rushed right down and hit the tree on the other side of the road."

Sodding hell. "But you said she's okay? The doctors have really looked her over?"

"Yes. Yes, don't worry about that. There wasn't enough time for the car to get going all that fast. She jarred her neck some, and they're getting her to lie still for a bit to make sure there's no major damage, but they haven't seen any reason to believe there is. I wouldn't be calling you if that's all it was."

My fingers tightened around the phone. "What do you mean? What else is there?"

"Well, ah... This is going to sound strange. But maybe you can make some sense of it." He paused. "When I heard the crash, I came running out of the house. There was a man standing at the end of the drive, looking at your mom in the car. I don't believe I've ever seen him before. He rubbed me the wrong way to begin with, just standing there looking and not doing a thing to try to help. And then as I ran by, he said..."

Dad's voice faded out. My heart had caught in my throat. "What, Dad?"

"He said, 'Tell Emmaline to watch where she walks.' I don't— It was so bizarre, and I had to help your mom, so I didn't stop to question him, of course. And then when I thought of him again, he was gone. It sounded almost like... like some kind of threat, but you've never been mixed up in anything to account for that."

He said it as a fact, but the question was implied. "No," I lied. "I have no idea what that could have been about. Do you think— did he mess with the car? Is that why—"

"It doesn't seem like it. The brake lines weren't cut or anything that suggests conscious tampering. The inspector said they should work just fine now, that it was some kind of momentary power failure."

As if something had sucked the energy out of them. No creature in the world could do that more easily than a dark fae.

I bit my lip. "Well, I'm really glad Mom's okay. You tell her to call me as soon as they're letting her move around more. And—do you remember what the man looked like? In case he comes around here or something."

"It's all a bit of a blur now, I'm afraid, but he was big, dark hair, probably around my age? If anything more comes of it, I'll let you know right away. And you take care, all right?"

"Of course, Dad," I said.

I lowered the phone to my side. It took a moment before I could breathe past the clenching in my chest. Darton and Priya were both staring at me.

"My mom," I said. "One of the dark fae got my mom in a car accident. Nothing serious, but it seems to be that they wanted to send me a warning."

Darton's eyes widened.

"A warning about what?" Priya said.

That was a good question. I frowned. "I don't know." After all, we were already holed up in here, effectively hiding from them. What kind of 'walking' had he meant to discourage me from doing? "Maybe he just wanted me to know that they know about my parents. That they can hurt them if they want to."

"Not a warning. A threat." Darton's hands balled. "They have to be trying to convince you to stop protecting me. That's the message, isn't it? Hand me over or they'll do worse?"

"The one that talked to my dad didn't say anything that specific. But a demand like that could be the next step."

I dragged in a breath. Sod it, I didn't even want to think about this. My first loyalty was to my king, always, but my parents of this life were still my parents. I didn't want them tormented by fae.

"You should go," Darton said. "Make sure they're safe. Deal with whatever dark fae is hanging around up there. I can handle a few days on my own here in the house."

I shook my head. He didn't even know the full story Ohanko had told us yet. "No. There are too many of them. The light fae said a dozen or so were hanging around here just a few days ago. Separating us could play right into Rhedyn's plans." And I didn't know if I could take on even one full dark fae on my own, without the tricks I'd built into the house. I was hardly prepared to go mobile.

"I could try to persuade the light fae to watch over your parents, to some degree," Priya said. "I don't know how willing they'd be to get involved, but—"

The buzz of an alert interrupted her. Darton made a face and dug out his phone. He clicked through to whatever message he'd gotten—and froze.

"What?" I said, my stomach lurching all over again.

Darton's mouth pressed into a tight, flat line as he stared at the screen. After a moment, he turned the phone to show me.

Someone had sent him a text with a video file. The written part of the message said only, *WE HAVE EYES*. Darton clicked to start the video playing, and I immediately stiffened too.

On the screen, Darton's sister ambled across the lawn outside what must have been her high school with a couple of friends. The camera tracked them down the street. Audrey and the other girls laughed and chattered, jostling each other playfully. They clearly had no idea they were being followed. At the corner, they ducked into a coffee shop, and the video cut out. But the message, and the threat held in it, remained.

CHAPTER FOURTEEN

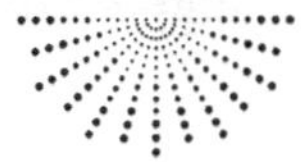

"IF THEY HURT AUDREY, I'll—I'll—" Darton's jaw locked with emotion. He flicked through his contacts list to bring up his sister's number, gripping the phone so tightly his knuckles were whitening.

"Is that... normal fae behavior?" Priya murmured beside me as Darton raised the phone to his ear. "Using human tech like that?"

"Not exactly," I said. My insides felt as if they'd tangled into one huge knot. "But it doesn't surprise me that the dark fae could adapt if they found a use for it. Machines and electronics appeal to their love of order."

"Audrey, when you get this, give me a call right away, okay?" Darton said into the phone. So she hadn't answered. He started to pace, tapping at the screen again. His second call went through. "Hi, Mom. Yeah, good, I, um— Is Audrey around? Oh, okay. Yeah, I know how much she loves window shopping. Right. Of course. I've actually— There was just something I wanted to ask her quickly. I've got to go, but I'll call again soon."

His hand fell to his side. He swiveled again, heading for the front door. "She's out at the mall with some friends. At least, as far

357

as my mom knows. If we drive fast enough, we can get up there in less than two hours. There's got to be something—"

I hurried after him. "Darton, we can't go. It's *you* they want, and you'd be giving yourself right to them."

"So what? We can't just leave Audrey there to... to whatever they're going to do to her. They already hurt your mom."

He grabbed his bomber jacket. Before he could start pulling it on, I grasped his wrist and tugged him to face me. His eyes were wild, barely seeing me.

"Darton. Art. *Arthur.*"

He made to pull away. I yanked off my gloves and caught his face between my bare hands.

At the contact, he went still. I held his frantic gaze, my heart thumping. "Arthur," I said again, and the panic in his expression retreated, just slightly.

"Merlin." His head dipped until his forehead brushed mine. I heard him swallow. "It's my little sister. She's only seventeen. She has no idea..."

"I know," I said, keeping my voice steady. "I don't want them to hurt her either. We won't let them. We're going to figure this out. But if we're going to do that, we need to stop and take a breath and think it through. You racing over there unprepared is *exactly* what the dark fae would want. We don't have to play into their hands."

"What else is there to do?"

"I don't know, but there's got to be something." I traced my thumb gently over his cheekbone. "You told me a couple days ago that you trusted me. You still do, don't you?"

He dragged in a rough breath. "Yes. Yes, of course I do."

"Then stay here with me now, and we'll come up with a plan together."

He nodded slowly. Then he tipped his head so his lips grazed mine. My pulse stuttered, but I let him have the kiss and whatever reassurance it gave him. When I didn't pull away, he pressed his mouth to mine a little harder. Hard enough that the stutter turned into a full out fluttering. Then he stepped back, leaving my skin flushed from head to toe.

Priya cleared her throat, her gaze trained purposefully away from our little embrace, and the blush in my cheeks deepened. But before we could move on from comfort to planning, she stepped closer to the door.

"I think I hear a car. Were you expecting anyone else?"

"No." I froze, listening. The growl of an engine reached my own ears, faint but growing. It must have already been coming up the drive.

Darton reached for the door, but I nudged him backward. "You're still staying in here for now," I told him. "Let me find out what's going on, and then we'll deal with everything else, as quickly as we can. I promise."

Wand in hand, I eased open the door and stepped outside. A dented burgundy Volvo was just pulling into the concrete yard. It parked about twenty feet away, which seemed a safe enough distance. The driver side door swung open, and my tension fell away.

"Hello there," said a familiar gruff voice as a familiar grizzled face appeared over the door. "I've been told a woman lives here who knows how to kill dark fae."

"Jagger!" Priya squealed, and dashed across the pavement to wrap the older guy in a hug he returned somewhat awkwardly.

I ambled over, a smile stretching across my face. "We didn't know if you'd made it out of the building."

The fae hunter waved his hand dismissively. "It'd take more than an exploding house to do me in. I had a hideout under the place—only big enough for one, or I'd have gotten you all in there too. It took a little effort getting back out of it, I've got to admit, but here I am."

A twinkle glinted in his eyes, but I thought I saw a new, thicker scar or two amid the spider web of pale lines that crisscrossed his face. Jagger had gone through a lot, and given up a lot, to help us.

"We still have your van, if you need it," I started, but he cut me off with a shake of his head.

"It seems like you've got more need of it now than I ever did." He peered past me toward the house. "And you've been busy in the last month. Is that a roof full of solar panels I see?"

My smile twitched higher. "I took a lot of inspiration from your handiwork. Here, come in. It's safer inside. There's at least one dark fae that's been lurking around the property. What are you doing here?"

"I joined up with a buddy a couple states over," Jagger started as we went in. He bobbed his head to Darton, who blinked at him in surprise. "I've been making the usual rounds with him, keeping an eye on things like usual, but I've kept a particular eye out for any situation that sounded like you might be involved. Couple days ago someone in the network pointed out a posting they'd seen that sounded possibly legit, asking for our help. I took one look at it and knew it was you. Wasn't hard to track you down after that."

He leaned against the back of one of the sofas and folded his arms over his broad chest. "So you've had some more dark fae dealings. Is this the same one as was chasing you before?"

"No," I said. My excitement at seeing Jagger alive began to wane. We were in so much more trouble this time compared to the last. "That one we dealt with. It's a long story," I added when he opened his mouth to ask. "What's really important is a whole group of dark fae have come with the intention of getting at us now. I think they've been brought together by... a particularly powerful fae who I had some difficult encounters with in the past."

Jagger hummed thoughtfully. "And you think my network might be able to help?"

"Maybe not. But I thought at least you might have information we don't. It seems that these fae came across from Europe. Probably Britain, from what I know about their leader. I'm guessing you have connections all over the world?"

"I know a few folks in the UK." Jagger studied me. "What

connections have *you* got over there that their dark fae would be crossing an ocean to get at you?"

I'd never told him the full story of who I was, or who Darton was either. It would only have complicated matters, and there hadn't really been time. There wasn't now either, as much as I owed the truth to him. "Another long story that I hope I'll be around to tell you about properly someday. But that's where I tangled with that one powerful fae, and from what we've gathered, she's the one who sent the others. Their methods of attack have been a little... unusual, though."

As quickly as I could, I laid out what we'd seen so far and what we'd learned from Priya's fae foster brother. Jagger nodded and asked a few brief questions, but mostly listened. When I got to the part about my mom's accident and the video of Audrey, Darton started pacing again. He didn't say anything, but his tension radiated off of him.

"It seems obvious they're making threats," I finished. "But they haven't given any clear indication what it is they want from us. It's all strangely vague for dark fae. There's got to be more to the picture that we just haven't caught on to yet."

"The kind of behavior you're describing does sound odd to me," Jagger agreed. "Unfortunately I'm not sure there's anything I can tell you that would shed more light on their intentions. That bunch has been keeping their heads down enough that I haven't heard any word about their activities through the wire. But a couple of my British colleagues have reported some unusual movement over on their side of the pond. Could be that's connected?"

My chest clenched. What were the chances it *wasn't*? "I wouldn't be surprised. What kind of 'movement' exactly?"

He took a small tablet out of one of his military coat's large pockets. "It wasn't anything striking enough that the details stuck in my memory. Let me look up what they've mentioned."

As Jagger brought up his sources, I sidled over to Darton.

"Whatever's happening in England, it isn't going to help us

here," he said quietly. "We still have to make sure Audrey's safe. And your parents. And mine. And—" He froze. "What if they go after Keevan and Izzy too? The dark fae have more reason to want to target them than our families—they helped us kill the mercenary."

"The dark fae don't have quite the same concept of revenge we do," I said. "They'd probably see the mercenary's death as a fair reflection of his abilities. But that doesn't mean they'd leave our friends alone." They'd already used Priya, after all. "Why don't you check in with them? Let them know to be extra cautious of strangers hanging around them. If they get really worried, they can always hide out up here."

At least they'd understand the danger. I had no idea how we could properly warn our families.

"Here we go," Jagger said. "Significantly heightened dark fae and vermin activity noted around the north end of Somerset, particularly in the vicinity of the Camroth Interchange. Sightings of dark creatures by passersby, unusual dying off of vegetation, human-like figures spotted walking beneath the freeway and then 'disappearing.' Taken altogether, they're sure some dark fae is expending a lot of power there."

"What have they done to stop it?" Priya asked.

Jagger grimaced. "Nothing so far. They're keeping up observation. Dispatched a few dark vermin that were getting particularly restless. No one's actually been hurt, and there's been no indication the dark fae plan to hurt anyone. When there are full fae involved, it's more likely to stay that way if we don't interfere. *We've* never found any way to outright challenge one." He raised his eyes to look at me.

My mind was still stuck on the location he'd mentioned. "Where exactly in Somerset is this interchange?"

"I can show you a map." His fingers skimmed across the screen. He turned it for me to see. "Not the most exciting locale."

I took the tablet from him and zoomed out so I could see the full lay of the land. My breath caught in my chest. My mouth opened, but in that first moment I couldn't force the words out.

I should have known. I'd suspected something close. But it was still a shock seeing it confirmed so blatantly.

"Em?" Darton said.

I forced the words out. "The Darkest One. That's where she's sealed. There are caves, under the ground there..." The images from my vision, when I'd tried to provoke one of Rhedyn, came back to me—the chill and the dark and the dripping water. The distant rumble. Cars on the interchange. "Rhedyn is down there. She's working to free her master. Right now."

His mouth snapped shut. Jagger looked between the two of us. "I don't know anything about a 'Darkest One,' but I'm guessing from the sounds of it this is pretty bad."

"I can't let it happen. If she gets out—"

"Your spell has held for hundreds of years," Darton broke in. "This one fae isn't going to be able to break it just like that. Right? Or she would have already. The others could be grabbing Audrey while we're talking about this. Our families—they're the people already in danger. We have to deal with them first."

I paused as his words wriggled into my head. The timing and method of the dark fae's "threats" had confused me from the start, but now the pieces were starting to draw together into an almost coherent picture.

"Maybe we don't," I said. "Maybe trying to deal with them will only encourage them to do worse. Think about how this all played out. I got that call from my dad, and less than ten minutes later you got the text about Audrey, and right after that Jagger showed up. The dark fae have been lurking around for *days*. That video of your sister—she was at school, so it must have been yesterday or earlier. But they waited until now to send it."

Priya's brow knit. "That is weird. What do you think it means?"

"I don't know for sure. But it's almost as if they knew we were going to get information from Jagger they didn't want us to have, or to respond to. They realized who he was and that he was heading here when there wasn't much time left, and threw everything they could at us. Like they were trying to get us to leave here before he arrived or to dismiss what he told us."

"How could they have known he was coming when we didn't?" Darton said.

Jagger's expression tensed. "About an hour ago, when I crossed the state line, I put your location into the GPS for the first time. Don't like those systems, but I knew I was going to need a little help finding the place. If the fae can send you texts, they could have some way of monitoring pings to this location. The account is registered to the car—they might have dug up some info on my friend that made them wary."

Darton swept his arm through the air. "So what are you saying? The car accident, filming my sister, those things don't mean anything? What's *stopping* them from hurting someone else?"

"We can," I said. "But not by running over there and giving them the chance to grab you, which I'm sure they'd love too. It's a game of distraction. There's no reason for them to play if we're not."

"What does *that* mean?"

"They've got two goals: Get you out in the open, or at least keep us distracted from what Rhedyn's doing. There's no point in trying for either of those if we've left the country." At his noise of protest, I barreled on faster. "You know I had that vision. Of your sword. It must have been telling me we're meant to go find it. Rhedyn was afraid of it. I remembered that. If we can manage to retrieve it, it must be able to stop her."

Darton's voice shook. "There are dark fae stalking my sister, and you want me to just abandon her to go on some hunt across the ocean?"

"It sounds like she'll be safer that way," Jagger put in.

"Yes," I said. "Darton, I can't promise anything, but the dark fae thrive on logic and order. Making chaos just for the sake of it is totally against their nature. If they don't think they can control us by hurting her, or anyone else, they won't do it. They'd get nothing out of it, not even satisfaction. And frankly, if we leave, they'll probably be too busy chasing after us to even consider it."

"I still don't—"

I grasped his hand with my still bare one. "Art. Remember what we talked about. We need a plan, and we need to be smart about it, or we're never going to get ahead of them. This is the best thing we can do. It protects our people here, *and* so many more. The Darkest One wants nothing more than oblivion for all living things. And she's had fifteen hundred years to stew over her defeat. She's not going to hold back when she gets out, and the light fae are out of practice defending against a force that strong. It's not just your sister and my parents. It's *everyone* in danger if we don't act."

Darton dragged in a breath. His fingers tightened around mine. His mouth twisted, and for a second I thought he was going to keep arguing. But when he spoke, his tone was resigned.

"All right. Then let's get out of here as fast as we can."

CHAPTER FIFTEEN

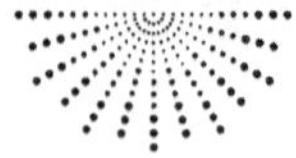

A KNOCK SOUNDED on the front door, and Priya sprang off the sofa. She joined the three of us already standing by the hall as I let our company in.

"The rescue squad is here!" Keevan announced, striding in with Izzy behind him. He took in our combined expressions, and his own darkened. "Ah, okay. No cause for celebration yet."

"We *are* here, anyway." Izzy looked to me. "What exactly do you need us to do? Are we smuggling you out of here or something?"

"No, we just want to confuse the trail." I handed her an opaque plastic bag containing Darton's "lucky" football jersey—smeared with his blood. He hadn't seemed happy about picking out two objects of great personal meaning to him or the blood part, but he'd followed my instructions without complaint. Even now, he was shifting his weight, just eager to get going. "You and Keevan will bring this in the van and head south. Jagger and Priya are going to take off to the north. And Darton and I will borrow Keevan's car to get to the airport west of here."

I held out my hand, and Keevan placed his spare key in it.

"Seems like you're making a habit of commandeering my car in one way or another," he said with a half smile.

"Well, this time you should get it back. I'll leave it in the airport parking lot and text you the exact location. The fae are just more likely to have taken note of the van and Jagger's car by now. You haven't been here since things got really bad." I turned to Priya. "How long should we give Ohanko?"

She checked the time on her phone. "I think we're good. He didn't think it'd take too long to lead the one dark fae here on a bit of a chase. We shouldn't have to worry about that one seeing us leaving now." She raised her head to meet my eyes. "I'll do everything I can to get the enclave on board making sure the others don't touch either of your families."

"And my colleagues have already confirmed they're on their way," Jagger put in.

"Okay," I said. "Then we're ready to go. Everyone, into the cars and out of here, and make it quick."

"Wait!" Keevan said. He grabbed Darton in a brief hug. "Look after yourself, man."

Izzy embraced Darton in turn. "Let us know when you're over there safely."

We wouldn't be safe over in Britain until Rhedyn was dead or locked away and the Darkest One secure once more, but I didn't see any point in rubbing that fact in their faces. They stepped back. Izzy's hand groped after Keevan's and squeezed it. He glanced at her, a hint of a flush shading his dark brown cheeks.

He really should just tell her how he felt already. But I didn't have time to impart that advice right now.

"Out, out," I said, hefting my bag and shooing everyone to the door.

We spilled onto the yard and dashed for the vehicles. Doors whined open and thumped shut. I dropped into the warm leather seat of Keevan's new Toyota and jammed the key into the ignition. The second the engine rumbled, I hit the gas.

Darton yanked on his seatbelt. He set his hand on the door for balance as we swung sharply around toward the drive. "Do you really think the trick with the shirt and the book is going to work?"

"Between your emotional investment and the physical essence in your blood, they'll give an impression of your presence. Enough that any dark fae sensing it will assume you're in that vehicle. In a few minutes, we'll be too far apart for them to compare."

I pushed the gas pedal harder as we reached the highway. Behind us, Jagger swerved in the opposite direction. The van roared up behind it. I raised my hand, not sure if any of them could see my farewell through the windows. Then we left them behind in the dust.

"All we have to do is get on that plane," I said. "Then there's nothing the fae can do."

"What if they follow us on?"

I shook my head. "A dark fae would never take that risk. Being that high up—that close to the sun—with no control over most of the windows? They couldn't tolerate it. They'll have arrived by boat, and that's how they'll have to get back. It'll give us a few days head start."

Not that Rhedyn wouldn't have a contingent of dark fae at her beck and call on the other side of the ocean, of course. But a dozen fewer was still good in my books.

The airport parking lot was a mass of cars, honking horns, and blinking lights. With the help of a twig and a few muttered words, a spot opened up for us not far from the shuttle stop. We grabbed our things and ran, catching the shuttle just as it pulled in.

As the shuttle carried us off toward the Departures terminal, I took a swift inventory of my things. Several wands, twigs, and bundles of herbs and salt filled my expansive carry-on purse. The additional supplies in my suitcase, tucked in with toiletries and a few changes of clothes, I hoped would be enough to see us through the entire trip. However long—or tragically brief—it might be.

Darton had a shoulder bag and a small duffel. He'd been so distracted while he was packing I think he would have forgotten to bring socks if I hadn't popped in and looked things over. He pulled out his phone, checked his messages even though he hadn't gotten any alerts, and returned it to his pocket.

Audrey still hadn't called him back.

All at once he went rigid. "Passport," he murmured to me, leaning away from the other shuttle riders. "I don't have my passport."

I waved his concern off. "That's an easy fix." I fumbled through my things for a scrap of paper and folded it. "Lick your thumb," I told him, turning to face him so no one else could see what I was up to. He did, and then swiped it over the paper at my gesture. I grasped one of the wands, closed my eyes, and murmured two verses under my breath.

When I looked again, I was holding a perfect replica of an American passport, complete with Darton's photo. He blinked at it and let out a hoarse chuckle.

"I don't know if I'm ever going to get completely used to how amazing you are."

"That's fine with me," I said with a teasing tug of his jacket's fur-trimmed hood. Just for a second, the tension looming over us seemed to recede.

The shuttle spat us out at the far end of the terminal. We hustled over to the baggage check. We'd just dropped off our suitcases and started toward the Security lines when Darton's ringtone blared.

His hand jerked to his pocket. He yanked out the phone and whipped it to his ear.

"Audrey," he said, so choked up I'd have been surprised if she couldn't hear his relief over the phone line. "Thanks for getting back to me. No, no, everything's okay over here. I'm sorry if I made you worry."

She must have started talking, because he fell silent. His face darkened. I watched him, my heart sinking.

"Uh-huh. Yeah, I can see why that would make you nervous. Why don't you— Why don't you stick around at home for the rest of the weekend, just to be safe? Have your friends over there if you want to hang out. Exactly. And if you see her around on Monday... Yeah. That's right. But let me know too, okay? Either way. I want to know."

He stopped just before the beginning of the line as he hung up, and lowered his head.

"What?" I said, as gently as I could. My nerves were jumping.

"It's nothing big," he said. "But, at the mall, she saw this woman watching her. Not for very long, but over and over again, all around the place, over a whole two hours. She says it felt like the woman *wanted* her to notice—like she'd keep looking just long enough for Audrey to glance over, and then the next time Audrey checked she'd have disappeared. Until ten or fifteen minutes later."

An uncomfortable itch nibbled over my skin. "Like maybe she was hoping Audrey would get nervous to tell someone about, so it'd get back to you?"

"That's what I'm thinking." Darton ran his hand through his gold-blond hair. "You figure it was one of the dark fae."

It wasn't a question, but I answered anyway. "That seems like by far the most likely explanation."

He looked to the Security lines and back toward the exits. His jaw worked. "They're there right now, *stalking* her..."

I touched his arm. "We already knew that. And I hate that they're scaring her. But you gave her good advice. And they haven't done anything but watch. As soon as you're too far away to intervene, they'll stop trying to provoke you."

His gaze slid to me. "You're sure? Absolutely, one hundred percent sure of that, Em?"

"Absolutely one hundred percent." I squeezed his elbow. "I promise, Art: What we're doing right now is the *best* way to protect everyone. We leave now, and Audrey's never going to see that woman again."

He swallowed thickly and nodded. "Right. Then this is still what we've got to do."

He hefted his bag onto one of the conveyer belts. I followed suit, a weight settling in my gut.

I didn't offer promises lightly. So I sure as hell hoped I hadn't just made one I couldn't keep.

CHAPTER SIXTEEN

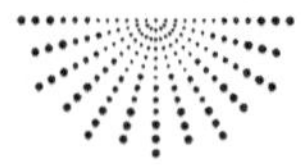

Car retrieved. No burn marks or shattered glass. Definite improvement over last time!

The corners of my mouth twitched up as I covertly typed in a response to Keevan's text. *Glad you two returned safe. Any fae sightings?*

One of the flight attendants walked by with a rattling drink cart. I tucked my hand closer to the hard plastic armrest.

Keevan was the last to get in touch. A couple hours ago, Jagger had confirmed he'd split up from Priya and joined a couple of colleagues heading east to my parents' hometown, and Priya had been in touch about an hour after that to say she was about to go into her enclave's territory to make her petition.

I'd also talked to my mom just before the flight had taken off. Hearing her warm voice, upbeat despite her minor injuries, had left my nerves a little more settled.

Keevan's response popped up on the screen. *Nothing definite. A couple came into the diner where we grabbed lunch and seemed to give us odd looks, but maybe they just thought we looked odd.*

I rolled my eyes. *Keep your eyes open and stay safe. This is the perfect excuse for you two to stick together in the next few days, you know. Maybe you could make a date of it.*

Shut up, Merlin, Keevan replied, with an emoji that was grinning as it stuck out its tongue.

I shot back one with a broad smirk and turned off the phone.

Darton shifted beside me. He'd managed to drift off after the attendants had brought dinner around, and now his head was slumped against the padded seat. His hair had fallen forward to shade his closed eyes. Typical Arthur, able to conk out anywhere if he took a mind to it.

I scooted a little down in my own seat and tried to relax into the stiff padding. After a moment, I let my head tilt sideways to rest against Darton's. The faint rasp of his sleeping breath tugged at my heart.

Right now, for these few hours, *we* were safe. No dark fae could touch us up here in the sky. But it wasn't long before we'd be coming to earth again.

If the Darkest One broke free, we'd be the first she'd want to destroy. It was by my will that she'd been trapped all those centuries, and she'd always wanted Arthur, for reasons she'd never bothered to share with me.

This could be the last time I spent with my king. I hadn't wanted to think it that plainly before, hadn't dared to even start to speak it to him, but I knew it was true with an ache that pierced right through the center of me. We'd barely had a month knowing each other again, Darton had hardly recovered a fraction of the memories inside him...

It wasn't fair. Our lives in tandem had always been cut so short. I wanted to see the Arthur of middle age, the Arthur turned elderly, the full life he would have built on that kingly foundation.

Well, maybe we would get that this time, just this once. This trip would be the first time I'd come close to confronting the Darkest One since I'd cast my spell and doomed us all to our bizarre, recycling fate. And I was arriving with ideas I'd never considered before.

I just wished I'd had more time to test those ideas, to experiment. Was I *ready* to face her? To cut her off from the world of the living for good?

I didn't know the answer to that question. I might not until I was standing there in her cave, with her and Rhedyn before me.

My eyes slid closed. I didn't sleep, but for a short while in the hazy airplane lights, I dozed. When Darton stirred against me, I jerked back into full alertness.

He tipped his face closer to mine, his nose briefly brushing my cheek in a sort of caress. Then he straightened up in his seat. He reached across the armrest for my hand.

I'd put my gloves back on, but the warmth of his skin still seeped through the fabric. I squeezed his hand back, a sudden lump filling my throat.

"Do you remember," he said quietly, looking at the back of the seat in front of him, "when we talked about why I would be king? Whether it was my choice?"

He'd been dreaming memories again. The description he'd given wasn't the most detailed, but I knew immediately what conversation he meant. The words penetrated my own store of memories and dredged one up to the surface. I let it slip into my consciousness.

The fire crackled. The skinned rabbit carcass sizzled over it on the makeshift spit, filling the air with a savory, smoky smell. I leaned back on my hands on my bedroll in the only position I'd found that didn't aggravate the dozen or so muscles protesting from a day spent on horseback. My prince poked at the fire with a stick and sat down beside me.

I might have minded the riding, but I didn't mind this part of traveling. When it was just the two of us, no need to mind my words or restrain my powers. When Arthur could let out his breath here and there too.

Back at the castle, his responsibilities piled up the second he passed through the gates, as if his arrival had triggered an avalanche. His father was shifting more and more kingly duties onto Arthur's shoulders.

Apparently the prince's thoughts had traveled along similar lines. "If we make good time, we should be home tomorrow evening."

I made a noncommittal sound. "Maybe we should find some very urgent matters to divert us along the way, then."

He shook his head at me, but he smiled too. "I need to be there when I can. If you don't like the court, you picked the wrong fellow to offer your services to."

"Humph." I lay back with hands behind my head. "Let me give that some thought."

"I'm only going to be busier once I'm king. I've been heading toward that role since I was born."

I peered up through the bowed branches of the oaks around us. The sky was purple with the deepening evening. "That's just the way it is, isn't it? You were born to the king, therefore you will also be king."

"Well, yes. Isn't that how it's always worked?"

"Around here, in recent times, I suppose. Do you ever wonder why? Why should it be set in stone like that? I don't see why simply being born should oblige a person to take on a position like that automatically. You still have choices."

Arthur gave a bark of a laugh. "Do I now?"

"Of course. You have some. You could run away into the woods if you wanted to. What is anyone else going to do about it? I'll cast some magic—they'll never find you."

He really laughed then. "I suppose you'd like that."

Part of me would. But another part of me knew he wasn't meant for a life as some sort of forest-bound hermit. My father wouldn't have prepared me for this mission otherwise. Whatever Arthur was meant for, it was big enough that it worried the fae.

"I have no preferences," I said blithely despite the knot that had formed in my stomach. "I will follow wherever you go."

The prince was silent for a moment. Then he said, "How many choices have you had, Merlin?"

The knot tightened. I made a dismissive face. "Some. Enough."

"Hmmm. Well, whatever choices I have, taking on the crown will be one of them. I want to be king, even with all the work that comes with it. I can do at least as much good as my father has. I have to try to, in any case. For the people. They need me more than the woods do."

The impressions faded back into the interior of the plane. I swiped my hand across my mouth. My prince had done so much *more* good than his father had. How much farther could he have gotten, if not for our dark enemy and that one bloody moment?

"Yeah," I said to Darton. "I remember."

He paused, still not looking at me. "Why—why did you argue against it? I thought you were all for my being king."

"What?" I pushed myself upright. Funny how our memories could cast such different lights on the same discussion. "That wasn't what I meant at all. I knew you would be great. It just bothered me that you never got a real chance to make that decision for yourself. As your friend, I'd have liked you to have the opportunity to do whatever you wished to, without feeling bound to any specific direction."

"Oh. Okay. I'm sorry." His mouth twisted wryly. He traced his thumb over the back of my hand. "I guess I haven't ever had a whole lot of control over my life, huh."

The lump in my throat rose higher. "No," I said. "But I'm still doing whatever I can to change that."

"I know." He drew in a breath. "And, in case you ever wonder, based on the pieces that have come back to me so far, I think I would have decided to follow in my father's footsteps either way. Even if there hadn't been any pressure to at all. It felt... right. I don't know how to explain it."

"You don't need to," I said. "I don't doubt it. It was who you were—inside, even when no one else was around to have a say."

We stayed like that, our hands clasped, until the attendants brought around a quick breakfast. I'd barely wolfed down the miniature muffin and rather sad looking omelet when the captain announced the plane was beginning its descent. A prickle of anticipation ran over my skin.

Jagger had arranged for one of his UK contacts, a mother and son duo who lived on the outskirts of London, to meet us at the airport. I guessed I'd find out from them what the most recent developments in Somerset were and what resources they could offer, and then I'd get to work hunting down that sword of Arthur's. Although I was more worried about what would happen *after* I located the pool of nightmares I'd seen in my vision.

A different sort of tingle passed through me as we shuffled with the rest of the passengers off the plane. A flicker of energy, with an almost probing sensation to it, sent my nerves twitching. My head jerked up. I scanned the plane, peering through the windows, opening my deeper awareness at the same time. Nothing fae-like caught my attention anywhere nearby.

My anxiety must be getting the better of me.

We made it through passport control and hustled to the baggage claim area. Our suitcases seemed to take forever coming out. I was just starting to curse myself for not finding some way to pack more lightly—but it was so hard to know what tools I might need here, and I had to be prepared for Rhedyn—when the first of them finally tumbled onto the conveyer belt. We hefted them off and jogged over to customs.

Thankfully we looked innocent enough that the officer decided against digging through my suitcase, sparing me the energy of diverting her from its contents. In the hall beyond, a line of people waited for friends or family to arrive. My gaze darted over the signs and stopped on one simply printed with *Emma & Darton*.

The woman holding it was middle-aged, with a bird-like face— big eyes framed by round glasses, a pointy nose and small chin— and a chin-length bob of straight, mahogany-brown hair. She was flanked by a young man I assumed was the son Jagger had mentioned. He'd inherited her hair, which he wore short and casually mussed, but high cheekbones and a strong jaw he must have thanked his father for.

"Emma and Darton," I said as we came to a stop in front of them. I offered my hand to the woman.

"I'm Mavis," she said with a brisk voice and a firm shake. "Glad to see you made it here unharmed. This is my son, Eric."

Eric gave us a little salute and a warm flash of a grin that quickly faded. "Let's get you out of here. There's been more trouble brewing just in the last hour."

CHAPTER SEVENTEEN

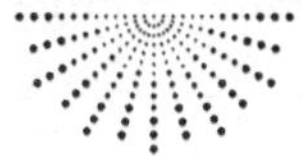

"Trouble?" I repeated as Mavis and Eric ushered us toward the airport parking area. My body had already tensed. Not that I'd been expecting we'd arrive to a relaxing holiday, but I'd thought I was going to have at least a minute or two to get my bearings before we were launched into the fray. "What's happened?"

"We have a colleague who monitors certain types of energy via satellite data," Eric said. "Starting just under an hour ago, he's been reporting some strange—*big*—surges that we know are usually associated with fae magic. It isn't close to our site of concern in Somerset, maybe four hours north, but that doesn't mean it isn't connected."

"It's bigger than anything we've seen 'round the interchange," Mavis added. "We've caught some reports on the 'net of odd lights and other visual phenomena in the area as well."

"Odd *lights?*" I frowned. "That wouldn't be dark fae, then."

"We actually wondered if there's some sort of conflict going on." Eric stopped at the back of a big green SUV. Like the two vehicles I'd seen in Jagger's use, solar panels covered its roof and lamps dotted the sides of its frame. He pushed the hatch open and swung my suitcase inside. "Maybe light and dark at odds—fighting with each other."

Darton heaved his bag in beside mine. "The light fae I've met haven't been very eager to fight."

"No," I agreed. They generally preferred to just stay out of any affairs that didn't immediately involve them. "But if the dark fae set on a bunch for some reason, they'd defend themselves. As well as they can." The light fae I'd seen recently had let many of their more forceful magical skills lapse from lack of practice. I hoped those here were better equipped.

Mavis opened the driver's side door. "I know your main concern was the goings-on at the interchange, but we feel this situation is more urgent. And like Eric said, the two situations could be connected. Unless you have a major objection, we'd prefer to take a look around the area up north first."

"I can understand that." I paused by the SUV's back door, sucking in my lower lip. I *definitely* wasn't ready to confront Rhedyn without Excalibur on our side anyway. And there was no reason I couldn't get to work on that part of our problem in a moving vehicle. "All right. We should get the full picture before we decide what to do next."

The inside of the SUV smelled like worn leather laced with a hint of herbal smoke. I took a deeper sniff. Chamomile and rose. They must burn a little in here regularly for the protective energies. I'd give these hunters points for knowing how to do that much. So many people in this day and age had completely forgotten all the wisdom of the past, even though some of it was totally sound.

I settled into the comfortable seat and tugged open my purse. The last time I'd been able to gather fresh twigs was during a brief detour just before we'd reached the airport. The life energy in those would be half faded by now, but there'd be at least enough left for a basic finding spell. I could collect some more at our next destination. Before we got too close to the possible fighting, preferably.

As Mavis drove the van out onto the highway, rain tapped against the windshield and roof. The sky overhead was a mass of thick gray clouds that blotted out all but the faintest glimmer of sunlight. I couldn't help grimacing.

Eric had turned in his seat to look back at me. He must have caught my dismayed expression.

"It's been like this three straight days now," he said. "The cloud cover hasn't let a single beam of sunlight in, all across the whole south of the country. I know we've got a reputation for the wet on this side of the pond, but honestly, it's pretty unusual for the weather to be this bad. It's hard not to wonder if there's a supernatural component."

I nodded, my hands clenching at the thought. "The dark fae could be directing the weather. Cutting off the sun will make it harder for the light fae—or me—to interfere with their plans. Less immediate power we can draw on."

"So they could do that then? Just conjure up a sky full of clouds."

"If they wanted to enough to give it the necessary focus and energy." If the fae wanted to, they could do a lot worse. "I guess like Jagger you two have mostly dealt with glooms and other dark vermin?"

Eric gave me a crooked smile. "There hasn't been much call for anything else. This is the first time I've ever seen the full fae make a big enough commotion to worry us. Mostly they leave us to us and them to them." He cocked his head. "So how does a lovely lady like yourself end up tangled up in all this fae drama?"

My own lips twitched, but more in amusement than appreciation of the compliment. I wasn't here to be *lovely* and I didn't care a great deal about being a *lady* either, for that matter. "Call it a birthright," I said. "It's probably best we leave it at that."

"Hmm. Jagger did say you're a mysterious one. But I do like a woman of mystery." He waggled his eyebrows playfully. "As you can see, I'm very charming. That's got to earn me at least a clue."

"Eric," Mavis said, sounding fondly exasperated. Darton coughed into his hand.

I resisted the urge to roll my eyes. "It doesn't really make a difference. All you need to know is that I'm very familiar with the fae, and what they're up to in Somerset is going to be very bad for all of us if we don't stop them."

He held up his hands. "Okay, okay, keep your secrets. But you never know. This charm might sneak up on you."

Darton reached over to rest his hand on my shoulder. His fingers pressed my skin tightly. I glanced at him, but his gaze was fixed on the back of Eric's seat. Well, really it was more of a glare.

"Don't you have energies to be monitoring or something like that?" he said, his voice tight.

Eric twisted a little farther to meet Darton's eyes. His own tone stayed friendly. "We've got a bit of a drive. No harm in passing at least part of the time enjoyably."

If we didn't shift the conversation, I had a feeling no one was going to be enjoying it shortly. I cleared my throat before Darton could reply. "*I* do have other responsibilities to take care of. I don't suppose you have a paper map of the country—or at least part of it—that I could use?"

"Of course," Mavis said. She motioned Eric to the glove compartment and smiled at me in the rearview mirror. "It doesn't take long in this line of work to realize you shouldn't rely on satellite reception for your directions."

Eric pulled out a stack of folded maps, some rattier than others. "You'd prefer the full spread of the country?" he asked.

"For now," I said. "I might need to narrow it down later."

He handed one of the more worn ones back to me. "What exactly are you going to do with that?"

"There's something we need to find before we take on the dark fae who's leading the activity by the interchange," I said. "And I need a better idea of where we should be looking. Think of it as a sort of dowsing."

I gave Darton's hand a squeeze. He dropped it without my having to ask. I took a deep breath and willed a calm to spread through my muscles while I expelled the air. The map crinkled as I spread it out on my lap.

I grasped one of the twigs I'd taken from my purse and murmured at it. Then I drew it across my palm. A thin red line split open in my skin, blood beading along it. The sting shot through my nerves. The twig crumbled. Eric inhaled sharply.

"I'm fine," I said. "I've done this hundreds of times."

"She has." Darton didn't sound as if he exactly approved of that fact, but I wasn't asking for his permission. Life blood gave every act of magic twice as much punch.

I gripped another twig between my fingers and closed my eyes. My arm swayed as I held it out over the map. "*On paper as real, show me the place I seek,*" I murmured in the old tongue.

Part of me was braced for questions from my spectators, but Darton knew well enough by now to keep quiet, and Eric appeared to be a fast learner. As I let go of those concerns, my mind raced back to my vision from more than a week ago. The sensation of plunging into sticky, churning shadows. The gleaming sword I'd spotted in their midst. *Excalibur.*

"*On paper as real, show me the place I seek,*" I repeated. My hand bobbed as the sense of that pool of darkness washed through me. A slight tug, to the left. Away. A little to the right again.

The marshy flavor of algae and rotted reeds coated my tongue, but a shiver of energy came with it. A sense of all the power in that blade, burning in the pool's midst, just not brightly enough to penetrate it completely. The sword needed Arthur's soul to reach its full potential.

A chill flowed up my drifting arm and bit into my chest. The sensation of darkness deepened. For a split-second, my mind fell away into the memory of my vision. My companions and the interior of the car spiraled away. I reached and reached and—

—slammed to a halt. The impact smacked me as if I'd hit a

concrete wall. A wave of pain and fear crashed through my mind, tossing me back so hard my eyes flew open and my hand jerked. The twig cracked and disintegrated as it hit the map.

I held myself still, breathing hard, my thoughts still rattled. I'd never been put off quite like that before.

"Em?" Darton said tentatively. He was staring at me, his face clouded with worry. Eric was staring too, his eyes wide and awed.

"It's okay," I said quickly, although it wasn't. The place in my vision, that pond of shadows and nightmares, *really* didn't want me coming there. But I had to anyway. It was the only chance we had.

The map had crumpled in my lap. I tugged it straight with my good hand as my fingers curled against the cut on my other palm.

My search hadn't been completely in vain. When the repelling force had struck me, my hand had jerked down—and smeared blood across a county in the northeast, near Scarborough. The spot it had been hovering over when the supernatural forces I'd been seeking had responded.

Thank the light for my reflexes. At least I had a general area to focus on now. When we were done here, I could head out that way. Closer, I could get a better lock on the pool's exact location. And I'd be prepared for its defenses next time.

"I've never seen anything quite like that," Eric said. "Are you some kind of magician, Emma?" His tone was still jaunty, but a thread of wonder ran through it.

"You could say that." I grasped a handful of twigs and murmured a few words to seal the cut on my hand. Then I folded up the map. "I don't think you'll want this back now that I've bled all over it."

"Nah, nah, we've got plenty." He was still watching me. "I have the feeling I'm really going to enjoy getting to know you."

"I don't suppose with your magical ways you can figure out what the fae are up to?" Mavis said from the driver's seat.

I grimaced. "Unfortunately no. I can sometimes glean pieces of information about distant events that are useful to me, but I don't have much control over how or when that happens. But the old-fashioned method of going and having a look still works just fine."

My gaze slid to the windows as I spoke. We'd left behind the London suburbs sometime while I'd been tracking my nightmare-ish pond. I wasn't sure how much time had passed in my reverie. It didn't feel like long, but sorcery stretched the mind in strange ways. All I could see beyond the road were grassy dells and a couple of farmhouses in the distance.

A sense of deja vu tickled over me. I sat with it, examining the feeling, as Mavis took one turn, and then another, the second onto a two-lane dirt road that sent pebbles rattling against the underside of the SUV. Forestland sprouted up on either side of the road. The tickle wriggled deeper into my chest.

I knew where we were going. Because I'd come this way many, many times in the past fifteen centuries, if not more than once in the last hundred years. The energies of this place were etched into my very soul.

Why wouldn't they be, when it was the place of my first birth? My original enclave—well, my father's enclave, more like—was the source of the disturbance the fae hunters had noticed.

Had Rhedyn ordered an attack on them for reasons only she could know? If she'd thought attempting to harm them would affect me anywhere near as deeply as going after my parents of this life, she'd been pretty impressively mistaken. For one, the light fae could defend themselves as need be on their own. And for another, I hadn't felt close to any of the fae living here by even the end of my first life. Well, except for my father, but he was long faded into the greater light.

That didn't mean I wouldn't intervene on their behalf if I could, of course. The enclave might not be my home anymore, but its inhabitants were far more my people than any of Rhedyn's were.

Several minutes later, Mavis pulled the car to a stop at the edge of a ditch. "This is as close as we can get in the car. I suppose we should watch from here before attempting closer observation. Our computer-savvy friend is still monitoring the emissions and so on. He says they're still fluctuating oddly, but no more than they were earlier."

I undid my seatbelt. "The rest of you are best off staying here anyway. I know the folk in these woods. I can go talk to them directly."

CHAPTER EIGHTEEN

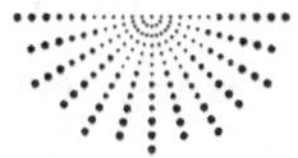

"You *know* these fae?" Eric said. If his eyes got any larger I wasn't sure his head would contain them. "Have you ever even been to England before?"

"A while back." I pulled a few of my wands from my purse. Light willing, I wouldn't need them. "Part of that long story."

Darton released his seatbelt as well. "Do you want me to come with you?"

I hesitated, meeting his gaze. He looked back at me mildly. I didn't think he had any great desire to chat with the fae kind—at the only other enclave he'd visited, he'd been either ignored or gawked at depending mostly on the maturity of the fae—but we'd developed an unspoken understanding around certain topics in the last few weeks. One of which being that I didn't generally like to leave him out of my sight when fae trouble was afoot.

I still didn't. But part of me balked at bringing him along to my father's enclave nearly as much.

He wouldn't be just a curiosity to them. Thanks to my father, Arthur and his rule had become entwined with the enclave's history —and not, from what I remembered from those return visits in my first life, in a positive way. The light fae preferred to keep themselves separate from humankind. They hadn't approved of my birth, and they absolutely hadn't approved of my father's coaching me to insert myself into the world of "lesser" people.

I had no idea what was transpiring around the enclave right now, though. If the light fae were under attack by the dark, Rhedyn's forces could easily stumble on the hunters' car and recognize Darton for what he was. It wasn't as if Mavis and Eric were prepared to deal with an onslaught.

No, as always my king was safer at my side.

"Let's go," I said with a jerk of my head. To Mavis and Eric, I added, "I'll try not to be long. Wait here unless it gets dangerous. If you have to take off, we'll get in touch to meet up as soon as we can." Jagger had given me Mavis's phone number.

"Now, just a—" Mavis started, but I'd already hopped out and shut the door. Darton followed suit.

It was still drizzling, but at least not outright pouring. I tugged my jacket's hood over my head and motioned for Darton to join me. Wand in hand, I leapt the ditch and tramped into the woods. Damp autumn leaves squished under my sneakers.

"Is there anything in particular I should be watching for?" Darton asked as the trees closed in around us.

My gaze darted over the landscape. The interlacing branches overhead held off all but a faint misting of rain, and a loamy smell filled my nose. None of the shadows pooled that around the tree trunks and shrubs looked more alert than the usual variety. Which was how they should be. In usual circumstances, glooms wouldn't come drifting this close to a light fae enclave even by accident.

"If you see something dark that's moving, shout," I said. "But I'll probably notice first anyway."

"Right." He squinted in the gloomy daylight. "How *do* you know this place?"

"It's my father's enclave." I clambered over a log. "My original father. I lived here up until a few days shy of when I first met up with you."

"Oh." Darton blinked, looking started. "I knew— I mean, you said you were half— Somehow I never thought about you spending all that time growing up with just the fae."

I shrugged. "I didn't know anything different back then. I'm lucky my father was as worldly as he was. Although I suppose I drove him to it, to some extent. You can't expect a half-human child to behave the same way and accept the same rules as a full fae. And he always believed in doing his research."

"So... is he still here? Do you have family waiting?"

"No. He was getting on toward elderly when I was born. He passed into the greater light a long time ago. And fae don't really have *family* the same way humans do. The light sort kind of... grow, rather than being born, and then they end up raised by the whole enclave. It's only when they mix with humans you get actual parents and so on."

Darton seemed to take a few minutes absorbing that idea, walking in silence. Then he said, "I'm not sure about these hunters Jagger set us up with."

"Mavis and Eric? What's wrong with them?" Nothing about them had struck me as particularly concerning. They'd put up with my weirdness calmly enough. I always appreciated people who could hold their questions in check.

Darton rubbed his mouth. "Eric comes across kind of pushy, don't you think?"

I glanced over at him, my own mouth twitching to contain a laugh. "Please tell me you're not jealous over a little half-hearted flirting."

He scowled at me. "It didn't sound that half-hearted to me."

"Ah, that guy strikes me as the type who turns on the charm at anyone who appears female and within the acceptable age range." I nudged Darton with my elbow. "It's not as if I have any interest in indulging him, Your Highness. I do have rather a lot of more important things on my mind."

"Obviously," Darton said. His shoulders relaxed a bit. He reached over and took my hand. I threaded my fingers through his, enjoying the contact even through my glove more than I really should have. I could be allowed one small indulgence here and there, though, couldn't I?

None of the forestland looked especially familiar, but that was the way of the light and the living—always growing, changing. We skirted a dense clump of saplings and navigated a muddy stretch of ground that sucked at our shoes. I had just a second to appreciate the feel of solid earth beneath my feet again when two glimmering figures appeared in our path.

"Son of Eóghan," the woman said. "Your companion must come no farther."

I halted, breathing deep and opening my senses. I couldn't feel even the faintest shiver of the enclave's boundary yet. Why were they stopping us so early?

"Neither of us is going to cause any trouble," I said. "Surely he can at least wait at the fringes?"

"I promise to be a considerate guest," Darton put in with a tip of his head. That small motion made both of the fae flinch.

I frowned. Before I could comment, the woman spoke again. "This is the ruling of the elders. We will not have him near our home. He may wait here or return to those who brought you."

I hadn't expected them to welcome my king with an embrace, but this reaction was rather extreme. From the set of the woman's mouth, she wasn't open to any negotiation on the subject, though. Light fae didn't have quite the same dedication to strict authority as the dark fae did, but they still carried a deep respect for the elders —those of the deepest roots, as they often put it. I scanned the forest around us again. There'd been no hint of dark fae presence here so far.

"I can't leave him in the middle of danger," I said. "I

understand there's been some sort of disturbance here—that's why I've come. Are there dark fae about?"

The light fae man's lips curled into an expression of disgust. "The shadowy ones are all busy elsewhere—past the forests, by the sea, under the earth."

Typical light fae poetic nonsense, but I knew how to interpret that much. They knew what Rhedyn was up to, then. But they hadn't bothered to do anything to stop her. That was typical too.

"He will face no danger here," the woman said.

"Will the two of you stay and make sure that doesn't change?" I asked.

They both looked at Darton warily, but the woman nodded. "We will await your return."

"I don't get it," Darton said. "What's the problem?"

"We'll only waste time trying to argue about it. They're not likely to budge." I squeezed his arm. "I'll be back as soon as I know what's going on. You stay alert. You've got the dagger still, don't you?"

He touched the hilt protruding from his pocket. He'd returned the weapon to that spot as soon as he'd been able to retrieve it from his checked luggage. It wouldn't get him very far if a full dark fae appeared, but it didn't appear likely we'd be facing any here after all. What were all those energy fluctuations about then? Maybe the hunters' colleague's system had simply gone haywire? That wasn't a comforting thought.

I hurried on through the woods, my hand tight around my wand. Even if there weren't dark forces about, the less time I left my king with only the uncertain protection of those two fae, the better. They hadn't looked like they wanted to come within ten feet of him.

As I approached the enclave, the sense of the boundary ahead rippled over my skin. I pushed onward, still scanning the brush— and hesitated. A big, old oak that stood about ten paces to my right triggered an immediate rush of recognition. Could it really be...?

I edged closer to it, my breath tight in my throat. The second I laid my hand on the gnarled bark, I was sure.

It was my father's tree. The one that had contained our home all those years ago. He'd always liked living close to the edge of the enclave, so that he could slip away for his field observations without facing too much judgment. The enclave's boundaries must have been redrawn since that time—perhaps several times—and they'd left this oak behind. No one had taken it over after my father had died.

Childhood memories from that first childhood, so long past, trickled through my head. Racing around this tree, daring my father to try to catch me. Using the life energy pulsing through its trunk to magically scramble up its towering trunk. Perching on the broad branches overhead and peering through the forest, watching the full fae come and go. Wondering what my life would be like when I was old enough to have responsibilities of my own. Until Father called me down for some new lesson or test.

I'd never given my human mother much thought. I'd never even met her to remember her, after all, and Father had rarely talked about her. As far as I knew, he'd sent her back to her people not long after she'd given birth to me, releasing her from the charm he'd placed on her—a much more potent charm than Eric's human sort.

After so many lives with fully human births, with at least somewhat "normal" families, I felt that empty space in my recollections now. Had *she* even remembered me—that she'd had a baby, that her son had been taken from her? Or had those nine months with my father in the enclave dissolved into a blur like so much of my many lives between then and now?

The breeze shifted with a wisp of wisteria scent, and an elder fae stepped forward through the enclave's boundary. His black hair fell in several long braids about his smooth but nearly translucent face. He studied me with pale blue eyes.

"Merlin," he said in a dry crackle of a voice. Apparently he was old enough or skeptical enough—or both—that he felt he could dispense with formalities.

He struck me as vaguely familiar, but not in a way I could pin down. I gave him a slight tip of my head out of politeness. "Indeed. If we've met before, you'll have to remind me. I don't keep good memories of my past lives beyond the first."

"Cormag," he said. "I was a friend of your father's—but your birth was before my time."

I made myself step back from the oak. "Well met. I suppose I should go speak with all the elders. I understand there's been quite a commotion here. You've drawn the notice of the humans, you know. At least the more alert among them."

No concern touched his placid expression. He held out his hand to motion me still. "I'm aware. It was our intention to draw mortal eyes this way. We knew they would draw you with them, like a current. Your light echoed across the land the moment you arrived here."

Oh, light save me. The light fae tendency toward flowery vagueness never got less annoying over time. "You were trying to summon me?" I said.

"As quickly as possible. To tell you to return to the place from which you came."

I blinked at him. Well, he wasn't beating around the bush now, even if he was still weirdly vague in his directness. "Technically," I said, patting the oak, "I came from right here."

Cormag frowned. "But you have no roots here now. And you will not set them down. You and your king must make passage across the ocean once more."

"Okay, yeah, no can do," I replied. "If that's all you wanted to say to me, I might as well get back to my king and take care of more important business."

I started to turn. Cormag cleared his throat sharply. "Merlin," he said. "Do you know why your father prepared you to follow the one named Arthur?"

I paused, glancing back at him. "I got the gist. The dark fae had been interested in his family line. Father was afraid they'd been meddling somehow, or that they would. He wanted me to be on hand in case they... escalated the situation."

"Surely you were aware the troubles ran deeper than that?"

I swiveled to face him again and folded my arms over my chest. "I only know what my father bothered to tell me, which honestly didn't include much detail. I'm pretty sure the Darkest One's attack took him as much by surprise as it did me. Which, by the way, is why we're here at all—to make sure she doesn't bring down even more death and destruction. It'd be nice if you showed a little more concern about that possibility."

Cormag's lips pursed. "If she does go free, your king will be the soul she's most eager to destroy. And we'd rather the aftershock play out on lands as far from here as possible."

"Or how about I just stop her from getting free in the first place? That sounds like a solution that works better for everyone."

"You don't appear to have had the greatest success at stopping her in the past."

My mouth twisted. "I have to *try*. I at least contained her for an awfully long time. It isn't just Arthur. Do you have any idea how many people she might—"

"Your father believed," Cormag broke in, "that the greatest disaster that might befall us *and* humankind was not the Darkest One's existence but what she might do if she claimed your king. The best for all would be if he passed from this world far from her, never to return. But failing that, we want neither of them nearby."

His bland selfishness sparked the frustration I'd been trying to suppress. It flared into outright anger. "Great," I said. "That sounds like the perfect plan. Make vague predictions of doom and expect everyone to fall in line. To protect you. Because obviously nothing matters other than making sure this particular enclave isn't disturbed."

Cormag gazed back at me steadily. "You are only distressed

because you do not understand what your magic has been harboring. I can clear that mist. Wait here."

He made a gesture over the oak's trunk and stepped through the bark. Apparently the magic that had formed my father's house inside hadn't completely dispersed.

I stayed where I was, shifting my weight from foot to foot, half tempted to stalk off while Cormag was gone. But whatever he had to show me, it might be of some use. I was already working from an immense shortage of information. If he knew something about the Darkest One I didn't, it didn't matter how self-centered he and the rest of his kind were being.

Cormag reappeared in front of the tree with a whisper of a rustle. He was holding six leather-bound books, each not much taller than his hand. He offered them to me.

"Your father's journals, as relate to the family line of your king. It was only recently, while I tended to this old tree, that I came across them. He had tucked them away, all but hidden them. Perhaps he was embarrassed of anyone seeing how much he'd indulged his obsession. I expect he meant to pass them on to you once the spiraling of your unnatural spell allowed it, but he never had the opportunity."

I accepted the journals into my arms. Tipping most of them into the cradle of my elbow, I opened the first. My father's cramped handwriting stretched across the crisp pages in faded lines—but not so faded I couldn't read them. The year and the names noted near the top of the first page told a long story on their own. My eyebrows rose.

"This was Arthur's grandfather's grandfather," I said. "Father was worried about his family for *that* long?"

"Longer still, as you'll see," Cormag said. "That time was only when he first began to commit his observations to paper."

"Okay." My lungs tightened. I'd known Father had been concerned, but I hadn't realized his interest in Arthur's lineage had run that deep for so long. "I don't suppose you could sum up the key points. It'll take me a while to read through all of these."

Cormag lifted his chin with a haughtiness he hadn't shown before. "I hope you will glean more from them than I could, with all of your mixing with humankind. But it was clear to me that your father was sure the dark fae's interest and intertwining in the strands of that ruling family would be catastrophic. And your king stood as the pinnacle of that catastrophe."

CHAPTER NINETEEN

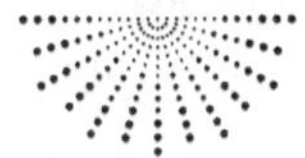

I saw Darton before he saw me. He was leaning against a younger beech tree, gazing pensively into the forest in front of him. The misting of rain had darkened his hair, so it gleamed more bronze than gold. His handsome face was pale in the dim light.

There wasn't a hint of a threat about him, unless you were the type of creature that ought to be frightened by the fae dagger in his pocket. He looked, in that moment, vulnerable and alone.

Alone. Where had the light fae sentries wandered off to? They'd given me their word.

I strode forward, and Darton's head jerked around at the snap of a twig underfoot. Two streaks of light flitted past me. Ah, so his unwilling protectors had stuck around, they'd just disguised themselves. What, did they think this "catastrophe" lurking in Darton would somehow rub off on them if they offered a little polite conversation?

I wiped at the moisture that had beaded on my face as I reached him. I had nothing left to say to any of the fae of this enclave anyway. I tipped my head toward the road. "All right, let's get out of here."

He straightened up and matched my pace, tramping back through the brush. "What happened? Are the light fae in some kind of trouble?"

"No. Well, no more trouble than they've stirred up in their own heads. The dark fae haven't done anything to them."

His gaze fell to the journals I was still clutching. "What are those?"

My gut knotted. I couldn't tell him about Cormag's insinuations, not when I hadn't had a chance to come to my own conclusions. Especially not when it would also require admitting that I'd lied to him all those years ago about why I'd come to him in the first place. I had his trust now—I needed to keep it.

"One of my father's friends passed on some of his old journals to me," I settled on. "There might be information about the Darkest One in them. I'm hoping I can find out more that'll help us take her on."

"So they're going to help us against the dark fae after all?"

I let out a choked laugh. "Oh, no. Not a chance. They don't seem to think there's any point in bothering with the attempt. They just want to make sure she keeps clear of them. What happens to the rest of the world—who cares?"

"They—what? Wow." He shook his head, seeming lost for words. Then he hesitated. "You don't think they're right, do they? That there's no point in trying to stop her?"

"Of course not. It's my spell that Rhedyn thinks she's going to break. You can forget it if I'm going to sit around and let that happen. I stopped the Darkest One once, if imperfectly. I can do it again—I've just got to figure out how. We didn't cross an entire ocean to lie down and give up now that we're here."

Darton nodded. "So it's just us again."

"Well, just us and whatever help the hunters can give us."

I watched him from the corner of my eye as we walked on, but nothing in his features or his gait gave me the slightest reason to worry. He was still Darton; he was my king reborn. My liege had been a lot of things, had shown all the mercurial emotions any human did during our times together, but the one thing I'd always known with bone-deep certainty was that he was *good*.

Did it even matter whether he contained some pending disaster I couldn't sense? If Cormag was right, if the Darkest One could create a catastrophe by getting her hands on Arthur's soul, then it would be catastrophic regardless of where it happened. We had a hell of a lot better chance of making sure it *didn't* happen if we stuck around and got in Rhedyn's way before she freed her master in the first place.

Giving in to the enclave's demands would just be signing a death sentence for a whole bunch of different people, which I cared about even if they didn't. No, we had to stay.

Stay and fight.

The SUV came into view through the trees ahead. I picked up my pace.

Darton glanced over at me. "You're looking very serious. Where are we headed next?"

I gave him a tight smile. "I'm thinking it's time we get that damned sword."

A hand shook my shoulder. I blinked and jerked awake, finding myself slumped in the back of the SUV. Eric was standing over me by the open door. The rain had picked up again, now drumming against the roof and the umbrella he was holding. The landscape beyond him was a blur of misty green. The damp trickled in past him and dappled my skin.

He cocked his head at me. "We're at the place you said to stop. It looks like you were able to get a little sleep?"

"Yeah." I pushed fully upright and checked on Darton. He stirred against the far window, where he'd propped his head to catch a few Zs of his own. A quick glance at the dashboard clock told me it was early afternoon. Still a few hours left of what amounted for daylight in this weather.

My father's journals lay in a heap at my feet. I hadn't wanted to set them on the seat between us in case Darton decided to flip through one and realized what they were really about. He might not have recovered enough of his former self to understand the archaic language—the fae had no written alphabet of their own, so my father had used human writing—but I wasn't going to count on that.

Not that my earlier skimming perusal of the journals had turned up any information that was much more specific than what Cormag had told me.

The dark fae had been interested in Arthur's family for several generations. My father had observed the Darkest One's minions venturing onto their grounds on various occasions. He'd noticed the visits increasing in frequency around each pregnancy in the family. He'd felt a sense of shadow growing around them. He'd watched the Darkest One assembling creatures and fae around her after Arthur's birth, as if she were preparing for some imminent event.

But he'd never uncovered any details. He'd hoped that I would, with my ability to blend into human society. He'd just never bothered to tell me that.

I'd known from our conversations back then that he'd been disappointed I wasn't reporting more, but he'd never told me what sort of *more* he was expecting, never given me any guidelines other than to watch for the dark fae in general. Maybe I would have come up with something more useful if he'd been clearer about his concerns. I might have some sensitivity to dark powers, but not on the same level as a full fae like him.

But he hadn't wanted to bias me. That much had been clear from the most recent journal. He'd been afraid if he said exactly what he thought the dark fae might be up to, I'd interpret signs that way even if they truly meant something else. He hadn't even written his ideas down for his own records. In every note that touched vaguely on his "suspicions," his discomfort with even continuing to entertain theories he hadn't been able to confirm bled through.

The scientist in my father, such a strange characteristic for a light fae, had caused us more trouble than good in the end.

After a couple hours of paging through those ancient volumes, I'd decided a more valuable use of my time would be catching up on some rest. Light knew I was going to need all my wits when we went for the sword.

"So, what exactly are we doing here?" Eric peered over his shoulder. "This place isn't much to look at."

"This is just a stopping point," I said. I rubbed my eyes, wiping the last remnants of sleep away, and grabbed the dried flowers I'd set aside in preparation. "We're close enough to our actual destination now that we can get a guide to show us the rest of the way there."

This spot, where I'd told the fae hunters to stop and wake me, lay in the middle of my bloody smear on the map from my earlier search. But I wasn't going to bother with the map this time. There was a simpler conjuring that should work, and that didn't require me extending my mind to that wretched place directly. I wasn't keen to experience the backlash again.

I cupped my hands around the marigold petals and leaned my face close. As I inhaled their fragile perfume, I reached back in my mind, searching for the emotion I needed. Something fraught and tangled, painful and yet poignant.

It wasn't hard to find the right image. My memory of my king's first near-death swam up. The courtyard crowded with revelers, the platform where Arthur had given his speech, the gaunt yet elegant figure of the Darkest One looming over him, cloaked in shadow. The metallic taste in my mouth as I'd run, heart thumping, knowing I couldn't move fast enough. The words sputtering up my throat. The crackle of energy, charred and electric, flaring around me.

The agony at the thought that I might lose him. That it would be my fault if I did.

My throat tightened. I exhaled that emotion into the space between my hands with a whisper. "*Like to like. Float and follow the roads home.*"

Holding the pained feelings in my chest, I breathed in and out with the same incantation until the energy tingled against my palms. I motioned Eric away from the door. He backed up a step, watching me avidly. I scooted to the open air and opened my hands.

A shimmering ball, whirling with pale blues, deep indigo, and a streak here and there of crimson, drifted away from my palms.

Mavis's eyebrows leapt up where she'd turned to watch from the driver's seat. "Well, then, that's something, all right."

"What *is* it?" Eric asked.

"Our guide," I said. The ball floated onward, a few feet off the ground. The raindrops passed through it without making it so much as quiver. To my relief, it stayed over the road—I hadn't been entirely sure that part of the spell would stick. As it gusted farther away, it started to pick up speed.

I reached to close the door. "Now we follow it. Let's go, before we lose sight."

The ball's faint glow stood out against the dim landscape. At the first crossroad we reached, it veered left. Mavis shook her head with a disbelieving chuckle, but she turned the wheel to stay on its trail.

The ball traveled faster and faster as it honed in on its target. Thankfully in this obscure corner of the country, with the inclement weather, no one else was on the road to see our bizarre procession.

Darton leaned forward in his seat as Mavis increased the gas.

He frowned at the windshield. "Is it going to take us right to the sword?"

"Well, yes and no. It's going to take us to the place where the sword is hidden." Where the dark fae must have chucked it once it had been out of Arthur's hands. Presumably hoping no one would ever find their way back to it.

"Which is the place full of nightmares that you talked about before," Darton said.

"That description was... not entirely accurate. I was trying to make a point when I said that." I paused, my skin prickling with the awareness that we had an audience this conversation. There were some things I didn't want to have to explain to the fae hunters on this short an acquaintance. But I could cover the basics without getting into trouble.

"I've mentioned to you before that the dark fae love order. They encourage death, and they enjoy the sharp, simple emotions that can lead up to it, like anger and fear. But when people are dying, a whole lot of other feelings can come into play that hover somewhere between light and dark, love and hate, joy and pain. Regret. Desperation. Longing. Emotions like that are much too chaotic for dark fae comfort. So when they take a life for themselves, they shunt anything like that off into a trash can of sorts."

"A trash bin of sad feels?" Eric said, his mouth twitching with amusement.

I glowered at him. "In practice it's more like a pond. The light fae—when they talk about it, which isn't often—call it the Pool of Turmoil. And you can laugh at the idea, but it's not going to be any fun going into the place. Other people's emotions can affect you even in regular conversation—and the ones in the pool are all packed in and condensed after thousands of years of collecting. Be glad you get to sit on the sidelines."

"I'm totally fine with sticking to spectating for this one," Mavis put in.

Arthur rubbed his jaw. "So if the dark fae throw all those emotions in this 'pool' because they don't like experiencing them, then can we at least assume we won't run into any dark fae while we're there?"

"Yes," I said. "Thankfully. But there are other sorts of creatures you wouldn't want to meet that enjoy the turmoil. And what's in a person's own head can be the most dangerous threat there is, if it's warped in the wrong ways."

Eric studied my face. "What's so special about this particular sword anyway?"

"It's magic," I said simply, and almost smiled at his consternated look.

"I get it, I get it," he said with an exaggerated sigh. "I haven't earned a spot in the secret club yet. I'll keep working on it."

"Ho!" Mavis exclaimed. "I think we're here."

The SUV eased to a stop. I looked to the windshield just in time to see my conjured ball flit off the overgrown dirt track we'd ended up on. It streaked across a rocky protrusion jutting up from the ground and disappeared over the other side.

I shoved open the car door and scrambled out, tugging my purse with me. "I've got to keep after it. There's no telling how much farther off the pool is. Stay here. And turn on the lamps so I've got light to return to. I might need it."

I dashed around the back of the SUV and clambered up the small, rocky hill. Footsteps thumped behind me. Darton caught up as I reached the crest.

"I think you meant 'we,'" he said. "It's my sword. I *have* to come, don't I?"

I wasn't completely sure he did, but I wasn't sure he didn't, either. And my glowing ball was disappearing through a notch between two boulders up ahead, nearly out of view already. "Come on then."

We hurried across the uneven terrain, scattering pebbles and shifting wobbly stones. The ground dipped and rose, and dipped and rose again. The rain pattered against my hood and dripped onto my face. I wrinkled my nose, pressing onward. Darton shrugged his bomber jacket closer around him.

"How much farther do you think— Oh."

We halted on a mossy peak. Below us, a thicker, darker mist than the one that had coated the moors churned within a ring of jagged rocks. A glinting black surface showed through the hazy currents. The ball plummeted down and disappeared into the pond.

"There you have it," I said, my body tensing. "The Pool of Turmoil."

"So we just dive right in?"

I shook my head. "It's not really water. We can walk right down into the hollow. But... it's going to be unpleasant. From what I've heard, the emotions don't just affect you in the present, they stir up awful memories from your own past. And transform them into moments even more awful. It's hard to tell what's real and what isn't. Most who've stumbled into this place never find their way out again."

"Ah." Darton crossed his arms over his chest. "But we've got some special trick to getting through it?"

"Just our smarts. I can't even count on my magic once we're in there. The pool could warp my intentions too. We just have to stay focused on our quest—on Excalibur—no matter what happens. Don't think about anything other than the sword. No matter what we think we're experiencing."

"All right," Darton said. "I'm ready. Let's get this over with."

He started down the rough slope. I had to bite back the words to call him back. To tell him to sit his butt down and let me do this alone after all.

He probably wouldn't listen to me even if I did. And as always, he was safer with me than on his own.

I skidded down the slope after him, catching his arm just before our feet hit the mist. "Darton," I said, and when he turned to face me, "My liege." He went still at the term of respect. I latched onto that opening. "I know the fae who made this place better than you do. I'm better equipped to fend them off. I want you to swear to me you'll let me take the lead, that you won't do *anything* without my go-ahead. Please."

Darton's mouth twisted. He hesitated, but then he inclined his head. "All right. I trust you. I swear."

He held out his hand to me. I curled my fingers around his, and together we stepped down into the mist.

CHAPTER TWENTY

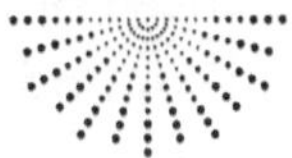

THE WAVES of hazy emotion lapped at my feet, my legs, my torso, and then my face as we edged down along the ridged bank of the pond. They seeped straight through my clothing, grazing my skin with chilly tendrils of feeling: a trickle of melancholy, a waft of anguish.

As I'd told Darton to, I schooled my mind carefully blank. Any thought that swam up I dismissed. I trained all my attention on the image of Excalibur I'd seen in my vision. There was nothing to see around us now anyway except shifting currents of energy in hazy shades of gray, from pale cloud-like tufts to shadowy dark streams. They coated my nostrils and throat with a damp, mildewy smell. I wrinkled my nose.

Darton's hand stayed clamped around mine. After several steps, it was the only solid thing I was aware of. The ground beneath us had faded away. Our feet seemed to walk straight on without touching anything beneath them. I dragged in a breath and exhaled sharply as a jab of desperation wrenched at my lungs.

"Are you okay?" I said. My voice came out warbled. I looked toward Darton, but the shifting haze obscured his face.

"So far so good," he said with a squeeze of my fingers and a ragged laugh. "Just think about the sword—and how much I'd like to have it right now, to slice through this stuff. I can handle that."

A silvery billow rushed at us, too fast for us to dodge. It washed over me and raced through my skin into my nerves. A sharp itching sensation broke out through my flesh, as if every muscle had fallen asleep. My pulse stuttered with a burst of adrenalin.

And then the haze parted ahead of us.

Two rows of figures stood around a long wooden table. They were leaning over the polished top, pointing fingers and snapping at each other in a cacophony of voices. At the head of the table, a young man with a crown resting on his gold-blond hair raised his hands.

"Order! Order, my lords!" Arthur's voice rang out. Darton froze beside me. I made out the pale, peaked face of my former self cringing near the doorway. I'd never enjoyed those political meetings. I couldn't even have said which occasion this memory was based on—they all had seemed to go pretty much the same way. Lots of yelling and fists knocking the tabletop and very little actual decision-making.

"That was me," Darton said beside me. Some of the color had drained from his face, but his eyes were wide. I couldn't tell if he was more shocked or impressed. Of course, he'd never seen himself —his original self—from the outside before. The memories he'd experienced had been from behind those bright blue eyes.

"It's still you, in the ways that matter most," I murmured.

The lords had settled down at their king's command, at least for the moment. They sat, frowning. One started to speak, and Arthur raised his hand, his expression firm. He'd always managed to evoke that commanding air when he needed to, even though I knew he didn't take much pleasure from drawing hard lines.

"A compromise should be possible," he said, and pointed to a map spread on the table. "Lord Damblin, your biggest concern appears to be access to the river, and Lord Salloway, yours is maintaining your quarries. We can account for both concerns, if we consider the boundary between your districts to be here." He drew his finger across the map. "Neither of you would lose anything you value. And there will be no more need for argument."

The first lord he'd addressed leaned back in his seat. "All right. I can agree that is fair. But if we run into further troubles, be sure I won't sit quietly about them."

Ha. Fat chance of any of them ever sitting *quietly*.

The other lord was shaking his head. Of course. When did they ever make any discussion easy for my king? I'd often thought he should just toss the lot of them out and rule the entire country directly, but when I'd remarked as much to Arthur, he'd pointed out even he would make a mess of trying to juggle that many concerns. *The lords serve a key purpose in administration, as frustrating as they may be.*

"There is still the matter of the farmlands along the river," the second lord said. "I will not have my realm placed at a disadvantage."

Arthur smiled patiently. "I think you will find my recommendation gives equal agricultural territory to both sides. Although if you have a suggestion you'd consider more fair, by all means, share it with us."

The lord frowned at the map, opened his mouth, shut it again, and grimaced. "I am not convinced, but I acknowledge that I can see no better alternative at the moment."

Darton leaned close to me. "This doesn't *seem* like a nightmare."

"Not yet." I hooked my arm around his. "Come on. We're not here for this, and you can be sure it'll sour soon enough."

I tugged at him, and he moved sluggishly, still staring at the memory playing out before him. And at that moment, the Pool of Turmoil decided to put the proof to my words.

"Excellent," Arthur was saying. "Now on the matter of—"

A lord at the far end of the table sprang to his feet with a shriek of chair legs against the hazy floor. "Why do we all just listen to this man—no, this *boy*?" he demanded. "What does it matter if he wears the crown? We all know he's too young, too untried, to truly understand the concerns we face. He never stood by his father's side here with us."

Well, that was blatantly untrue. My skin prickled. This wasn't just a memory anymore. The pool was skewing it into a nightmare.

"Now, then," Arthur started, holding up both his hands, but more of the lords leapt up before he could get another word out.

"Ruverton is right," spat out the lord who'd been agreeable just a moment ago. "You have no authority over us—none that you've earned."

"What have you ever done for us or this country, truly?" another sneered.

Okay, Darton *really* didn't need to see this. And I didn't want to find out how far and how fast it was going to spiral.

I hauled on his arm, and he stumbled. His gaze was fixed on the scene before him, his face even paler than before and his expression completely still, as if it held him transfixed. Maybe it did. I had no idea exactly how the pool worked its effects on the mind.

"He's a fool!" a lord shouted, flinging his hand toward Arthur. "He hasn't done a thing to earn that crown."

"We should take it from him. Find one who can carry it properly."

"Yes, yes, let us take the crown."

The hollering voices whirled around us as if lords had popped up on all sides. The ones at the table drew swords and daggers I hadn't seen until just then. "Good men!" Arthur yelled, lifting his arms, but the protest had no effect. The crowd of lords ran at him, their blades poised to strike.

"Come *on*," I hissed, and yanked at Darton again. His feet seemed to have melded to the invisible ground beneath us. I grasped his wrists with both of my hands and heaved, and all he did was list toward me, sidestepping to keep his balance. His eyes didn't shift for a second. Was he even *blinking?*

The figure of his first self vanished in the midst of the onslaught of lords like a gloom caught in the sun. The nobles spun around, weapons in hand, searching for a new target. Their glares caught on us as they noticed our presence for the first time.

Swine crud. We had to get out of here, *now.*

"Darton," I snapped. "Arthur!" I inhaled sharply. Then I drew back my hand and slapped him across the face.

The impact stung my palm, so I can't imagine it felt all that pleasant to his cheek. Darton flinched. His gaze jerked down to me. "Em," he said, with a flush of anger. "What—"

"We have to run." I pulled his arm, and this time his legs moved.

We plowed on into the shifting mists, the thunder of chasing footsteps echoing after us. Swung blades hissed through the air. "Stand and face justice!" someone hollered, but the voice was already fading. I waved aside the thicker currents of fog, squinting in the dimness, and finally drew to a stop.

Darton swiveled around beside me. He stared back the way we'd come. "That was— Did that really happen in our—"

"No," I said before he had to finish. "You were never set upon by a swarm of rabid lords. It's the tumultuous emotions of this place. Like I told you, they infect everything—including our minds if we let them. So let's not?"

"Right. Right." He turned back to me, shamefaced. Then he touched his cheek, which was still decorated with a splash of red in the shape of my hand. "Was assaulting me really necessary?"

I rolled my eyes. "Believe me, if I *assaulted* you, you wouldn't be standing around asking questions about it. And yes, I'm pretty sure a little smack was a better choice than letting you get run through with a dozen swords."

"But... it wasn't real. Would they actually have hurt me?"

"Did what you were seeing feel real in the moment?"

He paused. "Well... Yeah, I guess it did."

"If your mind believes it, then just about anything can do damage. Let's not stick around to test that theory out any further." I peered through the haze. We had a sword of our own to seek.

A glimmer of feeling grazed my chest. Not the strangled, twisted feelings of the pool, but something clean and bright. And sharp. I could almost taste the metal of the blade on my tongue.

"I can sense it. Excalibur. I think..." I turned slowly, reaching out toward that sensation. It was distant, wavering, but—there. "This way. The sooner we find it, the sooner we can get out of this awful place."

CHAPTER TWENTY-ONE

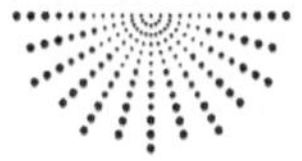

My FINGERS TWINED with Darton's, still clamped around his hand from our run away from the figmentary lords. I hadn't thought anything of it until, after a few strides, he disentangled them and pulled his arm away from me.

He walked on right by my side, but somehow that simple motion opened a distance between us. I glanced at him, searching his expression for a reason. My gut had clenched. I didn't realize how my mind had slipped until the mist fell away around a flash of color.

Cattle sod. I'd forgotten my own advice about keeping my head clear. I bit my lip, dragging the image of the sword ahead of every other concern, but it was too late. A scene had formed, bright and frantic, in front of us. My memory, this time. I knew it well, in part because I'd thought back to it so many times after it had happened, chiding myself for mistakes made then.

Darton jerked to a stop. What seemed like just a few feet away from us, men on horses charged about an oval ring. The horses' thundering hooves tossed up strewn straw and clods of earth. Beyond the white wall on the far side of the ring, men and women cheered and stomped against the wooden stands. The smell of sweat and damp horse hair drifted over me. It was a smell I had never missed one bit.

The men on horseback wheeled their steeds apart and cantered to opposite ends of the ring. The one at our left lifted his metal helm. Darton startled at the sight of his former face. Arthur—just a prince then, no more than a year or two older than Darton was right now—swiped his arm across his brow and tugged his visor back down. An attendant handed him a new weapon: a gilded spear. He spun it for show, letting it catch the sunlight. The cheers rose.

"I don't remember this," Darton said.

My mouth twisted. "That only means it hasn't come back to you yet. So far it's real. It was a tournament your father organized one year: battle games and the like. And you were the star, of course. I'm sure it'll come to you—properly, without the pool's meddling—eventually. We're better not lingering."

"But if this isn't my memory, it must be—" He craned his neck. "There you are." A little smile crossed his face. Despite myself, it sent a flutter through me.

I followed his gaze to my own original self, standing in the shadow of an awning by the lower edge of the ring, a stack of shields and weaponry beside me. My thick brown hair was mussed from all the rushing around before the tourney and, well, truth be told I was pretty sure it'd been messy most of the time. I hadn't bothered much with mirrors.

My thin hand was clenched around several twigs. My eyes tracked my prince as he swung his stallion around to face his opponent. In my present form, my shoulders stiffened. It was coming soon.

"Yes, there's me," I said. "You've seen me before. Can we—"

I tried to step away, but the memory surged around us. The horses barreled past us from both sides. The tent loomed at our right. Everywhere I turned, the past rose up to meet me.

I reached for Darton's hand again, shoving aside the pinching inside at the thought of how he'd pulled away before, but his expression stopped me. His eyebrows had lifted. Even with the thumping of hooves and the clanging of weapons around us, he was still watching that long ago version of me.

And the long ago version of me was watching Arthur.

The prince urged his horse faster, swinging his spear, and a grin sprang across my—Merlin's—face. Even in the shadow, my eyes lit up as if I were standing in full sun.

I swallowed hard. I'd never seen how I looked when I was focused on him. By the light, please tell me my affection wasn't as obvious as it seemed.

Darton let out a choked sound that might have been meant as a snicker. His jaw had gone tight. "Look at you, Em. You were mooning like a schoolgirl with a crush. If I didn't know better, I'd have thought—"

"Yes, yes. Very funny," I broke in. Now, in the present, my cheeks had flamed and my stomach knotted. "We can laugh about my ridiculous expressions some other time. First we need to find our way out of this mess."

"This time it's *your* mess," Darton pointed out. He started to turn, and hesitated. "What are you doing?"

He meant the me of the past, not me now. Because the figure standing under the awning had just palmed one of those twigs. Merlin tensed as Arthur swung his horse around in a whirl of dust. The prince's opponent jabbed out with a pike. Its tip sped toward a gap beside Arthur's shield. Merlin's lips moved in a silent litany— and the pike tip jumped an inch to the left. It glanced off the edge of the prince's shield.

Darton stiffened. The prince didn't appear to notice. His steed wheeled, and spear and pike clashed again. The massive man on the other horse pressed closer, and Arthur pushed back.

The memory spun. The colors streaked around us, and suddenly Arthur was charging at a different opponent, a slim sinewy fellow on a bay stallion, this time with a sword. His blade clashed against the other man's. They traded blows and broke apart. The other man kicked his horse's sides and urged it toward the prince before Arthur had quite turned around.

The prince's stallion sprang backward at the unexpected approach. Arthur jolted in his saddle. And in the corner of my vision, I knew without looking directly that my former self had snatched up another twig with another murmur.

Just a little nudge. Just enough to be sure the prince wouldn't fall. That's all I'd been thinking when I'd been struck by that jolt of panic. But it was also enough that Arthur had felt it.

In the vision before us, the prince flinched as he jerked himself back into balance. His head twitched toward the awning for just an instant before he kicked his steed forward to meet his opponent.

"Em," Darton started.

I shook my head. "Don't. I've heard it. Come—"

And then I was hearing it again. The memory collapsed, and suddenly all there was before us was me and him, Merlin and Arthur, face to face behind the equipment racks. The prince loomed over his wizard. His voice crackled with anger.

"What were you thinking, Merlin? Did you assume I wouldn't notice? Do you see me as that dim?"

I cringed inside my skin. "Darton..."

"Is this real?" he said quietly. "Everything we've seen so far—it really happened that way?"

"Yes," I said. "And believe me, the parts you're unhappy about I deeply regretted. Do we really need to see this?"

Merlin was stuttering, his face gone sallow. "Sire—my liege—I only— It's my job to help you. To support you. That's all I meant to do."

The prince's hands had balled, but I could see, as I hadn't had the wits to back then, how my obvious distress affected him. He kept his arms at his sides and eased back half a step. He'd been angry, yes, but he hadn't intended to make me feel threatened. Even justifiably furious as he'd been, he'd noticed and cared.

"It's your job to help me *when I need it*," he said. "And I don't need that help in everything I do. Do you really believe I can't handle myself in a simple tournament?"

Merlin winced at that. "Of course I don't believe that. You know how much I respect your skills."

"Then you have to remember that some things I must do on my own. Even if you're capable of assisting me. Riding, fending off a foe, those are areas I can succeed in completely on my own. I *want* to do them myself. To know when I've won, it's fairly—that it was just *me*, not some supernatural helper as well."

The real argument had ended there. I'd bowed my head and said my apologies, and my prince had cuffed my head lightly and told me to never to do it again, and I hadn't. At least, except on the battlefield, where his life mattered more than his pride.

In the Pool of Turmoil, my past face pulled into a grimace. "You're such a fool, Arthur. You can't ever see what's right in front of you."

I did not like the direction that comment seemed to be going in. I grasped Darton by the elbow. "Okay, we're veering into nightmare territory now. I'd rather avoid a repeat of the last encounter with various blades."

"What is that supposed to mean?" the prince snapped, advancing on Merlin. "What other secrets have you been keeping?"

Merlin's shoulders tensed. His chin jerked up. "None that you've earned the right to know."

Dear light, I did not want to see this. I swiveled, queasiness burning in my throat, and to my relief, Darton turned with me.

"Oh, shit," he said.

The ring and the stands I'd thought had faded away had sprung up again. And the spectators were streaming from their seats, waving their arms. With a pained whinny, one of the horses crashed through the thin white wall. A herd of stallions stampeded toward us, the tournament-goers gathering in a screaming mob behind them.

This time, I didn't need to drag Darton. As one body, we ran. I ducked my head, focusing only on the flight of my feet. And the sword. The sword with its distant glimmering that was humming a little louder with every step I took.

The currents of mist wavered and flickered with swaths of shadow and color. They dizzied me. Darton's feet skidded. I nearly fell at the jerk of his arm, but he caught me.

We paused for a moment, catching our breaths. We'd left the stampede—and our nightmarish argument—behind.

"Please tell me we're getting close," he said, a little hoarsely.

"Clos*er*, anyway, I think." I closed my eyes in an effort to pin down my sense of Excalibur even more firmly. The glint of its presence danced against my eyelids and tickled through my breaths. "Just don't think. Don't think."

I set off in what felt like the right direction. Darton hurried along beside me. "Don't think," he murmured to himself, his expression strained. "Don't think. Don't think."

The shadowy ground beneath us dropped out abruptly. We both stumbled, our arms flying out. I jarred my shoulder against a lump I couldn't see. With a grimace, I pushed myself onto my knees.

Darton was getting up too. He steadied himself with his hands pressed flat to the invisible surface. His eyes clouded.

"It's cold," he whispered. "So *cold*."

"Darton!" I said, but he didn't stir. He was already too absorbed.

Darkness take us. I raised my head, bracing myself for whatever awful memory awaited us now.

CHAPTER TWENTY-TWO

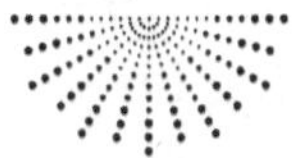

THE MISTS HAD CONDENSED into stone walls and pillars down the length of a massive, high-ceilinged room. It was empty—so empty the silence rang in my ears. An impression of thin sunlight streaked through the narrow, arched windows. My lungs clenched. I knew what I was going to see before I'd even turned my gaze toward the head of the room.

A large marble coffin sat on the floor, its closed lid carved with vines and figures around a blazing sun in its center. No one was around, but the silence was just the prelude to the funeral about to begin.

Arthur and I had been here in this moment, in our real history, but there was no sign of our past selves now.

Darton took a few hesitant steps toward the coffin. His feet thudded against the tiled floor. His hands balled at his sides and opened again, over and over.

"Father," he said.

I hurried after him. "Nothing good can come out of this. We should keep moving." *You don't need to live through this moment again.*

I remembered the real moment far too well, even after fifteen centuries. Edging along behind my prince as he'd walked up to the coffin. The wrench of my heart as he'd dropped to his knees and pressed his forehead to its side. The stuttered breaths as he'd tried to master his emotions.

The sickness had come on so fast. I still didn't know what had caused it or even what exactly it had been. But in the space of three days, the king had transformed from fit and able to a failing body heaving one final sigh. Leaving his son behind with a crown and a heaping of responsibilities he hadn't expected for years to come.

Arthur's strangled voice back then echoed in my mind. *I thought I'd have more time. There was still so much he wanted me to learn from him. So much I wanted him to see I could do.*

I had knelt beside him, not knowing what to say or do that would help, but feeling the need to show I was at least with him. Because he was revealing his pain to me. Because he trusted me enough that he hadn't hidden it—the way he would have to with every one of his subjects and the lords he ruled over when they poured in to pay their respects.

He'd shifted sideways to lean against me, and I'd raised my hand to squeeze his shoulder. For the first time, I'd felt as though I might be the stronger one, just this once. And he was letting me be. So I'd better do the best job of it I could.

He's gone back to the world that made him, I'd said haltingly. *He'll see everything you want him to. And you have your memories and his example to learn from. He knew that you were ready. I saw it, before he passed. He was more proud of you than anything else he's accomplished.*

Arthur had made a sound like a sob he'd tried to swallow. He'd rubbed his hand over his face and pulled away from me. But as he'd stood up, he'd grasped my hand in his and let himself meet my eyes even though his were reddened. *Thank you, Merlin.*

Here and now, I didn't for a second believe the Pool of Turmoil planned to show us that painful but poignant exchange. And I *really* didn't want to find out what it did have in store to replace it.

Darton had stopped moving, but he was still staring at the coffin. He must be caught up in his own memories again. I gripped his shoulder as I had then.

"Darton, we can talk about your father and his death another time. Out of here. Soon, if you want. But right now you know all that matters is— "

The lid of the coffin shifted with a grating sound. My voice died in my throat. Darton's back went rigid. We both gaped as the lid slowly, steadily rasped to the side, leaving a dark gap at the top of the coffin.

My heart thudded hard against my ribs, but I couldn't force words from my throat. There was a rustle, and a figure pushed through that gap.

Not just any figure. Arthur's father. It was the king's *corpse* that rose from that cold coffin. And not the body that would have lain there on that early day, but one with ragged rotting skin and hollows for eyes and fingers of bone dotted with only fragments of flesh. His formal robes drooped from his hunched frame, little more than stained rags. A stink of putrid decay wafted off of him.

He shuffled forward and swung a patchy leg over the side of the coffin. Stepping toward us. A low, wounded sound broke from Darton's mouth. His hand leapt out to grasp my arm. The contact startled me out of my daze.

"Let's *go*," I hissed, and jerked the arm he was clutching. Darton turned on swaying legs, but he followed me.

"God," he muttered under his breath. "God."

"You!" the dead king cried out behind us in a broken caw of a voice. "The wizard. I know you. I know what you did—and what you didn't. You couldn't wait to see me pass away so you could stand at the top by my son's side, could you? All that magic and you really couldn't find a way to cure me? You let me die. I know it."

Oh, darkness take me. This wasn't just Arthur's nightmare. It had latched on to my insecurities and regrets too.

"Don't listen to him," I said, urging us on down the long room that was starting to feel as if it had no end. A lump of guilt rose in my throat, but I ignored it.

My guilt had always been for Arthur, for failing him, not for any purposeful wrongdoing. *I* knew that, no matter what that nightmare tried to claim. I put my hand over Darton's. "I tried everything I could. I gave years of my life into all the magic that might have made a difference. I'd have given more if I'd thought of something else that might have worked."

"I know," Darton said. "It's just this place, doing what it does. There's nothing—"

He yelped and jerked around. Somehow the king was right behind us now, his bony hand clamped around Darton's other wrist. He loomed so close the fetid smell of his body clogged my nose. My stomach turned.

"You relied on this boy too much," the corpse rasped. "You let him take on responsibilities that should have been yours, shoulder burdens you should have been strong enough to carry alone. A king needs no one to prop him up. No one to hold his hand."

"Let *go* of me," Darton snapped, yanking at his arm, but the whites of his eyes shone with terror.

The king leaned even closer, his face only inches from this incarnation of his son's. "It's unhealthy. Unnatural. I am ashamed to even think—"

"Enough!" I slammed my fist down on the corpse's wrist. The bones shattered, the hand releasing Darton's wrist to thump onto the floor. The dead king shrieked and lashed out at Darton with his other hand, but we were already staggering away. Darton's mouth was clamped tight as if he were fighting the urge to vomit. I wouldn't have blamed him if he'd given in to it.

"Stop right there!" the king yelled after us. "You must listen. You never listened to me enough, my son. Not when it mattered."

"Just keep running," I said to Darton. Then I raised my head and my own feet skidded to a halt.

"Merlin."

A different figure blocked our way in the other direction. A figure tall and broad-shouldered, with a mane of tawny hair and burnished red-brown skin. I'd have said my father—the father of my first birth—looked as if he were glowing, but that wouldn't be completely accurate. He literally was glowing. Light seeped through his skin and blazed from his eyes. It seared over my face as it touched me. Darton sucked in a breath.

"Who—"

"You," Eóghan boomed at me. "Child. You never listened half as much as you should have. Look at you—tied to him in mind, heart, and soul. It's a disgrace on your kind."

His soul, heart, and mind were long dispersed into the light in reality. But even though my supposed father's words merely echoed the dead kings and I knew it wasn't really him, I couldn't stop the retort from leaping from my lips. "My kind is humans as well as light fae. As you well know. As you arranged to be the case. You *wanted* me this way."

"You were to *watch*." He slashed his hand through the air. "To learn. From a *distance*. You can't fix a disaster if you're so tangled up in it you no longer know where you begin and end."

The dead king was catching up with us again, his legs moving far faster than any body that looked like his had the right to do. "Never were strong enough. Never were smart enough," he was muttering, his hollow eye sockets fixed on Darton.

Darton squeezed his eyes shut. His fingers clutched at mine. "No."

I tugged him with me. We whirled together and ran to the side of the room, away from the ghosts intent on haunting us. Where were the sodding *doors*?

Both of our fathers kept pace, gliding over the stones with a hissing whisper that made all the hairs on my limbs stand on end.

"You ruined everything I'd worked for, centuries and centuries," mine was shouting now. "You'll bring about the downfall of both our peoples."

"Maybe I could have done a better job if you'd told me everything you actually knew," I shot back.

"I don't believe you," Darton was saying to the dead king, but his voice was shaking. "I don't. Shut up."

The ground tilted beneath our feet. I scrambled to keep hustling forward. Darton lurched. Our hands broke apart. I snatched after him, and the floor listed again. Trying to throw us backward to our pursuers.

And what would happen to us if they caught us?

"We're getting overwhelmed," I said to Darton. "We're letting them affect us too much—we're sabotaging ourselves. We have to drown them out."

The last word had barely slipped from my mouth when the room around us fell away. The floor swung up at a sharp angle. The walls crumbled away into dust around us, and shadows poured down from above. Darton and I both fell, jarring against the now-uneven tiles, and slid downward.

"No!" I caught Darton's wrist. In the darkness below us, the dead king reached up and grabbed his ankle. My heart squeezed. I let myself skid a little farther and kicked at the corpse's face with all my might.

The dead king plummeted—but so did we. I threw my arm across Darton's back, groping for some sort of hold with my other hand. We bumped and rolled down and down until wind started to whistle around us.

Darton's voice carried through it. He'd been murmuring, but now the words rose up.

"We're here for the sword. We're here for the sword. We're here for the sword."

Drown them out, I'd said. The words our fathers had said, the emotions latching onto us. I gulped air and joined him.

"We're here for the sword. We're here for the sword. We're here for the sword."

Our voices ringing out together sounded ridiculous, like a schoolyard chant. But as I shouted out the words again, focusing my mind back on that shining image of Excalibur, my fingers caught on a ridge in the surface beneath us. I clutched it, clinging to Darton at the same time.

"We're here for the sword. We're here for the sword."

My throat already felt hoarse. I didn't dare stop. Darton hefted himself a little farther up by another notch in the slanted floor. We heaved and scrambled, panting between recitations. And then the tiles cracked apart.

We thumped down onto the solid, invisible ground we'd walked on before. The mists had closed in around us. I swayed and caught my balance with Darton's elbow. He laughed for a second before resuming the chant.

"We're here for the sword."

His eyes caught mine with a triumphant gleam that shone past the stress marked across his face. I found myself smiling back, despite everything, as I repeated the words alongside him.

The sword. The sword. The tug inside me pulled harder. I veered right, and then left. The hazy currents parted around us, never letting us see more than a few feet ahead.

Then my toes jarred against something hard. I stopped, bracing myself, and looked up.

A laugh jolted out of me. Of course. How fitting. I was standing at the foot of a boulder nearly as high as my shoulders. And protruding from its bulging head was a broadsword glinting with light fae magic.

The sword in the stone.

I didn't think the dark fae that had sent it here had done so with any sense of humor, but that only made it funnier to me.

"Is that it?" Darton said, breathless. "Excalibur?"

"The one and only. We made it." I laughed again, with relief this time.

At the same moment, a hulking shape reared up over the hilt of the sword, and I realized we weren't finished here after all.

CHAPTER TWENTY-THREE

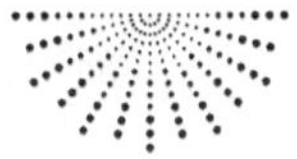

THE SHADOWY CREATURE towered over us. A crackling hiss carried from its mouth. I could barely make out its form through the mists, but what I could see was long and snakelike, with a flicker of a forked tongue.

Darton had tensed beside me. "What the hell is that?"

"Nothing good. But we have the sword now. You can handle anything with that."

I hoped.

The creature's head dipped lower, its hiss becoming more of a snarl. A narrow, scaly face, mottled gray and green like the mossy rocks around the pool, protruded from the haze. A fanned ruff twitched from its jaw up to its eyes, which were glossy black and narrowed at us. It bared an incredible number of jagged teeth in its gaping mouth.

Well, technically we didn't have the sword yet. I'd have felt a lot better facing that thing if Darton had been holding it in his hand instead of looking at it lodged halfway deep in that boulder.

Darton edged to the side, his gaze darting between the snake-dragon and the sword. The creature's head wove back and forth as if it were deciding which of us to lunch on first.

"Hold!" a low, frigid voice called out. The beast stilled. A figure that was little more than a silhouette appeared within the mist.

"Hello, Merlin. It took you long enough to make it this far. I've gotten bored."

My chest tightened. "Rhedyn," I said, not fully needing the confirmation.

I couldn't make out her features, but I heard her smirk in her intake of breath. Her physical form wasn't really here, I could tell now—only a projection of her presence. No doubt her corporeal body was skulking around in the Darkest One's cave still.

"Did you think I wouldn't know you were here from the moment you set foot on my ground?"

"I hardly think this entire country is yours."

"Mmm, we'll see. She's eager to return, you know. Our greatest one. I think she'll take everything she can, and that will be plenty."

The dark fae could be just as irritatingly vague as the light when they took a mind to be. But Rhedyn wasn't my concern right now anyway. We'd come here for the sword, and we'd leave with it, no matter what I had to do. That task felt even more urgent now that I could see she was apparently very keen to stop us from completing it.

"All that power and you're still afraid of one little blade," I remarked, and caught Darton's gaze. I twitched my eyes toward the sword, hoping he'd take my cue. We might as well make a grab for it while Rhedyn's pet was holding back. He backed up a step.

"The dark does not feel *afraid*," Rhedyn muttered. "Light fades. Darkness remains."

"So your kind is always telling me," I said, sidestepping to give Darton more room for his run at the boulder. "And yet here I remain."

"Not for long." Her voice slithered silky sharp from the mists. "The monster I summoned is eager to play with you. And as you can probably guess, he likes to play rough. I thought he was particularly fitting for this situation, don't you?"

I had no idea what she meant by that, but I didn't much care. We were going to have to kill the thing either way.

"If you say so. It'd have been a lot more interesting if you'd made the trip in person, you know. I've got a few things—"

Darton lunged at the boulder. His football player muscles served him well. He hefted himself up with a few quick jerks and grasped the hilt of the sword.

"Kill them!" Rhedyn snapped. Her shadowy form dissolved into the haze, and the snake-dragon attacked.

"Darton!" I called out in instinctive warning. The creature's head swung toward him, and he heaved at the sword.

It didn't budge from the boulder. I swore under my breath and snatched a twig from my pocket. I didn't know how my magic would react to this place, but I was quite certain of how Darton's vital organs would react to having all those fangs sunk into him.

"*Blast and back*," I shouted. A surge of wind smacked into the snake-dragon's face, but the mists drained away the impact. It barely flinched. I accomplished at least one goal, though. Its neck veered to the side as it focused its attention on me.

"Come on, damn it," Darton muttered. He wrenched at the sword again, and I thought I saw it shift an inch. What was the matter with the sodding thing?

The beast snapped at me. I leapt to the side just in time to avoid losing my head. My purse bumped against my back. I had a wand in my pocket and more in the purse, but after the puny effect my first attempt at a spell had provided, I wasn't in much of a hurry to waste them. If I could just keep the thing distracted until Darton got a handle on the sword...

The creature slithered around the boulder, revealing a tapering body supported in the front by two taloned feet. It swiped one of those sets of enormous claws through the air toward me. I threw myself backward with a wince at the snap of ripped fabric.

Shredded jeans had never been one of my favorite fashion choices.

Darton was still struggling with the sword. He swiveled, presumably aiming for a better angle, and the creature's spiked tail whipped toward him.

"Art!" I gasped out, too late. He flinched to the side, but the spikes caught him in the shoulder, hurling him off the boulder. He hit the ground with a thump and just barely tossed his arm up in time to shield his head. Blood bloomed across his shoulder and back where the spikes had dug in.

My pulse stuttered. The snake-dragon reared again, the fans of skin around its face rustling menacingly, and my mind went blank. Before I knew what I planned to do, I was leaping at the boulder myself.

I was no athlete, but I wasn't a total wimp. My fingers latched onto the nooks and crevices. "*Cast me far, cast me up,*" I whispered to the air beneath me, and that last shove was all I needed. I scrambled onto the lumpy top of the boulder.

The creature's head jerked toward me. I curled my fingers around Excalibur's hilt. "Em!" Darton called from below, as much a protest as a warning, but this wasn't the best moment for a debate about whose job retrieving the sword was.

The tingling of familiar magic—*my* magic—seeped into my palms from the hilt like a hello. So the sword recognized me too. Light willing, that was a good sign. I dragged in a breath and hauled at it with all my strength.

The blade slid free from the stone with a thin humming like metal scraped over smooth glass. I felt relieved for the instant it took before my body registered the weight of the thing in my hands. A broadsword was no amateur's dagger. Five pounds of hammered steel dragged at my unpracticed arms as I fumbled with it, nearly tipping me right back off the boulder.

It knew me, but the magic that had made it sing in my king's grasp didn't work for me. It was his soul, the link I'd forged, that powered it. So why hadn't it let him retrieve it?

No time for worrying about that now. The snake-dragon chomped at me. I managed to swing the sword in a clumsy arc between the creature and me. At the flash of the blade, it jerked to the side. Then its clawed foot slashed out at me.

I ducked and swiveled, but two of the talons cut across my arm. The sword's weight pulled me off balance. I teetered and half slid, half fell down the side of the boulder.

Darton had shoved himself to his feet. The sleeve of his jacket was streaked with red from the cuts on his shoulder, but his jaw was set hard. His fingers clutched the hilt of the light fae dagger.

The snake-dragon whipped around the boulder, intent on me. Darton leapt between me and it as I scrambled up. He sliced the dagger at the beast's face. The blade nicked its muzzle—it winced and bobbed its head with an angry hiss.

"The sword!" I shoved Excalibur toward him and fumbled for my purse. I had to have *something* in there that would help.

My hand closed around a clump of twigs. Darton heaved the immense sword off the ground. Even through the padding of his jacket, I could see the bulge of his arms as he took on its weight. He was strong, but his muscles had been built by football skirmishes, not wielding heavy lengths of metal. It would take more training before he handled any large sword smoothly.

And this sword still wasn't responding to him as its master. He jabbed it at the snake-dragon, but the creature just dodged and sprang at us again. I gritted my teeth against the pain stinging through my arm and thrust my handful of twigs toward the beast.

"Darkness begone!"

A burst of light flared from the twigs—and shattered against the mist drifting around us. Crackles of it echoed back at us, nicking my skin. The snake-dragon let out a sputter that sounded more like a sneeze than any real discomfort. Then it lunged its jaws toward Darton again.

He managed to smack the flat of Excalibur's blade against its nose hard enough to make it recoil, but he staggered backward a few steps too. Blood was still seeping down his shoulder. Without the magical connection and those years of training his former self had experienced, he wasn't going to have the agility he needed to make a killing blow. And I already knew I couldn't handle the sodding thing any better.

My grasping fingers dug deeper into my purse. Their tips brushed something... fluffy?

The rabbit skin. I'd tucked it and the amber stone in while I was packing, just in case I had the chance to continue my experiments.

Well, I couldn't think of a better time to experiment than now. It was either that or resign ourselves to being dinner.

I dragged out the rabbit skin, shoved it into my weaker hand, and fumbled for the amber. The snake-dragon gnashed its teeth and took another swipe at Darton with its claws. They clanged against the sword he'd raised to block them just in time. Darton's mouth had twisted with determination, but I could see the frustration creeping through his expression all the same.

I pushed myself upright and rammed stone and skin together. Before I'd had the chance to rub them more than once, the snake-dragon's gaze swept toward me. As if recognizing the threat I was about to pose, it smacked a taloned foot toward me.

I flinched backward, but one of its claws snagged on the rabbit skin. A yelp of protest broke from my throat as it wrenched the tool I'd been counting on away. I snatched after it, and the beast swiveled abruptly. The spikes of its tail whipped toward us.

Darton and I scrambled away, Darton panting but still clutching the sword. I glanced at him to check his shoulder, and my eyes caught on the ruff of his hood. My heart leapt.

"The fur on your jacket," I said. "Is it real?"

Darton's gaze jerked to me. "*What?*"

"Never mind. Just hold still. Unless you need to whack that thing." If it wasn't real, then this simply wouldn't work.

I grasped his hood and slammed the amber against it, rubbing furiously. Sparks crackled beneath the stone. A grin split my face.

"We've got this," I said, and turned to glower at the snake-dragon. "Come on, you ugly piece of cattle sod. Give us the best you've got!"

"Um, are you really sure that's a good idea, Em?" Darton said as the creature lunged around.

"Just stab it as hard as you can. The aim doesn't even matter."

He sucked in his breath and hefted Excalibur. The snake-dragon sprang. I whipped the amber against the fur ruff one last time and then snapped it against Darton's hand, just as he thrust the sword forward.

Electricity sizzled from me to him and up the blade. Excalibur lit with a flickering glow, and Darton plunged it into the snake-dragon's muzzle.

The blade sliced clean through the flesh. The sparks burst through the creature's body. It gave a wrenching cry as its limbs shuddered. Then it collapsed in a smoking heap beside the boulder.

Darton stared down at it, his breaths coming raggedly. The light washed out of the sword, burning away the dark blood that had stained the blade as it went. In an instant, it looked as if it held no magic at all.

CHAPTER TWENTY-FOUR

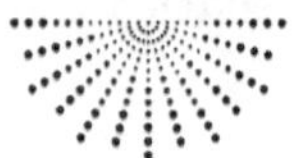

"There they are!" Eric hollered. I raised my head as I pulled myself over the last ridge of the rocky hills, and saw him and Mavis running over from the pool of solar light around the van. A sigh stuttered out of me. I wanted to sink down right there and let them carry me the rest of the way, but I did have a bit of a pride left, however small.

Darton paused beside me to wipe the sweat from his brow. The left sleeve of his jacket was soaked with blood from shoulder to elbow now, but he'd refused to release his grip on Excalibur. Hadn't even used the damned sword as a walking stick, as I'd have been tempted to do. But his face was nearly as pale as his knuckles where his fingers gripped the hilt, and I'd caught him swaying more than once during what had felt like the longest walk of my life.

At least the mists hadn't badgered us with any more warped memories leaving the pool. Excalibur had parted all those tumultuous emotions with a simple swipe here and there.

"My goodness, look at the two of you," Mavis said, and that was before her gaze fell on Arthur's shoulder. Her eyes widened. "Come on, come on, the both of you. Let's get you patched up before you bleed yourselves dry." She put her arm around Darton's back to lead him the rest of the way down the slope, ignoring his wordless protest.

"You didn't fare much better," Eric remarked to me, offering his own arm.

"I'm all right," I said. I didn't need the assistance, but I might have taken his elbow just for the break if I hadn't noticed the twitch of Darton's jaw. I waved Eric off and trudged the rest of the way by my own power.

The cuts on my arm were shallower than Darton's. I'd twisted the sleeve of my jacket to cover them, and only a little blood had managed to seep through. They still hurt like nettles dug under my skin, though. I'd have sealed his and mine with magic if I'd felt I could do that without collapsing, which wouldn't have done either of us any good for the trip back here.

In the stored daylight beaming from the van, my spirits revived just slightly. Enough that I could resist the urge to slump against its side as Mavis tutted over Darton's wound and then my own. She had strips of linen in the van which she wrapped around his back and shoulder and then my forearm, folded tight to reduce the bleeding.

"We'll take proper care of you back at the house," she said. "No arguments. That's where we're going now. You're not in any condition to be taking on more villains like this."

I wasn't sure I'd even been going to argue. I hadn't slept properly since what felt like at least a year ago, back in the other side of the ocean. The weariness filled my head, sloshing through my thoughts as if I'd been dunked in that ocean. A little sleep, and *I* could take care of us.

"House sounds good," I offered.

Eric cocked his head at Darton as Darton hauled himself into the van, pulling Excalibur after him. "That is *quite* the sword, mate."

Darton gave him a crooked smile that looked more pained than pleased. "Yes. Yes, it is."

The fae hunters' house, like Jagger's and the one I'd had modeled on his, stood off by itself on an isolated patch of land. Because this was England and closer in climate to our Pacific Northwest than Jagger's desert, like us they'd paved the yard around the house to eliminate shadows cast by grass or weeds, a sight that inexplicably pleased me.

The house itself looked slightly more homey than either back home: A chimney poked from its roof, and the sides of the building looked like wood. When we walked by, I touched one slat and realized it was actually ceramic.

"My mother believes that practical doesn't have to mean dreary," Eric said with an upward twitch of his lips.

The inside of the place looked like I'd have expected a stereotypical English cottage to, other than the absence of windows. Knickknacks cluttered the varnished shelves, and cushions lay across an array of oaken furniture. The kitchen, where Mavis insisted Darton and I sit for further tending to, smelled like fresh baked bread. I started to wonder if I'd fainted on the way back and this was all just a pleasant dream.

We unwound the hasty bandages and peeled off our jackets. The sting of my cuts confirmed that I was in fact fully awake. Darton sucked in a sharp breath as Mavis dabbed disinfectant over the gouges on his shoulder.

"I'm going to have to do some stitching on these," she said. "With your permission."

He set his jaw. "If they're that bad, go ahead."

Eric had been left to look after me, I supposed because I was the less urgent case. He grabbed the disinfectant from his mother and gave me a flash of a grin as he poured some out onto a clean cloth. "I'm only hurting you because I care."

I rolled my eyes at him. "Just get it over with."

He cupped one hand around my elbow as he wiped the cloth over the rents in my forearm. The sting prickled deeper, but it was bearable. His fingers squeezed reassuringly for a second before he let me go.

"I hate to see what the other guy looked like when you two were through with him."

My mind leapt back to the smoking mass of the snake-dragon. "Not great. We were thorough."

Eric chuckled. "I'll bet you were. No point doing a thing unless it's done right." Then he winked at me.

Darton cleared his throat. Mavis had just tied off her last stitch, but I had the feeling the tension in his face was in reaction to more than just her needle. "What's our next move, Em?" he asked.

I frowned as I considered. My head was still swimming with fatigue. He couldn't feel much better. And he wasn't likely to find his connection to the sword while exhausted and in pain.

"We'll work out how to confront Rhedyn tomorrow. It's no good rushing in when we can barely stand up." I turned to Mavis. "I assume this place has plenty of protections against dark kind."

She nodded. "It'd take a lot of effort to get in here. We're happy to put you up for the night. I already made up the spare beds downstairs."

"Downstairs?" My gaze dropped to the floor. Basements and avoiding darkness generally didn't mix.

She smiled. "The outer walls all through this place are two-layered. And in between the layers we stream stored sunlight against reflectors all night. You'll be secure enough down there, don't you worry."

"Of course," Eric said, "I happen to think *my* bed is super comfortable. And it's got room for two. Just pointing that out."

His mother cut a glance toward him, and he grinned easily. I wasn't even sure how much he meant the flirty advances. "Thank you, Prince Charming," I said. "But I do actually want to sleep."

"Well, if you change your mind, I'm down that hall to the left." He pointed.

Darton stood up abruptly. "She isn't going to be keeping you company tonight. Or any other night." His voice had gone harsh.

"Whoa, there!" Eric said, taking a step back with his hands up. "I didn't mean to step on any toes."

I touched Darton's arm, meeting his eyes for a second before I looked at Eric. "It's fine. But I don't think we're in much of a mood for joking around right now, after what we've just been through. We appreciate the hospitality given."

Nonetheless, Eric apparently felt it wiser to hang back while Mavis led us down to the basement sleeping quarters. Possibly he was right in that decision. Darton stayed close by my side as Mavis pointed to the foldout couch in the open main room and the twin bed in the smaller guest room beside it.

"I was figuring Emma would take the guest room, what with girls generally preferring their privacy more, but really the arrangement is up to you," she said. "There are some drinks and snacks in the fridge if you get peckish. But I think sleep is what you need the most now. I'll leave you to it."

The stairs creaked as she headed up. I rubbed my eyes. My stomach twinged, but we'd gobbled down some of the fae hunters' stash of energy bars on the drive to the house. That should hold me until morning.

I drifted over to the guest room door—and Darton followed. When I stopped in the doorway to give him a questioning look, he touched my shoulder. His gaze held mine, intent with some purpose I didn't guess until he spoke.

"Em," he said, and his voice was so thick with a different sort of hunger that my knees turned wobbly. His other hand rose to cup my cheek. He stepped so close my nose would have brushed his if I'd turned my head even slightly.

My breath caught in my throat. The familiar smell of him, warm and musky, drifted over me. I managed to keep my own voice steady. "Yeah?"

"Tell me you aren't even a little interested in that joker upstairs."

I gave a hitch of a laugh. "I couldn't be less interested. The only bed I'm at all inclined to be in right now is that one over there."

His thumb traced my lower lip. "Are you 'inclined' to have anyone join you there?"

I swallowed hard. It was so hard to think straight, to remember the lines I'd drawn and intended to hold, with him so *there*, touching me, wanting me. Harder still when I was so tired of fighting so many battles. I wanted him. I always did.

Maybe this was one of those times when the rest of my concerns didn't matter. I didn't think his proposition was just about him and me. His sword had rejected him. He was battered and wounded, inside as well as out. And now he had come to me.

How could I turn him away too? I could give him this, ease that hurt, even if it hurt me later.

"No one but you," I said.

Darton let out a ragged chuckle and pulled my mouth to his.

There was nothing gentle in his kiss. It demanded, claiming me. His lips worked mine apart, and his tongue swept in to meet mine. I melted into it, into him.

He groaned, his fingers tangling in my hair, and kissed me harder. His body pressed mine against the doorframe. I could feel him, every inch of him, including the hot length already hard against my thigh. His hands swept up under my shirt to caress my breasts. I whimpered into his mouth.

He dropped one arm to my waist to tug me away from the doorframe and shoved the door closed with his foot. I nudged him toward the bed. He pulled me with him, guiding me down to straddle his lap as he sat. The bandage on my arm shifted slightly as he freed me from my shirt, but I barely had time to wince before his mouth closed over my breast. The wash of pleasure chased every other sensation away.

His tongue worked over the nipple, drawing a moan from deep in my chest. I arched against him instinctively, seeking the pressure of his hardness between my legs—wanting it without all those layers of fabric still between us. Darton grasped my hip, matching my rocking rhythm with another groan. He turned his attentions to my other breast. Then he swung us around and flipped us over.

My head hit the pillow, and he sank over me, catching my mouth with his again. My hand trailed down his chest. It ventured over the hard-on bulging against the fly of his jeans. Darton gasped and bucked into my hand. Wanting. *Needing.* I curled my fingers around him, sliding them up and down against the thick fabric. He ducked his head against my shoulder.

"Em," he muttered. "God. You have no idea." He sucked in a stutter of breath, and every muscle in my body froze.

The sound drew up the memory of a similar one to a few hours ago. That suppressed snicker when he'd watched me—the first me, the me that should have mattered the most—watching him, my prince, my to-be-king, with open adoration. *Mooning like a schoolgirl with a crush. If I didn't know better...*

Darton had gone still over me. "Em?" he said. My throat constricted at the nickname. I could tell myself when he said it he was thinking of my real name, but right now... Right now he was only thinking Emma. Because he'd laughed to imagine Merlin could ever have wanted this, or wanted it with any hope of those feelings being returned.

Nausea churned in my stomach. I scooted out from under Darton and away to the side of the bed. My shirt was lying on the floor. I grabbed it, needing something to cover me. To make me feel a little less naked, even if my agony was written all over my face.

"We can't do this," I said. "I'm sorry. We just can't."

Darton sat back on the bed. His head bowed. He took one

ragged breath and another, as if he were struggling to get himself back under control.

"If it's that you don't really want to—that you don't really want me—you should just say so," he said in a low voice, still not looking at me.

A choked laugh escaped me. "It's not *that*. I've told you—"

"I know," he broke in. "But we keep doing this back and forth anyway. All kinds of dark fae know where I am. There's obviously no getting away from them. So it can't be just about how 'woken up' I am. I wish you'd just tell me the truth."

I didn't know how to deal with the rush of emotion that surged up inside me. Some of it was frustration that he sounded so wounded, that he was making this all about *him* and his insecurities when I—

And that was the other thing. *Tell me the truth.* The very thought of doing that, of admitting out loud what I hardly liked to let myself think, made my gut twist into a massive knot.

"Darton..."

He shook his head. "Don't tell me it's okay. Don't tell me it's nothing. I know something's wrong."

I swallowed hard, pulling my shirt all the way on. The way I'd kept quiet so long was ridiculous, wasn't it? I'd been nagging Keevan to speak up to Izzy about his feelings, while here I'd hidden my own for fifteen hundred sodding years.

Maybe it was time. Because who knew how much time we even had left.

I stood up and turned to face him. My arms instinctively rose to hug myself. "You want the truth?" I said.

Darton looked up at me. "Yeah. Please." But his body had tensed. He was bracing, because he was so sure that truth would be horrible.

Of course, in his mind it might be.

My fingers dug into my elbows. I closed my eyes for a second, drawing up the courage to put the words into speech. Then I opened them again to gaze straight into his. My voice came out ragged.

"The truth is I have loved you, utterly, always. From that very first life until now. And you—you have only loved *me* some of the time. Generally dependent on what body I happened to be inhabiting at that moment."

Darton's lips parted silently. He stared at me, apparently lost for words. I made myself hold his gaze.

"It *is* okay," I said, even though my throat had gone hoarse. "I feel what I feel. You feel what you feel—or don't. It's no one's fault. But I have to—I have to draw the line somewhere, for my own sake."

"Em." The nickname came out in a rasp. He didn't seem to know what else to say, still.

I let my arms drop to my sides. "I'm going to be here for you as I always have been. I'm going to do whatever I can to save you and to serve you after I have. You don't have to worry about that. But this"—I motioned to the bed—"wrenches my heart around too much. I shouldn't have let myself try. I'm sorry." I backed up a step. "We should both get some sleep. I can take the other bed."

I walked out, shutting the door behind me.

CHAPTER TWENTY-FIVE

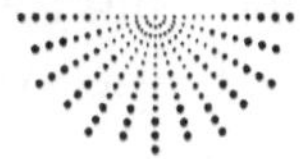

I flinched awake on the pullout couch, my heart thudding in alarm. For the first few seconds, that racing beat was the only sound I could hear. Had it been a nightmare that had woken me, and not some actual threat? I inhaled slowly, willing my pulse to slow—and a skittering sound carried through the wall beside me.

I pushed off the mattress, snatching up the wand I'd left close at hand. An eerie warbling rose and fell all around the room. The hairs on my arms rose. I didn't like the sound of *that* at all.

Something had found us. And given who we were and what we were here to do, I felt pretty certain it wasn't anything good.

Swinging my purse over my shoulder, I hurried to the bedroom door. I pushed it open with a purposeful thump. Darton startled out of his own undoubtedly restless sleep. He blinked at me.

"What's—"

He hesitated, and I saw the memory of our last conversation in the tensing of his expression, the twitch of his eyes. There wasn't time to hash out that awkwardness now.

"Come on," I said. "Something's here. I don't know what, but I think we'd better find out."

"Right. Right."

He threw off the blanket. Like me, he'd opted to sleep fully clothed, probably remembering how many hasty escapes we'd needed to make in the past. Just as well that I wasn't faced with any more bare skin than that.

I jerked my head toward the stairs, and he followed. The noises grew louder as we climbed the steps. We emerged onto the first floor to a wavering groan, a hiss, and then a piercing shriek.

Lights beamed all through the rooms, but the kitchen and living room stood empty. The front door hung ajar. A human-sounding shout carried through the gap. I pulled another wand from my purse, gripping two at once, and nudged the door farther open.

A ring of electric light hazed the concrete yard outside, ending several feet past the edges of the house. The space beyond it was choked with pre-dawn darkness. A darkness that moved. Shadow creatures shaped like all manner of animals stalked along it, their shapes rippling across the border of the light.

"Eric, bird, ten o'clock!" Mavis's voice hollered from around the side of the building. A dark hawk-like shape dove down from above, jittering as it passed through the light but holding together —until a burst of flame shot up, engulfing it.

A panther-like beast leapt at the door where I was standing. I whipped my arm out automatically. *"Darkness begone."*

Its shadowy form spasmed and vanished. My fingers stayed clutched tight around the wands. The building's light defenses weren't holding the dark creatures back completely anymore. And I knew from past experience that it was only a matter of time before they found some other way to turn the tables on us.

Mavis came running into view. She pressed a button on the bulky metal device she was holding, and a flare of fire hissed from its mouth. It seared across a serpentine creature that had been darting toward the house.

"What's wrong with the lights?" I called to her.

She whirled, her jaw tight. "It's been too long with too little sun. The solar panels didn't draw enough to hold us with sun power all through the night. We're running off the back-up generator now —and some of these vermin are apparently strong enough to brave that."

Swine crud. I glanced at the sky, but not a hint of dawn had tinged the clouds yet. And even once it came, it would take time before the panels gathered enough sunlight to bring the lights to full power. The rain was holding off for the moment, but the air was damp and heavy. The dark fae's conjured storm wasn't over yet.

Rhedyn must have sent these creatures after us as soon as she'd realized her snake-dragon hadn't done the trick. Or else—

My pulse stuttered. I shut my eyes for a second to tune out everything except my internal senses and reached out with my awareness to the south. If the Darkest One was already free...

No. The chill I'd been braced for didn't come. No sense of her unbound presence leaked across the countryside. She was still trapped—for however little time longer.

"It's our fault those things are here," Darton said where he stood just behind me. "Like at Jagger's place. We have to help fight them off."

I nodded, my mouth pressing flat. The last thing I wanted was a repeat of our experience at Jagger's house. The house he'd decided he had to blow to smithereens just to get us out safely.

"No more casualties on our watch," I said.

"Exactly."

At a shout from Eric, Mavis dashed back around the house. A second later, a winged creature that looked more like a pterodactyl than any living thing I'd ever seen in my lives swooped down toward the roof. I leapt forward, jabbing my wands upward.

"*Darkness begone.*"

Darton brushed past me. I spun around to tell him to stay back, and the warning caught in my throat.

He'd grabbed Excalibur from where he'd left it near the

basement door. The blade gleamed with unearthly power as he slashed it through the air at the edge of the light. He swung it as if it were part of his arm, part of him. The way he was meant to.

"Back!" he snapped at the dark rabble. "Get out of here, or I'll split you all apart."

He swept the sword toward them, and it cut through their shadowy bodies with a watery warble. The creatures hugging the fringes of the darkness scattered, several shattering at the touch of the enchanted blade. Darton sidestepped to press his advantage. A small smile crossed his face.

My heart squeezed, watching him find his rhythm. Watching the Arthur in him emerge. But I couldn't just stand around feeling pleased. This was my battle too.

I passed one of my wands to my other hand and strode closer to the edge of the light. Crossing my arms in front of my chest, I clenched my fingers around the sealed wood and pulled at the life energy inside it.

"Darkness begone."

I whipped my arms out in matching arcs. A blast of light rippled from the wands through the shadows. More dark creatures wavered and blinked away—but there were still far too many lurking around the more distant parts of the yard, lit up briefly by my attack.

Rhedyn hadn't bothered with glooms. Either she'd learned from the mercenary's mistakes or simply was wiser than him in the first place. The larger, more conscious dark creatures were wiser too. They weren't going to simply pour in at us in a mass for easy slaughtering. Now that we'd shown our power, they were regrouping where it would take much more power to reach them. Regrouping and considering the best way to outmaneuver us.

The wands had turned dead in my hands with the effort of my large-scale casting. I dropped them, and they broke into dust at my feet. I had a few more in my purse. More still in my suitcase back in the house. But I needed some of those to face Rhedyn. I had to be strategic too.

As if sensing my hesitation, the darkness around us shivered as a fresh wave of creatures slunk toward us. I dug out another wand. Eric loped over to join us, a flame-thrower fixed under his arm from a harness.

"Was that *you*, with the light?"

"Yep," I said. "And it looks like you might be about to get a firsthand demonstration." I eyed the creatures testing the edges of the light, wanting as many as possible close by before I drew on my magic again. The hiss of Mavis's flamethrower carried from behind the house. No, we weren't finished here yet.

Eric's head twitched toward the area where Darton was walking the fringe. Excalibur flashed as my king swung it through another beast that ventured too close. Eric's jaw dropped. "Holy shit. I'm starting to see why you went through all that trouble for that sword."

"Let's just hope between the bunch of us it's enough," I said.

The swarm of creatures was thickening. I took a step forward to increase my range. As I raised my hand, a rumble echoed across the sky. Thunder.

All the creatures in the yard flinched. They scattered in an aimless fashion for a moment before drawing back.

Oh. That was interesting. I should have realized. If a little static electricity could fry a gloom, how many of the dark rabble could a single lightning strike sear apart? I might be able to clear the whole area with just one more wand lost.

I raised my free hand toward the clouds, stretching higher with my senses. Up, up, toward those thickly congealed clouds. The weight of them pressed against me, stewing with gathered moisture. I nudged at them for any hint of a crackle.

But even as I brushed up against a tingle of electricity, the sensation pulled away from me. The clouds quivered and calmed, as if some other force had combed that building energy out of them. The taste of rot crept through my mouth.

Rhedyn's colleagues were working their magic even now. They didn't want a full-out storm interfering with their work. Without their presence, I might have summoned a lightning strike or two, but I didn't have the strength to push back against all of them.

One reincarnated half fae against who knew how many full—I didn't stand a chance, did I? I didn't have any chance at all.

The chill of that thought washed over me, and for an instant my mind simply froze.

"Emma!" Eric said.

I snapped back to the present, my hand automatically brandishing the wand. Eric was already flinging himself toward a pack of shadow creatures that had sprung at me in my momentary distraction.

Eric aimed his flame-thrower. The spurts of fire ripped through two of the creatures. The spell I spat out blasted through two more. But I hadn't been focused or had time to aim. The fifth, an immense hound-like beast, clamped its jaws around my forearm before I could speak another spell.

Cold seared through my flesh. I clamped my teeth against a cry and wrenched backward. The creature opened its mouth to take a deadlier chomp at me, but I was ready this time.

"*Darkness begone*," I gasped out with a flick of the wand. A spark of light flared around the hound. The hound's form crumpled in on itself and disappeared.

I staggered backward, clutching my wounded arm with my other hand to keep the wand steady. The dark creature's fangs had sunk straight through my sweater. I knew when I let myself look I'd find the skin marred with dead gray streaks to match the slashes I already carried from earlier encounters.

Footsteps thumped against the ground. Darton was rushing to my side, his face pale. I waved him back.

"We need you," I said. "You and that sword. We have to keep them back. I'm fine now."

"I can't..." He hefted Excalibur again, but not with the ease I'd seen just a minute ago. The muscles in his arms strained the way they had yesterday, when he'd stumbled with its weight. The blade's gleam had dimmed. What in sodding hell was going on?

"Just try. You've scared them plenty already." I pointed to the fringes. "It was working with you."

Darton's mouth tightened, but he nodded. He strode back to the edge of the fray, heaving the sword into the air as he went. But it was a clumsier motion now. The blade cut through the creatures pressing their advantage along the border of the light—and they only flinched away. The ordinary blade, without its magic activated, wasn't enough to end them.

Eric hurried forward too, blasting a few of the nearest creatures with flame, but it wasn't enough. We couldn't stop to figure out Darton's problem now. The next wave of the dark rabble's assault was still gathering.

But even as my fingers closed around the wand, an ache spread up my arm into my chest. It wasn't just Darton faltering. I was tiring out fast without the sun overhead to lend me more energy. We needed to end this fast, or we might not end it at all.

The dark creatures pushed forward again, and Darton stumbled back. He gripped the sword with both hands, his face set with the same anguished determination as when we'd faced the snake-dragon in the Pool of Turmoil.

But we'd gotten through that. Because we'd combined what powers we had.

I threw myself toward him. My first instinct was to reach for the amber stone I'd shoved back in my purse. But Darton hadn't bothered to pull on his jacket when he'd raced outside, and there weren't scraps of fur just lying around for my use.

Maybe that was for the best. I wasn't sure how to control the electricity all that well yet, and it would have taken quite a surge to blast it across the entire force around the house. I didn't want to hurt Mavis or Eric in the process.

I still had the light inside my wands and wound through the life inside my own body. Light that would sear apart the shadows but not our allies. Light Excalibur would respond to.

"Darton!" I set my hand on his shoulder. His muscles tensed at my touch. "We'll go at them like we attacked the thing in the pool. My magic and your sword's power, together. All right?"

He nodded, eyeing the creatures snapping at the fringes of the light. "What do you need me to do?"

"When you feel the energy coming, just swing the sword as wide as you can."

I thrust my hand into my purse, fumbling my fingers around all four of the wands I had left on hand. I might have to throw a year or two of my own life into the mix, but that was business as usual these days.

As I drew in my breath to cast the spell, a bear-like beast charged at us from the darkness. My heart lurched. I hardly had time to sputter out the ancient words.

"*Darkness all around be gone!*"

I grasped onto all the glittering energy I could catch hold of and propelled it through my body and down Darton's arm to the sword.

Sparks crackled behind my eyes. Excalibur lit up like a beacon. Darton was already slashing it through the air. The blaze of light that rippled off it whipped across the landscape around us like a sonic boom. Even soundless, it knocked the breath from my lungs.

Somewhere behind us, Eric gave a yelp, but at least it sounded startled rather than pained. All across the yard and on the fields now lit beyond, the creatures of the dark rabble crumpled and washed away.

Darton and I had been tired, and the shadowy animals were stronger than glooms, so it wasn't the thorough victory I'd been hoping for. But the scattered shapes that remained as the magical light hazed away staggered, limping, away. There weren't enough left that they were ready to attempt another attack, at least. And the new day's sun was just starting to tint the clouds along the horizon.

Darton lowered the sword. "They'll be back, won't they?"

"They will," I said. "And sooner rather than later. But I know what we need to do now."

He raised an eyebrow at me. "Oh yeah?"

I squeezed his shoulder briefly before releasing it. "We're going to get lightning on our side. And I know just who can help us gather it."

I also knew that they weren't going to be the slightest bit keen to pitch in, but I'd deal with that problem when we came to it.

CHAPTER TWENTY-SIX

SOMEHOW THE TRIP out to the secluded forestland we'd visited yesterday felt even lonelier this time. I peered past the sweep of the windshield wipers at the gloomy woods lining the narrow road. The tires of the car Mavis had lent Darton and me bumped over the ruts and stray rocks. The heating system was whirring away, but I felt as chilled as if I'd just stepped into the fall rain.

The drive was lonelier in a totally literal sense too. We'd left Mavis and Eric back at their house, which at least was in one piece and not a smoking ruin. When I'd asked Mavis about borrowing a vehicle, she'd smiled and said Jagger had warned her to make sure she had something extra on hand.

"I picked this up from a friend of ours in the business," she'd said, leading me to their garage at the back of the yard. "He is hoping to get it back."

"Well, I did manage to take decent care of Jagger's van," I'd told her. "And our track record with fae hunters here is already a lot better."

She'd shaken her head, bemused. "Are you sure the two of you should be going off alone? We committed to helping you through whatever you need to do to stop these fae."

I'd had to smile at her offer. "What we've got to do right now, I'm the only one who can handle it. But if we need your help again, believe me, I'll be in touch. If any other strange readings or whatever get passed on through your network, you give me a shout, okay?"

She'd nodded, and Eric had come over to shake hands and give me one of those jokingly flirty winks. Five minutes later we'd been on the road.

Now, Darton shifted in the passenger seat beside me. He had that sword in front of him, propped so the end of the blade rested on the floor and the hilt leaned against his chest. Every now and then he gripped the hilt and seemed to test it. His expression had been as clouded as the sky overhead for the entire drive.

"Are you sure this is our best option?" he said. "I got a bad feeling from those fae when we were out here before. They *really* didn't like me being around. Not that I think they'd hurt me or anything, but... Can we trust them?"

I grimaced. He didn't know the half of it. But I'd stashed my father's journals away in Mavis and Eric's house for safe-keeping, and I wasn't going to spill the beans about his vague worries to Darton now. "I know they were jerks. I don't like it—or them— either. But I think I can convince them to get on board for this one thing. And if they give their word, they'll keep it. We don't have a chance at pushing back against the dark fae on our own."

"But maybe we would if I could get this damned sword to work for me." Darton frowned at the blade. He hefted it again, careful not to gouge the dashboard, and his jaw tightened. "It doesn't feel right. It's like it doesn't *want* to cooperate."

"That's just how a regular broadsword feels," I said. "You'd have worked up to getting comfortable wielding over several years when you were training the first time. But if we can solidify your connection to the enchantment on it, that won't matter."

"If." He set the sword back down. "You were counting on me being able to do that from the start. You didn't think I'd have this much trouble."

"I had no idea what to expect. That sodding thing has been hanging out in the Pool of Turmoil for centuries. We'll figure it out."

Darton fell silent. He traced his thumb back and forth along the leather-wrapped grip of the hilt. He'd been quiet for a lot of the trip so far, but somehow this moment felt more ominous. As if the weight of the question he was working up to was leaking from him before he even opened his mouth. My fingers tensed against the steering wheel.

He inhaled slowly. "What you said last night," he said. "Was it true?"

When I hesitated, he glanced over at me, his gaze searching. A lump rose in my throat.

I could have dismissed the question. Pretended my feelings vomit had been an exaggeration brought on by the stress of the moment. But... I found as I turned that possibility over that I didn't like it.

I didn't want to take my confession back. It was out there in the space between us instead of bottled up inside me now, and suddenly I had a little more room to breathe, even if the breathing was a tad painful.

Darton—no, *Arthur*—deserved to know. I owed him at least that much truth.

"Yeah," I said. "It was."

He looked away, rubbed his mouth. "You never told me, back then. I don't think. I don't remember knowing, or having any idea..."

"No. I've never told you before at all. In any life before this."

His gaze jerked back to me. "*Never*? But I thought this... us..." He motioned between us as if the entirety of our bizarre relationship could be summed up in a wave of a hand. "I thought we'd, ah, hooked up in other lives before this. You made it sound like the attraction was normal."

My laugh came out hoarse. "There is a *small* difference between 'hooking up' with someone and professing your undying love for them. Just FYI."

"Well, yeah. I just mean... Why didn't you say anything, all this time?"

I swallowed hard. "You— No. It was me. I was afraid of how you'd react. I knew, back then, you would never have thought of *me* that way, and every time after... I've never known how much it was you and how much the spell."

I was still afraid. My pulse was rattling against my ribs. I kept my eyes trained on the road, but most of my attention was on his presence at the edge of my vision as he processed this information.

"Oh." Darton lowered his head as if to study his hands. "I can — From some of the things I remember, I can see why you might have been worried. The first time, anyway. But I really didn't have any idea. I'm sorry if I made things harder."

"Like I said last night, it's no one's fault. We feel what we feel."

"You also said that I only... In all the other lives, we've only ever gotten together like that when you were a woman?"

I wondered if he'd remembered something more, a sliver of sensation from some other existence between the first and now. I might as well be honest about that too. "No. It's been... Ever since we've gotten to be a certain age before the dark rabble would catch us, unless I've drawn a line, it's been pretty much always. But let's just say the times when I was in certain types of bodies have gone much worse than the others."

I only remembered one with any clarity, and even that was fragmented. A headlong rush from first kiss to fumbles under a blanket, alcohol tangy on both our tongues, and him waking up half sober some hours later, awkward and unsettled. He went to take a walk, to clear his head, so I had stupidly given him "space."

And in that space the glooms had found him. That was how I'd lost him, three of these cycles ago.

"Ah." Darton's brow furrowed, but he didn't seem to know what else to say.

"We don't need to talk about it anymore. Things are as they are. I've had plenty of time to accept that, even if I haven't done the best job of it." I tipped my head toward the sword. "You found your rhythm with Excalibur for a little while this morning. I saw how it responded to you. Whatever you need, it's in you."

"Just not enough," Darton muttered.

"Well, you're still coming awake. You aren't entirely... you. The you it's used to." I paused, thinking back to the moment in the fray when Darton's handle on the sword had slipped. Right after the one dark creature had attacked me. The gray gashes prickled on my forearm under my torn sleeve. "What was going through your head, when it stopped being easy? Or when you were trying to pull it out of the stone, back in the Pool of Turmoil?"

Darton leaned back in his seat, his expression pensive. "I was worried I couldn't do it, I guess."

"So it was doubts getting in the way."

"Maybe. I also..." His mouth slanted. "I don't know how to explain it. But this feeling came over me, when I was trying to pull it out, when I was trying to fight that dragon-ish thing, and today, when that monster attacked you... As if I *knew* I was going to fail you in some huge way, and it wasn't the first time. I was going to screw up all over again and let you down."

"Fail *me?*" I repeated, my eyebrows rising. "Art, it's not your job to look after me. So I don't really see how you could have failed at that. Failed yourself, maybe—whatever expectations you've got— but seriously, if we're going to talk about failure, should we get into my track record? We're only *here* fifteen centuries after our first lives because I've managed not to save us more times than I'd really like to count."

Darton made a dismissive sound. "You've kept us alive in the way that matters the most. We *are* still here fifteen centuries later. How much have I contributed to that?"

"That's not the point. My job was making sure you didn't get murdered by the Darkest One in the first place. The whole rest of this time I've been not-very-successfully trying to mop up the mess I made of that task."

"But you've fought, you've stepped up, you've done everything you could..."

"And you haven't?" I gave a disbelieving laugh. "Art, you don't give yourself enough credit. A couple of months ago you'd never have believed creatures like the things we've encountered in the last few weeks even existed. Yesterday you took on a snake the size of a house with nothing but a dagger. If 'doing everything you could' is the measure we're going by, I think you've got that covered."

Darton sucked in his lower lip. Abruptly I was remembering what those lips felt like against mine, which was really not what I needed to be thinking about right then. I trained my attention back on the road. The car's tires hissed through a particularly large puddle.

At least he knew now. I could draw my lines without having to lie anymore about why.

"It's always about me, though, isn't it?" Darton said after a moment, his voice low. "Even the first time, in our first lives, you came asking to serve me. You've spent so much of your life—your *lives*—trying to keep me alive."

"Well, yes. So?"

"How is that fair? For you to be tied to me like that, never getting to go after whatever it is *you'd* want?"

I shook my head. "You can't think of it that way. You— Do you remember that conversation we had on the plane? About being king, and whether you had a choice?"

"Of course."

"You said you did have a choice, and even if there hadn't been any pressure, you'd have made the same one, right?"

He nodded, and I drew in my breath. "I had a choice too. I always have one. I could walk away, do my own thing, make the most of the time I have doing whatever the hell I want until the cycle starts over. But I always choose you, without hesitation. Because *this* is where I want to be. So don't you dare tell me that's unfair."

Darton looked at me for a long moment—so long my face started to warm at his attention. He let out a rough chuckle. "What in the world did I do to deserve you?"

My mouth twitched. "Something truly horrid, I've got to think."

He blinked, startled, and then he cracked up. A second later, I started laughing too. It felt like a release of so much tension— tension that maybe we'd both been holding inside for far too long.

When we finally stopped, gasping for breath, I reached over and briefly gripped Darton's arm. "You had so much greatness when you started, Art. You'll find it again if we can buy you enough time."

His smile fell. "I don't know. You say that, but— Every time I sleep, that memory comes back. That woman—the Darkest One— stabbing me. I just stood there and let her do it and it's only because of you we got out of it at all."

It was my turn to stare at him. I slowed the car to make sure I didn't drive right off the road.

"Don't be ridiculous," I said. "You did a sodding lot more than that."

His brow knit. "I can't remember anything else. It's all hazy and her face and the pain. And you yelling."

My stomach clenched. "And that memory has been coming back to you *every* night?"

"Not the whole time since we met. I first remembered it, or at least pieces of it, in a dream that night when we were on the road, back home. I didn't have the same dream again for a while. But from around the time we moved into the new house, it's kept coming up."

"That would be around the time Rhedyn started paying attention to us."

He glanced over at me. "You think she has something to do with it."

"I think she could." My mouth tightened. "Because the way you're remembering it isn't accurate. And I don't think your mind would have distorted it like that on its own. It would be in Rhedyn's best interests to have you thinking of yourself as weak and helpless. Why didn't you tell me before?"

"I didn't know it was that strange. And..." His head dipped sheepishly. "I guess I didn't want to sound weak and helpless."

"Well, you're not." I paused, scanning the terrain around us. I hadn't seen any dark creatures since we'd left the fae hunters' home. This would only take a few minutes. And maybe it would make all the difference my king needed.

I eased on the gas completely and guided the car over to the shoulder. The engine sputtered out. I turned to face Darton. "Then I think you should see *everything* that happened."

CHAPTER TWENTY-SEVEN

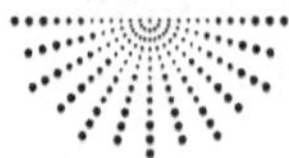

DARTON FROWNED AT ME. "How are you going to make me remember? I thought there wasn't any way to provoke a specific memory into coming back."

A hint of sunlight penetrated the thick clouds, but I didn't have any hope of that being suitable protection. I flicked a couple switches on the fae-hunter enhanced dashboard and the solar lamps blinked on all around the car. "I can't provoke a specific one of *your* memories. But I can let you see one of mine. If you're okay with that."

His eyes widened a bit, but I thought I saw more curiosity in his expression than apprehension. "All right. Are *you* okay with it?"

He was going to be seeing what I'd seen from right inside my head. With all the sensations and emotions that had passed through me in those moments. My body balked, but only for a second. There wasn't anything I'd said, done, or felt then that he shouldn't know. I'd already spilled my guts last night. Letting him see past the obscured visions Rhedyn had stirred up in his head mattered more than notions of privacy.

"I suggested it, didn't I? Hold on."

I pushed open the door and hurried through the drizzle to the trees along the side of the road. Birch, that would serve this purpose well. I snapped a good, solid twig off one branch. The tingle of fresh life tickled my fingers. I dropped back into my seat and extended the twig toward Darton.

"You hold the other end and close your eyes. I can take care of the rest."

He gripped the twig. I let our hands come down to rest on the cup holder between the seats. Dragging in a breath, I pushed my mind back through time to that last, painful memory from our first lives.

I'd thought back to it so many times, trying to remember the exact words I'd said, the energies I'd drawn on, that it surfaced almost instantly. The sudden clouds scudding across the bright autumn sky. The smells of roasting meat and fresh-baked pastries carrying on the breeze. The chatter, punctuated with shouts and laughter, of hundreds of townspeople in the midst of their celebration, not yet realizing it was about to come to an abrupt and horrible end.

I closed my own eyes. "*From my mind to his,*" I murmured, reaching into the twig. A shiver of its energy shot from my fingertips to Darton's, and I propelled the memory through it.

The crowd jostled around me as I edged across the lawn outside the castle, keeping half of my attention on the dais where Arthur was to make his speech and the rest roaming the figures around me for anyone suspicious. I hadn't eaten since my hasty breakfast, but even though it was mid-afternoon, my stomach didn't have room for hunger. It was pinched tight with an anxiety I couldn't quite explain, but nonetheless trusted.

Something awful was coming. And I wasn't sure I was ready for it.

A hush fell over the revelers as their king stepped to the head of the temporary stage. Arthur raised his hands and smiled that slightly crooked smile that never failed to make my heart leap, even now. A cheer rose up from his audience.

Less than a week ago, he'd sent the last of the enemy forces that had tried to invade fleeing home. It had been a long, painful war, but he'd seen us all through it, and it was over now. The relief in the crowd was so pungent I could almost taste it. Adoration for the man who'd accomplished it lit the faces all around me.

"My people," Arthur began as the cheer faded. "I can't tell you how overjoyed I am to be here with all of you, celebrating our victory over those who would have stolen our lands. We have all sacrificed and suffered, and now we all deserve to—

A cry split the air. I jerked around. The clouds were still thickening, and a figure had sprung from the shadows by one of the makeshift booths. He gripped the man in front of him by the head and neatly snapped his neck.

No. I hurried forward, pushing my way through the crowd. The people around the fallen man scattered with sobs and shrieks. Another shadow-clung figure and another wavered into view in the muted daylight. Their presence sent prickles over my skin. Dark fae, all around me.

The dark fae attackers lunged at the spectators with daggers and spears. A woman fell. A teenaged boy stumbled, clutching his bleeding arm. The fae who'd attacked him swung again—and Arthur was there, Excalibur gleaming in his hand, slicing through the fae weapon as if it were made of water.

"Back!" he shouted. "Back to the castle gates. My men, come to me!"

The castle guards who'd joined in the reveling were already hustling to flank him. The fae woman gnashed her teeth and sprang at him, dark sparks flaming between her hands. Before I could even spit out a spell to fling her back from a distance, Arthur had caught her with his sword. The shining blade cut through her dark-shrouded form, and she fell like a heap of fabric.

But more dark fae were emerging all across the lawn. Arthur raced to intercept a fae man who was aiming a blast of magic at a cluster of children. "Shield them!" I cried out. A barrier of light energy snapped into place around them, but the king had already leapt to protect them in his own way. The dark spell glanced off Excalibur and sputtered out in the air.

I brandished my wand to push farther into the fray—and a woman stepped out of the shadows right in front of me. Her ash-blond hair was pulled into a knot above her tan face. Her eyes glittered menacingly.

"Where do you think you're going, Merlin?" Rhedyn asked.

"Through you, if I have to."

That part of the memory was a bit of a hash as far as Darton was concerned. If I'd had a fast-forward button I'd have zipped past Rhedyn's snarking, the bursts of magic we'd thrown back and forth at each other. I'd been too busy tangling with her to pay attention to my king. Which was why, when I finally heaved her to the side with a massive blast of wind I'd redirected around her counter-strike at the last moment, I'd been startled and horrified to see Arthur face to face with the Darkest One herself.

The tall, gaunt woman loomed over even Arthur's substantial height. A smirk curled her lips. A civilian lay near her feet, his skin deathly blue.

The king's jaw had set tight. He'd raised his sword high, the muscles in his arms flexing. I hurled myself toward them. Just as he shifted to deliver the strike, the Darkest One's hand flicked out. The knife she held split the plated padding of his jacket—

I yanked myself out of the memory. The twig snapped between my fingers. Darton flinched. He rubbed a hand over his face as the borrowed images must have faded from his own mind.

"That was... That was really strange," he said. "Like watching a home video of myself, except it wasn't just a camera I was watching through, it was *you*."

I hoped nothing I'd felt in those moments had been too discomforting. At least I'd been more focused on watching out for threats than admiring my king's physique, which I might have done from time to time on other occasions.

"But you see, don't you?" I said. "You can hardly say you just stood there. You charged right in, you stopped the Darkest One's people from hurting so many of yours. You were faster to leap to the defense than *I* was. You can't be ashamed of anything you saw there."

And yet he was frowning. I started the engine again, knowing we had to get going, and tried to figure out what I could say that would make him understand. Before I had, Darton broke his pensive silence.

"I wish I could remember what I was thinking, right before— To get into that memory properly, the whole thing, in my own head."

"Why?" I pressed on the gas and turned us back onto the road. "Obviously you wanted to protect everyone. You were fighting off the dark fae. I don't think there's any reason to believe you had any mysterious motives for that."

"Well, no..." His frown deepened. "It's just, that last glimpse I got, before she stabbed me and you pulled us out... There was something about the way I was holding the sword." He touched the hilt of that same sword where it leaned against him now. "The angle of it, or my grip. I'm not sure. It didn't look right."

"After watching you in battle innumerable times, I feel confident saying that you knew how to hold a sword properly."

"I know. That's why it seems significant." He shook his head. "Maybe I'm just overthinking it. Or I misunderstood what I was seeing. You were pretty far away, and it was just a glimpse. And I'm not really an expert on swords now. It's not like it matters at this point."

It might, but not enough that I wanted to delay our current mission any longer. "If it does, I'm sure it'll come to you, like the idea about the lenses finally did. In any case, you can see, can't you? That you saved so many lives, made so many better—and that was just on that one day. I've had centuries to catch up with your record of heroic deeds, and I'm still working on it."

"Okay. I get it." He relaxed back in his seat, and for the first time the corners of his lips curled a little upward. Remembering how brilliant he'd looked with that sword, I hoped. But then he added, "I'm sorry."

"What for this time?"

He laughed. "I'm not sure. It just felt important that I say that. Everything I should be sorry for, I guess."

"Well, consider yourself forgiven."

He looked as though he might have been about to say more, but at that moment a light fae woman sprang onto the road in front of us.

CHAPTER TWENTY-EIGHT

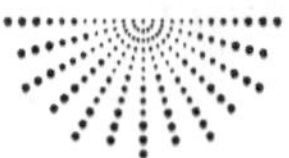

I HIT THE BRAKES. The tires squealed on the slick road, but the car jerked to a stop a foot shy of the fae woman. She didn't even flinch. I supposed if she'd judged the threat too much, she could have flashed away in an instant.

I shoved open my door and leaned out. "What are you *doing*?" We were still a half a mile distant of where I'd planned to stop to hike to the enclave. And while I'd expected a certain amount of resistance from my light fae brethren, nearly getting us into a road accident wasn't an approach I'd been prepared for.

The fae blinked her doe-like eyes at me. From her faint glimmer, she was a youngish one. But she didn't bow. I'd gotten more respect back in the New World than here in the place where they should have recognized me most.

On second thought, maybe that was the problem.

"You were told to leave," she said in a calm, silvery voice. "You and... him. You're not meant to be here."

Well, we could debate who got to decide where I was "meant" to be ad nauseam, but I didn't think it would be very productive getting into that subject with her.

"Stay here," I said to Darton. I switched on the sun lamps and pushed myself right out of my seat. The fae eyed me as I nudged the door shut and came around to speak to her face to face.

I leaned against the car's hood. "I need to speak to the elders," I said. "Cormag can come along if he likes, but I want at least two of the others as well. If protecting the enclave from the Darkest One and her plans here matters so much to them and the rest of you, I have a proposition they'll want to hear."

"*That one* is not to come any closer to the enclave," she replied, flicking her hand toward Darton.

"That's fine. You get a couple of your people over here to keep an eye on things, and I'll go talk to the elders wherever they want. But I *am* going to talk to them. You can't keep me out of the enclave if I want to get to it. I have roots there. The forest knows me, even if the rest of you don't like that."

She raised her chin with a little sniff, but she darted away, I assumed to deliver my message. Gritting my teeth, I got back into the car just long enough to park out of the way of anyone who might pass by, not that this road appeared to get a lot of traffic. I hadn't seen any other vehicles either time we'd come out this way. No doubt the enclave had set wards to encourage the average person to head in other directions.

"Is everything okay?" Darton asked.

"They're about as friendly as before. But I think I've gotten myself an audience with a few of the fae who can make the real decisions, and that's all I need to get started. Hang out with your sword some more. See if you can get better reacquainted."

He gave me a crooked smile and didn't protest when I got out again.

The light fae woman reappeared a minute later with two youthful companions in tow. "The elders say they will hear your proposal," she said. "As long as you go alone. We are to wait here to ensure no darkness passes this way."

I wasn't sure if she meant Darton or the dark fae who might

come looking for him, but either served my purposes fine. "All right. Where should I find them?"

She pointed toward the woods. "Straight to the mothering ash, then seaward."

Directions in poetic form. I managed not to roll my eyes. "Thanks."

It took about a quarter hour of tramping through the forest before I spotted the "mothering ash." The large, aged tree loomed over a sapling on either side, clearly sprung from its own seeds. And seaward would be... I checked my sense of the sun and swung left. I guessed I was supposed to just keep walking until I bumped into the elders.

I was just starting to wonder if they'd decided it would be more worthwhile to watch me wandering around trying to find them than to actually talk to me when I spotted four shimmering figures amid the trees up ahead.

Cormag stood in the middle of the group, but the others were even more elder. They created a pool of natural light in their little clearing, streaming from the filmy edges of their bodies. In the dim daylight, it was as if a miniature sun had settled in the middle of the forest.

Cormag's face was tensed. "I thought you understood everything after our last conversation," he said the second I'd reached them. "I was as clear as I knew how that we cannot tolerate—"

"I know, I know," I interrupted. "The dark fae got their dirty fingerprints all over Arthur's family line. Maybe there's some stain that's lingered. I haven't seen any sign of it since you brought it up, but sure, I'll accept it's possible. That's exactly why I'm here."

Cormag scowled. One of the elder women stepped forward with a beckoning gesture. "Tell us what it is you seek here, Son of Eóghan. Your father was wiser than most, and I hope some of his forbearance has passed onto you."

I was pretty sure my father had vented on more than one

occasion that he felt it had skipped me entirely, but no need to get into that right now.

"You want me and my king gone," I said. "I understand that. But we *will* not leave until we've done everything we can to prevent the Darkest One's release. I was the one who imprisoned her. Keeping her in her prison is my responsibility. I assume you all can understand that."

"After all this time," Cormag tried again.

I shook my head. "Nope. I'm not getting into that argument again. We're staying and fighting, and there's nothing any of you can really do about that, is there? Unless you want to play dark fae and kill us."

The shudder those words provoked told me there wasn't any chance of that. I crossed my arms over my chest. "So the only questions left are whether the Darkest One will get free and snatch up Arthur's soul or whether we'll stop her. You'd prefer the latter, wouldn't you? And you *can* make a difference there."

"We will not fight your battles," the other woman said. "Our kind defends our ground, but we do not stir up conflict elsewhere."

"That's fine," I said. "I'm not asking you to go anywhere. But it's been wearing on you, hasn't it, all those clouds up there?" I pointed toward the sky. "No one in the enclave can have been enjoying that weather. And you have to be able to tell it's the dark fae keeping the sun hidden away."

"You want us to push back the clouds?" Cormag said.

I smiled. "No. I want you to crack them open. That'll be easier anyway, won't it? There's lightning brewing in them already. The dark fae have been calming it, but it's got to be a tricky balance. If the enclave works together, you can tip it. I want a full-blown thunderstorm over north Somerset by the end of the day. You get me that, I can destroy the fae working to free the Darkest One, no one touches my king, and this ends happily for everyone."

The second woman peered down at me haughtily. "Why should we expend our energy for one who has so little concern for our own wellbeing? You are bringing the poison straight to she who wishes to spread it."

"If she gets out, she's going to find him one way or another." I waved a hand in frustration. "But fine, fine, it really bugs you that this catastrophe might go down on your doorstep. I don't want it to happen here—or anywhere—either. That's what I'm trying to stop here."

"But if you fail..."

"I won't fail, if I have the lightning on my side." I hoped.

Cormag's eyes narrowed. "Even if the Darkest One escapes after all, there is one way to still protect us. To protect all those you claim to care about. If the king's soul passes from this world before she can grasp it, she will lose it for good."

I paused, my back stiffening. If Arthur died, he meant. Died for good, not just tumbling back into our cycle of rebirths. If the binding part of the spell was broken, the rest would fracture in turn. But there was only one way I could guarantee what Cormag was asking.

I raised my chin. "Is that what you need? My word that if she emerges, I'll take his life before she can?"

The fae's lips curled in disgust, but Cormag inclined his head, and none of the others argued. They couldn't bring themselves to destroy a life, but they could tacitly approve of me doing it. Bloody hypocrites.

I swallowed hard. I'd been ready to end Darton's life a few weeks ago when we'd faced the mercenary, if we'd lost control over that situation. But then I'd assumed I would be simply throwing us back into our cycle, *preventing* my king's final death—not bringing it about.

What if the magic the Darkest One had worked on Arthur all those years ago had faded away over the centuries? What if he wasn't a disaster waiting to happen after all? I *hadn't* felt anything catastrophic in him, ever. They wanted me to agree to kill him without even knowing whether it was really necessary.

"If you swear you'll sever his light before the Darkest One can spread her poison from it, we will bring your lightning," the first woman said. "I swear that."

Her words rang with a magical finality. She was bound to them now. I could have everything I needed, if I just agreed to this. This horrible task that I'd never have to consider as long as we took down Rhedyn in time.

With the lightning and the sword, we'd have all we needed. Without the enclave's help, we were almost certainly lost anyway.

"All right," I said, my voice rough. "If the Darkest One walks free, I will sever Arthur's soul before she can. I swear it."

I pushed a sliver of the life energy pulsing through my body into the last words. They spilled out into the air and solidified in my chest at the same moment. The oath hung there over my heart like a lump of stone.

The elders bobbed their heads. "It is spoken. It is so."

I clamped my lips back together, praying that the dread swelling inside me was only nerves and not an omen.

CHAPTER TWENTY-NINE

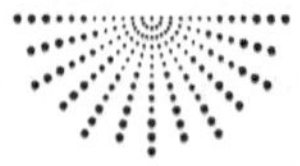

"OKAY." Darton gestured with his phone. "Keevan has finally gotten a hold of his sister. *I'm pretty sure she thinks I'm crazy or involved in some kind of wacky science cult at this point. But I got all her physics Ph.D. lightning expertise out of her.*"

My hands tightened on the steering wheel, but the corner of my mouth quirked up. I could practically hear Keevan's voice in Darton's recitation of his words. "And what did she say in her expertise?"

Darton leaned back in the passenger seat. "He's getting into that... *Apparently there isn't a whole lot you can do to attract lightning, if for some insane reason you'd want to. I'm hoping your reasons aren't completely insane, Art.*" He chuckled. "I'm thinking it's probably a good thing Keev isn't around for this little expedition."

"Ah, he rose to the occasion just fine last time around." But, true, last time around we hadn't been messing with lightning bolts.

"*Anyway, unless you're a skyscraper or something, you're not likely to change the direction of a lightning strike unless it's already really close to you, she says. Within a few feet or so. But if it is coming down really close anyway, it will tend to hit the highest thing around. So if you're by a tree in a big open space—or by yourself in a big open space —you're more likely to get 'lucky.'"*

I nodded. "Okay. I think I can handle the getting it close part." My affinity to the light would make it easy to call down the energy once it was ready.

"If the light fae come through with provoking the lightning in the first place, right?" Darton frowned. "Are you completely sure we can count on them?"

"They seemed persuaded by my arguments," I said. And by my oath, which I hadn't mentioned to Darton.

I glanced over at him. At the living embodiment of my king. He was peering at his phone now, waiting for Keevan's next text, looking every inch the modern college guy—the kind of guy who shouldn't have needed to worry about summoning lightning or fae magic.

The kind of guy whose possible murder I shouldn't have hanging over my head.

Darton had never asked for any of this. He'd been born with my king twined inside him, and he hadn't even known *that* until last month.

But he was still here. We'd gotten this far. I didn't have to fix all my mistakes right now. All I had to do was interrupt Rhedyn's meddling and shore up the bindings holding the Darkest One in place for a little longer. Buy us a little more time. The rest I could figure out afterward.

There was no *if.* I simply was going to do it, no other options allowed.

"You were right about the metal idea," Darton said. "*Any kind of metal will act as an attracter too. The bigger the better. I hope that helps. And that I'm not going to see any reports from England about some dude getting fried.*"

I laughed at that. "Tell him I'm the one who's going to be channeling the lightning."

Darton's fingers tapped against the screen. "He says he'd rather you didn't get fried either."

"Well, that's comforting. I guess we should be looking into buying a lightning rod."

He sent off one last message to his best friend and brought up his mobile browser. "You haven't heard anything worrying from Priya or Jagger back home, have you?"

I shook my head. "Our families are fine. The dark fae that were hassling them haven't made any moves since we left. It sounds like most of them have taken off—probably on a boat headed back here."

"But they won't get here in time."

"Not if we can end this today."

"Right." He skimmed through his search results. "There's a home improvement store in the next city we'll be passing. According to their website, they carry lightning rods."

"Perfect. Then we'll make a little detour." My heart started to thump. One more stop, and then we'd be returning to the ground where this all began to face our greatest enemy.

Darton had seemed calm enough strapping the lightning rod on its side on the car roof, which was the only way we could figure out to carry the thing, but when we exited the car a couple hours later, he eyed it as if he were worried it would start shooting lightning at us right there and then.

"Are you *sure* you won't get hurt with this spell?"

"Maybe a little," I admitted. "But a little hurt beats death and mass destruction."

"Yeah." He still looked pensive as he helped me undo the cables that had held the rod in place. I'd parked at the far end of the lot behind a country flea market a short hike from the overpass—the closest I could get the car to Rhedyn—but a few passing shoppers noticed and shot us odd looks anyway.

Just wait until they saw Darton hauling out his broadsword.

A sprinkling of rain dappled our faces and then faded. The damp breeze pressed against my face. A gathering tension reverberated through it, carried down from the churning clouds overhead. A hint of ozone tickled over my tongue.

The light fae were working their magic. The crackling power of the storm was building, almost ready to burst open. And I needed to be in the right spot when it did.

"Come on." I pointed to a low, bare hill just south of the overpass. "That looks like a good spot to tempt lightning."

Darton gave a hoarse laugh, but he heaved Excalibur out of the car with a smooth sweep of his arms. The blade beamed. He shifted his stance, angling the sword out in front of him as if ready to do battle, and the light lit in his eyes too.

"This is my sword," he said, and for the first time, he sounded as if he fully believed that.

"It is," I said. "And I think we'd better take it elsewhere before a whole lot of people other than Keevan decide we're crazy."

He lowered the blade as we left the parking lot behind and tramped toward the hill. My arm burned with the weight of the lightning rod, which was nearly twice as tall as I was. I leaned it against my shoulder for balance and pushed onward. My other hand dipped to my side, checking first for the two wands I'd shoved in my pocket for easy access and then for the rest of the supplies in my bulging purse.

The moisture on the wet grass soaked into my sneakers and chilled my feet before we'd made it more than halfway up the hill. The wind picked up, hissing over it in a way that reminded me too much of the snake-dragon Rhedyn had sent after us in the Pool of Turmoil. Light only knew what she'd throw at us this time.

But this time my king had his sword, really *had* it, and the most intense blast of light nature could provide would soon be at my beck and call. We had a chance, and I was going to wring it for all it was worth.

As we continued up the hill, the rumble of the cars on the overpass reached me. The twisting roads, raised up on steel frames so they could be routed over and under each other, spewed the vehicles traveling on them off in a bewildering number of directions. The hill lay in a wide V between two of those adjoining highways.

I squinted at the shadows beneath the nearest branch of the overpass. An unearthly tremor ran over my skin. Somewhere down there, the Darkest One was sealed away in the stone. Somewhere down there, Rhedyn was battering my ancient spell with her dark magic. I wished we didn't have to be here—I wished she'd never shoved her way into these lives of ours. But at the same time, an ache almost like homesickness had filled me.

My spell had propelled the Darkest One away from the spot where she'd confronted Arthur before sealing her away, but not terribly far. We were some half a day's ride from the site of my and my king's former home. We might have sat on this hill, fifteen hundred years ago, to break for lunch on the way back to the castle.

Maybe the same sense of nostalgia had struck Darton, because he sucked in the cool autumn air and said, "Somehow this feels like I'm *returning*, even though I don't remember ever being here before."

"Some part of you does," I said. And then my voice fell away, because a cluster of shadowy figures had emerged from the dark spaces beneath and around the overpass.

Maybe two dozen dark fae were striding toward us, with a host of dark creatures charging alongside them. My jaw went slack. Darkness take me—and it very well might.

I grasped Darton's arm and tugged. "Let's get the higher ground while we can."

We scrambled the rest of the way up the hill, our feet skidding on the slick grass. The end of the lightning rod thudded against the ground as I flung it out in front of me like a walking stick. We hadn't quite made it to the crest when the first warbling of dark magic sounded behind us.

I whipped around, drawing my wand and snapping out a spell at the same moment. My blaze of light crashed into the dark fury of energy that had been rippling toward us.

Both spells shattered apart in a spray of mingled light and shadow. My muscles trembled. I dropped the lightning rod and grabbed my other wand to hold it at the ready.

A few of the swifter creatures had already clambered up the hill. Darton slashed at them with his gleaming sword, and they fell, crumpling into the grass. A small, determined smile had crossed his face.

Yes. That was what we needed.

I hollered into being another blast of light at the brigade of dark fae heading our way. It swept over them, rippling their shadowy clothes. They didn't even stagger, but they did at least slow down.

I didn't have any hope I could destroy even one of them with just my own power, but as long as they were busy defending against my assaults and attempting to attack us, they weren't focusing their attention on the clouds. My enclave could work their own magic even faster.

A few of the dark fae spat spells toward us, but I cast those away between pants for breath. This bunch had been picking away at the Darkest One's bindings and holding their storm steady across half the country for days. They'd drained most of their energy by now. I couldn't have survived against even a couple of full dark fae who had all their power, but a bunch of exhausted ones? I might just be able to hold them off.

I hadn't seen Rhedyn yet, though. And she was not just full fae but ancient, with all the power that came with that age.

A thicker wave of shadow creatures was barreling toward us. Darton glanced back at me. "Together?"

I hadn't tried combining my magic with the full power of Excalibur before. The blade was practically singing with its connection to my king's soul. Voices rose by the base of the hill. The dark fae squadron was starting up the slope. I sprang forward, clapping one hand against Darton's back with the wand between us.

"Darkness begone!"

Darton sliced the sword through the air, and the light blazed from its edge all the way down the hill, glowing brighter and brighter as it streamed on. It burned away every one of the dark creatures the fae had sent after us. The dark fae gasped and cringed, but stayed standing.

Both of my wands crumbled, drained of energy, but a fresh surge of confidence filled me. The two of us, together with the sword, were more powerful than they'd expected. And we had more power yet to come.

I snatched another wand from my purse. The dark fae at the base of the hill were pulling closer together, their murmurs echoing in a joint spell. I preferred not to give them the chance to finish it. "Again!" I said to Darton, gripping his shoulder. He nodded and swung the sword once more.

The blade arced with a brilliant glitter, and I pushed all the energy in the wand through me into that motion. *"Beams of light, twist and hold."*

The light that seared off of Excalibur's blade this time twined into a thick rope. It whipped down the hill and snapped tight around the huddled fae. A few tried to spring out of range at the sight of it, but the light spiraled on and on, winding loop after loop around every one of them.

Darton stared at the mass of struggling bodies. The shadows that clung to them licked and cringed away from the gleaming binding.

"How long can you hold them like that?" he asked.

I tossed away the now-dead wand. "They'll be able to work

themselves free in a few hours, I'd guess. But in a few hours we'll be long done here."

Or long dead by Rhedyn's hand—or her master's.

I paused to take a breath, and that was my mistake. In the instant while my guard was slightly down, three dark fae who must have circled the hill and crept up the opposite side sprang at us from behind.

One of the men leapt at Darton with a lash of dark magic and a knife. The other and the woman came at me.

Throwing myself onto the ground, I tumbled away from them. I didn't have time to grab another wand. My fingers dug into the grass. That thin green energy flowed into my palms. I snapped it up like a shield as the woman swung a whip of shadow at me.

"*Carry them, like to like!*" I called out. A wind whipped up from the grass and slammed into the man. It tossed him down the hill, right into the knot of trapped fae at the base. His pained grunt gave me a small twinge of satisfaction.

The woman had managed to dodge the blast. She lunged at me again, words in the old tongue spilling from her mouth. I battered away her smack of magic with a flail of my arm and a wrenching at the life energy inside me. Good-bye to another couple weeks of life.

Beyond her, Darton was matching blows with the other fae, Excalibur's blade deflecting knife and spells alike. The clouds overhead crackled but didn't split. So sodding close.

The fae woman flinched at the sound. I took advantage of her brief distraction to snatch at my fallen purse. The woman had just whipped her hands up to throw another spell when I spun with my second-to-last wand, calling up the wind again. The surge of air tossed her down the slope after her companion.

A chill quivered up through the ground into my body, as if from somewhere deep below. From the cavern where Rhedyn was unwinding my work. The Darkest One's will was seeping through even stronger now. Was she that close to breaking free?

Pulse racing, I shoved myself to my feet. Darton was just

swiveling to track his attacker's parry. The dark fae man leaned close and muttered something as he sliced out with his knife.

Darton smacked the narrow blade away, but his expression stuttered as if he'd been slapped. The glow that had lit both his face and the sword dimmed. My stomach lurched.

I scrambled over as he tried to swing the sword again. Its weight dragged at his arms, and his mouth twisted. The fae man cackled. He gathered a whirl of shadow between his hands—and I kicked his feet out from under him.

I grasped Darton's wrist. "I've got you." He let Excalibur drop toward the dark fae who was springing up again, and my fingers clenched around my wand.

"*Carry him, like to like,*" I said, channeling the magic through the enchanted sword. The wind stirred with the swoop of the blade. It sent the fae man careening down the hill to join the others.

"Art," I said, but I never got to ask the question on my lips. The ground shuddered and pitched beneath us. I fell to my knees, snatching at the suddenly crumbling soil.

The lightning rod. I couldn't lose it. I hurled myself up the hill over the sudden landslide. Pebbles and clods of dirt fell away under my scrambling feet. My hand closed around the metal post. I jerked around to call Darton to me, and the rod started to slide down the hill too.

Darton had dug his sword into the ground, but as I glanced over, the hill spit it back up. I caught his arm as another quake jostled us closer together, but then we were just hurtling downward side by side.

Down toward the dark space that gaped even wider now beneath the underpass. Movement stirred within the shadows as we tumbled toward it. A cold laugh carried from their depths, and then Rhedyn's raspy voice rang out.

"So glad you've come to meet me, Merlin."

CHAPTER THIRTY

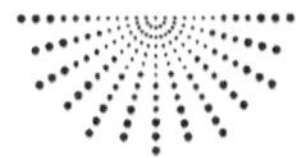

THE LANDSLIDE JERKED us to a stop a few paces shy of the base of the hill. Darton staggered to his feet. He hauled Excalibur with him, but the sword's blade was still dull, his arms still straining. Whatever that damned dark fae had said to him had clearly shaken him badly.

The blade had shone a little more for me, recognizing my magic, when we'd faced Rhedyn's snake-dragon. At the crunch of footsteps over gravel by the cave just below us, I scrambled up and grasped the hilt.

"Let me take the sword."

Darton stared at me. He opened his mouth with an expression that told me he was going to protest, but then a figure appeared at the cave's opening, and his grip loosened. I heaved the sword toward me and turned to face Rhedyn.

For the first few seconds, *I* could only stare. She wasn't the blond, tan-skinned fae I'd faced more than once in the past. It was her—I could sense it in the tendrils of shadow clinging to her like hazy vines—but this body was shorter, more solid, with a head of black curls and eyes nearly as dark.

A human body.

Rhedyn smiled at my surprise. "Not what you were expecting, wizard? I learned from you—how to cling on after death and find a new home, as you have so many times. It took longer to work the magic than I'd hoped, but here I am now."

That was why. That was why *everything*. Why I hadn't sensed her in so many lives before. Why it had taken so long for her to build up enough power that her efforts were finally affecting us. A human body would restrain some of the natural fae powers of her soul.

She must have been working to free the Darkest One through my entire current life, at least. Wearing down the barriers so more and more influence could seep out, until our mercenary had sensed it from across the ocean and made me realize something worse than usual was happening.

I didn't know whether to be angry or grateful for that. Darton could have had more time to live his life properly. But if the mercenary hadn't stepped up, Rhedyn might have carried on like this, scraping away at my spell, never worrying about me, until she'd broken the binding and we'd all been in an even deeper mess than we were now.

Thunder rumbled overhead. Rhedyn kept her smile, but it tightened. So very close. If I had the sword, I wouldn't even need the lightning rod. I could channel the lightning straight through Excalibur.

"It doesn't matter what body you're wearing," I said. "It won't stop me from doing what I need to do."

Her lips pulled back into a full-out sneer. "If you really think you can, go ahead and take your best shot."

I wrenched the sword off the ground. My magic sang through it, but not enough to really lighten its weight. Gritting my teeth, I swung it at her. "*Darkness begone.*"

I hadn't expected to do much more than propel her backward anyway. Her power might be dampened by the body she was in and all the magic she'd expended working at the Darkest One's prison, but I was working with a human body too, and full fae trumped half any day. But before the words had even fallen from my mouth, Rhedyn shoved out her hands with a snapped spell of her own.

Energy radiated from her body. The hill shook, and the ground tipped. She raised her arms. With a groan, the entire crest upended and poured down in a mass of earth toward us.

"Em!" Darton grabbed my arm and yanked. I stumbled with him, clutching the sword. He pulled me under a small, rocky outcropping on the hillside, just as the avalanche cascaded over us. In an instant, we were buried in that small pocket of air and darkness.

My breath stuttered. I pushed back against the more stable ground behind us until I was sure the dirt had finished falling. Darton crouched unmoving beside me. I couldn't see him, but his shoulder pressed against mine, hitching a bit with each inhale.

"Well, this is going smashingly," I muttered, and he choked out a laugh.

"What do you always say? 'We'll figure it out somehow'?"

"That sounds like me." I closed my eyes, not that it made much difference in our earth-bound prison, and started to reach my awareness out into the hillside to get to work on figuring things out. Then Darton's arm slid around me, tugging my mind back to him. To us.

"Em," he said, his voice rough. "Merlin. I don't remember if I ever said this before. I know I didn't say it enough. Maybe it *isn't* enough, in the end, after everything you've told me. But I want you to know that you have always been the most important person in my life. All of them. I'm pretty sure I can say that for the ones I don't remember too. And I will always stand by you, no matter what comes. No matter how this ends."

He hugged me tighter to him. I pressed my face to his shoulder, closing my eyes again, this time against the tears threatening to spring up. The ache that filled my chest now was only painful because of the thought of losing this. Losing him.

"It's enough," I said, past the lump in my throat. "It's always been enough." My liege. My greatest friend. "Now let's get out of here and show that dark fae what we're made of."

I grasped Excalibur's hilt with my free hand and shoved it into the loose earth that had covered our makeshift shelter. *Batter and blast.*

Energy blazed through the sword with a crackling power no wand had ever offered me. The barrier in front of us burst apart in a spray of soil. I threw myself forward, feeling as much as seeing Darton charging forward beside me, the fae dagger in his hand.

A blast of dark magic sizzled into my face. I jerked to the side just in time to only feel the singe across my cheek. Rhedyn was hissing words under her breath. I swiped the dirt from my eyes and dodged another shadowy projectile. The clouds overhead outright boomed.

I swung the sword, sending out an arc of light that forced Rhedyn backward a couple of steps. A half light fae against a full dark fae might not be much of a contest, but add a magically enhanced sword to the mix, and I had a sliver of a chance.

A flicker crossed the sky. The lightning had come. That would give us much more than a sliver. I just needed it to come down to us. To come down to us and blast our enemy away.

"Em," Darton said. He held out his hand. "Let me?"

His hair was plastered to his head with the damp and his face was smudged with dirt, but in that moment he looked every inch the stalwart king. My heart skipped a beat.

This was his battle too. He'd told me over and over again that he trusted me, had shown me he did so many times. He'd given me the sword bound to his soul just a few minutes ago, because I'd asked. Did I trust him to know he was ready to wield it? To stand by me as he'd promised.

Yes. With all my heart, I did.

I thrust the sword toward him, swiveling in the same movement to search the hillside for my fallen lightning rod. Rhedyn snapped out a spell, and Darton whipped the blade to shatter it. A gleam lit within the sword from hilt to tip.

"Are we ready?" he asked me.

"Almost." There. The metal staff with its pointed top protruded from the earth just a short dash above us. I hurled myself upward over the still crumbling soil and wrapped my hands around the rod. With a heave, I freed it.

I needed more than this to call the lightning to me. I needed a source of power.

My gaze fell to the matted grass at the base of the hill, just a few feet from where Rhedyn stood. I'd have to sacrifice height for that, but no matter.

"We need to close in," I shouted to Darton. He nodded and pressed on down the hill, cutting off every blast of shadow Rhedyn threw his way with a slash of his sword. Her eyes narrowed. She stood her ground, hurling another spell at him, and another. But I thought I could see her tiring more. Her arms shook, just slightly.

I skidded the rest of the way down the hill, landing ungracefully but on my feet on the flatter ground at its base. Rhedyn's army of dark fae was still thrashing at the binding of light I'd cast around them, but she either didn't have the energy or the interest to try to free them.

She whipped a searing ball of shadow my way, and I leapt to the side. Darton charged at her at the same moment, jabbing his blade at her stomach. She batted it aside with a swift muttering, but her face had pinched with strain.

She'd given up so much of her strength trying to free her master. And despite it, the Darkest One was still sealed beneath the mountain, stirring but stuck.

The clouds above let out a massive rumble. It was time to finish this. To prove that we could.

I stabbed the lightning rod's base into the ground and dropped down with my knees braced on either side of it to hold it upright. Digging my hand into the limp grass, I flung out my other arm. "Arthur! Now!"

He parried one last surge of Rhedyn's magic and dashed over to me. The sword sang in his hand as he extended the other to clasp mine. I tipped my face to the sky, clenched the grass and his fingers, and cried out with every shred of life in me.

"*Light of the skies, blaze to me, blaze true. Break the darkness and cast it away.*"

The clouds boomed and flashed. Not one but three streaks of lightning raced down to meet me. They snapped against the head of the lightning rod in a single mass of energy. The rush of light and electricity smacked into me, rattling my teeth. I held it with all my strength and balled my will around the coursing, shuddering power. Then I threw it from me into Darton, into the sword he held.

Darton thrust Excalibur toward Rhedyn. Light blazed and arced all around its blade. In that last instant, I thought I saw Rhedyn turning to flee and catching herself. She spun back toward us, meeting the blast of pure light energy with her arms raised as if in surrender.

The immense bolt seared straight into her gut. Her lips jittered, but her body fell. She slumped over on the ground. Her eyelids stuttered, her eyes gone pure black right through the whites. Her arms lay spread in her last pose, now limp with death.

A wisp of shadow drifted up from her chest. My pulse hiccupped. Oh, no, I wasn't letting her essence flee again to cling to some other human form. I swung the lightning rod down, calling on the last flickers of electricity still humming through it, and tossed them at that wisp.

It sizzled and popped in a burst of sparks. And with that, my old enemy was fully gone from this world.

CHAPTER THIRTY-ONE

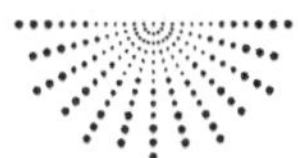

I dropped the lightning rod. My skin stung as it fell to the ground. I raised my hand and found myself staring at a bubbled scarlet burn streaked across the center of my palm and the inner knuckles of my fingers. My nerves were jangling as if a shot of that electricity were still bouncing around inside my body.

A wash of relief swept those uncomfortable sensations away. Rhedyn was gone. The Darkest One was still bound. We'd done it. Again.

A laugh I couldn't pretend wasn't a bit startled jolted out of me. Darton gripped my shoulder.

"Is it done?" he said hoarsely. "Is she— Are we safe now?"

Not even hardly. I dragged in a breath. "Not yet. Rhedyn has still weakened the seal that was keeping the Darkest One locked away. I have to do my best to rebuild it." I glanced up at the sky. "Maybe the lightning can help with that as well."

Maybe, if I absorbed a little more of that power, worked it through my will, I could create a binding that didn't require the tangling of our souls to hold it in place. And then we could really be done, for good.

I raised my hands to reach out to the sparking clouds—and an ear-splitting *crack* rang out from the cave before us.

The earth jumped and broke open between us. From the depths of the darkness in the cave, a screech pealed out, as pleased as it was furious. My heart stopped.

"Em?" Darton said, his eyes wide. He threw his hand toward me. The chasm in the ground between us gaped wider. I scrambled and leapt across, catching hold of him just before the edge crumbled under my heel.

"It can't— *She* can't—" I was mumbling, but I knew even as the protests spilled out that it wasn't true. The image of Rhedyn with her arms spread flashed through my mind.

I'd destroyed her, but she'd turned her death into a sacrifice to her master. And that last burst of sacrificial magic had been enough for the Darkest One to wriggle free.

Before the thought had even finished passing through my mind, a tingling raced over my skin. An itchy tingling, as if a layer of my skin were sloughing off. I stared down at my arms, and then at Darton, who was shuddering as if he felt the same thing. The itch dug all the way into my chest, between my ribs, pinching and scratching. I choked on a breath.

My spell. Fifteen hundred years of binding, of deaths and rebirths, of finding each other. The Darkest One had finally wrenched it all apart.

With another *crack*, the entrance to the cave shattered apart. A wave of darkness spilled out, crashing toward us like a tsunami, surging up toward the clouds to sputter against the flashes of lightning. My lungs seized up.

I couldn't fight her. I'd never been able to fight her. The only way I could save my king was to get him far, far away. But I was capable of that.

I threw my arms around Darton and called out a spell down to the depths of my fragile, mortal life. The wind whipped up around us, whirling us away. It tore away my sight. My mind spiraled into darkness. I felt us land, stumbling on grassy ground. Heard Darton's voice saying, "What— Em, where are we?"

"Somewhere safe," I mumbled. "Momentarily." Then the effort hit me over the head, and I blacked out completely.

SOUL'S BLADE - BONUS SCENE

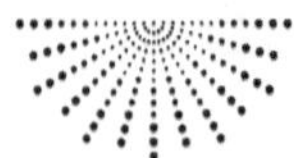

WHAT DID the dark fae say to Darton in the final battle to shake his confidence—and how did he regain it, for good this time? This bonus scene gives you Darton's point of view of the events from the end of chapter 29 through the beginning of chapter 30...

I'd taken those fencing club lessons back at school. I'd mowed players down on the football field. But nothing had ever felt quite like the heft and the slash of Excalibur in my hands when its magic responded to my presence.

The blade clanged off the dark fae man's knife and shattered the spell he'd tried to toss at me with his free hand. Light streamed off the sword's gleaming surface and coursed through my arm to light up the inside of my chest with a heady glow. I swung again before spinning to the side to dodge a swift jab.

My attacker followed. He lunged at me, snatching my arm. "And they called you king," he hissed with narrowed eyes. "Do you even know how to fight without your wizard's magic propping you up? I look forward to seeing him witness me gutting you. Light fades; darkness remains."

He sliced out with the knife at the same time. I heaved the sword to block it, but its glow had dimmed. Faded, like the dark elf had said.

I gripped the hilt tighter. I'd ruled long before I'd had this sword. It was my soul that powered it as much as Merlin's magic, wasn't it?

But maybe it wasn't. How many fae had Em already dispatched while I still couldn't overcome this one?

I wrenched at the sword with a grimace, and the fae man whipped up a ball of shadow in his hands. Then Em was toppling him with a swift kick. Her fingers curled around my wrist. "I've got you."

I didn't want to have to accept her help, but I needed it. I lowered the sword to point it at the dark fae as he shoved himself back toward us, and she raised her wand.

Words in that ancient language of hers, from before even the time of my first life, spilled over her lips. The sound of her spell-casting always sent a shiver through me that was both exhilarating and unnerving. Excalibur jerked in my hand, and a blast of wind flew off of it to hurl our attacker down the hill.

As if in protest, the ground lurched under our feet. I stumbled, skidding down the slope as the earth crumbled. Em dashed over the scattered soil toward her lightning rod—away from me. My pulse stuttered.

I rammed the sword into the earth to stop my downward tumble. It held for a few seconds, and then the hill expelled it with another quake. Em caught my elbow, and we careened together to the base of the hill in the midst of the landslide.

A chilling laugh rang from beneath the underpass. "So glad you've come to meet me, Merlin."

I swayed to my feet, lifting Excalibur with me. Its weight dragged at my arms. Em thrust out her hand and grabbed the hilt.

"Let me take the sword."

Every nerve in my body protested. Excalibur was *mine*. I had to make it work, somehow. But before I could even form those words out loud, a woman strode out from the mouth of the cave, power crackling around her.

I let go of Excalibur, and Em swung it up, ready for the battle I should have been able to fight for her.

"Not what you were expecting, wizard?" the woman taunted. This must be the henchman of the Darkest One, the one we were here to stop. Her next words blurred into the rumble of thunder from the clouds above us. My heart leapt.

Our storm. Our lightning. It was coming. That was all Em needed.

What I needed… I didn't have a clue.

"It doesn't matter what body you're wearing," Em retorted. "It won't stop me from doing what I need to do."

"If you really think you can, go ahead and take your best shot," the woman said.

Em heaved the sword and spat out a phrase I'd heard enough times to recognize: the spell that shattered darkness. The woman's hands shot out as she shouted something else I didn't understand. The hill behind us groaned and shook. My head snapped around in time to see the entire peak rushing toward us in a tsunami of pebbles and soil.

"Em!" My gaze caught on a slab of granite protruding from the hillside just above us and to our right. I snatched her arm and pulled her with me, throwing both of us into that meager shelter a second before the avalanche hit.

Dirt flooded the open space in front of us. We squeezed back against the surface beneath the rock, huddled in the sudden dark. Our breaths rasped as the ground shuddered again and finally stilled.

"Well, this is going smashingly," Em said, so petulantly a laugh jolted out of me.

"What do you always say?" I asked. "'We'll figure it out somehow'?"

"That sounds like me."

She went silent for a moment. I couldn't see her in the darkness, but I could feel her—her shoulder pressed to mine, the quiver that ran through it.

My throat tightened. Maybe it didn't matter who saved who how many times, or what powers Merlin had lent to my cause before and Em now. This woman—man—this wizard, friend, fellow soul had given everything for me and my cause. And I couldn't say for sure I'd ever expressed how much that meant to me.

My arm slid around Em's back of its own accord. "Em," I said, and her head turned toward me with a rustle of hair. I swallowed the lump in my throat. "Merlin. I don't remember if I ever said this before. I know I didn't say it enough. Maybe it *isn't* enough, in the end, after everything you've told me. But I want you to know that you have always been the most important person in my life. All of them. I'm pretty sure I can say that for the ones I don't remember too. And I will always stand by you, no matter what comes. No matter how this ends."

I squeezed her to me with those last words. Em tucked her face against my shoulder with a shaky exhale. She'd moved to me, not away from me. Right then, that was all I could have wanted.

"It's enough," she said raggedly but so earnestly the truth rang through her voice. "It's always been enough. Now let's get out of here and show that dark fae what we're made of."

She spat out three words in her magical tongue, and the soil in front of us burst apart. We hurled ourselves out onto the open landscape as one being.

Magic sizzled past us. Em swung Excalibur with a blazing glow. A streak of lightning flickered against the clouds, and my breath caught.

Em looked toward it too. She needed to reach toward that

electricity, to bring it down on the woman still intent on destroying us. Which meant I needed to play my part to.

Looking at my oldest friend, I knew all I had to do was take the chance.

I held out my hand. "Em. Let me?"

She blinked at me for a second, and then a small smile crossed her face. As if she didn't have the slightest doubt in me. Had she ever doubted? I didn't think so. Suddenly it seemed ridiculous that I had.

She heaved the sword to me and scrambled up the hill toward the lightning rod. As I grasped the hilt, a flood of shimmering power raced through me. The blade shone as I sliced apart the fae woman's next spell. Excalibur flashed through the air like it was lightning itself, made to soar at my command.

Because it was. I was Arthur, and this was my Excalibur. Hell yeah, they'd called me king. I *was* a king, down to my bones, down to my soul. And no dark fae could take that from me.

DRAGON OF DESTINY

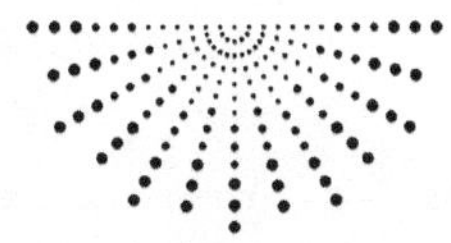

LEGENDS REBORN #3

CHAPTER ONE

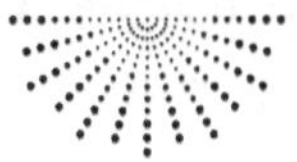

A FRANTIC VOICE pierced through the blankness in my head. "Em? Em!"

Normally I wouldn't have objected to waking up with my head cradled in the lap of the guy I'd been in love with for fifteen hundred years. It might actually have been a plus. The trouble was, as soon as I opened my eyes to Darton's whitened face staring down at me, I remembered why I'd been knocked out in the first place.

The images rushed up: The ear-splitting *crack*. The shudder of breaking earth beneath my feet. The itchy pull of the binding spell tearing away from my body. The wave of darkness sweeping from the cave as the Darkest One charged forth.

I'd failed. Sodding hell. Despite all my efforts, the most powerful of the dark fae had broken free from the prison my half-fae magic had kept her trapped in for the last fifteen centuries. No doubt she was very peeved. And who was she going to want to inflict her rage on first? Me, the wizard who'd sealed her away, and the current incarnation of my king, whose soul she'd been determined to twist to her malicious purposes all those years ago.

I'd used the last bit of my exhausted magic to apparate us away from her, but I'd been too panicked to give the spell much focus. Where exactly had I gotten us *to*?

I pushed myself into a sitting position. My hands pressed down into soft, cool grass. Darton kept one hand by my elbow, as if he thought I might need further steadying. A reasonable concern. A rush of dizziness sent my thoughts spinning. I closed my eyes until the sensation subsided.

We were sitting in an open field. The breeze that licked past us smelled like autumn, damp and earthy. Across the field, the sunlight glimmered off the surface of a small pond. Weeping willow trees lined its bank. I blinked.

Oh. Not exactly the place I'd have chosen if I'd been thinking straight, but I guessed this was fitting.

"Do you know where we are?" Darton asked. The rising wind ruffled his gold-blond hair.

I nodded as I heaved myself onto my feet. "This is a park not too far from my parents' house. I played here a lot when I was a kid. We're just outside Boston." Apparently I still associated my most recent childhood home with safety. At least it was plenty far from Britain and the Darkest One. For the time being.

Darton stood up too. He bent to grasp the hilt of his sword. He'd been clutching Excalibur when I'd grabbed him to whisk us away. At least we still had that enchanted weapon, after all the trouble we'd gone through to retrieve it.

"Boston?" he said. "What do we do now? What exactly *happened* back there?"

I winced. Right. He didn't know yet. The knowledge sat heavy in my chest. I'd failed a lot of people by not stopping the Darkest One, but no one more than my king.

"Rhedyn offered herself up to the lightning at the last second," I said. "She sacrificed herself. To free her master. The Darkest One snapped my spell, the one that was keeping her bound. She's out now."

Darton went still. "Out? Then..."

"Then she'll be coming after you. Which is why I got us out of there." I rubbed my hand over my face. I'd lost my purse and my bag of supplies in the chaos. I had no phone, no wallet. Nothing but the now rather muddy sweater and jeans I was wearing. I glanced at Darton. "What do you have on you?"

He shook himself out of his daze and reached for his pockets. His phone's screen stayed dark when he tapped the buttons. He grimaced. "It had a little power an hour ago."

"Lightning plus magic might not have been a good combo for the battery. If we're lucky, it's not completely fried."

He patted his other pocket, and his frown deepened. "My wallet's gone. It must have fallen out—maybe during that landslide. Damn."

"So we've got no money and no means of communication. Perfect!" I reached my awareness out into the air, testing my magical sensitivity. Every nerve in my body ached in protest. No way was I hopping us to the other side of the country, to our house and all the supplies I had stashed nearby, by my power alone.

Which meant there was only one reasonable course of action, as much as I balked at it. "I guess we'd better drop in on my parents. Their place is about a twenty-minute walk from here."

Darton looked down at himself. In the middle of the battle, Rhedyn had sent a landslide over us. It had left as much dirt smeared all over his sweatshirt and jeans as I had on my clothes. "This isn't exactly how I'd have wanted to meet your mom and dad for the first time, but it sounds like we don't have much choice."

"Yeah." I wanted to say they'd seen worse, but for all my childhood weirdness, I was pretty sure showing up out of the blue and caked with mud—as a grown adult of twenty, no less—was going to make the top of the list. "Come on, Art."

Little shivers traveled up my legs as we started walking. My breath started to catch in my lungs before we'd made it to the road that ran alongside the park. That last apparating spell had really drained me, and my brief "sleep" had hardly left me recovered. All

I wanted was to curl up in a bed and really sleep, for at least a week.

But I wasn't sure I could afford to sleep at all with the Darkest One on the loose. How long would it take her to figure out where we'd gone? What was she going to do to all the people who stood between her and us?

A sharper shiver raced down my back. We definitely weren't going to stay at my parents' house long enough to find out. I'd already gotten them into enough trouble. Just a few days ago, one of the Darkest One's fae minions had gotten my mom into a minor car accident, meant as a threat to me.

Darton held the sword close at his side when a car cruised by. "I feel kind of conspicuous. How much do your parents know about... all of this, Merlin and King Arthur and the rest?"

"Nothing," I said. "And we're going to keep it that way. All they know is their daughter Emmaline is a little odd and sometimes knows more about things than it totally makes sense that she should. It's basically never a good time to tell your mom and dad that you're not their kid but the reincarnation of a legendary wizard they probably don't even believe really existed."

"Ah. I can see how that would be tricky." He gave me a wry smile that looked slightly pained. "So, just so I'm prepared, what's our story?"

Good question. "Hmm... We can say it's some kind of college club hazing ceremony. The ringleaders drop people off in pairs, and then we have to use our wits to get back to campus. As long as we sound like we're fine with it, my parents won't ask too many questions. We just won't stick around too long."

It might be good to stop by anyway, just to look for any lingering dark fae influence in the area. As far as I knew, the Darkest One's minions had left our families alone after we'd ignored their threats and headed overseas. The fae hunter we'd gotten to know, Jagger, had called up a few of his colleagues to keep an eye on things here just in case. But I'd feel better checking with my own senses.

The road swerved to the left, meandering past a few blocks of well-spaced suburban houses. The yards and driveways grew steeper with the rising hill. I scanned the lawns ahead of us as we came up on my parents' home, a two-story colonial in pale peach-toned brick. Thanks to the time difference between here and Britain, it was still early morning on this side of the ocean. Late enough that Mom and Dad should be up, but not so late that they'd have left for work yet.

A rental car was parked at the top of their steep driveway—theirs must not be back from getting repaired after Mom's accident. No one stirred around the house. This late in the fall, there wasn't much to do in the gardens anyway. I didn't see any sign of the fae hunters either. Of course, they'd know better than to be totally obvious in their surveillance.

I showed Darton where he could stash Excalibur in the depths of the hedge, since I had no idea how we could explain why we were carrying around an ancient sword on top of everything else. Then I walked up the front steps and rang the doorbell. It felt strange, requesting entrance like a stranger. My keys had gotten lost with the rest of my stuff back in Britain.

Dad answered the door. His thinning hair, the same dark brown as mine, lay damp from his shower. His eyes widened at the sight of me.

"Emma! We weren't expecting you. Are you all right?" He paused, the corners of his mouth creasing with worry as he took me in. "You look as if you've had a rough time." His gaze slid farther, to Darton. "And who's this?"

"Emmaline is here?" Mom's voice carried from deeper in the house. She hustled over, bringing her cup of tea with her. A thick neck brace held her heart-shaped face stiffly straight. "My goodness, honey. I'd say this is a wonderful surprise, but if there's been some sort of trouble—"

"No, no," I said quickly, with a faked laugh and a casual wave of my hand. "We're fine. Just a crazy club activity that got a little out of hand. You know how college adventures can end up. This is my friend Darton, who was my partner for the weekend. We're kind of cheating by showing up here, but as long as you don't tell anyone..."

As I'd expected, my lack of distress put my parents at ease. And they'd always fretted a bit about whether I was making friends. The idea of me being in some kind of adventurous college club would probably make their day. Yeah, Dad's lips had already curled into a little smirk. He and Mom had gotten into way crazier escapades when they were my age.

"Come on in, then," he said. "Do you need something to eat? We just finished breakfast."

The tension wound around my stomach pinched too tight for the thought of eating to be appealing. But I wasn't going to get my energy back by starving myself. "That would be great," I said. "First I think we should get cleaned up, though. I wanted to grab a change of clothes and a few things from my old room. Dad, would you mind lending Darton a pair of pants and a shirt?" Dad was a little shorter and a little broader, but we couldn't afford to be picky.

"We can put your things through the wash," Mom offered. "I'm taking the day off, but even if I wasn't, you could stay as long as you like."

"Oh, no, we'll have to get going to make sure we don't get caught out." I winked at her, burying my guilt over the lies. They were safer the sooner we were out of here.

"Well, come on then, young man," Dad said, clapping Darton on the back.

I hurried up to my childhood bedroom, which my parents had left intact for summers and holiday visits. The pickings in my dresser and closet were pretty sparse, but anything clean was better than the muddy stuff I currently had on. I grabbed an old, faded pair of jeans and a sweater that had developed a hole in the sleeve.

After a quick stop in the bathroom, my bladder was relieved and the dirt streaks gone from my face. I shoved my messy hair into its usual ponytail. A shower would have been amazing, but I wasn't sure we had time for that.

Back in my bedroom, I dug into a box I'd left tucked in the back of my closet. An emergency stash for circumstances like this— not that I'd ever really thought I'd be having a showdown with the Darkest One in this life. When you've gone through dozens without your biggest fear becoming a reality, it starts to feel a little less real.

I grabbed a purse I hadn't used since high school and stuffed in the few wands and baggies of herbs and salt I'd left here, as well as my spare credit card. There. Now I wasn't totally helpless.

As if a few handfuls of herbs and the wave of a wand would do much good against all the Darkest One's coiled power.

The floor creaked as I was straightening up. Darton stopped in the doorway, looking a little comical in the baggy khakis that bared his ankles and the checkered button-up shirt he'd borrowed from my dad. But still handsome. You could deck that guy out in a garbage bag and he'd make my heart flutter anyway.

There definitely wasn't time for thinking about *that*. Anyway, he knew how I felt now, how much I'd always felt, and I knew it wasn't the same for him. Better that we'd put the whole subject to rest.

"So this is where you grew up," he said.

"This time," I couldn't help saying.

He arched an eyebrow at me before taking a step inside. "It's hard to imagine you being a kid. I guess I never knew you as one."

His gaze swept through the room. I felt suddenly exposed, even though my king already knew me better than anyone else in the world.

My duvet had a deep green vine pattern that had appealed to the sensibilities of my light fae side. The books I'd left behind on my now-dusty shelves included a bunch of science-y nonfiction, which was odd for teen reading but not embarrassing, and several historical romances, which were *definitely* embarrassing. An herbal, slightly smoky smell still clung to the walls from all the incantations I'd cast over the years, hoping to provoke the vision that would lead me to my king. A black smear marked the floorboards where I'd once dropped a lit candle.

Darton nodded to one of the band posters tacked over my bed. "Justin Bieber fan, huh?"

I made a face at him. "Past tense. I *was* an actual teenager along with everything else, you know."

He gave me a teasing smile, and sod it if my heart didn't flutter all over again.

Enough nostalgia. We had bigger problems to tackle.

We walked downstairs to the smell of frying eggs and fresh toast. "Mom," I said. "You really didn't have to. Are you even feeling okay?"

"I'm perfectly all right!" she insisted, waving the spatula. "I'm not sure I even need the neck brace, but I wasn't going to argue with the doctor. It's not as if I was in some huge crash—I was barely out of the driveway."

"Right," I said skeptically, and paused. "You haven't seen anyone suspicious around here since then, have you? Dad said some weird guy made a strange comment to him."

"Nothing suspicious at all," she said. "And the mechanic told us it was a random system failure—unusual but not impossible."

Definitely not impossible when magic was involved. But when she shoved the plate of eggs and buttered toast into my hands, I reached for the fork automatically. I'd barely eaten anything all day —and by British time we'd have been well past due for lunch now.

"This is wonderful," Darton said to my mother. Mom beamed. Dramatic music and a serious news reporter voice trickled from the living room. I ambled over to find my Dad sitting in front of the TV.

He motioned to the screen. "Quite the storm."

What appeared to be an atmospheric pressure display was showing on the TV, but I'd never seen colors quite that stark. The broadcast cut back to the reporter. "After several days of stormy weather all across England," he said, staring solemnly at the camera, "winds are building to unprecedented levels. Some areas are already experiencing hurricane-like conditions. Residents have been advised to follow local alerts, but hospitals are already filling with injured civilians."

My stomach dropped. I put down my plate on the side table. Darton had come in behind me. He lowered his fork, his face paling, and caught my eye. I gave him a slight nod.

The Darkest One was already making her presence felt. How many more people was she going to hurt along the way?

CHAPTER TWO

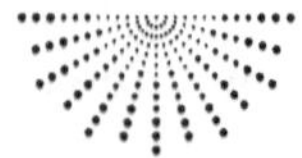

A BATTLE RAGED AROUND US, *but the heaving bodies were little more than a blur. The shouts and clatter bled together into a shapeless din. The taste of iron lay on my tongue, and a chill coated my skin. The blue sky darkened above us. And a figure shifted across the field like a traveling shadow.*

The Darkest One. I reached for my king's arm, but Arthur was suddenly across the battle from me. The clamor rose. The blur of bodies churned between us. I threw myself into it, but the dark fae lady loomed over him already. Gray mists curled around her tall, slender body. Her arms shot out so quickly he didn't even have time to move. She dug her thumbs through his chainmail into his chest and wrenched him apart.

His body split open with a burst of shadow. His head lolled, bloodlessly pale. A scream of protest jarred in my throat. I raised my hand—

"Em." Darton's voice, like my king of old's but not quite the same, broke through my sleep. He gripped my shoulder with a quick shake. My eyes popped open. A narrow, gray space came into focus around me.

The plane. We were in the same stuffy plane cabin we'd entered a few hours ago, stiffly padded seat beneath me, recycled air filling my lungs.

Darton was eyeing me closely. "We just landed. And you... seemed like you weren't all that happy being asleep. You were jerking your head back and forth like you were fighting with something."

A flicker of the nightmare rose in the back of my head. "Don't worry about it," I said, waving him off. "Just a bad dream. Have to expect a few of those, these days." But my chest still felt tight.

It hadn't been only a nightmare. The images had come from a vision. The vision I'd had of my king's death, fifteen hundred years ago, five years before the Darkest One had nearly made it come true. It had been the first warning I'd gotten. I'd tried to heed it. And still, here we were.

The second we were allowed off the plane, Darton pulled out his phone. My dad had lent us a charging cable, and the battery had proven to be in working order. Darton skimmed through the news feeds as we made our way through the terminal in the state I'd called home for the last few months.

I patted my pocket to make sure the twigs I'd stashed for quick access were still there. I'd been able to present a couple of slips of paper as our ID cards when we'd gotten on the plane, but the illusion would have worn off shortly after we'd gotten into the air. It hadn't been worth wasting my still-limited energy to maintain that magic if I didn't have to. In my current state, casting the spell to make sure everyone ignored Darton's sword, which we couldn't exactly check, had been exhausting enough.

"The storms in Britain are still building," Darton said. "They've totally shut down the London subway system. They're evacuating a bunch of towns and cities along the coast." He shook his head, his jaw tight. "The news articles are already reporting six deaths they attribute to the storm."

"She could have done a lot worse already, if all she cared about was killing lots of people, and fast," I said, keeping my voice low. This wasn't the sort of conversation I wanted anyone overhearing.

"So what do you think she does want?"

"I have no idea. I've never been able to understand how dark fae minds work. From what we're seeing, I'd say for now she's just playing around. Collecting energy from people's fear and pain. It's been a long time since she's been able to affect anything in the world. She's stretching her muscles."

Darton shoved his phone back in his pocket. "And what happens when she's done stretching?"

I hesitated. "Probably she comes looking for us. So we've got to get ready."

A jittery itch crawled up my arms under my skin. I rubbed them through the sleeves of my sweater. I'd dozed a little on the plane, but it wasn't that long a flight. Apparently my body still hadn't recovered from this morning's jump across the ocean.

"We can grab a rental car to get home," I said, pointing Darton toward the sign. The drive would only take an hour from here. Then I'd know Darton was at least somewhat protected before I got on with other business.

The guy at the rental car desk gave us a bit of an odd look, I guessed for our lack of luggage, but he led us to a car quickly enough. "I'll drive," Darton said after the guy had left us. He set Excalibur in the back seat. "You should rest as much as you can after everything we've just been through."

I had the urge to argue. I should have been looking after him, not the other way around. But if I'd learned anything during our adventures around Britain, it was that Darton could protect himself a whole lot better when he held on to his confidence. And he could do *that* a whole lot better when I showed I trusted him to handle whatever our current situation threw at us. So I made myself simply say, "Thank you," and settled into the passenger seat.

I really *did* need that rest, after all.

As Darton maneuvered the car out of the lot, I leaned my head against the cool glass of the window and closed my eyes. I was tired enough that my mind started to drift without any effort. But the little twitches running through my body kept jolting me back into consciousness. My fingers curled of their own accord, as if needing something to grasp.

I had those few wands in my purse, but that didn't feel right. Was my body responding to some instinct I didn't quite understand?

The muscles in my arms coiled tighter with each minute. I found myself gritting my teeth. Okay, this was definitely not restful. I tried to inhale and exhale slow and deep, but the tension didn't ease.

Something was wrong. Something I couldn't ignore.

I opened my eyes in time to see a sign for an upcoming rest area off the highway. I pointed to it. "Let's pull off there. Something feels... off. I don't want to go any farther until I figure out what."

Darton took the next exit. "Do you need me to do anything?"

"Grab some food from the vending machines?" I suggested. "I'm just going to search around with my magic."

He parked at the edge of the lot near the squat dun building that held bathrooms and a small seating area. I stayed in the car when he got out. Less likely to draw attention that way. I pulled one of the wands from my purse and sat with it resting on my palms in my lap. I didn't want to draw much energy from it, but it'd be good to have it on hand.

Closing my eyes again, I let my awareness seep out into the world around us. My fae-enhanced senses swept over the rest area and across the highway and the landscape beyond.

The itch in my muscles had already started to subside. Maybe my instincts had been responding to something we'd been heading toward? I stretched my senses west, watching for any hint of dark power. The Darkest One might be playing around in Britain at the moment, but she had plenty of underlings on this side of the pond.

A shiver ran over my skin. A small but steady stream of glooms were heading our way from various directions. The scraps of dark fae vermin were still more concentrated than usual around our state thanks to the fae mercenary who'd sent them on a hunt after us just a few weeks ago. And now they were on a new hunt. A few had already nearly reached the rest area.

Glooms weren't much to worry about on their own, but in large enough numbers they could do plenty of damage. I'd cast a protective shield around Darton before we'd left the country, but it must have worn off with all the magic we'd encountered since. And the soul of my king inside him was certainly a lot more woken up than it'd been before.

Not much I could do about that, but I could cast a new shielding spell on him. It'd be an awful irony if glooms got him before the Darkest One even showed her face on this side of the ocean.

I got out of the car and ambled over to a sapling near the edge of the paved walk. By the time I'd collected several twigs from it, Darton had rejoined me. "Do you need to work some more magic?" he asked.

"I want to redo that spell I put on you in the hotel room a while back." A fresh jitter ran through my limbs. Yeah, stopping here definitely hadn't solved the problem. "The glooms are reacting to your presence again. Come here. We don't want someone calling the cops on a couple of weirdos playing with blood."

Darton grimaced, but he followed me into the single-stall handicapped bathroom. A dank, sour smell filled my nose. Muddy footsteps and a puddle of what I hopped was water marked the floor. Not exactly ideal spell-casting circumstances, but I couldn't afford to be picky.

I scattered the twigs around us on the floor and murmured a quick incantation to sever a lock of Darton's hair. He slung his hands in his pockets and inclined his head as I broke open the skin on my palm. Seeing me do blood work always made him squeamish.

Apparently it made me squeamish today too. My nerves were twitching even harder now. The glooms weren't *that* close, were they? I tensed my arms to keep them still as I pressed the lock of hair against the cut. A murmur in my first language spilled over my lips. I drew the power from my life's liquid and the green pulse of the twigs. Then I brought the tip of my wand to my hand, circled it against my palm, and waved it in another circle around Darton.

A tingle raced over my scalp as the magical barrier formed around him. At the same time, my hands started to shake. They wanted to move—to fling out? To reach for something? My tongue quavered too, attempting to reject the words of my casting. What the hell was going on?

I barreled on through my discomfort. *"Like mist conceal, and never reveal."* The spell wouldn't be enough to hide him from the Darkest One when she decided to look for him—it wouldn't even discourage a particularly determined regular fae, as we'd discovered not long ago—but it'd divert the lesser creatures at least temporarily.

Darton closed his eyes when I pressed my bloody palm to his forehead. The threads of my magic pulled tighter around him. There. That would do for now, at least. I could do a more thorough job of the spell once I had more supplies on hand. Assuming we had the chance before the Darkest One and whatever she had planned came calling.

"Okay," I said. "All done. Wash up." I let him go to the sink first while I tucked away my wand. The twigs had disintegrated into a circle of dust around the stall. I smeared it with my foot. No need to advertise that magic had happened here.

That strange, itchy energy kept wriggling through my bones. Whatever my body was worried about, casting this spell hadn't reassured it. I frowned as I switched places with Darton at the sink.

My hand flinched away from the soap dispenser for a second before I got it under control. Hog's balls, this was annoying.

Well, I'd done what I could. I dragged in a breath, willing myself to relax, and turned around. Darton moved to open the door. And my body suddenly sprang into motion without consulting my mind at all.

My arms snapped through the air toward Darton's back, my hands jerking up so my palms pointed toward the area behind his heart. Power pulsed from my soul and onto my tongue. "*Seize and—*"

I had to bite my tongue to cut off the spell before I finished it. A chill flooded me. Darton glanced back at me the second before I wrenched my hands down. He looked at them and then my face.

"Are you okay? Was there something else you needed to do?"

I swallowed hard. *Yes*, the urge echoing through my limbs said in answer to that second question. *Yes, yes, yes.*

Oh, light have mercy. I'd forgotten. Before we'd gone to strike down the Darkest One's allies in the hope of keeping her contained, I'd struck a deal with the light fae enclave that used to be home to my father—and me, fifteen centuries ago. In exchange for their help summoning a lightning storm, I'd sworn an oath to the elders.

If the Darkest One walks free, I will sever Arthur's soul before she can.

"It's nothing," I said quickly. I crossed my arms over my chest, jamming my hands under my elbows. "Let's get out of here."

The Darkest One was walking free all right. And the oath bound me whether I was thinking about it or not. I hadn't given an exact timeline, but clearly the threat was already great enough for the power of that binding to try to force me to act.

If I didn't figure out how to control the oath, *I* would kill Darton before the any of the dark fae did.

CHAPTER THREE

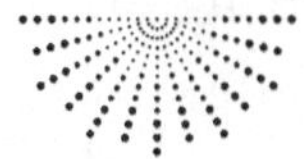

WE REACHED our house in the middle of its lonely concrete yard in the late afternoon. The shadows of the trees along the country road were already stretching long, but the boxy structure we currently called home cast no shadows at all, thanks to the flood lights that had automatically turned on with the fading sunlight.

"Looks like everything's still in working order," I said with forced cheerfulness. "I guess nobody saw any need to mess with our house while we weren't in it."

Despite the reassurance of the lights, I kept one of my wands in my hand on the way past the door. Motioning for Darton to stay close, I walked through each of the rooms.

The furniture we'd bought less than a month ago stood exactly where we'd left it. The faint smell of oil and garlic from the last meal I'd cooked here lingered in the kitchen. No signs of any dark fae presence or anything else worrying appeared. Other than the continued jumping of my nerves whenever Darton moved closer to me.

Sodding hell. I should never have made that oath. Of course, if

I hadn't, then we might have had both the Darkest One *and* her most loyal lieutenant still to deal with... Argh.

The safer I made Darton, the less I'd feel the impulse. If the Darkest One couldn't kill him, then I didn't need to. No one could argue with that strategy. But if I was going to make this house any safer than it already was, I needed more supplies. I'd already emptied this place in our dash out of the country a few days ago.

I came to a stop in the living room after my search of the house was done. "All right. I need to go out to my storage locker to bring back some more magical materials." And maybe some of my journals too—had I ever written about dealing with oaths? I couldn't remember anything like this coming up before, but then, my memories of all but my first life were awfully hazy.

"Sure," Darton said. He headed to the front door.

I shook my head. "No, I want you to stay here. The house has way more protections than the car. The sun trap stopped a full dark fae before. And I'll only be gone a few hours."

Darton frowned. "I trust *you* more than I trust a building. Half the stuff here only works because of your magic."

"Well, you've got your nifty magic sword to defend yourself now too." I nodded to Excalibur, which he'd been carrying from room to room with us.

His frown deepened. "Do you really think we'll be in that much danger here? We just got back. How quickly can the Darkest One follow us?"

I bit my lip. "Not instantly. She doesn't have any connections here to make the leap by magic. But she's not the only thing we have to watch out for."

"If any dark fae things attack, I'm sure I'll be safer if I'm with you."

I'm not, I thought but didn't let myself say. I looked down at my hands. The hands that had moved to stop Darton's heart less than an hour ago.

That was what my feelings came down to, wasn't it? I was

more afraid of the oath that was riding me than of the dark rabble or any other of the dark kind. What if the impulse to kill Darton hit me more strongly next time? What if I *couldn't* control it?

The spell that had bound my and my king's lives together, kept us reincarnating after each successive death, had been broken in the Darkest One's escape. If he died, by anyone's hand, there was no returning.

Darton was watching me, his expression puzzled and determined. "*You'll* be safer too," he added. "The dark fae are afraid of Excalibur. We took them down so much easier when we could work with both your magic and the sword."

"It might not be enough," I started, but that line of argument wasn't going to be enough either. He was right. We were both safer from dark powers with our own powers combined. And to explain why that wasn't enough, I'd have to tell him about the oath. How much would he trust me then?

I trusted myself, didn't I? I'd caught myself in the bathroom before I'd hurt him. And now I understood what was happening inside my body, so I could stay more aware of it. The only reason the oath had worked on me as far as it had was that I hadn't known what I had to defend against. It couldn't take me by surprise like that again.

"All right," I said, as breezily as I could manage. "Have it your way. But prepare for extreme boredom."

The bland beige building of the storage facility made a gloomy picture in the deepening evening. We stepped out of the rental car —I'd insisted on doing the driving this time, to keep my hands busy—and I led the way up to the main doors.

A gloom glided toward us along the edge of the building. The thicker patch of darkness amid the shadows was moving fast enough to catch even Darton's eye. His head jerked around a second before I waved my wand at it. *"Darkness begone."*

The dark vermin shuddered out of existence. If only I could tackle the actual fae and their queen that easily.

I tapped in the code, and the door unlocked with a beep. The inner hall always smelled strangely like stale bread. I hurried past the rows of garage-style doors to the one I'd moved my stash to after a vision had brought me to this part of the country looking for my king. My keys might be lost somewhere back in Britain, but it only took a tiny twig and a few murmured words to open the padlock.

I pushed the door halfway up and ducked under. Darton followed. His eyebrows rose as I shoved the door back down to give us privacy.

"Wow. You really do like to stay well-prepared, don't you?"

"I've had a lot of time to collect supplies and not too much need of them until recently," I said. "I'll try to make this quick."

I grabbed a couple of the duffel bags I kept there for purposes like this and started stuffing them full of pre-enchanted wands, bags of dried herbs and flowers, various types of salt, incense and candles, various semi-precious stones that might come in handy, and a knife to replace the light fae dagger we'd also lost somewhere in our battle with Rhedyn. Like that one, its handle was made of magic-sealed living wood. But it didn't come close to the craftsmanship the full fae were capable of when they bothered.

My life would really be a lot easier if they bothered more often.

Here and there I paused with an instinctive urge to leave some behind. For next time. My hands balled, and I shoved more into the bags.

There wasn't going to be a "next time." No more rebirths. No certainty that no matter what happened, I'd find my king again. This was the last life we were going to get, however little might remain of it.

Darton meandered amid the shelves, stopping to finger a folded cloth, to sniff a bunch of herbs dangling from the top of one shelf. He wrinkled his nose. "It reminds me of the apothecary shop. At least, as well as I remember that at all."

"I don't suppose you've had any other incredibly helpful memories?" I said. His recollection of visiting the apothecary in our first lives had led us to the brainstorm of using lenses to amplify the power of sunlight. That idea had allowed us to destroy the dark fae mercenary who'd attempted to grab Darton for his own purposes, and powered the sun trap in our house.

"Not so far." Darton rubbed his mouth. "I still can't even remember why I was looking into the dark fae without talking to you about it. I mean, it's one thing to want to help on my own, but having seen what I have now, I'm pretty sure I was smart enough to realize I'd accomplish more with your knowledge on my side."

"You grew up back then knowing you'd be king," I said. "You weren't used to having to hold yourself back for anyone else. Besides, knowing *me*, you might have asked and I just told you to leave it alone and let me handle everything."

Although I didn't actually recall Arthur ever coming to me asking what strategies I'd looked into for defeating the dark fae. He'd listened well enough when I'd talked about them, but he'd seemed willing to leave that conflict to me while he dealt with his many totally human opponents. I'd never realized he'd wanted to tackle that part of our problem himself.

"Hmm," Darton said, sounding unconvinced. "I'm sure I could have pressed you into talking if I'd tried hard enough."

That was also true. I'd always had trouble denying my king anything.

I moved to my stacks of musty journals, some dating back hundreds of years. A pang ran through me at the thought of the different set of better-cared-for journals I'd left behind on the other side of the ocean. My father's friend Cormag—the elder who'd insisted on the damned oath—had given me a set of my father's journals that detailed his observations and thoughts on the dark fae influence on Arthur's family line. It hadn't made sense to bring them to our confrontation with Rhedyn. I'd left them with two of Jagger's fae-hunter colleagues for safe-keeping, thinking I could come back for them.

I hadn't expected to be making *quite* such a huge or hasty exit.

It would have been good to pour over those more thoroughly right now, but the truth was that nostalgia and family ties aside, they hadn't offered me much useful information in the skim I had been able to give them. If my father had figured out anything that could definitely have changed Arthur's fate, I'd have known about it.

Darton crushed a few leaves of the herb between his thumb and forefinger. A sharp, bittersweet smell drifted through the air. His gaze had gone distant.

"You said Rhedyn let us kill her. That she sacrificed herself so that she could free the Darkest One. Right?"

"Yep. A sneaky trick. We were going to kill her anyway, but she stopped fighting at the last moment. Giving herself over so she could tap into that magic." I made a face and opened up one of my journals to check the contents.

"So she could just make that choice in the moment, because she wanted to? Did she need any magical materials for that? Or is it something the fae can just naturally do?"

"Sacrificial magic is completely internal," I said. "It's about the shape of your will and the strength of your intention." I paused, glancing up. "Why are you asking?"

Darton shrugged. "I just wondered. Obviously it's not something we'd want the fae using against us again."

It wasn't something I wanted *him* thinking about either. Darton could be a little too eager to prove himself a hero sometimes. You'd think years of princely and then kingly valor would have satisfied that urge. It wasn't as if a twenty-year-old college guy could match that kind of past. But so far that fact hadn't stopped him from trying.

Which was why I loved him, wasn't it?

That was another line of thinking it wasn't wise to go down. I bit my lip, poked through the rest of the stacked journals, and finally grabbed a couple to add to my bags. I wasn't sure they'd be useful, but they seemed like the most likely.

The duffels weighed heavily on my shoulders now. "Okay," I said. "I think we're done here."

Darton held out his hand in an offer. I let him take one of the bags off me. I swung the other behind me and heaved up the storage room door. The bag bumped against my hip with each step as we walked down the hall. Fifteen hundred years of stockpiling and experimenting... and it still didn't feel like anywhere near enough to sustain us through the battle ahead.

CHAPTER FOUR

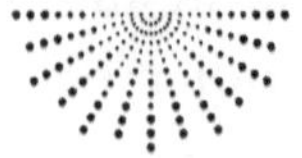

The newscaster's solemn voice carried from our TV. "This catastrophic storm shows no sign of abating. Many coastal areas have completely flooded, but the intense winds are making further evacuation difficult both by land and by sea. Rescue teams are doing as much as they can under these extreme conditions. Still no agreement from meteorologists on what might have caused this truly bizarre and horrific weather over the United Kingdom."

The five of us huddled on the couch and loveseat winced together at the video footage of telephone poles toppling in the gale. On the TV screen, shingles flew away off a nearby house's roof. The pelting rain colored the entire image in shades of gray.

No lightning, of course. The Darkest One wanted her torment to be as grim and gloomy as possible.

"So all that was stirred up by just *one* of these faeries?" Keevan said, his eyebrows high.

"The oldest and most powerful of all of them," I said. And probably not quite at her full power yet. She was just warming up. My stomach listed queasily. "Plus she'll have all the lesser dark fae in the country pitching in."

"Man." He rubbed his hand over his dark face. "That's just— Shouldn't you be over there, like, fighting her or something? Isn't that what wizards do?"

"I'm the only wizard I know, and I can't match that." I waved at the TV. "If we're going to stop her, or at least contain her, we're going to have to be incredibly smart about it. She'll show more of her hand soon." I hoped... and also dreaded. I couldn't imagine she'd wait much longer before coming after me and Darton.

"But all those people..." Izzy shuddered where she was perched next to Keevan, her pale auburn waves drifting over her shoulders. "What about the light fae? Those enclaves you talked about, here and over there. Can't they do anything?"

I made a face. "The light fae generally don't care about anything they don't have to care about. The ones affected in Britain will be doing what they can to protect themselves—and not wanting to expend any additional energy trying to get into some sort of fae war. The ones here won't see any reason to get involved, since it isn't affecting them. They're not exactly philanthropists."

Beside me, Priya twisted her hands in her lap. "My old enclave might be willing to do *something*. They did help monitor what the dark fae were up to around here last week." My former roommate had grown up with the light fae as a sort of changeling, until they'd brought her back to the human world to be adopted. And to be fair, her bunch *had* stepped up when we'd needed them. But keeping an eye on things and waging war were pretty different requests.

"I'll keep that in mind, when I have a better idea of our best strategy," I said. "The other enclave I'm familiar with around here wasn't even willing to keep us protected on their own territory, so they're definitely not getting involved in some huge conflict off of it."

The news broadcast moved on to the next big story. "With the International Peace Summit approaching in just one week, the Windy City's hotels have already started to fill with citizens from all around the world, eager to have a voice in their leaders' conversations. The summit is scheduled to be hosted at Chicago's Fairning Convention Center in—"

Darton switched off the TV and stood up. "We'll do what we can, when we can. Let's get the table set. The food should be here any minute."

The rest of us ambled with him to the kitchen. He'd texted his best friends last night to let them know we'd gotten back in one piece, for now, and I'd reached out to Priya. After all the five of us had already been through together, I guessed I shouldn't be surprised that they'd all insisted on coming right over after classes to confirm the whole "in one piece" part in person. But all their visit was leading to was a whole bunch of uncomfortable conversations.

"Wouldn't it be better if you were at least closer to where the dark fae are casting their magic?" Izzy said, grabbing glasses out of the cupboards. "I mean, so that when you know what to do, you can act right away."

I turned away from her to place a stack of plates on the table. "I don't think there *is* any safe way of getting into Britain at the moment." Maybe flights were diverting around the storm to land in France or other countries closer than we were right now... but the closer we were to the Darkest One, the more I'd feel that impulse to fulfill my oath. Even now, the itch scrabbled faintly under my fingernails. Darton hadn't let me go off to my storage locker on my own—he sure as hell wasn't hanging back here while I flew across the ocean.

Thankfully my king was also quick to defend my reasoning, even if he didn't know all of it. "Em jumped us back here in five seconds flat," he said, handing Keevan another Coke from the fridge. "If we need to get somewhere, distance isn't going to be a problem."

"Is there anything *we* can do?" Keevan asked. "I mean, I'm still not cool with evil faeries and crazy magic and all that, but you know if you need someone to have your backs, we're here."

Izzy and Priya nodded. My heart squeezed. I'd never really had friends in any of my lives before—no one except my king. I'd never been able to let anyone else in on the secret of who I was. It was scary... but also kind of wonderful.

"If anything comes up that I can delegate to you guys, I'll let you know," I said, and I meant it. We wouldn't still be here at all if it weren't for them.

For a moment, the room went quiet except for the faint clink of Priya setting cutlery around the table. I suspected we were all trying to think of something less dire to talk about. And apparently failing, because when Keevan cleared his throat, what came out was, "Are you two staying holed up in here again for the time being, then? No classes, no football practice..."

"At this point, I'd probably be putting everyone else at college in danger by showing up there," Darton said. "I don't like it, but that's just the way it is." He caught my eyes with a meaningful look.

We'd argued over the last couple weeks about how much of his regular life he'd have to leave behind for his safety. How much he didn't want to leave it behind. But that had been before the dark fae had threatened his sister and nearly blasted us into pieces.

"Well, we'll keep our eyes open around campus," Izzy said. "If I see anything strange, I'll let you two know right away." She'd proven especially sensitive to glooms and other dark vermin that normally passed beneath human awareness.

"The campus crusaders!" Keevan announced, slinging an arm around Izzy's shoulders to give her a quick hug. She laughed and elbowed him. He let go of her sooner than I'd bet he wanted to, given the puppy dog look on his face as she turned away. I wasn't the only one around here who had it bad.

A cool prickling ran over my skin. I froze and focused on my senses. The feeling wasn't the same as the oath's itch—I could still feel that too. This was an impression wafting in from beyond the house's walls. Something was present out there that I didn't like. I knew I didn't like it very, very definitely, even without knowing what it was.

The prickling didn't have the pungent flavor I'd have expected if the Darkest One herself had suddenly vaulted to our doorstep, impossible as that was anyway, but my heart started pounding. "Something's outside," I said.

The others fell silent. "The Chinese delivery guy?" Keevan ventured with a weakly hopeful smile.

I shook my head. Whatever it was, I didn't get the sense it was *moving*. It was just there. Waiting. Somehow that unnerved me even more. It almost felt as if the presence *wanted* me to notice it.

Priya shivered. "I, uh, suddenly don't feel so well either." She rubbed her arms. "What's going on, Emmaline?"

The house's protective systems hadn't tripped. The baggie of salt I'd replenished and returned to my pocket wasn't trembling in warning of a dark creature crossing the boundary I'd drawn around the house. Whatever was causing that sensation, it was keeping a healthy distance. For now.

I swallowed hard. "I'm not sure, but I think I'd better check. The rest of you stay in here. Keep the door closed until I'm back."

"Em," Darton protested. I walked past him to the wand I'd left in the basket by the coat rack for exactly this sort of situation. My fingers curled around the warm wood. The pulse of life and magic inside it soothed my nerves just slightly.

"I don't know what kind of danger we might be facing yet," I said. I'd spent all day putting down every protection I could think of around the house, but some of them were untested. They might not be enough to hold an attacker at bay, depending on what was out there.

Darton jogged down the hall to his bedroom and emerged a second later with Excalibur in his hands. Held upright, ready to strike, it glowed with its connection to his soul. I'd enchanted that sword for my king centuries ago in our first lives, and it still lit up for him like no one else.

"Holy shit," Keevan said, his eyes widening. "You didn't tell me you brought back souvenirs."

Darton's lips formed a crooked smile. "Everyone, meet Excalibur. I'm pretty fond of it, mostly because the dark fae don't seem to like it very much."

That was an understatement. Okay, maybe I *was* better off with Darton out there with me. We had worked together, sword and magic, awfully well back in Britain.

"Fine, fine," I said. "But stay close to me and to the door. The lights aren't potent enough to completely repel a full dark fae, and I don't know if the rest of my spells were enough to do the trick."

He listened to me at least on that count. I eased open the door, stretching my awareness ahead of me. Nothing close. Nothing in motion. I slipped outside, and Darton joined me.

We stood shoulder to shoulder as I kicked the door shut behind us. He held the sword poised, his eyes intent on the darkness beyond the flood of the solar lamps. It was only mid-evening, but the contrast made the space beyond the ring of light nearly black.

But only nearly. My salt pouch shuddered a second before a shape shifted near the edge of the light. I tensed, my hand clenching around my wand. Words of a spell leapt to my tongue.

A face framed by tendrils of shadow swam into view at the edge of our protective light. Brown skin, pale eyes, a mocking smile. The salt's vibrations intensified. Another figure emerged, and another, standing several feet apart, all around the house. Not the Darkest One, no, but her minions. We were surrounded by a circle of dark fae.

They didn't move any closer. The sun-powered lights might not have been able to stop them completely, but they'd still drain the fae's power. Maybe my herbs and salt and the rest were enough to hold them in place. Or maybe they weren't here to take Darton quite yet anyway. Their master was still making her preparations, wasn't she?

"We see you, halfling wizard," a pale-faced woman sneered. "We know your weaknesses."

Another chuckled. "Consider this a reminder that we can take what we desire whenever we want."

"The Darkest One is rising, and when she arrives, you will crumble in front of her."

"How does it feel to know you've already failed?"

That last remark and the smirk that followed it cut deep. I swallowed hard and nudged Darton backward. "Stand around puffing yourselves up all you want," I called to them. "We've got better things to do than listen to your rambling."

They stayed where they were until I'd hauled the door open. Then I felt, like an exhaled breath, the pressure easing as they faded farther back into the shadows. But they didn't leave completely. No. They were still waiting along the fringes of the forest beyond the field.

I'd felt them like that before, hadn't I? So long ago the memory rose up like a mist in the back of my mind.

The horses' hooves clopped along the packed dirt road. A thick, piney scent carried on the breeze from the dense forests on either side. An autumn chill laced the air, but the voices of the soldiers around my king and I were light with pride and relief. Even Arthur was smiling, in a weary sort of way.

We'd won. We'd finally pressed the invaders back far enough, sent them fleeing, left them so wrecked that they shouldn't think it wise to return for a very, very long time. The country was safe. The people had been protected. What wasn't there to celebrate?

A prickle crawled across my back. I wasn't the only one who sensed it. My mare, who was calmer than most horses in the face of my half-fae nature, shied a few steps to the side. Arthur glanced at me with eyebrows raised, as if to question whether I'd managed to lose what little horsemanship I'd gained over the last several years at his side. He couldn't feel that waft of unease.

They were here. I tugged my mare back into the line, but my gaze searched the shadows between the close-spaced trees. Something cold and cruel was watching our procession, out of the reach of the setting sun. Something fae. And only one kind of fae would give me that impression, like the edge of a cool blade scraping down my spine.

My fingers clenched around the reins. Words clogged my throat. Let's race our way out of here, I wanted to say. Let the horses run until they're ragged. Until we've left the watchers far behind.

But as happy as our army was, it was exhausted too. I felt the dark fae marking our passage all down the road, too many to easily pass by. We'd beaten one enemy, but another one was still waiting to bring the battle to us.

And when they wanted to, there would be no outrunning them.

CHAPTER FIVE

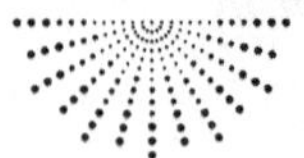

DARTON and I stumbled into the house and shoved the door closed. The thump shook me completely out of my memory of that long ago ride.

Our three friends stood at the edge of the living room, staring at us. Darton lowered his sword, his knuckles white. "What do we do now?"

"To the fae?" I grimaced. "Nothing. Not yet, anyway. They'd probably like it if I started wearing myself out throwing spells at them. They're following the same M.O. as their master. Stirring up fear and pain. That was all they wanted—to taunt us."

To taunt *me*, mostly. The fae on both sides had always seen me as something of an abomination because of my father's light fae blood mingling with my mother's humanity, but the dark found it particularly repulsive. Totally contrary to the sense of order they were so fond of. And my soul's habit of leaping from one new human body to the next struck them as even more unruly.

Well, too bad. It wasn't as if I was looking for their approval.

"What the hell happened out there?" Keevan said.

"Dark fae," Darton said. "All around the house. They said a

528

bunch of stuff, but they didn't come at us or anything." He froze up. "I need to call my sister."

He took out his phone and brought up his little sister's number. My arms twitched. I dropped my wand into the basket. Too much dark power, too close. The oath's hold was tingling through me more sharply than before.

"Hey, Audrey! How's it going? Ah, come on, can't I check in on my little sister now and then? Yeah, yeah. So everything's been fine there? Okay, good. Good. I know. I'll see you at Thanksgiving."

Darton lowered the phone looking only partly relieved. He was more protective of his sister than just about anyone. Maybe because he'd already had to save her life once, though not for fae-related reasons. When we'd first been getting to know each other, he'd told me the story of how he'd had to drag her out of a pool when he was twelve and do CPR to restart her breathing. A moment like that stayed with you.

But all the moments he and I had shared weren't enough to calm the oath's demands. I stepped away from him, toward the kitchen. Distance. If I could just get a little distance from him, let the sense of the threat fade...

"I don't think the fae will bother us while we're in here," I said to our friends, fighting to keep the strain out of my voice. "But if you all want to leave... or if you want to stay the night so you don't have to go out there while they're lurking around, it's up to you. We can put you up."

"Yeah, it's no problem," Darton said. To my dismay, he followed me over to the kitchen island. The closer he was, the more my nerves jittered through my limbs. Urging me to turn on him, to snap out a spell or slash the knife in my back pocket across his neck. To end his life before the Darkest One could use it for her own ends.

I grabbed a glass and kept my hands busy filling it with water. What if we weren't safe even tonight? I didn't think the Darkest One had started the journey from England across the ocean yet—

did she really have enough power to keep that storm raging without being present? But I could be wrong. The dark fae might be expecting her to make her appearance before the sun rose.

What in light's name would I do then? Swine crud and cattle sod. I wasn't ready. I didn't have any idea how to become ready.

My hands started to shake. "Emmaline?" Priya said gently.

"I'm okay," I said. "Just thinking it through." I gulped the water and set the glass down before I could spill it. The cold liquid pooled in my stomach.

I had my wands, my knife, and all my other supplies. Every magical protection I'd ever used or imagined was in place around and inside the house. There was no building more secure in the universe.

If we had to make a last stand, there was nowhere better to do it.

The thought of the Darkest One appearing in a gust of magic on our doorstep sent another tremble through me. "Em," Darton said. He stepped closer and touched my shoulder.

My lungs seized. My hand leapt to my knife. The urging of the oath ran through my muscles and closed my fingers around the hilt. It whipped my arm back in front of me, my hand clutching the weapon.

No. I clamped my teeth together and wrenched myself to the side, fighting for control. Every nerve in my body was screaming at me to spin back toward Darton, to let the knife do the work I'd promised Cormag.

No, no, no!

"Em, what's going on?" Darton said, oblivious. He started to move around me—toward the sodding knife. My hand jerked. I gasped, and my arm shot out.

I could only think of one way to interrupt the compulsion. With a heave of my muscles, I yanked the knife out of its arc toward Darton's throat—and into the palm of my other hand.

The magic-enhanced blade sliced right through skin and sinews and out the other side. Pain lanced through my hand and up my arm in a sharp, searing bolt. It left my body shuddering, but it washed away the oath's frantic itch. All I felt was that flare of agony.

"Emma!" Izzy yelped. Priya darted over. Darton had already caught me, his arms around my shoulders as I staggered. My head had started to spin. Possibly because of the blood streaming from my punctured hand to patter across the kitchen floor.

"What can I do?" he said, low and rough by my ear. "What do you need?"

"Is it really *her*?" Keevan asked. "Did one of those evil faeries get in her head like that one did to Priya before?"

"It's me," I mumbled. "I'm sorry. I need to clean this up. Come with me, Art?"

I cradled my arm against my sweater, the blood soaking into the wool fabric, as Darton ushered me to the main bathroom. There, I rested my wrist on the edge of the sink so I'd bleed into the drain. I eyed the knife warily. The pain had started to dull into a throbbing burn. But the blade needed to come out. That wasn't going to be fun.

"Is there anything I can get from your rooms—all those supplies we brought back—" Darton said.

I shook my head. "Just hand me a towel. Whichever one you like the least."

He laughed hoarsely and opened the cabinet. I took the towel he passed me and laid it under my hand. Gritting my teeth, I grasped the knife's hilt and jerked it out.

A fresh spasm of pain clouded my vision. Darton flinched. I tossed the bloody blade in the sink with a clatter and tugged the towel tightly around my palm to stifle the flow of blood. Then I snatched a few twigs from my pocket and murmured a quick incantation.

"Seal the skin and flesh beneath. Stopper the blood that flows."

I didn't have the concentration to do a perfect job of it. I could feel even as the muscles knit back together that they weren't perfectly aligned. This hand wasn't going to work the same unless I redid the healing at some later time, with a clearer head. But at least it wasn't emptying all the fluid out of my body anymore.

I could have said a few more words to numb the pain, but I wanted it to keep hurting. As long as it was hurting, I had control. I'd really prefer not to have to stab myself all over again.

"Are you going to tell me what happened back there?" Darton said quietly. He rested his hand on the small of my back.

I closed my eyes for a second. The dizziness and the pulse of pain set off jagged sparks behind my eyes.

If it had gotten this bad, I had to tell him. He had to know, so he could protect himself from *me*.

I inhaled shakily and looked up at him. "There's something I didn't tell you before. I thought I could keep it under control—I didn't want you to worry."

Darton's brow knit. "What are you talking about?"

It hurt almost as much as my hand admitting this. "When I went to my father's old light fae enclave to ask if they'd summon the lightning for us... They didn't want to. They were upset that we were even still in the country. They know that the Darkest One is particularly keen to get her hands on you, and they were worried... that you being here, her having the chance to kill you, might make things even worse."

I still hadn't told him about my father's suspicions, about the hint of darkness even I had sensed woven into his soul. He'd had enough trouble keeping his confidence steady without having to worry about danger lurking inside himself.

"And?" Darton prompted.

"And so I swore an oath to them, in exchange for their help. I gave my word, with a magical bond, that if the Darkest One got free despite our efforts... I'd kill you before she could."

I winced as I said it. How could he see my actions as anything other than a betrayal?

Darton stared at me. "I didn't think we had a chance otherwise," I barreled on. "I figured if we didn't manage to contain her, we'd both be dead anyway. But we didn't and we aren't, and the oath... It isn't happy that I'm ignoring it. Especially when the situation we're in starts to feel particularly risky."

"Like right now," Darton said.

"With the dark fae. Yeah. The oath almost took over. But I figured out a way to cut off the impulse." I held up my roughly bandaged hand with a crooked smile.

Darton leaned back against the sink counter, his head bowing. He rubbed his forehead. "You should have told me."

Guilt pinched my gut. "Like I said, I didn't think it mattered. I figured we'd either keep the Darkest One imprisoned and the oath would be moot, or she'd get out and kill us immediately. It's not something I'm *proud* of. I didn't want you thinking about it, about what I'd said I'd do, while we were fighting Rhedyn."

"And after?"

I dropped my gaze. "And after I felt like swine crud for having taken the oath in the first place. I thought I could keep overcoming the urge. I didn't realize it was going to get this bad with her not even nearby." I paused. My throat closed up. "I'm really sorry. You know the last thing I want to do is—"

"Of course I know," Darton said. He motioned to my bloody hand. "You'd always jump in front of a blow coming for me. Even if you were the one dealing it." He didn't sound all that happy about the fact. "I even understand why you didn't want to talk about it, especially considering all the trouble I was having just getting that damned sword to work with me..."

Yeah. And the shamed look on his face right now was exactly why I didn't want to burden him with any more troubles than I'd needed to. "Well, you know now. And I know... to be more careful." My stomach twisted. I didn't really think that was going to be enough.

My king must have seen that too. "Where do we go from here?" he asked.

My stomach twisted. I'd wanted to pretend the oath had never happened. To squash it down and keep going. But that didn't seem like such a wise approach anymore. How could I *ever* confront the Darkest One if a little taunting from her minions could make me attack Darton?

If I was going to save my king, I had to tackle the oath's sway first.

"There has to be a way to break the oath," I said. "I'll figure that out, whatever I have to do, and then we'll be ready to take on the Darkest One." Ha. Sure, it'd be that easy. But Darton's stance relaxed slightly, as if he believed we could do it.

Maybe I could use some more confidence too.

"For now," I added, "I think we'd better go out there and find a decent explanation to give to our friends, before they start to think I must have bled to death in here."

Darton nodded. "Better not to tell them about the oath?"

"Maybe not in excruciating detail..."

He touched my face, tracing his thumb over my cheekbone. The intentness in his eyes washed away the lingering pain. My breath caught.

"I know we can get through this," he said. "I know you'll be right here beside me, and I'll be right here with you."

I leaned into his touch, allowing myself that brief moment of comfort. Wishing I didn't feel even more terrified of what lay ahead of us than I had just ten minutes ago.

CHAPTER SIX

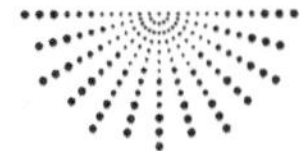

FOR THE FIRST hour of the drive to Priya's former enclave, Priya cranked bouncy pop music in the car. I was grateful to let it fill the space between us. There were too many things I didn't want to talk about. She hummed along with it, tapping her fingers against the steering wheel. But not far from Seattle, she turned the radio down a few degrees and glanced over at me.

"So how does a person, or a fae, usually undo a magical oath?"

Not a question I wanted to contemplate. "They usually *don't*. Generally speaking, the only way to get out of fulfilling a magically charged oath is to die before you have to."

"Oh." Priya's eyebrows leapt up.

"I'm hoping to find a different strategy," I said dryly. "With a little luck, your light fae friends will have some other ideas. I've actually never been bound by an oath before, so I haven't done a whole lot of research into that area." And the human databases of the present day? Pretty sparse on legitimate magical theory.

After a long night spent pouring over those internet resources, I'd decided visiting the fae was my best course of action, at least as a first attempt. They'd know more than anyone about how the oaths of their kind worked. And the trip would put a little distance between Darton and me if the compulsion hit me hard again.

Not that I liked leaving him on his own. But the dark fae hadn't made the slightest move against us all night, so it seemed unlikely they'd try to breach the house now with the sun shining bright in the cloudless sky. Whatever the Darkest One had planned, if she'd even made a real plan yet, she was taking her time.

"How's your hand?" Priya asked.

I ran my thumb over my palm. I hadn't healed it well enough to avoid scabbing. A mottled line marked the center of my hand, front and back, where the knife had pierced through.

I couldn't blame the knife, of course. I'd put it back in my pocket this morning.

"I've felt better," I said. "But it's only a little painful now."

"I know what it's like, having some other force take over your body. Making you do things you don't really mean to do. If you want to really talk about it, not just that hand wave-y explanation you gave us last night, I'm happy to listen."

I grimaced at the windshield. "It's complicated. But I can promise you it's got nothing at all to do with the dark fae." Other than as a trigger. "The light fae can be just as cruel sometimes in their own way."

Priya shrugged. "I don't love all of the ones I've met, but I've never seen one call up a catastrophic storm over an entire country either."

"Fair point." I tipped my head back against the seat. "Generally speaking, the dark fae don't do that either. This one's just 'special.'"

She drove in silence for a few minutes before she said, "You really don't know if you can beat her, do you? Even if you figure out what she wants. Even if you're really smart about it."

My pulse stuttered. "No," I made myself answer. "I don't. Maybe I can't."

"Do you have to fight her at all? Can't you just... I don't know, find some really good hiding spot and hang out there?"

I had to laugh at that. "No. I don't even like that I'm hiding away right now, just letting her get away with everything she's doing. Standing back while she's hurting all those people. If I thought I had *any* chance of stopping her right this moment... It's my fault. I wasn't fast enough dealing with Rhedyn. I didn't stop the Darkest One from getting free."

Priya shook her head sharply. "But you were the one who managed to shut her away in the first place! It's not like you made her go around and do horrible things. She was already being awful back then, and you came along and gave the world, like, a fifteen hundred year respite. As far as I can tell, you've done more than your share."

"She'd probably be a lot less angry right now if I hadn't shut her away," I pointed out. "Anyway, who else is going to step up? The light fae over there clearly can't, if they've even bothered to try. Regular people don't stand a chance. So that leaves me. And Darton with his magic sword. It started with us and her, so it only makes sense it's going to finish that way."

Priya sucked in her lower lip. Her voice came out quiet. "What happens if she just kills you two?"

I hugged myself. "I don't know. I'm trying not to think about that."

"Well, I'll ask the elders here to help you any way they can. I don't know how much they'll listen to me, but I've got a little sway. Ohanko will be there. He'll speak for us."

She pulled off onto a grassy patch by the side of the road. Ancient trees loomed over us. Like every enclave I've visited, Priya's adoptive one lay deep in a wild patch of countryside. The better to keep humans away without being too obvious in their repelling.

I could smell the light fae presence in the air as I got out of the car, like a faint sweetness lingering several hours after cookies have come out of the oven. Priya set off through the forest, picking her way over tree roots and around the underbrush. After just a minute, the canopy of evergreen pines and cedars closed overhead, leaving us in only dim, filtered sunlight.

Winter was nibbling at the edges of the atmosphere. I tugged my jacket tighter around me. The dark fae loved the coldest season. Shorter, darker days. Life gone dormant. So much of the world still and orderly. Nothing like the chaos of new spring growth. Maybe the Darkest One was holding off on her grand catastrophe until then.

"We're almost there," Priya said, motioning to a tree that must have been a landmark for her. Several steps farther, the tingle of the enclave's protective boundary washed over me. It would have repelled most regular human beings, but it didn't appear to affect Priya. The fae must have adjusted their magic to make her a welcome visitor despite her biology.

A lean, long-haired young man stepped out of a sunbeam to meet us. A faint gleam shone in his bronze skin. He bowed to me with the same respect he'd shown when we'd first met last week.

"Hey, Ohanko," Priya said. "Thanks for coming out to meet us. Are the elders ready to talk?"

He made a pained expression that didn't offer much hope. "They have agreed to meet with Merlin. They were hesitant to discuss how we might get involved."

Well, they figured we were coming to ask them to battle the Darkest One. They might be overjoyed when I told them I was here on a much simpler errand. "That's fine," I said. "I'd actually like to talk to them alone, at least to start."

"Are you sure?" Priya said.

At the same time, Ohanko gave me another deep bow. "But of course, Daughter of Eóghan. Should you need any assistance, just call on me."

I bumped Priya's arm with my knuckles. "I'll be fine. I've been talking to light fae types for hundreds of years longer than you have, remember?"

Ohanko motioned for me to follow him. The trees within the

enclave were spaced more sparsely, so warm streaks of sunlight dappled the ground. I drank it into my body as I walked behind the fae man. I might not light up like they did, but I still felt and welcomed the sun's power.

Ohanko led me to a large clearing. A dozen stones the height of stools stood in a ring at its center. Most of them were already occupied by light fae so translucent I knew immediately they were the elders. Ohanko directed me to one of the free stones. I sank down onto its hard, smooth surface, and the younger fae faded back into the trees.

The elders peered at me from around their circle. Their bodies were so filmy it was hard to make out much difference between their features. Their hair and skin faded into the light beaming down from above. If I tried to focus on any one of their faces for more than a second, my eyes started to sting.

They'd been part of this world for an awfully long time. I wasn't sure if that was to my benefit or not. Obviously this enclave hadn't seen much disruption over the years. That might have fortified them—or made them even more wary of conflict.

"Welcome, daughter of Eóghan," the woman nearest me said with a voice like a tinkling bell. "We understand that you come to us with a request for help."

That was as straightforward a statement as I could hope for from a light fae. "Yes," I said. "And thank you so much for agreeing to hear me out. I'm sure you'd like to keep out of this mess around the Darkest One as much as possible. I promise I'm not going to ask you to do anything that involves her, at least not today. I'm hoping you can advise me on a different matter."

One of the elder men bobbed his head, his silky hair drifting around his face. "There are many paths that may lead to the same destination," he said. "We cannot see the end without the beginning."

Yeah, that was more the kind of conversation I expected from these types.

"Right," I said. "So here's the thing: I swore an oath to a few light fae in Britain. I promised to do something that I didn't think I'd ever be in a position to have to do. But... things worked out differently than I expected. Circumstances changed. And now doing that thing, it wouldn't actually make things better. It would make them so much worse, for everyone."

"That is unfortunate," the first woman said. "The winds of life are always shifting."

I nodded as if that remark was in any way helpful. "Yeah. So, I'd rather not follow through and cause even more problems. Since it's light fae magic that went into the oath bond, I thought maybe you all would have some idea how to dissolve it."

The elders exchanged a glance around the circle. They didn't try to hide their discomfort at my suggestion. It flickered through their glow like a passing shadow.

The elder man who'd spoken before turned to face me again. "To give one's sacred word, it is a root dug deep. Cutting it off can only do harm."

"Well, that's not necessarily true," I hedged. "I mean, what if that root had a sickness take to it? And then if you cut off the root, you're actually saving the rest of the tree from dying. That's the kind of situation we're talking about here."

My adapting of his metaphor seemed to impress him at least a little. He pursed his lips, but he'd tilted his head in consideration. A couple of the others leaned closer to murmur to him and the elder woman who'd spoken first. I waited, trying to look responsible and deserving. Not like someone who made oaths willy nilly without consideration of the consequences.

I was trying to save the world from having the Darkest One inflicted on it, I thought, biting back the urge to say it out loud. *If your kind weren't so bloody self-absorbed, I wouldn't have* had *to make wretched oaths like that one just to get some help.*

The woman shook back her shimmering hair and met my eyes.

"It is not something any of us has ever attempted," she said. "But we will examine you and make a decision then."

"Sure," I said, my spirits lifting. They were actually going to try. "What do you need me to do?"

They consulted each other a few minutes longer. Then the man gestured to the middle of the ring. "Sit in the midst of our energies, and we will see from all angles."

Fair enough. I walked to the center of the stone circle and hunkered down on the soft grass. The combined presence of the light fae warmed the air enough that the ground here wasn't even cold.

Several pairs of glowing eyes honed in on me. I closed my own, a quiver passing over my skin. Exactly how much were they going to see?

A wash of light passed over me, flashing softly behind my eyelids. Then another, and another, as if it were the ocean's surf sending its waves toward me. A warmth bloomed throughout my body. A honeyed scent trickled into my lungs as I inhaled. The quivering spread across my scalp and into my head. It tingled through my thoughts.

Were they releasing me even now? Wearing down the tie between me and Cormag? I could almost taste the release on the tip of my tongue.

Then a faint cry split the air. I looked up, startled. Another fae woman was staring at me, the glow around her body dimmed and shivering. The man who'd asked me to sit there turned his head away with a jerk. His neighbor shook his head over and over, muttering something to himself. The waves of light and warmth fell away. Abruptly, I felt chilled.

"What?" I said. "What's wrong?"

The woman who'd addressed me before held out her hand. I let her help me to my feet. As I sat back on my stone, she looked down at her lap, her brilliant face creasing before she found the words.

"I am still not sure if we could touch the cord that binds you," she said. "But we do not want to. We fear more what would happen if the oath is broken than if it remains in place."

What? I bit my tongue before I could snap the question at her. "How can you say that? You don't even know—"

"We know," she said, even and solemn. "We saw. The one you serve has a sickness of a sort in him, yes, but it's not because of your oath. It's already in the core of him. You swore to defend the world from it. Can you not see that doing so may be the right thing after all?"

She looked at me, her eyes pleading. My throat closed up. My hands clenched, but I couldn't summon any real anger, not when her expression was so distraught. She didn't like saying this to me. She was only saying it because she couldn't bear not to.

She believed my king was meant to die.

"How can you condone it?" I said. "Killing an innocent person..."

"He has lived more than his fair share of lives already, has he not?" she said. "And how many other innocents might be swept up in the tide of darkness if the one you fear takes him first?"

"I don't know! I don't know what she did to him."

"Perhaps that is the answer you should seek then," she said. They all stood up to leave, not one giving me another glance.

CHAPTER SEVEN

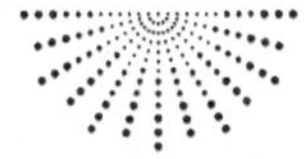

THE WARM, salty water of the bath lapped at my arms. I lowered them deeper into the bathtub, breathing in the tang that wasn't quite like the ocean. Too much chlorine in the tap water for it to be an exact imitation. But it was real sea salt I'd laced the tub with, along with a sprinkling of burnt frankincense.

It didn't matter what the light fae had said. I'd learned something from them anyway. The oath was a thing they could see inside me, a thing they'd felt in my mind. If they could grasp hold of it and comprehend it, then I could grab it too. Grab it and hopefully snap it, if I'd picked my tools right.

The purifying bath had seemed like a reasonable first step. I'd cleanse myself as much as possible from any outside influence. Let nothing remain but me and the oath. Maybe the immersion would even wear it down a little before I got to the real work.

I'd been soaking long enough that my fingertips had pruned. I rubbed my thumb against them, grimaced, and climbed out of the tub. I pulled on my undyed cotton bathrobe and ambled out to the supplies I'd laid on the floor in my bedroom. I'd ordered Darton not to disturb me unless there was a total emergency. After seeing my face when I'd gotten back from the enclave, he hadn't even tried to argue.

I whispered to the sticks of copal incense set around my circle of twigs. They started smoking. The crisp, woody scent curled into the air. I set a black onyx stone on both of my knees to strength my will and resolve. A pile of bay leaves waited in front of my crossed legs, ready to accept the energy I planned to shed.

I brushed my hands over the stones and inhaled deep. The copal smoke seeped into my lungs. I exhaled it and scooped the bay leaves into my cupped hands. Closing my eyes, I turned my awareness inward. Deep, deep into my head, where the oath wound through my thoughts.

There. I couldn't see it, but I could almost hear it. Like a faint humming just a little too distant to pinpoint. But the itch beneath my fingernails shifted when the humming did, in time with the beat of my heart. If I could just find the threads of it, pick them apart...

"*Let me see what I seek,*" I murmured in the old tongue. "*Bring distant ties to visibility.*" Keeping my focus inward, I reached out to the life energy in the twigs at the same time. It thrummed into me. My nerves jittered alongside it. The tug of the oath's compulsion rippled through my muscles and squeezed at my lungs.

"No," I said. "*Let me find it. Let me grasp it. Let me—*"

I hauled at the energy around me even harder, slamming it against the magic twined through my head. That was the wrong move.

The burst of energy hit me like a punch. My thoughts spun, and the oath's power lashed back. My hands jerked, the bay leaves scattering. A flood of light seared behind my eyes. My body listed. I tumbled over, and the world went dark.

Everything was dark. I couldn't feel my body, not even my breath. I was floating, still and numb, in a blackness that might have been as vast as the universe or as shallow as my bathtub. I tried to turn, to feel, but there was nothing to move. Nowhere to move it to.

I'd knocked myself out into some kind of vision. But usually my visions hurtled me toward whatever they wanted me to see. They didn't just toss me into a random void. What was the point of this?

How did I get *out* of it?

Cold tendrils started to wrap around my consciousness like trickles of frigid water. I would have shivered if I'd had a body to shiver with. I still couldn't see anything, but a drifting sensation crept over me, as if I were gliding very slowly downward. Down and down and down, without any impression of what was slipping past me.

Was this some kind of trap the light fae had worked into their oath, to punish me if I tried to break it? It didn't *feel* like light fae work, but Cormag had struck me as being a little on the sadistic side. The only thing I knew was I didn't care for this situation at all. Was there some way to knock myself free?

I stretched and pushed my awareness, but that didn't seem to get me anywhere. I just kept drifting on. To where?

A thin crackle of laughter sliced through the darkness. The chill deepened, twisting around my mind. I sensed without seeing a gaze fixed on me. A gaze even more icy than the tendrils that tangled around my thoughts.

The presence expanded until it loomed over me, until it filled the blackness all around me, as if it had swallowed me up. I was pinned in place by it. My entire being strained to get away.

It was *her*. I'd know her essence anywhere.

"There you are, little wizard," said a voice that was both low and crisp. It echoed all around me. "Did you think you could run from me? Such a pathetic specimen of both fae and humanity. I've been waiting a long time to have you in my grasp. Don't worry. It won't be much longer until I'm there in the flesh to fully enjoy your torment."

The tendrils sharpened into frigid claws. They scraped through my mind, severing thoughts and sparking panic. I tried to cry out with a mouth I couldn't find. Some part of my will remained, an unbroken thread in the midst of the Darkest One's game. I held onto it tight. It was only a vision. I could endure this. She couldn't break me with an ocean between us.

Only I wasn't completely sure of that.

"Do you think you can defy me again?" she said. "Oh, halfling abomination, you know how many years I've had to contemplate the many ways I can take my revenge. Your death will be slow, slow and horrible. That's a promise. Your king's, though? You don't need to worry about him. That life I intend to snap fast. The better to unwrap that beautiful present inside."

Her laugh carried through the darkness again. *No*, I thought. *No, no, no, no, no.* I wouldn't let her. I'd make it through. I couldn't think any farther than that, not with her icy fingers digging deeper and deeper into my consciousness. *No, no, no, no—*

"No!" The shout broke from my lips. I flinched awake, my elbows smacking out against arms that held me in place.

Darton's arms. His solid football player frame was wrapped around me. His warmth and his citrusy, earthy smell washed over me.

I blinked at the scene around me. Most of my twigs had disintegrated into dust, and that dust was smeared in violent streaks all across my pale floorboards. Bay leaves scattered the room as far as I could see, as if a gale had whipped through the room. The onyx stones had both shattered. Dark shards speckled the floor around me like shiny black teardrops.

"Hey," Darton said. "Hey. I'm here. You're back. It's okay."

My mind tripped back to the memory of the Darkest One's presence swallowing me up, and my throat constricted. No, it wasn't. Nothing about this was remotely okay. I *had* failed, so badly. I couldn't even make *myself* safe for my king, let alone anything or anyone else. Even as my body came back into focus, that sodding itch was tickling up my arms. Reminding me of the oath I hadn't fulfilled.

I'm not going to, I thought at it, with a defiance that was more like a teenager sticking her tongue out at her parents behind their backs than anything really convincing. *You can't make me.*

Other than it probably could, if I let it go on long enough. If I didn't sever it soon. Not that I had any clue how, despite my best efforts.

Darton's arms shifted around me, tugging me closer. I let my head tip against his chest. My bathrobe had loosened during... whatever had happened while I was lost in that vision. The soft fabric gaped to the swells of my breasts and bared my legs halfway up my thighs. His hands rested so close to that naked skin...

A different sort of heat swept over me, embarrassment and longing mixed. "I told you not to come in," I muttered.

Darton sputtered a laugh. "Unless it was an emergency. Believe me, it sounded like one. You were yelling out stuff I couldn't even understand, other than I think I heard my name in there at least once, and when I came in you were shaking on the floor. You couldn't seem to hear me at all. You wouldn't open your eyes. It's been—I don't know, but a long time, since I came in. Where *were* you?"

"A vision," I said, the irritation draining out of me. Light help me, I must have terrified him. "I'm sorry. I had no idea what was going on outside my head. It didn't give me anything useful. The Darkest One showed up personally to add in a few more taunts."

Darton's body tensed against mine. "Oh." He lowered his head, his cheek brushing my temple. "Are you all right? Did she hurt you?"

"No. Not really." A splinter of a headache was working its way through my skull, but that might be my own fault for messing with the oath. "She said she'd make her way here soon. At least that means we can be sure she's not here *yet*." What was her idea of "soon," though? She might mean tomorrow or a year from now for all I knew.

I started to push away, but Darton's embrace tightened. "No," he said. "You stay right here a little longer. Lord knows you need more than five minutes to recover before you go charging off in some other direction."

I made a muted sound of protest. "I still have that wretched oath to break."

"I'm just asking for five more minutes. I don't want my wizard completely run ragged. How are you going to come to my rescue then?"

He said the last sentence jokingly, but I heard the hint of bitterness in it too. "Seems like you're the one coming to my rescue," I said. That earned me a chuckle that sounded a little less strained.

"I try." He shifted me against him so we were almost facing. His fingers stroked over my hair. Then they dropped to cup my cheek. His lips brushed against my forehead. Almost a kiss. My pulse kicked up for reasons that had nothing to do with the enemy whose grip I'd just been in.

"Art."

"I know." His mouth grazed my skin again as it moved. A delicate, teasing heat. Almost begging me to lift my head so my lips could meet his. "I'm sorry. I know we can't— You have no idea how hard it is not to even be able to kiss you."

My heart fluttered. I set my jaw. I had to say it. "To kiss *Emma*."

He swallowed audibly. "I'm not sure I know how to tell one part of you from the other anymore."

Maybe he couldn't, but I could. I could tell the part he'd never have wanted to kiss back when we'd been only ourselves. My soul had been in a body that didn't suit him. Just because that had changed didn't mean I didn't remember. And conditional affection... No.

I'd learned over and over how much that hurt. He understood now. I'd been honest with him. *I have loved you utterly always,* I'd told him a few nights ago, after he'd accused me of rejecting him, of not caring enough. *And you have only loved me sometimes.*

That was the crux of the problem, wasn't it? I'd never even known whether his affection and attraction meant anything at all or whether they'd only been conjured by the spell that bound us together, the closeness it created.

Of course, *that* bond was broken now. And he still wanted to hold me, to touch me like this. But it had only been a few days. Maybe this was only habit, an echo that would fade with the magic over time.

I'd let myself hope too many times. Even all the way back then, when I should have known there wasn't a chance. A memory swam up, as if I needed the reminder.

"There's nothing wrong with taking advice from others, Your Highness. I'd never suggest as much. Gods, I hope you listen to my advice now."

"Then what exactly are you suggesting?" Arthur's voice rang cold from the private alcove where one of the local lords had stopped him for this little chat. It was just down the hall from the king's chambers, which was where I'd been heading when my fae-sharpened hearing had caught their conversation from down the castle hall. I stood now with my back braced against the hard plaster of the wall and my stomach twisting.

"He always has your ear. He's always at your side. I've seen you change your mind after a few words from him—"

"Because I trust him," Arthur interrupted. "Because he has proven himself right time and time again. He's earned that trust."

"My point is only that the extent of his influence... it's concerning. You want to be seen as a king who rules with his own mind first."

"And I do," Arthur said, his voice absolutely icy now. "My mind tells me that my rule can only be stronger with Merlin's support. If you have proof that he's caused any harm, by all means, bring that to me.

But all I'm hearing at the moment are vague and baseless assumptions."

The lord muttered something else, but I could tell he'd been dismissed. I murmured a hasty distraction spell. He stalked past me down the hall without a glance in my direction, totally oblivious to my presence. Arthur strode into his chambers, shutting the door a little harder than necessary behind him.

My heart had squeezed. It wasn't as if I didn't know my king trusted me, valued my assistance. But hearing him defend me so firmly and absolutely left me a little short of breath. I gathered myself and continued my own walk to his chambers.

"Good afternoon, my liege," I said breezily as I ambled in. No need to remind him of that troublesome conversation.

Unfortunately, my king knew me far too well now that I'd spent more than a dozen years in his service. He turned where he'd been standing by the chair near the door, and the second he caught my expression, he grimaced.

"You heard," he said.

"Heard what?" I said. He cocked a skeptical eyebrow at me. "Oh, well, there might have been some lordly blathering carrying down the hall, but it didn't sound like anything I should worry myself about."

Arthur shook his head. "It really isn't. If they could see everything you can do..."

"Hmm, let's not push things too far. I spent most of my first year here afraid you might decide to send me to the chopping block for sorcery."

He winced. Then he reached out to grasp my arm, just below the elbow. Not an intimate touch by any means, but these days, even a faint brush of one of those capable hands was enough to make my pulse leap. I steeled myself against my internal reactions. I couldn't let them show. He couldn't know that.

But he stepped closer, until there was less than a foot of space between us. His voice dropped low, making my heart thump even faster. "You do know you never have to worry, don't you? I'd rather *have you at my side than twenty of those preening lords. How can they understand loyalty when they barely know how to demonstrate it themselves?"*

"I know," I said. The words came out quiet. My king smiled. His gaze held mine. The rattle of my pulse echoed in my ears. For one instant of insanity, I almost thought his hand would rise from my arm to stroke my cheek, to draw me closer, to—

He stepped back, his eyes jerking away. "Well, maybe if you played the fool a little less, they'd see why I respect you."

My head reeled for a second before I caught myself. "Ah, but then you'd be even more bored during those bloody conferences."

"That's true. Forget I said that." He smiled again, with a distance that was only friendly. Damn my sodding overactive imagination.

That was all it'd ever been. Hope feeding my imagination. Wanting to read more into a kind word, a warm look. We'd been best friends, or as close to it as liege and subject could be. I hadn't *needed* more.

Darton tipped my head so he could tuck it under his chin. I let out my breath, the twist of longing and tension in my chest relaxing now that his mouth was no longer quite so close to mine.

"I don't want to hurt you," he said. "I've done that too many times already without meaning to."

"I know," I said. "This is enough, Art. It really is. As long as you're by my side, I'm happy."

I'd be a whole lot happier if I could count on keeping him there.

And I still had an awful lot of work to do toward that end. I started to straighten up, and this time Darton let me.

I'd just eased off of his lap when a pounding on the front door resonated through the house.

CHAPTER EIGHT

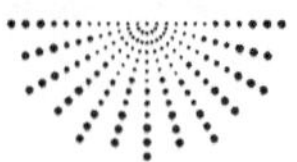

"You weren't expecting anyone to stop by, were you?" I said, yanking open my closet. I grabbed a sweatshirt and jeans at random and tugged them on, modesty be damned. Darton was enough of a gentleman to avert his eyes anyway.

The knocking rang through the house again. "No," Darton said. "Keevan and Izzy had exams to study for. They'd have called or texted if something important came up. And it's not like I'm talking to anyone else about what we're up to here."

"Right. Well, let's see who's hassling us tonight. I'd have hoped we were too far off the beaten track for door-to-door solicitors to bother." At least we could assume a dark fae army here to make good on the Darkest One's promise wouldn't have bothered with knocking. I was pretty sure of that.

Darton followed me into the living room. I was about to wave him back, to keep his distance while I opened the door, when a voice carried through it with the next knock. "Emma. Darton. If you're in there, don't leave an old friend hanging."

It was Jagger's voice. I hadn't known the grizzled fae hunter very long, really, but considering he'd blown up his house to save the bunch of us not that long ago, I figured he'd earned the right to call himself an "old friend." A smile leapt to my face as I hurried the rest of the way to the front hall.

Jagger was just turning away from the door when I opened it. His head jerked back around, his face lighting up under its spider web of pale scars. He grinned. "Good. I figured the car meant you were around."

He hadn't come alone. An even more recent friend stood beside him. Eric, the young fae hunter who'd come with his mother to give Darton and me a hand when we'd arrived in Britain, ran his hand through his dark hair. He gave me a sheepish smile. "We meet again."

My eyebrows shot up. "Oh. Hey. When did you get here? *How* did you get here?" With the tantrum the Darkest One was throwing over his country, it couldn't have been easy to get out.

I stepped back to let them in. Eric shrugged, gripping the strap of his shoulder bag. "The network can create opportunities most people don't have. I made it over to France and got a flight from there."

"And I'd just made it back in town," Jagger put in. "One of my buddies reported he'd seen you stopping by your parents' place, so I knew you'd made it home relatively safely." He gave me a questioning look.

The fae hunters had been invaluable allies, but I hadn't given them the full story of my identity, or Darton's. They didn't know why the dark fae were so interested in us, only that the fae's determination in coming after us obviously wasn't good for anyone. So far it had seemed simpler not to complicate things by getting into legends and so on. Talking through the explanation with Keevan and Izzy had been hard enough.

"We made it back by the skin of our teeth." I motioned for them to sit in the living room. Darton was still standing by the sofa, his expression hesitant. He'd gotten along with Jagger okay, but he and Eric... There'd been a bit of a clash. "You should have told us you were coming."

"I tried," Jagger said. "But it seems your old numbers aren't doing me any good."

Oh. Right. Which was the exact same reason I hadn't reached out to him or Eric earlier. I'd gotten their phone numbers, but they'd been in the phone that was now being thoroughly rained on and wind-blasted back in Britain.

"Sorry about that," I said with a grimace. "It's been... kind of a chaotic few days. What's going on?" My gaze shifted to Eric. "Why did you come all the way over here? Have you seen any activity from the dark fae—I mean, other than the obvious storm? Is your mother all right?"

He nodded. "She sends her best. We were pretty worried about you for a while there. But then Jagger mentioned you'd turned up back on this side of the pond... It sounded like this dark fae queen has a particular bone to pick with you. I figured she'd be heading this way before too long, so maybe you could use some extra help."

It seemed like a long way to come when he hadn't been able to help all *that* much with the actual fae-fighting even on his home turf. Maybe he simply hadn't been able to tolerate sitting around in the middle of that storm, not knowing what was going on. But it was a generous gesture anyway.

"You're probably right about her intended direction," I said. "As, er, you may have figured out, we didn't quite succeed in our plan the other day. We stopped the dark fae who was trying to free the Darkest One, but not soon enough. She's totally free now. We've just been regrouping, observing, deciding on our best steps for trying to contain her again. I... I'm really sorry." The country she was tearing through had once been my home, but it was currently Eric's.

"Please. I've seen what a force of nature you are when you put your mind to something." Eric gave me one of his flirty smiles. "I'm sure you gave it your all. I can only imagine matters would be much worse if you hadn't intervened."

"Well, that might be true." I glanced at Darton, but his gaze was focused on me, not Eric. His expression had relaxed. A little jealousy had reared its head thanks to Eric's flirtatious nature before, but that was also before I'd confessed my eternal love to my king. I guessed he felt a little more secure in my affections after that.

Jagger leaned forward, resting his sinewy elbows on his knees. "The whole fae hunter network is on high alert. The second we can act against the dark fae, we will—in any way we can. But the folks over in the U.K. have been pretty much overwhelmed. They haven't even been able to determine what part of the country your dark fae menace is throwing her magic from, there's so much of it whirling around in the atmosphere."

"And the atmosphere is doing plenty of whirling of its own on top of that," Eric said.

"I think the storm should let up before much longer," I said. "Unfortunately that'll be when she heads this way. I've laid all the protections I could think of around this house. A bunch of really determined dark fae, or a really powerful one, could still break through, but we're about as safe as we can get. Beyond that... I'm still working on a solid plan."

"If you need to put your head together with anyone..." Eric said, his smile returning. I managed not to roll my eyes. To my surprise, he turned to Darton next. "And you have that fancy magic sword of yours. Is that here? There was something I wanted to discuss with you about it. Maybe better as a private conversation to start, man to man."

One of Darton's eyebrows arched. "You want to have a private talk about my sword?" he said, not quite suppressing a note of snark.

Eric looked unfazed. "Unless that's a problem."

Darton glanced at me. I shrugged. I might have insisted on

being in the loop, but they were only going to walk to the other room. If it was important, Darton would fill me in when they were done talking. He wouldn't enjoy me babysitting the conversation. Anyway, it might be good if they put *their* heads together a little, in a constructive sort of way, after all the knocking heads they'd done last week.

"All right then." Darton got up. He led the other guy into his bedroom, where he'd stashed Excalibur.

What could Eric possibly have found out about the sword *I'd* commissioned and enchanted that we didn't already know? And that he felt he needed to talk to Darton about privately? I looked to Jagger, but he spread his hands.

"First I'm hearing about it," he said. "I thought you'd want to know, though, that my guys didn't see anything worrisome around your parents house while you two were away."

I'd already guessed as much, but it was still a relief to have it confirmed. "Give them my thanks for keeping watch. And thank *you*. I'm sure I've set some kind of record for amount of trouble caused in under a month."

Jagger laughed. "Ah, it's worth it. After chasing after the occasional stray shadow varmints here and there most of my life, I'm finally getting to take on the big guns, if only from the sidelines. I'm glad to be involved at all."

"Well, your help is more than appreciated."

"Let me get that new number of yours," he said. "I don't want to be left out again."

I took his phone and typed in the number for the disposable I'd picked up. "I'd guess the people in your network who monitor all those dark energies have noticed more fae activity stirring all over the place, not just in Britain."

"You'd be right. Lots more activity. Lots more partial sightings. Nothing extremely intrusive, but it's clear this dark fae lady's influence has a wide range."

"That'll all end if we can deal with her," I said. "I was wondering—"

A *crack* rang out, so loud and sharp it seemed to snap my eardrums. A... gunshot?

From Darton's bedroom.

I threw myself to my feet. There was a thump. Someone shouted. And with a few murmured words, I apparated across the entire house to appear at the foot of Darton's bed.

CHAPTER NINE

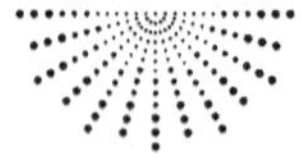

MY FEET HIT the floor with a jolt. Darton and Eric were tussling by the door, Excalibur on the floor near their feet. Eric had a pistol clasped in one hand. He tried to swing it toward Darton. Darton shoved his arm to the side, but his own arm faltered. Blood was seeping through the fabric of his shirt over his shoulder.

I didn't have time to find a wand or even a twig. Wrenching at the life energy inside my body, I spat out a phrase. *"Melt it, meld it."*

A bolt of energy hit the gun. The pistol's barrel warped in on itself, the opening collapsing. Eric stared at it in shock. Then he swung its blunt surface at Darton's head.

I dashed forward to catch his wrist. Jagger burst in the door at the same moment. He shoved Eric against the wall by his shoulders. "What the hell are you doing, kid?"

I turned to Darton. His mouth was twisted, his hand clamped to his bleeding shoulder. Beyond him, a dark circle showed where the bullet had dug into the wall.

"Let me see," I said.

He shifted his hand. Blood smeared his fingers. "I don't want you using any more of your own energy to heal me," he said through partly gritted teeth. "I can wait long enough for you to get a wand."

I eased back the torn fabric of his shirt. The bullet had grazed him, taking a chunk of flesh with it, about a quarter of an inch deep and an inch across. The wound was bloody and painful, but nowhere near fatal. Easier to patch up than what I'd done to my hand yesterday.

"It's the right thing to do," Eric said raggedly. He grunted as he struggled against Jagger's hold. "We have to think about protecting *every*one."

"What in light's name are you *talking* about?" I snapped. Patting myself down, I found a spare twig in my pocket. I gripped it and murmured to seal the skin over Darton's wound. The twig crumpled in my hand. "What happened?" I asked my king. After what Eric had done, I didn't trust *his* account of the situation.

"I turned around to pick up the sword," Darton said. "He must have had the gun in his bag. I looked back just as he was about to shoot." He glanced down at Excalibur with a slanted smile. "I should probably be thanking that fencing training. I managed to smack his arm to the side with a quick block. Didn't even realize what I was doing or why until after instinct kicked in."

"As long as he's alive, he's a danger to the entire world," Eric said. His words rippled into me, setting off the itch in my muscles. The itch of the oath. I stepped toward him, my eyes narrowing and my arms crossing over my chest to hold the urge in check.

"Where did you get that idea from?"

He stopped struggling, evidently realizing that fit as he might be, Jagger had at least fifty pounds, most of it muscle, on him. Instead he just glowered at me.

"You left behind those journals," he said.

Journals. My father's journals. The ones where he'd written out all his observations and fears about Arthur and his family. A chill raced down my back. It hadn't occurred to me that the people I'd left them with might read them. It hadn't occurred to me that they *could.*

"How much did you even understand what's written in those?" I said. "It's Old English—it makes *my* head hurt going through it." And I'd grown up on the language, as distant as that first growing up now was.

"There are skills it's useful to know if you want to be effective in our line of work," Eric said. "I've got a passable grasp, and my mom's nearly fluent. When I got the gist, I brought them to her to confirm."

I thought of Mavis with her kind smile. My gut knotted. "Did she know you came out here to kill Darton?"

For the first time since I'd appeared in the room, a hint of uncertainty crossed Eric's face. He scowled. "No," he admitted. "She has no idea. She thought it was for you to figure out. But you obviously aren't willing to do what's necessary. You care more about him and the time bomb lodged inside him than whether the rest of us have a chance."

My father's journals had been all about Arthur and his family. But he'd made notes in the last one about the cycle of rebirth I'd gotten me and my king wrapped up in. Notes to me, warning me that he believed the darkness would have clung on to Arthur's soul no matter how many reincarnations it went through. After everything Eric had seen me do, the way he'd heard us talk to each other, he must have put those pieces together too.

"Em," Darton said behind me. "What does he mean?"

Sodding hell. This was not how I'd wanted to have this conversation. "I don't think I want to discuss it with *him* still here," I said, matching Eric's glower. "You can count yourself no longer welcome on our property. You have no idea what you're messing with, and I do. You could have asked a few questions before you came charging in."

"And maybe I'd have tipped you off. I didn't even manage to get the job done as it was." Eric's head sagged.

Jagger scowled at him and then glanced back at me. "I'm sorry I brought this delinquent into your home, Emma," he said. "Let me do the honors of taking out the trash. I'll give you a shout when he's well away from here."

Keeping a tight grip on Eric's arm, he walked the younger man out of the room. My shoulders didn't sink back down until the front door thudded shut behind them. Then the breath rushed out of me. I sagged onto the bed.

Darton rubbed his mouth. "A time bomb?" he said, his voice hesitant.

The knot in my gut came back, twice as large.

"Sit down. This is going to take a while."

Darton eased himself down on the bed, wincing as his wounded arm bumped it. My hasty healing spell hadn't fixed him completely. He tipped onto his back to stare up at the ceiling. His jaw had tightened.

"Okay," he said. "Hit me with it. The whole story this time, if you don't mind."

I bit my lip and looked away. "This isn't something new I've been keeping from you. I mean, I didn't tell you about it, but... I've always not told you about it."

I thought he'd already been lying still, but his body went even more motionless at that. "Since how long ago?"

My chest clenched. "Since always," I admitted. "Since..." My head bowed. "Art, I never told you the whole reason why I came looking to serve you in the first place."

"Oh." He paused. "But you didn't do anything wrong while you were with me. You always *did* serve me. How bad can it be?"

"Well, I... I had a lot of arguments with my father about my methods. Working with you changed my mind about what was really important. I hadn't had a chance to form my own opinions before. All I'd had was what he said and the knowledge of the enclave to go by. I was always honest with you about how *I* saw things. Just not about how my father wanted me to."

"Your father who was a light fae."

"Yeah." I pressed my hand to my forehead. "You know I was always worried about the dark fae hanging around. That they would try to talk to you, or just watch... You aren't the first in your family that they've taken an interest in. My father had observed their interactions with your ancestors going back several generations."

Darton frowned. "He thought we were colluding with them?"

I laughed shortly. "Oh, no. That wouldn't even have occurred to him. A dark fae would never lower themselves to align with human beings. But he was sure they were planning to use one or more of you for some purpose. He noted signs of magical ceremonies being carried out. Saw them lurking around the castle. Noticed a faint energy that seemed to grow across each generation..."

"What kind of 'energy'?"

"I—I don't have all the details. *He* wasn't even sure exactly what they were doing, and I didn't have time to read through all of his notes after I got his journals. But he believed the dark fae had placed some sort of dark enchantment on your family line. Something that was passed on with each generation and that grew in strength as it did. And the signs he saw made him believe that you were the culmination of whatever they were planning."

Darton was silent for a long moment. "That's why she came for me. The Darkest One. The dark fae hadn't ever attacked the kingdom like that before, had they?"

I shook my head. "A direct assault isn't their usual strategy. But I think she had something larger planned. Something she wanted to... release from your soul."

He set his hand on his chest. "That dark enchantment your father thinks they were casting. It was inside me—it's still inside me?"

"I've caught glimpses of it when I've worked other magic on you," I admitted. "Not enough that I thought I needed to worry. I mean, as far as I knew, whatever it was, she's the only one who could activate it. So as long as she was bound, it didn't affect us anyway."

"But that's why your enclave was so nervous around me. Obviously. That's why they made you swear that oath." His gaze slid back to me. "That's why even part of you wants to kill me. Before the Darkest One can get to me and set off... whatever this 'bomb' inside me is."

"No part of me wants to," I said firmly. "We've managed to stay ahead of her for fifteen hundred years and we'll—we'll find some way of fighting back now. I'm not giving up. I'm not giving up on *you*."

Another silence settled over us. Darton's brow furrowed. "Some of the things I've remembered from back then make a little more sense now. There've been a couple of people I had the feeling must have been dark fae—the way they looked at me, talked to me... Like there was something in me that they wanted."

I couldn't help perking up. "Did they say anything about what they expected from you?"

"No, nothing like that. If I'd known I should wonder, maybe I could have prodded. If you'd told me there was something to prod about."

A lump rose in my throat. "I thought you'd cast me out if you knew why I'd come. I was meant to be, well, a spy more than anything else, for my father's research. And a plant within your castle to try to prevent the Darkest One's plan from coming to fruition, of course. It seemed more important that I was there with you than that I was completely honest." My voice dropped. "That's the only thing I ever kept from you. Well, that and... the exact nature of all my feelings for you."

"All right. And what do we do about it now?"

"I don't know."

He stirred, swiping his arm across his forehead. "I need to think a little. On my own."

I probably didn't deserve even that polite a dismissal after what I'd just admitted. I bobbed my head and slipped out of the room. In my own bedroom, I leaned back against the wall. A burn filled my eyes. I dragged in a breath and swallowed the beginnings of a sob.

Of course he was upset. That was why I hadn't told him about the dark fae's doings over all this time. I had to allow him those feelings. If my omissions ruined things between us, well... our friendship had always been living on borrowed time, hadn't it?

The sense of loss rolled over me, bringing an ache between my ribs, but one clear thought came with it. I hadn't been completely truthful even just now. I *did* know what I had to do.

I'd been going about this all wrong, trying to combat the oath instead of the reason for it. I'd never wanted to look at the darkness inside my king too closely. It was the work of the Darkest One and her underlings, built up over hundreds of years. There might be no hope at all of me even pricking at it.

But I had to try. If I could untangle her fingerprints from his soul and wrench her enchantment out of him, the oath wouldn't matter. Her power wouldn't matter. We could take her on directly, magic and sword, without needing to fear what she might do with my king.

Between me and her and Eric and everyone else who might come calling... Tackling that dark curse was the only way Darton was going to make it through this catastrophe alive.

CHAPTER TEN

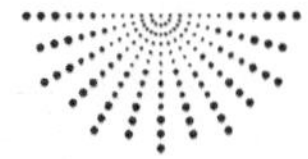

I PUT the kid on a plane back to France, Jagger told me by text. *That seemed like the safest option for all involved. Have you and Darton sorted things out between you?*

He didn't ask any questions about who we were, or how we'd come to be this way, or anything like that. Had Eric told him what he'd figured out about our past lives? I guessed if he had, Jagger had decided it wasn't really his business. Or at the very least, that he trusted me to work my way out of this mess more than he trusted Eric's preferred strategy.

For the most part, I typed back. *No permanent harm done.* Physically, anyway.

A knock sounded on my bedroom door. I pushed myself upright. "Come in."

Darton eased the door open. He stepped over the threshold and stopped there. His striking blue eyes were shadowed.

"There's nothing else you haven't told me?" he said.

Guilt jabbed me in the gut again. "Nothing," I said. "I swear it. *May the light strike me down if I lie.*"

He caught the gist of the old language enough to glance at the ceiling as if to check for a lightning bolt about to take me up on the request. When none appeared, he sank into the chair at my desk and swiveled it to face me.

"So this dark fae magic," he said. "It's been in me all this time?"

"I'm sorry," I said. "So sorry. I gave you a bunch of excuses earlier, but none of them are enough. I should have tried to deal with it sooner. I wanted to think it wouldn't matter... but obviously I should have known it would."

I hadn't wanted to deal with the possibility that once I looked at my king's soul that closely, I'd realize I couldn't do anything to fix it. I was *still* scared of that.

"Can you get it out of me?" Darton asked, getting right to that point.

I gave him a pained smile. "I can't answer that without knowing exactly what it is. The magic is buried deep. The Darkest One and her underlings didn't want anyone seeing it, let alone poking at it. But I'll do my best. Come here?"

For a second, my breath caught with the fear that he was too upset with me to want to even sit next to me. But he got up and settled on the edge of the bed. I turned, taking his hand in mine.

"We don't need some big magical ceremony for this?" Darton said without looking at me.

"Not for an initial look around. My soul knows yours pretty well by now." All of it except the part the Darkest One had touched, anyway.

I palmed a few twigs in my other hand and closed my eyes, focusing my awareness on the skin-to-skin contact of his hand in mine. The pulse of life flowing through his body. The warm earthy smell of him that filled my nose, tugging at me to lean closer. I ignored that impulse and the rising itch running through my fingers.

His pulse turned into a glow. A glow with a tremor of darkness running through it. I reached my mind toward that shadow. "*Delve deep, delve clear,*" I murmured.

The hint of it flickered away from me. I stretched my awareness farther into the glow. Glimpses of Darton's memories and Arthur's shimmered past me. For several minutes, I waited. Finally, the shadow surfaced again. It seemed to catch sight of me and flinch away, flitting as fast as a minnow in a stream.

"*Come forth to be seen*," I crooned to it. It only slipped away faster. In a second I couldn't see it at all. I hesitated, watching, as Darton's heart beat on. The tremor of darkness stayed hidden this time.

I drew myself out of my meditative state with a sharp inhale. Darton was looking at me now, studying my expression. "Did you see it? What *is* it?"

"I don't know," I said. "I couldn't get close enough to—"

My hands jerked. I shoved them back into my lap, ramming my thumb against the palm I'd stabbed yesterday. A bolt of pain shot up my arm, and the oath's urge faded. Darton looked down at my hands warily, but to give him proper credit for bravery, he stayed where he was.

"It wasn't good, though, obviously," he said.

"I think we could have been sure of that already." I took another steadying breath and folded my arms over my chest to better restrain the itch. "My magic hardly touched it. Actually, it seemed to *repel* it, if anything... Whatever they've conjured, it knows that it should only show itself to dark sorts. My own nature is probably repelling it. Which means my usual tricks aren't going to work."

"So you can't do anything?"

"No." I paused. *My own nature.* So how could I overcome that? What else? "Maybe I can make it believe I'm a dark fae." I glanced around the room. "But for that, I'm going to need a different sort of supplies than I've usually collected..."

The crisp autumn leaves crunched under our feet as Izzy and I strode along the narrow forest path. The branches were all but bare now, just a few browning strays clinging on. Though the breeze that brushed over us was dry, a damp tang of rot was starting to creep into it already. Soon all those leaves would be mulch for next year's growing.

"I swear there are a bunch of willows out here somewhere," Izzy said, shoving her pale auburn hair behind her ears. "It was last year the hiking club came out here, so I don't remember *exactly* how far along they are..."

"It's okay," I said. "I'm just glad I already knew someone who had the scoop on the nearby forests."

She tucked her gloved hands into her pockets. "I'd have thought with all your magical senses, you could have tracked a tree by its vibes or something."

The corner of my lips quirked up. "Oh, I can. But only if it's alive." I'd already used that method to find a nice clump of the other plant I needed to add to my stockpile, aconite, in all its highly poisonous glory. "For my current purposes, I need to scrape bark from a willow that's dead—and has been dead for at least a few months."

"That sounds... ominous."

"Usually the best way of dealing with dark magic is to overwhelm it with light," I said. "But sometimes you need to be a little sneaky. Lull it into complacency with something familiar." Izzy's eyes widened, and I gave her a tense grin. "Don't worry, I'm not planning anything horrifying."

I was still keeping the darkness in my king's soul a secret from everyone except Darton. After he'd told me about Izzy's hiking club inclinations, he'd paused and asked if I could avoid telling her exactly why I needed these new materials. *I know it's not my fault the dark fae did this to me,* he said. *But the thought of my friends knowing... I wish you'd told me sooner, but I guess I can see why it wasn't a subject you wanted to discuss.*

He'd still been a little awkward with me before I'd left. An ache spread through my chest at the memory. We'd come so far, learning to trust each other. I hoped I hadn't broken that trust too much.

Izzy pushed aside the branch of a sapling that had sprouted across the path. "Honestly, I don't know if I even mind horrifying if it means you can take care of this 'Darkest One.' The way she's practically tearing apart all of England... It's awful. Sometimes you have to fight fire with fire?"

"Something like that," I said.

We hopped stones over a shallow creek. "This looks familiar," Izzy said. "I'm pretty sure the big stretch of willows wasn't too far from here. There were enough of them that I think there's got to be at least one fallen."

"One is all I need."

A gloom drifted by, following the shadows along the edge of the stream. Izzy tensed an instant after I saw it. She'd always been the most sensitive of Darton's crowd, but for her to notice it that quickly, it was obviously a lot more potent than usual. The Darkest One's influence was spreading far and fast.

I snapped a twig off a nearby shrub. *Darkness begone.* The gloom wisped away, and Izzy exhaled.

"There've been more of them again," she said. "Floating around campus. They're even more visible than they were the first time, when you said that mercenary was giving them extra energy. I've seen people getting freaked out by them. Not that they have any idea what they're seeing, but moving shadows is going to creep anyone out."

"Maybe I'll have to go do another cleanup of the grounds," I said, but I didn't really believe I'd have time for that. The glooms weren't likely to hurt any regular human beings. Unless the Darkest One started commanding them to. Now that was a horrifying thought.

Izzy fell silent for a moment, studying the forest and the path ahead. When she sucked in her breath, I could tell from the sound she was nervous about the question she was about to ask.

"I've been thinking," she said, in an even softer voice than usual, "about the Darkest One, and everything you've told us about her... You knew she was a threat all the way back in your first life, right? You knew she wanted Darton—Arthur... You know what I mean."

"I knew the dark fae were keeping an eye on him." My thoughts dart back to that long-ago vision of the Darkest One ripping into Arthur's body. "And I was worried about her in particular, yeah."

"But even with that... I'm not saying this to criticize or anything, really. It's not as if I'd stand half a chance at stopping her. But when she did come, back then, if you *could* have just destroyed her instead of the whole binding spell, you would have, wouldn't you? You sealed her away because that was the best you could do."

My throat tightened. "That's a fair read of the situation. The direction I took was also partly due to how quickly the attack happened and how little time I had to think." But I'd had plenty of time to think about how I'd defend my king from the Darkest One before she'd arrived, and I hadn't come up with a definite solution any of those times either.

"Mostly she was too powerful," I added. "She's the most powerful dark fae there is, and I'm only half-fae myself. Creative strategy can get you a long way, but..." I shrugged, my heart heavy.

Izzy bit her lip. "So... If that was the case back then, and you haven't had as much time to prepare now..."

Ah. It wasn't hard to figure out what she was asking, as much as she obviously hated to. "I don't know if I'll be able to take her on properly this time, no," I said. "I just can't think about that. I have to try. Maybe I can at least seal her away again. Maybe I can find a way to get her attention off Darton, at least, so whatever she's planning that involves him, she won't be able to do." If I could rid him of his curse, that would throw a wrench in her schemes.

"And Darton will help fight her."

"Of course. In some ways he knows *more* than he did back then, so he'll be able to do more." I hadn't been enough to stop her on my own, but maybe the two of us together, both with a full understanding of the threat...

But how could I let him get close enough to the Darkest One to fight her while her influence was still tied to his soul? No. The spell I was going to attempt had to work. I had to release him from the darkness she'd woven into his soul, or we were screwed. It was that simple.

"Oh, look!" Izzy pointed ahead. The drifting branches of a weeping willow had come into view. We hurried along the path. The breeze passed through the grove with an eerie rustling. But as we ventured into the midst of the willows, my gaze caught on a prone trunk a short hike down the path. My spirits lifted, and a real smile crossed my face.

This was the first time I could think of that I'd been happy to see something dead, but I'd take my victories where I could.

CHAPTER ELEVEN

"You went all that way to gather this stuff, and now you're going to burn it?" Darton said.

I poked at the shavings of dead willow bark I'd gathered in a small pile in our concrete yard. "Reduce it down to its most basic, orderly state. That's the whole point. Anyway, I've got more if I mess up the materials somehow."

I had to be careful not to add extra elements to the mix. That meant no matches and no chemical lighters. And no light fae magic.

I knelt down and struck the rocks I was using as flints against each other. One, two, three—there. I got a spark. It leapt onto the finer shreds of bark beneath my hands and caught. The flame sizzled over the pile as I straightened up. A thin, acrid scent drifted into the air.

"And this will convince the... whatever... inside me that you're a dark fae?"

"That's the idea." I glanced over at Darton. He was trying to keep his voice casual, but tension showed all through his posture. I was about to go digging deep into his soul. We both knew there wasn't any other option, but I couldn't help saying, "If you've changed your mind, we can just leave it. We can just make sure the Darkest One never gets the chance—"

"But we can't really make sure she won't." Darton shook his head. "It's fine. I want her magic out of me. You can't do that unless you know what *it* is."

The scraps of bark had been small enough that the fire had already consumed most of them. I stirred the ash with my poker. "I'll be done here soon. Why don't you go lie down where we decided and relax as well as you can. That'll make my job easier."

"Right." He turned to go with a jerky motion. It tugged at my heart.

"Art," I said. He looked back at me. "It's going to be okay. Whatever it is, we'll deal with it. Like always. Isn't that what you always say?"

His mouth twitched into a small smile. "I guess I should be glad you do listen to me every now and again."

The door thumped as he went in. I watched the flames crackle lower over the disintegrating bark. That little smile had warmed me more than the fire did.

When the fire had sputtered out completely, I took out my bag of dried aconite petals and scattered them in the ash. Then I scooped some of the mixture into a bowl. With a stone pestle, I ground petals and ash together into a fine powder. The scent that rose off it, tart and prickling, made my stomach turn.

There was darkness here, all right. My fae senses cringed at it. Well, they'd just have to tolerate it for a little while. I had work to do.

Inside, the cup of chervil tea I'd brewed had stopped steaming. That herb was the only one I'd already had on hand that I thought might be useful, to thin out the light fae essence running through my veins. I drank it in slow gulps. The delicately sweet flavor seemed at odds with the smoky smell still clinging to my clothes.

I left those clothes on—the willow smoke could only help my cause—and carried my bowl of powder into the guest room.

We'd pushed the bed into the corner to leave as much open floor space as possible. Darton lay on the polished wood, shirt off, his arms resting at either side of his well-muscled chest and his eyes closed. He was breathing deep and even, but the twitch of his jaw as I came in told me he was far from sleeping.

I knelt beside him and rolled up my sleeves. The willow ash and aconite powder was faintly grainy and still warm under my fingers. I smeared it up my forearms to the elbows, rubbing it in until my skin looked darker than Keevan's. Then I coated my face with it, eyelids, nose, lips—everything. Next a ring around my neck and down past my collarbone to shield the energy of my heart. The only impression I wanted to give off during this exploration was that of the deathly darkness that characterized my opposite in fae kind.

The itch in my hands had faded. Maybe the oath thought all this work was going toward bringing death to Arthur's soul. Well, at least that'd be one less distraction.

I dragged in a breath and leaned forward to set my hands on Darton's bare chest. His heart beat against my palms from beneath those firm muscles. And all through his body, the energy of his soul quivered. I let my eyelids fall shut.

"I travel in, I travel well. Darkness, come to meet me."

My sense of the energies inside Darton expanded. I glided on into them, as if into a vision.

A pulsing light filled the space around my awareness, forming the walls of a tunnel. I moved onward through it, my senses on high alert. Little traces of shadow flickered here and there amid the glow. I could see them more sharply now. They gleamed darker for me as if welcoming me.

Come to me, shadows, I thought without speaking. I had no real voice in this inner realm. *Let me see you in all your dark glory.*

I had the sense of something stirring, up ahead. A faint waft of cold cut through Darton's natural warmth. I was closer, far closer than I'd managed to get before.

The tunnel turned and twisted, as if someone had knotted it here. The speckles of shadow grew larger and seeped even deeper. I braced myself as I ventured on. Whatever dark curse the fae had conjured inside Arthur's soul might not be racing out to greet me, but it wasn't fleeing either. I could feel it hovering, waiting, with a quiver that was almost curious.

I turned another corner—and whatever breath I had in this strange space fell away. A shadowy shape sat coiled in the space ahead of me. The thrum reverberating off it gave me the same icy chill as the Darkest One's voice in my vision. I could almost feel her fingers reaching off of the thing to smear her frigid essence on my skin.

That was it. My king's curse. If I could touch it, scry out the purpose of it—

I took another step closer, and the thing raised its head. A wave of horror crashed over me, sweeping all my thoughts away. I froze, numbed with panic.

I didn't need to touch that thing to know what it was. The head that peered down at me was narrow and sharp, with puffs of smoke trailing from its two wide nostrils. Slanted eyes shone with a darkness so complete I couldn't focus on them for more than a moment. Scales gleamed all along its shadowy length as it uncoiled its sinewy body. Claws like obsidian cut into the glow of the soul around us. Folded wings stirred by the line of spikes running down its back.

A dragon. I was looking at a dragon. A dragon shaped entirely from dark fae magic, some two hundred years of it, all packed into this tiny gap in Arthur's soul.

But it wasn't tiny in essence. The power humming inside it was enough to leave my head ringing. Bottled up and waiting to explode—like the time bomb Eric had called it.

All the Darkest One had to do was rip Darton open and set this thing free, and it would unfurl its cruel shadows over humankind with a wallop that would put shame to the storm now raging over Britain.

The stories called Arthur "Pendragon." As if they'd known somehow. How absurd. Light help us, how the hell was I supposed to conquer *that*?

A hysterical giggle bubbled through my mind. The dragon shifted toward me with another wave of its cold, concentrated energy. It stabbed through my awareness as if I'd been splashed with liquid nitrogen. It barred its fangs, gathering its breath for whatever horrible sort of flame a creature like that could produce, and the last shreds of self-control holding me in place vanished.

I flinched away, tumbling away from the shadow, through the glow, and back into my now-quaking body. The chill raced after me. No. No. I clenched my fingers as more shivers raked my body.

The Darkest One's laughter echoed in my ears. The ice of her energy ached under every inch of my skin. Not just a curse. A monster. A monster so vast I could hardly comprehend it.

A whimper crept from my throat. I clamped my mouth shut, but Darton's eyes had already blinked open. He sat up. "Em."

My arms shot out of their own accord. My hands clamped around his neck, thumbs poised to channel the killing energy straight into his throat. My lips parted, the oath's urge burning in my mouth.

No. I hadn't gone through that horrible journey just to give in now. I tried to wrench my arms away, but my muscles wouldn't obey. Air stuttered from my mouth. My tongue shifted. I couldn't even drag my thumb to the side to press it against my wounded palm. But I had to feel something, something other than this drive to snuff out the life in front of me—and the beast contained within it.

Darton stared at me. He gripped my forearms, but I already knew he couldn't have dislodged my grasp now, football player muscles or no. The warmth of his touch bled through my skin, and

I did the only thing I could think of. I yanked him forward and pulled myself to him at the same time, catching his mouth with a kiss.

It had only been a few days since we'd last kissed. Since we'd last... almost everything. But somehow it felt as if I'd been waiting ages to feel his lips against mine again. As if I'd gone nearly mad with the lack of them. He kissed me back, hard and hot, setting off sparks all through my body. My hold on his neck loosened.

Darton cupped the back of my head, his fingertips tracing over my scalp. I tipped my head to angle the kiss even deeper. To drink up every drop of pleasure it could offer, before we had to stop.

Because we did. When the itch of the oath had completely dampened, I eased back. My body was still quivering, but for a very different reason. Darton let out a shaky breath. His hand slid away, but only as far as my shoulder. He ran his thumb over the peak, and that single contact was enough to leave me longing to throw myself back into his embrace.

"Em?" he said. I thought I heard the same longing in his voice, but there was confusion too. "Are you— Was that okay?"

Hadn't he noticed I was the one who'd initiated the embrace? I laughed, a little roughly. "A minor exception to my rules. I figured it was better to kiss you than to kill you."

He touched his neck. My fingers had clutched him hard enough that the skin there was mottled pink. Guilt knotted my stomach. "I'm sorry. I was overwhelmed, and the oath took over—"

"And you stopped it. Even then you stopped it." He let out a huff of breath that was almost a chuckle. "Even when you've got a magical oath compelling you to hurt me, I can trust you with my life."

The only urge I was fighting now was the urge to kiss him again, which had only gotten stronger with that comment. I took his hand from my shoulder into mine, twining my fingers through his. We were still in this together, my king and me.

He bowed his head toward me, and my heart skipped. His lips

only brushed my cheek with the briefest of pecks. Then he tugged me to him so I was leaning against his solid frame. He looked down at our twined hands.

"You said you were overwhelmed. You found the dark magic inside me, then? I'm guessing it's pretty bad."

He was braced for the news. It still took me a few seconds to open my mouth, and another several to find the words.

"The dark fae conjured a dragon. Bit by bit, it must have been. Shaping it and feeding it more and more power. For now, it's just a ball of energy hidden in your soul. But if the Darkest One gets her hands on you..."

"She'll release it," Darton finished for me. "A dragon. A fucking *dragon.*" He pressed his hand to his forehead. "I don't even know what that means. Is it going to burst out of me someday, all *Alien* style?"

I'd kept up with modern culture enough to understand the reference. "No. It's not a bodily thing. It's all dark energy pulled into a form. If she never gets the chance, it'll just stay there, dormant, until... well, until you die."

"But we can't count on staying ahead of her that long. So what do you do about a soul plagued with dragons?"

I hesitated. "I'm not sure. I've never dealt with a dragon before. It's not something light fae are inclined to construct."

Darton's fingers tightened around mine. "It scares you," he said.

"I'll try my best," I said quickly. "There has to be something—"

"Right." His voice had gone brisk and distant. "And if there isn't, and the Darkest One comes—how bad exactly will it be if this dragon gets out?"

I wet my lips. "I can't know for sure. But... they were feeding it with power, all through your first life and the lives of your ancestors. The Darkest One wanted something that could rain more destruction down in an instant than even she can on her own."

"So it'll be *worse* than what she's already doing."

"A lot worse," I admitted. "From what I felt of the thing, it could lay waste to this entire state—people, animals, plants, everything destroyed—in a matter of minutes."

Darton sucked in a breath. I heard him swallow. Then he said, "Maybe you *should* kill me then."

I jerked away from his chest to stare at him. "*What?*"

His jaw set. He looked back at me steadily. "Maybe your old enclave was right. Maybe Eric was right. The Darkest One could decide to go through with her plans for me any minute now. As long as I'm alive with that thing in me, she can. But if I die, if my soul passes away, the dragon dies with me. Doesn't it?"

"Yes," I said, "but—"

"No but. I don't want to be responsible for millions of people dying. *I* don't want to die, but I'm not going to kid myself that I'm that important."

My chest clenched. My fingers curled around his, as if he might slip away from me right now, just by saying that. "You are to me."

"Em. Merlin." One side of his mouth slanted up, but the shape it made was too crooked to really call it a smile. He touched the side of my face, leaning in so our foreheads nearly touched. "You've done so much for me already. Kept me going all this time. Don't you think maybe it's time you let me go?"

"I'm really not good at that," I said. "As I think the last fifteen hundred years should prove. Art—Arthur. I don't want you to be turned into the Darkest One's weapon either. If it comes to that, if I know we don't have a chance... I'll do what I have to do. But I don't believe we're there yet. I *do* believe there's a chance. I swear to you, on all the years we've spent together, I'm not giving up on you yet. Don't give up on me?"

Darton made a choked sound. "Of course not. Don't say it like that. You know I—" He faltered. "What's next, then? Where do we go from here?"

CHAPTER TWELVE

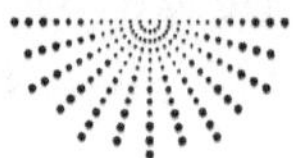

"Dragons, huh?" Jagger turned the wheel of the fae hunter van he'd lent to us and now temporarily reclaimed. The wheels bumped over a pothole in the near-abandoned dirt road with a lurch and a squeal. "Just when I thought I'd seen everything. You do like to top yourself, don't you?"

"Believe me, I'd rather not have in this particular way," I muttered. Sunlight wavered over us from between the sparse trees along the side of the road. Its intermittent light wasn't enough to provide any comfort. "Thanks for coming back. I mean, after everything you must have heard from Eric..."

Jagger's mouth flattened into a grim line. "He's not a bad kid, but he could do with a little more thinking before he acts. If you are who he says you are, then I can't see how he or I are better equipped to handle the situation."

He left that statement between us like a question, for me to confirm or deny. I opted for the middle ground.

"I'm sure any ideas you have about that are highly distorted by time and imagination. The stories don't get a whole lot right."

Jagger gave a bark of a laugh. "Emma, I have spent more than a minute in your presence. You don't need to tell me *that*."

I braced myself for the sorts of questions Keevan and Izzy had asked when they'd found out—about what Arthur and I *had* been like, about our long series of lives and rebirths, about the spell that had thrown us into that cycle. But Jagger just left it at that. Maybe I'd been silly to keep it from him in the first place. He'd never been the dramatic type.

"I prefer not to shout it from the rooftops," I said. "As you've probably also already figured out. So with this expert of yours—"

"By all means," Jagger said. "But so there's no misunderstanding, I wouldn't exactly call Hugh an 'expert.' He, er, is mainly known in the network as a kook. The guy spends all his time obsessing over creatures the rest of us didn't have any reason to believe existed, despite all the things we had seen. I'm not sure anything he thinks he knows is any more true than those stories you mentioned."

"That's fine. I couldn't really expect anything better than that." How could I when *I* didn't even know what to do about a dragon? The Darkest One must have been amused with her cleverness, taking human nightmares and letting them guide her magic-making. I'd heard of dark fae-formed dragons in my first life, but those had been brief conjurings designed more to scare than do any real destruction. The dark lady had truly outdone herself.

Jagger turned down a drive even narrower and bumpier than the road we'd been on. A small stone house stood at the end, spotty forest all around it. One tree leaned over so far it nearly touched the mossy shingles on the roof.

My eyebrows rose. "Doesn't worry much about dark fae access, does he? No floodlights or solar panels?"

Jagger brought the van to a halt. "Like I said: a kook. From what he's said, he doesn't do any actual hunting, just 'observing.' So I suppose he's never pissed off a dark thing enough to find out what it's like when they follow you home for payback."

Like many times before, I had to bite back the question of how exactly Jagger had gotten those scars on his face. It'd been some kind of dark creature's doing—I had no doubt about that. I also suspected the creature that had done it had done worse to someone else, someone Jagger cared about, at the same time. But he'd never volunteered the information, despite my occasional vague prodding. If he wasn't going to make a fuss about my secrets, I could do him the same courtesy.

The house's door opened as we climbed out of the van. A short, pudgy man with wire-rimmed glasses peered at us from the front step. For a second I thought he was wary. Then he rubbed his hands together, and I caught the excited gleam in his deep-set eyes.

"Jagger," he said in a slightly raspy tenor. "And you must be Emma. I understand you've come dragon-hunting." He gave me a flash of a smile.

"That's one way of putting it." I glanced around. The terrain by the house was a mishmash of shadows. It made my skin crawl even without seeing anything definite crawling in it. "Should we go inside?"

"Yes, of course. Come on in."

Hugh swept back inside, leaving the door wide open. No, this guy clearly had no worries about dark vermin following him home. It was a damned good thing after a fair bit of waffling I'd decided to leave Darton at home, on the condition he kept his sword in arm's reach.

Besides, I didn't like the way Hugh was already sizing me up. Like I was a specimen rather than a person. It reminded me too much of the way the fae looked at me sometimes, as if they were trying to figure out how my half-fae soul could have come to be in this completely human body. I doubted he could have seen the dragon in Darton anyway—it'd been hard enough for me to reach it—but he no doubt would have tried, by light only knew what methods.

"I understand you're the dragon expert in the network," I said, matching Hugh's academic tone. "I was hoping to hear some of the results of your research. In particular, about how a person gets rid of a dragon."

"Hmm." He sat in one of the armchairs in the cramped living room and took off his glasses to rub them with the hem of his shirt. The place smelled of dusty leather, probably due to the stacks of old books on the shelves that filled one wall. I stayed standing, not trusting the wooden chairs that remained. The woven seat on one looked ready to unravel the next time anyone put their weight on it.

"Tell me a little more about this dragon," Hugh said, putting his glasses back on. He folded his hands in his lap. "General appearance? Behavior? Where did you happen to find it?"

He was taking this all very calmly. Exactly how many actual dragons had he run into before? Jagger had given me the impression Hugh's research was purely speculative.

"It was formed by dark fae energy," I said. "Like all of the dragons I'm aware of, which to be fair isn't a large number. Long and scaly, beady eyes, fangs and sharp claws, wings. You know the deal. Based on the smoke it had coming from its nose, I'd say definitely some sort of fire-breathing. They've encouraged it to stay still and quiet for now, though. It's all burrowed down in my—my friend's soul."

"In their *soul*," Hugh repeated.

"Yes," I said. "It's complicated to explain, but the fae have basically twisted a little portion of his life energy into a sort of home for it. Fed it from their own energy somehow. And I'd like to get rid of it."

"Right." Hugh gave me an odd little smile. Then he glanced at Jagger. "I know the rest of the network doesn't think much of my work, but this is a bit much, isn't it? Haven't you got better things to do than resort to pranks?"

Oh. I bristled as the realization hit me. The kook thought my story was so ridiculous he'd decided *I* was a kook. Hog's balls.

What, did he expect me to have brought the dragon with me on a leash so he could inspect it?

"Hugh," Jagger said in his gravelly voice, "I think you should listen to the girl. She knows what she's talking about. I thought you'd be happy to put all that research to use."

"I would be if you'd brought me something other than a farce."

I cracked my knuckles. At the sound, Hugh's head jerked toward me. I gave him an even smile. "What exactly would you need for you to believe I'm not joking around?"

He blinked at me. "Well, I— Some sort of evidence of your story, I suppose. A better explanation of how this dragon came to be. Honestly, dark fae conjuring dragons in people's souls is nothing I've ever—"

"Fine." He wasn't getting a full explanation, especially not when he'd just proven he wasn't likely to believe that either. The whole story wasn't any easier to swallow. But I could show him proof that he was dealing with someone who knew more about fae dealings than he ever would. I didn't like to have to show off my magic as if it were a parlor trick, and showing him what I needed to wasn't going to be *fun*, but I didn't have time for all this blathering.

I pulled a couple of twigs from my jacket pocket. "Take a close look," I said, "because I'm only going to draw this for you once." I clenched my fingers around the twigs and held out my arm, my hand turned toward the ceiling. "*Picture from memory, take shape, take form,*" I murmured, reaching back to my memory of Arthur's dragon.

The air above my hand shimmered. The energy I was drawing from the twigs balked at my command. I was asking that life to imitate a vision of death, which was the last thing it wanted to do.

"*Picture from memory, take shape, take form,*" I repeated. Sweat beaded on the back of my neck as I trained my will on those wisps of energy. They whirled, darkening with the sharpening of my attention. They were visible to my spectators now. Hugh inhaled with a hitch of breath.

I ignored him, training my mind even more closely on the image of the dragon. The memory sent a chill down my spine, but I ignored the discomfort. I wasn't going to stop until the kook was well and truly convinced.

The shadows rippled into a more detailed form. The illusionary dragon uncoiled its body over my hand the way the real one had moved when I'd encountered it. Its teeth even flashed when it opened its mouth. It shuffled its wings, peering at Hugh.

A prickling started to dig down into the roots of my teeth. I gritted them, holding the illusion for a few seconds longer. Then I snapped my fingers, and the shadows dispersed.

Hugh was frozen in his chair, his jaw slack. He looked from the spot where the dragon had hovered to me and back again. I decided to sit down in the slightly less ramshackle chair after all.

"That's what it looked like," I said. "Although I expect its actual size when not imprisoned will be a lot larger than this house. Now what can you tell me about it?"

"Well, I— How did you do that?"

"I know a few fae tricks," I said. "Enough to recognize a dragon when I see one. Enough to know my friend is in a whole lot of trouble if we don't get rid of it. And an awful lot of other people will be in trouble as well."

Hugh paused. His gaze turned thoughtful. "Is this at all connected to that strange storm that's been attacking Great Britain for the last few days?"

"Only so far as the fae causing that is the same one who orchestrated the creation of the dragon," I said. "We'd really rather it wasn't inside him when she comes to collect."

"All right. All right. In his *soul.*" His chuckle sounded a little frantic. "Unfortunately I'd imagine the easiest way—"

"If you suggest anything that involves getting rid of my friend to get rid of the dragon, I'll be very tempted to get rid of you," I said matter-of-factly.

Hugh paled. "N-no. Of course not. Let me see." He stood up

and went to his wall of books. He pulled one leather-bound volume out, paged through it, considered a few of the pages, put it back, and repeated the process a few more times. I waited, tapping my fingers against the chair's wooden arms. Jagger leaned against the door frame, looking mildly amused by his colleague's distress.

"I don't believe I've ever heard of a dragon formed in someone's soul before," Hugh said after several minutes. "Not even in the more outlandish stories. I assume you don't want to simply *remove* it..."

"No. It's not going to do anyone any good out on the loose either. I need a way to destroy it without moving it—or to at least weaken it." Maybe the latter would help me get to the point where I could do the former on my own.

"All right. Well, my research *has* given me some insight into dragons formed by energy. In fact, I've always believed those reports sounded the most authentic." The academic's enthusiasm had come back into his voice and his eyes. "There are of course the traditional methods of dragon-slaying involving swords and other weaponry..." At my grimace, he nodded. "Obviously this would require more of a... metaphysical approach."

"That's what I was thinking," I said. "But I want to be careful that the methods I use do actually weaken it rather than simply annoying it. It didn't look like a very forgiving creature."

"Understandable, understandable." He wet his lips. "Unfortunately, as I said, this isn't a situation I've encountered before. But I can tell you what I have found out about dragons' general inclinations. They seem particularly drawn to flow—of an even, orderly sort, being dark creatures. Many modern sightings have taken place near trains, trolleys, and other vehicles that tend to move along a clear path at a steady pace. They also seem to enjoy rivers and streams."

"I'm not seeing how that's going to help Emma slay one," Jagger put in.

I waved him off. "Let me figure out how to piece it together." If

I could piece anything together from what Hugh's questionable sources had taught him. I turned back to the scholar. "What else? Anything at all. There's no way to know what idea might at least point me in the right direction."

"Well, perhaps for that reason—the appeal of a steady flow—dragons also seem to be drawn to... blood. And respiration."

"Which flow through the body, in an orderly way—under ideal circumstances," I said. "Got it."

He nodded. "Dragons are almost like fish themselves, needing to be in continuous motion when they're active. Trying to restrain a dragon in any way tends to have unfortunate results. I assume yours is subdued rather than contained."

Lurking, waiting. "Yeah, that describes it pretty well."

"What else, what else..." He frowned, looking away. "There are some accounts that myrrh smoke can send them into a stupor, but I wouldn't rely on that. They're known to be fickle, shifting their attention easily, and difficult to tame. Their weakest point is generally thought to be either their throat or a particular point on their belly, which I suppose might hold true even in metaphysical terms..."

He fell into a silence. I waited a few minutes before I said, "Is that everything?"

"There's relatively few accounts of dragons at all," he said with an apologetic shrug, and waved toward his shelf. "I've spent more of my time on less impressive creatures. But I can say this." He paused, holding my gaze. "I've visited a site that was apparently the target of a dragon not much bigger than a sparrow. The destruction that creature wrought, if that is indeed what wrought it... If this one is as large as you say, I hope for all our sakes that something I've told you today is useful to you. Because the last thing I'd want to see is that creature getting loose."

CHAPTER THIRTEEN

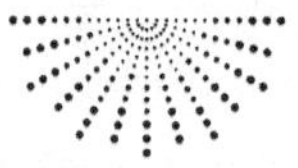

JAGGER KEPT his own council until we'd climbed back into the van. "Is any of that rambling going to do you any good?" he asked. "I can't promise his information is at all reliable."

"I know," I said. "It gives me a starting point at least. Would you mind—I think I'm going to... meditate for a little while, in the back. To see if I can connect what he said to any of my own observations."

"Be my guest," Jagger said with a sweep of his arm.

I squeezed between the two front seats and sat down on the carpeted floor between the shelves of fae-hunting equipment. Jagger started the engine. The van rocked as he turned it around to head back up the pocked driveway. My body swayed.

Maybe lying down was a safer bet. Especially seeing as I planned to slip far back into my memories, where I'd barely be aware of what was happening outside.

I sank back on the floor. The bristles of the carpet prickled against the back of my neck. I didn't need any magic to travel back into my memories—they were already in my head, after all. Concentration would do the trick just fine. I dragged in a slow, steady breath, trying not to think about how appealing a dragon might have found that sensation.

There'd been several times I'd witnessed the dark fae interacting with Arthur. My father would have seen many other encounters, and maybe he'd even written about them in his journals, but Eric hadn't done me the favor of bringing those back along with his murderous intentions. So I had to make do with what I had in my own memory.

I let my mind drift back toward the sensations of fifteen hundred years past. The chalky smell of the plaster in the castle halls. Roast meat sizzling over a spit for hundreds of royal dinners. Hoof beats as my prince and then king dragged me off on some new quest. The lilt of his voice, low and measured. Always trying to help his subjects in any way he could.

Always listening, patiently, even when he shouldn't.

The woman was standing by the side of the road, a basket covered with a scrap of cloth slung over one arm. Her face sagged with apparent weariness and her clothes were torn, but it was a feigned distress. Shadows licked higher on her feet and deeper into her eyes than was truly natural. When she looked at my prince riding up to her, they shivered in anticipation.

She had more power in her toenail than the average human did in their entire body.

"My liege!" I said, but as always Arthur was ahead of me. His horses never balked at his taps of his heel or tugs of the reins. He drew his current stallion to a stop in front of the woman.

"What brings you out here, good woman?" he asked. "It's a long journey from the nearest town."

"I don't mind the walk," she said in a thin voice. Shadows unfurled with it from her mouth, too dim for my prince's eyes to catch. "Are you the prince? Arthur? I'm sure I'm no one important enough for you to trouble with."

I didn't believe for an instant that she hadn't known exactly who he was before we'd even come into view. She'd been waiting for him. And she couldn't have picked a better ploy to keep him there. At the suggestion that he might think himself too high to bother with a peasant, he immediately slid down from his saddle. He didn't see any threat, just a harmless peasant.

Swine crud. After a few jerks of his head, the gelding I was riding finally agreed to stop behind the prince's steed. I scrambled down after my prince. My feet hit the ground with a jarring thump. The gelding snorted as if mocking me.

"Every person in this kingdom is important to me," Arthur was saying. "If you have any concerns at all, I'd much rather you told me than didn't."

"Oh," the woman said, suddenly coy, "I don't have any troubles big enough to complain. It's enough just to know we matter to you."

She took his hand and bowed down over it, as if in a gesture of supplication.

I cleared my throat sharply. "My liege," I said. The prince looked over. I gave him that look, the look he really should have been familiar with by now. His shoulders tensed slightly, but he still smiled at the woman as she straightened up. Too sodding confident for his own good.

"I appreciate your kind words," Arthur said, warming up to an excuse, but the woman waved him off before he had to produce it.

"You have business to attend to, of course. Think nothing of it. Stay well, Your Highness."

The hint of sarcasm in her tone had nagged at me even then. But now, studying the memory, I focused more on her bow. The way she'd tipped her head over Arthur's hand. Her chest had contracted—I hadn't paid special attention to *that* detail in the moment back then.

She'd exhaled over his knuckles. Had she been passing energy into him that way? I hadn't seen the dark fae work exactly like that before, but then, I hadn't dealt with dark fae conjuring monsters in people's souls before. Hugh had said dragons responded well to the rhythmic, flowing bodily functions like breath, after all.

I inhaled deeply and sent my mind drifting back again. There'd been that one time we'd run into a whole group of fae...

A chill raced up my spine before we'd even reached the cluster of tents. There was no fire lit to provide light or heat for the "band of travelers" the local townspeople had complained to Arthur about, even though evening was settling in. Shadows drifted over the tents from the scattered trees, undulating before my eyes. My hands tightened around the reins.

"Those are dark fae, sire," I said. A flicker of that old vision, the one that had predicted his death at the Darkest One's hands, darted by behind my eyes. My chest tightened. "Maybe it would be better to leave them be. The townspeople didn't say they'd actually done anything wrong. Confronting them may cause more harm than letting them finish their business."

My king glanced back at me. "If they haven't been doing anything wrong, there's no reason to avoid them, is there? I have my sword and you have your magic. I'd like to know why they're venturing so far into human territory."

I couldn't think of any good reason for a bunch of dark fae to be hanging about here. But I also knew that Arthur wasn't a big fan of caution. "Stay on your horse, stay wary, and be ready to ride at the first sign of trouble, all right?"

"Don't worry, Merlin," he said with a grin. "I'll keep you safe."

He turned back toward the camp, and I rolled my eyes at his back. He didn't even know half the times I'd saved his hide. For the sake of his pride, I didn't rub those moments in his face. But I wasn't keen to add to that number.

The chill deepened as we came up on the tents. I shivered, but my king didn't appear to be affected. Maybe because it was a cold that only touched my fae senses. The flavor of it brought back my vision of Arthur's death again. Was she here? I scanned the figures moving to greet us. Shadows clung to all of them, but none of them emanated the cool power of their great lady. I wasn't sure if I was glad of it or more wary. My nerves tingled.

She was nearby, I'd nearly bet on that guess. This glade didn't look like the place in my vision, but those visions weren't always completely literal. I eased my mare closer to Arthur's stallion.

"Your Highness," one of the assembled fae said. "What an unexpected visit."

"I got word of a camp that had settled here, and I wanted to discover what your aim is," Arthur said. "War is brewing. Many people are wary of strangers."

"Completely understandable," the young man said with a nod. "We apologize if we've caused any distress. We've been traveling for a long time, and merely stopped here for a few days to gather our bearings. We'll be moving on to our home in the south tomorrow."

Because they'd only stopped here in the hopes of gaining the king's attention, I suspected. The fae man doing the speaking cut his gaze briefly toward me, with a flash of a smirk. He knew I recognized what they were.

"Our loyalty is to you and this great country, of course," he said, turning back to Arthur. "We give you our utmost respects."

He bowed his head where he stood beside Arthur's horse, by Arthur's leg. The others gathered close, stepping up to Arthur and bowing in turn. The first man stepped back, rubbing his thumb against the palm of his hand.

The chill of that encounter followed me out of the memory. I stared up at the ceiling of the van. The hum of the engine did nothing to soothe my nerves.

They'd all exhaled by him, the same way the fae woman had. I hadn't put it together at the time because I hadn't thought to watch for their *breathing*. And that one man—that gesture with his palm —something about that felt familiar. Where had I seen that before? I closed my eyes.

The smells of straw and manure drifted down the town street from the stable where we'd left our mounts. My prince picked up the pace of his strides, no doubt eager to make it back to the castle before dinner. You'd think he was fifteen and not twenty-five the way he ate

—like a bottomless pit. I hurried along behind him, debating whether the discomfort of the ride would cancel out the joy of feasting for me.

A horse-drawn cart rattled by and stopped with a clatter. One of the wheels had popped off the frame. Arthur leapt to help, catching one of the sacks of produce near the back of the cart before it could tumble out. I moved to join him, but I froze when the driver hopped down. He swept his hand over his dark hair, and wisps of shadow followed it. My back tensed.

"Bit of bad luck there," Arthur suggested. "I can help you get that wheel back on."

"Thank you kindly, sir," the dark fae-playing-farmer said. He knelt down to grasp the wheel. When he started to lift it, he gasped. It thumped to the ground, and he raised his hand. Blood streaked down the palm.

"Damn. You'd better bind that," my prince said. "I think I have a handkerchief that'll do the trick." He reached to his pockets.

"I'm sure he—" I started, but Arthur had already produced the cloth.

"You're too kind," the dark fae man said. He bowed his head and reached for the handkerchief with both hands. The wounded one twitched around Arthur's as if to brush against it.

"Hey!" I said, pushing closer. But the back of Arthur's hand was unmarked. The fae man mustn't have touched him. He was wrapping the cloth around his palm now. He tied it and bobbed his head again. His thumb rubbed against the wounded spot on his palm through the fabric, as if he were pressing the pain deeper in.

At the time I'd thought the strange gesture he'd made was some kind of tic, nothing important. But Hugh had mentioned dragons and blood too. Had the dark fae man smeared some onto Arthur's skin with a magic to send it straight through to feed the dragon? And his bow—I'd be willing to bet he'd exhaled over Arthur's hand at the same moment.

Had the fae man at the camp passed on blood to my king

somehow too? That rubbing of the palm... It could be tied to their magic.

It had to be tied back to the Darkest One somehow. Had she ever approached him directly back then, before the last near-fatal time? I'd seen her. I'd spoken with her, unpleasant as that experience had been. I frowned, reaching back into my memories once more.

Cheerful voices and laughter carried across the fields outside the castle. The smells of fresh baking and cut fruit wafted through the air. Jangling music assaulted my ears from different directions. It seemed half the country had arrived to celebrate their new king.

Arthur sat on his temporary throne on the dais, nodding and saying a few words to every person who stopped to give their blessing. His smile was warm and his face bright, but I recognized the restrained weariness in the way he held his head. It was only one month since his father's death. Long enough for the festival not to seem insensitive. Not long enough for him to have completely recovered, as devotedly as he'd thrown himself into his new role.

I watched him from my little nook out of the way between two of the stalls selling sweets and breads. The first few months of his ascension felt the most dangerous to me. I had a wand tucked up my sleeve and another in the satchel slung over my shoulder. How many twigs were tucked into various corners of my clothing, I couldn't count.

A quiver passed over my scalp, a sensation like the sun disappearing behind an unexpected cloud, although the actual sun was still shining brightly. My gaze jerked away from my new king. It caught on a figure standing in the middle of the crowd, which thronged around her without touching her.

She stood there, still and unmoved, like a stone protruding from a frothing sea. The darkness of her bled into the shadows beneath the people's feet and between their bodies. A haze drifted over her face as if she wore a veil of shadow.

My stomach knotted. The chill of the fae woman's presence burrowed deep into the center of my body. But I couldn't just stand here. She could make everyone else avoid her, but she couldn't escape my notice.

I squared my shoulders and strode over. Her eyes slid toward me when I was a few steps away. She smiled thinly and looked back toward Arthur.

She was watching my king too. Of course she was.

"What are you doing here?" I said, in the boldest voice I could summon. "You're not welcome."

"No one else seems to mind," the dark fae lady replied. Her voice was shadow too, low and smoky. It licked my ears with its chill.

"No one else sees what you are. You don't let them."

"And how much do you let them see what you are, halfling?" she said silkily. "Isn't this an occasion to pay our respects to our new king? Why can I not do the same?"

She kissed her palm and exhaled over it as if to blow the kiss to him. My arm shot up, the wand flying into my hand. But Arthur didn't so much as wince. The Darkest One let out a cool chuckle.

The din faded. The rush of bodies around us fell away. It was only me and her and darkness falling. My jaw dropped. The Darkest One loomed over me, her hair streaming from her head like black water, her eyes flaring with a blue flame.

"I see you, little wizard," she said. Her voice warbled, echoing into my ears as if from every direction at once. "I see you and I'm coming for you now."

I opened my eyes with a gasp. The van. I was still lying on my back in the van.

The suspension was jostling less now—Jagger must have gotten us off the back roads and onto the highway. I scrambled to the feet and peered out one of the windows, letting my fae senses solidify my sense of place.

We'd been on the highway for a while. We weren't far from my house now. Good. Because my heart was thudding away and a cold sweat was tingling over my skin.

That last part hadn't been a memory. The Darkest One had

sensed my investigations into the past and broken straight into my mind.

I pulled myself between the front seats and dropped into the passenger one. Jagger had tuned the radio to a classical station, the volume low so it wouldn't distract me. I pushed the button to switch stations.

"Don't care for Bach?" the fae hunter said lightly.

"I want to check the news." Hip hop. Pop music. There. A reporter was speaking in a crisp voice. She finished commenting on the ongoing preparations for the World Peace Summit in Chicago and started talking about a recent earthquake in San Francisco. I pressed my feet against the floor to hold back the urge to squirm in my seat.

Finally she got to the story I'd been waiting for. "Citizens of the United Kingdom may soon be able to breathe a sigh of relief," she said. "The unprecedented storm that has raged over the country for the last five days is finally showing signs of abating. Wind speeds have dropped by half in the last few hours, and rainfall has ceased over much of the country."

Jagger glanced at me. "What does that mean for us?"

I sagged back in my seat, setting my hand over my churning stomach. "The Darkest One is tired of playing games. She's on her way to find us."

CHAPTER FOURTEEN

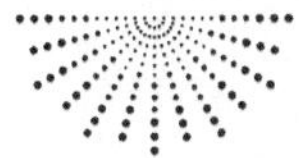

I ADJUSTED the position of the carved obsidian bowl for what was probably the hundredth time. The holly-handle knife lay where it should beside me. I'd drunk my chervil tea and smeared myself with dead willow ash and aconite again. I'd even wiped a small portion over my tongue, teeth, and the insides of my cheeks, careful not to swallow the semi-poisonous powder. My stomach churned with the feel of it anyway. My fae side was not pleased.

Everything was as it should be. Except I wasn't entirely sure about any of this.

"How exactly is this supposed to get rid of the dragon?" Darton asked. He was sitting up in the circle of twigs I'd laid around us, his arms folded over his bare chest. I wasn't even sure he needed to be shirtless for the spell I was about to attempt, but it made sense that having fewer barriers in the way would be better. It said something about my mental state that even his sculpted body in all its glory didn't hold much appeal at this particular moment.

"I don't think the ritual will be enough to fix everything all at once," I said. "But the process will weaken the dragon. I think. We'll just keep going until I feel it's stopped working, or it gets painful for one of us. And then, if it seems to have done some good, we can have another go after a little recovery period."

"And then the Darkest One won't be able to use the dragon?"

"If we can weaken it enough, it won't be able to do what she wants. And the oath will lose some of its grip on me."

"So it's a win-win situation then." He gave me his usual easy grin. The one that could still make my heart flutter, despite all the worries whirling in my head.

"As long as it works. And as long as we can reduce the dragon's strength enough before she arrives." Like all dark fae, the Darkest One should abhor the idea of plane travel, so close to the sun that could kill even her at the right intensity. Most likely she was traveling by boat, the fastest one she'd been able to hitch a ride on. Which gave us maybe two days before she showed her face on this side of the ocean.

Not anywhere near as long as I'd have liked, but I guessed I should just be glad she'd never bothered to travel over the ocean in her earlier life. Hopping from one place to another through magic, like I had done to get Darton and myself away from her, required an emotional connection to your destination. She couldn't care about someplace she'd never seen.

I picked up the knife. "Okay. Let's get started." Waiting around was only giving my worries more time to dig in their roots.

I pricked the skin of my palm where I'd stabbed myself the other night. The blade slid into my flesh easily, just half an inch. I wanted a steady but slow trickle of blood. Draining myself dry wouldn't do anyone any good.

Darton grimaced. "Are you sure that part is necessary? You said that in the memories you looked back on, you didn't actually see any of the fae using blood."

"No," I said, "but I saw enough to think it played a part. And even if *they* didn't use blood, dragons are supposed to respond to it, and it makes any magic more potent. Now be quiet and lie down."

"I thought it was the king who got to give the orders," he

muttered, but he lay back as I'd asked. His chiseled chest rose and fell with his breaths. I shifted my weight over my knees and rested the heel of my bleeding hand on the edge of the bowl so the blood would collect there unhindered.

Flow, steady and orderly. Breath and blood. If the fae could cast their dark energies *into* Arthur that way, I should be able to dredge them out. It sounded reasonable in theory, at least.

The glow of my king's spirit ran all through Darton's body, but when I focused with my fae-touched sight, it shone brightest around his heart. So I'd aim my efforts in that area.

I leaned forward, dipping so low that my lips almost touched Darton's skin above his rib cage. My hair, bound in its usual ponytail, slid against my neck. The warmth of his body tickled over my cheeks. I closed my eyes, sending my awareness down into his soul. Into that bright space with its flecks of shadow, the traces showing where the dragon had passed.

"Darkness, come to me, come through me," I murmured. The bitter flavor of the ash paste filled my mouth. I parted my lips and sucked in a long, steady breath, willing those thready shadows to creep from his soul toward me.

A wisp of darkness drifted into me. It prickled over my tongue like a shard of ice. I channeled it into my lungs with the air I inhaled, and pushed it on with the thump of my pulse, out through the dribble of blood seeping into the bowl.

Yes. Only a tiny shred of the dark power wound into Arthur's soul, but I'd taken it. Sucked it out of Darton like poison from a snake bite. I just had to keep going.

I eased my head an inch to the side and inhaled again, reaching out to the darkness. Another icy shard drew a frigid line over my tongue. It stung my lungs and then my veins as it traveled through me, but the pain disappeared with the flow of my blood into the bowl.

I smiled. The Darkest One thought I was helpless, did she? She had no idea what I was capable of when it came to protecting my king. I'd break down her dragon bit by bit, however long it took.

I continued breathing at a steady pace, careful not to lose my rhythm, shifting slightly with each new breath. Dragging the dark poison out of Darton one wisp at a time. When the fragments started to shudder and balk, I paused and repeated my spell. *"Darkness, come to me, come through me."*

The speckles stirred again. Deep within the passages of my king's soul, I felt the dragon unwinding. My body tensed, but I kept my breath even as I sucked down another shot of dark fae power.

The beast stayed where it was. With my next inhale, the thread of darkness seemed to unravel straight from that sinewy form. My heart leapt with a rush of exhilaration as its energy streamed out of me through my blood.

I refocused, willing my body to relax. Steady, even flow. This only worked as long as I appealed to the dark energy's preferred state.

I leaned even closer to Darton, my lips grazing his chest, as near as I could get while still leaving room for breath. The more darkness I could pull out with each inhale, the better. The sting of the alien energy passing through me barely pained me now. All that mattered was watching the taint of darkness gradually release from his soul.

I crossed his heart and made my way down the other side of his rib cage. I'd just taken what might have been my hundredth breath when a faint groan escaped Darton's throat. I jerked my head up, my eyes popping open. Had I hurt him?

Darton was gazing up at the ceiling. His face was flushed, but he didn't appear to be in pain. "It's fine," he said without looking at me. His voice came out slightly ragged. "Don't worry about it. As long as it's working, don't stop."

Don't worry about it. I didn't understand what he was talking about until my gaze traveled down the length of his body—and stopped on the tented fabric of his khakis.

Oh. *Oh*. That hadn't been a groan of discomfort at all. I'd been so absorbed in the spell-casting, it hadn't even occurred to me what other sorts of effects the ritual might have on Darton. More concrete effects. I was practically kissing every inch of his naked chest. A spark of my own heat flared between my legs. Not that I intended to tackle *that* problem.

He'd told me not to stop. Maybe this was feeling like the worst kind of teasing to him, but that was better than the torments the Darkest One wanted to inflict on us.

I checked the bowl. It was only a third full from the red stream trickling down my fingers from my palm. I wasn't even a little lightheaded yet. I could dredge out a whole lot more darkness yet.

Darton kept his reactions under control as I steadied my breath and leaned in again. I shifted, breath by breath, down his rib cage to just above his belly button, and then back up the center of his chest. His musky smell seeped through the acrid scent of the powder that coated my face. I trained all my attention on the shine of his soul and the threads of shadow I was unwinding from it.

I hadn't seen the dragon, but now that I was aware of it, I could sense its movements. It wound itself tight and uncoiled itself more than once as I drained away those shreds of the energy collected in it.

Then, as I inhaled yet another time, it lashed out with a swipe of its tail.

The bolt of energy smacked me in the solar plexus. My pulse stuttered, and an ache swelled through my abdomen. I sat up, my breath gone shaky. My head swam. When I clutched the side of the obsidian bowl, my fingers dipped into what had to be nearly half a quart of blood.

Okay, maybe that was enough for one session.

Darton had closed his eyes. "Em," he muttered. "Gods, Merlin." A fresh wave of heat washed over me. I didn't know what he was responding to now, what we'd just been doing or some memory only he could see, but he was obviously still turned on. And he'd spoken to *me*, not just to Emma.

"My liege," I said cautiously. "I think we'd better take a break from this. Your dragon isn't especially happy with me right now. And I could use that recovery time."

I said a few words to stop my palm's bleeding, but didn't seal the wound. No point in wasting the energy when I'd be reopening it before the end of the day. Darton pushed himself upright, adjusting his slacks, as I reached for the bandage I'd left just outside the circle. He coughed, still flushed. Still having some trouble meeting my eyes. "So, ah, did it work?"

"I captured some of the energy. I'm not sure how much of a dent I made, but at least the process accomplished something."

I patted the bandage in place and reached for the bowl. Darton's gaze followed the motion. He grimaced at the sight of its contents. "Are you sure *you're* okay after all that?"

"I've been studying human biology for centuries," I said. "I know exactly how much blood a body can stand to lose. Now if you'll excuse me, donation clinics recommend juice and cookies for a reason. I've got to stock up on fluids and energy for the next round."

"The next round," Darton murmured to himself, with a rough chuckle and a shake of his head. He scrambled to his feet to follow me. On his way out the door, he grabbed his shirt from where he'd draped it on the dresser. "I don't feel any different. Can you sense anything different with the oath?"

That was a good question. I paused, turning as he caught up. A glance downward told me his, er, enthusiasm for the situation had waned, and with that apparently his embarrassment. He looked at me questioningly when I raised my eyes. I tested the impulses running through my body.

Urge to grab the front of that shirt and yank his mouth to mine? Check. Urge to run my hands over *his* body until he was groaning my name again? Double check. Urge to snuff the life out of him…? Hmm. The now-familiar itch nagged faintly at my fingers, but without much oomph. I wasn't sure if that was because of all the other sensations running through me or because my king's soul had been downgraded in threat level, but I'd take it.

"I think it's a little better," I said. "I definitely don't seem inclined to kill you any time in the next hour or so."

Darton laughed. "Well, I guess I'll take that." He opened his mouth again as if to say something else, but he didn't get the chance. Because in the same moment, the ceiling over the kitchen collapsed with a hail of rushing shadows.

CHAPTER FIFTEEN

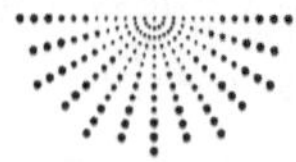

DARTON LEAPT BACK, but a wave of dark magic was already crashing over us. It crackled cold over my skin and shrieked in my ears. I threw my arm toward Darton, groping for him, but my fingers only touched frigid air. I hurled myself in the direction I thought he'd gone, and finally my body collided with his.

His arms closed around me. "What's happening?" he shouted by my ear over the roar of the shadows.

"The dark fae," I said. "They've broken past my protections." I'd set aside my salt pouch so it didn't disrupt the ceremony, so I hadn't felt them cross the barrier outside.

They were coming for Darton. The Darkest One was on her way, and her minions had arrived to snatch up my king and deliver him to her. My heart thumped. "Where's your sword?"

"By the door."

"Then we run for it."

We dashed together, stumbling in the swirling darkness, toward the front of the house. My wand. Where was my wand? I'd set the one I'd been carrying on me aside for the ritual too, for the same reason. I should have picked it right back up when we'd finished. How could I have been so careless?

There. The energy in one called out to me like a beam of light through clouds. There was the wand I'd set in the basket near the door.

Excalibur gleamed as Darton grasped its hilt. I spun around.

Shadowy figures swept through the haze toward us: The dark fae, following the path their magical assault had broken open.

"*Darkness begone!*" I hollered, channeling all my intention through that wand. Light exploded through the room. The shadows splintered; the dark fae that had been running at us staggered backward. Only for a moment, but that was all I'd known I could hope for.

I grabbed Darton's elbow as the wand crumbled apart in my fingers. I'd used every shred of energy stored in it with that one spell, but it'd been worth it. "Come on!" I said, and yanked the door open. We hurtled out into the concrete yard.

The sky that had been clear and bright when I'd returned from my trip with Jagger now churned with dark gray clouds. They blotted out all but the faintest hint of sunlight. Dark creatures, filmy beings shaped like panthers and wolves, stalked along the edges of the yard, not strong enough to break through my protections.

Not *yet*. The Darkest One was coming, and her power was already sweeping over this country. My fingers dug into Darton's arm. I spun and tugged him toward the van Jagger had left in our possession.

If you can't fight 'em, flee from 'em.

A chant was ringing out from inside the house. I wrenched at some of my own bodily energy—goodbye, another three months of my life—and cast it out with a hasty spell. "*Shield us, save us, press back the darkness!*"

A quiver of energy shot up around us. It formed a gleaming ball of light, as if we were rodents in a giant, glowing hamster ball. And not a second too soon. A bolt of sizzling shadow smacked into its surface and burst apart. Icy fragments seared over my skin, but they didn't do half as much harm as if the bolt had hit me dead on.

Darton swung out his sword, shattering another bolt of magic streaming toward our shell. Then he turned and ran with me the last steps to the van. I hauled open the back doors, and we charged through to the front seats. I dropped into the driver's seat. A jolt of panic hit me.

"The keys. I didn't grab them from the basket." I'd been in too much of a hurry to get us out.

"You're a wizard, Em," Darton said. "You're *Merlin*. Can't you convince the engine to start some other way?"

Right. I didn't have a whole lot of practice with mechanical magic, but the principles were the same. And I couldn't have asked for more motivation.

The van rocked as some dark force struck it. The dark fae were almost on us. I hit the switch to turn on the flood lamps, hoping their sun-filled light would buy us an extra second or two, and shoved my hand into the cup holder between Darton and I. The twigs I'd stashed there during my drive with Jagger met my grasping fingers. I snatched a handful and pointed them toward the ignition.

"*Spark and sing*," I ordered the transmission. The engine roared on. Okay, that was a little more energy than I'd intended, but I'd take it. I grabbed the steering wheel and slammed my foot on the gas.

The van peeled down the driveway with a screech that suggested we'd left a lot of tire on the concrete. We careened through the ring of dark creatures that had been stalking around the edges of the yard. All those nearby leapt at us in a rush. Their shadowy forms burst apart as the van's sun-powered lights hit them, but the wave of them was so forceful it rocked the vehicle anyway.

I jerked the wheel to follow the curve of the driveway toward the main road. A clot of darkness shot toward us in the rearview mirror. I braced myself half a second before the spell hit the van with a wallop.

Bulbs popped with a tinkle of cracking glass. The glow around the van dimmed. I had just enough time to mutter a curse before a pair of shadow creatures like giant eagles dove at us from above.

They slammed into the windshield at the same moment. The van's lights were still bright enough to shatter them, but not before the thrust of their energy had split a crack down the middle of the glass. Heart thudding, I swerved onto the highway, so fast we nearly spun.

My lips started to move of their own accord. A few words had spilled out before I caught myself—caught the spell they meant to cast. A choking enchantment to smack Darton in the throat. My stomach knotted. The itch dug into my hands even as I clenched the steering wheel with all my strength. My arm twitched. Another blast of dark magic hit the back window, blackening it.

I didn't know if we could make it. Maybe there wasn't anything I could do but grab Darton and think of some other place to apparate us to where the fae couldn't quickly follow. But the second I let myself reach toward him, I had the feeling I'd be driving magic into his heart, stealing the breath from his lungs—fulfilling that awful oath. They were right on our heels, and the urge didn't believe I could stop them from completing their mission.

My elbow jerked to the side. I gritted my teeth, biting down on my lip hard enough to draw blood. That sting wasn't enough. With every ounce of self control I had in me, I released my left hand from the wheel just long enough to press my thumb into the knife wound I hadn't bothered to seal.

I winced, but the jolt of pain that radiated up my arm was worth it. The oath's urge dulled enough that I could breathe. Darton looked over at me, his eyes widening.

"Em," he said. Then, without waiting for any response, he reached over and rested his hand on my leg.

A shaky laugh spilled out of me. He must have remembered the other way I'd tamed the oath's urge. His thumb traced a gentle line across the top of my thigh, and the heat of it flared up my leg to the core of me, despite everything going on around us. Maybe even because of it. Adrenalin could make quite the enhancer to physical attraction.

A slash of dark magic cut across the road in front of us—literally. The pavement snapped and gaped in a half-a-foot chasm. I jammed my foot harder against the gas, thinking maybe we could hop it.

Before I got the chance to find out, another dark bolt must have hit us from behind. The van jostled and listed to the side. One of the wheels gave a dull *thump thump thump* against the ground that told me the tire had blown out. We were coasting to a stop.

I pumped the gas pedal, hoping I could squeeze a little more speed out of our momentum. No such luck. I slammed my hand into the cup holder to grasp the last of my twigs.

A wave of shadow swept toward us and crashed into the side of the van. The vehicle swayed and skidded. With a screech, it tipped over into the ditch.

I clutched the wheel, but I still fell half out of my seat on the impact. The top of my head smacked the ceiling. I dropped down onto Darton, who'd had the smarts to put on his seatbelt during our mad rush away from the house. The passenger window shattered. Darton grunted as my hip hit him in the gut.

"Sorry," I mumbled. "Sorry." We had to get out of here. The dark fae and their creatures would be swarming us, getting closer every moment we lay here. I squirmed away from Darton as he fumbled to detach his seatbelt. My hand throbbed. My head ached.

There wasn't any other answer now. I had to use the magic, had to whisk us away from here, as far as I could. What were another few years of my life gone anyway? It wasn't as if I was going to live more than a few minutes if we stayed here.

Where to go? Not back to my parents. Campus was too close. Maybe the desert, near Jagger's former house. Could I summon enough connection to that place to port us out there? I grasped Darton's arm and closed my eyes, dragging up every impression I'd had of dry earth and blazing sun—

"That's far enough, you monsters!" someone hollered outside the van. My head jerked up.

"What?" Darton said, looking as startled as I felt. A crackling, hissing sound that was almost familiar split the air.

No, it was completely familiar. I'd heard it when Eric and Mauve had taken on the dark vermin that had come for us at their house. It was the flare of flamethrowers spewing their fire. And another sound, too, that I definitely *didn't* recognize, but something about the warbling sizzle of it made my spirits lift.

I grasped the back of the driver's seat and hauled myself up to the door that was now above us. With a heave, I flung that door open. Darton gave me a leg up so I could poke my head out of the van.

Two rows of vehicles, all of them fitted with outer lamps like the van, had formed a blockade from one of the road's gravel shoulders to the other. Their passengers had streamed out of them to surround the van. Several of the men and women wore harnesses with flamethrowers attached. Others held devices I hadn't seen before, with a large spherical chamber at the back and a narrow rod at the front.

A bear-like dark creature charged at a young woman wielding one of the new weapons, and she pulled the trigger. A streak of electricity discharged from the rod. It zapped the bear right in the chest, and the creature exploded into fragments of shadow. Sodding hell, what was that thing?

Jagger stood at the front of the crowd, holding one of those electro-guns. He waved it at the surge of darkness that was swelling down the road toward us. The figures of at least two dozen dark fae glided toward us with strides hastened by their magic, flanked by a mass of dark vermin so dense I could barely tell where one creature ended and another began.

"Just try me!" Jagger shouted. It was his voice I'd heard earlier. But I'd never heard it like that before, so harsh and raw. He was angry—and terrified. Not that I could blame him.

I *could* get my act together and pitch in rather than sitting here like some damsel waiting to be rescued.

I hauled myself the rest of the way out of the van. "Pass me the sword," I called back to Darton. He held Excalibur up to me, hilt first. I hopped down with it to give him room to clamber out after me. My head swiveled, taking in the lay of the land.

The dark creatures had already nearly surrounded us. Jagger and the others—more of his fae hunter colleagues, I assumed—were torching or electrifying any that came within a few feet of their protective circle. Their chill carried on the breeze with a smell like slush mixed with rotted leaves.

My gaze snagged on a sapling at the edge of the forest on the other side of the ditch. Darton jumped down beside me, and I shoved his sword back into his hands. One of the fae hunters barbequed a snake-like creature that had just slithered past the sapling. I dashed over to her.

"Cover me?" I said, waiting only an instant for her nod. "*Darkness begone*," I yelled at the closest creatures and clamped my jaw against the jerk of my soul. At least I was only giving up a few weeks rather than the years I'd been looking at a couple minutes ago.

I leapt forward and snatched at the sapling's branches. With a murmured apology, I snapped two, and then another two, and another, dodging backward just as a hissing ball of dark magic whipped toward me. It vanished in the stream of the fae hunter's flamethrower.

Clutching my plunder between my hands, I hustled back to Darton. He'd joined the fae hunters facing the thickest onslaught, Excalibur gleaming in his hands.

"My liege!" I said. "A little assistance?"

He sliced through a snarling shadow fox and jogged backward to me. "The great wizard needs *my* help?" His grin was far too tight.

"Shut up, Art," I said. "Magic plus sword was a fruitful equation the last few times we tried it. I'm all for sticking with that strategy."

He glanced back toward the fray. The fae hunters were keeping the dark fae's magic and minions at bay, but the fae themselves looked unharmed, only frustrated. I felt the prickle of all those narrowed gazes seeking out me and my king.

"Can you kill them all?" Darton said, sounding uncertain. Which, fair enough, I'd had plenty of trouble simply killing *one* full fae not that long ago.

"Probably not," I said. "But in light of that fact, I figure we'll set our sights a little lower. Knock them unconscious and bind them up like I did on that hill near the overpass. That'll at least buy us some time."

What we were going to do with that time, I hadn't figured out yet, but that could come later.

I shoved all the branches I'd gathered under my left arm. My palm was bleeding all over them, but that was okay. A little extra life energy leaking into the magic would only give it more oomph.

The green energy pulsing within the just broken branches thrummed against my side. I breathed in deep and grasped Darton's shoulder by the crook of his neck, where my fingers could meet his bare skin. Waking up more memories hardly seemed like a reason for concern given everything else we were already facing, and I wanted as direct a connection as possible.

Darton readied himself without my needing to say anything. He raised his sword, his arms tensed, the muscles in his shoulder bunching under my grip.

"Three, two, one," I murmured. "Now! *Darkness begone, darkness fall! Light knock the sense from their darkened minds! Bind them to the ground they fall to.*"

As I shouted the words in the old tongue, Darton swung the

enchanted sword. The power I was drawing from the fresh branches washed through me, into him, and blazed from Excalibur's blade. It seared across the landscape in every direction, whiting out my vision. Several of the fae hunters yelped or gasped.

I lowered my hand from Darton's shoulder, blinking the haze from my eyes. The remains of the branches fell in a shower of dust by my feet.

The road ahead of us, the forest on one side, and the field on the other were all washed clean of shadows—other than those cast naturally. And those still wisping around the dark fae that had collapsed in the wake of my spell. Their bodies dotted the pavement, the shoulder, and the grassy dip of the ditch. A line of glowing light arced over each of their unconscious bodies.

I didn't know how long my spell would hold them in place once they woke up and could put their own magic to work, but like I'd told Darton, it gave us time.

Jagger let out a rough chuckle. He strode through the group of his colleagues to greet us. "Looks like we showed up just in time."

I glanced around at the cluster of fae hunters. "Why *were* you on the way to our house?" They looked like they'd come prepared for full-out war.

Jagger shrugged. "After having that talk with the kid from overseas the other night, I thought we should provide whatever protection we could. Add a human factor to your security systems."

"Ah." I rubbed my forehead. The feel of the gritty paste of ash and aconite still smeared there made my nerves cringe. "Well, I think the house is a loss now. We're missing a pretty big chunk of our ceiling."

"Maybe not quite in time, then." Jagger grimaced. "I wish we'd made it here a little sooner."

"Better than not at all," I said. "We were practically goners." I nodded to the weapon he was holding. "Have you come up with some new gadgetry? It looked like those electric guns worked well."

"Oh, these?" He patted the rod by his side. "This idea I got thanks to your story about channeling lightning. You mentioned the shock had to be natural for it to affect the dark varmints. One of our more inventive members came up with a design that uses a slightly more sophisticated version of your fur and amber approach to create the current."

Huh. My attempts to combine physics with my magic had gotten us pretty far already. Maybe there were more possibilities to delve into there.

Jagger took another step closer, squinting at me. "What have you got on your face, Emma? Did the fae do that?"

I moved to swipe at the caked powder with my sleeve, which turned out to be a fruitless attempt. One sleeve was mottled with blood from my palm and the dust of the branches I'd sapped the life energy from. The other was flecked with slivers of glass from my scramble out of the van. I lowered both arms.

"I was doing a spell that needed me to suppress my innate energy," I said. "To give the impression I have a totally different nature."

And it had worked. Both times, the dragon had let me approach it, even though it had fled during my first attempt. I'd managed to convince it that I was a dark fae, an ally instead of an enemy, simply by covering myself with the right materials...

"Where do we go now?" Darton asked. He was eyeing the slumped fae warily. "Obviously we can't stay in the house anymore."

"No," I said. "But I think I have an idea about that, that should keep us under the radar for at least a little while. Long enough for us to come up with a longer-term plan. I think I'd better just grab a few things from the house before we abandon it completely."

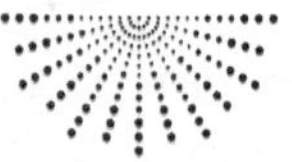

"*Light and warm us, softly,*" I said, pinching my fingers against a twig. It burst into a glowing ball that floated toward the ceiling of the pitch-black room we'd come into. A thin heat took the edge off the stony chill.

The light revealed the smooth granite floor, the granite walls with their slabs of doors shutting away the mausoleum's silent inhabitants. The hairs on my arms were already standing on end, but my nerves jittered with a deeper shudder. The fae energy inside me did not like this place at all. But that was exactly why we needed to be here.

Beside me, Darton made a face. "It's definitely got a lot of atmosphere... Are you sure this is the best place for us to spend the night?"

He kept his hand tight around Excalibur's hilt, but I set down my duffel of supplies. I'd left some of what I'd scavenged from our ruined house with the fae hunters, but I didn't trust that we'd be safe here without some help.

"Death is the dark fae's arena," I said. "Stillness and silence and gradual decay. This whole cemetery stinks of it. With a little

614

enhancement, it should mask our life energy from any dark fae looking to finish their attack. The same way my powder masked my light fae essence from your dragon."

"It's not *my* dragon," Darton muttered. He sat down in the middle of the room, as far from any of the individual tombs as he could get. His shoulders had tensed. He rubbed his hand against his chest as if a muscle there pained him.

My own muscles were still jumping, but not entirely because of the way my senses cringed away from all this evidence of death. The oath's itch had been creeping back through our entire journey here. Now it wriggled through my arms and nibbled at my fingers. I flexed them a few times, trying to work the impulse out of them. Then I grabbed my supplies to keep them busy in a preferable way.

The bitter smoky smell wafted from the bag of dead willow ash and aconite when I opened it. I dipped in my hand and sprinkled the powder along the edges of the room. If having this stuff smeared on my skin could convince a dragon filled with masses of dark fae energy that I was one of its kind up close, then surely it could confuse any fae looking for us from afar, especially with the entire cemetery's energies clouding us too.

Any regular dark fae. The Darkest One knew my soul and my king's too well. Once she arrived in this country, there'd be no hiding from her.

Darton set his sword down beside him. He rubbed that spot on his chest again.

"Are you all right?" I asked him.

"I've just been feeling a little... off, since the dark fae attacked us," he said. "I don't know how to describe it exactly. It feels as if there's a knot in my chest, that's... twisting around? Every now and then. The feeling is stronger when I'm holding Excalibur. The fae didn't cast some other spell on me, did they? It's not really *painful* or anything—just strange."

He was keeping his voice calm, but his jaw clenched after he'd finished speaking. It might not be painful, but it was bothering him. Why wouldn't it? After what we'd been through, any strange sensation could be the beginning of a new catastrophe.

I completed my circuit of the room and set down the bag of powder. "Let me have a look." I sat down across from him and touched his chest where he had.

His body was as warm as ever against my palm. The glowing life energy pulsed through it—and a hint of something shadowy coiled around it at the edges of my awareness. A familiar motion.

"It's the dragon," I said. "Having all that dark magic thrown around nearby must have stirred it up."

"So your spell before to weaken it didn't work after all?" Darton said. He reached for his sword, as if he could fight the creature inside him with that.

"I'm sure it did," I said. "But that thing's been fed on generations of dark fae energy, and I can only sap away so much at a time. Weaker doesn't mean it's not still plenty strong. But we can keep working on that. I should do the ritual again. This is the perfect spot for it. I brought the supplies so we could. When I'm done, it'll probably have settled down again."

Darton paused and then inclined his head. "Fine." He glanced around the room, his eyebrows arching slightly. "At least this place should put a damper on any, ah, embarrassing and unnecessary reactions. Are you sure you've recovered enough from the last time? I mean, with the blood loss?"

My own cheeks flushed a little at the memory of how his body had responded to the ritual a few hours ago. "We had some rest in the car on the way here," I said. "I finally got my juice and cookies and a whole lot more of a meal on top of it. I'll be fine. You just get yourself ready."

He pulled his shirt over his head and folded it into a makeshift pillow. I reached for the powder again. I'd washed up when we'd made a quick pit stop at a gas station, but a fresh coating would do the job best anyway. I rubbed it between my hands, over my forearms, and all across my face. Around my neck, down my chest. A careful swirl of it around my mouth.

Darton had lain back when I turned toward him. My gaze shot to a purple-black blotch that marred his skin across the left side of his rib cage. Right where my hip had collided with him when the van had tipped. I winced.

"I'm sorry. I didn't realize I battered you that badly."

"Hmm?" Darton raised his head a few inches. He brushed his fingers over the bruise. "It's okay. I've had a hell of a lot worse after a football game."

"Maybe we should start having you wear that padding everywhere we go," I said.

He managed a chuckle and a smile, even though I could see the tension in his eyes. He rested his head back on his folded shirt. "A bruise shouldn't interfere with what you need to do, should it?"

I shook my head. "No problem. Just tell me if anything starts to hurt. More than it already does, I mean."

I set the bowl by my side and picked up the knife. I wasn't really sure I was in the best state for spilling out more blood. I hadn't exactly been keeping track of how much I'd lost during the fight with the dark fae. But there was nothing more important than weakening the dragon.

Nothing I had any hope might save us, anyway.

My palm stung as I sliced the cut open again. The pain was duller than it'd been before—I wasn't sure if that was a good thing or a bad thing. At least it still prickled over the urging of the oath.

I'm trying to fulfill the most important part of that promise, I thought at it. *Making sure nothing in my king poses any threat to anyone.*

The oath didn't seem to care about my explanations. I aimed a silent expletive in Cormag's direction and settled myself into the meditative state the ritual required. Slow, even breaths. Slow, even pulse. Drip, drip, drip of my blood into the bowl.

I bent over Darton as I had earlier that day. Inhale, dragging in those wisps of shadow clinging to his soul. Exhale, feel them flow through my veins to the bowl. Over and over, sinking deeper into the shimmer of his soul with each repetition. Sharper flickers whipped past my internal sight. The dragon's tail, lashing just ahead of me. A flap of constrained wings. The dark energy quivered through the glow with a restlessness I could taste.

No doubt the creature sensed that its master was approaching. Its time of freedom was almost at hand. And even bottled up in that concentrated form, the power the beast contained made me wince. I'd drained a little of that energy last time, definitely, but nowhere near enough. How many more blood-lettings would it take?

How many did we have time for? How many could my body handle?

I wet my lips and breathed in again, careful of my lips over the bruise on Darton's abdomen. Whatever it took, I could handle. If I drained myself dry while draining that beast, oh well. My life wouldn't matter much if I didn't.

The tender spot on the top of my head where I'd hit the van roof started to throb. My thoughts swam through my head. In and out. In and out. I could stay focused on that, even if my head was starting to feel as if it was going to float right off my body. A little more might make all the difference. I wasn't stopping until I had to.

Shadows wavered behind my eyes. It took me a moment to realize they reflected the clouding of my own mind, not the dragon's movements. My body had dipped farther, my lips brushing Darton's sternum. For a second, I felt as if I would tip right over into him, down into his soul, into that cavern of light where the dragon lurked.

I jerked myself upright. The granite walls around me spun. I closed my eyes and opened them again, willing the world to settle.

A thin ache crept up my arm from my still bleeding palm. The bowl was full of my blood.

"Em?" Darton said, sounding concerned.

"I'm all right," I said. I might have been more convincing to myself if my tongue hadn't felt detached from the rest of me. I shut my mouth and swallowed hard. *"Seal and stop,"* I mumbled to my palm. *More* bleeding definitely wasn't going to help.

Another wave of dizziness passed over me. I swayed and braced my hands against the floor. Breathe in, breathe out, like before. But this time for myself.

Darton pushed himself upright to grab the bag of supplies. He opened a bottle of apple juice and pushed it into my good hand. "Thanks," I managed. I tipped it to my lips and let the tart liquid flood my mouth. One swallow, another. Refill my body. Bring it back down to earth.

I fumbled for the cloth and water I'd set aside and wiped the powder from my skin. The light fae energy inside me pressed back toward the surface with a feeling like a sigh of relief. It still twisted away from the feel of death around us, but that was a more distant discomfort.

Darton passed me a granola bar next. I wolfed it down despite the clenching of my stomach. I needed that energy too. Because I'd be doing this all over again in the morning if I had any say in it.

My body still felt slightly insubstantial, but I managed to stand up without shaking like a leaf. With careful hands, I got out the funnel and glass jar I'd brought. The blood I'd collected was run through with dark fae energy. That energy could serve us now. Using it felt like thumbing my nose at the Darkest One and all her efforts.

I poured half of the bowl's contents into the jar and quickly sealed it. Then I walked the circuit of the room again, dribbling the rest of the blood alongside the line of ash powder. Even more darkness to cloak us in our hiding spot. The Darkest One could be here as soon as tomorrow night. We were going to need all the rest we could steal.

Darton watched me circle the room. "You took a lot," he said.

"We don't have a lot of time for spacing out attempts," I said. "I've got to drain as much of the dragon's energy as I can when I can. Look, I'm perfectly fine." Other than the fact that my head was still throbbing and also filled with that floaty feeling. But hey, the oath's urge had been completely drowned out by those combined sensations. I could look on the bright side. "How about you? That knot in your chest—is it still bothering you?"

He touched the spot over his sternum. "There's a bit of pressure there still," he said. "But that twisting feeling, like it's *moving*, is gone. That's a good thing, right?"

"I tired your dragon out," I said with half a smile.

Darton opened his mouth, looking like he was going to protest my use of *your* again, but then his expression settled into a resigned smile of his own. I set down the bowl, and he held out his arm to me. "Come here?"

I wasn't sure what he wanted, but I'd never been good at saying no to my king anyway. Besides, this standing up thing was definitely getting old. I sat, and he eased me down beside him so we were lying together on the hard floor. He tucked my head under his chin. I couldn't resist snuggling closer to him, letting him wrap me in his warmth. The musky, earthy smell of his bare skin filled my nose.

Darton made a pleased hum into my hair. He tugged me even closer to him with his arm around my back. Then his body tensed. "If this is too much... I just—" He swallowed audibly. "I'm not going to try anything. I just want to feel you."

He didn't have to explain any more than that. The same need was running through me. As if my old soul inside this young body wanted to reach right through both our skins to his. It couldn't, not exactly, but I could get us a little bit closer.

Without letting myself second-guess my decision, I squirmed away from him just enough to peel off my sweater. Darton let out a hitch of breath as I lay back down. Our bodies aligned, bare skin to bare skin, nothing covering me from the waist up except my bra. I draped the sweater over us to hold in the warmth. But there was nothing chilly about the heat that seemed to burn everywhere my skin touched his. A flame of desire shot down through my belly.

I shut my eyes against it. I didn't have to give in this time. I could simply enjoy the closeness without needing it to be something more. No, not more, just *else*. There wasn't any such thing as more when my king was already giving me everything he could offer.

Darton's hand brushed over my hair. His pulse, thudding against my ear, evened out. I rested my fingers on the soft curls of golden hair that ran down the middle of his chest and let my mind drift on the memories floating up.

The memories our close contact was waking in Darton would be even more potent, coming to him for the first time. His breath tickled my ear. "Do you know," he said, his voice gone distant but still affectionate, "the first time I met you—the first you—I thought you were so earnest and calm. All politeness and bows and waiting to see what I'd ask of you."

"You *thought*," I said. "Are you suggesting that impression was wrong?"

"Well, it obviously took you a while to get comfortable being yourself and let loose that sarcastic tongue of yours. And I definitely would never have imagined just how grouchy you could get."

I made a disgruntled sound. "Only after you put me through a long muddy ride in the rain or something equally horrific."

"Yes," Darton said lightly, "I probably deserved every spark of that temper." He tipped his head, lapsing into silence as another memory must have swept over him. When he spoke again, it was with a chuckle. "And you did have an odd sense of humor at times. Why did you enchant Lord Barimeld's clothes to smell like pickles?"

A snort escaped me. I'd almost forgotten that little act of

revenge. I'd never told Arthur exactly why back then, because he hadn't been there for the conversation I'd overheard.

The sun danced over the forest floor between the shadows of the leaves. I settled myself in a patch of it, examining the patch of coltsfoot I'd found. The tiny yellow petals tickled my fingers as I snapped one of the flowers off.

The tramp of horse hooves carried through the woods. I went still, murmuring a quick concealing spell.

Two horses walked into view, one carrying a man I recognized as one of the lords currently visiting the castle, the other his servant. The lord was speaking in low, harsh tones.

"It really is ridiculous, all that running about from town to town, getting involved in every tiny peasant concern. You'd think he's a laborer, not a prince."

I bristled. The servant's head bobbed in automatic agreement, his gaze vague as if he was lost in his own thoughts and hardly listening. "Yes, m'lord."

"Someone should set him back a few paces. Remind him that he's as human as the rest of us. Trip him up in front of the other lords so they stop looking at him like he's some kind of hero, and not just a spoiled brat whose head's got too big."

"Yes, m'lord."

The lord tsked his tongue. "You're helping with the serving tonight, aren't you? I've still got some of that mushroom powder left. Lace a little in his cup, and let's see how he talks when we've loosened his tongue."

"Yes, m'lord... M'lord?"

"Yes, that's the perfect plan. He won't know what hit him. Now the way you'll need to play it..."

His voice trailed off as the horses wove on through the forest. I glared at his retreating back, my hands balling into fists.

The lord had never gotten his chance to drug my prince, of course. I'd dashed straight back to the castle, snuck into his rooms, and found the packet of dried hallucinogenic mushroom in one of his trunks. I'd burned it to a crisp. And then I'd enchanted his entire wardrobe with a thick briny smell as if it'd all been pickled. With all the angry energy I'd put into that spell, I suspected the stink had stuck on for at least a month.

I started to formulate a vague excuse and caught myself. No. No more lying to spare my king the discomfort that would come with the truth. This might be a little thing, but I owed him my honesty after all the bigger truths I'd kept from him so long.

He was stronger than I was, when you came down to it. Maybe all this time it'd been my own discomfort I was trying to prevent. Wanting to feel I'd kept just one small weight off his back, with all the other responsibilities he'd had bearing down on him.

"Lord Barimeld was an ass," I said. "I overheard him scheming about how to undercut you. So I made sure he didn't and figured out a suitable punishment. And kept a close eye on him whenever he was at the castle again. It obviously worked, though, because he played nice after that incident."

"Ah," Darton said. "I remember wondering about his sudden change in attitude. He must have thought I'd found out about his scheming and sent someone to undercut him myself."

"Almost the same thing," I said. "We were a united front."

"We were." He ducked his head closer, his lips grazing the top of my forehead. His voice dipped too. "You know, over the years a lot of people gave me a piece of their mind about how closely I worked with you. But I've never regretting trusting you, not for one moment, Merlin."

I smiled, my heart swelling with a glow to match the magic ball I'd conjured. Right then, skin to skin, warmth to warmth, I couldn't imagine a greater bliss than lying there in my king's arms. He needed me. I was here for him, like I always was. Like I always would be.

My eyes drifted closed. "Is it safe enough here for us to sleep?" Darton murmured.

I nodded against his shoulder. "I laid down a ring of salt just in case. If any dark fae *do* come out this way, we'll know. But all they should be able to see now is the darkness around us."

"That doesn't sound like it should be comforting, but somehow it is."

He managed to scoot even closer to me, his breath rising and falling in a deeper rhythm. But my eyes had blinked open. I stared past him at the wall, thinking of the lines of dark energy I'd drawn around us. Like a cage. Like a trap. A memory flashed through my mind of the fae hunters' electro-guns and their crackling light. My heart leapt.

"I think I know how we can stop the Darkest One."

CHAPTER SEVENTEEN

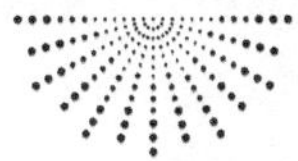

Keevan looked over his shoulder three times as he eased the storage room door open.

"I don't think you need to be quite that nervous," I said under my breath. "You have a key. No one's going to think we're breaking in."

"A key I stole from my sister's apartment," Keevan whispered, and groaned. "Why do I always let you talk me into the craziest things?"

"Hey, don't put the blame for this on me," I said. "From the way I remember it, *you* volunteered."

"Okay, fair. But if I've developed an addiction to adventure, *that* is definitely your fault."

"Less talking, more checking out the inventory," Howard said. The third member of our party, a thirty-something guy with long black hair in a ponytail nearly as long as mine, was the fae hunters' local technology expert—the one who'd invented their electro-guns. And possibly the key to my plan for dealing with the Darkest One.

We slipped into the room and shut the door behind us. The still air had a slightly floral smell, as if someone wearing a strong perfume had recently walked between the stacks of equipment. Keevan flicked on the light.

The stainless steel shelving units that filled the room were piled with all sorts of lab supplies for the physics department's use. I poked at one box and peeked inside another, but I didn't know exactly what we were looking for. I'd come up with the concept, but the logistics of the mechanical arts were far from my specialty.

"Let me know if you see any spools of wire," Howard said. "I'll have to check to make sure the conductivity is appropriate."

"Roger that," Keevan said, giving him a salute.

"I don't want you to get into any trouble," I said to Darton's best friend. "If there was an easier way..."

He waved me off. "It's for Darton. Which means it's not a problem. The college has a crapload of stuff, obviously. And you've saved the place at least once, so you probably deserve some payback."

While that might be true, it was also true that the campus wouldn't have been in danger in the first place if Darton and I hadn't been here. But Keevan clearly had enough on his mind with this criminal turn. He paced the aisles with a slight jitter in his step.

Howard had drifted toward the back of the room. He picked up a metal tube with some sort of circuitry protruding from one end, frowned, put it down, and checked another. "None of these is an ideal voltage."

"Is there one close enough to what you think we'd need?" I asked. No, this was our one chance to overcome the Darkest One. We couldn't skimp. "Grab whatever you can make do with, but if there's something better you can't find here, make a list. I've got funds. We'll track down whatever you need."

At least, I hoped we would. We didn't have much time for searching out lab equipment suppliers and the like. It wasn't as if we could just waltz into a Wal-Mart to grab what we needed.

"Emma and her bottomless bank account," Keevan said. His tone was teasing, but my gut twisted.

I *had* saved an awful lot of money over the decades, across my most recent lives. Computerized banking had made keeping track of my funds between each death so much easier. I hadn't had much to spend it on, most of the time, so it'd just sat around accumulating interest. But the last couple months had put quite a dent in my savings, between replacing cars and custom building entire houses at a rush rate and last-minute international flights. If I kept going at this rate, I'd be penniless by next year.

But I had enough to get us through this, and that was all that mattered. It wasn't as if we were going to get another do-over. If I didn't spend that money keeping Darton and me alive now, then no one was ever going to spend it.

"How much electricity do you think we'll be able to keep flowing in a continuous circuit?" I asked Howard. "You said we should be able to flood the entire surface of the trap with it, and reduce the amount of energy lost to almost nothing. But there must be limits to what the materials can handle, right?"

"Oh, I can build something sturdy enough that the strongest dark creature out there couldn't stand the touch of," Howard said. He picked up a jointed metal rod, gave it an approving nod, and stuffed it into the duffel I'd lent him. "The trickiest part is going to be getting a natural source for the volume of current you want in the first place. The guns I rigged using static are only capable of a small fraction of that power. But I've got some ideas to tackle that difficulty."

"Ideas you can get working in less than twelve hours?" I said. I had no idea how long it would take the Darkest One to reach us even once she hit the east coast, but we couldn't count on her taking her time.

"I'll work as fast as I can work," Howard said. "Ah, these will be useful." He scooped up an entire box of something that clinked as he dropped it into his bag.

"Hey!" Keevan said from the other side of the room, where his restless feet had taken him. "I think these are the coils of wire you were asking about."

Howard hustled over, and I ambled along behind, wishing I had the knowledge base to be of more help. My studies had followed my light fae inclinations toward the sciences of life: biology and chemistry. Machines tended to be more the domain of the dark, with their orderly construction. But there were areas where mechanics and the chaos of light could interact. It just wasn't going to be as simple as calling down a lightning bolt this time.

Not that the lightning bolt had been simple. I rubbed my arms in memory of all that wild power coursing through me.

Howard started examining the coils of wire one by one, dismissing most of them. Keevan wandered over to join me. "So Darton didn't want to join our little field trip?" he said.

"Oh, he would have if I'd agreed to let him," I said. "But he's a heck of a lot safer back in the mausoleum."

Keevan raised his eyebrows at me. "That doesn't sound like the Emma I know. You've always been pretty strict about keeping him right by your side."

That was before the itch of that deadly oath had started pricking at me. And before entire armies of full dark fae had gone on the attack. "There are too many fae looking for him now," I said. "The second he steps outside the barriers I set down, they might sense him. When we were just fighting glooms, that was one thing, but I'm no match for the average dark fae on my own."

"Right," Keevan said. He'd help me destroy the first—and only—full dark fae I'd ever killed, so he should know. But he still sounded doubtful.

The twist in my gut tugged tighter. I *didn't* like leaving Darton behind, and I knew he didn't like it either. Before she'd even set foot on this country's shores, the Darkest One was managing to tear us apart.

"I don't see you bringing Izzy along to make her a criminal accomplice," I pointed out, keeping my voice light. Keevan and I didn't always see eye to eye, but I did have sympathy for his crush—and his reluctance to reveal it. After all, it'd taken me fifteen hundred years to come clean about mine.

"The more people with us, the harder it'll be to avoid getting noticed on the way out," Keevan said. "I just didn't tell her. You think she'd listen to me if she decided she needed to be a part of this? I don't have any great wizardly knowledge to make my arguments convincing."

"*You've* never been very good at listening when other people tell you there's danger up ahead either."

"Fair." He rubbed his face. "That doesn't mean I'm not going to try to protect other people from danger when I can. Unlike you, we're not going to get to start over if this all goes wrong."

At that comment, my entire stomach balled into a knot. "Neither are we, this time," I said.

Keevan's head jerked around. "What? What happened to your special reincarnation spell?"

I hadn't realized he didn't know. We'd told him and the others about the Darkest One getting free. I'd assumed the other consequences were obvious.

"It was all part of the same magic that was keeping the Darkest One shut away," I said. "A big tangled mess of an enchantment. When she broke free, she broke the spell—all of it. We're just ordinary one-lived mortals now... who happen to have very old souls."

"Oh." Keevan looked vaguely ill. "I thought— You've got no more safety net, then."

"That's one way of putting it." Just thinking about it made me feel sick too. I turned back toward the shelves. "All the more reason we need to make sure this plan goes off without a hitch."

Howard strode over, hefting the now-bulging duffel bag. "I've gone through the whole place. I think I've collected everything here that we can use. I have some bits and pieces back home that we can add to the mix... We may just have enough."

That wasn't quite the level of confidence I'd have liked to hear. "Remember," I said. "Anything else you need, let me know what it is, we'll track it down as fast as we can." I had at least the rest of today. The Darkest One couldn't have caught a boat faster than that.

We ducked back out into the basement hallway. Keevan locked the door and shot a guilty look at the key before tucking it into his pocket. "Thanks," I told him. "If you want to dash right back to your sister's place to return that—"

He shook his head. "I'm coming along with you two. Darton must be going stir crazy, cooped up in a cemetery of all places. I don't have classes until the afternoon. I can keep him company while you all work on that crazy contraption."

A thread of worry ran through his usual playful tone. "Of course," I said. "I'm sure he'll appreciate that."

Neither of us wanted to say what we both knew: This might be Keevan's last chance to spend any time at all with his best friend. If my "crazy contraption" didn't work...

No, I wasn't going to think that.

We hurried through the hall and up the stairs to the doors leading to the parking lot. The fae hunter van we'd taken looked a lot like the one I'd borrowed from Jagger—the one that the dark fae had pretty much destroyed yesterday—only even bigger. Howard yanked open the back doors and scrambled into the workshop area he had set up behind the seats.

"You want this done fast," he said. "So I'll get right to work."

"Perfect," I said, with only a small twinge of relief. We still had so much to do. And I didn't even know yet if my imagined invention would work once we'd put the thing together.

I got into the driver's seat and turned on the ignition. As I drove toward the parking lot's exit, my gaze roamed over the buildings and green around us. This campus was where I'd spent most of my waking hours in the last few months. Where Darton had gone to school like a normal college guy for the last two and a half years.

All the uncomfortable feelings inside me condensed into one huge lump just below my heart. I'd told him—no, I'd *promised* him —that I'd give him as much of a normal life as I could. I'd wanted him to have at least a little more time to be Darton instead of a fae-hunted king. I'd barely given him a week before that plan had fallen apart.

But if my contraption did work, if I could contain the Darkest One like I had before, after that—

The handheld radio mounted on the dash crackled. Jagger's voice broke through the static. "Emma and crew, are you there?"

Keevan tugged the radio out of its holder. He glanced at me and I nodded, my hands tight on the steering wheel. "We're here," he said. "Heading to the cemetery now."

"Good," Jagger said. "Make it fast. The dark fae are on the move—and it looks like a bunch of them are heading this way."

CHAPTER EIGHTEEN

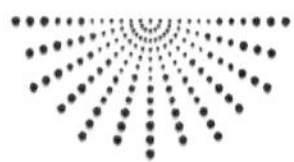

A TRUCK HONKED at me as I whipped the van into the lane ahead of it, but I didn't give a sow's ass. In normal circumstances, it was nearly an hour's drive from the campus to the cemetery where Darton was holed up. If I had my way, I'd cut that time in half.

"We're watching the energy readings on the ground here," Jagger was saying over the radio. "Our scanning system has picked up some major fluctuations moving toward the cemetery from a few different directions. They're still en route."

"Thanks for the update," I said, jerking the wheel to veer around a slower moving car. "If you can stay there, standing guard as well as you can, that would be great. And be ready to jump in the cars and take off. Now that they know we've holed up there, we can't stay. Darton is still in the mausoleum, right?"

"Hasn't left it for a second, though he looks like he'd like to take a chunk out of those fae with that sword of his."

I'd bet. My hands tightened around the steering wheel. If Darton hadn't stepped outside my ring of protections, I didn't think it was my king's soul that had led the dark fae to us. It was

632

too convenient that they'd honed in on the cemetery only after I'd left.

They must have been watching for traces of my hybrid light fae energy too. Closely enough that they'd caught on so soon after I'd left that they'd been able to figure out where I'd been leaving from.

I'd led our enemies straight to my king.

I pressed the gas pedal even harder. The van lurched forward with a fresh burst of speed. Something clanked as it fell over in the back, but Howard didn't complain. Keevan gripped the inner door handle.

"I'm thinking we'll protect Art a lot more effectively if we get there in one piece," he said, shooting a plaintive look my way.

"Just keep your seatbelt on," I told him. My fae senses were alert to every movement around the van. I sensed every opening a second before the cars even turned their signals on. I wasn't letting us get into an accident, but I wasn't going to let traffic laws slow us down either. I'd already stretched my awareness ahead of us to confirm there were no cops patrolling along this stretch of highway.

The new pouch of salt I'd stuffed in my jeans pocket hadn't stirred. No dark fae or vermin had crossed the warning boundary I'd laid around the cemetery. I still had time.

A hill dotted with dark pines came into view up ahead. The cemetery was right on the other side. I swerved around another truck, ignoring the rude gesture the driver made, and tore along the open stretch of road ahead of me. Keevan let out a shaky breath.

"I guess if I ever need a getaway driver, I know who to call."

As we came up on the cemetery entrance, I saw a couple other cars pulling into the drive—cars mounted with the fae hunters' standard flood lamps. Jagger had summoned all of his colleagues to hold this ground.

I jerked my chin toward Keevan, and he pressed the talk button on the handheld radio. "We're almost there," I said. "Two minutes tops. Get Darton ready to run for the van. I'll get him out of here, and we can figure out where we're going after that once we're no longer surrounded."

"Sounds like a reasonable plan to me," Jagger says. "I'll let the guys with him know to be ready."

I took the turn into the cemetery so fast the van skidded, tipping onto one set of wheels just for an instant. Keevan made a face like he'd swallowed a frog. We roared down the lane, turning left at the split.

The cemetery's road only got us within a hundred feet of the mausoleum on the top of its grassy slope. Several fae hunter vehicles were already parked at the foot of the slope. I slammed on the brakes as soon as we reached the closest available spot and leapt out, snatching my wand from the cup holder as I went.

Jagger waved to me from the truck he was standing by. I nodded and started jogging up the slope.

Darton and a couple of fae hunters, one holding a flamethrower and the other an electro-gun, appeared at the entrance to the mausoleum. Cattle sod. I should have told Jagger that they needed to stay in the inner room, with all its barriers, until I reached him. The blood and ash I'd laid down wouldn't stop the dark fae from reaching Darton, but it might have prevented them from figuring out exactly where in the cemetery he was.

Too late to worry about that now. Darton eased a step ahead of his companions, Excalibur gleaming in one hand, our bag of supplies slung over his other shoulder. I felt the moment he spotted me, his gaze snagging on me like a thorn on a sleeve. He blinked. An expression I couldn't read crossed his face, his eyes widening and his jaw twitching as if he was somehow surprised to see me, but at the same time a faint flush crossed his cheeks.

I didn't have time to puzzle out what could be wrong. The pouch of salt shuddered so hard it nearly jumped out of my pocket. A wave of cold air washed over me, stealing my breath with its sharpness.

"Watch out!" I shouted, throwing myself up the slope faster.

Not fast enough. Shadowy bodies shot through the air toward my king so fast they were little more than streaks through the air. I drew in my breath to shout out a spell, and one of the dark fae had already slammed a fist writhing with dark magic into the face of the hunter holding the electro-gun. The other hunter raised his flamethrower, but two fae grabbed his arms, ripping the weapon out of them and hurling him down the slope toward me.

I dodged his tumbling body with a silent apology. *Shining shield, fend off the shadows!* I hollered, snapping my wand through the air. At the same moment, two of the dark fae threw a clot of churning darkness toward me. Our spells shattered against each other like a firework of light and shadow.

"Where did they come from?" someone was saying down by the cars. "How did they—"

Darton swung his sword. He caught the closest fae in the gut. A bolt of soul-driven light seared through the blade, and his attacker fell with a spasm. Darton whipped the sword to the other side, catching another. His arms moved with the weapon like they were one being, exactly the way he was meant to fight.

But even my king's valiant soul and an enchanted sword weren't enough to fend off a concentrated assault of dark fae. I shouted out another spell, and one of the fae still standing leapt in front of Darton to smash it. Another wrenched a shroud of shadow over Darton's head from behind.

Darton slammed back with his sword, but the fae rammed a knee into his elbow, hard enough that I heard a bone snap from twenty feet away. His fingers flinched apart. The sword fell.

No. My king's name caught in my throat. I spat out another spell, putting everything I had into the casting. A blaze of light swept forward from my wand. My nerves prickled with the life energy I'd expelled into it.

The wash of light careened toward the dark fae. In the instant it crashed into them, I could see nothing but searing white. Then several shadowy bodies reeling, two toppling with their heads between their hands... but no sign of Darton.

Panic rushed through my body, drowning out the thumping of footsteps on the slope behind me. I scrambled forward. My wand had burnt out with that last effort. I dropped its crumbling length and grabbed twigs from my sleeves.

As I snapped out spells to keep the dark fae disoriented, the fae hunters caught up. Flames and electricity blazed. The dark fae staggered away from our onslaught. With a series of faint *pops* that I felt in my eardrums, they vanished into the air.

Leaving nothing at all behind.

I stopped at the spot where my king's sword and our bag of supplies had fallen. Excalibur lay in the grass, looking far too dull without his soul's light guiding it. The ground was trampled with the indents of frantic feet. But there was no trace of Darton or the fae that had grabbed him.

The dark fae must have magically apparated away with him before my spell had hit. There was no way of telling where they'd jumped to.

My shoulders sagged. "Emma?" Jagger said, coming up beside me. I dragged a breath into my suddenly raw throat. The last of my twigs tumbled from my shaking fingers.

"He's gone," I said. "They took him. He's *gone.*"

CHAPTER NINETEEN

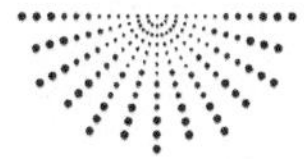

"We can tap into satellites all over the country," Yasmin was saying. "The level of energy dark fae give off when they're doing this amount of casting, we'll always pick it up. We'll narrow down their possible locations. I promise."

The fae hunter seemed to expect some sort of answer. I made myself nod. She was perched in the bed of a pickup truck, computer open on her lap, a swirling map that didn't mean anything to me filling its screen. I looked away from it across the cemetery. I couldn't concentrate on anything in front of me for more than a second.

Darton. Arthur. My king. The dark fae would be carting him off to the Darkest One right now. She might not have reached this country's shores yet, but light only knew how much of a head start they'd gotten on us. And we didn't even know where they were now, where they were going—anything that might have given us a direction.

I pushed away from the truck, paced to the other side of the road, spun myself around, and walked back. Keevan was standing near the van we'd arrived in, his arms folded over his chest, his eyes even darker than usual. Jagger watched me from where he was leaning against the hood of the truck. All the fae hunters were standing around, waiting to find out what we'd do next. Waiting on me. And I didn't have a clue.

I'd never lost my king to the fae before, not like this. And when the dark vermin had overwhelmed us in the past, that had always been the end. I'd never been able to do anything other than give up.

But I couldn't give up now. The fae would keep him alive. They *needed* him alive, for their lady's plan to work, whatever exactly she meant to do with that dragon inside him. I had to keep my head, stay grounded. Pull all these people around me together.

I dragged in a breath and propped my arms on the side of the truck. The swirls I'd seen on the laptop's screen before had condensed into several brighter dots speckling the western half of the country. Yasmin frowned, swiping her long bangs back from her narrow brown face.

"Those points of energy all formed at approximately the same time," she said. "It takes a lot of magic to teleport like you said those fae did, I guess?"

"Yeah," I said. "It's one of the most tiring spells there is."

"I don't understand why they'd be scattered all over the place."

I did. "The magic only works if you have an emotional tie to the place you're jumping to," I said. "Dark fae... they don't get emotionally attached very easily. Most of them probably couldn't magic themselves to anywhere except the place they consider their home ground. And the ones that attacked us had come from all over."

But all from this side of the country. It wasn't good, but it could have been a little worse. Okay, maybe I was grasping at straws.

"The one that took Darton apparated maybe half a minute before the other ones," I said. "And it would have taken more energy for the fae to bring someone with him. Can you figure out where Darton ended up with that information?"

Yasmin made a face. "Unfortunately the readings only give us a general idea, nothing fine-tuned. We only just figured out how to detect magical activity at all in the last ten years. It's a work in progress. I'm sorry."

"Not your fault," I said. No, it was mine. I hadn't made it back here fast enough. I hadn't protected my king well enough. I'd failed, and this time there was no starting fresh.

This time, losing him might mean losing not just his life, but millions of others. I'd failed my oath too, or nearly so. Its itch scraped at the inside of my ribs, nagging me with a bitter pressure.

Jagger must have been listening in on our conversation. "We've got to come up with a plan of action somehow. Are there any other factors we could look at?"

I considered, tapping my fingers against the side of the truck bed. "Well, if they were being strategic, which dark fae tend to be, they'd have wanted Darton grabbed by the fae who could take him the farthest from here, so we'd have the most difficult time giving chase. But that's assuming the fae who grabbed him is the one they planned to have do it. He did take out a couple with his sword first."

Yasmin circled a few of the dots on her screen to highlight them. One at the farthest point south, another to the southeast, one almost due east from here, and one in the northeast near the border to Canada. "If they *were* following strategy, we'd bet on it being one of these."

"That sounds about right." Identifying those spots didn't narrow down our options in any very useful way. The northernmost dot and the southernmost were a couple thousand miles apart. "We can't split up to chase down all of those fae. Whoever finds Darton won't have the manpower to get him back."

"Let me look at overall patterns of movement across the last twenty-four hours," Yasmin said. "Maybe that will give us more of a clue. They'll be taking him to the lead dark fae you were talking about, won't they?"

"Probably."

She leaned forward to peer at the screen as her fingers raced over the keys. Several ripples creased the fainter swirls that still dappled the entire map. "Hmm." She pointed to a ring of darker ripples in the northwest. "This is the movement we saw this morning, toward the cemetery. But here"—she gestured toward the Midwest—"there's been a broader but fainter pattern of movement. It looks as if quite a few dark fae or creatures, or both, are gathering."

She typed in something else, and the ripples moved. At the sight of them shifting across the map like surf on the ocean, my stomach tightened. Why would they be converging around the general area of—oh. Sodding hell.

I didn't want to believe it. Maybe I'd read the map wrong. "Can you do some kind of analysis to see what point they're all heading toward?" I asked.

Yasmin nodded. "We can't predict perfect, of course, but with them coming from a few different angles, we can determine the general center point... Huh. Looks like they're coming in toward Chicago. That's an awfully populated area for fae to hang out."

"Yeah," I said, a rasp creeping into my voice. "That's why they want it. That's why the Darkest One wants it. It's not just people. That World Peace Summit that's been all over the news—it's happening in Chicago. Leaders from all different countries..."

She wanted to destroy them all. Release the dragon and rip apart any pretense of peace. Leave dozens of countries scrambling without their leaders. All the pain, all the fear. She'd just drink it up, wouldn't she?

She must be loving this modern world, where she could strike a blow to human life all across the globe in the snap of her fingers.

Keevan ambled over. "The Summit starts in two days," he said. "So that means we've got two days to get Darton back, right?"

I blinked at him, and he grimaced at me. "I do pay some attention to current events." At the sound of a car engine down the road, he raised his head. "Oh, hey. The rest of the gang is here."

What? I glanced past him, and my heart sank. A car I recognized as Keevan's parked behind the row of fae hunter vehicles. Izzy stepped out on the driver's side, clutching the key. Keevan must have given her a spare for emergencies. I guessed this qualified. But I didn't want to have to look her in the face and tell her I'd lost her friend and former boyfriend, the guy as far as I'd been able to tell she still carried a torch for.

Priya hopped out on the other side. The two of them strode over to us. "I called Izzy to tell her what was going on," Keevan said, his tone defensive even though I hadn't questioned him. My expression must have been tense enough to give away my discomfort. "I figured she'd want to know. And she was hanging out with Priya on campus."

"It's okay," I said. Not really. Not at all. But at the same time, all three of them had been through a lot with Darton and me. They did deserve to know.

"What's happening?" Priya asked as they reached us. "Have you figured out where the fae took Darton?"

"Not yet," Keevan piped up, to my sudden gratitude. "We're working on it. We have determined that this Darkest One lady is planning on blowing up Chicago while the World Peace Summit is on. And that's how my life goes these days."

Izzy rolled her eyes at him and turned her gaze on me. Her mouth was tight with worry, her hands balled in the folds of her flowing skirt. "Keevan said you don't think they'd hurt Darton. He should be okay as long as we get to him in time?"

"Definitely," I said. "The Darkest One needs Darton alive to use him the way she wants to." Which didn't mean her minions wouldn't do him any harm at all. They'd at very least broken his arm in the attack. But Izzy didn't need to hear that. The thought already weighed on me like a boulder on my back.

She raised her chin. "Okay. Okay. Let me know if there's anything I can do. I know you'll find him."

Her certainty sent a jab of guilt through my chest. I wouldn't have had to find him in the first place if I hadn't lost him. But apparently she wasn't blaming me.

"What have you got so far?" Priya asked. She sidled over to check out Yasmin's laptop.

The fae hunter pointed to the screen. "These points are our best guesses of which fae whisked your friend away. We're still considering other possibilities for narrowing it down."

Izzy and Priya's arrival had diverted my attention. I focused it back on the map. "If the Darkest One is meeting the rest of her minions in Chicago, they'll be bringing Darton there. So it wouldn't make much sense for them to have taken him south. One of these two points would be most likely." I motioned to the two points farthest east from us. "Unless they're trying to throw us off the trail."

"That doesn't sound like the usual dark fae M.O. to me," Jagger said. "Granted, you've got a lot more experience with them, but from what I've seen they tend to be awfully... direct."

"Absolutely." I pressed my hands together. "Okay. Let's not sit around talking anymore. We head east, staying about halfway in between those points in latitude. Yasmin, you can keep checking the data for other patterns that seem meaningful. If we haven't been able to—"

A chime sounded from the open van Keevan had left. It took me a second to recognize it. My new cell phone—a text alert. Who would be texting me? No one had my new number except the people standing around me...

And Darton.

I dashed to the van and hopped in to grab my purse. My hand shook as I pulled the phone from its pocket. Keevan, Izzy, and Priya hurried after me.

"Is it him?" Izzy asked. "Does he know where he is?"

"It's from his number," I said, my pulse hiccupping. "But it's not exactly coherent." He'd typed out *Em* followed by a short string of letters that didn't form a word in any language I was familiar with. Other than my name, it looked like a butt dial more than anything.

But maybe that made more sense than anything else. "The dark fae probably didn't think to check him for a phone. It's not like they're in the habit of kidnapping humans and having to worry about that. But he wouldn't want them to see him using it. He must have tried to type something blind."

They'd have him bound somehow too. He might not even be able to see his surroundings. I remembered the shadowy shroud his captor had pulled over his head. Even if he *had* been able to see, the dark fae's territory would be out in the wilderness somewhere. The chances he'd be able to tell us how to find him were slim.

But he was alive. And well enough to type something. Even though I'd known they wouldn't kill him, having that confirmation sent a flutter of warmth through my heart.

I couldn't let him down. We had to get to him.

"If he's still got his cell phone, and it's on, there are ways of tracking the phone's location," Priya said, her eyes lighting up. "At least, if those crime TV shows are accurate."

Yasmin perked up where she'd been watching us from the truck. "They are. I can tap into that network. Let me see your phone?"

I jogged over and handed it to her. She examined the text and Darton's listing in my contacts. Then she bent over her computer again. The keys clattered under her fingers. A different map popped onto the screen, this one dotted with what I guessed were cell phone towers.

"Let's see where he pinged," she murmured. She typed in one last strand of data, and three of the dots shone red. She zoomed in and then flipped back to the map where she'd been tracking dark fae energy. "And now to compare..."

Darton's self defense must have thrown off the dark fae a little —or else they hadn't been quite as strategic as they could have been. The cell phone data put him at a dark fae arrival point that was a little closer to us than the two outliers to the east, smack in the middle of Wyoming.

Still a long haul from here. But now we knew where we were going. A spark of hope lit inside my heart.

I wasn't sure if I could say I'd found Darton, but he'd found me.

"There he is," I said. "Let's go get him."

CHAPTER TWENTY

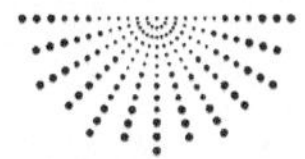

"Here, this part isn't too difficult," Harold said, handing two metal rods to me. "Fit the joint on the end of this one into the middle of that one."

My hands closed around the smooth metal cylinders, warm from their many hours in the van's workshop space. The floor rattled under us with the roar of the engine.

We hadn't stopped since we'd taken off after Darton this morning, other than to fill up on gas when the tank got low. After a few hours spent checking my silent cell phone over and over, and probably driving Yasmin batty asking her over the radio if she'd seen any change in Darton's phone position or the dark fae energies, I'd decided my own energy was best spent working on my trap.

We still needed it, if we got Darton back. If I was going to believe this entire mission wasn't hopeless.

I twisted the joint to work it into the second rod. Keeping busy did distract me from my worries. There was something vaguely reassuring about having equipment to grasp with my hands. Equipment that I knew might end up trapping the Darkest One where she couldn't hurt a single soul. Howard was fiddling with a more delicate mechanism that he'd said he was designing to modulate the flow of electricity.

The work distracted a little, but not enough to completely avoid my thoughts. As I set the rods down, the memory floated up of Darton's reaction when I'd told him about my new plan.

So you're going to make a trap for the Darkest One... and I'm going to be the bait. This sounds a little too familiar. He'd shaken his head with a wry smile.

Hey, it worked last time, I'd pointed out. *And with a little luck, this time you won't have to cut open your arm to tempt her over.*

We'd been able to joke about it, as if our lives and light knew how many millions more didn't depend on it. The threat had still been distant enough then. But night had fallen outside the van's windows. If I'd peered through the glass closely enough, I'd have been able to make out stars. For all the speed limits we'd broken, we were only just coming up on Darton's last identified location.

I left Howard to his work and leaned between the front seats, where Jagger was driving and Izzy navigating, to grab the radio. "Hey, Yasmin," I said. "Still no movement?"

"Nothing recent that I can see," Yasmin said. "Just the same few miles of travel we saw before. They don't seem to be in any hurry."

"Better for us," Jagger said.

Izzy looked up from her phone. "Why do you think they're staying there? I thought you figured they wanted to get Darton to Chicago."

"If they can't jump all the way there, they'd have to haul him by normal means," I said. "Maybe he's making it difficult. Or maybe they decided it isn't worth expending the energy. They don't *need* him in the city until the day after tomorrow. My best guess would be they've got another fae coming to meet them who can apparate with him closer in one quick leap."

We just had to get to him first.

Izzy bit her lip and turned back to her phone. "Who are you texting?" I asked.

"Keevan. If he's not talking to me, he'll badger his driver so much I think they'll toss him out of the car."

Keevan and Priya were each riding in other vehicles. It hadn't made sense for us all to cram into the same one. But it didn't surprise me that they'd be getting restless.

"Darton wouldn't have expected you to come, you know," I said. "You're missing classes, you've got exams coming up... You didn't sign up for this."

Izzy lowered the phone to her lap. "Sure we did," she said. "We're his friends. He's in huge trouble. That's more important than exams."

"Taking on the dark fae—it's going to be harder than anything we've faced before."

She shrugged. "You didn't expect us to be able to help the first time around. But we did, didn't we? You couldn't have stopped the mercenary that was after him without us. Maybe that'll happen again."

I couldn't argue with that reasoning.

Another text alert popped up. Izzy glanced at it and laughed. She clapped her hand over her mouth as if she thought she shouldn't have let the sound out. But it was nice to hear it. Nice to know someone could laugh.

"He's just... You know how he is," she said, waving her hand vaguely. But her mouth was still curved in an affectionate smile. I watched her for a moment, gaze fixed on the screen as she replied.

Maybe Keevan's situation wasn't so hopeless. The guy really should speak up already. Or else Izzy should, if she was starting to catch feelings there too.

After all, there was no telling whether any of us were going to survive the next hour, let alone the next week.

"Emma," Howard called. "I think we're ready to test out the conductive functioning. I'll need a hand for that."

"Right," I said, swiveling. "Of course. Just tell me what I should be doing."

He'd fixed most of the poles I'd helped join together across the walls and ceiling. Several others crisscrossed the floor. In one corner, he'd built up a generator housed in a black box, four times the size of the chambers fixed to the electro-guns. Mounted on the opposite wall was a control panel with a row of buttons and switches.

"When it's completely ready, I'll have it automated," he said. "For now, I want to take things slow. I'm going to build up the current in the generator, and you release it through the framework as I tell you. We're working with the switches for now. One at a time."

"Got it." I positioned myself on a rectangle of bare floor between the rods. "Should I be worried about getting electrocuted?"

Howard chuckled. "Just stay right there and you'll be fine."

"Should *I* be worried about getting electrocuted?" Jagger said from the driver's seat. "I know what you mad scientist types are like."

Howard just smirked at that. "No need to worry. I've padded all the outer edges with insulation."

That wasn't especially comforting given that I was standing *inside* the framework, but he seemed to know what he was doing. I braced my feet in case the van rocked, setting my hand beside the panel for extra balance.

"Okay," Howard said. "Initiating the electrical cycle now."

He turned a dial on the black box. A hum, thinner than the rumble of the van's engine, carried from it. It rose in frequency until it tingled at the very edge of my hearing, a thready whine that probably would have made a dog whimper.

"First switch," he said.

I jabbed at it with my thumb. The whine rang louder. My body tensed, but nothing zapped me. Howard studied a tablet he'd hooked up to the system and nodded as if satisfied with what he saw.

"Second switch."

That one stuck a little when I pushed. I gave it a good poke, and it clicked over. The whine rose with it. I rubbed my ears. Earplugs would definitely have been useful right now.

The framework around me looked exactly the same as before. "Is it working?" I asked.

"Everything's proceeding as expected," Howard said. "It's not supposed to put on a show. You want to catch this fae, not entertain her, right?"

I glowered at him. "I was just asking."

He turned the dial on the box and tapped something on his tablet. The whine expanded to a piercing note that was almost a squeal. Izzy winced.

"I can smooth out the connections once we know the basic functioning is in order," Howard said, which I guessed meant we wouldn't be tormenting the Darkest One's ears while also imprisoning her with electrical energy. "Third switch."

I flipped it, and a quivering energy raced over my skin. Something was radiating through the rods by my feet now. I was starting to feel the power of it, fast and heady. And bright. No, the Darkest One wouldn't like this at all. We just had to amplify the electricity enough that she couldn't break through.

A faintly acrid smell tickled my nose. I turned my head, trying to place it. Was it just a bit of exhaust from outside?

"Fourth switch," Howard said. I nudged it up, and the squeal leapt into a screech. Izzy yelped and covered her ears. I flinched.

And the rods across the floor crackled, emitting a puff of smoke.

Howard swore and wrenched at the dial. The screech faded, and so did the crackle. I waved at the smoke to disperse it, my stomach knotting.

"I'm guessing *that* wasn't the reaction you were hoping for."

Howard shook his head. "I think I'll be able to build up the charge as intense as you need it, but the framework has to be able to carry it without frying. Maybe if I double up the wiring... We're going to need to take it apart so I can do a proper job of it. Why don't you start on that side? The rods shouldn't be too hot there."

Hog's balls. I gritted my teeth against a surge of disappointment and grasped the rods on the wall next to me. It was a little much to expect this experiment to pay off on the very first trial run, wasn't it?

But how many more trials would we have the chance for before we'd run out of time?

"How far off are we from Darton's location now?" I asked.

Izzy consulted her map app. "At the speed we're going right now, about half an hour."

Almost there. Almost to my king. I had to focus on that.

I twisted and detached the rods with an efficiency I'd built up through the day's practice. Howard pulled out one of the heavy coils of wiring he'd taken from the college supply room. When I finished my part of the job, I rolled my shoulders and suppressed a yawn. I couldn't afford to be tired right now. We had not one but two big battles ahead of us.

"Take a left at that intersection up ahead," Izzy told Jagger. He was just slowing when Yasmin's voice crackled from the radio.

"They've jumped again! The cell phone signal moved too."

Sod it. I dashed to the front. "What do you mean? Where have they gone now?"

"Looks like they took a leap to the west end of Iowa. I guess we're adding a bunch more hours to this trip."

I closed my eyes. Iowa. Damn it. We were going to have to drive right through the night. And that was assuming the fae didn't manage to teleport Darton even closer to Chicago—or right to the city—before we caught up with their new stopping point.

"I'm thinking we are going to need your help, at least with the driving," I said to Izzy.

"I can keep at it for a few hours longer," Jagger said. "This won't even be the longest drive I've done."

"Yeah," I said. "But a few hours longer isn't going to get us there. We'd better sleep as well as we can so we're ready when you need to tap us in."

And ready to run into the first of those battles if we got our chance.

CHAPTER TWENTY-ONE

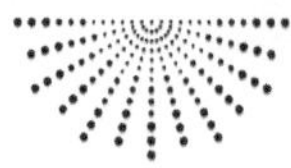

THE ELECTRO-GUN FELT UNCOMFORTABLY bulky in my grasp. "You need to put harnesses on these like you've got for the flamethrowers," I said.

"That's coming soon," Howard said from the driver's seat. "You're lucky we've got those at all. I had to throw them together in less than a day."

He'd taken over the driving from me as dawn had crept up over the land around us. We'd crossed into Iowa forty minutes ago. Treed hillsides rose on either side of the road in the thin sunlight. To the best of Yasmin's detecting skills, Darton hadn't been apparated again. Of course, I'd seen how quickly the dark fae could slip from our grasp last night.

"You set the generator spinning by pushing this button here," Jagger said, adjusting my hand on the weapon. "And then when you press the trigger, you'll get your jolt of power. It's not the most elegant contraption I've ever seen, but it does send the dark varmints running."

"So I've seen." I handed the gun to Izzy, who'd joined us in the back. "Are you okay carrying one of these when we storm the dark fae camp?" If we were able to this time.

She took the weapon from me awkwardly, fitting her hands into the spots Jagger had demonstrated on me. "I think I can handle this. It's a little less scary than one of those flamethrowers. And anything that keeps the dark fae running *away* from me sounds good to me."

I couldn't argue with that sentiment. With nothing left to do with my hands, I re-checked the spread of wands I'd laid out for the seventh or so time. I'd propped Excalibur against the wall behind them. Light willing, I'd be putting it in my king's hands in fifteen minutes' time.

"Still no movement," Yasmin reported over the radio. I was pretty sure she'd slept sometime during the night, but every time I'd checked in for a report, she'd been there on the other end. "We're coming up on the location now—as close as we can get by car, at least. From satellite footage, it looks like they're hiding out in some caves about a mile off the nearest road."

Howard turned the van, following her directions. I tucked a wand into both of my sleeves, others into my pockets, and kept one in my hand. "We wouldn't want to drive too close anyway. We'll have a better chance if we can sneak up on them."

The dark fae wouldn't pay much mind if they sensed my human companions. They barely saw people as anything different from the animals of the forest. To mask my light fae essence, I'd smeared more of the willow ash over my skin. It itched at me, but not as much as my nervousness about the fight ahead of us. Or the prickle of my nearly broken oath, digging into my gut like a particularly vicious thorn.

I haven't gone back on my word yet, I thought at it. *The Darkest One doesn't have him.* We wouldn't get into how close she was to setting her hands on my king's soul.

Howard eased the van to a stop. He clambered into the back to grab his own electro-gun. I hefted the sword in my free hand. We slipped out the back in silence, congregating with the other fae hunters who'd parked along the road. They all stood solemn and quiet, watching me for direction. Even Keevan had the sense to keep his mouth shut.

I stretched my awareness over the uneven hillside. The wind hissed through the bare branches of the oaks and hickory trees, rustling the needles on the firs. To my senses, it was laced with a sharper cold than the regular autumn chill.

The dark fae were here. Only a small group, from the feel of them. And in their midst, the pulse of my king's soul came to me.

There. Darton was so close. My heart wrenched. Now that I was near enough to feel his presence, I could have jumped straight to him with my magic. But then we might both end up caught instead of just him. I needed my allies with me.

I motioned with the sword in the direction I could feel the cluster of dark fae. The others readied their weapons. Dragging in a breath, I stepped off the road and into the hillside forest.

It would have been a tiring walk even under regular circumstances, up and down the sloped terrain—and mostly up. Carrying a sword meant for a practiced fighter and going on no more than three hours sleep? My head was spinning by the time the fae energy grew strong enough ahead of us that I raised my wand to motion our company to a halt. I took a moment to catch my ragged breath. Sweat was trickling down my back under my sweater despite the chill in the air.

The dark fae were barely stirring in their caves. I didn't taste any concern or wariness in the air. They probably couldn't imagine that a group of mere humans could have figured out a way to trace their magic. The fae liked to think themselves so mighty compared to the rest of us, but if they'd paid more attention to what the human beings around them were doing, they'd have been a lot more prepared.

This once, it worked in our favor. We had the full element of surprise.

I waved the fae hunters and my friends closer to me. "I'm going to magic myself over to Darton," I murmured. "If he's conscious, we should be able to knock them back between the two of us and the sword. If he's not... I'll do the best I can on my own. Either way, we'll need the rest of you running in there to have our backs and scatter the fae. There are probably glooms and other dark vermin around too, so keep your eyes open."

Jagger and several of the others nodded. I turned back toward the vague shape of the cave openings I could make out through the trees. My king's presence, so much stronger now, wound through my chest. *I'm coming.*

"Here I go," I said, and switched to the old tongue. "*Wind carry me to the place of my heart.*" Darton might have looked at me strangely if I'd called him a "place" in his hearing, but the truth was he was the closest thing to a real home I had.

I twirled my wand. The wind whipped up around and through me. And with a lurch—much less disorienting than crossing an entire ocean, thank the light—I was stumbling on cold stone ground in the darkness of the cave.

One of the dark fae standing nearby gave a cry. Darton was slumped by my feet. I snapped out a lash of light, jerking the sword through the air at the same time. The five fae gathered around me staggered back a step, and the spell lit up my reborn king.

His hair was damp from the cave's moisture and matted at one temple with scabbing blood. A coil of shadow bound his wrists and ankles. The arm the fae had broken rested at an unnatural angle. But his eyes were open and bright.

"*Darkness begone,*" I spat, gesturing to his bonds. They fell away —and the dark fae charged at me, shouting spells of their own.

Darton shoved himself upright and grabbed Excalibur from me with his working hand. It lit up with an eager flash. He stabbed the blade into the bolt of dark magic blasting toward us and smashed the energy apart. I bent down to grasp his shoulder so he didn't have to try to stand just yet. He lifted the sword, already knowing what we needed to do.

"*Darkness begone, darkness fall! Light knock the sense from their darkened minds!*" I yelled. A thunderclap of light blazed through the cave. Two of the fae toppled. The other three had conjured shadowy shields around themselves. The light slammed into them, shattering the shields and throwing the fae backward, but not quite hitting them.

The three of them started to press forward again, but a crackling rang out on the other side of the cave. My allies had reached us. Flames leapt and electricity shot out all across the cave entrance. My grip on Darton's shoulder tightened.

"Again?" he said, his voice creaky. It pained me to hear it, even as his determination squeezed at my heart.

"Let's show them what they get when they mess with my king," I said.

He chuckled roughly and heaved himself onto his feet. I shifted my hand from his shoulder to the bare skin at the back of his neck.

"*Darkness begone, darkness fall!*" I hollered, my own voice hoarse. Darton sliced the sword through the air. Another wave of light crashed through the cave. It smashed into the remaining fae, sending them flying right out of the cave into the midst of the fae hunters.

Excalibur dipped in Darton's hand. He swayed. I caught him with an arm around his back. "Hey," he said, sounding slightly dazed. He leaned his head next to mine. "My wizard."

I laughed, but something about his tone made my throat constrict. It was so tender. How hard had they hit him in the head? I touched his cheek as I steadied him. His broken arm hung useless at his side. I bent over it and murmured a few words to knit the bone. It would still be too painful for him to swing the sword with it quite yet, but it was a step in the right direction.

"Your wizard, as always, sire," I said. "And right now I recommend we make sure these fae are well and truly beaten."

He carried his own weight walking to the cave's opening, mostly, but he moved stiffly after the many hours of lying bound. "You got my message?" he said. "I tried... I couldn't manage much. And then they saw me moving and tied my wrists tighter. Took the phone off me too."

"I got the message," I said, "inarticulate as it was. It gave us a better idea of how to find you. Apparently they held on to the phone, because it led us right to you. And here we are, back together."

"I tried to fight them off, in the cemetery."

"I know, my liege. You felled two of them, did you realize? It'd be a little much to expect you to conquer an entire dark fae army. You might be an excellent king, but you're not a god."

His mouth twitched with a hint of a smile, but his expression still looked pained. "It shouldn't always be you," he murmured.

I didn't know what he meant by that, but we'd reached the edge of the forest then. "Art!" Keevan hollered, and slapped his arm around his best friend. Izzy hurried over too. The fae hunters had spread out through the woods around the caves. They looked as though they were patrolling rather than actively fighting now.

"The fae?" I said.

Priya loped over to join us. "They took off when they saw what they had to contend with out here." She hefted her borrowed flamethrower with a grin. "I've never seen a fae look quite that disgruntled. It was really very satisfying."

They'd be more than disgruntled. They'd be furious—and panicked at the thought of the Darkest One's displeasure.

"They'll have been waiting for others to join them, to take Darton the rest of the way to Chicago," I said. "We should get moving before those reinforcements, or others, show up."

"Chicago?" Darton said as we headed down the mountainside toward the road. His legs were steadier now, but he wavered a little on the rocky ground. "Why would they be taking me to Chicago?

Where are we *now*? I haven't seen anything except shadows and trees for... however long it's been."

"The World Peace Summit," I said. "It looks like the dark fae are gathering around Chicago to meet the Darkest One." A shiver passed through me. They've probably *already* met her by now. She herself could be sweeping toward us at this very minute, ready to claim her long-awaited prize. "I think that's where she's planning on unleashing... her plan." I caught myself just shy of mentioning the dragon. He'd asked me not to tell his friends.

"Oh," Darton said. He swallowed audibly. Probably processing the thought that the monster lurking inside him could be poised to destroy one of the largest cities in the country. He wet his lips. "But we're going to stop her."

"Of course we are," Keevan said. "That's what we do."

"Emmaline has been working with one of the fae hunters on this trap for the Darkest One," Priya said, with a brightness that sounded a little forced. She knew it wasn't going to be easy. "Something to do with electrical currents and I don't know what else."

Darton lifted his head. "You got that thing working?"

Well... "It's getting closer," I said. "And, sorry, you're still the necessary bait."

He gave me a crooked smile. "That seems to be what I do best." He held my gaze for a beat longer than usual, his eyes searching mine. I didn't know what for.

Keevan cleared his throat. Izzy motioned to the scabbed cut on Darton's forehead. "Did they hurt you anywhere else? I think the fae hunters have medical supplies. I guess they'd need to in their line of work..."

Darton touched the patch of dried blood and made a face. "They mostly just kept me tied up. Even this is really my fault. I hit my head on a rock while I was trying to break free after they first grabbed me. I think they added something to their magic after that, so I couldn't move at—"

A cry rang out through the forest from below. Most of the fae hunters had gone ahead of us. My pulse stuttered. I grasped Darton's hand, and we pushed faster through the forest.

I had my wand ready as we burst from the trees, but there was no battle to join when we emerged from the trees. The fae hunters were hustling around the line of parked vehicles with more sounds of dismay. My gaze caught on shattered glass glinting on the pavement.

Several of the flood lamps on the cars had been smashed. One had a gaping hole in its windshield. Another's hood was completely caved in. The dark fae had battered our transportation as they'd fled.

I turned, and a yelp escaped my own lips.

One of the van's back doors was hanging sideways from one hinge. The other was folded inward. Howard stood there, his hands shoved into his hair, his stance defeated.

CHAPTER TWENTY-TWO

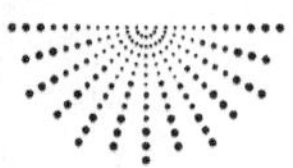

I DASHED TO THE VAN, dragging Darton with me. Even if I couldn't see any dark fae at the moment, I wasn't leaving him out of arm's reach. I wasn't giving them another chance to grab him.

As we came up on the back of the van, my heart sank all the way to the soles of my feet. A blast of dark magic had consumed most of the interior. The rods were crumbling, eaten away by a sudden rust. The black box that had housed Howard's generator lay strewn in little pieces across the floor. Wires had melted together into a shapeless blob.

Our trap looked like a pile of old junk.

Howard pawed through the mess, his mouth pressed tight. "Can you salvage *anything*?" I asked. My voice came out raw.

He shook his head. "I'll have to start over from scratch. I don't know where I'll get another conductor like the one I had in there... I constructed those at home. I've got other ones there..."

But his home was a day's drive away, he didn't need to say. We didn't have a day. We might not even have an hour.

I exhaled shakily. That trap had been our one shot. I didn't have any other plans left. We had Darton, but no real way to protect him. No way to stop the Darkest One from doing whatever the hell she wanted.

Jagger walked over. He studied the ruin of the van and folded his arms over his chest. "Is it still drivable?" he said.

Right. Because the only thing worse than having lost our chance at imprisoning the Darkest One again would be losing Darton again, right here, because we didn't have any means to escape her minions.

Izzy had already opened the driver's side door and hopped in. The engine rumbled and then sputtered out. Whatever magic the dark fae had thrown at the vehicle as they'd charged past, it had wrecked the van all the way through.

"How are we getting out of here then?" Keevan asked.

Jagger let out a huff of breath. "We'll manage. They didn't hit all the cars. They haven't knocked us down yet. But I'm thinking we should be getting out of here *fast*?"

He glanced at me. As if anything I'd contributed so far had gotten us closer to real safety. I swallowed a slightly hysterical laugh. "Yeah. Out of here and fast sounds good."

"All right. We've got people one state over we've been in contact with. They're already heading out to meet us. We'll pile into the cars that are still working and meet them halfway. I'll see if they can scrounge up a few extra vehicles while they're at it." He paused and gave my shoulder a quick squeeze. I had no idea how despondent I must have looked to provoke that gentle gesture from Jagger of all people.

"We'll regroup," he said. "We're not beat, and we won't be."

He could say that, but from where I was standing, it sure as hell felt like we were. The Darkest One had no doubt already landed on America's shores. I'd barely managed to weaken the dragon in Darton. We were out of time and out of options.

But there was nothing to do but go forward and hope some other answer came to me on the way. Jagger motioned us toward the truck where I'd first met Yasmin. Darton and I climbed in the back with her and a couple of the other fae hunters. She'd already gotten out her laptop.

"Let's go!" she said. "I'm not liking the readings I'm seeing here."

Jagger waved his arm, and the truck and a few of the cars pulled onto the road. The driver gunned the engine. I watched the wrecked van until we turned the corner, leaving my last great plan behind for good.

We had our rendezvous with the local fae hunters at a farm near the state border. The windmill creaked as its tattered blades rocked back and forth in the breeze. Weeds choked the fields beyond wooden fences that were half collapsed. Not much chance of us being spotted here by anyone who'd find our activities suspicious, but the whole place had a deathly atmosphere that left my nerves prickling.

Only four new hunters joined us, but they'd managed to bring one vehicle apiece, partly thanks to a quick bank transfer I'd made through my phone. They'd picked up a couple of RVs for sale at a used dealership. "That'll make sleeping on the road a little less painful," Jagger said, as if he thought we could just keep driving and somehow that would fix everything.

But what else was there to do? As the hunters bustled between the vehicles, redistributing supplies and discussing routes, I took a bottle of water one of them had passed me and wiped the powder from my face and hands. Then I rinsed out my mouth. Between the aura of death and the literal poison in the ashy mix, I'd been feeling increasingly queasy. Painting myself in darkness definitely wasn't a permanent solution.

When I was done, I handed the bottle to Darton. He drained the third of water left in the bottom. I brushed past him to flick on the truck's radio.

After a few attempts, I found a station with a news show. The hosts chattered away about a political bribery scandal and a deli meat recall. Then the weather anchor came on.

"We're seeing quite a sudden cold front sweeping the east coast this morning," he said. "Temperatures have dropped to around fifteen degrees below the expected average at this time of year. It's not clear what caused this sudden shift, so meteorologists are having difficulty predicting when it might pass."

Darton rested his hand on the small of my back and leaned his head over my shoulder. "Do you figure that's because of the Darkest One? No storms this time?"

"I'd stake my life on it," I said. "She's here. And she can't resist strewing discomfort to lead up to the main event. But a full-out storm would mean planes can't fly in all those world leaders for tomorrow."

"If we can stay ahead of the dark fae until after that... I guess there isn't much chance she'd give up?"

"No. Not much chance at all." I grimaced. "The summit is supposed to last for an entire week. I don't know if we even can stay ahead of all of her minions that long. And if by some miracle we did, she'll find some other way to use you. She's been waiting fifteen hundred years for this moment—more if you count the time before. A small delay isn't going to put her off."

As if on cue, the news show switched focus. "Anticipation is building for the massive World Peace Summit. Crowds gathered near the O'Hare Airport to watch the presidents from France, China, and Brazil arriving. The event will kick off with a public forum held in Lincoln Park tomorrow afternoon."

I shut off the radio. Hearing that news didn't help me. We couldn't outrun the Darkest One forever. We couldn't take her on with flamethrowers and electro-guns. Between Darton's sword and my magic, we couldn't do more than knock out regular dark fae, so we certainly weren't stopping their high lady with the tools we currently had. What was left? What was I missing?

Or maybe there wasn't anything.

The oath's itch crept up my fingers into my hands. I shoved them into my jacket pockets and turned away from the truck. I was exhausted. I hadn't eaten anything since yesterday. Maybe the newcomers had brought some food to give me the energy I needed to keep resisting.

I took one step toward the nearest RV, and an icy finger traced down my back.

My body stiffened. I held my breath, taking in the sensation, as the frigid tendril pierced deeper inside me. A hum of dark magic ran through it. A magic and a chill I knew better than I'd have liked to.

It was her. The Darkest One was searching me out. Because she knew she'd find Darton with me, of course. And she'd found me. Practically tapped me on the shoulder from afar.

I tried to grasp onto the thread of her magic with my own awareness, but it yanked away from me. I stretched my mind after it as it trailed into the distance. The chill vanished, leaving only the regular fall damp in the air around me.

From afar, yes. She wasn't close enough for my half-fae senses to find her. But that was a small comfort. She'd pinpointed my location. We had to get moving. I had to throw her off somehow. I had to—

In my panic, I lost my grip on my body. I swung around, my arms jerking toward Darton. He caught them by the elbows as if thinking I'd turned to him for an embrace. The heels of my hands rammed into his chest. Words sputtered off my tongue.

"Break and bur—"

No. I couldn't make my arms budge, but my neck moved. I smacked my face into the roof of the truck, cutting off the spell less than a syllable shy of rupturing Darton's heart. Pain jarred through my jaw and into my skull, snapping the oath's hold.

Darton grunted. My stomach lurching, I wrenched my arms

back to my sides. He pressed his hand to his chest, just below where my palms had struck him. His mouth twisted.

A little of the spell had slipped out. I'd hurt him. My throat choked up. "I'm so sorry. Let me—"

I cut myself off, jerking my hands back from reaching for him. As if he'd want me trying to help after I'd done the damage. But Darton blinked at me, and then his face fell. As if, somehow, he was more bothered by my pulling back than the fact that I'd almost killed him.

I touched his chest tentatively, digging the fingernails of my other hand into my palm to hold back the oath's urge. With a quick murmur, I found the problem. My fractured spell had cracked two of his ribs.

At least I could knit those back together. Ramming my nails deeper into the wound on my palm, I whispered a few words to seal the bones.

"Are you okay?" Keevan said, coming over. I dropped my hand from Darton's body and stepped back.

"Sure," Darton said. He prodded the spot without so much as a wince. "Em was just healing me up."

He didn't say I was the one who'd hurt him in the first place. Keevan wouldn't even guess, considering where we'd just found Darton. He'd assume it'd been the dark fae's doing.

But even his kidnapping had been *my* doing, hadn't it? I'd led them to the safe place we'd made, even if inadvertently. I'd taken the oath that was preventing me from being able to keep him by my side without risking him more. And now the Darkest One was using me as a target to track him down.

A different sort of chill passed through me, one that twisted my stomach with guilt. Maybe I'd been going at this problem all wrong. I'd been so focused on us getting through this *together*... But that didn't really serve my king, did it? By all evidence, he was safer without me. I'd been clinging to him for my own sake. For my own longings.

I'd taken another oath, all those centuries ago. I'd sworn to protect him with my life. It hadn't been magically binding, but it meant more to me than the words I'd given Cormag and his light fae cronies. I'd followed Arthur across all those centuries and all over two continents meaning to fulfill it.

Now was the time. I couldn't think about how I felt, only what was best for him. What would keep him alive and away from the Darkest One.

"I have to go," I said.

Keevan cocked his head. "Yeah, I think Jagger's people are almost done strategizing. I'm supposed to tell you we'll be moving out in a couple minutes."

"No, *I* have to go. I can't stay with the rest of you."

Darton stared at me. "What are you talking about, Em? Do you really think we can handle it alone if—"

"Not *we*." My hands balled by my hips. "You'll stay with the fae hunters. I'll lay down some barriers that should make it hard for the dark fae to trace your energy before I go. It's me they can track the easiest, not you. They've used me to get to you before. I can feel the Darkest One herself trying to reach me already."

"No." He shook his head, his voice hard. "No, not a chance. We're in this together, Em. There has to be a way to rebuild your trap, or to keep ahead of the dark fae, or..."

He trailed off, because what other possibilities were there? I gave him a pained smile. "Even before the fae wrecked the trap, we couldn't tell if it was going to work. And we can't run for the rest of our lives. I came all this way, all the times before and now, to make sure you have a life. I'm not backing down from that mission now. I'll do whatever I have to do."

"So, what, you're going to take on the ruler of all the dark faeries by yourself?" Keevan said. "I mean, I've got a lot of respect for you, Emma, but weren't *you* saying before how impossible that is?"

"Maybe I was thinking about it the wrong way." I'd been

thinking like a light fae. But all the good moves I'd made in the last few days, I'd accomplished by letting darkness seep in. Maybe the way to defeat the Darkest One wasn't by clashing with her. Maybe there was some way I could sidle close and then yank the ground out from beneath her feet.

I had no idea how. But I did still have a little time. I could go, and watch, and hope the right strategy would come to me.

Jagger ambled over to us. "What's going on? It's time to head out."

"Emma says she isn't coming with us," Keevan said.

"What?" Izzy's head jerked around where she was standing farther down the lane. She marched over. "What are you talking about?"

Darton was still focused on me. "This is crazy," he said. "You can't— What if they find me anyway? You know we won't be able to fight them off without you here."

"I'll be where she'll be bringing you," I said. "If it comes to that." If I couldn't stop her first. The immensity of that task settled over me. I focused on my resolve, but my body betrayed me. My legs wobbled. I set my hand on the side of the truck to steady myself.

Jagger's eyebrows rose. "You don't look like you're in much condition to walk across the farm, forget battling dark fae queens."

"We can help," Izzy said. "If the problem is the dark fae tracking you two... You should stay with Darton, Emma. Can't we use the same strategy as we did when you were going to the airport? Take some of your things and drive off in different directions to confuse them? That'll be better than you just taking off."

"Yeah!" Keevan said. "I'm totally up for that, and I'm sure Priya would be too."

I hesitated. That trick would muddy the trail at least a little bit. But it wouldn't solve our problems for long.

"Please." Darton touched the side of my face, so gently my heart started to melt. His voice dipped. "At least stay until you have a definite plan. Get some rest, make sure you're thinking straight. We'll talk it through. Please."

"You two can have first dibs on one of the RV bedrooms," Jagger said, but that last *Please* from Darton had already broken me. Was I kidding myself? My thoughts were too scattered in my exhaustion.

"Okay," I said. "I'll grab a few things that you three can take, Izzy. We'll get moving, and I'll sleep, and then we'll see where we're at. But if I'm going, I'm going soon."

CHAPTER TWENTY-THREE

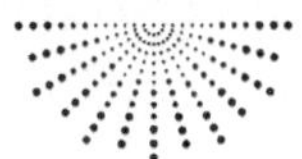

THE SLIDING DOOR clicked shut behind Darton and me. I sank down onto the end of the narrow double bed. The RV's engine rumbled beneath us as the driver pulled out of the farm. I pulled the shade closed over the window. I'd insisted on marking the outside of the vehicle with my ash mixture before we'd left, but I didn't trust that to be enough of a shield. Not for very long.

We had a head start. None of the fae had been near us. Keevan and Izzy had taken off in his car, Priya in one a fae hunter had lent her, carrying the most meaningful items I could give them marked with our blood. And Yasmin could keep us away from any hot spots of dark fae activity. They shouldn't be able to catch us for at least a few hours. I could get that rest I'd promised I would.

But my nerves were humming way too loud for sleep to seem likely.

Darton laid his sword on the floor by the door and sat down beside me, leaving a few inches of space between us. My hands twitched. I swallowed hard.

"Maybe you should sleep on one of the bunks up front. I don't know how much control I can keep after I've drifted off."

"I want to stay with you until you're asleep," Darton said. "I want to make sure you *do* go to sleep."

"So you're my babysitter now?"

He narrowed his eyes at me. "If that's what you need. You're not going to be saving anyone if you're about to collapse on your feet."

He might have had a point there. I sighed and flopped back on the bed. A faintly spicy lavender smell rose off it. Apparently the previous owners had been potpourri fans. At least the mattress was decently firm.

Darton was watching me. His expression had gone odd again, that uncertain look I'd noticed when I'd been coming to him in the cemetery.

"What?" I said. "Are you waiting for me to ask you to tuck me in?"

A smile crossed his face, but it faded quickly. Okay, something was definitely bothering him. Before I had to pry it out of him, he dragged in a breath.

"I've been remembering a lot more over the last few days," he said. "From my first life. From being Arthur."

"Excalibur probably helped with that," I said. And moments like lying half naked in each other's arms. A flutter of warmth passed through me at that memory. I squirmed away from it, farther up the bed to where I could rest my head on one of the thin pillows. "And? Did a new great plan come to you?"

"No." He looked down at his hands and then turned to face me. There was something so haunted in his eyes that my heart started to ache. "But I need to tell you something. I don't know if it'll make things better or worse or— I don't know. But before you go making decisions about running off on your own, before the Darkest One maybe catches up with us, or anything... I think you need to hear it."

"Okay," I said, bracing myself.

His Adam's apple bobbed in his throat. "You told me not that long ago that—that you've always loved me, but I haven't felt the same way. I thought, from what I'd remembered so far, that had to be right. I wasn't ever going to bring it up again. I saw how hard it's been for you. But I—"

His voice faltered. He seemed to gather himself and pressed on. "The more the pieces come together, the more I see how it was for me in that first life. The more I *feel* it. Maybe your confession dragged that part of my past up, or maybe it's how intense the last few weeks have been, or... I really don't know. But I know what I remember. It couldn't be more clear."

My heart was thudding now. I shifted upright on the bed, drawing my knees in to my chest. "What are you talking about, Art?"

His fingers curled into the bedspread, but he held my gaze steadily. "I'm talking about flirting with a beautiful lady during a dance in the castle and finding myself thinking how much I'd rather be bantering with you. I'm talking about missing you when you left my chambers for the night. I'm talking about catching myself wondering how it would feel to really *touch* you, with more than a playful swat here and there. I'm talking about the dreams—gods, the *dreams*."

He shook his head. "Some part of me had to know it meant something. But it didn't fit how I'd expected to feel. It didn't fit anyone's expectations for me. So I kept squashing down those thoughts, those feelings. Telling myself it wasn't more than close friendship, telling myself my mind was playing tricks on me. Pushing you away when I couldn't convince myself quite enough." He lowered his gaze then and rubbed his brow. "I owe you so many apologies."

My chest had gone fizzy. I couldn't do anything more than gape at Darton for a long moment. My heart thumped dizzyingly on.

Had I already fallen asleep? Maybe *this* was a dream. Because what he was saying, it sounded like he meant—

No. I would have known, back then. I would have seen, surely...

"I don't understand," I said weakly.

He raised his head. I could have fallen forever into the deep blue of his eyes. "How was it you put it? I've heard *those* words echoing so many times in my head. Em. Merlin. I have loved you, utterly, always. I just had my head too far up my ass to admit it, even to myself. I didn't want it to be true, back then. As if it was something to be ashamed of." He winced.

"I wasn't interested in *men*," he went on. "I was in love with *you*. And you happened to be a man, at the time. I don't know why I found it so hard... And all the times after, all the rejections I've obviously subjected you to..."

"Arthur." His name fell from my mouth, soft and light as a petal. He smiled at me, as if hearing that was all he needed. The fizzing in my chest softened too, into a slow unfurling of emotion, like a flower blooming. I'd thought I'd loved this man, this soul, utterly, in every one of my lives, but I'd never loved him quite as much as I did in that moment.

"I don't know how I can apologize properly," he went on. "I'd understand if you still want to keep your distance, if you feel that you're better off—"

A laugh bubbled from my throat. I shot across the bed with one quick scoot to grasp the front of his shirt.

"Art," I said, "shut up."

And then I kissed him.

We'd never kissed like that before. Tender and gentle, hard and passionate, we'd pretty much covered the bases. But without entirely realizing it, I'd always been holding a piece of myself back at a distance. As if I could pretend that it was only Emma, or Martin, or any of the other lives before who was getting swept up in the moment, while some part of Merlin remained untouched. Unshaken.

Not that it had ever hurt less that way.

Now I felt as if I'd thrown my whole self into the meeting of our lips. All of me, offered up for however he wanted to make use of me. Although I could think of particular uses I'd especially approve of.

A hungry sound reverberated through Darton's chest. His fingers tangled in my hair as he kissed me deeper, unraveling my ponytail. His other arm wrapped around me, pulling my body flush against his. I ran my hand down his chest and then up under his shirt, reveling in his heat and the coiled strength of his muscles.

He pulled back an inch, but couldn't seem to resist planting his lips on my cheek, the corner of my jaw, before he managed to speak. "I'm sorry. If I hadn't been such an ass—"

"It's okay," I said. "I forgive you. Enough talking. Do you have any idea how long I've been waiting for you?"

He chuckled low in his throat. "About fifteen hundred years?"

I growled at him and yanked him back to me. His hands slid up my torso as we fell back on the bed, his thumbs tracing the curve of my breasts. I gasped into his mouth.

It wasn't just okay. It was fantastic. It was perfect. There was no spell binding us. No doubt about who exactly he wanted. Just the two of us coming together, as if we'd always been meant to.

He pulled my sweater off over my head as he kissed his way down the middle of my chest. "Em," he murmured. "Merlin." A shaky breath stuttered out of me. I tugged at his shirt, and he peeled it off. But that wasn't enough. I wanted all of him, now, while I could have him. A thread of urgency thrummed through my pulse.

That was why he'd told me now, wasn't it? He might not get another chance. *We* might not get another chance to make something real out of the words he'd said.

He tossed my bra aside and dipped his head to take one nipple into his mouth. I swallowed a moan. That sliding door hadn't looked especially thick. My breath turned into pants as he teased his tongue from one of my breasts to the other.

I pulled him back up for another kiss. My thighs splayed around his hips. He rocked against me, and a shudder of pleasure shot through my body from between my legs.

"Merlin," he said, his nose brushing mine, his gaze locked on my eyes. "Tell me you want this. Just because I— We don't have to—"

His voice was so raw and desperate it only turned me on more. "I've never wanted anything more," I said. "Don't you dare stop."

He kissed me hard, his tongue slipping into my mouth to caress mine. His hand slid down my side and along the waist of my jeans to navigate the button and the zipper. I squirmed and kicked them off as soon as they were loosened. My fingers grazed down over his sculpted body and curled around the rigid length pressing against the fly of his pants. He groaned into my hair.

"You have no idea how many times I've imagined being inside you."

His muttered words sent a fresh wave of heat through me. I yanked at his zipper. The sooner we made those imaginings a reality, the happier I'd be. He jerked off his pants and made short work of his boxers as well. The heel of his hand settled over my sex, rubbing me through the damp fabric of my panties. I bit my lip, arching to meet him.

"Off," I gasped out. He didn't wait to be asked twice. Then he leaned over me, his erection sliding over my wetness. I gripped his hip, and he took the hint. With a sharp exhale, he slid inside me, all the way to the hilt.

I couldn't bite back the moan that escaped me then. I burrowed my face in the crook of his neck as he found his rhythm. It felt as if every part of him were touching every part of me, outside and in, and I only wanted to somehow get closer. Memories from our first life together swam up in my head, but I ignored them. None of them could come close to the bliss of this moment.

Darton's thrusts quickened. Pleasure shuddered through my body. It built and built with every plunge of his hips, every caress of his hands. He lifted my hips, fitting us together even more tightly, and the sudden burst of pressure sent me over the edge. I clenched around him, my fingernails digging into his shoulders. My lips parted. "Arthur."

He groaned and rocked into me a few more times. Then he slumped over me with a satisfied quiver of breath.

Without a word, he rolled onto his side and gathered me against him, tucking my head under his chin the way he had in the mausoleum the other night. I nestled closer, my legs still entwined with his. His earthy scent filled my nose.

"I love you, Em," he said softly. "Merlin. I love you." As if he thought by saying it over and over, he could make up for all the years before. Well, maybe he could. The words set off a warm glow in my chest.

"And I love you, my liege. My king." I kissed the base of his throat. "My Arthur."

He tucked his arm around me, encasing me in warmth. His happy sigh tickled past my ear. That was the last sound I heard before exhaustion dragged me down into sleep.

"Is it only the fae who can do magic?" my prince said. "That doesn't really seem fair."

We were standing by one of the castle's parapets, looking out over the surrounding lands. The air still held that summer mugginess, but I could taste the dry cool of autumn at its edges. Fall was on the way.

"A hawk can fly," I pointed out. "A fish can breath underwater. Human beings can make tools with their hands. Why shouldn't we have our own special strengths? Believe me, there are plenty of weaknesses to go alongside them."

Arthur raised an eyebrow at me. "What, like a perpetually sharp tongue and an absolutely horrid track record with horses?"

"Those are just my weaknesses," I said. "And I happen to think a sharp tongue is an asset."

"You would."

I ignored that remark. "Anyway, magic doesn't only belong to the fae. It's part of all life. It's just that the fae have by far the easiest time calling to that energy. But in extreme circumstances, any creature can be capable of more than their nature. Do you remember seeing that scrap of a woman lifting an entire cart to get at her child?"

My prince made a noise of agreement. "So that was magic?"

"Well, not exactly. But it was tapping into a strength she wouldn't normally have. The same thing can happen with magic. If a person's willing to give themselves over to it, to sacrifice their own life, there's no power that can compare."

CHAPTER TWENTY-FOUR

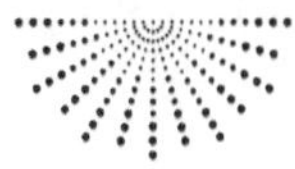

WHATEVER NOISE WOKE ME, it was already over by the time I was awake enough to think. All I heard was dull silence around me.

Silence. That was wrong. Why wasn't the RV moving?

Darton's hand had slipped down my side to my hip as we'd slept. He was still out like a log, slow breaths drifting over his slightly parted lips. I eased myself away from him and off the bed, grabbing pieces of clothing as I went.

From the glow seeping past the window blind, it was still daytime, and not late in the day either. Voices filtered faintly through the wall from outside. I couldn't make out the words, but their tone was harried. My stomach knotted. I picked up the wand I'd left by the bedroom door and slid aside the door as quietly as I could.

The RV was empty. Worrisome sign number two. I padded down the length of it and nudged opened the door. Cool air and bright mid-day sun greeted me outside.

I understood part of what was going on right away. We'd pulled into a rest area to refuel. The other fae hunter cars and trucks were scattered around the two RVs. I guessed everyone had gotten off to grab some food and use the restrooms. But that didn't explain why a bunch of them were clustered at the far end of the parking lot. A couple of the hunters were gesturing with sharp jabs of their hands. Jagger made a sweeping motion toward something in the distance.

Then Yasmin noticed me hurrying over and said something that made them all fall silent. They turned to watch me approach. My heart sank as I drew to a stop in front of them. Something was wrong. So wrong it prickled up through my consciousness and stole my breath.

"What's going on?" I said.

Jagger swiped his hand over his mouth. "Your friends," he started, and hesitated. I'd never seen him look so downcast.

My friends. "Keevan? Izzy? Priya? *What?* Just tell me."

Howard piped up. "Dark fae took them. The damned creatures used one of their phones to text a message and a photograph to Jagger as proof."

My heart stopped. Like the video a dark fae had sent Darton of his sister. But then the fae had only been following Audrey. He hadn't touched her. "Why would they— What would they want—"

No. I didn't need to ask. The dark fae didn't pay a lot of attention to human activities, but they understood the basics of human nature well enough.

They'd threatened our families before, when they'd wanted to shift Darton and me to their will. That hadn't worked. So they'd gone for the only other people around we cared about. Easy targets, who wouldn't have been carrying weapons, who would have expected any fae that followed them to step back when they realized Darton and I weren't around. A lot easier targets than attacking the king with his wizard standing guard.

The Darkest One figured there was an easier answer than sending her minions chasing after us across the country. She'd found the perfect way to make us come right to her. As soon as Darton heard Keevan and Izzy had been taken—

My hands clenched. No. I couldn't let that happen. There

would be no reasoning with him. There'd be no stopping him. These weren't just vague threats—our friends were literally in dark fae hands. He'd go after them. The king in him wouldn't allow him to do anything else.

Unless he never got the chance.

My body went still. There was my answer. The thought of him waking up and finding himself alone sent a twinge through my gut. But he'd understand, eventually. He'd know I'd done it for him.

That hadn't just been a memory that had tickled past the edges of my sleep. It'd been a reminder. Sacrifice was the most powerful magic. The fae mercenary had used it. Rhedyn had used it. It had always been there within my reach, except I hadn't been willing to face the consequences. I hadn't been willing to leave my king.

Better to leave than to see him killed. Better that than killing him myself. The itch this morning's bliss had subdued crept up through my arms again. I rubbed my hands over them.

"The fae have taken them to Chicago," Yasmin said. "It's obviously a trap."

"Obviously," I agreed. "But we can't just leave our friends trapped there. I was already planning on going." Jagger started to speak, and I shot him a hard look. "I've rested. My head is clear. I know what I've got to do. Darton's friends and mine were my responsibility. *He* is my responsibility."

Jagger frowned, but he inclined his head. "You have to do what you have to do, Emma."

"Thank you." I sucked in a breath. "What I need all of you to do is not tell him. And don't let him leave that room on the RV. Someone can bring him food. He can pee in a bottle. Whatever. I'm going to lay down all the cloaking magic I can. If you can keep him there, they won't find him before I've ended this."

"Do you really think he's just going to accept you disappearing and us not telling him anything?" Jagger said.

"I think doors have locks and he doesn't have any magic to get past them," I said grimly.

The pickup truck had been carrying my main duffel. I stalked over, dug into it, pulled out the jar of shadow-tinged blood from the last time I'd worked on my king's dragon. With the jar in one hand and my wand in the other, I slunk back onto the RV.

Darton was still deep asleep. I couldn't help stopping for a moment to look at him, his arms and legs spread akimbo on the bed, his face gentled by sleep. Even with the blinds closed, the faint light that crept into the room sparked in his gold-blond hair. He had a lot of rest to catch up on after the horror of that day and night in dark fae hands. I hoped he'd sleep a long while yet, for his benefit as well as mine.

He was going to be angry with me. I was absolutely sure of that. But he'd also be alive, and after a while hopefully he'd be able to see that mattered more.

I opened the jar, dipped the end of my wand into the collected blood, and drew a streak of it along the bedroom wall. *"Darkness stretch and darkness hide,"* I murmured. A splinter of pain shot up my arm at the shadow-working, but my magic complied. The dark energy I'd drained from the dragon shimmered up to the ceiling and down to the floor. I dipped the wand back in and drew the line longer, repeating the chant.

The hardest part was tackling the stretch of wall over the bed. I leaned over Darton, reaching my wand across, and he shifted onto his side with a murmur. I froze in place. He hugged the bedspread to him, his brow knitting, but his eyelids didn't even flutter. After a long minute, I finished my reach and slipped around to the other side.

When I connected the line to its tail, the dark shimmer snapped into place around the entire room. A crackling discomfort had spread all through my nerves. Sweat dampened my forehead and the back of my neck. I swiped at it with my sleeve. Then I gave myself one last look at the man my heart had always belonged to.

"Live long and well," I whispered. If I could have made that a spell, I would have.

Jagger was waiting for me outside the RV doors. He took in my weary state with only a crook of his lips.

"This is for you," he said, holding up a key. He motioned to a navy blue sports car parked on the other side of the rest area's lot. "It's full of gas, and it's one of our guy's private vehicles, so you won't stick out like a sore thumb in one all covered with lamps and solar panels. I figured you'd want to get where you're going as fast as possible."

I hadn't even started to think about how I was going to get to Chicago. My throat tightened. "Thank you," I said. "I mean, not just for this—for everything—"

He cleared his throat to cut me off. Were his eyes looking a little misty? "Don't get started with that," he said gruffly. "You know we're good. And I think you'll also be wanting this." He hefted an electro-gun and handed it to me. "I know your magic gets you pretty far, but there's nothing wrong with having backup."

The tightness became a full-out lump. It took me a second to speak. "Thank you, again. You take good care of my king, all right?"

He smiled properly then. "You know I'll do my best. Blew up my house for the two of you already, didn't I? And hey, I'll tell you what. If you can manage to do what you've got to do and still make it back, you can have the story of my scars the next time I see you."

A grin touched my lips despite myself. "Sounds like a deal."

I stopped at the truck again to grab my duffel. I checked the side pocket quickly to confirm my spell-worked knife was still there. Then I tossed everything into the back seat of the sports car —other than the electro-gun and a fresh wand, which I decided to keep in easy reach up front.

Okay. I had everything I needed.

Most of the fae hunters had gotten back into their vehicles now, but they were all watching me. Light only knew what they were thinking of this plan. I gave them a quick wave, because some acknowledgement seemed only polite, and then I slid into the driver's seat. The engine hummed on with a buttery smoothness.

I wasn't going to kid myself. There was almost no chance I'd get to take Jagger up on his offer. I wasn't coming back. But this sacrifice was what my life had been meant for. All my lives. How lucky was I that I'd gotten to have so many of them, frustrating as they'd often been, in the first place? How lucky was I that I'd gotten to know my king over and over, despite the lonely parts in between?

Darton had told me days ago that maybe I should let him go. He'd been right, just not in the way he'd thought. I had to stop clinging to my time with him and go to meet my proper fate.

I hit the gas and turned the car onto the highway toward Chicago.

CHAPTER TWENTY-FIVE

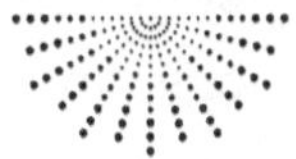

Even if the fae hunters' data readings hadn't pointed us toward Chicago, I'd have known the dark fae had gathered around this place before I even hit the city limits. A supernatural cold stretched across the state for dozens of miles around, too thin for the steel shell of the car to keep out. I shuddered as I slowed into the urban traffic, wishing I could murmur a few words to warm the space. But any light fae magic might bring my enemies running right to me.

The first part of this plan required stealth. The second part... I hadn't quite figured out yet. I was hoping the first part would give me the pieces I needed.

The cold wasn't only in the fae energy saturating the air. A real, physical chill had settled over the city with the deepening night as well. The pedestrians on the sidewalks hurried along with coat collars high and hats pulled low. Frost dappled the edges of the windows. A bitter wind warbled past the car as I drove through the suburbs toward the city core.

From what I was hearing on the radio, the situation on the east coast was even worse. All the major lakes had frozen solid. It had hailed in New York City, chunks of ice big enough to shatter windshields and store windows. But the Darkest One didn't want to make this city too inhospitable. She wouldn't want to scare off the world leaders or the audience she wanted her dragon to devour.

The chill sank deeper into my body until I couldn't stop shivering. I parked on a downtown street, my senses alert for any fae physically nearby, and got out of the car. Walking got my natural energies flowing through my limbs a little more, keeping the cold at bay. And I didn't want to come up on the dark fae's urban enclave too fast.

I wandered the streets until I had a clear sense of it: The dark fae had taken over a section of parkland down by the lake. It looked like a recent installation: a series of neatly winding hedges stretching across a broad span of stone tiles. Just the sort of orderly lines that would appeal to dark fae sensibilities.

I watched from a few blocks away as people ambled toward the hedge garden as if meaning to take a stroll along the paths—and then veered away without a change in expression. A magical barrier like the ones the light fae put up in their woods was "encouraging" the locals to take other routes.

Figures stirred among the hedges, but I couldn't make out any of them clearly. If the Darkest One was there right now, she was out of my view. I'd have been able to sense her essence at the briefest glance. But I could feel her presence in the city in the sharpest jabs of the frigid air against my cheeks and hands.

The fae probably already had some idea I was in the area. All their previous actions suggested they'd been keeping an eye on my movements. But the Darkest One wanted me and my king to come *to* her. If I didn't push the matter, I could hope she'd be content to wait for my next move.

And *she* might have been, but a few minutes later, it became clear not all of her minions were of the same mind. Three figures shrouded in shadow, two male and one female from what I could make out of their features, slipped away from the hedge garden and headed my way.

My back stiffened. I wasn't ready for a confrontation. And how the hell was I ever going to get close enough to take on the Darkest One if the other fae perked up before I was near enough to even see her? I'd used up almost all of my willow ash—

Oh. The thought struck me like a zap of electricity. There was the inspiration I'd been looking for.

Instead of trying to paint myself into a dark fae, I could simply step right inside one, couldn't I? There'd be no better disguising my true nature than that.

The dark fae were approaching steadily. I faded back down the street, making for my car. If this was going to work, I needed to do it as far from the other dark fae as possible. No one could suspect the switch.

My fae senses tingled as the three followed me. They were only half a block away when I hopped into the car. I pulled onto the road and drove away from them as if I meant to flee. But I didn't challenge the speed limits even a little. I wanted them behind me but keeping up.

They fell back in the first minute, but after that they kept pace. They must have been tracing my energies the way I followed theirs at the edge of my awareness. I led them on a winding path through the city core and south into an industrial area that was even darker and nearly vacant this late at night.

When I hadn't seen or sensed another being in five minutes, I pulled over outside an abandoned warehouse. I picked up my wand and the electro-gun. Then I got out of the car and leaned against the hood to wait.

My followers emerged from the shadows by the street corner a moment later. They fanned out, the woman coming straight at me and the two men moving to circle around me. I held the electro-gun down by my side where it wasn't quite as noticeable. These ones might not have been in the groups that had engaged the fae hunters before. They might not even know what the weapon I held could do. Surprise would always work in my favor.

"What are you doing, fae-in-a-human-suit?" the woman said in a hiss of a voice. "Where is your pet king?"

"Do you really think I'm going to answer that question?" I said. "How stupid do you think I am?"

The dark fae sneered, which meant pretty darn stupid. "I'm sorry to disappoint," I said. "If you want any info from me, you're going to have to drag it out of me."

"A process I suspect I'll enjoy," the woman said, and lunged. Her lips moved at the same time, spitting out a spell. I jerked my wand to dispel it, snapping a line of my own at the same time. The man at my right whipped a lash of dark magic toward me too. As I whirled to meet it, the third fae joined in.

I wanted them closer. I had to hold on before I showed my entire hand. I cast a bolt of light in one direction and dodged the other spell. It clipped me in the shoulder, sending a searing chill down my arm. The electro-gun slipped an inch in my grasp before I caught it. But the fae were closing in on me, exactly the way I wanted. I bit back a whimper and swung the weapon into the air.

"*Darkness fall and darkness dull,*" I shouted, gripping my wand and pressing the gun's trigger at the same time. As I spun around, a stream of electricity slammed out all across the street, urged on by my spell. It smacked all three fae across the head. They crumpled to the ground. Not dead—I wasn't using my one hope at producing that level of power on these lackeys—but unconscious, and hopefully for a while.

The exertion had left me panting. The wand had turned dark and brittle. I tossed it aside and grabbed a fresh one from the trunk.

I was getting low again. And this was the last of my supply anywhere. But then, I didn't expect to be needing them again after tonight.

I walked to each of the fae, keeping the electro-gun and the wand pointed at them. Over the two men, I cast a binding spell across their arms and mouths with a little zap from the gun for extra oomph. If they woke up sooner than I hoped, it would take them some time to break free from that spell.

Then I chucked the weapon in the car and bent down beside the dark fae woman. "I can promise you I'm not going to enjoy *this* at all," I said to her limp form.

Gritting my teeth, I dragged her to the car and pushed her into the back. To give this plan the best possible chance, I couldn't be finishing it here at the scene of this crime against dark fae kind.

I drove farther into the industrial district until I came across an alley so narrow I could only just squeeze the car into it and so dark I couldn't see more than a few feet inside. I pulled in until the darkness closed around the car. Then I flipped on the overhead light so I could see what I was doing.

The dark fae woman lay motionless as I dug a stick of incense and the knife out of my bag. With a snap of my fingers, I lit the incense and set it, burning, on the dashboard. Then I tipped the driver's seat back as far as it would go and held up my left arm.

I'd studied human anatomy for enough years that the spread of muscles, tendons, and bones beneath the skin were more familiar to me than my current face was in the mirror. I knew exactly where and how deeply to cut.

A slow bleed, that was what I wanted. I didn't know how long it would take me to get to the Darkest One. If this body died too soon, I might not be able to use the sacrifice against her to full effect. Eight hours—that should be enough.

I dug the blade into my skin. My breath hitched at the sting. A thin line down the wrist, just enough to let the blood start seeping out.

"*I give my life to take another's,*" I murmured, putting all my conviction into the words. "*I give my light to squash the greatest darkness. Lend me the power to shatter her shadows.*"

A tremor ran through me. I couldn't tell whether it was the

magic's acceptance of my sacrifice or just my body objecting to its death. Maybe both.

I sagged back in the seat and closed my eyes. As I inhaled, the herbal smoke of the incense filled my lungs. My soul loosened within its shell of flesh. I cast myself up—and into the sprawled body behind me.

My spirit cringed the second I dipped into the dark fae's shadowy body. Every inch of her being made my consciousness burn. But that was why I needed her. All that dark essence would disguise my small soul hiding inside her.

Her own awareness stirred faintly as I settled into her mind. I could control her body easily, if not comfortably, while she stayed unconscious. If my knock-out spell faded before I'd done my job here, my sight-riding was going to become a lot more difficult.

So I'd better get going.

I opened her eyes. There was Emma's body, slumped in the driver's seat, dribbling blood onto the car floor. Nausea trickled through my spirit without reaching the dark fae's stomach. *Her* essence approved of that sight.

Testing the woman's limbs, I eased myself onto my feet. The sunroof opened when I gave it a sharp yank. I climbed out, slid down the back window, and walked out of the alley.

I had an appointment with the Darkest One to keep, even if she didn't know it yet.

CHAPTER TWENTY-SIX

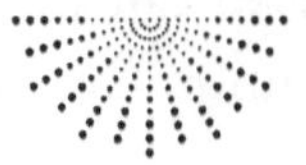

EVEN WITH MY new dark fae suit, as the woman I was wearing had so poetically referred to my human form, it would have been stupid to go charging into the middle of a crowd of dark fae. I ambled up the sidewalk across from the park slowly, watching the activity in that makeshift enclave.

The walk from where I'd stashed my car had given me plenty of time to familiarize myself with this body and its reflexes. The dark burn still nagged at my spirit, prickling through all my thoughts, but dully enough that I managed to ignore it. I could appreciate the fact that the wind's chill seemed to brush right past my dark fae shell. No wonder she hadn't thought anything of walking around with nothing more than a thin trench coat over her old-fashioned blouse and slacks.

My hand drifted to the trench coat's lower right pocket. My fingers ran over the hard line of the narrow shard of glass I'd picked up on my way. I couldn't have brought my light fae enchanted knife with me and expected no one to notice, but that temporary blade would work just as well.

I passed a few dark fae who'd wandered farther across the park's lawns. None of them gave me a second glance—or even a first, in most cases. The dark fae liked order, and they usually found it much easier to maintain if they kept to themselves,—unlike the light fae, who preferred to live in groups with all the chaos that came with clashing wants and personalities.

In my original time, the dark fae had all given respect to the Darkest One, but they hadn't banded together in anywhere near these numbers. She must have called on every dark fae that could reach this end of the country in time for her grand act of destruction.

As I approached the hedge garden, a dark fae elder who was more shadow than figure stepped out to meet me. My host's heart jumped in response to my apprehension, but the man merely looked me over with a curl of his lips and said, "Straighten your shirt. Our lady wants to see us at our best."

Ah. My host's blouse had gotten a little rumpled in our fight. I smoothed her hands over the cool silk, and the elder nodded approvingly. There was no hint at all in his expression that he'd sensed anything off. No wonder. The dark energy encasing me felt as if it was outright gnawing away at the edges of my soul.

That didn't mean the Darkest One wouldn't notice. A little more time for my soul to settle in before I sought her out would work in my favor. Especially because I had another concern to address first.

"Has the king come looking for his friends yet?" I asked.

The elder frowned. "Have you not eyes? If he were here, our lady would make no secret of it."

I could also appreciate the dark fae tendency toward speaking their minds instead of rambling off into vague poetics. I clasped the fae woman's hands in front of me, resisting the urge to twist my fingers together. A dark fae wouldn't fidget. "Perhaps if we caused them more distress, he might feel the urgency of the situation."

"Humans don't sense feelings that way," the elder said. "They are duller than most animals. He's barely fit to hold our lady's conjuring. But he will come. They also have no self-control."

He drifted away without giving me a chance to ask any more questions. Well, he hadn't been all that helpful anyway. I drifted along the fringes of the park, looking for another opportunity.

Maybe a fae a little less mature, a little more eager to please. The body around me wasn't *that* young. I'd guess, from the gritty tingling of the energy around me, she had at least five hundred years. Who could I exert a little authority over here?

Ah ha. A slip of a fae man with only the thinnest shadow clinging to his skin was entertaining himself by blackening the leaves on the side of a hedge, one by one. He smirked to himself in delight as he killed another. My light fae sensibilities shuddered, but I made myself walk up to him.

"You there," I said in a firm, even voice. "I heard we're holding humans at our lady's request. I have a taste for fear tonight. Where are they tucked away?"

The young fae blinked at me, looking startled that anyone had bothered to so much as talk to him. Then an even more wicked grin split his narrow face. "I saw them brought in," he bragged. "They're in the basement of the boarded-up bar down the way." He pointed, and then raised a careful eyebrow at me. "Perhaps I could join you."

I gave him my best darkly imperious stare. "I prefer to indulge alone."

The young fae deflated. Then he turned right back to his hobby of murdering leaves, so I left him to it without the slightest bit of guilt. Other than maybe over my inability to rescue the hedge.

A few blocks down the street, I spotted a bar that indeed had plywood boards nailed across its windows. Someone had spray-painted various swear words and a comically large penis on the wall. Lovely. I ducked around back to the alley there.

Glooms coated the bar's back door and windows, but they parted when I stepped toward them. Apparently this dark fae body got me full access. I knelt down to peer through the barred window that gave a view into the basement. If our friends already had dark fae company, I'd have to strategize around that.

It appeared the dark fae hadn't thought a full guard was necessary. The glooms and whatever magic they'd cast around this place would keep any wandering human beings away for the time being, and probably would have stopped me from tracing the three figures inside if I'd been trying to by my usual means. All the full fae wanted to be on hand for when the big show started, no doubt. Keevan, Izzy, and Priya were alone in the dim concrete room.

They'd been locked up in separate cages like the kind you might have crated a large dog in, a foot of space between them. Shadow magic coiled around the locks and the borders of the room. Priya was huddled in the corner of her cage, hugging her knees, but her eyes were open and wary. Keevan and Izzy had pressed up against the sides of their cages closest to each other.

When I first looked in, they had their arms stretched between the bars, hands clasped in the space between them. As I watched, Keevan murmured something to Izzy. She nodded, and he raised his hand to caress her cheek. She leaned into his touch, her lips forming a tight smile.

My heart squeezed. Maybe that was just friendly comfort. Or maybe Keevan had finally found the courage to tell Izzy how much he cared about her. Either way, I was torn between gladness for them and a pang that I was never going to have another moment like that with Darton.

I couldn't afford to waste time on mourning what was done, though. If our friends were still prisoners when I took down the Darkest One, there'd be nothing stopping her minions from killing them—in light knew what sort of torment—as revenge.

I eased open the back door and crept down the steps to the basement. All three of my friends tensed as I reached the bottom of the stairs. Keevan and Izzy pulled apart. Keevan shifted forward in his cage, as if he thought he could somehow defend her from behind those bars.

The less I said, the better. I started with Priya's cage, closest to me. She stared at me as I dipped my hands into the shadows binding the lock. They wisped eagerly around my host's dark fae hands, and my spirit winced. Ignoring the deeper jab of discomfort, I twisted the dark energy to my will. It fit into the lock —and clicked the mechanism over.

Priya's eyes grew even wider when I tugged the door open. She braced herself against the back of the cage, but I left her and moved to Keevan's. As I bent those shadows, an acid chill hazed over my thoughts. I gritted my teeth against the burn and moved on to Izzy's cage.

By the time I'd unlocked it and swung the door open, my mind was reeling. It took all my energy to pull myself stiffly upright.

"Go," I said, pointing to the stairs. "Get out of here, as far as you can."

Priya had already edged out of the cage. Keevan and Izzy followed suit, looking bewildered. Priya's forehead furrowed. My former roommate took a step closer to me, her eyes narrowing.

"Emmaline?" she said. "You're in there, aren't you? It's got to be you. This doesn't make any sense otherwise."

Swine crud. "Do I look like an Emmaline to you?" I said, motioning to myself. "Weren't you listening? You have to get out of here before anyone else comes."

My refusal to admit who I was didn't stop Priya from beaming. Keevan's expression relaxed too. Izzy grabbed his hand.

"What can we do now that we're out?" she said. "How can we help stop them from getting to Darton?"

Sodding hell, his friends were stubborn. "If you want to help Darton, the best thing you can do is make a run for it," I said, dropping most of the pretense. "You're the bait. You're the only reason he'd come here. Find him and the fae hunters, and show you're okay so he'll stay put."

Keevan made a scoffing sound. "While you're running around here in someone else's body with who knows what kind of crazy plan? I don't think so. If you're here, then Darton will be coming too."

I didn't intend to be here much longer, but if I told them that part of my plan, I had the feeling they'd insist on sticking around too, while trying to talk me out of it. Instead I motioned to the stairs again. "It doesn't matter. Just get going. I don't know how often the dark fae have been checking on you."

Finally, they started moving. Keevan and Izzy hurried up the stairs. Priya paused for a second to bob her head to me.

"Whatever you're doing, good luck with it, Emmaline," she said in her bright voice. Then she darted up after the others.

I looked around the room, but I couldn't see any way of hiding their escape, not without using my light fae powers and drawing so much more attention to this spot. As soon as anyone came by, they'd realize someone had let the prisoners out. I'd just have to hope that fact would work in my favor. If the dark fae were busy trying to figure out where their hostages had gotten to, they'd be less likely to notice me making a move on their "lady."

My friends were already out of sight when I emerged from the bar's basement. I wandered down the alley, which ran behind the backs of several stores, and meandered around the next few blocks. Gradually, I made my way back to the park. The roundabout route both gave my soul time to recover from the dark magic work and should have prevented anyone who saw me return from realizing where I was coming from.

I ambled by the hedge garden again. None of the dark fae drifting between them looked at me with any suspicion. Time to work my way closer and figure out where exactly my ultimate target was lurking.

I headed down one of the walkways between the hedges—and my host's pulse hiccupped. Panic flashed through my mind. Her spirit was twitching, deep in her head beneath my awareness. I hadn't managed to knock her out for anywhere near long enough.

The sense of her soul, like a fizzing thundercloud beneath my mind, stabbed up at me with a sudden blow. I pressed down at her with all of my will, but that left my control over her body shaky.

Her feet stumbled. She fell against the side of the hedge. I wrenched her upright while still grappling with the angry spirit trying to unseat me.

If I'd been alone, I could have risked a quick spell to silence her, even for just a little longer. I staggered around and found two older dark fae studying me.

"You seem unwell," one said with a frown. "Is something the matter?"

My tongue tangled before I manage to wrestle back full control over it. I stomped down on the fae woman's spirit with all the strength in my soul.

"I'm fine," I said. "Completely fine. Just not used to being in such a large crowd. I think I'd better step aside for a few minutes to clear my head."

The excuse might have worked if my host's soul had been just a little weaker. I made to stride past the two fae and their apparent concern, and she smacked my consciousness with a punch of energy that threw my coordination off all over again. I jammed my will back down on her, but at the same time her body swayed. It fell to one knee.

The other fae grasped my arm to help me up. "You look more than just overwhelmed to me," she said. "We'll take you to our lady. Whatever's wrong with you, she'll know how to cure it."

CHAPTER TWENTY-SEVEN

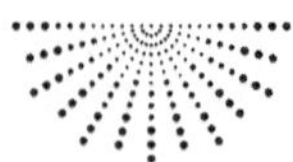

TAKE YOU TO OUR LADY. The words echoed through my mind with an even deeper cold than that brought on by the dark fae presence around me.

The older fae ignored my hasty attempts at humbleness —"Really, I'll be all right. She has so much to occupy her without bothering with me."—and ushered me farther down the paved paths between the hedges. There was no way I could protest more, not without giving away that I wasn't supposed to be there at all. Any real dark fae would have seen a chance to be attended to by the Darkest One as the highest possible honor.

The chill in the air, both supernatural and physical, thickened as we went. It seemed to enliven my host's soul. She shoved at me, and I shoved back, only just managed to keep my feet moving one step after another at the same time. Her eyelids stuttered. Her mouth opened and closed as she tried to speak. I snapped back control at the last second.

I could still do this. Maybe I hadn't meant my plan to proceed quite like this, but I'd wanted to reach the Darkest One. I'd just have to make do with the circumstances I'd been given. All that mattered was keeping my head—my host's head, really—long enough to see my intention through.

We came around the end of a hedge. A wind whipped over me that jittered through my host's nerves and nearly froze my spirit solid. Breath caught in my host's lungs with both her awe and my horror.

The Darkest One had fashioned herself a throne of sorts out of dead, twisted branches from the hedges. Its jagged form sat by the edge of the stone tile dais that overlooked the lake.

My greatest enemy perched on it, her narrow eyes glinting as dark as the water beyond her. They were the sharpest part of her body. The rest of her ancient figure seeped like living shadow over and between the brambles in the hazy shape of a tall, elegant woman. Her gray hair drifted around her wavering face like a storm cloud on the verge of bursting. Power thrummed off her even as she sat completely still.

"What's this you've brought me?" she said in an arch tone. Her voice was as cool and dry as autumn leaves long fallen.

"Apologies for disturbing you, great one," one of my supposed helpers said with a tip of his head. "This young one appears to be experiencing some strange distress. We hoped you could find the cause and see it gone."

The Darkest One shifted forward, tendrils of shadow streaming off her body as they clung to her throne. Her hazy lips pursed. My host's soul squirmed beneath me, wriggling and jabbing to try to break free. I rammed her down with a mental pummel, and her body stumbled forward. But that was okay, because I still had enough coordination to dig my hand into her coat's right pocket. My fingers closed around the long shard of glass.

"I bring a gift," I gasped out. "For my lady. *Shatter this body, shatter her darkness!*"

As the words spilled from my lips, I whipped the blade of glass out of the pocket and stabbed it at my host's throat. A surge of magical energy swelled through my mind—

And the dark fae spirit hurled herself at me in the last moment. Her arm jerked just an inch to the side. The glass sliced across the side of her neck. Pain lanced through the flesh, but I'd missed the killing blow.

"*Halt*," the Darkest One said before I could regain control. A magical vice locked around my host's body. My host's lips froze, parted. Freezing air tickled over her tongue. My soul shuddered, and the Darkest One's magic clamped around it too.

I couldn't even attempt a leap back to my own body if I'd wanted to. I couldn't do anything except hold there, staring. Together, my host's spirit and mine watched the Darkest One approach us through unblinking eyes.

I wanted to cringe back from that dark, fathomless gaze, but I couldn't so much as shiver. My greatest enemy stopped a few paces from where my host stood like a statue. She cocked her head, shadows trickling to the side with the movement. Her lips curled into a smirk. She let out a low chuckle.

"My dear Merlin. You've finally shown your face. Well, not your real face, but it's your soul that matters the most, isn't it? The same soul that sealed me away for all those wretched centuries. But what *have* you done with that ridiculous human body you've been inhabiting?"

Her gaze fell to the shard still clenched in my host's hand. The edge of it had broken the skin of the fae woman's palm. Blood was beading along it and dripping down its length, untethered by the spell that had frozen the rest of her body.

"Ah," the Darkest One said. "Even you would know better than to try to make a sacrifice solely with someone else's life, wouldn't you? We can't have any of that mischief here. You won't be dying until I say it's time, little halfling abomination."

She drifted forward, reaching out her hand. Every ounce of my being screamed to pull away from her, but her spell held my host's body and my soul fast. The Darkest One's fingers grazed my host's thick bangs and settled against the fae woman's forehead. She murmured a few words under her breath.

A pinching sensation ran through my spirit. I'd have flinched if I could move. The Darkest One massaged her fingertips against my host's forehead as if drawing something loose from the skin.

I felt, with a shiver of understanding, what she was doing. She was tracing the thin cord of belonging that kept my soul connected to my body even at this distance, the one that would have pulled me back to it if I'd been able to let it.

After a moment, the Darkest One stepped back. Her shadows coiled around her gauzy limbs. She looked at the two fae who'd brought me to her, who were now standing nearly as motionless as my host in their shock.

"I need you to retrieve something for me," she said, and rattled off an address that I had no doubt was that of one of the buildings I'd parked the blue sports car in between. "Find the body, bring it here quickly. I want it alive."

The fae nodded with nervous jerks of their heads and swept off into the shadows around the hedges. The Darkest One turned back to me. We were alone now—well, the two of us and the dark fae woman whose soul was as frozen as mine.

"You do seem to have some sort of obsession with trying to be what you're not, halfling," she said, waggling a filmy finger. "It'll never lead you to anything good."

I'd done all right with that approach for fifteen hundred years before now, but I couldn't open my host's mouth to point that out.

"Uncomfortable, isn't it?" she went on, her near-black eyes peering into my host's as if she could see the shimmer of my spirit through them. "Being trapped, unable to move, unable to speak, cut off from the world and from your magic? It's only been a few minutes, and you're already hating it. Imagine spending fifteen centuries in that state, little wizard. Imagine how much you'd hate the one who did that to you by the end of it."

Her voice had stayed cool, but a crackle like breaking ice crept into the last sentence. Oh, light save me. I could imagine, and whatever she felt was probably a hundred times worse even than that. And now she was going to take it out not just on me, but as many living things as she could.

She had me. I couldn't see any way out of this. I had no magic without a voice, without the ability to even move. My enemy wasn't likely to accidentally let me out of these bindings. What could I even hope for?

"So I think I'll keep you in this state for a good long while," the Darkest One said. "You might as well get to witness my greatest work, which I'll be putting on even greater display now that there are so many more humans in such a small space." She grinned. Placing a chilly hand on my host's shoulder, she turned us toward the other end of the dais where it ended at a grassy field. A temporary stage had already been set up at the far end of the broad lawn.

"That's where so many of this world's human leaders will be gathering tomorrow," she said. "And all the other humans who wish to catch a glimpse. I'll crack open your king and watch all those mortals swallowed up, and you will watch it too. What a triumph. And it'll only be the beginning."

She'd given herself a front row seat with that throne. But she wouldn't get my king. *That* was the best I could hope for. The fae hunters would keep him far away from here... long enough for her attention to waver and for me to get another chance?

I wasn't sure that would happen in another fifteen hundred years.

The Darkest One stood gazing over the field in silence for what felt like a long time. The wind stirred the shadows so they rippled around her. That horrible grin stayed on her face. Was she picturing her triumph, playing it out in her head?

Fabric hissed against the ground behind me. The Darkest One shifted my host's body as she moved to meet the arriving fae.

The two she'd sent after my body had returned victorious. They were dragging my limp figure by the arms. One of them had bound my left wrist with a strip of cloth. Drying blood stained the hand below it. But not enough. Not enough to have transformed my life's energy into a killing blow.

"Excellent," the Darkest One said. She motioned for them to prop my body against the nearest hedge. My head lolled. She jerked it upright and spoke a few magic-tinged words to freeze it in place the way she had my host's.

"All right, halfling. Time for you to take your proper place."

She spat out a phrase and whipped her hand between my host's body and my own. With a lurch, my soul shot back into its home. The world outside swam before my eyes as the sensations of my body came into focus. Stiffened limbs, thumping heart. The acid taste of panic in my mouth. An ache on my wrist. I was just as frozen as before.

"*Free,*" the Darkest One said, and the fae woman I'd been riding jerked back to life like a puppet whose strings had been abruptly grabbed. She stumbled and caught her balance. Then she dropped to her knees in front of her lady.

"Greatest one, I fought her, I stopped her. I—"

"You let her take your body and use it as a weapon against me," the Darkest One snapped.

Her hands shot out, so quickly I couldn't tell whether they actually touched the fae woman or merely cast magic around her. The woman's head wrenched sideways with a sickening crack of her neck. Her body tumbled over like it had when I'd flung my spell at her—except not. Because this time she wasn't waking up.

The Darkest One swept her arm through the air. The wind rushed over the fae woman's body and flung it over the edge of the dais into the lake. My stomach roiled.

The Darkest One wiped her hands together. "That's done now. All we have left to do is wait. I've gotten a lot of practice at that. You couldn't stop me, could you, Merlin? Not forever. Every delay comes to an end. Light fades, and darkness remains."

No, I wanted to scream at her. My voice was locked in my throat. Was this what my efforts to protect the world from her darkness would come to? It might have been better for everyone if I'd let her draw forth her dragon all those centuries ago. One ruler destroyed, one country in chaos, instead of dozens.

But she couldn't know the outcome for sure. The light hadn't faded yet. She didn't have my king.

As if she could read my thoughts, the dark fae chuckled. "Do you doubt me? Don't you worry, halfling. The king you've made a fool of yourself over is coming. He's already on his way."

CHAPTER TWENTY-EIGHT

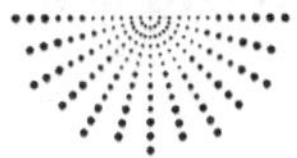

THE SUN ROSE UNBEARABLY SLOWLY, and yet far too fast. With its first gleam over the horizon on the lake, it woke me from the uneasy doze I'd managed to fall into. As its beams stretched across the park, spectators spilled into the field around the stage where the World Peace Summit would open its series of talks. The Darkest One lounged on her throne, watching them with a languid smile.

Darton hadn't come. She didn't look concerned, but that might be a front. Or maybe it didn't matter to her that much when exactly she dealt out her wave of destruction.

I could hope that she'd been bluffing when she'd said he was on his way. She'd wanted to torment me, of course. She'd known that was the best way.

Or she'd been telling the truth, and he just hadn't gotten here quite yet.

If I could have stretched my awareness beyond my body, I might have been able to determine the answer. But the spell that kept my body frozen also made a prison for my mind. I couldn't feel anything with my fae senses beyond the boundaries of my skin.

Posh black cars started to park along the road beside the park, down near the stage. Presidents and prime ministers followed a path marked through the swelling crowd, flanked by security officers. Cameras flashed. The murmurs rose.

No one in the audience paid any mind to the swarm of dark fae just a couple hundred feet away from them. The Darkest One's magic and their excitement for the event were working together to keep them distracted. She probably could have been setting off fireworks over here and they'd barely have heard a sound.

When all of the seats on the stage had been filled, the World Peace Summit's host stepped up to its edge with a microphone. His cheerful voice rang across the field, totally at odds with the apprehension that filled my body. He grinned at the crowd, said something about appreciating their enthusiasm despite the chilly weather, stirred up a few laughs. Then he presented the first topic of conversation, and the various national leaders started to say their bit one by one.

The audience pressed closer to the stage as more people trickled into the park to join them. No Darton. No triumph. The sun shone bright and clear in the stark blue sky. Cold as I was, its beams managed to bring me a small warmth. Just for a minute, the dread that was twisted inside me began to relax.

Then the Darkest One stood up. Her head turned away from the stage, toward the downtown buildings visible over the hedges behind me. I'd have followed her gaze, but my head was still locked by her spell. All I knew was that the smile that curled her thin lips squeezed the air from my lungs.

A few of her underlings hustled over to consult with her in low voices. Their lady never stopped smiling. She motioned them away with a flick of her shadowy hand.

"Let them try. They cannot enter. When you see the one I need, bring him to me. We will keep this neat and tidy."

A neat and tidy reign of destruction. How typically dark fae.

Every nerve urged me to move, to leap at her, to race to find my king, but of course I couldn't move so much as the tip of my finger. The Darkest One turned her smirk on me.

"And now you see exactly what your king is made of, halfling. Or should I say, what I have made inside him. I expect all those centuries of stewing have only made it more—"

The air seemed to hiccup. A shock of electricity smacked into me with the zap of a static charge. Yelps and grunts burst out all through the hedge garden. The Darkest One merely twitched, her lips pursing. My body flinched.

It flinched—it moved! I didn't know where that electric jolt had come from, but it had shocked me free from the dark magic that had bound me. The Darkest One's gaze jerked to me. Before she could spit out the words to renew her spell, I threw myself down the path between the hedges.

The muscles in my legs ached from holding the same position for hours. The dark fae amid the hedges were running this way and that. I staggered among them, snatching at the sides of the hedge. The brambles bit into my hands, but twigs snapped off in my grasp.

The air had filled with a familiar hiss and crackle. The fae hunters' weapons. They were somewhere to my right—they'd managed to launch an attack.

And Darton had to be over there with them. That thought filled my entire mind. I had to get to him before the Darkest One did.

One of the frantic dark fae noticed me running past. He hurled a bolt of dark magic at me. I dodged it, stumbling into the hedge. The chill of it seared past my temple. Ears ringing, I ducked and shouted a spell back at him. One of my twigs crumbled into a blast of light. It sent the fae reeling backward, and I dashed onward.

The sweep of electricity through the hedge garden must have dissolved the spells warding people away too. Human voices carried over the hedges. A fae hunter I recognize but couldn't name charged into my view, zapping the dark fae in front of her with an electro-gun.

Another fae sprang at her from behind. She whirled around, only just managing to catch the spell he was whipping at her before it caught her with full force. It shattered around the stream of electricity, but the shadowy shards cut across her face. She cried out.

The three fae around her closed in. "*Darkness begone!*" I yelled, grasping another handful of twigs. A wave of light rocked the fae, giving the hunter time to whirl with her gun. I couldn't stay to make sure she could keep holding her own. My king needed me more. Wishing her luck and speed, I scrambled down the next path.

Voices were hollering all around me now, human and fae mingling together. Another wave of expelled static electricity rushed over us, leaving my nerves jittering and the fae flinching backward. But it wasn't enough to stop them. I darted around another bend in the path to see a fae hunter sprawled on the ground, his eyes deathly wide, a clot of shadow clogging his mouth.

My stomach turned. I had to find Darton. Where the hell was my king?

As if in answer, the warble of a sword singing through the air— the song of a blade in harmony with the soul that held it—reached my ears. Excalibur. And it would only sound like that when one specific person wielded it.

A cluster of dark fae appeared behind me. They propelled a surge of dark energy my way. I plunged my hands into the hedge. "*Let me fly!*"

My magic tossed me up and over the brambles. I landed on my hands and knees, the swing of a gleaming blade bouncing sunlight into my eyes. Darton was standing some ten feet down the path, Jagger at his left and Yasmin at his right. A stunned dark fae lay at my kings feet, but more pressed close to them.

Darton slashed out with his sword while Jagger blasted their attackers with flames and Yasmin sent out a bolt of electricity. It wasn't quite enough. One of the dark fae's spells smacked Jagger in the head. He squeezed the trigger of his flamethrower for one last spurt of fire, but he was already staggering backward.

I threw myself forward. "*Shield him, save him,*" I said, my fingers closing around my handful of twigs. A flare of light arced over Jagger's falling body. He crumpled—unconscious or dead, I couldn't tell—but the next bolt of darkness aimed at him shattered against the shield. The bubble of light wavered. It wouldn't hold very long against a dark fae onslaught.

"Em!" Darton dodged one spell and smashed another with a swipe of his sword. He sidestepped closer to me. "You're all right."

"Only relatively speaking," I muttered, and barked out another flash of light to fend off a dark fae's attack. "*You* won't be. You're not supposed to be here. I told them—"

I had to stop talking to cast up another temporary shield of light. Darton jabbed at a dark fae who pushed too close, and the fae flinched away, clutching her chest.

"I'm the *only* one who's supposed to be here," he said, breathless from the exertion. "I remembered—I know what I need to do. This is my battle, Merlin. It always was."

What in light's name was he talking about? "You don't understand," I said. "You can't fight her. You have no idea how much power she holds."

Darton let out a raw chuckle. "But I do. I've got it inside me. Where is she?"

"No. You're not doing this. I'm getting you out of here."

I reached for him, ready to pull him to me and shout the words to apparate us away like I had before. Darton pushed me back, gently but firmly. "No. I refuse. I have to do this, Em."

"You *can't*—"

Another electric sizzle washed over us and rattled the words from my mouth. Thankfully, it rattled the dark fae that were rushing at us even more. They faltered, and Yasmin took the opportunity to blast them with a much more concentrated jolt.

I gripped Darton's arm as he swung Excalibur. My magic sent a scythe of light spiraling through the air in the wake of his attack. It smacked into the dark fae and tossed them over the hedge.

"What *is* that electric pulse thing?" I said, rubbing my arms. The hairs were standing up all over them.

"That thing that just hit us?" Darton whirled to face a few fae that were springing at us from the other side of the path. "Howard came up with that. It takes a while to generate enough power for the electrical field to hit the whole area even briefly. Otherwise he'd just keep it going the whole time. But it's handy, isn't it?"

"It might be the only reason we're not already dead." I snatched up more twigs and called my magic into Darton's next strike of his blade. I couldn't give him enough power. The dark fae stumbled backward, but they were already shouting out more spells. I shoved my hand deep into the hedge, clasping my fingers around one of the thicker branches.

"We've got to hit them with everything we have," I said. If we could knock out all the lesser dark fae, maybe I could get Darton out of here before the Darkest One descended on us. I didn't want to abandon the fae hunters to be slaughtered. But if he could see we had a real opening to escape—

"Ready," Darton said, bracing himself with his sword raised. I clamped my other hand onto his shoulder. I opened my mouth.

And a wave of darkness burst over us with a shuddering force. The shadow's thrust wrenched me away from the hedge and from Darton. He tripped, clutching Excalibur as he caught his balance.

The hedges in front of us crumbled into ash as the Darkest One drifted down to stand before us.

"*Halt*," she said. Her magic snapped into place around me again, holding my body rigid. Darton froze too. The Darkest One smiled and stepped toward him.

CHAPTER TWENTY-NINE

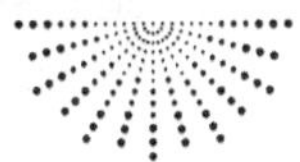

"Oh, ambitious human king," the Darkest One cooed. "I've waited so long for this moment. And you've so kindly come right to me. Did you really think you stood a chance? Look at you and your wizard. You've got nothing that's a match for my power."

It was difficult to argue with that while her magic bound us, helpless, but Darton somehow managed to glare. The Darkest One snickered, amused by his anger. My lungs seized as she brushed her shadow-laced hand over his gold-blond hair in a gesture that could almost have passed for affectionate. Affection for the monster she'd grown inside him, maybe.

When her magic had thrown me away from the hedge, the branch I'd been gripping had snapped off with me. I still had it clenched in my rigid hand. Its green pulse of living energy tingled against my palm. If I could just break free long enough to say a few words of a spell...

I pleaded with my nerves, but I couldn't convince a single twitch of a muscle.

The Darkest One spun around with a sweeping gesture. All of the hedges between us and her throne crumbled away. Bodies lay scattered on the ground between the ruined brambles. Most of them were human forms. The dark fae edged closer, watching eagerly.

The Darkest One waved her arm again, without even looking at us. Her magic propelled our frozen bodies forward. We drifted along behind her as she stalked back to her throne. She stopped us with a sharp gesture when she was standing in front of it. Then she turned, her fathomless eyes glittering amid the shadows that formed her face.

"Watch and know how useless you are, little wizard," she sneered. She stepped right up to Darton. My heart wrenched so hard it might as well have burst out of my chest. The Darkest One raised her hands—

And another wave of static electricity shot across the hedge garden.

The spell binding us shivered apart. I leapt at the Darkest One, my muscles coiled, the branch clutched in my hand. Darton brandished his sword. I whipped my arm around, ready to dredge up every shred of magic I could find in my body. But my hand jerked toward Darton.

In my panic, I'd forgotten the oath. The itch of it surged up through my arms and clawed over my tongue. *Kill him, kill him before she takes him.* A spell sputtered over my lips. My fingers clenched tighter around the branch as they jabbed it at his chest.

I closed my eyes and jammed my teeth down into my tongue. My feet tangled under me. The taste of blood, sharp and metallic, flooded my mouth. My body kept hurtling toward my king—until the Darkest One smacked her fist into my skull.

I staggered backward, reeling from the blow. Pain filled with dark sparks of magic radiated through my head. The oath dulled, but so did my mind.

The Darkest One loomed over Darton again. He backed up, holding Excalibur between them. She flicked the tip of the sword's blade with fingers trailing shadow and laughed.

"You think too highly of your halfling abomination's work, soon-to-be-fallen king. Do you really think this little sword can hurt *me*?"

Darton hefted the sword over his head. Just as he had all those centuries ago when he'd faced our greatest enemy for the first time. When I'd given him that memory through my eyes a week ago, he'd commented that the angle had looked odd. Now, seeing it as I struggled to set my thoughts back in order, the shape of his stance suddenly made sense. Oh. No. *No.*

I opened my mouth to form that protest out loud, to throw whatever spell my addled mind could produce between the two of them. But right then Darton glanced at me. My king's soul shone back at me through his eyes. The way he'd looked at me yesterday when he'd told me he'd loved me. Utterly.

Always.

I stopped, understanding washing over me. This was his battle. I'd tried so hard to fight it for him, but he'd seen the full picture for what it was.

Darton shifted his gaze back to the Darkest One. "No, I don't," he said. "But the sword isn't for you. It's for me. Me and *my* dragon."

Confusion stuttered across the Darkest One's expression. Then her eyes widened.

My king heaved his sword in a downward arc and plunged it into his chest.

The Darkest One shrieked. She snatched at Darton's body as it crumpled, as if she thought she could catch his life before it left him. And maybe she could have, if all my king had meant to do was end that life.

But it wasn't. A shadow plumed around the blade where it protruded from his chest. The wind whipped up over the dais, shoving me back. It whirled the shadow larger, faster, wings spreading, claws extending.

The dragon swelled over the entire hedge garden, casting its darkness across the lake and field as well. The icy chill of its presence pierced my skin. The audience around the platform scattered. Screams and frantic babbling filled the air.

The Darkest One threw her hands toward her creation. "You are *mine*," she hollered. "Mine! You will obey my commands. Destroy them!"

She pointed at the field, but the dragon born of my king's sacrifice swung its massive head toward her. Its eyes glowed like hot coals in its vicious face as they fixed on the fae woman who had once been its master. Its jaws yawned open, revealing a row of gleaming fangs.

The shadows clinging to the Darkest One shuddered with what looked like panic, but she refused to believe she'd lost even that close to her end. Words in the dark fae tongue spilled over her lips. She whipped her arm, and a wave of shadow careened from her into the beast. The power of it rasped frigid over my skin.

The dark magic washed right through the dragon's enormous form without so much as a quiver. The beast flapped its wings with a gush of cold wind and slammed its jaws down over its creator.

The Darkest One's last screech vanished with her into the beast's mouth. Nothing but a few wisps of shadow remained, settling like dust on the dais.

The dragon roared, a thundering sound that reverberated right through to my bones. It swept around toward the Darkest One's underlings, who were standing around us motionless and gaping. As it dove toward them, they snapped out of their daze. The dark fae rushed away in its wake. But the dragon was too fast and huge to outrun. It snatched up one here, two there, in its fanged maw.

I heaved myself toward Darton. My king lay slumped on his side, blood pooling beneath him. I clutched his shirt, tears burning in my eyes. Not a hint of breath stirred his chest. Grief surged up from my gut to my throat, choking me.

"You stupid sodding idiot," I told him. The tears spilled out, streaking down my cheeks. I moved to bury my face against his body, but a sudden heightening of the screams across the park made me raise my head instead.

The dragon had finished with the dark fae in the hedge garden. With no more of our enemies left to devour, it appeared to have reverted back to the Darkest One's whims. It was soaring toward the stage and the fleeing crowd beyond it. Smoke streamed from its nostrils. A flap of its enormous wings shook the walls of the stage.

My work here wasn't done. I swallowed down my grief and shoved myself to my feet. I had to finish what my king had started. It hadn't been only my battle, but it wasn't only his either.

I picked up the branch I'd dropped in the chaos. It wasn't going to be nearly enough. Gripping it with both hands, I reached inside me to the thrum of life energy flowing through my veins. All of it, all of it, if I needed to. What did it matter if I lost decades? I'd been granted plenty of life already. The people the dragon meant to consume had barely gotten one.

"*Creature of darkness!*" I called out. The energy I was gathering inside me pitched my voice high and hard. It split the air.

The dragon veered toward me. A quiver of recognition rolled off of it. Of course it knew me. We'd met more than once in Darton's soul. We might as well be old friends.

"*Darkness must be consumed,*" I said. "*The only darkness that remains here is you. Swallow yourself, swallow it all. Fulfill the purpose you were tasked with.*"

With those words, I flung all the magic I could gather toward the beast. It tore from my limbs and chest like an uprooted tree. Pain lanced down the center of my body. I staggered, barely able to breathe. Yeah, that had been at least a couple decades right there.

The spell hit the dragon. It shuddered and lashed its tail. As I sagged to my knees beside my king, my gut clenched. Had my effort been enough? I reached down into myself again, right to the core, ready to pour every last shred into my next casting.

The dragon whipped its tail back and forth again—and caught the tip in its jaws.

My own jaw went slack as I watched the creature chomp down. It tugged and snapped, pulling even more of its own body into its maw. The wind whirled around it, pulling tighter. Its glowing eyes flared. It started to spin with the wind, coiling in on itself. Its mouth opened and caught its hind legs with its fangs.

It wrenched itself even more sharply around, until it looked like little more than a blurred ball of shadow. I lost sight of its limbs and wings in the haze. Its body undulated and contracted. It whirled faster and faster, shrinking so fast now that the air shrieked. Then, with an awful sucking sound and a wallop of wind that made my ears pop, it was gone.

I sagged over Darton's body, all my strength having fled my own. His face was still warm under my hand. I gazed dizzily down at the wound on his chest, the blood streaking the blade I'd enchanted fifteen hundred years past. One thought broke through the roar in my head.

He wasn't the only one who could be a stupid sodding idiot. I'd sworn I'd save him, and damn it, I would, with whatever life I had left.

I wrapped my arms around his still form and kissed his cheek. "*I love you,*" I murmured in the first language we'd ever spoken to each other, the first language I should have said those words to him in. But there wasn't any time left to regret that. I closed my fingers around Excalibur's hilt and dragged it from Darton's chest, wincing at the renewed gush of blood. Then I rolled him onto his back and pressed my lips to his self-inflicted wound.

"*Live long and well,*" I ordered him. With the last bit of energy in my limbs, I pushed myself to the edge of the dais. The lake's water lapped the shore beneath me.

"*For my king,*" I said, and tipped myself over the edge.

My body plunged into the frigid water. Some distant part of my brain woke up with an urge to save myself, but my body was already too exhausted to fight.

The water closed over me. My vision hazed. As the liquid

seeped into my lungs, my awareness drifted away from me to the body still lying on the dais. To flesh knitting and sealing. To a breath rasping down Darton's throat. I'd given my sacrifice, and the light had accepted it for my king. A smile crossed my face.

Then the blackness took me.

CHAPTER THIRTY

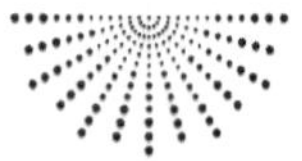

PAIN. Hard and heavy, slamming through my chest. Air choking my throat.

My lungs heaved. Water spewed out of them, searing up my throat and over my tongue. I coughed in short, hacking bursts, and wretched again.

Everything hurt. My muscles ached. My rib cage throbbed around my still-stuttering lungs. A sharp jab of a headache needled my temples.

My eyes blinked open of their own accord. A face loomed over mine, blurring and then coming into focus. Darton's. Flushed with exertion, his shoulders tensed. Blue sky above him. My fingers clenched and found soft grass between them. The breeze shifted, and a shiver rippled over me. Wet fabric clung to my chilled skin from shoulders to feet.

"Where's that blanket?" Darton said, his hand jerking toward someone behind him. His blue eyes never left mine. A second later, he was spreading a stretch of knitted wool someone must have handed him over my shaking body.

"Em," he said, touching my cheek. "Em, can you talk to me? Do you understand what I'm saying?"

I dragged in a shudder of a breath. My lungs protested at being put to use, but the fog in my head cleared slightly. "Yes." My voice seemed to scrape my already raw throat. I winced and tried again. "What happened?"

Another face appeared beyond Darton's. Jagger. He was holding his arm at an unnatural angle, his expression tight with pain, but he was alive. "What happened is Darton dragged you out of the lake and gave you the most impressive performance of CPR I've ever seen. How you ended up in the lake in the first place, I'm not so sure."

CPR. "He has a badge for that," I said inanely. "Boy Scouts." Jagger just gave me a puzzled look, but a smile flickered across Darton's face.

"If you remember that, you mustn't have been too far gone."

"Enough to make sure *you* weren't a goner," I muttered. I squirmed but failed to maneuver my body well enough to push myself upright. Darton eased his arm around me and helped me sit up.

People were milling around the field in apparent confusion. As you'd expect when a massive magic dragon had just terrorized a major city park and then eaten itself. A few of the other fae hunters were standing nearby, patching up wounds and eyeing Darton and I cautiously.

I was alive. The fact of it hit me out of the blue, as if it hadn't already been obvious. I'd sacrificed my life for my king, and he'd brought me back in turn, in his own way.

"You know," I said, tugging the blanket tighter around me, "I'm pretty sure we can only get away with something like this the once. No second chances."

"I think I'm okay with that," Darton said. "As long as there aren't any *other* hugely powerful fae enemies you've just forgotten to tell me about."

"Enemies, no. People I've generally irritated... Let's not start counting."

Darton chuckled, with an abruptness that seemed to surprise him. He snapped his mouth shut, but his smile remained. He traced his fingers over my forehead, brushing damp strands of hair back from my face. His gaze softened.

"You know," he said, "when your hair's wet, you really do look like him—like you. The first you."

When he'd made that observation before, it hadn't led to quite the reaction I'd been looking for. But the same question tumbled from my mouth anyway.

"Do you like that?"

Darton's smile tightened. My pulse skittered in a sudden panic. Then I saw him blink his eyes, hard. It wasn't a lack of emotion that was making him pause. It was too much of it.

"I do," he said roughly. "I like you every way you could possibly look. As long as you're looking back at me."

The tension seeped out of me. In that moment, I'd have been perfectly happy to snuggle into his warmth for the rest of the day. But I had the feeling this wasn't quite the place for it. Still, I could sneak in a quick cuddle before we had to haul ass back toward home.

I leaned into him, nestling my head against his shoulder. "I don't think you need to worry about that. You're my king, and I'm your wizard. You're stuck with me whether you like it or not."

CHAPTER THIRTY-ONE

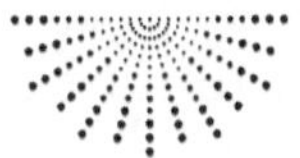

Three months later

My saber glanced off my sparring partner's blade. He parried it to the side and jabbed his saber toward me. I dodged the blow, distracted him with a quick feint, and landed a tap in the middle of his chest.

"Point!"

He chuckled. "You're too fast for me."

"Hmm. Maybe you just got too used to having a magical sword that did half the work for you."

Darton pulled off his fencing mask with a grin. "I suppose that's possible. You'll just have to beat proper discipline back into me. Some other day. Lucky for me, practice is pretty much over."

I rolled my eyes at him, and then lifted my own mask and did it again so he could see me this time. The gesture didn't stop Darton from stepping closer and leaning in for a kiss. The brush of his mouth against mine sent a rush of heat through me, still as potent as the first time we'd locked lips last fall.

Coach cleared his throat. Darton pulled back with a sheepish smile that provoked just as much of a flutter in my chest as his cocky grin before. Seeing Coach's expression, I decided not to give in to the urge to kiss that smile too. We had plenty of time for kissing—and whatever else we felt like getting up to—outside of practice.

Darton caught my hand to squeeze it, and we parted ways to our respective change rooms.

When I emerged from mine a few minutes later after a hasty change into street clothes, I found Keevan and Izzy waiting in the hall. They were talking to each other, their heads leaned close in conversation.

Izzy gave me a little wave when she saw me. Her hand stayed tucked around Keevan's elbow. He beamed at me. He'd been beaming at pretty much everyone and everything since they'd gone on their first date back in December.

"What's up?" I said as they strolled over.

"Oh, I borrowed a book from Darton that he said he needed back for some assignment." Keevan held up the book in question, which from the title was some sort of legal text. "Figured I'd stop by now. Ah, there's the man I'm looking for."

"Hey!" Darton said, coming out of the change room. Keevan gave a little bow as he handed over the book, and Darton accepted it with a grimace. "Don't you start."

"Just giving you the respect you're due, Your Highness," Keevan said with a wink. I had a feeling it was going to be years before he ran out of king-related humor.

"We were going to grab some dinner at that new Italian place just off campus," Izzy said. "Did you two want to come with?"

"Not tonight," Darton said. "Priya's coming over so she and Em can have their weekly cooking extravaganza."

"And I've got about a million assignments to get through." I made a face. "I'm still getting back in my professors' good graces after skipping out for all those weeks. Maybe we can hang out sometime this weekend?"

"Definitely," Izzy said. "I'll text you."

Keevan slung his arm around Izzy's waist as they ambled away. Darton and I set off in the opposite direction. He shook his head. "I've got to say, I never saw that coming. The two of them getting together, I mean."

I nudged him with my elbow. "It took you fifteen hundred years to figure out your own feelings. I'm going to have to say picking up on chemistry is maybe not your forte."

Darton made a non-committal grumbling sound and took my hand, twining his fingers through mine. "I figured it out in the end. That's got to count for something. I just don't see why he told *you* and not me."

"Ah, well, that's where you have to realize that he didn't so much tell me as I dragged it out of him. But it wasn't that hard to see."

As we crossed the courtyard, my gaze caught on a scrap of floating darkness that *would* be hard to see, for anyone on campus except me with my fae-touched sight. I tugged Darton to a halt and palmed one of the few twigs I tucked into my pockets every morning.

The dark fae had left us alone since we'd bested the Darkest One. Now that the dragon was gone from my king, Darton wasn't useful to them as a tool. Without their mistress urging them on, I suspected they valued keeping their own lives over seeking possible vengeance. Few of them had lived long enough to have met her more than a couple days before her demise anyway. And since the spell that had bound her to our lives was broken, the glooms didn't have any interest in Arthur's soul either.

But it didn't hurt to be prepared. And there was no point in letting dark vermin wander around, potentially stirring up minor mischief.

"*Darkness begone*," I murmured. The gloom wisped away. Darton squeezed my hand a little tighter when we started walking again.

"Our lives are never going to be completely normal, are they?" he said.

The words sent a pang through my chest. I'd tried so hard to give him *normal* before. But when you were a reincarnated wizard attending to your reincarnated king...

"No," I said. "Probably not."

He shrugged and gave me a smile that melted my regret. "I'm okay with that. Normal *all* the time would get kind of boring."

We crunched through the thin layer of snow on the campus green and turned onto the street leading to the apartment he and I had moved into right after Thanksgiving.

"I've started thinking," Darton said, with a hint of hesitation that told me my opinion was going to carry some weight. "Instead of going all-out with the law thing as a career... I might like to try my hand at politics. I mean, I do have a little experience, even if it's not very recent. And, well, the idea just appeals to me."

I rubbed my thumb over the back of his hand. "That sounds great." He'd never seemed all that enthusiastic about becoming a lawyer—he'd picked it to follow in his dad's footsteps, not out of any real passion. "Maybe you won't end up with a castle, but I'd bet you can make a meaningful impact, just like back then."

"I might as well try, at least."

Priya was waiting for us in the building's lobby, where it looked like she'd just stomped the snow off her boots. She hefted a bulging grocery store bag. "I found the *perfect* recipe," she told me. "You are going to totally chemistry-geek out over it, Emmaline."

I laughed. "I can't wait."

In the apartment, we headed straight for the kitchen. Priya pulled out her phone and brought up one of the most complicated curry recipes I'd ever seen. The thought of the challenge set my thoughts buzzing.

Darton leaned against the counter next to me. "Is there anything I can do to help?"

My mind flashed back through the centuries to my king's attempts at cooking stew over a fire while we were on the road. "Nope. Definitely not."

"Hey," he said, holding up his hands in mock-offense. "I can handle a pot and a spoon. I *did* kill the greatest dark fae ever, in case you've forgotten."

"Right. By killing yourself. Not the sort of strategy you can replicate on the regular. Also, cooking is a *slightly* different skill set from combat."

"Fine, fine," he said, grinning. "I'll just provide the moral support, then."

I grabbed the spices we needed off the rack and started grinding them with a pestle. Priya got to work chopping the veggies. Darton stayed there next to me, his arm grazing mine when I shifted a little closer. The warmth of his presence spread through my body with a glow that felt almost like magic.

This was our life now. This apartment, those classes, fencing practice and hanging out with friends. I couldn't remember the last time I'd felt actually... content. Maybe I never had, even in that first life. The looming threat of the dark fae had always been there in the back of my mind.

We only had this one life left. I had no idea where it was going to take us. But all that mattered to me was that this time, we were going to get to really *live* it.

DRAGON OF DESTINY - BONUS SCENE

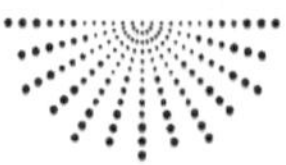

I'd like to have thought that I'd been, if not a brilliant king, at least moderately smart. The way my advisors had talked to me in my memories seemed to indicate they'd thought so. Merlin had always acted as if I were full of great insight. And my decisions, by and large, had served the realm well.

So how had I managed to be so oblivious to my own goddamned feelings?

In every fragment of the past that drifted through my dreams while I lay cuddled next to Em, I caught glimpses of the love I'd unconsciously tried so hard to smother. There was the day when we'd gone down to that one village to check on the lambing, and the sun had turned the dark waves of Merlin's hair so glossy I'd barely resisted brushing my fingers over them. When he'd beamed at me even brighter than that sun, I'd made an excuse to linger there an hour longer than was really necessary, just to have this moment together before the responsibilities back in the castle dragged me away from him.

There was the dinner when one of the serving women had started flirting with him, leaning her bosom against his shoulder each time she'd topped up his drink, and I'd missed half the conversation around me watching Merlin flush red and stammer some awkward response that could just as easily have been eager nerves as reluctance. Somehow I'd convinced myself it was coincidence that I'd suddenly needed him to check over all my armor for dark fae magic the moment we were done eating.

There was one of those dreams from back then, all heat and sighs and trembling limbs, the satisfaction and relief of finally feeling that slim but lean body under mine. Jolting awake with a lurch of my stomach and an erection so hard it was painful.

Just good friends. Just the bond of a ruler and his greatest confidant. Ha. *A sodding idiot*, that's what Merlin would have called me.

But he'd never known. I'd lied to myself and in that way lied to him, over and over, until—

I'd told him now. Em knew. She didn't hate me, and she was Merlin, so I must have done something right. Even if it still filled me with a pang to think of all the interludes like this one we might have shared from the beginning if I hadn't let prejudice cloud my mind.

I shifted on the bed, my brain still foggy, and realized Em's sleeping form no longer lay next to me. The vibration of the RV's engine carried through the mattress. I guessed she might have gone to use the bathroom or grab some food for us.

Those were perfectly reasonable explanations, but as I rolled over and propped my shoulders on one of the pillows to watch the door, a nervous twinge ran through my gut. With each passing second that Em didn't reappear, my stomach clenched tighter.

After what I estimated to be at least ten minutes, more than enough time for anyone to be finished doing anything out there, I scrambled into my clothes and reached for the door.

The handle jarred when I tried to open it. I frowned and tugged again. It still didn't budge. The tension in my abdomen wrenched through me.

She'd wanted to go. She'd wanted to go and take on the Darkest One all by herself and—

God, no, Merlin, you can't do this, not when we've just— You're not meant to do this all on your own.

And if that queen of the dark fae killed my wizard, I wouldn't follow. We wouldn't return. I'd be left with a half hour of bliss and endless lifetimes of regret.

I rattled the door, my hand sweating against the handle. "Hey! Who's out there? Keevan? Izzy? Jagger? You can't keep me locked in here like this!"

No one answered. I moved to the bedroom's single window, but the sight of the landscape slipping by outside made me pause. The sky had darkened to a deep purple-blue. It was evening already. How long had I slept?

More to the point, I wasn't sure I could fit through that little rectangle in the first place, and I was even less sure I'd survive the tumble afterward. The door it was. So I was damn well going through it.

I cast around and discovered Em's one mistake. She'd left Excalibur resting on the floor where I'd set it down when we'd come in. Of course she had. She wouldn't have wanted to leave me completely defenseless.

Which also meant I could defend myself against my wizard's sodding idiocy.

I snatched it up, inhaling sharply at the rush of the sword's power washing over me. The room only gave me about seven feet to the back wall, but I'd take what I could. I steadied myself there, sword raised, and then hurled myself at the door.

Excalibur's blade sang through the air, driven by all the determination I had in me. It sliced right through the thin aluminum and severed the lock mechanism in two. I kicked the door, and it swung open with a clatter.

Jagger stepped out to meet me as I strode into the hall. He took in me and my sword, and his mouth curled into a slanted smile.

"'Doors have locks,' she said," he muttered, sounding as much amused as annoyed. "Clearly she doesn't know you quite as well as she thought."

"Where is she?" I demanded, even though I already knew. "How long ago did she leave?"

"She headed off to Chicago, like she wanted to from the start," Jagger said. "She's got a few hours' head start on us… and a much faster vehicle. And also I promised not to let you go anywhere near that city and the dark fae gathering there."

I gave the older man a look that felt as if I'd carried it forward from my kingly past, one that wasn't taking his refusal as an answer. "I don't give a shit what you promised her. She's my wizard, and we're not letting her throw herself at that fae army alone. Point this vehicle in the right direction, or I'm getting off and finding my own."

"Are you sure that's a good idea?"

I could tell from the slant of his gaze what he meant. That prickling pressure inside me that I'd been able to ignore for a while stirred, just a little. My hands clenched.

"Em has weakened the dragon. And if we don't go out there and help her do this thing, the Darkest One could kill her and then come for me without her around to help. Do you really think we'll stand a better chance that way?"

Jagger sighed. "No. I figured it was going to come to this. Come on. I don't like backing down from a fight like this either. But the situation's gotten a little more complicated while you were sleeping. I can fill you in on the way there."

The muscles holding me braced released. I almost staggered

with the bump of the wheels over a shallow pothole before I followed Jagger to the front of the RV.

We might still get there too late. I might still lose my Merlin. But I'd do everything I could to stop that dire fate from coming true—and whatever happened, the Darkest One was going to fall at my hand.

❦

After a long talk with Jagger and a whole lot of swearing toward the dark elves that had grabbed my friends, I found myself back in the RV's bedroom with its ruined door. We still had a ways to go before we'd reach Chicago, and after all the chaos of the last few days, this afternoon's nap had left me still groggy. I needed to have all my wits for the battle ahead.

A little of Merlin's sharp bright scent lingered on the blanket. I burrowed my face into it, an ache squeezing my chest. But eventually sleep did find me.

And with sleep came the dreams.

The laugher and music of the victory celebration swept around me where I stood in the middle of the field. So much joy, and yet a prickle of apprehension crept over me.

The dark fae were coming. I knew it.

That remark Merlin had made years ago, that had come back to me in the last few weeks as the stress of protecting me has shown more and more in his eyes, rose up again. If a person's willing to sacrifice their own life, there's no power that can compare.

My hand came to rest on my sword instinctively. If it came down to that, if it was the only way I could do my duty and protect my *people from this threat, so be it.*

I went up to give my speech. The people cheered. The dark fae attacked. Bodies fell and dark magic swirled, and as I sprang into the crowd to charge at those wretched figures, a gaunt woman rose up among them like a ghoulish specter. She stepped toward me.

So much cold power reverberated off her that I didn't need to ask. This was the Darkest One. Her eyes glittered, and her lips curled with a smile that looked far too pleased.

I couldn't defeat that. I couldn't conquer it. The certainty of those facts sank like a stone into my gut.

But I could end her anyway.

I hefted my sword high, setting my hands so that with one swift arc, I could stab it straight into my own heart.

And I woke up, gasping like a fish out of water. My skin was clammy with sweat. I sagged against the mattress as my frantic pulse slowly evened out.

The intensity of the memory faded, but the understanding that had come with it didn't. I reached toward the sword I'd lain at the other side of the bed and touched Excalibur's hilt.

If a person's willing to sacrifice their own life, there's no power that can compare.

There was a monster in me. Maybe it was time I owned it, before the Darkest One and her minions had the chance to. Even if that meant I went to my final death with no more than this afternoon's half hour of bliss.

Merlin could still live on, if we got there in time. Em could have a life of her own that wasn't bound to serving me. Even as my resolve sent an ache through my chest, that thought gave me a twinge of satisfaction.

"I know," I whispered, to my wizard who wasn't there to hear me. "I know what I was trying to do. I know what I have to do now."

LEGENDS REBORN - BONUS SCENE

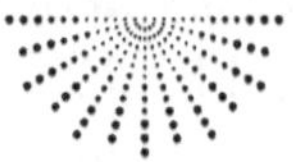

Enjoy this little glimpse into Emma and Darton's future, set twelve years after the events in the main series…

I heard Priya's voice before I'd finished opening the door: "There she is." Followed by a squeal and the patter of my daughter's feet.

"Mommy!" Madelyn cried as I stepped inside. I dropped my purse and caught her in my arms, swinging her around. At five years old, with a slender frame she'd inherited from me, she was still light enough that I could do that without much of a strain.

I hugged her, tucking my face next to her soft curls, which were a bright gold-tinged brown I figured she could mostly thank her father for. Speaking of which… I glanced at my best friend.

"Darton isn't home yet?"

Priya shook her head. "He called about a half hour ago, said he had a few more things to go over at the campaign office. That boss of is his working him hard, huh?"

"That's politics," I said. I couldn't help reflecting from time to time that in some ways it'd been a lot simpler when people just got the king they got, no campaigning required.

"I need to show you the picture I made for you," Madelyn informed me. I set her down, and she scampered off toward the living room of the modest bungalow we'd moved into when we'd decided to start trying for a family.

"So, this motherhood gig still seems to be working out well for you," Priya said, slightly teasingly. "From all-powerful wizard to maternal superstar?"

"Still a wizard," I said. "Which does come in handy when someone's *absolute most favorite* toy gets lost or a scrape is bleeding a little more than I'm comfortable with."

I wasn't sure I had the words to convey the joy that lit up in me at the sight of my daughter hustling back to me, a paper clutched in her little hands. I hadn't been completely sure, given my odd situation as an old soul *and* a half-fae residing in a younger body, that I even could have kids. Maybe I wouldn't have another. But Madelyn had only taken a few tries to come into our lives, and even through the early sleepless nights and the tantrums, I'd treasured her presence with all my heart.

We'd made this wonderful new life together, my king and I, and it was nothing short of magical watching her come into her own.

"How was your meeting?" Priya asked after Madelyn had explained the intricacies of her marker drawing to me.

"Oh, it was good, just a little more arguing than I like. But I'm used to that." I straightened up, rumpling Madelyn's hair. Because of the wealth I'd amassed across my various lives, I didn't *need* to work. But I didn't do well with inactivity, any more than Darton did. I'd started volunteering my historical expertise at the local museum… not that they always took my recommendations in stride.

Well, who could blame them? The books they'd learned from

paled in comparison to first-hand knowledge, but I couldn't exactly tell them how I'd acquired that.

"Any exciting plans for tonight?" I said to Priya as she grabbed her things.

"Not tonight, but tomorrow I'm seeing that guy again—the one you gave a thumbs up to? He's cooking me dinner. We'll see how long I last before I can't hold myself back from the kitchen." She winked with a grin. Priya had ended up turning her enjoyment of cooking into a longstanding chef position and now a professor role at a prestigious culinary school.

I wagged a finger at her. "Don't scare him off now."

"If he's scared off that easily, he's not the right guy for me," she said primly, but she was still grinning.

"If things keep going well, you'll have to bring him around the next time Keevan and Izzy are in town," I said.

"Oh my God. Did you see the pics of their new place in Brooklyn? So sweet."

When she left after a little more of a chat, Madelyn gave me a solemn face. "No Daddy before bedtime?"

"I guess not," I said. "Or…" A smile leapt to my lips. "If he can't get here in time, what do you say we go to him?"

Madelyn pumped her fist. "Yeah!"

I texted Darton as we got into the cab. *Is anything you're currently doing an emergency?*

No, just the usual, he wrote back a minute later. *Why? Do you think there's an emergency somewhere?*

Oh, just wondering.

Why does that make me nervous, Em? he replied, with a smirking emoji to show he was teasing.

Even after all these years, the sight of the nickname brought a flutter of warmth into my chest. He'd told me, ages ago, "Every time I say or write that, I'm thinking *Merlin.* But this way no one else needs to know that."

I have no idea, I wrote now. *I've certainly never gotten you into any trouble that I haven't gotten you out of… eventually.*

Madelyn and I got out in front of the rather drab building where Darton was helping a new candidate run for state governor. I dipped my hand into my purse, curled my fingers around the wand I made sure to always carry, and murmured a few words to distract all attention from the two of us.

My skin itched as we slipped into the building and past the cubicles to the walled offices at the back. Madelyn skipped along beside me. No one gave us a second glance, or even much of a first glance. We made it to Darton's door unnoticed.

He raised his head at the swing of the door with an expression as if he were bracing himself for a heap of additional paperwork. His eyes brightened in an instant. I kicked the door shut behind us. "Surprise!"

"Em, Maddy." He pushed away from his desk and scooped up our daughter, tugging me in a moment later for a joint hug. "What's the special occasion?"

"Just that you need to take a break," I said. "I think we should have better scenery than this, though."

"Em," he said, with a look that was both affectionate and wary.

"I'll make sure no one notices you're gone, and I'll have you back in fifteen minutes. Don't you think you deserve fifteen minutes?"

"Please, Daddy," Madelyn said.

Darton laughed. "Well, I obviously can't say no to that."

I wrapped my arm more tightly around him and Madelyn, gripping my wand with my other hand. *"Away from here, where green things grow,"* I whispered.

A magical wind whipped up around us, and with a jolt we were landing in a secluded little grove in our favorite of the city's parks.

Twelve years wasn't enough to erase fifteen centuries of learned caution. I scanned the trees and flowerbeds in a heartbeat, checking for any unnatural twitch of a shadow. No glooms and certainly nothing larger lurked on the park's terrain today.

Not that I encountered them very often these days as it was. It'd been months since I'd last banished one of those scraps of semi-sentiment darkness. The dark fae themselves had stayed well away since the death of their queen. I wasn't sure whether they were more wary of me or of the enchanted sword Darton kept in a case under our bed, sealed to prevent explorations from curious little hands.

Madelyn squealed happily and rolled on the thick grass to peer up at the evening sky. Darton kept his arm around my waist as we eased down with her. For the first few minutes, we just sat like that, my head tipped against his shoulder, his thumb tracing a soft line up and down my side. Madelyn exclaimed over a ladybug and an intricately veined leaf, and then drifted a short distance from us to pluck clover to chain into a necklace.

"Maybe I should tell her to make it a crown," I said.

The man who would always be my king chuckled. "That might come with a little more explaining than I'm ready to do yet." He brushed his lips to my cheek. "Thank you for coming. I did need this. I wish things hadn't been so busy the last few months. You know once the election is over—"

"It'll all calm down," I finished, giving his hand a reassuring squeeze. "I do know. It's fine, Art. We knew going in that your schedule was going to be hectic. You're following your dream—and my dream has always been to see you through whatever you set your mind to." I paused, a sudden swell of emotion constricting my throat. "I have more of you now than I ever did before. How could I complain?"

"Em," he said, his voice thick, and stole a quick kiss, so tender I wished we could linger in it. "*I* can complain. I want to see you and Madelyn as much as I can. There's just so much else I feel like I should do too, especially since I'm lucky enough to be here at all."

"Exactly," I said. "I wouldn't want you any other way. I fell in love with a king."

The corner of his mouth twitched. With the light as my witness, I'd swear he was as handsome as he'd ever been, even with the faint lines starting to gather where his eyes crinkled. Sometimes I couldn't do anything but sit in awe of the fact that I'd now known him, been with him, in this existence for as long as we'd had together in our first lives.

Darton's gaze went distant for a second before it slid back to me. "I was actually starting to think I've built up enough experience that next year I could make a go of running for a prominent position myself. Campaign for myself instead of for someone else."

Excitement shivered through me. I'd been wondering when he'd take that step. "Of course," I said. "You should go for it."

"It'll mean even longer hours."

"We'll make it work. Maddy and I will come and surprise you whenever we can. Regular people in this line of work find a balance—we should be able to too."

"You'd think so," he said wryly. And then, sounding almost shy, "I was also thinking… it might be nice if you joined me, however you feel comfortable. Campaign manager, strategist—any title you'd like. Make it a family endeavor."

The shiver of excitement turned into something soaring. I couldn't stop the smile that stretched across my face. "Like old times?"

"Like old times." He beamed back at me, clearly pleased with my reaction. "You know I'd never have been much of a king without you by my side every step of the way."

I raised my eyebrows at that. "And *you* know that's not actually true. But, I will concede that I may have contributed a significant amount to exactly how successful you managed to be. One can only imagine how far we might get without villainous dark fae lurking around waiting to strike."

Darton laughed. "Is that a yes?"

I snuggled closer to him, holding my arm out to Madelyn as she bounded back to us. "It's an 'Absolutely, and now that you've offered, there are no take-backs allowed.'"

My husband, my king, and my only love nestled his head next to mine. "There's not a single moment with you that I'd ever want to take back."

"Mommy," Madelyn said. "Do *you* know how to do this?" She twirled one of the flowers she'd plucked by the stem and then pressed that stem to the ground. Before my widening eyes, two small leaves sprouted on either side of it. When she released her fingers, the new plant stayed upright. I nudged it, feeling the pull of roots now stretching into the earth. My daughter's face shone with pride.

"Well," I said. "That's really something." I touched her cheek. "You know not to share anything like that with your friends at school, right?"

"Of course," she said with a scoff, and rambled off again.

"So..." Darton said as we stared after her. "I guess we know who she takes after more, huh?"

I hadn't been sure light fae magic was hereditary in my particular peculiar situation. There'd been a few hints here and there, but that trick with the flower—that was pretty undeniable.

"Somehow I have the feeling our lives are about to get a lot more interesting," I said.

Darton chuckled and nuzzled my hair. "I wouldn't have it any other way."

ABOUT THE AUTHOR

Eva Chase lives in Canada with her family. She loves stories both swoony and supernatural, and strong women and the men who appreciate them. Along with the Legends Reborn trilogy, she is the author of the Witch's Consorts series, the Dragon Shifter's Mates series, the Demons of Fame Romance series, the Their Dark Valkyrie series, and the Alpha Project Psychic Romance series.

Connect with Eva online:
www.evachase.com
eva@evachase.com